Simon Louvish is a biographer of comedians and author of satirical and outrageous fiction. He is a film screenwriter and teaches film at the London Film School. His film biographies include, *Chaplin: The Tramp's Odyssey, Mae West: It Ain't No Sin,* and *Monkey Business: The Lives and Legends of the Marx Brothers* (all published by Interlink). Interlink published Louvish's novel *The Silencer* to high acclaim.

DREAM
OF AGES

BY SIMON LOUVISH

Interlink Books

An imprint of Interlink Publishing Group, Inc.
Northampton, Massachusetts

First published in 2021 by

Interlink Books
An imprint of Interlink Publishing Group, Inc.
46 Crosby Street, Northampton, MA 01060 USA

and

Studio 11A, Archway Studios
25-27 Bickerton Road
London, N19 5JT UK

Library of Congress Cataloging-in-Publication Data available
ISBN 978-1-62371-923-4

Printed and bound in the United States of America

VOLUME 1

THE GREAT GRAMBY

"I should have died in California..."

Je cherche mon frère...
Ich suche nach meinem Bruder...
Io sto cercando mio fratello...
Busco a mi hermano...
Caut fratele meu...
Szukam mojego brata...
Я ищу моего брата...
...יחא תא שפחמ ינא

I am searching for my brother, in the dim first light of the dawn breaking over the hill across the valley that I can see from the chair. I can see it only at a slant, from the bed, but if I move the old carcass from the bed to the chair I can see it in its academy frame. The light glimmers, and one can see first of all only the outline of the hill, and then the terraces on which the gravestones are set, rank after rank, step after step, ringed by the stone fences that might have been set to cultivate orchards but instead guard human remains.

Most of the dead who lie in this soil facing me are soldiers, mostly young men who have been killed fighting this country's wars, from the mere privates who had barely left their mothers' wombs to the generals who died festooned with ribbons of this war or that, this campaign or the other, among them one of Sarah's grandsons who flickered as a brief candle and burnt out, in some desert or field. My sister herself lies on the other side of the slope, out of my sight, among some other elders, far from their ancestral earth, or close to their own, the same dust. I know that my brothers do not lie under this earth, but I still look out, wondering, particularly at this hour, when the first shafts of the Jerusalem sun reach out between the harsh blocks of the new city's concrete jungle.

They say that I have lost the power of speech, or more accurately, that of utterance, as I do not respond when they thrust a notebook and pen into my hand, nodding and pointing, except for a few slow dabs. That part of the brain has shut down, and I am not sure I miss it, as I have always spoken most clearly in pictures. I still have the old cinematographer's routine, even with the window, of checking out the four corners of the frame—top left, top right, bottom right, bottom left, to get the composition proper. In fact, I have always preferred the old-fashioned academy frame, later the "television" frame, though that had forbidden zones on all four sides, before that too widened, though not yet to the full "letterbox" of CinemaScope—remember the capital C and capital S, the trademarks, before everyone went the same way.

I have outlived so many it is a miracle that I can still stir. But I still speak, though, in my illusion, it can only be Yakov who can hear me. The others are either beyond reach, or silent. But there is always Yakov—Vassily. The Great Gramby. If anyone still lingers, it is he. I remember as vividly as yesterday his greatest trick—the Lazarus act, the raising of the dead, a trick even Lafayette, or Houdini, couldn't conjure. That was Gramby's specialty. In Paris, at the Medrano. Or was it the Folies Bergere? Three certified doctors in white coats would come on, carrying the coffin, from which they would produce the corpse in swaddling sheets. Three members of the audience would be invited to certify death, doctors preferably, but any other person of authority would do. They would hold the dead pulseless hand and show the clear mirror to the audience. The coffin would be closed again, and nailed shut, in the witnesses' presence. It would be lifted off the stage, by four muscular assistants, dressed in loincloths and Gramby's signature turbans. Then Gramby, dressed in pristine white, from tip to toe, from gloves to shoes, the red diamond glittering in his immaculate headcloth, would begin to whisper, softly, and then with a rising timbre, his occult intonations, the patchwork song of half remembered lullabies, semi-Latin, cod-Romanian, shards of Greek, liturgical ripples of Hebrew, slivers of Aramaic and Syriac, some Arabic he had learned off Hajji-Ali, gobs of church-Russian, and the invented tongue we had ourselves used loose in the fields, along the riverside, hiding in the tall wheat as the Moldavian boys and girls clattered past in their carts, with their spades, hoes and scythes... sometimes his song would break into a twisted phrase of the old Ukrainian tones, rippling in the wind, and then a sudden shout as his voice rose, startling the audience, waking them from their reverie, hurling a shard of light through the smoke that billowed across the stage and over the coffin and its attendants, and then he would dance about, calling and crying, stamping his feet, waving his hands, tearing off his gloves, which would miraculously change into white doves that fluttered off up into the flies and vanished, drawing all eyes up, while the magician rolled out his final, thundering commandment, and the attendants clustered round the coffin, pulling out the nails with their claw-hammers, tearing off the lid, and then a slow, pallid hand would emerge, waving softly as the smoke cleared, and the spotlight turned upon the wizard, who moved forward, extending his hand to the Resurrected, who was slowly drawn out, clad in white robes which were wound away to reveal the man, in a pristine dark suit, waistcoat and sharp pressed pants, who would pick up his hat and cane from the coffin and make his gracious bow. Or was that later? Before that, it was the woman, dark and mysterious, clad in her black diaphanous gown. What was her name? Alma. As the audience applauded, the "police" would rush in, supposedly searching for the stolen corpse. But since it had already come to life, there was nothing for them to investigate.

My brother, Yakov. If anyone could survive death, it was he. I know Sarah is long in the ground. Ze'ev, the Wolf, disappeared long before him, somewhere along the Trans-Siberian railway. Kolya still seethes in his abiding eminence at Michigan, but speaks only to the dead, not the rest of us. And Judit, Judit, almost the youngest... Judit of the sparkling eyes, queen of the Shanghai matinees... the wind in the wheat fields... far away. There were great distances, in those days. The cry of the long distance engine...

the Chattanooga Choo Choo... I almost said that out loud. My son, Asher, brings his ear close to my mouth, in case I am actually saying something. But what I have to say can't be recorded. It can only be thought. There is a comfort in this, because it means that everything that can be said can be said, without the necessity of explanation. It can simply form, float, and evaporate.

The youngest of us all was Isaac. He departed when I was eight years old, having glimpsed with eyes that were barely open just the first two years of our century. Maybe he was clairvoyant, saw the other ninety-eight, and closed his eyes again.

My younger son arrived, I think, some weeks ago. He still moves like an angry arrow, hungrily searching for a target. He is the son of my dotage, like Kolya in his pristine anger, with the same flying mop of black hair and moustache that matched the look of Georgian brigands, whom the young firebrands admired in those days. The men of action, ungrown boys, who felt the world at their fingertips and urged it to move, at their bidding, in an essential obedience to their will... the globe, spinning on Charlie Chaplin's finger... but even then, it was not an ephemeral thing, for them, they felt the planet's weight in their bones, urging the flesh to rise up and move it, the ball of grimy, hairy mass stubbornly cleaving to its own orbit... just one more push! Just one more push!

Now I can hardly push Charlie's balloon, and that with only the left arm, the right having finally lost its cunning. Vassily! Vassily! I need your white gloves to make their passes over my carcass, mumble your mumble jumble in the secret song of the wheat fields and call out your diamond fakeries... hoshanra kalamalakam khushmantush balakala balakala! The smoke billowing across the creaking wooden boards, the shiny oiled bodies of the Arab "djinns" hired from the porters' union of the Port de Clichy, the young black boy who had been with him from the old days was long grown up by then, or was he still there, playing the saxophone, blowing his horn, in one of those dark spotlit dives? I can see the shot, glistening faces, in the semi-darkness, unmodeled, harsh noses, gleaming eyes, fingers twitching, and in the center, the artist's face, thrown back and bathed in sweat, the white sleeves flowing from the dark waistcoat.

The four corners of the frame: top left, top right, bottom right, bottom left... in the old cameras, the old warhorse, the Mitchell BNC, the image you saw in the viewfinder was not exactly the same as the composition seen by the lens. It was separate, so the camera operator had to make the adjustment instinctively as he looked through. Back in those days, you felt the weight of the work, as the massive cranes cranked you up and up. Rising and rising like gods. The deity himself beside me, DeMille, the long peaked cap shielding his bald pate, and the booming voice bellowing over the two-foot megaphone that could drive his words like nails into the skull of every extra mulling about in the vast set below. Payday for every extra in Hollywood. The chaff of Jerusalem, in rags, robes or old sacks sewn by the legion of girls in the costume department, pushing their way through herds of sheep cluttering down the steps of the plasterboard temple; old men hanging about in corners clutching their staffs, nodding their glued on beards; the kid pulling a calf across the line of centurions marching up under the ancient arch, the moneylenders waving their arms over the tables and stools strewn with every piece of gimcrack gewgaw garbage culled from the prop stores, old bangles, lucky charms, phials of Egyptian magic potions, Assyrian cardboard jewelery, goblets of fake gold and silver, ceramic vases and pots, coins of the realm duly stamped with the portrait of Caesar, or was it Augustus? Titus? Julius? DeMille himself?—the voice booming from the heavens: "That boy with the sheep! I said go right! Go right! Not left! Jesus, Mary, and Joseph!" And there was the studio head, H.B. Warner, the prince of peace in the maelstrom, making his way determinedly up the ersatz alley with the apostles struggling to keep up behind him, pushing past the centurions, striding up the steps to the moneylenders and scattering them aside, turning over the tables.

"Cut! Cut! Cut!"

The boy with the sheep was not even in the frame in that shot. That was the close shot next. So many things take place in the margins, in the corner of the eye, where there are only swirls or echoes of the bygone or might-have-been. All the forgotten ghosts, who might just return. Hoshana khashbalabash malaktam malakabam! My elder son arrives now, the Sad One, who stands by the bed and prays for me, swaying about and supplicating the Lord on my behalf. A grandfather himself by now, if not more, gray-haired and bowed-down with burdens. He wanted to put the leather straps on me, the phylacteries, around the right arm and the little boxes on my arm and around my head. The box on my head is to remind me that all my thoughts are subservient to God's will, and contains minute scrolls, scribbled by savants, proper calligraphers who must utter prayers before any stroke of the pen. Talakabam talakbam! But I have long transgressed in all directions. The arm straps have to go on my right arm, which is completely useless, but my regular attendant, Gil, who is, unusually, a local rather than the Catholic Filipinos who tend to us ancients' needs—charity comes from afar, nowadays—refuses to put them on me unless I clearly give my assent, which my elder son claims he has seen me provide with a nod of the head, or a blink, but which the carer knows is only his delusion. My elder son, Yitzhak, named for the dead child—we have several of these Isaacs in the family—is not happy, and sways about, mumbling and muttering. He trails a full crew of earnest middle-aged men in gabardine suits and black hats and various loads of beards, with their wives in tow, shtetl ladies transplanted to their supposed salvation, bringing along their offspring, boys with little skullcaps and bright eyes, girls dressed in readiness for obligations of which they have yet a scant inkling, who sit around, asking strange questions and bringing me wrapped sweets and halvah. One or two of them, I think, already have babies of their own; they seem to grow as I watch, like speeded-up vines.

Know from where you are coming and where you are headed. While the elder prays, the younger sits, impassive, reading the evening paper. He is angry because it appears that another war has been unleashed, in Lebanon. Tanks and soldiers have crossed the northern border to crush our enemies. I have no say in the matter.

I cannot see them. I have not experienced them. They do not gleam in my viewfinder. He is probably anxious that he might be called up, even though he has spent the last ten or fifteen years away, and must be nearing the tail end of the recruitment age, while the elder is angry because he is too old to contribute anything but his prayers, or because he is always angry, even in repose. Perhaps he believes I have a different destination from the elect, or perhaps there are too many pin pricks of everyday tribulations that preclude the calm that he so dearly seeks. I don't know. One sits and the other sways, while I watch the dead soldiers on the hill. Am I a stranger here? People gather around, whispering to each other that I am the last one of my brood, saving Kolya, come home to die with my forefathers. But I am far from home, and my forefathers are nowhere near here. Other tanks, other soldiers, rolled over their graves, blotting out their crumbling bones.

I should have died in California. The paradise of dreams. The streams of youth, pouring in by cart, by bus, by Model T Ford, by the Chattanooga Choo Choo pulling in to the station. When you got off the train, you could smell the orange trees and gaze at the calm beauty of the rolling, green mountains. So fair, so fair. I am perhaps the last generation for whom this was not memory but a pristine rush that caressed hopeful faces. What remains locked, and what is open. Everything that we thought we lost we made anew in those orchards. No more the valley of dry bones, no prophets' nightmares of revenge. Back in the lost village the Moldovan girls still dance. The golden braids curled about their heads, the festive blouses rippling in the wind, the songs rolling across the fields. Like the babies settled about my bed, in a semicircle, looking at Methuselah. They are innocent of their fathers' sins. In good time, they will accumulate their own.

Top left, top right, bottom right, bottom left. Inside the frame, things could be controlled. Subject only to the caprice of the editors, the cutter, the director, the producer, the studio heads, and even then the negatives, at least, can be preserved, with foresight— DeMille preserved almost all his films when he decided he would be world famous, several years before the fall, and even then, a half dozen of the early ones were lost, which we had labored over in the first two years, feeding them into Lasky's maw... but he kept the bulk, so future generations could gasp and gape at his genius. Unlike the rest of us, he was king of his castle, the man in the chair, the jack of all trades... It was DeMille who gave me, on my fifty-fifth birthday I think it was, the little package of stills, lobby cards and poster photographs of Judit's Shanghai career. Like a pasha, he had engaged a flunky, who traveled on company business to China just after the war. He had just completed one of his clinkers, *Unconquered*, with Gary Cooper, and was smarting over the drubbing the critics gave him, especially over Boris Karloff as the Indian chief. We were bent over the first storyboards and artwork for *Samson and Delilah*... the planned model of the Philistine temple, the great stone god of Dagon, the fish-faced deity. The Japanese had gone, but the communists were advancing all over China. I told him my little sister had been an actress in Shanghai, before the war—the messenger couldn't find her, but came back with a dossier of strange-colored delights and designs. Vignettes of the Russian Lotus of Shanghai in romantic poses with some unknown companion. The same pose, on a cigarette card. A smiling calendar photo for 1935. The same image in a black slinky dress on a label for "Devil Brand Five-Color Firecrackers." He said her name was Ju Yuanjun, which meant Chrysanthemum Goddess. Soon after that, the communists took China and Samson pulled down the temple of Gaza with the miniature stone god of Dagon. Asher used to spread the set out on the carpet when he was small, gazing at the strange pictures. I remember there was a tiny booklet of photo stills, of a black-and-white thriller, *The Rose of Shanghai*. "That's your Aunt," I told him, "my kid sister, Judit." He promised to go and find her someday. But it all somehow got mislaid when the old playthings were put aside and the Wollensak 8-millimeter camera replaced everything else, the tiny windows of color film that only he could make out, with the brightness of youth's naked eye.

The Rose of Shanghai. I was left with one label, from a box of

Creme de Lait Facial Cream. She is seen with her black hair with middle parting, pencil-thin eyebrows and lipstick, slanting eyes, Chinese but unmistakably a Gorevits of Celovest. She has a pink rose behind her ear and a yellow-and-green-striped muffler or scarf. She is holding an old Bakelite black telephone, the acme of modernity then, listening rather than speaking to whatever voice is crackling from the other end of the line. Or perhaps the line is silent, and she is persevering, waiting for a sign of life, some communication, having smoothed her fresh face with the delicate product pictured exquisitely at the bottom right frame. Her eyes, I remember, gazed out into the distance, with some confidence that a voice would emanate from the air. I try to speak, but nothing emerges.

Ya yichu moego vrat... I am searching for my brother. Yakov, Vassily. He is the magician. He can pull all the threads together. The soldiers across the valley are dead, and cannot be brought back to life. Iris out. Black frame, dotted with flecks and scratches. Then the reel's end. I have to descend to the vault, down the spiralling steps of crumbling brickwork and stone, to the cellars, which have hopefully not been flooded, where the older, rusty cans might still contain stock that has not yet turned to dust on the spool...

"Can you get those damn mules to crap right of stage for a change?"

Keith's Orpheum Theatre, Columbus, Ohio, January 9, 1915

Ace Harrington — Vaudeville 'go-fer' (assistant):

You can tell that Bill Fields was nervous. He had never had to share the stage with the Four Marx Brothers before. Fields was used to getting the headliner treatment and they were muscling in on his act. He had that big billiard table that came in the cargo car and he always made sure there was a big crowd to watch him unload it at the back of theater, driving the poor porters on with his cane. "Gangway! Gangway! This is private property! Prince Herzenhoofer of Upper Westphalia lost it to me on a bet on twelve sets! Don't touch it, it's embossed with mother-of-pearl..." He would grumble all the way to the storeroom. But the Marx Brothers were carrying some pretty heavy baggage themselves. They had huge thirty-foot flats and the prop of a whole side of an ocean liner for the first act and a mansion on the Hudson for the second. Their show was called "Home Again" and was supposed to last for twenty minutes, but sometimes they dragged it out to thirty, adding gags and jokes that they had just thought out in the interval, or pretended they had. They had been playing this act, under different titles, for four years, and the peeps always came back for more. It was four against one, not counting the supporting cast of fifteen, and their mother, who sometimes joined in, or at least looked on, to blow them kisses and lead the claque from the back. So it looked like the big star was beat.

It was said they could steal the show from Houdini, which was not a name I was allowed to say around Gramby, or back of him, since he had ears like a cat. He would keep clear of all the pre-show hoopla and make sure he got the equipment prepared before anybody else so that only his own crew saw the setup. On the day of first nights he'd be at the theater by 6 a.m., when the other acts were only dreaming of breakfast. We'd go through everything most meticulous, just him, me, the new Girl, Hetty, and the Gross brothers, who doubled as baggage men and whatever duo the boss could think of to liven the show. During the time I was with the act they'd been the Magic Mahoneys, the Electric Brothers, the Karmi Sutras, Jig and Jag, the Singing Bodeens, the Missing Links, the Wild Men of Malaya, Jehenum and Max, the Fratellinis, Pedro and Pablo and even the Van Hoffman Sisters, joint winners of the Leipziger Geshuftenplatte—the All-Prussian Women Wrestlers' Plate. They were gentle souls who had been steelworkers in East Berlin, Connecticut, before joining with Gramby at Hartford, when he was with the Columbia wheel. Under the protection of their cast-iron arms, we had nothing to fear. Especially the Girl, and Zuleika before her. In fact, I suspect they were not brothers at all, but men who fancied each other that way. I was too young to fig-ure those things, as I was only twelve years old when I joined, but I always thought they acted funny, giving each other long looks and sighing deeply. In the night they were quiet, except sometimes I would hear them moan, like remembering some age old pain.

Those were the days, in the profession, in vaudeville, when you didn't ask where people came from. Ninety-nine times out of a hundred, if you bothered, they'd tell you some cock-and-bull story. Houdini was in real life called Ehrich Weiss, Chief Running Bull was really Herschel Feigenbaum and his Wild West Indian riders all came from the Bronx. Blitz the Human Fish had once been an accountant. Ching Ling Soo was Bill Robinson. The Great Lafayette was born as Sigmund Neuberger. You always had to be somebody else. When Gramby started, the first moniker that he took up was Finnegan, the Boy Wonder. Being Irish was really popular in New

York City, and he had learned the patter and some old songs from a couple he met on the boat called Mick and Rosa O'Reilly. Rosa was Italian, but she had married her husband in Cork. They worked the English music halls and made friends with some Americans who were on tour. Gramby told me they used to drink with Bill Fields in Sheffield, the steelworkers' town. Somehow they scraped together their hundred dollars and got on the Liverpool ship. They were trying to get on the swish new liner, *Titanic*, but even the steerage was too expensive. Lucky for them. You never know what cards fate is going to deal you. Except the card sharps, who have it all sewn up.

The Girl is sliding in and out of the panels of the Magic Wardrobe, an old prop that always gets big laughs. Hetty is new in the game and I am the one who is asked to show her the ropes. Gramby has that glassy look in his eye that tells me he is still dreaming of Zuleika. But she has been gone for more than a year now with Hatem Ali's Arabian Riders. Zuleika of the india-rubber bones—she could fit in any compartment. This new Girl is small enough, but she can't fold up the same way.

"Maybe we'll have to stick to the mind reading," Gramby mutters to me, "vot do you think, Ace?" He still hasn't tamed that Russian accent. Most of the time, he has the Yankee twang down pat, but one hour with Julius Marx doing his "Vas ist das?" act and he's back all the way to the shtetl. Or whatever they call it back there. I wouldn't know—everybody expects me to spout my best Uncle Tom patter when I get into the Mystery Cabinet. That's when I'm not playing Mowgli, the dumb Indian boy from *The Jungle Book*, who's brought back alive out of the Traveling Trunk. In the two years I've been with Gramby I've come back from Borneo, from the Hindu Kush, from Tasmania, Ubangiland, the Barbary Coast, Ethiopia, Patagonia, the Kongo, even as the Little Chinese Chimney Sweep, and I still haven't been out of Brooklyn except on tour with the show.

Now Gramby told me this story, one day when he was serious, wearing that long look, looking backwards: When he had got on the boat, he told me, he was called Yakov Gurevitch, and he put himself down on the list as a Russian. He was not actually from Russia but from a province on the border with the Austrian Empire that was called Bessarabia. He showed me these places on the atlas, and they seemed close enough when you looked at the big map but quite far away when you looked at the details. So he changed his name for a while to Haji Ali, the Bessarabian Conjurer, till he found out that quite a lot of people knew Bessarabia was not in Arabia, and there were three other Haji Alis. The most famous of them was a regurgitator—he used to swallow walnuts and then drink water and swallow more walnuts and then spit out the water first and the walnuts afterwards. He was a headliner for some time, till it all began to wear on the audiences, who wanted a tad more variety.

Anyway, when Gramby arrived at Ellis Island he put himself down as Vassily Gorevich, which was on his document, and then he kept the Vassily, after he dropped the Irish and the Arab labels and took on Gramby, which he took from a map of Canada that somebody had left in the dressing room. Actually it was called "Granby," but the map was smudged. And this stuck. He was seventeen years old when he came, and he was eighteen when he became the Great Gramby, which is when I came to join the show. I saw them unloading the boxes of magic things off the cart at Miners Bowery and just went in and asked for a job. I told them my father had been Magick Bones in the Ethiopian Virginia Minstrels till he had been drowned in the Delaware on his way to play for President Taft. The young Russian who I thought was the teaboy but turned out to be the act said I had real chutzpah. He liked my "get up and go," so he hired me.

The shows were a good place to go, in those days, as a black person. In those days the word "negro" meant no harm, when today it is just another insult. People don't know what being in-sulted means anymore. They get in a rage when somebody hurts their feelings. In those days you had to keep your wits about you to stop being lynched, or beaten to a pulp by some hotheads. You had to play the fool, like Stepin Fetchit in the movies. He made a couple of million dollars out of shufflin' about, talking slow like half his brain was missing. I had dinner at his house once, when he was famous. In fact he had six houses and sixteen Chinese servants and twelve cars that he was always boasting about. He lived high on the hog in Hollywood and gave wild parties that lasted for three or four days, but that still couldn't make him white. As blacks, we were the only ones who could not change our skin and put on other faces. I can't count how many doormen and bootblacks I played in those early days, and then again between music gigs, till I met up with Gramby again in Paris.

But I am moving too far ahead of the game. We are still in Ohio, in the freezing winter, with the wind coming out of the northeast and whipping the snow into the city, painting Broad Street white with just the black tracks of the tramlines. Gramby went back with the Girl to the hotel for his regular morning rest, though he made sure everybody knew she was safe in her own bunk with the other girls, and I was allowed my half-day off to hang about the other acts getting together. The Marxes were not in yet, except Leo, who came in early to grab the trade papers. He used to devour *Variety* like it was the Bible, every story a mysterious miracle. His straight man today being Fink, the Mule act man, who was putting his feet up in the dressing room after feeding his little beauties their hay. I had helped him a bit, so he took out a jug of some Kansas hooch, which he passed around.

"You hear this, Finkie?" he says. Sometimes he is in his act as the Eye-talian, sometimes he is just himself, when you hear all the Brothers talking alike, including Arthur, who is supposed to be a mute, though at one time he was also an Irishman. "Do you believe this? 'Lady Satan,' a three-act comedy drama by Leroy Drug, a New York newspaper man, is to be given a 'tryout' with a New England stock and a view toward a road production later.' We should use his-a name in our show."

"It's those cokeheads in New York who are writing that copy," said Fink, who was a very quiet man with a huge nose that the mules followed all over the stage as if it was itself stuffed with oats.

"'The Lorch family of acrobats,'" Leo reads, "'who were recently held in London as alien enemies, have been released and are playing at the Hansa Theatre in Hamburg.' Just as long as we stay out of this war, boys. Its a sickness, it's all over the world. Did you read this? 'Jerry Daly, for many years manager of the John Robinson Circus privilege car, was shot and killed in Havana, Cuba, late last week.'"

"They are trigger-happy, those Spanish," says Fink, shaking his head. "I played in Mexico City, at the Alamo Plaza, and they started shooting in the air during the acts. They thought they would panic the mules, but they are professionals, they just carried on all the same. But one poor boy was killed when the spent bullet dropped down plumb into his brain."

"You don't say. Everybody is a smartass." He turns to me, flicking a new page. "Your boss should look out, there's fakers everywhere. Listen to this: 'Long Tack Sam is the lead in Hammerstein's...' That shmo is as Chinese as I am. He starts with the Oriental spear juggling after a Chinese in clown makeup has done the cymbal spinning, and the act goes right down the list: magicians, contortionists, plate spinners... 'He brings the most laughter with the Johnny drawl, done excellently by this Chinaman, who appears to be fluently possessed of several languages: American-English, German, French, and Yiddish.' But he is just another pisher off the boat. Itski Tillimzoiger from Yehupetshlaf."

"Every dog knows its own spoor." Bill Fields barges in, shaking his top hat off his head and catching it just as it rolls off his arm. He lays his grab bag on the ledge and seats himself majestically in front of the mirror, feeling his bulbous nose. "I hear the house is pretty full tonight. News of my coming has evidently preceded me. This happened last week in Cincinatti. They were so packed in they couldn't applaud horizontally, they had to applaud vertically."

"You don't say..."

"In Omaha, before Christmas, they were jammed in so tight they couldn't laugh hah-hah-hah, they had to laugh hee-hee-hee..."

"Thassa so bad," says Leo, gazing at his own reflection. "Could be a line for our opener. Use it for Grouch."

"Trade secrets, my boy, trade secrets."

"Say Bill," Fink finally looks up, "I read last week in the trades that you was signing with Ziegfeld for the new Roof Garden, with the Keatons and Cantor. You and Joe Jackson an' Gertie Vanderbilt. Sounds plush."

"Plush is not the word for it," Fields rubs his proboscis thoughtfully, "we are rising to the manor born, Fink old boy. Farewell to the dust of the road, the ceaseless jog of the bogeys, the chain-gang bunks of the red-eye, the fetid sheets, putrescent goulash and Mrs Windleshmeer's bony shanks of Roach House... good riddance, and not a day too soon. And speaking of bony shanks, how are your own little darlins doing? All ship-shape and earning their hay?"

"Matilda was a tad under the weather last week, but she's all pepped up and chipper tonight."

"Just do me a favor eh, Finkie old chum—can you get those damn mules to crap right of stage for a change? My assistant is a sensitive little thing, poor girl, she doesn't take to the sheer vulgarity of the profession the way we old folks do. We did a show last month in Kansas City Missouri, with Chasen's Chimps. Those fellas shit straight from the high wire—poor girl got a dollop right in her left eye. I wasn't put out myself. I just potted the little turds into the left pocket of the table. But she didn't like it one bit."

That night in Columbus was a last stand for Bill Fields in the vauds. The Marx Brothers came on with their crazy patter and their guys-and-dolls mooching and dancing. The first scene was set in the Cunard docks in New York where Julius the Grouch, as old Schneider, comes off the gangway and is greeted by Leo in his fake Italian: "I would-a like to say-a goombye to your wife!" and Julius says: "Who wouldn't?" Milton played the straight man who dances a little, and Arthur comes on as the boob, shaking hands and rattling all the forks and spoons he has swiped on board out of his sleeve. Then he chases some dames around the stage. In the second scene, the "Villa on the Hudson," Arthur chased more dames, played "Waltz Me Around Again Willie" on the piano and then Leo played "Chopsticks" on the keys. Then Arthur chased the showgirls again. When the curtain came down the whole house was howling, and they had precious little left to give when it rose again on Fields and his billiard table. He did his usual crafty shtick with the twisted cue and the balls and then juggled his cigar boxes, most elegant, but only got a polite smattering. He took it one more night and quit, calling in the manager and telling him: "I've blown my wrist. I'll sue this house for malpractice. You'll never see my face here again." He didn't need it, since he had signed pretty solid with Ziegfeld, and never looked back. As they say, the rest is history...

Gramby's act closed the show. It's a bum listing, because if the punters are tired they just get up and go all through your best routines. Everybody except the Marx Brothers on that night had to keep to their ten or fifteen minutes. Gramby had to fight to get fifteen, in those early days. The act went well enough, Hetty and me got in and out of the cabinets without a hitch, and Gramby in his blindfold guessed some startling facts off a man in the back that we had paid two dollars to volunteer earlier in McDonagh's bar.

After the opening show, we all trudged out into Broad Street under slow-drifting snow. The city was covered in white, the tram tracks long disappeared, all of us floundering as we made our way to our hotels. Most of us were doubling or tripling up at O'Malley's, but Fields was putting up at the Chesapeake, in grander surroundings, with his new girl. I hear he was married once, and his wife was his sidekick, catching the balls that he pretended to drop in his juggling. But then they had a kid, and she wanted to give up, but he kept on the road and they separated, and sent each other letters filled with anger and frustration and rage. I sure hoped I wouldn't get like that, because I dreamed at night, I am afraid, of Zuleika, and what would happen if she had come with me, not with Gramby, though that was a dangerous thought in those days, and still is, as I recollect those days now. He never touched the New Girl, who was sharing a room with three of the Marx company girls, but I could feel, in the night, that we were strangely dreaming the same dream. He was upstairs of course, in a room of his own, and I was billeted downstairs with the negro boys, the bellhops, except I had their room for myself because they sat up with the Marxes, playing cards and gambling with Leo, who lost every cent to them but still slouched off happy. He was not called Chico then, but when I next came across them, they were already Groucho, Gummo, Harpo and so on.

It was a strange time. Not because so many strange things happened but because we didn't know, quite then, how strange things would become. January 1915. There was a war in Europe, I only knew that because Gramby told me, but, on the wheels, nobody took much note of it until four months later, when the penny dropped and the U-boats took down the *Lusitania*. We were playing the Colonial in Sacramento, and the manager stopped the show in the middle of our act to tell the crowd that news had just come over the wires about this ocean liner that had been sunk by the Germans off the coast of Ireland, with two thousand people on board. There was shock in the theater, and Gramby was struggling with the Girl trapped half in and half out of the wardrobe. The show went on, but there were no laughs left in the audience. Poor Herman Schmidt led his tame bear, Shorty, on the stage, but the audience growled and he led him back off again. Everybody went to bed without getting drunk. But back in Ohio we were still innocent yokels with no idea of the world off our stage.

"And it ain't a fit night out for man nor beast..." Fields' drawl fading as he struggled off through the drifts, heading for the bright lights of fame. As we headed the other way, the city grew quiet, and all you could hear was our labored breathing as we trudged along like a worn-down chain gang. The Keith circuit had an old slogan: "After breakfast—go to Keith's; after Keith'—go to bed!" It was a hard life, but folk like the Marx Brothers and Fields and

Fink, who was hard-headed as his mules, were obsessed—they loved the life and hated it, and moaned about it all the time, and cursed the managers and the agents and the booking office and the band that played out of tune and the cops that kept harassing the folks on the road and the hoteliers that kept peeking in the bathroom to make sure you didn't make off with the towels. But they kept at it, day by day, night by night, week in week out, like bedbugs in Pullman coaches.

I was not sure why Gramby took it. He was not one of nature's born entertainers, not by the tales he told me, sometimes, on long train rides, or nights, in his room, when he snuck me up to share a nip of the sauce. "A man should not drink alone," he said, both of us knowing so many who did, and did not last the course, though plenty of those who drank together went under. The grand model was Duffy and Sweeney: they were a nut act that knocked each other about and had an old Irish patter. Duffy would tell a stupid story while Sweeney dozed in a chair. Then Sweeney would wake up and slap Duffy in the face, then they would swing at each other, and start all over again. The story goes that they are both drinking in a bar when Sweeney keels over and falls stiff on the floor. Duffy just downs his next round, and comments to the barman: "I like a man who knows when to stop." As luck has it, it was Duffy who keeled over first, found dead in a doorway at the corner of Eighth Avenue and 42nd Street in New York. But that was a long time later. Gramby, like Fields, used to ration his drinking, so he wouldn't get the shakes when on stage.

"Mick and Rosa, they got me started," he would tell me, nights when he was in the mood. Or on the train, when we couldn't afford sleepers and I would come up from the black coach, on the pretext of sorting his clothes. "What a big country," he would say, "and no borders between the states. When there's a state line, you don't take no notice. Back in the old country, we couldn't travel more than fifty kilometers and we was in the Ukraine or Austria. Of course, you could cross there, but you would be stopped if they didn't like your accent, or if you spoke Russian or Moldovan.

Yiddish you got by in all the Jewish places. The Russians and the Austrians, they always wanted papers. Then if you got to Italy or France, you was free. One day, Ace, I will take you to Paris. You will not believe it. Color doesn't matter there. In show business it's free and easy. And people serve you in the cafés. You want to be served by a white flunky? Stick with me and it will all happen."

I never had a father, so I guess Gramby was it, though he liked to see himself as my big brother. He had three other brothers, he said. "One is God knows where, somewhere in Poland, he is older than me, my younger brother got caught in the czar's army, poor kid, and is fighting somewhere, or maybe, God willing, he got away. We pray that he is alive. My elder brother, he is safe, he is a big shot in California, he shoots the movies, you know, the flicks, with the camera. You must meet him. He has all sorts of crazy ideas, you never know. One minute he wants to save the world for the workers, the next he is in the nightclubs, with Mabel Normand. You know her? She is in the Keystones, with Fatty Arbuckle. You remember, he came to our show, in Denver, you remember, on the Pantages wheel... Very polite, moves as if he weighs nothing, you wouldn't think he kicks people in the bum and falls over and jumps across cliffs and so on. It's all illusions. The little magic box. We will get there one day, you will see."

One night, when he was not even hard on the rye, he got tearful about his sisters, who were left behind. The older one, Sarah, she was the eldest child of his father, who he once told me was the Wise Man of the village. A rabbi. He was "the ringmaster," Gramby said. When he cracked his whip, everybody danced to his tune. Sarah and the youngest child, Judit, were still in the Old Country. In the shtetl. According to Gramby, Sarah was married to a "son of a bitch." I think he said she had a child who died young. But maybe he was talking about Mick and Rosa. When he got dreamy, you were never quite clear where he was. I got the point that he had been soft for Rosa, but nothing happened. He once caught me tight round the ear, it wasn't vicious, he just really wanted me to listen: "The first rule in life," he said, "you never betray a friend. You hear me?"

"I hear you, Mister Gramby."

"You call me Vaz. You don't mister me. If I let you down, you can come in the night and cut my heart out, because it is no use to man or monkey. You get that?"

"I get it, Vaz."

"No, you don't. I don't mean that if I leave you in the cold one day because there ain't dough enough for a good spot for the two of us, or if I screw up with the cabinet, or if I shout at you and say, 'dumb black boy, I never met a clumsy bum like you in my life!' or I curse you, or kick you in the bum when you deserve. I mean if I really betray you. One day, when somebody does it to you, you will understand."

But then, when some people who talked like that from the booze might break down and bawl, he would fall asleep, as if there were some things you just had to wipe away. I think that's how he took the magic. You took all the things that screwed up your life, all the ugly stuff, and waved your hand, and there it was, flying out of your sleeve as a pigeon, or an endless flow of colored silk, or a dozen packs of cards all exploding with kings, queens, jacks, diamonds, and spades. That was how I got to be "Ace." My aunt, who raised me, if you could call it that, told me I had been named Assa, for Assa-El, "healer of the Lord." My dad, somebody else told me, because she wouldn't, was a preacher who scattered his seed among his female flock as if he alone was given the commandment to multiply and fill up the land. Then he skedaddled, and was never heard of since I was less than one-year-old.

I told this to Gramby, when I got to trust him, and he told me never to miss a negro prayer meeting, so that I might go and smell him out. "Use your nostrils," he said. "You will sniff your father on the coldest wind. This a man knows. As a son of a preacher myself, I know what it is like. There is an aura, you can almost taste the ectoplasm, there is something that stays long after death. But the ghost is already in the body long before the end. That is the real magic secret. In Yiddish we call this the 'dybbuk.'"

27

I didn't like the sound of the 'dybbuk,' but in any case I did not go to black revival meetings. I didn't want to meet my father, or see him, or smell his smell, or taste his taste. The only preacher meeting that I ever went to was of the famous lady, Aimee Semple McPherson, who came in a circus tent in Philadelphia and preached to ten thousand people all at one time. Because she was a woman, and I thought she had the real secret of life, like my aunt who had died when I was twelve, just before I lit out for the road. But then I was just a kid, and did not know how complicated life can really be. And she was talking about Jesus, who was a man, despite how holy he was. He was no use to me.

Next morning, in Columbus, the bellhops hopped early, tireder than me with all their gambling with Leo, who always let them win his pennies because he knew how little they earned, and I stayed under the sheets. It was like Christmas and New Year's to stay in bed rather than jerk around like a rag doll on the night train. After the first day, Gramby only needed to check his gear in the afternoon. But I would come up to his room just after a snatched breakfast with the cook, to fix up his costume and check all the secret pockets with the invisible props that had to appear when they were supposed to. He would sit at the table in his scarlet gown with his turban on, and the special cards—the magic pack, what they called the tarot. He played them in the magician's manner, spreading them out quickly, then disappearing them into thin air, then plucking them from whatever part took his fancy that day: the mouth, the ears, the groin, the armpits. This time he had just fanned out the first seven that turned up: the Wheel of Fortune, the Upended Man, the Tower Struck by Lightning, the Fool, the Hermit, the Lovers, and the Sun.

"The wheel," he says. "Not bad at all. A good start. Luck and positive energy. We can take heart from that. The Hanged Man, that is double-edged—transformation, perhaps for good or ill. Present sacrifices could bring benefits. The Tower inverted. Not a good sign. It could mean imprisonment, that sheriff from St. Louis may be close on our trail. Vot do you think, Ace? On the other hand, the Fool simply reminds us of who we are. A new beginning, the unexpected, an important decision. But here the Hermit counsels prudence. Ve need to be calm and stand back from our immediate circumstances. Then the sun is reversed. Trouble and strife, maybe a broken contract. Misjudgement, delayed happiness. Vot else is new? But the lovers are upright. Perhaps this is for you, Ace? Some kind of testing moment, vunce again a decision to be made between two paths."

He turns to me with that innocent look he has adopted in the last few months on the stage: a wide-eyed innocence that suggests all his powers derive from some other source. It is not me who makes things happen; I am just a channel for an outer power. I am a blank page. It is you, the audience, that writes the future on it, though you are ignorant of your own power. The aura that accompanies the Great Gramby, whatever else is packed in his trunk. Or maybe he was just trying on me the old hypnotist trick that he was always talking about, the one the Great Hermann had worked from Berlin to Brooklyn. At times like this, the illusion of age fell from him, and I could see that he was not much older than me.

"There's sausages for lunch," I told him, "the bellhops told me its today's special." Mrs Voskonsky, the cook, was an Old Russian Believer, she was planning a treat every day, and a meat pie on the twelfth of January, because it was the Old New Year's Eve.

Gramby passed his hands, and the pack vanished.

"Go to lunch, Ace. I'll grab something later."

He opened the inkpot, dipped the cracked nib, and started writing the first page. I think he was writing a journal of some kind. I never got quite sure. I myself could only read very slowly at that time. He had begun teaching me a few months before. "I need you to read the notices," he told me, "I don't want to read all that crap myself, but you can just tell me the headlines." I went down to the dining room. The players were already at the table, laying into the food as if it was their last supper, even without Christ. Fink called me over and piled a few wieners on a plate for me. Mrs O'Malley, who runs the show since Mr O'Malley upped and died of whatever he was for certain to die of, looks gimlet eyed at his transgression. To her, every mouthful the vaudevillians take seems like a bite from her soul.

When we leave the hotel, the white blanket shines under a beautiful and clean sky-blue day. The nags have drawn the snow-plows up the High Street and the trams are moving smoothly up and down the tracks, the dark coats of the city people like moving inkblots over the road. Gramby joins us, with the Girl, checking the pulleys and slides as ever before the first show of the day. The stalls are filled with parties of excited kids, in bright striped jackets under their little coats and furry hats, allowed off school for the day because their classrooms are too cold. They adore Fink's trained mules, who kick and dance and pretend to have breakfast around a table, reading the papers. They scream at the Marx Brothers, and want to eat Arthur alive. They snigger at Fields, because they don't understand that his mistakes with the balls and the cue are the act. It's the last straw for him, and he packs his bags. But they sit rapt and quiet as Gramby comes on in his white costume, the tasseled jacket and pants, the pure white turban with the gleaming red jewel. The limpid gaze, as if he's sleepwalking onto the stage. The magic silks fly around him like a flock of enchanted birds. The cabinets work like a dream. Hetty and me appear and disappear and then appear again without missing a cue. But I noticed that as he stood at the edge of the stage, the soles of his feet would rise, just a fraction, a bit higher at each performance, till he was almost on the tip of his toes, like a dancer, willing himself maybe to take off, to rise up and hover over the stage, just a millimeter, then another, then perhaps fly out over the audience, not by the invisible tricks of the trade but by an unexplainable flair.

After Bill Fields left, the porters carrying his billiard table, muttering and moaning, the manager gave us five more minutes for our act. Gramby sent me out to buy a brazier, and we practiced the Burning Money gag. The magician gives the Wild Boy Mowgli—that's me—a big wad of money and I burn it in the brazier. Then he pulls the bank notes out of my hair, my loincloth, the Girl's hair, and then he goes into the audience and pulls it from people's lapels and sleeves. It's all trick money, except the three genuine bills that he keeps palming and producing. Then there is a beautiful one-thousand-dollar bill that was made up by a rogue printer in Boston who was so tempted by the job that he started producing for real and was sent up to the Big House for five to twenty. Gramby plants a sheriff in the audience who climbs on the stage and insists on examining the note, jangling a large pair of handcuffs the while. Then Gramby makes it disappear into his ear. It gets a great laugh, but a real sheriff got on the stage once in Baltimore and made a fuss, so we dropped the cash-burning act for a while.

So we carried on, from Columbus to Cleveland, Toledo, Detroit, Chicago. Chugging on by the train from Madison to St. Paul, then doubling back to Springfield, then on to St. Louis and Kansas. We went south to Oklahoma City, Dallas and Austin, where the audience is all rednecks with huge hats who are ready to cheer you to the sky when they like the act and burn down the theater if they don't. Then we went up through El Paso to Albuquerque and way up to Denver, where we caught the Western Pacific to Sacramento. We shared the stage with so many acts they all come in a blur: Burns and Acker, the Moneta Five, the Cowboy Minstrels, Boganny's Bakers, Mae West and Deiro the Accordionist, the Keatons, whose act was now starring the boy, Buster, because his Dad was too boozed up to get on the stage. All the Chinese acts, Irish acts, Dutch acts, horse and mule acts, monkey acts, dog acts, Spatz's Cats and Rats, the Skating Bear, Singer's Midgets, the Fridkowskys, Herschell Hendler, Martell's Manikins, who told the future, Captain Spaulding—"the man who was hotter than Vesuvius"—he was my favorite, he ate live coals and belched fire out of his mouth and his ass at the same time. There were so many acts and so many venues those days you could spend a couple of years touring and not play the same theater twice. Edging closer and closer to the West Coast. After Sacramento and the *Lusitania* news we were low for one night, but the show went on as we reached the coast at San Francisco. The next few days' newspapers were full of angry headlines talking about "Mad Dogs of Europe," "Prussian Savages Drunk with Blood," "Vengeance" and "War." People were beginning to be afraid that America would be sucked into the European battlefields, in which soldiers were dying like flies. Gramby was white enough without his makeup. It was difficult for us to enjoy the city, which had risen up from the Great Earthquake only nine years ago. People told us how the whole city had burned down. Fink told us that he had been caught in the middle and rounded up for corvée labor, pulling out the dead from the ruins. But all I saw was busy crowds in the streets, saloons busting with action, and whooping audiences filling the aisles.

Gramby could have booked for another week, but he was eager to go on south. At our hotel on Turk the reception had sent up a letter that arrived for him on the fourth day. He didn't show it to me but sent me to the station to book tickets for three on the afternoon train to Los Angeles after our last night at the Orpheum on Market. The Gross brothers would join us later when we began our booking at the L.A. Colonial a few days later, while they earned a week's pay with the Fridkowskys. But he wanted Hetty and me to go with him.

I become so used to traveling on the train that I forgot the wonderful sights that you could see out the windows, though these were pretty poky in the black carriages. The trips were so long I took to playing Chinese checkers in the baggage car with the Girl. It was a nice embossed set, with all the little china tiles, that Gramby had got from one of the Manhattan Comedy Four, I'm not sure if it was from the Irishman, the Italian or the Jew. This passed the night, and in the morning we went to check out the windows and saw the shadow of the train play on the valley, and the sun hitting the mountain range to the west. Pretty soon we were getting closer and closer to the ridges, and then, from San Luis Obispo, the train pulled up into the hills, all the way to Santa Barbara. Gramby joined us to peek out at the Pacific breakers rolling in to smash against the shore. "As far as we can go, Ace," he said to me with a kind of regret, an admission of limitations. "The next land from here is Japan. Then China. One day, Ace, who knows, one day..."

We got off the train together at Santa Barbara for the stop, me carrying his bag, so we could sit on the bench together. Hetty went off to get some hot dogs. He brought out the letter. It was written in a writing I couldn't understand at all. It looked like magic squiggles.

"Cyrillic," he said. "It's from my brother, Boris. It's in Russian writing. He calls himself Bill here. William. We called him Berl, or Boris. We have three different names, each one of us. One for us, one for the gentiles, one that's new. Here in America, we all use the new. We must all be magicians, making our own story. You will have to do the same thing. You are from here, you are from there, everyone sees you and thinks they know you. But only you know yourself. This is the best magic. You will become an expert."

I was excited, because I was going to meet Gramby's brother and hear all his Hollywood tales. The man who carried with him the whiff of real freedom to make his own dreams. The friend of Fatty Arbuckle, and Mabel Normand, and Pickford, and the new clown, Charlie Chaplin, and all the Mack Sennett crazies. The Keystone Kops, who couldn't even arrest themselves, I loved them. All the people who ran about in the mountains, fell off cliffs, raced in motor cars, flew in daredevil aerial contraptions, kicked each other in the ass and hit each other over the head with mallets, or rode up the Rocky Mountains on noble steeds, meeting the Indians. We had seen some Indians riding the trains, keeping mighty silent, but the only Indians we got to talk to in the shows turned out to be Greeks, Italians or Jews.

We rode the rest of the trip in anticipation, hanging out the windows till the conductor sent Hetty back to the white coach and me to the crowded negro carriage. I dozed off and missed the whistle blowing for the Union Station till the porters came, and I scrambled up to rejoin my boss.

I found him with Hetty, just off the steps of the carriage, as the crowd surged around, the porters passing down the baggage, people greeting their friends or relations off the coaches, shouting, yelling, kissing and bawling. He was holding the hand of a tough-looking, sturdy man who looked about thirty years old, with a good jacket and watch chain and a new brown fedora, a brown face burned in the sun. Gramby turned to me, and I hurried up for his bag, but he took me by the arm and pulled me up to present me.

"Ace, I want you to meet my brother. Boris, this is Ace, who sees everything whether he admits it or not."

"Ace," he said, "that's fine. I'm glad to meet you. Welcome to Los Angeles." He held out his hand to me, which was a little strange, since we were still in America, not in Paris. But I took it gladly. It was a firm handshake, very un-Gramby like, certain and hard. I looked up at them both, but they looked very different. At first-sight you wouldn't think they were kin, just two strangers who had met up for some mutual business, as people did in these great new cities of the nation that was always moving on, always ready to perform its own miracles, blazing new trails. But they talked, suddenly, in that strange language, which I had of course heard on the road, because here, in the new world, everybody was a stranger of some kind, with their own story of what they had been before. And I saw that the way they stood was very similar, legs firmly planted, a bit splayed, as if they were neither of them sure that the ground would hold them properly, or that they could keep their perch on the world. And I saw the look between them, one that kindled a memory of another place that had been forgotten but was conjured out of the air between them as soon as their eyes met in the crowd…

*

"Stormy clouds delirious straying..."

Boris:

Of our mother, I remember her hands, which were always soft, though I am sure they were hard from all the kneading and cooking and scrubbing that had to be done before my sister, Sarah, was big enough to take over these women's duties, and I remember two smells: a strong whiff of boiled soap, and the tshulent, of which I can picture the pot, bubbling on the hard black stove. But of our father, I still keep the abiding image of the Face—huge and encompassing, in the summer gold and large as the sun, in the winter like an immense full moon, pitted with craters and strange valleys, but also covered in forests, the great black foliage of his gargantuan beard. And even well into adulthood, I could never look at the full moon without imagining these woods concealing its lower half, and the black skullcap that crowned the top.

He was always present, always hovering over me, although I recall from the more advanced, today we would call them adolescent years, that he was always busy, up in his room, the library, where he took refuge and received no visitors, and even my mother only entered when absolutely necessary, either on command or special request. It was a dark place, where my father sat at his immense desk, or so it looked to me, looming up as one pattered softly in, and illumination came from a set of tapering candles, at night, or, in daytime, especially in the summer, a shaft of light that pierced through from the rather small window, much like the Rembrandt painting "The Scholar Reading," I believe it's called. (DeMille called his silent movie technique "Rembrandt lighting," after the head office complained that only part of the actors' faces were lit in some of the early films, and the audience would only want to pay half the money, but after he made up the term they said, Oh, that's all right, for Rembrandt they'll pay double; so the legend goes, but in fact I had remembered my father when we set up those flickering scenes.)

I remember the house as large and all encompassing, but it was probably small and narrow. My father needed his larger room on the second floor because he kept not only his books there but several cabinets which held documents and deeds and family records that were entrusted to him by the town's residents. They had the only locks in the village, apart from the lock I once saw on Golomb the butcher's secret box, where he probably kept his ill-gotten gains from bribery and dirty dealings over improperly cer-tified meat, and where we boys were convinced he kept shrunken heads of animals or even humans on which he experimented in the dead of night, since even we imbibed the legends the gentile children heard from their parents about the secret blood rituals of the Jews. Other people thought my father kept under lock and key the prayer shawl and whiskers of the sainted Ba'al Shem Tov, the Master of the Good Name, the founder of the ecstatic movement, which his own grandfather had personally shaved from the saint's chin as he took his last breaths before passing to the Next World. My father had several keys tied to his belt, which jangled as he walked. My sister Sarah said that they were the keys to the Garden of Eden, but that was in her own early ecstatic phase, before her brief marriage to Zonenshein, the Soroki rabbi's son.

The ground floor was the Material World, the world of mundane life, noise, mess, joys, suffering, shouting, cooking, eating, fighting, discord, friendship, love. There was the kitchen with the grand samovar and oven, full of clanging pots and ladles and steam, the adjacent room with the large table where we ate, learned, performed all the rituals of Sabbath and the holy days, and the two small rooms, one for the girls, Sarah and baby Judit, when she arrived, but which Mother often slept in when the rabbi was involved with matters of the spirit and business upstairs, and the "prison dormitory," the boys' room, where we slept on bunks, Zev and I on the bottom bunks as the seniors, while the kids, Nathan-Kolya and Yakov, dangled their bare smelly feet at us from above and cluttered our lives. It was no wonder that we dreamed of the fields, and what lay beyond them over the river, beyond the forest, over in the forbidden lands.

Our house was the center of the village, as the main rabbi's abode, although there were two other rabbis officiating at either end of the town, west and east. The next house to the east was the butcher, though there was a patch of field between us where we kept the chickens and our horse, Dimitri, the pampered member of our household; he was supposed to pull the cart but preferred lying about dreaming in the hay. Occasionally he would give us rides, when he felt like it.

The house to our west was the cobbler's, Kotik's, and the strong smells of leather and saddler's soap wafted from one side to mingle with the butcher's odors from the other. Only after the cobbler's house was the bet midrash, the town's main building, which doubled as the prayer house and school. The synagogue was on the ground floor and the children's school, or *heider* ("room"), was on a kind of mezzanine. Zev and I, as the eldest, called it the Dungeon, as the scriptures were drummed into us there by the voice and cane of the third town rabbi, Druk, whom we called the Knout. We had our own small, putative revolutionary cell, which we called the Novembrists, as the anti-czarist Decembrists was already taken. We cut our hands and mingled our blood in an oath to end his tyranny as soon as possible, break up and burn his knout and tie him to the "Baba Yaga tree" whose strange occult branches loomed over the river bend at the western end of the town.

People do not understand this, but ours was an agricultural town. It was not the dark, destitute, Caligari-like setting of the legendary shtetl but a bright, sunny outpost of one of the more successful reforms of the czar's own policies of the late nineteenth century, carried out by the zemstvo, the local government set up by Alexander the Second, the "liberator" and emancipator of serfs. The policy was aimed at encouraging the Jews who were not wanted in the main urban centers of the empire to live in rural communities, sponsoring agricultural colonies, with grants of land and proper supplies of farming implements, livestock and feed. Celovest, our home town, was formed I think sometime in the late 1870s, just before Czar Alexander was assassinated by the Narodnaya Volya, the "people's will" movement, which had been trying to shoot or blow up the czar for years. That was, I believe, in 1881, but my father did not arrive in the village until 1888, some time after the first great pogroms that followed the czar's killing had abated but displaced large numbers of Jews from Kiev and Odessa and many smaller Ukrainian communities. He came from a small genuine shtetl near Vinnitsa, with his wife, Hanna, and the first baby, Sarah, who was just one year old. I was the first child born to them in the village. It seems he was called there when the local rabbi, whose name I can't remember, died, after serving the town since its foundation.

Some migrants from Bessarabia in New York once sent me a draft of studies they had put together about our province's Jewish communities. They had found old census figures of the villages between Soroki and the major center of Belz, north of Kishinev. In our own village, the count, at the turn of the century, was 3,215 souls, of whom only three were goyim: the Shabbos goy and jack-of-all-trades Mihai, the customs officer and the policeman, of whom I recall only his formidable moustache. The rest were all Jews, of whom about 300 families were farmers and the rest various tradespeople and artisans. We had, apparently, 165 horses, 320 chickens, 54 goats and 35 carts in 1898. And their own memories were full of vaguely recalled characters such as Itsik-Shmerl the conjuring tailor, whom I suppose may well have influenced Yakov, Mottel the blacksmith, Chayim the janitor, Tsvantsig the goldsmith and Moishe Rosenberg, the town's richest merchant, who appointed himself chairman of the town's Revolutionary Committee the day after the 1917 revolution. But by that date I had long flown the coop.

My mother was of a mystical bent, and she would often croon

over the cooking pots, passing her hands over the chicken wings and muttering strange incantations that were partly in Yiddish, part Russian, and part some invention of her own. She had dealings of her own in her "shopping," buying stuff from the peasant women who went around the towns on the Christian festive days, and Zev and I would spy on her huddling with the Moldavian women and their baskets. We imagined she was part of some intensely forbidden and dangerous witches' cult that was in direct contact with the Baba Yaga and other ancient peasant spirits, and drifted away at night, when the rest of us and our father were asleep, on broomsticks, to the Romanian mountains west of Bukovina, where the devil often visited after his Sunday dinners with the Emperor Franz Joseph in Vienna. But we dared not speak out about this, in case word reached our father, who would banish her back to the Ukraine or conduct an exorcism that would extract her "dybbuk" and leave her crippled and blind. When we initiated our younger brother, Yakov, into our deadly secret, he took the whole thing much too seriously and bawled in his sleep for two weeks, till we had to tell him we had made it all up, swearing an oath on the Torah. But we both felt swearing this false oath contaminated our own souls, causing a complete rift from our faith and leaving us open to the forces of apostasy and evil, which we began to relish.

In fact, my parents were both devout adherents of a miracle-working rabbi, the savant of Sadagura, Rabbi Israel Friedman, whose father, Rabbi Abraham Jacob of Ruzhin, had established a dynasty in the small town of Sadagura, north of Cernowicz, then in the Austrian Empire, which had thousands of followers and was the most influential rabbinical "court" of the age. The rabbi's followers built a vast mansion in the small town and endowed themselves with luxuries, riding about town in richly furnished carts, dressed in pure white robes, but the rabbi himself lived in small room behind the synagogue, from which he rarely emerged, speaking to his followers in whispers, praying with intense inward devotion, groaning and bending like the bough of an immensely ancient tree. Or so my father described him to me, for he had been in his presence once, and was touched by an almost blinding white light that emanated from the rabbi's soul, which he could only liken to a divine embryo that could only grow to adulthood when all evil was cleansed from the world. He promised us that on our fifteenth birthdays, two years clear of our bar mitzvahs, he would take us on a pilgrimage to the rabbi's court. But, in the event, when I was fifteen, other matters interfered.

When I was fourteen, just after my birthday, evil was manifest in our region in the most palpable manner. We had just celebrated the Passover, and the Christian Easter was due some days later, when news came through of a terrible pogrom against the Jews in Kishinev, which was the central city of our province. The pretext was a classical "ritual murder," which had supposedly been enacted on a young Christian boy, who was found dead in a field. The rumor spread that his blood had been taken for the Jewish matzos. A couple of years before I might have tried taking a dab of my brother Zev's blood to sprinkle in the mix, to test this out, but now that I was formally a Man, I had to take things more seriously. The Russians had apparently sent some doctors from Odessa who exhumed the boy and certified that the body had no open wound. But on Easter Sunday, after the night-long Saturday prayers in the Orthodox churches, a great gang of Christians spread through the city and attacked the Jewish houses, smashing windows, breaking in and looting. When the local police stood by and did nothing, the gangs became more bold, and returned to the same houses with axes and knives. Terrible barbarities were carried out and several dozen people massacred.

The entire area was up in arms. In every Jewish village, including ours, the people gathered to discuss defending themselves against attacks, and meetings were held of the young bloods, the seventeen- and eighteen-year-olds, who were not interested in supplications to the authorities. We had good relations with the Moldavians around us, or so we thought, often too good, in the view of the parents of the boys who hid in the river rushes to watch the Moldavian maidens pass by on their feast days, with their loose white blouses, flowers in their hair, and singing, or worse, the girls who stood quietly at their windows, looking at the peasant boys. There was one tavern in the town, a den of fearful vice, according to my father, where the two communities sometimes met, and where vodka battled with religion. But Zev and I could only peek in the window.

That was my first direct encounter with Leibel Grossman. Grossman was the senior town blacksmith, and Leibel was his eldest, a strapping lad who could wield the hammer as well as his father and would perform feats of strength on Purim, when he dressed up, or rather undressed, as Samson, and wrestled with chains. He said there was a famous Jew from America who had performed in Berlin, who could break out of chains and locks and handcuffs with enormous ease. He had a magazine which Yudik the Traveler had brought back from Germany with a photograph of the near-naked man, his muscles bulging, breaking the chains with his chest. He had an Italian name: Houdini, but everyone knew he was a Jew. Of course I didn't believe that. The only strong Jews were those who had a license to perform goy-like feats, by reason of their professions. The rest of us just had to scrabble along, mumbling our daily prayers. Leibel wanted me to go with him into the tavern, but I knew my father and my mother were both dangerous sorcerers, who manufactured chains rather than broke them, so I cried off, and in any case, Zev was too small and was with me every minute of the day.

After Kishinev, Leibel organized the village defense forces. I was roped in, as by that time I was ready for service, and to test the parental chains. Two boys came up from the city, who were members of an illegal group that they called the Yiddische Bund. They deployed not only clubs and axes but guns, pistols that they obtained from other revolutionaries. We met on the riverside, in a secret meeting, where they displayed their weapons. They told us the Jews could not fight the Christian pogromists on our own. We had to think beyond our village, beyond our region and the province. This was the first time the word "revolutsya" was

41

uttered in our tiny speck of land. They said there were great matters brewing, great deeds that were about to be done, far from our shtetl, in Moscow, St. Petersburg, Kiev and Odessa. This was a glorious enterprise that would unite all working people, not only throughout Russia but the world. Workers were rising in Poland, in the Austrian empire, in Vienna, Berlin, Paris, London, waving aloft red banners of proletarian freedom. Two Jews called Karl Marx and Friedrich Engels had written massive books, longer than the Bible, in which they analyzed the secret workings of the world of capital and classes, and predicted the risings that would sweep away the old world of empires, of poverty and exploitation and would make all men brothers, and all women sisters, in the great explosion that would smash all fetters and chains. There would be no divisions between rich and poor or Jew and Christian; all could worship freely or, even better, delve deeper into the commonality of man. I was not sure what this meant, but I had an inkling, which a glance from Leibel endorsed, that this led to a fundamental break from the world of my father and his eternal, unchanging, unchangeable path.

As an immediate first step, we drilled in military formation, with sticks and staves, up and down the riverside and across the bridge and through the main street of the town, up to the cobbler's house, within sight of ours, and back again. The peasant boys sat around on their carts and looked at us, waving and laughing. It must have been just after the Easter Monday. Either no news had reached them of the Kishinev pogrom or they just didn't care. At every Easter, the goyim would ride through the village, shouting out "Christ is Risen! Christ is Risen!" But we would merely shrug, or nod, or ignore them, or mutter, in the old saw from Sholem Aleichem: "So I heard, from Berl Isaac!" And they would just ride on. When they got drunk, we just stayed at home, and my father would read from the midrash. Live and let live.

No one attacked our village. But Leibel went off to the city, leaving his younger brother Mottel with the hammers and horseshoes, and did not come back till eight months later, in the harsh winter, when the snow-covered the fields and houses, leaving us huddled in our rooms, wrapped in our own thoughts and dreams. One day at *rosh hodesh*, the new month, he rapped on the window of our boys' room, and summoned me out into the drifts. We trudged down to the storehouse behind his father's workshop, where they kept the old wheels and carts.

He had a rucksack with him, from which he took out several books as well as a number of pamphlets adorned with flags and symbols, with exhortations in larger print to uprisings and protests against oppressive laws, the pogroms, and the czar himself. These appeared to be more dangerous than the pistols we had been shown before, and I devoured them avidly, shivering among the cartwheels. But he was more keen that I should read the books that he insisted I should read, which were fresh editions of his favorite Russian authors.

"You must know your country," he said. "Celovest is nothing, just a hole in the ground. We are just maggots, Jewish maggots, goyish maggots, looking for a corpse to eat. This is life. Feed your heart and mind."

On my father's shelf there were books. Some were old, with scuffed covers and crinkled pages, some were relatively newly printed, with beautiful binders and titles that appeared of glittering gold; all were volumes of holy writings: the five encased copies of the Humash, the Five Books of Moses, the volumes of the Torah, Prophets and Scribes, the many volumes of the Mishnah and Talmud, the Shulchan Aruch and other later commentaries, and some volumes that he had on the top shelf that my mother once told me were of the Zohar and other more "difficult" texts. But they were all of the Holy Tongue, with the relevant commentaries of the Talmud; none were in the vernacular, the jargon or Yiddish, and only one, a book of accounting, was in the Russian language. We were, of course, taught the Russian, in the lyceum school that convened in the meeting hall behind the bet midrash, and which was mandated by the rural zemstvo legislature. Presiding over this was

Rabbi Barenboim, and my sister Sarah's husband, Zonnenshein, until his untimely death from a chronic lung infection, though he too was a rabbi's son. The town's elders were careful to entrust our secular education to the devout, although there was talk among the merchants of opening a Higher School, a technicum, at some future date. This was after all, they said, the twentieth century, and even in czarist Russia there were universities, and new mercantile possibilities, and modern factories, and trains, which one day would reach our village, and motor cars, which we had never seen.

In the school there was a library, or rather, a small cabinet of books, which were mostly textbooks, though there was a set of volumes by Count Tolstoy. The compact four volumes of the masterpiece, *Voyna i mir—War and Peace*—sat there, waiting for our minds to ripen enough to even desire to open up the pages. But we were too young, we were told, to experience the world. It was a world enough in our father's house, the world of our own spiritual treasures.

Leibel's knapsack contained other treasures that opened up the universe. These were the books, he said, which contained the full bloom of the human mind. There was Mikhail Lermontov, *Geroy nashego vremeni—A Hero of Our Time*. There was a slim volume of Pushkin, poetry, so well thumbed by Leibel there were food stains on most pages. There was Turgenev's *Virgin Soil*, which he said was his Bible and would explain to me more than any other example the realities and challenges of our times. There was a book by Fyodor Dostoevsky, whom I remember my father mentioning once as the devil incarnate, an extreme anti-Semite who proselytized for the Orthodox church while spreading poison about sons who murdered their father in cold blood. Leibel's volume was called *Crime and Punishment*, and also featured murder.

I had, before this cascade of treasures, only opened one secular book, miraculously written in the holy tongue but totally profane. My sister Sarah owned it, and kept it secretly among her feminine garments. It was called *Ahavat Tsion—The Love of Zion*—and it was by an author called Abraham Mapu who wrote in Hebrew about ancient Israel at the time of the prophet Isaiah. She said it was the most beautiful telling of the tale of our origins. I found it to be romantic and boring, but then I was just thirteen. Nevertheless, I kept her secret from our father, who forbade this kind of literature in our home. But by fifteen, in 1904, I was ready for Pushkin:

> "I have lived to see desire vanish,
> With hope I slowly came to part,
> And I am left with anguish only,
> The fruit of emptiness at heart..."

Who did I desire? Wherefrom my anguish? What was the hope? I had no idea, but I felt it keenly. Bodily stirrings, down by the river, as the shiksas bent down in the fields, baring their soft brown arms. There were hints of this in the classroom, but the only remedies that were proposed were contemplation of holy matters, the sayings of Rabbi Akiva or the Ba'al Shem, or thoughts of purity of soul, along with regular bathing, but not in solitude. My brother Zev sometimes complained: "You're moving your leg all night again. I can't sleep." You'll be moving your own leg pretty soon, I thought. But the feeling that I was becoming an idiot, about to sprout with suppurating sores and buboes, and expire before I even reached the age of sixteen became stronger and stronger, until Leibel brought me Lermontov and the poet:

> "He is blessed who lives in peace, and distant
> From the ignorant fools who call,
> Who provide his every instant
> With dreams or labours or recall..."

I particularly warmed to the "Goblins of the Steppes":

> "Stormy clouds delirious straying,
> Showers of snowflakes whirling white,
> And the pale moonbeams waning
> Sad the heavens, sad the night!
> Cloudward course the evil spirits,
> In unceasing phantom bands,

As their moaning and their wailing
Grip my heart with icy hands!"

I longed to be with Lermontov's hero, Pechorin, the young officer of
loose morals who wandered about the mountains of the Caucasus,
fighting with demonic Chechens and Cossacks, bedding their
women, seducing and abandoning rich princesses, fighting duels
and drinking through the night. I longed to be him. I would gladly
have abandoned my home, my family, my faith and my mother's
tshulent for one night on the slopes of Gud Mountain, in a Cossack
"stanitsa," baying at the full moon. I was convinced I was born to
be a Rumanian werewolf, of the kind my mother sometimes told
tales of, as a reason we were not born as goys.

I was dying to fornicate, but I did not quite realize it at the
time, and it was only by Leibel's rebellious example that I ever got
to the forbidden fruits, the red apples of the Tree of Knowledge,
which had caused the fall of mankind. I suppose he was my
serpent, but I loved him, he was the elder brother I never had.
Eventually I met Dostoevsky's Raskolnikovs, and his nihilist demons and tormented parricides, who dreamed of slaughtering the
father czar.

Leibel left after a few days, leaving me alone with the books
that I stored under my bed, in a pact with Zev that he would keep
my secret as long as I read Pechorin's adventures to him nightly.
By then Yakov was ten years old and another pair of ears, while
Kolya was only eight, and immersed in his initiation into the
Talmud at the *heider*. Judit was a tot of four, physically attached to
our mother, while Sarah came in and out to help with the chores.
Zonnenshein was ill, and would die a year later. Sarah had not
become pregnant by him. Father was, as fathers were, restless for
an heir and began looking at me with a new frown, which did not
bode well. Twice I caught my parents huddling with the matchmaker, Zeidel, a typical hag with a glass eye and a strange whistle
when she walked, which seemed to emanate from her backside.
Luckily, in midwinter, it was hard to tell the girls from the boys;

everyone moved around like a heavily wrapped package, and my mother vetoed most of her neighbors' daughters as either mentally deficient or not high-born enough for her Bereleh. I knew she was my secret supporter, since I knew she knew we read in the night. My other confidante was Sarah, to whom I lent both Pushkin and Lermontov. I had no idea how far they would send both her and Zev.

In the summer I know my father sent a message to another rabbi down the road, in the next village of Markolest, who was said to have a healthy daughter. But she was still just fourteen. In the old days they might have married her off two years earlier, but I was saved by modernity. At the new year of 5664—still in 1904—my father told me he expected an engagement by the next summer. The matchmaker was drinking tea in the kitchen. I resolved to waylay her in an alleyway on some dark night and dispatch her with the woodcutter's ax, but she eluded me. I could sense my days were numbered.

But four months later, in January or February of 1905, Leibel appeared again, looking somehow much older, with his hair grown down to his shoulders and a wild look in his eye. He told me stunning news, which had not yet been written about even in the *Bessarabian Gazette*. There had been an astonishing incident, thousands of miles away, in Saint Petersburg, which heralded the end of the czar. Hundreds of thousands of workers had marched on a Sunday towards the Winter Palace, bearing a petition for a new constitution. An orthodox priest headed their procession, to emphasize its peaceful intent. The police gendarmes however fired on the crowd and then charged on their horses, cutting down men, women and children with sabers. The main streets of the city were bathed in blood, and it was said that thousands had perished. A general strike broke out the next day throughout the city and strikes spread to Moscow and other cities. Everywhere in Russia the masses were in turmoil. The czar was said to be quaking in fear in his palace. The masses had lost their fear of the police. Revolution was nigh, and spreading south. Pretty soon, it would be on our doorstep.

I looked around and nothing was happening. The cartwheels had gathered frost instead of dust in the blacksmith's storehouse. Outside, wheel-less carts were covered in snow. There was no sound, except the occasional shuffle and cough of someone who had to step out for a quick errand between the houses. From the storeroom, I could see the top story of my house, with the chimney belching out the smoke from the kitchen oven. I told Leibel my father was planning to marry me to the rabbi's daughter of Markolest, who was of a respectable lineage, albeit one that did not seem to trace any further back than the usual Ukrainian boondocks. He told me to come with him to Odessa and took out three new pamphlets—freshly printed revolutionary protests. They were so fresh I could actually smell the newsprint, even in the cold, but what caught my eye was not by the words but the pictures, which immediately altered my world.

They were cartoons, garish caricatures, printed in bright colors that I had never seen or imagined before. One depicted the czar as a hyena, baring his jagged, blood-stained teeth over a stream of corpses floating in a blood-red lake. Another showed Death, with his scythe, in gendarme uniform, cutting down a seething mass of people. There was a huge dragon-like beast with the face of the crown minister, Count Witte, slavering over the body of a half-dressed woman labeled "Mother Russia." I felt as if my head had come off and was floating, with popping eyes, over a landscape that reverberated with my most secret dreams.

"There is a group of students in Odessa," he said. "They were in the Bund but have now joined the General Social-Revolutionary Action Committee. We are going to publish our own journal. It will be called "Bayonet." The whole city will soon be rising. Will you come with me?"

We went to Odessa. We couldn't go before Passover because late snowstorms blew in from the steppes, burying the roads under six-foot drifts and isolating the villages. We joined the able-bodied men, young and old, and even women, who spent weeks chopping firewood, pulling carts of goods whenever possible from Floresti and Belz. Leibel fumed, but there was no news coming through of any place closer than Soroki. Someone had heard from Kishinev that things were quiet there, which was all the news the Jews of our province ever wanted to hear. But when Passover came the sky cleared, and the temperatures began to lift. I told my father I was called to the Black Sea port by representatives of the Bund who had to organize self-defense squads in the provinces when the unrest that even my father had now heard of spread to our areas. We had our first argument. He told me I was the man of the house and had my obligations where I stood. I told him that if I was a man now, at sixteen, I would stand where I chose. I could see the woe in his eyes, as he realized this was too late to start beating his children when he had never done so before. My sister Sarah told him I had to go, and, as my mother had begun to shrink from her mythological frame slowly into her manifold woes, he had taken to relying on my sister, and felt guilty that his famous foresight had not included a foreknowledge of her young husband's ill health. He went up to his books. I told Zev he was the man now. His bar mitzvah was due later that year. I promised to be back to celebrate it. I took Turgenev and Raskolnikov and some supplies for the road.

This was a long journey in those days. Where are we now? We take taxi-cabs to the airport and can climb on board massive steel-winged machines with gigantic engines that power us from state to state in less time than we would take to reach Belzi, forty-five kilometers down the road, let alone Kishinev, 100 more to the south. There was a train that reached Kishinev from the Austrian border, which is today Rumania, and from which one could go further east, south to Bucharest, or to Belgrade, or even Budapest and Vienna, as I later found out. But Bessarabia, Bessarabia... Caught between two giants: The Russian Empire to the east, the Austrians to the west. Czar Nikolai and Franz Joseph. Different kinds of moustaches. Everybody who wanted to display authority had to have one in those days, from emperors to policemen, sprouting out from the nostrils like bristling eagles' wings.

It took us two weeks to reach Odessa, crossing the Dniester at Tighina. It was a radiant day. The great river rippled in the sunlight, evergreen forests shimmering on either side. Two Bundist comrades in Kishinev had joined us, Ivan and Irina. She was my ideal come alive, black-eyed and determined. I floated in my dream. We rode in carts of hay towards the big city. The fields gave way to huts, the huts to houses and smallholdings, the houses to streets, and then suddenly the wheels clattered on the unforgettable sounds of cobblestones, and the harsh clanging in the morning of the trams ringing their bells.

Odessa! The wide boulevards, the majestic buildings with their white columns and golden pediments, the great squares of the Palace of Justice, the city cathedral, the gleaming onion domes of the Panteleimon church, the monument of the Empress Catherine, the Opera House, the Radetzky monument, the parks, the Gardens of Arcadia, the bustling central station and the grandeur of the harbors: the Praktinya, the Androsovski, the Kharantina, the great quays jutting out into the deep blue waters, huge crowds surging across the railway lines towards the vast iron ships that docked and sailed, chugging and hooting, off across the Black Sea to the Crimea or, so much farther, towards the straits of the Bosphorus to head out towards the Mediterranean or even the Far East. Soldiers climbed in endless tramping rows up gangplanks to head to the far reaches of Siberia to replace those who had been decimated in the Russian-Japanese War, those reluctant servants of the czar whose bones lay so far from their home soil, in Manchuria, a place I could hardly begin to imagine.

The big city! At the time, it hardly occurred to me that there might be bigger cities elsewhere in Russia, or further off, I could only imagine that Paris, Berlin, Bucharest or Vienna must be much like this. Give or take the port. Everything within it seemed to preen and spread its feathers like an imperial peacock: I am here! it cried out, I am grace, I am beauty, I am nobility incarnate! But at the same time it was a city teeming with injustice, and unrest, and trouble. A mixture of Russians, Ukrainians, Jews, Greeks, Italians, Germans, Poles, Armenians, Tatars. Out of its half million inhabitants, less than half were Russians and Ukrainians, and nearly a third were Jews, more than a hundred thousand. Here were some of the most advanced people in our community, teachers, professors, writers, scholars, engineers, artisans, scientists. It was only when I was here that I heard their names, from all the smart young students around me, among whom I felt like an awkward, mawkish hick, a country idiot with straw in my ears: Asher Ginzberg, who was Ahad Ha'am—"one of the people"—Shlomo Yakov Abramovich, who was the great Yiddish writer Mendele Mocher Sforim—"Mendele the Bookseller"—the poet Bialik, and all sorts of people who were already household names, except in my household, where only one name could be held up for notice, apart from the Sadagura rebbe, whom I was now fated to never set eyes upon.

In later years, people asked me about this, but I told them I met none of those persons, some of whom were dead before I got there, others who had gone elsewhere, and yet others, who were not of our circle. For the first time, I was not among Jews only, but hurled about in a great vortex of talk and action, among Bundists, social revolutionaries, Social Democrats, constitutionalists, anarchists, even Zionists, of whom there were already a few, indistinguishable from the rest. I felt lost. The black-eyed temptress was whirled away from me immediately. I had to read more. I had to do more. I had to wear spectacles, even if there was nothing wrong with my eyesight. I had to grow my hair even longer. I had to grow a beard, urgently. I had to spit in the street and curse like a peasant. I had to distinguish between the Bolsheviks—majoritarians, and the Mensheviks—the minoritarians. They all looked and sounded alike to me, but they had apparently split only the year before at some party congress in Belgium. I had no idea where Belgium was, and was too ashamed to ask anyone whether it was in Hungary or in Rumania.

The Bundists congregated in an apartment on the second

floor of a building in the Yelabetskaya street, off the main Preobrazenskaya, not far from the central station. There was a bakery downstairs, which doubled as an armory, as the proprietor, whose name I can't remember, was an old Ukrainian narodnik who hated Jews but hated the czar even more. He was willing to keep pistols for the "young comrades," as long as they promised to only shoot gendarmes. "Aim at the uniform, not the man," he said. Which made no sense, but kept him happy, along with the vodka.

There was a certain air, a buzz, a hum that you were certain you could hear, communicating from one person to another, a look that passed between like minds, who were legion, massed in protests, or just rapidly passing in the street with hurried glances, or in the trams, on the bridges, even on the park benches. It was the dress that marked you out: anything that was poor, awkward, not quite properly fitting, ragged, threadbare, with a button hanging off, or a frayed belt, patches on the elbows, a cloth cap. Except for the Tatars; you could never tell if they were bourgeois or proletarian. But you felt that the streets were emptying of those who walked with a more dandyish air, with a neat waistcoat, a gleaming watch fob, perfectly pressed pantaloons, shiny shoes or spats, a cane or top hat, not to speak of an overcoat in the evenings. Women twirling umbrellas, leaning on the arm of a well-turned-out Lieutenant of the Guards, would be shown home early so that their beaus could report for night duty and prepare for the unknown of the next day.

Something was going to happen. There were daily reports of strikes, riots, arrests, killings, massacres, in different parts of the empire. Here at last I could be told what had been happening since that day in January when the priest Gapon led the masses of Saint Petersburg into the hellfire of the Winter Palace guards. In Kazan, police had shot a hundred students. In Baku, in the Caucasus, there had been a strange massacre of Christians by Cossacks. In the Russian villages, peasant women left their hearths to demonstrate with their husbands and sons. And Jews were everywhere in peril, shot down, bludgeoned and murdered by the Black Hundreds, the bloodthirsty assassins organized by landowners and clergy, armed by the police and spreading terror wherever the spirit of resistance and revolution stirred.

What could I do? How could I contribute? In the village, I had dreamt so often of vengeance, of burning Reb Tsunts, the teacher, of cutting off the head of the matchmaker, of emulating Raskolnikov for the sheer villainy of the deed. But when they put a pistol in my hand, I trembled and handed it back. "What does he do?" asked the leader, "Grisha" Gershon, a palefaced youth with warts but an air of utter certainty. Leibel Grossman answered, "He draws pictures."

It was true. I had begun scribbling in a school notebook to while away the hours we spent in the blacksmith's storeroom while the snow flowed down outside on the village and Leibel was hogging his well-thumbed copy of Karamazov. If God is dead, nothing is forbidden. Even graven images, mercy upon us... I was leafing through Leibel's uncanny pamphlets and fitting the various monsters to our local faces—the teacher, the cobbler, the butcher, the town gossip Finkel, and so forth. I even put my own father's face on a lion that signified the Homeland aroused, but I tore that quickly out and scattered it in tiny shreds in the snow. One must not blaspheme too close to home. But I was learning how to use lines, and shading, and foregrounds and backgrounds, and how to make characters lunge forcefully forward off the two-dimensional drawing towards your eyes.

And so I went down to the basement of another building, on a workshop street the other side of the station, to join the writers and printers, who were preparing the new youth journal of the resistance movement, the Zarevo, or "dawn." (There were several other journals of that name, I should point out, the most famous being that of Moscow, which did not publish till the following year.) Unlike the more famous ones, we did not have color blocks, and had to make do with black ink. I adopted the image of the czar as a hydra, with his tentacles crushing cities and people from Moscow to Warsaw, Samara to Kursk, Nizhni, Yekaterinburg and

Kiev. In one of my cover drawings there was a small side tentacle that stretched forth to a smudge of faces in the shape of Bessarabia and a tiny dot of a village house that was just out of reach—our own; but nobody noticed the allusion. They liked the idea that the czar's moustaches became snakes that were devouring young women, although the editor, a young Armenian, Gatom, suggested that the victims should be naked, to increase the shock value and circulation at the same time.

He clapped me on the shoulder. He knew, without my having to confess to him, that I had never seen the naked body of a woman, if one discounted a very brief glimpse of my mother getting into the tub when the door to my parents' quarters was not properly closed. Of course I averted my eyes quickly, lest I risked the much more blasphemous prospect of seeing my own father unrobed, the sin for which Noah's sons were cursed. Many years later, when I looked up at the ceiling of the chapel in Rome where Michelangelo had painted that very scene, I inadvertently shuddered, my father's teachings flooded back to me suddenly like the depicted deluge. I was fixed to the spot, gazing upward, while something within me was urging my feet to unglue and run away from the sacrilege. But back in Odessa, there was nothing to inspire me in the required direction, although Gatom did take me to the Museum of Art, which contained many works of the Russian and Ukrainian artists, such as Levitsky, Kiprensky, Repin, many beautiful landscapes and portraits of nobles and peasants, but not much skin apart from fleshy cheeks and noses or the occasional buxom maiden's arm. There was no choice, Gatom declared, but to get me a sitter, a model such as those of Western painters, or the art schools in Saint Petersburg or Moscow, where young or not-so-young girls were paid to sit or pose for the students as they made their first etchings of human anatomy in the raw. It was a perfectly chaste and proper performance, he said, laughing at my evident regret.

Perhaps, I imagined, the sitter might be the black-eyed girl of my long hay ride, but she was instead a somewhat shy Ukrainian blonde girl, somewhat more spindly than the living icons of my

Bessarabian fantasies singing out in the summer wheat fields. She was herself a student of fine arts at the Odessa University, a very serious girl, a social revolutionary, Tanya, who shook my hand before disrobing quite casually and sitting on a bare chair in front of me in the basement kitchen, where I set up my sketching pad and pens, willing the blood to rush to my head instead of elsewhere. She sat quietly, reading Trotsky's leaflet on the All-National Insurrection as the Culmination of the Struggle of the People over their Age-old Foe, which had just been printed in Kiev, while I sketched her thigh lines and torso and edged in towards her breasts. These I had to augment and fill out using one of the more lush Saint Petersburg covers of Count Witte as a vampire pecking the corpse of a fallen virgin as a guide. When I showed her the result she laughed and gave me a strong pinch on the cheek that made it stay red for nearly an hour.

She ran into me the next day, at the printing works, and invited me out for a walk in the Alexandrovsky park, which was nearby and had a fine terrace restaurant featuring some relatively cheap pirozhki enjoyed in a delicate landscape of chestnut trees and ornate benches. It was a place of rest, where one might imagine that indeed nothing was happening in the fine city of Catherine the Great's historical victory over the Turks, who had ruled here for two hundred years.

We ate the pirozhki and drank tea, and walked down the wide gravel paths and sat on the benches in the sun, close together but not quite touching. I could not look at her in her student cap and uniform without seeing the fair form underneath, so I looked ahead, at the rotunda of the restaurant. She asked me if I had met Trotsky or Lenin, the real leaders of the revolution that was now as inevitable as the blazing summer that follows the spring. I said that I had only met some local leaders, who flitted about, and only knew Gatom, and Leibel, and mostly the Bundists, who had their own organization. But she said I should read Leon Trotsky's leaflets, which were full of fire and certainty, and full of calls for city-wide "soviets" that would work with the peasant organizations to unite to form the grand Constituent Assembly, which would, with the aid of the mutinous common soldiers, force the czar out of power. While the peasants were not yet ready for socialism, the unquenchable force of the people united would fuse the rural and urban proletariats into a single social-democratic army that could accomplish the final task. She told me that Trotsky was also a Ukrainian, born not far off in Kherson province, and that he had been exiled in Siberia and had escaped to Europe and London. He was also, like me, a Jew, called Bronstein. She said that if I was to play my own part in the revolution I would have to choose my own name. She suggested Satirik ("satirist"). But that was far too bold.

Apart from all other problems, I had not told her that I had just turned sixteen, whereas she was at least eighteen. I had managed to fake a more mature appearance by aping Leibel's aggressive posture and the way he walked confidently down the streets of the city as if he was a genuine Kosmopolit. A man of the world. I began smoking cigarettes without coughing. They made me sick but I persevered. I began drinking coffee, which was available in a couple of Moorish-style places along the Preobrazhenskaya. One day in early June I put my arm around Tanya's shoulders in the park. I could not imagine a greater thrill, even storming the gates of the czar's own palace would not have brought me that lift, the sudden flush of blood to the heart. She put her blonde head upon my shoulder for a brief while, then laughed and sat up.

"Are you prepared to die for the people?" she asked.

"I am."

I would have said anything to have her put her head again in the crook of my shoulder but it wasn't an entirely idle boast. The hum of like minds binding in the crowd that flowed in ever-increasing marches and demonstrations was becoming more intense, and news continued to come in of more strikes and more repression spreading from town to town. I was spending more and more of my time in basements, as Gatom found me a way to earn my daily bread at the printing works where larger brochures and journals and even books were printed, so that I learned the rudiments of the trade, a sweaty tussle with the chunks of metal endlessly to be rearranged in their blocks amid the overwhelming smell of printers' ink, something I could never quite scrub off but Tanya pretended to endure gladly—the smell of honest labor, she declared, but not quite nuzzling up to me as closely. The printers, however, were often out on the streets themselves, among the militants. But the revolutionaries were not the only ones marching. Ukrainian nationalists also paraded their own flags and icons, and even supporters of the czar marched, with young boys carrying aloft the portraits of Nikolai and his czarina. The streets themselves seemed to be on the move, the cobbles stirring to many thousands of footfalls, even as the "normal" life of the city still somehow continued in daylight; the trams passed each other over the arched bridges, people still walked their children and dogs on a Sunday, pirozhkis were still served in the parks.

On one Saturday evening in May, Gatom, Tanya and I and a couple of the other students took a night off from the printing to go to a special picture show at the municipal theater on the Alexandrovskaya place, where an enterprising engineer called Leizer Popov had brought a projecting box and a few reels of "kinematographs" that had arrived by ship from Paris via Constantinople, at the other end of the Black Sea. The theater was packed because there was said to be a reel of film depicting the war between Russia and Japan, which was still raging in the Far East. But the day of the showing, we were told when we arrived, the police had entered the theater and impounded the reel, though they had left three other moving pictures, after unspooling them on the floor and examining the tiny rectangular frames. One half of the theater started shouting "Down with the police!" and calling for an immediate march on the police headquarters, but the other half shouted "Show us the films!"

I remember two of the three reels vividly. One was a fast-paced Italian comedy showing a cook pelting his customers with spaghetti, raising happy laughs, but the other two were like lightning bolts inside one's brain. The French film was a fantastical tale, half drawn and half acted, about a group of scientists who fly in a rocket ship to the moon, where they encounter a strange race of creatures and barely escape back to Earth with their lives. It was colored, by a magical process we couldn't imagine, in garish yellows, reds and blues, and held the audience completely spellbound. The second picture was merely black and white, but American, and portrayed a gang robbing a train. At the end of the picture, the bandit's face loomed hugely on the entire screen as he pointed his gun at the audience. Several women screamed, and some men pulled their own guns, firing at the screen, upending the seats and setting off a fight between the groups of revolutionaries, nationalists and monarchists, who were luckily separated by red-armbanded stewards of the Bund, who were attending the show en masse. We all scattered out of the theater before the police could arrive and begin smashing skulls right and left.

I don't remember if there was a piano player, as we were so entranced by the pictures: Méliès' *Voyage dans la Lune,* and Edwin Porter's *Great Train Robbery...* the miracles of a new age of change, speed and unleashed imagination... Ten years later I met Ed Porter in Hollywood. He was working for Adolph Zukor's Famous Players Film Company, but nobody wanted a veteran in those days, it was all go for the young pioneers. Maybe it doesn't pay to be too smart too early, you have to be lucky at the right moment. He soon left to set up his own manufacturing company, making and selling the motion picture projectors. The Simplex, that was his speciality. A smoother flow through the spindles and gears. Some great yarns though, of the old days. I told him I first saw his famous picture in Odessa, during the 1905 revolution, but we didn't know when we were speaking then that within a couple of years there would be another, the one that actually worked. Méliès I never met. He made hundreds of those trick films but lost his title to them. Somehow he was totally forgotten and screwed. His films were pulped, and I think he ended up running a toy shop at the Montparnasse station.

Honor after death—I never saw the point of it. In fact, I didn't want to die for the people at all. I wanted to live, to live, goddammit! To see the underdog triumph, and a fair world rise up on the rubble of the putrefied old. But as things got hot in Odessa, I came to believe it was there that I would see my own end. The gendarmes became more violent in suppressing demonstrations and began firing on the crowds. One night all work was stopped at the printers' and we staggered out into an ominous dawn, a sheen like the artificial hand-coloring of Méliès spread over the funnels of the ships docked at the port. Tanya found me in the crowd and told me that at Ivanovo the women textile workers had marched on strike and the troops had fired on them without discrimination, killing both women and children. All male and female workers were coming out in the city. Odessa was in full-fledged revolution.

People often asked me what it was like. They wanted to know the inside story. Was it like the posters, sturdy toilers and sailors rearing up, with the red flag, bearing the vignettes of Marx and Lenin? Were you on the ship? What did you think would happen? And most of all, Were you on the steps??

DeMille asked me that when we went together to the first screening in Los Angeles of the famous *Battleship Potemkin*. Who more than DeMille knew the stunning power of the Image unfurled, the kingdom of fantasy, the Story, the moment, the Big Lie...?

But it was all true. Or most of it. There was a red dawn, at which, as people gathered, there was that strange feeling of newness, something different in the very air. It was mid-June, and hot, but with the morning smell of the sea. The sailors, however, were still on their ships. They had committees, which had sent delegations, but they were still under military discipline. It was war time. There were rumors, rather than news, that the entire Russian fleet had been sunk off the Manchurian coast, but no one knew if this was true or not. Such as it is, there was a great sadness for the sailors, and all the soldiers, workers' and peasants' sons, who went off to the other end of the Earth to fight for the czar's Siberian dreams. It was all very far away.

The city was elevated above the docks. Separated from the city by the railway line were four great wharfs that carried cargo on and off, and were still running, I think, on the day of the muster. Our attention was concentrated on the factory workers who had poured out, filling the grand boulevards. Because of the shootings, more and more of the young men were armed. Rebellious soldiers had supplied us with rifles. But there was, we knew, an army of shock troops waiting, armed and disciplined, Russians and Cossacks, who had no concern for the Ukrainians and even less for Jews. The Bund was very active, but they could not defend the Jews locally, since we were spread through the city.

As one might expect, everyone had their own militias. The social revolutionaries already had divisions, though whether they were "left" and "right" or clusters around certain leaders was unclear. I had to stand with the Bund. I looked for Tanya, but I could not see her on that first day. She would have been with the students.

There was no great waving of flags. That was for demonstrations, not fighting. Everyone knew what had to be done. There was never any picture of Lenin or Stalin or Trotsky or even Marx on our flags. That all came later. None of us knew who Stalin was. I never saw Trotsky, but he was one of us, only twenty-six years old, I think, then.

If you "move with the people" it is quite different. You are not led. You simply move, like one organism, in the same direction. If you stopped to think what direction that should be, you would be lost, and the organism would fall apart. You just moved. We flowed towards the City Hall on the Primorsky boulevard, which runs along the cliff top just above the port. There were two rows of guards lined up outside but they were local lads so we just let them alone on that day. There didn't seem to be anyone inside the building but we left it alone. We gathered above the steps then, which led down to the Praktikskaya dock. Some cargo vessels were there, but no battleships. We held a meeting at the statue at the top of the stairs and heard speeches. Then we moved back towards the city center. There was no shooting that first day.

I was assigned to the unit that was tasked with feeding the strikers who were allied with the Bund, mainly from the garment trade. People brought food from home but we had to open a supply line to the peasants who came in from the villages with supplies. The markets were still working. That took up much of my time. We slept on bags in the streets and central squares, ready to defend the city if and when the Cossacks marched in. Down below the cliff, army detachments were still guarding the port. On the third day, we crossed paths with the students and I met up with Tanya. I thought she would be glowing with enthusiasm but she was somber. She knew so much more than I did about the world, about her country, she had read so much, she had her great surges of enthusiasm, then she would fall back into pensiveness about the difficulties that lay ahead. Even on a balmy summer night, it's not easy to keep up the rush of enthusiasm that hurled you first into the streets. All the talk about being willing to die echoed differently when you thought that this choice might come in the next few hours. I wanted to make love to her and I think she might have wanted to as well but there was nowhere it could be done. We couldn't sneak off back to the printing works or the bakery or her apartment, where several dozen students were living in five or six rooms. Her own home was in the country, to the east, where she had parents who were probably praying to icons every second of the day.

So we sat up all night and talked. We talked about the revolution and the possibilities of a New Life and a freedom neither of us could define. We only knew that we wanted it, in whatever form it might appear. We were ready for surprises and wanted a life in which one woke up every morning to an unknowable future, one that was full of challenge and adventure. She wanted to travel all over the world and see Moscow and Saint Petersburg and Vienna and Berlin and Paris and London. She wanted to go to Spain, of which she had seen pictures as a small child and had developed a fantasy of being the first woman bullfighter, though she might be sorry for the bull. The bull was magnificent nature in the raw, a force that could only be vanquished in body but not in spirit. She seemed to have had a childhood full of fantasy animals and places, which were brought to her by an uncle who had traveled in

Europe and the Far East. He had pictures of white Siberian tigers and Indian elephants and a bear from China that was black and white and soft as silk. She was achingly sad for the sailors and soldiers dying in Manchuria and said the greatest work of the revolution was to abolish war between nations. This could only be accomplished by a world government that would be created when the working class rose up in all the advanced nations, as Marx himself had predicted. I had never read a word of Marx but happily agreed. As the night wore on I felt as if we were an old couple who had been together for more than thirty years, and fantasized about us sitting on the porch of our dacha, in the summer moonlight, overlooking the Dniester, with a horse munching hay in the stable. She wanted to know my story but somehow I could not tell it, so I made up a tale in which my father was a merchant's agent who had traveled a lot to Bukovina and Galicia but not much further afield, a man always bent over his books and concerned with money and daily matters; I could not explain to her that my father was a Jewish priest. But she said one's parents were one's parents, we could not escape our families but we had a duty to construct the new world, even if the separation was painful. She had two brothers and a sister and I told her about my Zev, and Sarah, whose husband had died of the typhus, and about little Vassily, who cried when we tried to exorcise our mother of her belief in spirits and demons. Our parents, she said, were of the old world, and she knew how difficult it would be for them to adjust to the new.

We fell asleep, or rather dozed on each other's shoulders and in the first rays of morning her comrades came and called her away. There was talk of the troops moving in towards the university and everyone was being called to man the barricades. I ached to go with her, but my Bundist friends were all about me. We said we would meet in the same place the next night if we could, but we didn't. My group had to rush off towards a Jewish area which had been attacked by some thugs in the night, and there were rumors that armed gangs of the Black Hundreds were ready to launch a pogrom to divide the city's nationalities and start internal fights. For the next two nights we sat in vigil at the entrance to courtyards, but the thugs stayed away.

On the third day, in the morning, Gatom came running with vital news from the factories that everyone was going on strike. The masses had grown so vast in the streets that the few leaders with any authority, moral or otherwise, were losing their grip on the situation and there were riots in several places as people were running out of patience and some wanted to rush the army and the port, and seize control of the city. The pot had boiled over and no one was in control. At the same time, it was rumored that there had been mutinies on several ships of the Black Sea fleet, which were sailing from their port in Sebastopol, in the Crimea, towards Odessa.

Historians pieced together the story later, but when you are in the thick of events you have no idea what is going on. DeMille asked me about it: the rotting meat, the ship's doctor glaring at the swarm of maggots, proclaiming the meat is all fit, the sailor's sudden defiance, the threatened shooting of the mutineers. That was just a movie C.B., I told him. Who the hell knows the truth? We only knew the story that went around, that the crew had mutinied and taken over one of the battleships, the *Potemkin*, which had sailed into the harbor. Everybody started going down to the port to see the red flag flying on the mast. I went down with a crowd of young people and students and we all stood on the wharf cheering the ship, which loomed with its massive twin funnels and cannons like a friendly monster that had suddenly materialized out of our most vivid dreams. We gathered at the top of the nine or ten flights of steps and flowed down them to the dock. There were no soldiers or guards that we could see at that moment. The sailors stood on the deck and astride the cannons and cheered and waved back at us, but they still stayed on board. A delegation was huddled on the wharf with several of our own Social Democrat leaders and delegates from other factions. I looked for Tanya but could not see her. There were about a thousand Tanyas in the crowd, all waving handkerchiefs and cheering. Then the crowds parted as the sailors brought the body of the shot sailor off the ship. Most of the crowd crossed themselves, except the Bundists, and then they sang the "Marseillaise." "The Internationale" was already known then, but nobody knew the Russian words. Or perhaps my own memory is muddled. Even Eisenstein couldn't mythologize that, as his movie, twenty years later, was silent.

It seemed, for a moment, for a few hours, that we held the New World in the palm of our hands, but we could not all be Boris and Tanya, holding hands under the stars and telling each other our dreams. Someone has to stand up and say: "This is what happens next." But, as one looks back, it is clear that our mulling about the cliffs above the docks simply allowed the troops and the Cossacks time to march in to the city center, down the Preobrazhenskaya and ride the railway carriages directly into the port. Some of the students ran up to say the poorer people from the Moldavanka, the plebeian part of the town, were looting the warehouses. Rumors began to spread that martial law had been declared. But we were preoccupied with the grand theater of the slain sailor's funeral, wrapped in the red flag. What was it like? What was it like? Moods change in an instant. One minute, elation, the next, bewilderment, then panic. A great mass of people running down the boulevard, crashing into the funeral procession like a human wedge, pushing thousands back against each other, old people falling, children lost underfoot. Shouting and wailing. Then the gunfire, like a string of firecrackers spreading out and echoing off the white facades and ornate balconies of the elegant imperial buildings. Sudden screams, and the heavy angry shouting of the invaders, and the clattering hooves of horses, and a bellowed, jeering chant, followed by more screams and total confusion. My group of Bundists, with a youth called Itsik Mandel seizing some kind of command, pulled back out of the crowd to find a vantage point along a crossroad, those with guns pulling them out and looking for the source of gunfire. There were five or six of us, two with rifles. I had nothing but an iron bar dropped by someone who had been prepared at some stage and then lost his wits.

This is what I saw: A woman with a shawl, running, in her hands some kind of package, not a child, but probably a wrapped loaf of bread. Scrabbling for it, she fell under the boots of running men. I pushed through the throng and dragged her out. She was some kind of middle-aged Armenian or Greek, and she simply clapped me on the arm and ran off without her bread. Two young boys, probably twelve or thirteen, with schoolboy caps, ran forward between the legs of the withdrawing crowd, waving two children's catapults. I saw them climb up the ledge of a shop and perch above the fleeing heads. One of them let fly with his slingshot, in what direction or at whom who could tell. I saw a group of young men and some girls, running up with rifles ready, waving to us but cutting past the crowd towards the direction of fire. Then I saw them for the first time: the Cossacks, some with their fur shako hats, some with army caps, pressing forward on horses, slashing with sabers. Itsik Mandel aimed his rifle. But the crowd was pushing him back. He fired, but I don't know at what. He ran ahead and we tried to follow, but the crowd pressed the rest of us back. We became separated. I never saw him again.

I seemed strangely paralyzed, unable to run forward or backward, but the other comrades grabbed me and we ran back along the less crowded street. They knew an alleyway that cut through the houses and would come out the other side of the Cossacks, where we could join up with Itsik or find a vantage point and shoot. I didn't know if they had any bullets. The whole affair was too sudden for logic. It was as if we had been preparing for several months for something we never expected to happen. We foresaw it, but only in words, speeches, pamphlets, slogans, cartoons. It was all very well to draw an image of the czar's demons, wielding the knout on a symbol. Facing it in real life was quite different.

We never made the alleyway, because the crowd was pressing in all directions, pushing us back to the port. But as we ran back there, a sudden set of thunderous claps rang out with deafening force, and explosions sounded inside the city. Smoke billowed out and suddenly fires were raging.

The *Potemkin* had fired on the city. What they were trying to do, it turned out later, was to fire on the troops, or the police head-quarters, despite having no idea where it was. We were all running around like chickens in a burning hencoop. I have no idea what took place on the steps. When DeMille asked me about Eisenstein, I said it was impressive, but not in line with the facts. First of all, the soldiers would have been coming up, not going down the steps, because they would have been dropped off by the trains. Everyone had left the steps to march with the funeral. In any case, what was that woman doing there with the pram? It was a revolution, goddammit, not a Sunday outing. But he just laughed and said "Calm down, Boris. It's only a movie." The up and the down. The clashing lines of force—the diagonal bayonets of the soldiers and the horizontal lines of the steps. After all, art is also reality.

Later we heard that hundreds, maybe thousands of people were shot in those three days. I don't know. That night was full of fires. We had one practical thing that we planned for: When in doubt, fall back to the bakery. Leibel was ther. He grabbed my arm immediately and told me we had to go to the south quarter because the Black Hundreds were attacking the Jews. To confuse the revolutionaries, and prevent the Ukrainian nationalists from joining in, they had been spreading rumors and handing out leaflets for days, saying the Jews were responsible for everything that was happening and wanted to ruin both the Ukraine and Russia for financial gain. God help us, they might have printed the leaflets in our own printing house, in the intervals between our own shifts. We gathered a band of about twenty Bundists and found our way around the burning streets and the running crowds towards the most heavily populated Jewish district, where the road was already littered with broken furniture thrown out of the houses, broken glass with blood on the shards, torn prayer books and praying shawls, men and women's clothes, children's shoes. There was a body in the street, a woman in a black dress, whose headscarf had come off and her white hair was bloody against the cobblestones. She was dead, having clearly been thrown out of the window of the second or the third story. A man came out of the house, and another followed. Two hulking brutes, in military boots over baggy pantaloons, black bearded and shaggy haired, with thick noses and fleshy, vodka-soaked faces. The first had an army saber that was glistening with freshly shed blood. This time, Leibel had supplied me with a gun, a large and heavy machine pistol. The two other lads with me had the same. All four of us lifted our guns and blazed away at the murderers like the Western bandit in the American film. I am sure I emptied the clip, which would have been five bullets. The man's face exploded like a shattered watermelon. The other lads fired on at the bodies. We ran inside, but there was nobody left alive in that house. Three men, two women and four children, one of them just a babe in a cot.

On the other hand, perhaps I just dreamed it. I could not have been there, at that time, at that moment, in the hub of those great events that were to me just a bewildering whirlpool of pictures, acrid smells, terrible sounds. The camera grinds on from shot to shot. If one is flawed, it can be retaken. One need never be satisfied with second best. In the early days, even for a DeMille picture, stock was precious, and one only needed to print those takes that might be used in the rough, if not the final cut. Maybe I was sleeping the entire time in my father's house, in my childhood cot, that had been replaced by the longer bed that was still too short for me two years after my bar mitzvah, and left my feet dangling over as I moved my leg, keeping my poor kid brothers awake. "Berel, you're shaking your leg all night." It's not all that is shaking, my brother.

I had to leave the city. Leibel pulled, dragged, carried me bodily out while the fires still raged all around us. The rebellion was crushed. A putrid smell spread through the city like sulphur seeping from the pit of hell. I cried, I shouted "I want to kill them all!" Or something like that. I had lost control of my muscles, I stumbled everywhere and my hands were trembling, my head wobbling, my eyes saw only a blur. Leibel and two others, there was a girl there, but I don't remember her name—some Feibel, or

Greta? Neither blonde Tanya nor the black-eyed temptress with whom we had entered. They carried me onto a cart and we hid in a hay pile as some bearded peasant creaked out to the fields in the dawn. The army was still busy in the city. They were not concerned with comrades escaping; they had as many corpses they could cater for. As in the Paris commune, they had no need to sift the loyalists from their enemies. Everyone who looked poor was a target. Jew, Christian, Social Democrat, nationalist or any of those of no affiliation whatsoever who were just caught in the open.

In the morning, the countryside was quiet. The rich wheat fields seemed to be awaiting summer harvest with the eagerness of life unblemished by the human disease. Some women were in the fields with their sickles, and some carts rumbled by as if nothing was happening elsewhere, down the road, where new worlds were dreamed.

I was in a fever and could not stop retching, trying to drive the horrible stink from my lungs and breathe in the soft balm of the hay. Leibel and the other three cradled me like a child, which I suppose I still was, or had been, till the last three months. I could see the guilt in his eyes for plucking me away from the comforts and ignorance of my home.

We crossed the countryside west as we had traveled east, by the local roads, bumping over rutted pathways almost invisible in the lush fields. North, south, east and west, the land seemed never ending, flat and gorgeous, with the clear blue sky slowly dispelling the pall of the murdered city. *Der heim*. Our ancestral land. Not, as some people try to tell us, some distant biblical past that we dreamed of, not Zion, but the old village. This is the landscape we dream of, which my sister Sarah, in her own trancelike voyage fifteen years later, thought we could implant into Palestine.

We crossed the river at another point, near Talmasc, with barge haulers dragging our boat up against the current like the serfs of Repin's famous old painting. Then we walked, due west, to Kavshan, and then, on a local Jewish blacksmith's wagon, to Tsimishilie. We brought the news of Odessa with us like a black cloud, spreading it north to Kishinev, where the local Bund took us in. But I could not remain in this renewed atmosphere of rushing students, shouting, declaiming, planning imaginary expeditions, erecting barricades for a repeat of the massacre two years before... Home! Home!

It was late July, I think, when we rode up, Leibel and I, in the cart from Belzy, down the familiar main road into our town. I was recovered by then, but was a different person from the frenzied and rather idiotic youth who had rushed off towards an unknown paradise. Like an Adam who had found his Eve, but lost her. There were too many serpents, and certainly not enough apples to go around. She was seared into my mind, and I would see her in every one of the blondes who marched by in summer convoys, with their hoes over their shoulders, singing the Moldavian songs. As I watched, I always imagined that one of them turned to me and threw me a familiar glance, just to tease, and then gave a shrill laugh and moved on.

My mother stood at the door of the house with Sarah, Zev, Yakov and Kolya, who was already nine, and little Judit, the five-year-old. A whole family, can you believe it? They had been told we were on our way. I was gathered in, like a misplaced sheep. My father was in his study. I went up, gingerly, step by creaking step. Oddly enough, his great bulk had shrunk. Where I remembered a giant sitting at his desk, with a massive back like the Greek Atlas who held up the world, there was just an old man, with a beard more than half gray, the black skullcap pasted to his thinning hair, tired eyes and a trembling lip. I was not surprised that he did not recognize me. I was much thinner, and I stood differently, in a more defiant mode, I thought. I had not grown a beard, but there was a fuzz on my upper lip and round my chin that I could noticeably feel. I sensed that there were many things he wanted to say to me, but he just shrugged and pulled up one of his books, the standard siddur, or prayer book, which he carried with him every day to the bet midrash and was as well thumbed as any volume that could be imagined.

"Na," he said. "At least the boy comes back before Tisha B'av."

My father had the knack of saying many things in one moment. He did not like to waste words. There were enough words in the holy books to last any Jew as many lifetimes as Methuselah, and beyond, from the beginning of time till its end. We could observe the day of fasting and mourning for the fall of our Temple, one thousand and eight hundred years ago. I did not tell him that I had another temple to mourn, and that the smoke of its burning was still in my nostrils. But I knew then that my homecoming could only be temporary, and that the scalding fire would come closer, and that this house, which had been my refuge, was only a tent on my own journey, which had hardly begun.

"I've gone this far, I might as well go through with it."—Julius Marx

Ace Harrington's Vaudeville story continued:

Gramby was booked for two weeks in Los Angeles in the summer of 1915, but his brother persuaded him to take a break from the tour so he could try out a role in the movies. The director, DeMille, was always busy, and was preparing to shoot an extravagant picture, based on a French opera, that was set in Spain and featured gypsies, bandits and bullfights. He had just shot a picture set in New York, on the Tenderloin, about poor people trying to fight poverty and crime in the slums. He had already shot movies that were set on the frontier, on Indian reservations, in the frozen North, in the south of France, in Virginia during the Civil War, in Bulgaria and in the Arabian sands. He was everywhere and nowhere, because they were all made on the Lasky ranch, which was just up a way on the Hollywood Hills outside the city. Boris told his brother he was going to pitch DeMille a picture based on a magician who escapes from Russia during the war.

We hung on for a while, staying in a house Boris had rented at Silver Lake, up near Edendale, where Mack Sennett had his comedy studio. It was a very pretty country, and the roads wound like lazy snakes up hills that were so steep you could toboggan down on a board. Boris had a car, a new Model T Ford, which was powerful as six horses but still couldn't make it more than halfway up the hill, so we had to leave it and climb up a huge flight of steps from the next ridge down. From the top we could look out over the hills that led to Griffith Park, where most studios shot their Western movies.

Still, Gramby needed to work, and he didn't fancy hanging around with the novices hoping to take twenty-five bucks a week tumbling and clowning at the Sennett works, so while the director toiled away at his preparations for the saga *Carmen*, we moved out to a hotel downtown, walking distance from the Orpheum. There was a vacancy in the midsummer rotation and we got another week with the act. By the luck of the draw, the Marx Brothers had hit town at the same time, and we all met up again. Their show was funny as ever, and they never ran out of energy, so we joined them most nights in Groucho's room for an all-night pinochle game. The Gross brothers were rooming with a German twin act just down the road, and Hetty was taken in by a dog act, the Polonskys, whose ma traveled with them and took in strays.

I could get into any room in the hotel by wearing my bellhop uniform, so I would join Gramby and the boys for the card game. I was on their roster since I showed them a whole load of card tricks Gramby taught me that even Julius—Groucho—didn't know. Gramby sat cross-legged on the floor like a Turk and pretended I had learned it all by myself.

The brothers were just as wild as they had been in Ohio. Artie was doing something he shouldn't with a black maid who worked at the hotel, and when he heard we were going to work in the pictures he said she had told him that *The Clansman* was still playing in the city. This was the picture that had been the sensation of the country for five months, but since we had all been on the road continuously since January none of us had seen it. It seemed there was a big scandal, because the black groups had said it was an insult to every colored American and should be banned. As it happened, we had a break coming up on Sunday, as the Orpheum was booked for a special one-day sheriffs convention, so Artie suggested we could all go out together and see what all the fuss was about.

It was funny that Artie talked so much, when later, as Harpo, he would be known as the one who never speaks. But he was a real gab in those days. Julius and Leo, who would be Chico, talked just as much, but Milton (Gummo) was pretty quiet. They had a little brother, Herbert, who would be Zeppo, who wanted to come on the stage with them but was only fourteen at the time, just about my own age.

The problem was, if we wanted to see the picture with the chambermaid, and with me, we couldn't go to the white show, which I think was still playing at that time in the giant Clune's Auditorium, but had to go down Central Avenue to 20th Street, to the Rosebud, a black movie house that was showing the movie despite the ruckus, because every sensation made money. The best solution—Artie had it all figured out—as for the brothers to black up and turn up as negroes. They had done it before, apparently, in Chicago, to get into a blacks-only card game, which ended, for some reason that was never explained, in Leo playing the piano for six nights in a brothel on the South Side. He couldn't get the color off for two weeks, he claimed, and had to join Lew Dockstader's minstrel show for the season.

The brothers were like that; they tossed their stories about between themselves like dodgeballs, each one taking over where the other left off. The only exception was Milton, the serious one, who tried to concentrate on the game. He cried off the blacking and said he would stay at home and read a good book. Gramby also cried shy. I think he was not sure at all about the whole idea of the movies, despite his brother and DeMille. All he wanted to do, I'm sure, was to be around his big brother for a while and find that missing link that I always felt he was grappling for on the stage when he pulled invisible pigeons from hats.

We played the rest of the week to happy audiences, and even got the brothers into our act, the only time on stage that this took place, with Gramby putting me in the cabinet and Julius, practicing his blackface, coming out of it. It got a big laugh, but nobody seemed to recognize Groucho so we were all set for Sunday. It was a warm, close evening but still daylight when we set off for the 8:30 show at the Rosebud. Our hotel was eight blocks from the theater so we walked, the five of us, Groucho in a kind of Mexican suit with huge lapels and big buttons and an old fedora, holding hands with his chambermaid, who was called June and was a mass of giggles all the way. Chico looked like a longshoreman on leave, with his hair slicked down with Mrs Keeley's Anti-Kink Pomade, which all the black folks were using in those days. Artie just looked weird, having decided to go out with the bright red fright wig that he wore on stage, but he tucked it into the back of his pants before we went into the theater. But people used to dress up in all sorts of queer get-up in those days to go to the picture houses and the "jass" clubs that I was really aching to see in the city, where nobody cared if you were black or white, Anglo or Mexican, or anything in between.

As it was a Sunday night the streets were pretty empty; people had been to the negro churches that were on every corner—the New Hope Baptist Church, the New Zion Mission, the First Holiness Church, the New Church of Zion and so forth—but there were groups around the diners and saloons at the more busy junction of Central and Walnut, where the big circular front of the Rosebud rippled with colored lights. Two men in neat suits were standing there with placards that said: "CLANSMAN: INSULT TO OUR SPIRIT" and "GOD'S MERCY ON DIXON, GRIFFITH. HARMONY AND LOVE WILL PREVAIL." There was a steady trickle of people going in, so we totted up our fifteen cents each and edged in. A couple of people did look at us a bit suspiciously, as if we might spell trouble, but we shuffled very quietly into the rows of seats at the back, the only noise coming from our party being the rustle and crack of the peanuts Groucho had bought in a paper cone. There were two ushers who were about my age in smart uniforms buzzing up and down, shining their torches in the auditorium, which was already pretty dark. A spot of light shone down on two musicians at the left side of the curtain, a piano player and a boy with a saxophone who looked maybe a year older than me. They were both dressed in striped suits, and joking between them and testing the keys and belting a few toots as the hall filled out.

I was used to the bands that always played in the theaters in between the acts and added their licks to the shows. They were the "pit boys," who mostly played ragtime, but they would also let fly with

Italian overtures, German tunes, Irish jigs or some wailing Jewish music when the need arose. The man who tickled the ivories always amazed me, and I could spend hours just looking at his fingers as they whirled over the black and white keys. At one time I liked the drums, because they made the loudest noise, but I was resolved, already then, when I could have the time, to learn to play like that. But what really gave me a thrill, in the picture house, that special evening in Los Angeles, was the boy with the sax. I had seen some movies, mostly the Sennett comedies and Ince Westerns, always with a single player with a standard piano or the special enhanced ones with added bells and whistles and honking noises that would stand in for voices. I saw a full-length Western in St. Louis with a full organ music that I later found out was Cecil B. DeMille's *The Virginian*—I remember the hero's line to the villain, "When you call me that, Trampas, smile!" Those were all intertitles in those days. But I didn't know what to expect at all from *The Clansman*, apart from the warning that it ran for more than two and a half hours, with only one interval. I was told that the big white Clune's Auditorium, which could seat more than two thousand people, ran the picture with a full orchestra and a special score that was composed and written on sheet music that was an eighth wonder of the world, but here in the puny Rosebud, with its four hundred seats, which were comfortable, none of those picture houses was old and shabby yet, we only got the one pianist and his sidekick, the saxophone wailer. But what licks! The kid really poured his guts out, as the curtain swung open and the photoplay began.

Everybody knows big movies now, but nobody, rich nor poor, knew what to expect at that time. Mr. Griffith's movie had opened in February, but with all the fuss and bother he had changed his title by July, so now it read "THE CLANSMAN—BIRTH OF A NATION," and there was a long title that read "A Plea for the Art of the Motion Picture." I looked it up since, and it said:

"We do not fear censorship, for we have no wish to offend with improprieties or obscenities, but we do demand, as a right, the liberty to show the dark side of wrong, that we may illuminate the bright side of virtue—the same liberty that is conceded to the art of the written word—that art to which we owe the Bible and the works of Shakespeare."

I could not read very fast at that time, so I didn't get past the word "improp—" whatever it was, and skipped to the word "Bible" at the bottom, before the title changed, so I got the impression that it was something about the Ten Tribes of Israel, or some such scriptural tale. But instead the picture opened with some black slaves who had been brought from Africa, so I thought it might be a geographical story. Then the picture settled on a very fine house, which the titles told us was owned by the Camerons, a rich white family in Piedmont, South Carolina, who are being visited by two brothers who are their friends from the North. They are all laughing and fooling together, and there are two young white girls, Margaret and Flora, the "Little Sister," who both looked pretty, pale and underweight. The older Cameron brother falls in love with a picture of the brothers' sister, Elsie, who was the star of the picture, Lillian Gish. I had seen her in the pictures before, and she was pretty frail too. So far I hadn't seen anyone that could match Hetty, who was plain but getting curvier every month, or Eva Tanguay, who we had seen in Chicago and was past thirty but had a figure that could stop a clock at five hundred yards. But it was quite pleasant enough.

The people up on the theater screen didn't move around that much, or jump over cliffs or drive into gullies in motor cars, like in the Sennett movies. Instead, we saw their faces closer up and could see what they were thinking. The kid saxophonist was serenading his way into our hearts, making us believe the people were real up there, so that you could almost believe you heard them speaking, although there were no words. There was a dear old gentleman, who was the father, who was worried because he read in the newspaper that the North was going to fight with the South. I wasn't sure north or south of what. I had heard something about the Civil

War, because there was an old duffer, O'Finnegan, who ate bullets and then spat them out on a plate, who told stories on the stage about the Battle of Bull Run, but I thought maybe he was one of those Mexican matadors. In those days you never asked what a film was about before you went in to see it, you only needed to know, as Groucho would always put it, like the old-timers wanted to know about any show: "Is it sad or high-kicking?" You wanted to know if you were going to laugh or to cry. Or to gasp at the acrobats and magicians.

The film got more exciting when war was declared, and the Southern family all got together at a grand ball when the army marched in, and they spread out the Confederate flag. I was a New York boy and knew nothing about it, but I often saw it when we toured places like Richmond, Virginia, Charlotte, North Carolina, Atlanta, Georgia, Birmingham, Alabama or Jacksonville, Florida. I thought maybe we were in another country, like Canada, which had a leaf on its flag. I could see that black folk there were more separated, but sometimes white folk would treat you more kindly than in the northern states, where they treated everybody like dogs. There is a difference between a pat on the head and a kick in the ass, though I would not like the NAACP to pick me up on that. But there were precious few black or near-black faces in the picture till much further on, apart from the Africans at the start, who didn't seem to have anything to do with the story. There was a scene of President Abe Lincoln signing a paper with all his ministers, and everybody in the theater applauded. Then suddenly there were battle scenes, and we were off. The pianist began to play louder and louder chords, as if he was attacking the keys with a mallet, and the saxophonist drew sounds of horror and pain out of his instrument that cut me right to the heart. You could feel everybody leaning forward in their seats, completely caught in the action. There seemed to be thousands and thousands of people in the scenes, tiny dots across the battlefields, and balls of fire and smoke, which the saxophonist carried all the way into our ears, mouths and eyes. Now we were among the soldiers, wounded and dying, crying out for help. We could figure out now that the boys in the first part were fighting on different sides, and were going to fight each other. The two young Northern brothers are killed, and the older brothers from each side meet in the battle. The older Cameron, "the Little Colonel," leads a desperate charge to stick the Confederate flag in the mouth of a cannon. By this time the Marx Brothers around me were bobbing and feinting, swinging their fists as if they were in some catch-as-catch-can wrestling ring. Groucho was shouting "Attaboy! Up the Rebs! Make those Yankees eat shit!" while Artie was whooping like an Indian. I thought we would all be thrown out, or lynched, but everybody was caught up in the great swell of emotion, as if it was all happening for real.

It was hot in the theater and we were all sweating, but we calmed down a little for the scene in the hospital when the Little Colonel meets Lilian Gish, who is his nurse. Some of the girls in the audience were weeping, but Groucho was just biting his nails. I looked around at the other people, and my eye caught a newcomer who had just entered from the back. I could only see by the light from the screen, but there was something familiar in the way the man walked in, very delicately, and sat down in a vacant aisle seat. The theater was only about two-thirds full, so I could see him isolated, taking off his cloth cap. Once again the gesture was familiar. But the scene was switching to the Little Colonel, released from hospital and returning to his shattered home. It was very sad, though I had gathered by then, by the flags, that he was on the wrong side. Then we were back with Lincoln, arguing about the end of the war, and then Lincoln went into a theater to see a play and got shot. That was something I had heard about, that he was the president who freed the slaves and was killed by a white man. Everybody in our theater groaned.

The lights went up for the interval, and I sneaked another look at the man who had walked in so late. I could only see the back of his neck and part of the left side of his face, but I was pretty sure who it was. The way he had come down the aisle, almost like floating, with bird-like steps, and the cock of his head, as if listening out for any unusual sound or vibration from this as well as other worlds. I knew it must be Gramby. Quite cleverly, he had made himself up more brown than black—a mulatto look. I had never seen him do that before; he preferred to go the other way, to white out his face so that when he opened his brown eyes, they flashed out like dark pools on the moon.

Since he clearly didn't want to be noticed I made no move towards him and said nothing to the others. The audience was milling out, towards the foyer and the peanut and hot dog stalls. June noticed that Groucho's makeup was running into his suit, so she took a couple of dollars off the brothers and I went out with her to get some dogs. In the foyer, several white cops were idling at the street entrance who had not been there before. June bought the hot dogs and came up whispering to me that there was going to be trouble in the second half of the show. She heard people talking about some kind of protest. But it was too late to walk out, and in any case, we were all hooked on the story.

In the second part of the picture, things began to get ugly. It took me some time to figure out that the troublemaking Silas Lynch, who wanted to build a black empire on the ruins of the Old South, was supposed to be a black man, rather than a white actor with lousy makeup. Then there was a hysterical woman blacked up even worse than Groucho, who was mad because Mr. Lynch was besotted with Lillian Gish and wanted to make her his queen. There were two old black servants who wanted to help the whites, but another white actor with mud on his face was an ex-soldier who was stuck on the Little Sister and chased her through the forest onto a cliff. "She will be in hot water pretty soon!" boomed a sonorous voice from my left that could only have come from Groucho. But the audience was restless and muttering. Then the poor girl fell to her death and the Little Colonel, vowing revenge, hit on the idea of making up white sheets to scare the blacks and start up a whole army of "knights" with big crosses and pointed hoods. I guessed he was the "clansman" of the title. The clansman started riding around the country, scaring blacks, and then they all gathered in a grand army to rescue Lillian Gish, who had been tied to a chair by the evil Silas. I thought this was terribly exciting, but felt a kind of grim pressure coming from Artie on my arm. He tried to shush Julius, but you could never silence Groucho, who said in a loud voice that could be heard all through the theater, "This is fucking bullshit!" I could see Gramby, as it was certainly him, several rows down, turning around.

Something had also changed with the music. Instead of playing the excitement of the chase and the tension of the white family besieged by the negro soldiers in their shed, the pianist was hitting the keyboard in a completely tuneless cacophony, producing a sound like a train engine that was falling apart, while the saxophonist blew up a storm of high notes like a hyena being flayed alive. Then some more people got up in the front rows and unfurled a large banner which we couldn't see, and began chanting, "Freedom! Freedom! Freedom!" One of them had a bullhorn, and he stood up, with the Ku Klux Klan in full gallop projected across his face and torso, and shouted: "They killed Abraham Lincoln and now they want to kill our rights! Afro-Americans died for our freedom and we are not giving our freedom up! We will not accept race hatred in our streets and in our theaters! Stop this moving picture now!" The close shot of Lillian Gish with her gagged mouth splayed all over his shirtfront like a luminous ghost.

"Down with whitey! Kill the Klan! Kill the Klan!"

Despite Artie, Chico and June tugging at him, Groucho was in full voice. I could see Gramby moving towards us, trying perhaps to reach and pull me away from the madness, but right then one of the men at the front pulled out some metal object that exploded with a loud bang, spewing out a thick curtain of smoke. A woman screamed, "Fire! Fire!" and everybody made a charge for the back. We burst through the lobby, and I could see the white policemen turning around to face us, with their clubs raised and mouths open. But we seemed to cut through them like butter, spilling out onto the broad pavement and upending the hot dog stand outside. Hands gripped for the sizzling dogs and I saw Artie, eyes wide with childish delight, stuffing two wieners into his pockets. People were shoving and shouting, and the men with the placards ran forward, as if their moment had come. And then Gramby materialized by my side, grabbing my arm and pulling me away, back up the road, away from the scrum and the three brothers, who were plunging in as if there was a ball to retrieve. I tried to turn back to see how they were doing, but two police cars rushed up just across us and disgorged a mob of club-swinging cops.

"Just walk away, Ace, just walk away."

He stopped, some blocks up, at an open diner, whose customers were spilling out to see what the cop cars were doing rushing south, followed by the clanging bell of two fire engines rattling down, festooned with helmeted men like a Keystone movie. He set me down on a stool and went into the restroom, emerging two minutes later with his face scrubbed clean, white as the pope. Back at the hotel, he took me up to his room and took the tarot pack out from his case, opening up the Major Arcana. We got the High Priestess, the Lovers, the Heirophant, Temperance and Judgment. Wisdom, serenity, pleasure, desire, affinity, the heart, temptation, respect, maturity, discipline, moderation, transcendence, healing, forgiveness, reconciliation, resurrection, renewal.

"What do you think, Ace?"

"I don't know, boss."

He sighed. "You don't need to pretend with me, Ace. The devil is in the rush for new experience. The magic of the motion picture. My brother thinks I can succeed there. But he is a modern technician. I am an old fashioned practitioner of an old fashioned craft. You know, when my brother left our village he left me a box of his magazines. You would not understand them. Caricatures of old monsters. The czar, the Russian priests, the Black Hundreds, not like your black people, Ace. Black in their souls. Did I tell you? I never saw a black person till I reached New York. At Ellis Island, when they took us off the boat. I thought they were maybe people who got tar stuck on them in the voyage. We were the black people where we came from. But my brother also left me an old photograph he had got from a newspaper. A naked man in chains. That was Houdini. Then I found a book of magic tricks. *The Turkish Masters*. It was in Russian. Did I tell you this story before? Anyway, this is my trade. We are good at this, you and I. Not at this jerking and mugging up for the flickers. If I did it I would like to use the machine. You know, you can do tricks with it also, not just to photograph action. You can stop it, make it go backwards and forwards. You remember the French movie we saw once? A man throws his head up again and again on the music bars and plays his head like a conductor. But still people know it's a trick. On the stage, they are not so sure. Maybe he is doing it for real. They think it's mirrors but they can't see the glass. You tell them how it's done and you're finished. When Ching Sing Loo has the assistant shoot the bullet in his mouth to catch in his teeth, the audience sees it happening in front of their eyes. It is real. It can go wrong. Maybe one day he will die. Maybe one day the knife thrower will miss his throw. Maybe the acrobat will fall from the wire and break his neck. It is not all fake."

"I want to learn to play music," I said.

He lifted the Judgment card towards me. The angel in the heavens, with his trumpet, looked down at naked beings, coming out of their graves.

"Of course," he said. "Everybody wants to do this. It is the Great Trick. One day I will show you how it is done. But you can perform little tricks along the way."

He picked up the Lovers. Adam and Eve, by the Tree of Knowledge, with the Serpent coiled in its branches. He gave that little shiver I knew so well, the tremor that says, Leave me alone. I left him sitting cross-legged on his bed, looking inward, his eyelids fluttering, in a posture that suggested flying into the dark inside his head and down to the servants' quarters, just by the separate entrance at the back of the house...

Provisional Title:
THE MAGICIAN
Scenario by C.B. DeMille and
William "Boris" Gore

Opening title: "The lives of ordinary men are sometimes interrupted by extra-ordinary events.

Such an event is War, which disrupts the calm process
of Life and shatters Hopes, Dreams and Desires. When
Emperors and Tyrants fall out, it is the helpless who
discover in Themselves new Powers which enable them to
Rise above the Flames..."

Second title: "The summer harvest..."

Scene 1: A field of wheat in a southwest Russian valley.
Peasants, women and men, gather the wheat. Scythes cut
through the stalks. A farmer, Andrea, leads a horse
and cart. He is introduced in a title:

"Andrea—a man of the Valley."

By his side is a young girl, with a headscarf:

"Irina—his sister, who dreams of the City."

The scythes cut—

Long shot: The farmers are streaming towards a platform towards the top of a hill. It is a village fete.
The summer celebration. Up on the platform a troupe
of entertainers is performing: There are clowns, musicians with fiddle, drums and cornet, a strongman
straining against chains, and—

Title: "The Magician"

He is dressed in a white suit, with a Turkish turban.
Two white doves are perched on his shoulder. But he has
a strong face, that of a peasant farmer himself. He is
regaling the audience with his introductory speech. As

he talks, a Dancing Girl emerges from a booth at the back of the platform. She begins to perform her dance as the musicians play—

Title: "Natalya, the Strongman's daughter"

All seems merriment and festivity—women sell their goods from baskets—the men wrangle over the sale of a horse—

Cut to—

Scene 2: Interior of farmer's house, a simple wood home, with plain furniture and a large table, at which an old man is bent before an open book. The man is heavy-set, with a short gray beard and black fez-like cap—

Title: "Gavrilov, Andrea and Irina's father—a Scholar"

Beside him are two smaller boys, Felix and Yakov. Their mother, Sonia, is at the stove.

Back to the Magician, who extracts a hen's egg from the dove and swallows it, then pulls it from the cornet player's instrument and cracks it on the drummer's head. A tiny sparrow flies out, to the applause of the crowd.

In the fields, the scythes continue to play—

Cut to—

Title: "Far from thoughts of peace—the Assassins"

Scene 3: A city road junction. Four men with guns lurk by a wall on the junction.

An ornate and open carriage comes by, marked with the double-eagle crest and preceded by several uniformed horsemen: the Guards.

In the carriage, a richly attired nobleman with a plumed hat and his wife sit back, comfortable and satisfied in their position.

Title: "The Archduke tours his new province."

The Assassins rush forward, firing at the Archduke, who is hit by the bullets and slumps forward. His wife is also shot. Guards rush and grapple with the Assassins.

Scene 4: In a palatial room, an old man festooned with medals and braid sits, his great white moustaches trembling as he hunches over his vast desk signing a decree, while a row of Generals wait eagerly behind him.

Title: "The Emperor signs."

Scene 5: Cannons fire, soldiers advance, rifles at the ready. Smoke covers the battlefield, the soldiers march on. Boots crush the growing wheat into the ground. Bodies begin to fall in the field.

Scene 6: The quiet valley is now full of the rush and turmoil of the army bivouac of Russian troops quartered at the village. At a desk in the field, the czarist commander, Colonel Shlekhov, a grizzled and ruthless bully, is haranguing a row of able-bodied peasants drafted for the war. Andrea is brought before him. The Colonel hands him his induction papers and he is dragged away by the jeering guards.

Above the field, Natalya and the Magician watch from the steps of their caravan. Natalya's father, the Strongman, comes out of the caravan, in uniform as a sergeant, rifle slung over his shoulder.

Title: "Off to kill Austrians!"

He looks dismissively at the Magician:

Strongman: "She's in your charge now!"

Scene 7: Cavalry men ride into the valley. The peasant women mill about, looking for their husbands and sons. Andrea and a group of fellow draftees come out of a tent, awkwardly pulling at their ill-fitting uniforms. Irina rushes up and embraces him.

Andrea: "Don't worry. This can't last long! I'll be home soon."

The cavalry riders push away the women. The sergeants draw the men up in a ragged order as the Colonel stands on the slope to address them:

The Colonel speaks, his mouth opening and closing, as horses' hooves paw the ground and men shuffle their boots, which are mostly badly wound straps of cloth. The sunlight glints on their bayonets. A dog wanders, bemused, among the drafted men, looking for its master, and chickens cluck and wander between their feet.

The Colonel: "No longer a rabble—you are now SOLDIERS of His Imperial Majesty—Father of us All—Our Holy CZAR!"

His sword waves in the sky.

Camera rises over onion-shaped domes in far-off cities—from Actualities: great phalanxes of clergy blessing the czar, Nikolai the Second, and his czarina, while a gaunt bearded monk stands at his side—Rasputin. Vast armies march down the streets of the cities, while, in Close-Ups, terrified and anxious faces of men and women watch from windows.

Cut to—

Scene 8: The Interior of Papa Gavrilov's house. His wife, Sonia, and the children, Felix and Yakov, sit by the samovar while a group of Elders huddle with Gavrilov round the table. One of the Elders, Piotr, speaks—

Title: "News from the Front"

Insert scenes of dead bodies lying across blasted trenches, defeated soldiers, with their hands raised, taken captive by the enemy—

Titles: "Five thousand taken prisoner at Tarnov... the Germans advancing through Poland... the Austrians are crossing the Dniester River... Russia is losing the War..."

Scene 9: Exterior—outside the house, in the moonlight. The Magician and Irina are meeting. Her face is turned up towards his as his hands clutch hers.

Irina: "Is there any news of Andrea?"

The Magician shakes his head. They climb the hill and look out over the performers' caravans. Natalya, seated on the steps of her caravan, looks out.

Irina: "So peaceful, the valley—"

The Magician: "We should leave. The war will soon be here."

It is her turn to shake her head, inclining it towards the house.

Irina: "I can't leave them. My life is here."

The Magician shakes a white dove out of his sleeve. But instead of flying, it just hops along the ground limply.

In the underbrush, we see the glinting eyes of a fox.

Archive note: Missing scenes 10 to 14.

.   .   .   .

Scene 15: The huts in the village are burning. The armed are dragging Papa Gavrilov and several other Elders out onto the crushed field to join a row of other villagers whose hands are tied behind their backs. A line of soldiers with rifles ready is forming. The boy Yakov runs calling—

Yakov: "Father! Father!"

The mother, Sonia, is fighting with the guards, who drag her away.

The soldiers raise their rifles—

The camera moves by the row of faces of villagers who have been sentenced to die—

Title: "'Deserters' and 'Collaborators'"

Sonia pleads with the Colonel

Sonia: "We are Russians—like you! We are all Children of this Earth!"

The Colonel raises his hand—

Irina breaks free of the concealed group and runs forward across the field—

Irina: "MURDERERS!"

The Colonel looks around. Gavrilov lunges forward but—

The Colonel's sword drops—the rifles fire their volley—the condemned fall—the Magician stands up, his eyes, startled and open, looking into…

the eyes of the Colonel—

Irina turns, but—

A blast of shell fire hits the field on which she is standing—

The soldiers of the execution squad are thrown back—

The Colonel's sword is shattered—

The Magician, in Big Close-Up, turns around—

Armored vehicles appear over the top of the hill—the Russian troops run—

Title: "The Austrians!"

Scene 16: Disciplined soldiers march down the slope of the hill. The Russian soldiers rise with their hands up in surrender. Colonel Shlekhov hesitates, over the dead body of Irina that lies before him. Then he, too, raises his hands.

Title: "One month later"

Scene 17: A barbed-wire enclosure surrounds a field of barrack huts, with watchtowers looking over it. Soldiers in Austrian army uniform and headgear patrol the wire and man the watchtowers. A sign in German fades into its English translation:

"*Prisoner of War Camp 19. Entrance Forbidden.*"

Men in very ragged Russian uniforms walk about in small groups, some smoking cigarettes, others muttering to one another. Some sit in corners, playing cards. Others are washing their rags in large tubs set in the dismal courtyard between two barracks. Inside, others lie on their bunks, listless, looking up at the bare rafters.

Title: "Despair"

Scene 18: In another room in the barracks—the officers' hall—a gambling table with about a dozen high-ranking prisoners and Austrian prison warders playing cards over a pile of banknotes. There are bottles of vodka and fine glasses as the officers, with their jackets loose, enjoy life far away from the battlefield, Colonel Shlekhov raking in his winnings.

Title: "Money knows no borders."

Scene 19: At the camp gate, a truck rolls up with a new batch of prisoners— civilians, moved from one post to another, hurried through the gates by the shouting guards. Among them, the Magician, clutching a small case of his belongings. The group moves in, under the watchtowers.

Scene 20: The Magician is ushered into a busy hut

full of other prisoners, one of whom recognizes him immediately. It is Andrea, who comes up and embraces him before moving a fellow prisoner from the bunk next to him so they can be close.

Andrea: "Have you seen mother? And the children?"

The Magician: "We have been moving from place to place, like cattle."

Andrea: "And Natalya?"

The Magician shakes his head, he does not know.

Andrea's lips move close to the Magician's ear.

Andrea: "Shlekhov is here..."

The Magician's eyes blaze luminously in the dark.

Scene 21: Night—strong searchlights move over the camp grounds, illuminating spots of light... A couple of senior guards, emerging drunk from the splash of light spilling from the hut with the gambling table, wave to the guards on the watchtowers. They huddle together, smoking cigarettes. Then one parts from the others, and, staggering, his coat loose, he moves towards his own quarters—

As he passes the corner of one of the huts, two figures dart out and grab him around the throat—he falls into shadow—

Out of the shadow, he seems to re-emerge, but, as the searchlight passes over his face we see that it is the Magician, in the guard's uniform. Behind him, other prisoners emerge to drag the body into the hut.

Led by the Magician, Andrea and two other prisoners of war creep up to the guard's hut.

Scene 22: Inside the hut—the drunk guards are struggling to take off their boots, staggering against one another. The door opens—a figure with a rifle comes through. The befuddled guards are captured by the prisoners and tied up with their own belts.

Scene 23: In the courtyard—the huddled group of prisoners inches forward, along the walls of the barracks, as the searchlight streams. Several of the lads begin shinning up the wooden supports of the watchtowers. Meanwhile, the Magician and Andrea approach the gambling den.

Scene 24: Interior, gambling room—the table full of upturned vodka bottles, glasses and mugs, the vodka soaking the banknotes. There are only four players left—two very drunk Austrian officers, a Russian officer and Shlekhov, his tunic open, his face running with sweat, he is pushing forward towards the Austrians—

Shlekhov: "You LOST! I lost my country, but—" His hands rake in the money. Then he looks up, startled—

The Magician and the other prisoners are at the door. Bleary-eyed, Shlekhov sees their faces as swaying, distorted demons—

The Magician's face, still distorted:

The Magician: "A man should die on his own soil!"

Cut to—

Scene 25: The home province, with its ruined houses and empty fields.

Title: "Homeland"

The burnt shards of houses, skeletons of horses and cows, little mounds of graves, with simple wooden crosses, or a Hebraic inscription...

Scene 26: On the hill—The Magician stands upright against the sky as smoke billows behind and before him. He looks forward, his eyes open again in that blazing look that sees all.

Title: "Magician, where is your magic?"

Close up on his eyes—

Title: "Sorceror, where are your spells?"

He closes his eyes. The smoke swirls thickly.

Scene 27: As the landscape dispels, a different one appears. Instead of the charred ruins of war and the scattered corpses—the wheat fields are restored, the houses standing sturdily, the harvesters' carts wheeling across the paths, the girls in their pristine blouses climbing down to the field—a soft white smoke rises from the chimney of the family house.

Scene 28: And yet another army—the smoke is too heavy to make their uniforms out—Russians or Austrians?

Rising from the ruins of the house—Mother, her face blackened. She is helped up by the boys, Felix and Yakov—pulling their mother, away into the fields, they run.

All groups merge into the thick black smoke—

The cannons roar again, belching fire—

Scene 30 (?): The Magician, on the hill, trying desperately to shake something from his sleeve—anything—but nothing emerges.

He turns away, walks down the other side of the hill, away from the fires.

A small figure, becoming smaller as the camera pulls back, to show the rolling hills, the burning forest—the carcases and skeletons—

He walks further—another hill—perhaps beyond it...?

Title: "Life strives to Live—War's Power passes—

All Life is Magick—in a New World"

Note scribbled on endpapers in DeMille handwriting:

"prelim. Boris better behind camera than desk

File in 'pending to '16."

*

The day after the *Clansman* riot, Boris appeared at our hotel with an offer from DeMille to play a role in his new "Spanish" picture. He was to be Miguel, a gypsy fortune teller, whom the heroine Carmen consults on her fate. He was to have several scenes, and at least four close-ups, with DeMille's signature "Rembrandt lighting" and a crystal ball. Recalling the cards of the night before, Gramby spread the tarot, the first card being the Wheel of Fortune, which decided him to remain in Los Angeles at least until the fall.

Boris motored us to the Lasky "ranch," heading up from Silver Lake along Sunset Boulevard and then way up into the hills on the other side of Griffith Park. It was a beautiful journey, and although we got to set out that way often, in the early morning, when the daylight was still just a hazy dream, I sometimes fancied that it was Gramby's magic, rather than the Vista Mountain roads, that took me there, and then, when we left, it would always vanish, folded up like a pack of his cards. As we approached the location, the morning sun would shoot over the peaks and shine right on the houses and towers and walls that were built into the folds of the hills. Seen closer, they were a real jumble of styles: an old-style Western saloon, a row of picket fences in front of neat new stuccos, some low clay huts that might have been Mexico or biblical Palestine, and then, just around the next fold, a whole part of Manhattan, with the signs for 42nd Street and the lights of the theaters, the soda fountains and coffee shops and diners, and people walking up and down and jiving as if they had just stepped out of the nearest dance hall or the new-fangled automat.

The biggest construction of all was the front and inside part of a giant stadium, stretching just so far in a hollowed-out valley and then stopping, as if sawn in half, with all the scaffolding and the building work showing around the edges and a big gateway with Spanish houses, topped with flags and banners that were set fluttering by huge fans that could make wind or blow dust. Later on I would see that they could also blow a sheet of storm rain or millions of little scraps of paper that would be pretend snow. The half stadium, Boris told us when we first set eyes on it, rounding the hill, was the bullring, the centerpiece of the biggest picture that Mr. DeMille had made so far.

Mr. DeMille was a storm all of his own, rushing up to us the minute Boris had pulled his car into the parking lot through the main gate, heading for Lot No. 12. He didn't wait for us to stop, but jumped up on the running board and leaned in, his shining bald head shooting through the open window like a bullet:

"Conference in ten minutes! The fucking bastards sent the wrong bulls!"

I thought he would be some grizzled veteran, eight foot tall, with a Stetson hat and one of those big cigars bosses like to chew, but he was much younger, about thirty-five, and chunky, the same height and size as Boris, who was about a head shorter than Gramby. He was always angry, and often shouting, though he would stop in mid-bawl and run up to his target, man or woman, fling an arm around their shoulder and whisper like a lover into their ear. He treated everybody, young and old, like children, except the boss himself, Jesse Lasky, who would come on the set like a dapper gentleman just dressed for the club, in a sharp suit and fresh hat and his nails manicured, though I noticed his hands showed signs of a working man, some time back. Gramby told me he had been in vaudeville for twenty years and had come up the ranks, playing a cornet in his own band, touring the wheels like everybody else. Now he owned the studio and was a millionaire. He never shouted at anybody, but liked to stand around, watching, the classic man with cigar, and would sometimes call over his personal sidekick, Valdemar, and tell him something. He was the one man DeMille never argued with, and even if the director was angry with the chief, he would just stand beside him and sizzle, muttering his curses to himself.

DeMille dressed himself in a weird getup, halfway like a laborer ready to set out to dig ditches, his sleeves rolled up and his pants rich with large pockets from which he took his gauges and a big shady glass on a strap, half like a cowpuncher with tall boots just about to leap up on his horse and gallop off for the big roundup.

DeMille hauled Boris into his main shed, where he had a big table that everybody sat around while he laid down the law and chastised his minions. I just got a peek of it from outside. He flicked an eye at me for a split second, and gave Gramby about three more: "Mr. Jacob Gore? See Carl, lot fourteen." We wandered about the sets, walking down the Spanish alleyway in which the builders were setting up a row of mock-adobe houses, with stables and a saloon and stalls for an outdoor fruit and vegetable market. All very lifelike at three angles but showed up the wooden slats and boards that held it all up from behind. At the end of this the grand stadium rose up thirty feet or more to the sky. And inside the wide entrance, which was still unfinished, a small army of workmen hammered out the long benches on which the hundreds of extras would sit, when the right bulls would finally trot out.

"Ah, Seville!" said Gramby. "You would want to go there someday, Ace. The real bullring is still there, you know. I was going to go there with Boris, when he was coming to Paris, but the plan changed and we only met when he got here. But one day, Ace, we should go there. Where things are real. Here it is all make-believe. But so much hard work, to build the facade. You know what I mean, Ace? What we do on the stage we can do with pennies. We have a box, and some furniture, and some well placed wires, and colored smoke, and we can make entire worlds. The magic is in the audience's head, not on our stage. But they need it all ready made. Thousands and thousands of dollars, to make people believe. If they close their eyes, or just drift away in their seats for a few moments, it is all there. This is the world of the machine. You can see it with Ziegfeld. Make all the pretty girls line up in rows, put hats with street signs and 'sky-scrapers' on their heads and make them go around like automatons. Boris likes that. Boris believes in the machine. If you can control it, it will not control you. This is his theory. Socialist electricity. But I am not a believer."

And the cards? But Gramby was full of paradox. At the time, of course, I didn't know that word. I believed in what I saw in front of my eyes. I had been inside the magic cabinet enough times to know nobody was being transported to Abyssinia, to Mastrashastra, to Patagonia, Hankow in China, or Samarkand. I always stayed huddled in my corner, just under the stage level of the Orpheum in Kansas City, or Poli's Theatre Philadelphia, or the Pantages in Salt Lake. So I began to think that maybe those places weren't really there, but were just dreams that were conjured up by Gramby's pack of "carrot" cards, which was the way they seemed to be for me. The Fool, the Emperor, the Lover, the Hermit, the Hanged Man, the Devil, the Tower. My aunt used to talk a lot about the Devil, and she tried to scare me so much that I came to want to meet him, just so I could see if he was as scary as she made out. But I hadn't seen the Devil yet, just a lot of poor sons-of-bitches who thought they could lord it over the rest of us, or who liked to inflict pain, or to kill. Palookas. But what my time with Gramby taught me was that it was no use imagining you were some place else, safe in the jungle with Mowgli the Jungle Boy and his animal friends, or Br'er Rabbit, because you were always just crouched in that ball, in the "magic" compartment, breathing steadily and trying not to cough or sneeze.

We finally found Carl, the casting man, on that morning, or he found us, wandering around the fake Spanish stalls. He got Gramby to sign on a contract for two weeks' work, just dressing up as the fortune-teller, blacking his face up and mumbling over a fake crystal ball. He was a kindhearted man, so he took me on also, just as a face in the crowd, in the night scenes, when the star of the show comes up the mountain trail to the "gypsy village," which was set in a glade. It was spooky but nice, with the great electric lights all around us dimmed and split up by shutters mounted on poles, so that only narrow shafts could shine on our faces as we sat around and waited for the shot to be taken. Mr. DeMille, it turned out, had two cameramen, Boris and "Wick," who went around managing the lights and moved the camera in different scenes. They had three assistants, who took measurements, got the actors together and rehearsed the scenes. Only when it was all ready would the Director himself march up, with his "chair boy," the kid who carried a chair behind him all the time he was working and just put it down wherever the Director decided he wanted to sit. It was a real skill, but I wasn't so sure I wanted to try it, because if you got it wrong the Director would fall down flat on his ass, and I wouldn't want to be on his wrong side when that happened. Not that I ever saw it happen. The chair boy always got it right. You always got it right for DeMille, or your ear would be blasted as if you had got the last trump from God Himself.

In the meantime, while waiting, the "gypsies" would sing a medley of Polish or German songs, or the lead chieftain, Adolfo, with a genuine beard the size of a doormat, would warble a Jewish tune he had sung when he had been a cantor, a religious singer, back in the Old Country. Gramby said he had the best voice he had heard since his own father sang at the Passover festival, when

95

he was a child. Now he made a living playing "gypsy" chiefs, vegetable vendors, angry fathers, or the kind of villains seen in the Sennett comedies. He was quite good at fights, other extras told me, and had once bitten a fellow actor's nose off in a fake brawl.

Gramby told me the story of the picture, which was about Carmen, the cigarette girl. I thought that meant she would be like one of those Gibson Girls shown on the poster ads, smoking a Lucky Strike. But Gramby said she was a poor but beautiful girl who worked in a cigarette-making factory and was loved by two rivals, an army man and a bullfighter, who were ready to kill for her. I thought the star must be the most desirable woman on Earth, but it turned out she was a thirty years old opera singer from New York, who looked like somebody's mother. It showed me right then that I couldn't understand the moving pictures at all. There didn't seem no point in a singer being hired for a silent picture, though in those days of course there were no silent or talking pictures, there were only the pictures, and the only sound was the live orchestra, for the big hits, and the guy or gal at the piano... As it turned out, the big star, Geraldine Farrar, was a real sweetheart, a trouper who didn't turn up her nose at the drudges, but mixed in with the extras as well as the principal players and wasn't scared by the Director either. She treated him just like one of the boys. He still treated her like a child, but she was, she admitted, a kindergarten kid in the moving picture business and was pretty eager to learn. Many times, when the crew was waiting, and DeMille and Boris and Wick and his prop people were fussing over this or that arrangement, she would haul up and belt out an aria from one of the shows she had starred in on Broadway, like *La Traviata* or *La Boheme*. We got practically the whole of *Aida* hollered out over the Hollywood Hills. It was all completely new to me, but I was surer and surer that my own future lay somewhere in music. Not in singing, at which I was useless, but somewhere on the sides, fingers playing the keys, or where that saxophone boy at the Rosebud sobbed out his pain and anguish at Griffith's offense to our race.

96

The movies were shot fast in those days, the actors rushing from set to set, and with no sound recording; it didn't matter that the hammers clattered all through the shoot. The big movies, like Lasky's and DeMille's, gave you relative silence while the cameras rolled, but in the Keystones, as we saw later, the builders were going at it all day, not to speak of four or five pictures being shot at the same time, with different directors bawling into megaphones at the same time. The chaos just added to the pitch of the scenes, and instead of taking down the scenery, it cost Sennett less just to have general mayhem or even a fire to trash the set when it was finished and done with.

After the gypsy scene, we got to be extras in the bullring sequences that wrapped up the movie, the big moment when Carmen is confronted by the officer, Don Jose, who fought and killed a fellow officer for her, after she turned him down for the bullfighter, Escadrillo. He catches her just outside the bullring and stabs her to death, so that nobody else can have her. Gramby told me that in the theater, after she gets stabbed, she still sings, but with DeMille we just got The End. The whole bullfight, which I thought would be the whole point of the picture, just flashes by pretty quick in the background.

The night I saw the film was certainly different from the quick dash down the skid row area to see *The Clansman* with the Marx Brothers in disguise. A gala premiere. That was another piece of real magic. Nobody needed a disguise there, at the Hollywood the-ater, with all the crowd surging, and the police cars and flashing lights and the stars arriving in their black tuxedos and the women's shimmering gowns—and there was I, beside Gramby, who had put on a pure white India-style suit, with scarlet cuffs and his best on-stage turban with the glittering fake diamond on the fold, the Girl, Hetty, looking more pretty than she ever looked on his arm, me shoehorned by Boris's maid, Matilda, into an adult tux, and nobody looking askance that I was the only black face going in to this luxury white theater. I could see quite a few Mexicans dressed as if the old world was still alive and kicking and no Pancho Villa and Zapata had replaced the old rancheros. Everybody cheered as the Star arrived, looking like the Queen of Broadway, with a kind of silver crown. The mayor was there, and the chief of police, and maybe even the governor of California, and all the studio heads. Boris pointed them out to us: Laemmle, Tom Ince, William Fox, Sam Goldfish, Mack Sennett, Colonel Selig, Jesse Lasky and DeMille together, and Cecil's brother, William, who had written the scenario for the movie, and in between them a tiny midget fellow who Boris told me was Adolph Zukor, the most powerful man in Hollywood. And there was a little, quiet man in a quite ordinary suit who everybody cheered to the skies. I couldn't believe it when Boris told us it was Charlie Chaplin. He lifted his hat and bowed around as if the whole thing was for him only, but he was too far away from us for me to run over and shake his hand and tell him how happy he had made me, and almost everybody else in the country, I guess, with his Essanay funnies. Gramby held me by the shoulder and whispered something in my ear, but there was too much noise for me to hear it; I think it was: "Enjoy the moment, Ace. Taste the lollipop, and then move on."

But he lingered. As we watched the film we realized that Gramby's grand moment with the grand opera diva from New York only lasted for one shot, and all close-ups of his muttering over the prop crystal ball, in Rembrandt glimmer, had been cut out, leaving her instead laying the cards. And we had about five seconds to try and look for our faces in the bullring crowd. Nobody cared. The sweep of the story, the high drama of those dashing characters, the energy of the grand diva, despite her age, and the beauty of the scenery and the shots—they were colored and tinted in different tones for day or night, action or tragedy. Along with the crashing chords of the orchestra that played with the picture, all the chaos merged in the succession of moments that were all of the absolute present, that sucked in both the future and the past. The film was much shorter than Griffith's epic, and DeMille didn't use the great camera movements that we remembered from the Klan riding shots, but there was something in it that was very enticing for the audiences of those early days: a kind of thrill at the very close scenes between the men and the Girl, the glowering looks and the feeling that they might just be about to get down and make it right there in the tavern, right on the table, while the gypsies shouted and egged them on. It was a new thing in pictures, and something that DeMille would do again, just a few weeks later, with another new movie, *The Cheat*, which was about a Japanese character who brands a white woman who owes him money. That one caused a real scandal, but Gramby and me were not in that show.

Still, Boris wanted us to stay on, and we did appear in another DeMille movie, a comedy Western about a funny kid from the Bowery in New York who gets sent west by crooks to fake a gold strike, with a big star of those days, Victor Moore. Later he became an old sack of a guy. We were in a saloon scene. Gramby wore a big Stetson and sat playing poker with three other yeggs, just in the background. I was in the corner as a bootboy, but I don't think I got in the shot. All you could see of Gramby in the picture was the back of his neck, behind the hero.

Boris still hoped that DeMille would make his movie, his scenario on the War in Europe, with characters that were kind of like his own family, although the Magician was very different from Gramby, and DeMille made him change the family from Jews to Christians because he said the Jews were always making trouble about the way they were presented in pictures. "Leave 'em alone," he said. "It's not a big audience. Movies are for the masses, not politics." Lasky was a Jew like most of the producers in the business, but he didn't want to make the picture either. He had a system that worked for him; mainly he bought up stories that had made money either as books or as stage plays and made them into movies. The dollars rolled in.

Gramby stuck around, I think, because he had an idea of his own that he got from looking at the tricks of the movies. On one of his visits to the studio, Boris had taken us into the cutting rooms and shown us, on a tiny screen, with a hand-wound machine, a very old movie that he said he had first seen ten years before, in

Russia made by a Frenchman who had been a magician himself before he started making the pictures. It was a trick film in which a music conductor seemed to take his own head off and throw it onto a kind of washing line that was like sheet music, and then do it again and again, about a dozen times, and then he conducted the heads, which were all singing on the lines. It was something he called stop-motion photography, but it looked like pretty good magic to me. Gramby's idea was, if you made a whole movie about a magician and his magic tricks, you could do this on the grand scale, and do things that no magician had ever done on the stage, like vanish whole cities, or trains, or battleships, or make stories like those of Jules Verne. Boris said the Frenchman had made some pictures like that, but it was right at the beginning, when movies were new, and they were all very short and pretty old-fashioned. But he did say, if Gramby stuck around, that he could try and write a story for him, if he had the time.

But there was never time with DeMille. There were five different productions, at least, that DeMille was planning, as well as a dozen more that were planned by other Lasky directors. There was a race, after *The Clansman*, for movies that could be bigger and better, and the Griffith film, they said, was making millions because of all the fury about it. Tom Ince had a plan for a big war picture, and Griffith himself was going to make another big epic: building the entire ancient city of Babylon out in the desert somewhere and employing every single extra in California, even those who were on crutches or in wheelchairs. So DeMille had his own big picture for the Lasky ranch: the story of a French heroine, Joan of Ark. I was, as usual, the innocent fool. I knew about Noah's Ark, so I was really looking forward to seeing all the animals. But it was a different story. Like *Carmen*, it was set in Europe, with a huge fortress and thousands of soldiers with swords, spears and riders in armor.

Gramby fretted in the house on top of the hill, with its flight of stairs leading down to the next road, which he often exercised by going up and down to keep from becoming bone idle. Once Boris called, telling him to go down to Alessandro, to Mack Sennett's studios, where the boss was willing to listen to a proposition about a testing picture for the magician idea, so we went down, all three of us, Gramby, me and Hetty, who was still sleeping with him at the time. It was one of those things you noticed but didn't pay any attention to, vaud people doubled up all the time. We went to the gate and were shown through the busy lots—Sennett was expanding his studio to at least double the size, part of a deal he had made with Tom Ince and Griffith, which they called the Triangle Film Corporation. It was big business all the way. But Sennett was still the kaiser in his own kingdom, presiding over the clowns and tumblers from his tower, rising high above the administration blocks. In true form, as we had been warned, he received us in his bathtub, his rangy torso just deep enough in the suds, while a flunky kept his constant cigar lit.

"You do magic?" he barked out at Gramby, who didn't bat an eye at the treatment, wearing his most inscrutable look. "Let's see it." Boris had warned us, so Gramby just stood there, and one of the doves, Angy, I think it was, fluttered up from behind his collar. She moved around his shoulder, cooing, and took something in her beak from Gramby's mouth, and then flew over to perch on the bath. Sennett took the folded piece of paper from the bird's beak and handed it to a flunky, who opened it up and said, "It's a contract."

"How much is he getting?" asked the boss, totally unmoved.

"Three hundred a week," the flunky read out.

"I'll give you two-fifty for one month," said Sennett, "but I don't want to see birds coming out of anyone's ass. I want to see girls coming out of pies and jumping through walls. This is about sex and violence, goddammit! The Maharajah's palace! The Black Hole of Calcutta! What do they call that stunt—suttee! The princess is going to be burned on the prince's pyre. You're an American, Buck Stanton, from Kansas, a cowhand who can rope five steers at the same time. You get into the palace disguised as the court sorcerer, Abdul, Jafar, who the fuck cares, the intertitlers write the dialogue afterwards, you magic her out of the fire, the natives go doolally, the Thuggees chase you all over the lot. You make them vanish one by one because you have Professor Otis Muggins setting up those trick trapdoors—is Mack Swain free? Get Jake and that new kid, Harold, get 'em to write it up. What happened to the elephant? Did some mug here send it back? What kind of assholes do I have working for me here? Isn't anybody on the fucking ball today?"

He looked at Hetty. "Can you dive from a board thirty feet up from the pool?" he asked.

"No," she said, "I don't think so, Mr. Sennett."

"OK. You're hired too. And the boy, what's your name? Don't bother telling me. You can be the funny kid who works the trapdoors. I'll give you fifty dollars and you can look through the hole these fuckers who work for me rigged up outside the girls' showers. No touching though. Can you roll your eyes around ten times? Now scat! Take 'em to costumes."

But that didn't work out either. The Maharajah's palace burned down in an accident before the movie could be started. Mack Swain wasn't available to play the part; he was too busy playing his usual character, Ambrose, with his partner, Walrus, a funny bullet-headed guy with an enormous fake moustache whose real name was Chester Conklin. The elephant had been sent back to the zoo, and Sennett lost interest in Indian magic trapdoors as he became obsessed, the next week, with stunt tricks with airplanes. "Can you fly one of those gizmos?" he asked Gramby. "I want it to fly between two chimneys, clip both the wings off, and land in the reservoir upside down, leaving Mabel stuck on the chimney." But Gramby couldn't pilot a car, let alone a plane, so he had to earn his contract by playing majordomos in hotel dramas, the sort of comedies in which Fatty Arbuckle fell into the lobby drunk and started a romance with the maids. Once he played a comic fireman, who doused the entire hotel set with his firehose so that everybody was washed out of the building, and Mabel Normand floated down the stairs in a bathtub. Sennett was big on bathtubs. He tried to do the same scene with a bear, but the bear turned out to be less tame than it should have been and rampaged through the set, chasing Al St. John up a lamppost. It was a good scene, and was kept in the movie, but the bear got docked a week's pay for breakages.

I loved the whole thing, and might have stayed there forever, if they had let me, but, as one thing leads to another, I found my way back to the young saxophonist who had wooed me with his siren call back in June. Under the wacky surface of the Keystone studios, there was a huge amount of hard-sweated labor for lousy wages that the workhands had to deal with "backstage." There were a lot of navvies, both black and white, Irish, Germans, Italians, Polish, Mexicanos and Southern negros who had drifted west. There was one man called Johnson, who supplied the crews and players on the lot with the wherewithal to keep going under the pressure, mainly weed and cocaine. The whole Keystone lot, in fact, and for all I knew all the studios, were floating on a nose-candy sea. Gramby knew about it, and kept warning me and making clear he would kick me square back to the sewers I'd come from if I got hooked, but he knew he couldn't keep me from trying. Life is tough, even in the funnies.

Johnson got his supplies from the "jass" bars that had sprung up all over town, but mainly in skid row, downtown Los Angeles, at the time. Later they said it was a New Orleans sound, but from what I knew, it came from Chicago. It was not ragtime but something else, without any limits, that seemed to come from inside, unguarded, not something that could be bought or be sold. You couldn't think of it advertised in *Variety*, under the heading of "Ten Great Songs Everybody's Singing"—like "Circus Day in Dixie," or "When I was a Dreamer," or "Over the Hills to Mary" or "Wrap Me in a Bundle and Take Me Home with You"... This was not something you could wrap in a bundle at all. It wailed out like the boy at the Rosebud, telling you something about all the pain and the longing and the life and death that lay inside you, coiled like a snake, waiting to uncoil and bite. Or it was just the blues. Later people said it was slave music, that it had the tones of far-off Africa, where we came from, under a different sky and sun. But I didn't know anything about that. I only knew that when I packed in with the crowd on a Saturday night in the basement of Sam Remo's on skid row, at Fifth and Central, I was just merging with the slow beat, the trembling of the cornet, the strum of the bass, the sudden call of the trombone or—and there he was, the boy with the sax, the same face, the same piercing call.

Everything was a haze, in that moment, and the smell of the weed was so pungent inside the hothouse that for all I know I was there for an instant, or for ten hours. I seemed to just sit there, on a crude stool, till Johnson's brawny arm pulled me away, with the other Keystone hands, since he had got what he came there for, and we just piled out and took the night car north, back to Edendale. Some of the men peeled off to a flophouse, but Johnson took me back to the studio, all quiet and ghostlike in the night, the sets lying idle, the western street eerie, as if everybody was holding their breath behind closed windows for the gunfight that would start there at dawn, or for Ben Turpin to come rattling along in the gloaming, twiddling his gun and falling over a hitching post. Or was Ben Turpin much later, at Keystone, when I was long gone, and I am remembering a movie, not the real thing? It's so easy to mix them up. But it was all new, those days, new sights, new sounds, new smells, new experiences, people making up things as they went along, pioneers of jokes and stories, glad mornings when you could sense the dew, the brightness of the sky just waiting to dazzle, the raw energy of the mad men and women around you, full to the brim with pep and pizzazz, raring to go, run, jump, pratfall, kick each other in the pants, crash a tin lizzie over a clifftop or jump out of a window onto their head just for a gag and a few happy bucks. The days when anything could happen.

It would take me five years to meet up with that kid saxophonist with the reddish hair and the marvelous licks, but that's another story. That time, that golden winter in Los Angeles, I was still stuck with Gramby at Silver Lake. The only change in our little circle, with Boris setting out at dawn to cross the mountains to his magic castles, was that we lost Hetty to the Keystones. Of all of us, she was the one that got a contract with Sennett for the long haul—two hundred dollars a week to play dippy dames and funny maids and pratfalling tomboys in the funhouse. She appeared with all of them: Fatty Arbuckle and Mabel Normand and Mack Swain and Wallace Beery and Gloria Swanson, who was only about seventeen, I think, at the time, and Louise Fazenda, and those crazy boys of the Keystone Kops. I remember them, Hank Mann and Al St. John and Slim Summerville and Ford Sterling, who was the chief—he had been Sennett's big shot before Charlie Chaplin, but Charlie had already flown the coop when we came; he didn't want to be trussed down in the kennels for two hundred fifty a week and was climbing the ladder to the very top of the tree, where he shone up there, laughing from the sky. Those were great days. But Gramby was left down on the ground, despite the cards, despite the rosy dreams. He stacked up the basic pay and then stopped, and so I stopped with him, because we had been together for a long time by then, and I had grown from being a child fool to being a wily kid who smoked reefers in the backyard when he wasn't looking, not as if he didn't know, after five years in vaudeville, though the stage folk were a straighter folk, who moved in their own groove, ruled by habits, routines, customs, old traditions, and were set in their ways. They could also be drunks and hopheads, but they needed their heads clear for the work on the stage that you couldn't fake, or sham, or re-take. Everything you did, even magic, was out there before hundreds, sometimes thousands of eyes that could see, more often than you thought up there, right into your soul, and it was that tension, that shuddering tremble that you knew was the life force that kept you going, repeating the same gag, the same angles, the same motions, over and over again, because you were in a hairsbreadth between success and failure. At any moment, a mistake, a fumble, a misstep, and it would all come crumbling down. The original house of cards...

So I took the streetcar with him, daily, down to the vaudevillians' hotel, to mingle with the folk who were playing the Orpheum that week—all the usual miscreants, the Tumbling Demons, the endless double acts, Adair and Wyant, Barto and Clark, Leonard and Willard, Duffy and Sweeney, Pipifax and Panio, Sullivan and Mason, McManus and Carlos, Ball and Chain, all the forgotten names. The Honey Girls, the Soldier Men, the Cycling Brunettes, the Four Melodious Chaps, the Suffragettes a La Carte, The Three Keatons, the Tetsuari Japs, the Langdons, the "Enchanted Forest," Swain's Cockatoos, Fink's Mules again, and Norris Baboons. He would sit in the lobby and devour *Variety*, picking out the latest novelties or travesties, muttering to himself or to me: "Jennings and Evers, Singing and Talking. Whadayaknow, Ace? Another blackface act... the world is waiting... Kuy Kendall and Girlies, well that always works... 'the girls come on with the cakewalk tango, then a Rose waltz and a Grecian number closes...' Who knows, Ace, who knows... Another Chinese act—Manchurian Trio... spinning plates, juggle, balance heavy ornamental articles... 'a neck drop is utilized for the encore...' Come back Long Tack Sam... What do you think of this, Ace? Van Hoven calls himself 'the Dippy Magician,' a full-page ad here—'To whom it may concern—realizing the predatory tendencies of irresponsible artists, and in order to protect my material in both hemispheres, I have made arrangements with Will Collins in London and Edward S. Keller in New York to play twenty weeks on each side of the water every year... my material is copyrighted and patented and all piracy or other infringements will be ruthlessly prosecuted to the full extent of the law...' Have you ever heard of this galoot?"

He was obviously chafing at the bit. But he was still reluctant to cut off from Boris; I could see there was something between them that was what he called an aura, a link that was strangely remote even when they were together in the same room, though they almost never touched each other, except for the handshake or a quick squeeze of Boris's hand on Gramby's arm. Gramby had a kind of fear of contact; it was not a matter between us of race or color. He edged away from anyone, and the affair with Hetty—that was way out of anyone's sight; I might glimpse her in the bedroom, sitting up, for a flash, before the door closed, and once she came out of the bathroom in her pajamas, but she pretended she didn't see me. It was something to do with the past, the other world, the Old Country, the village, the world that Boris half-invented when he wrote his scenario that never got made.

I got cheered up myself when I read that the Four Marx Brothers were edging closer to us again and were playing the Orpheum at San Francisco, when another arrival, up the coast, took Gramby over the edge: Houdini was playing in Oakland. He was not only doing his usual act, the chains, the handcuffs, and the "milk-churn" escape, but had also performed one of his open-air spectaculars in the main street of the town. Suspended upside down by his feet from the seventeenth floor of the Tribune building, in a straight-jacket, he freed himself and hauled himself up the chain over the heads of twenty thousand people, who filled the street and stopped all the traffic. It was on the front page of the *Examiner*. Gramby didn't say anything, but his lips were pursed in that look that I knew meant even the cards were not needed to point the way ahead.

Winter was beautiful in Los Angeles. The sun preening in blue skies as if forever. DeMille dreams still beckoning on the magic mountain on the other side of the park. Keystone frenzy unbound beside the king's bathtub. But two days later, Gramby called me again to the streetcar ride down the hills, past the lake and Echo Park towards the hubbub of downtown and into the lobby of the Cameo Hotel, where two familiar figures, the Gross brothers, strong and dapper in new suits, stood up to greet us, and beside them, a shy young blonde girl with jewel-green eyes stood demurely, waiting for her turn in the lights.

"The Unraveling"

Asher:

My father retreated slowly from life, withdrawing over a period of three years from the chair by the window of his room at the care home to the bed, and then from each one of his failing faculties to the flutter of eyelids and the slow move of the glistening pupils that signaled some kind of deliberation. Most probably, I thought, the last reflex of the cameraman that he always repeated to me as his mantra: Check the frame: top right, top left, lower left, top right. If the frame is correct, all's well, or, at least, you can make a start.

My father was always old, since I was born when he was just two months short of his fifty-eighth birthday, which means I was conceived in the joy of his alliance with his second wife, my twenty-eight-year-old mother, when he was fifty-seven. I grew up feeling that fathers were always ancient, with gray hair and a face full of brown wrinkles. When schoolmates saw him around me they assumed he was my grandfather and often envied me, since grandfathers were more placid and malleable. Which I suppose he was, in his own restrained way, since he found it, I think, rather difficult to square my infancy with the adulthood of his firstborn. In the end, it was only he, the eldest, Yitzhak, the religious one, who was at his side when he died. I can picture them both: my father, dreaming those endless dreams that encompassed his astonishing ninety-five years from the village to the rolling hills of Hollywood and onward to the Land of the Fathers. Depending how far back you wished to go, if you leapt over the uncharted centuries where genealogy long peters out to the certitudes of the Book that my brother spent weeks, months, years reading to him in the hope that a realization of the divine imperative would dawn in those wandering eyes, at the last moment. I never asked him whether he thought it finally did. We had very little to talk about, my brother Yitzhak and I, since my childhood, when his awkward role as an older brother who was old enough to be my father himself was soon deflected by his own embrace of God, a suitable spouse, and the row of little boys with sidecurls and little girls destined for recycled formulas bounced out of his wife's loins, my flock of nephews and nieces.

The family tree. Yitzhak was the obsessive. He wanted to know. He gathered information. He went to conferences of Holocaust remembrance and retrieval of the world lost to the gas ovens of Auschwitz-Birkenau and all the rest. He joined a group of survivors of Bessarabia, mainly veterans of the main city, Kishinev, who were gathering the annals of the old communities that had been scythed down in the killing years, 1941 to 1943. They were gathering material for a big book that would contain every available record of the ancestral hearth, its birth, its formation, its statistical details, its properties, its livestock, its produce, its geographical contors, roads, alleyways, rivulets, its housing stock, its inhabitants from Aaron to Zwiegel, their professions, their causes, their personal qualities and peculiarities, who flopped, shuffled, dragged their feet or walked tall from the house of learning to the burgeoning Zionist societies from whom these stalwart souls had emerged, bursting through the chains and death houses of Nazi Germany to carry their faith in burning brands of resurrection across the sea into the promised land. Most of this I found out leafing through my brother's copy of their occasional bulletins, occurring long after the last Gurevits had departed from the river Dniester's plateau. Celovest, in general, figured very partially in their research, as whatever memories were carried by my Aunt Sarah and Uncle Kolya were being kept for Kolya's magnum opus, and my father mumbled something about having written his own account some decades earlier, in Los Angeles, but was not very keen on revisiting the consequences of all those opened wounds. After 1945, when the Russians marched in to Bessarabia, there was nothing found but ruins; the village itself was destroyed, the old homes ploughed under, and as far as we knew, nothing left to mark the fact that anyone had ever lived, worked, flourished, failed, enjoyed or suffered there at all.

I was even less keen than my father to take on those old ghosts, the legions of the victimized and the eradicated. As an uprooted child of California, I had a different legacy: The lobby cards my dad had ceded to me on my sixth, or was it seventh birthday, the framed set of his collected glories—the color ones were, I later found, extremely prized, deriving from the days when the color was just a trick to entice the customers into the theater for what were mostly black-and-white films. These strange pictures of costumed stars of films I could never see because they were almost all twenty, thirty, forty or even fifty years old at a time, in a country that screened new films that were certified as popular by their releases in far-off England, or Paris, or Greece, it made no difference to most people what languages they were in; they were all foreign, and accompanied by double rows of subtitles in Hebrew and French, the lingua franca of culture. And these could only be seen if one's parents took one by the hand to the cinema—the *kol noa*—the "moving sound," for which there were about twenty theaters in Tel Aviv, quite a few within walking distance of our old ramshackle apartment. It was, more often than not, filled with relatives, who either lived nearby or passed through on trips by the scattered units of the clan dotted about the country, whom I could escape by going out on the roof terrace, as we were a top floor apartment, four floors up the steep and elevator-less stairway, past all the doorbells of the neighbors most of whom seemed to have been living on the block since before I was born: the Nahmanis, the Rosenbergs, Mrs. Abulafia and daughter, the Habibs, Ben-Arieh Katarina and Adam, and F. Dobrynin, whom we all decided was a long-term Russian spy, though what he spied on no one could quite pin down, since he only left the flat to shamble slowly down the two steps of stairs with an old string bag, to limp stolidly down Sheinkin to Allenby and return within at most two hours with the bag stuffed full of groceries. We were convinced they were secret messages collected from all his fellow moles in the shops stretching down towards the beach. But on the roof terrace one could ignore all that, and gaze over the flat rooftops of the older part of the city towards that hazy sun, which touched the tiny strip of the sea and sand that we could glimpse between two blocks above the Carmel market. One didn't need to see the sea since one could smell it, wafting up from the west, balmy on days of blessed breeze, salty close on the stifling days of summer, when the terrace became a baking oven, and one leapt over it in bare feet like a cat on a scalded stone.

The road was called Lord Melchett Street, after a British chemical industrialist and Zionist philanthropist of the 1920s and '30s, we were told, though it was not very long or memorable, and contains nowadays not a jot of parking space. But it was a leafy, quiet bastion then, and one could shoulder one's little bag of towel and bathing suit and pad down in about fifteen minutes to the beach. I was not myself a sea urchin, but preferred my father's celluloid dreams, kept for years in an old shoebox that no one else was allowed to touch, till I transferred the cards to a large format album with proper celluloid pockets to protect the collection, which was by then beyond price. I knew their names by heart and probably knew them better than the old colleagues who used to drop in from the other side of the world, from Los Angeles and New York, to sit in the open parlor around the circular glass table, sip coffee made in mother's old brass Arab finjan and gossip about the old days. Even if they were old, when I tested them they confessed to only the vaguest knowledge about Elliott Dexter, Leatrice Joy, Rod La Rocque, Richard Cromwell, Helen Burgess, Victor Varconi and other DeMille stars, though they did recall, at least by name, Claudette Colbert, and Charles Laughton, and Henry Wilcoxon, and Gary Cooper, and Jetta Goudal and even Joseph Schildkraut, who appeared together with his father, Rudolph Schildkraut, in *The King of Kings*.

Most of my lobby cards were from DeMille movies that my father had worked in, though he had other credits as well: with John Ford, Raoul Walsh, Tod Browning, Ernst Lubitsch and a host of others I only came to recognize much later. But I was fixated on those marvelous faces—strong, dashing, beautiful, cunning, heroic, villainous, young and old, from the fresh cherub Jackie Coogan as Tom Sawyer, with fat Eugene Pallette as the Duke, to old guys like Guy Kibbee or H. B. Warner, who was DeMille's Jesus Christ, and others who were probably not that aged except to a ten-year-old. And the ladies: Colbert, Gloria Swanson, Barbara Stanwyck, Loretta Young, Hedy Lamarr, Paulette Goddard, all shiny hair and flushed cheeks and slinky bodies, or staring out in tragic poses like the girl in prison clothes in one of the DeMille films, *The Godless Girl*, which I never saw until I was sitting at the large viewing desk in the American archives of George Eastman House in far off Rochester, New York, decades later, unspooling a rare, fragile print. Her name was Lina Basquette, and I was probably the only kid who had ever seen that name on a lobby card or poster since 1929.

Those were the companions of my childhood days, till I grew up a little and graduated to Westerns, when I had to stockpile more pictures that were sent in by my father's friends in California—pictures of Alan Ladd, and Randolph Scott, and grizzled old Walter Brennan, and John Wayne, and Robert Mitchum, and Ben Johnson and other unlikely contenders from the antiques: W.S. Hart and Tom Mix and Harry Carey... Woody Strode—he was big and black and stood out. I was very curious about him, but my dad had never worked with him. His stories always curled back not to the stars but to the great cinematographers of his own time, names like Gregg Toland, and Karl Struss, and Bill Clothier, and Burnett Guffey, and Loyal Griggs, and James Wong Howe: "the Chinaman." I had no idea what they did that was so great and different from all the others, but he took me when I was twelve to the local studios at Herzliya, just outside Tel Aviv, to show me the sound stages and the immense Mitchell BNC camera, which swooped and soared like a mechanical flying elephant on its expanding steel crane, with the cameraman seated behind his instrument like a blessed charioteer of the gods. One day, I thought, all this will be mine...

At a time when other kids got bicycles, I got a three-lens fully windable Wollensak 8-millimeter cine-camera, with interchangeable wide-, medium- and long-length focal lenses, and a Eumig projector, which had a set of pulleys and levers through which you could thread quarter-inch magnetic tapes so that a soundtrack could be recorded and synchronized. I had already experimented, using the lobby-card archive box with a rudimentary projecting device that could throw the image of a single 35-millimeter frame on the wall. Dad advised but let me sort it out for myself. I could use the frames from film strips that a man with a stall at the Carmel market sold for one piaster a frame, presumably cast out, or requisitioned from the movie projection booths, from offcuts of jammed reels or entire cans set aside of films that only had one run and would be unlikely to be re-shown. My favorite was an entire mini-spool of technicolor glory showing an army of cavalry knights, both men and horses lavishly costumed, with chain-mail armor and helmets and white waistcoats with the red cross emblazoned on each, advancing, frame by frame, until they reached a blaze of yellow, purple, blue, green, and red banners fluttering over the stands of a medieval joust, which was just about to start when the celluloid reel ran out... Later on, I realized the movie was *Ivanhoe*, that the man with the dark beard was Robert Taylor, the tall helmeted figure was George Sanders, and the black-haired girl was Elizabeth Taylor, but there were just a few frames of her close up, at the end. (1952—cinematographer: Freddie Young!) One by one, the selected frames appeared on the white walls of 4d Lord Melchett, just between the framed card of Charlton Heston wielding the Tablets of the Law at Mount Sinai—a gift from Dad's old boss, in his grand apotheosis, and a photograph of Aunt Sarah, Dad's eldest sibling, standing in a peasant smock with a hoe in her hand and a rifle slung at her shoulder, side by side with the first prime minister of the State of Israel, David Ben-Gurion, and his wife, Paula, a fellow follower, along with Sarah, four decades back, of the anarchist Emma Goldman. Between those two options, my own dreams unfolded, of the castle on the hill, the grand adventure of England, the country of jousts, Robin Hood, King Richard the Lionheart and Winston Churchill, whose hand Dad had pressed once, alongside DeMille, during a visit the ex-prime minister made to California, where, he said, he had always wanted to meet the director of *The King of Kings*.

According to Dad, the great man told them, "I cried like a baby! The scene at Golgotha! Judas and the hanging tree! Healing the blind boy... Of course, we can't all be like that."

London was not like that either. No knights, no jousts, no massed rides to the rescue of unrequited love, though chain mail would have come in useful. The dark sky, the drizzling rain, the pressure of anonymous millions, Jo Lyons tea rooms, meat and two veg, two slices of bread and dripping, still available in the late night cafés of the Covent Garden market, long gone, replaced by tourist nirvanas of street performances and souvenir stalls, but then still the larger stage for the London School of Film Technique, a haven of a different sort. Dad offered to get me into UCLA, the jewel in the crown of Californian film schools, seeing as I was blessed with an American passport, and old friends would help to pay for the education of the next generation of Gore "lensers," as *Variety* stockpiled its phrases. All would be well in the best of all possible worlds, but I held out for the London school, and in the end the Master couldn't argue, since it was three times cheaper. Best not to live one's whole life in the shadow.

Nevertheless, they all saw me off at the airport. It was a big deal then, early September 1968. The world was not yet a single global hive buzzing with frequent flyers, the vapor trails of the carrier planes more familiar than clouds, the sky's rumble a constant background. There had been a local war the previous year, in which I played my part, however trivial, with the army unit's Arri 16. Kolya arrived on eve of battle, from his academic perch in middle America, a kind of stern nemesis, very tall, the tallest of the

Gurevitses, and with a face that was most often fixed in a kind of somber frown, a disapproval of most of what occurred before his eyes or in the interrogation room of his intellect, that stark and, I always imagined, monkish cell in which, like a scholar of old, he hunched over a great oak desk piled with scrolls and manuscripts, with an immense black feather quill and two baskets or trays on either side, one containing a small pile of "values" (*arachim* in Hebrew) that he considered both necessary and valid, and which were worth defending to the death, against all odds, material or ideological, and were forever true and eternal, and the other, full to the brim and overflowing, a paper mountain scraping the ceiling, of Values that were False, mendacious, fallacies, deceptions, strategic and overwhelming errors of historical judgement, moral quicksand, in which the best minds, faltering for but a fleeting moment, would find themselves mired so helplessly that they were unable, even in the flash of recognition of their mistake, to extricate themselves, and led to inevitable extinction. To counter this, he had sequestered himself by force of will and judgement in his fortress house in Ann Arbor, Michigan, in whose university department of history he had been a recognized savant since the mid-1950s, and in that leafy retreat he had wrought his mighty treatise, "Jew Hatred Through the Ages: from Babylon to the Third Reich," a title he struggled mightily to preserve from the university's mild suggestion that he deploy the more academic concept of anti-Semitism. But he refused this, in edition after edition, as he expanded the work from five to ten volumes and then on towards the twentieth and even beyond, hauling in the latest excretions of racial ethnic religious hostility from reaches as far apart as Argentina and Indonesia, including of necessity and choice the entire Arab world, having mastered language after language in his search, from all the usual Latin and Germanic nuances to Arabic, Malay, Persian and Swahili, as well as a smattering of Chinese and Japanese, although he announced, to great astonishment in the world of scholars, that he was not including the latter in his roster of Jew-hating nations, since, although they held that

Jews were different, and were eager recruits to the fellowship of idiots who believed in the Protocols of the Elders of Zion and the theory that "the Jews rule the world," they did not consider this a defect, but something to be emulated and admired. For this, he was denounced as "as close to a crackpot theory of history that a distinguished scholar can devise" by Michiko Kakutani in *The New York Times*, though that was much later, in the 1980s.

In 1967, Kolya—Nathan Gurevits to the rest of the human race, he never took on my father's Americanization—was still considered an eccentric maverick by the bulk of the Zionist academics, a curiosity, a man so extreme in his revisionist politics that after a decade of fighting both intellectually and physically for the rightist Irgun Zvai Leumi—the National Military Organization—and settled and borne a son and two daughters for the cause, he chose, in anger and disgust at the socialist government's acceptance of German reparations—the post-Third Reich's compensation for Nazi atrocities and looting of Jewish wealth and lives—to leave the country, denouncing its government as a "travesty in the best traditions of Stalin" and settling in the United States, with his wife, Tsvia—who lucky for him was of the same persuasion, since they had fought shoulder to shoulder in the underground and were a poster couple for the national insurrection—and their three children. He visited once, after 1956 and the Sinai campaign. He appreciated the required martial spirit, though he still denounced it as a collaboration with the imperialist hypocrite powers of Britain and France, and then, in June 1967, he again temporarily set aside his disdain for the Labor Zionists and their "Communists-for-a-rainy-day" apparatchiks. This was the first time I met my cousin Adi, Adir Gurevits, soon to be Gur-Arieh—"lion cub," who had come to be recruited to the armed forces, having just passed eighteen, since he had been allowed back for a few years to attend school in the Holy Land and we had kicked shit together in the streets out of range of his parental terror. He seemed a diffident lad, stuffed to the gullet with his father's opinions but with the assertive posture of the Gurevitses, that swaggering walk and a kind of eagle eye that took in things at a glance and appeared to store them, in case they were needed for future use. I had no idea how far that would lead him.

The gathering at the departure lounge of Lod Airport was a curious round-up of the remaining family guard. My father and mother were there, and Aunt Sarah, whose husband, Moshe, had died two years before, Sarah looking more and more like an old Russian babushka who had spent too much time in the sun, till she was brown as one of those Sephardi matriarchs who marched their brood in and out of stations, bringing the strong whiff of Fez and Casablanca to the Mediterranean west. She had become more mysterious, as time went on, and her role as the Memory Queen of the old days and the pioneering spirit of the Third Ascension had diminished and faded into sighs and long silences, or shaking of the head, or the long perusal of the trade union newspaper, *Davar*, with its vast blocks of indigestible words and almost no pictures, which still connected her to at least the vestiges of what the old folk thought they had been trying to achieve in the name of progress, justice and peace. I remember being terribly embarrassed when she appeared at our school, at assembly, to deliver her standard talk on the ravages of life in old Palestine of the 1920s, the hardships of the communal life, the embrace of poverty, the struggle against the Arab rebellion of the 1930s, the days of the spade and the gun, the grand heroism of Zionist toil...

Everyone noted the strangeness of this reunion, in a cafeteria wedged between those departing, presumably briefly, to taste the fleshpots that still tempted even the best, and the arriving, curious tourists, or sheepish groups that may or may not be new immigrants harvested for absorption and the speed-learning of the Ulpans, the studios that taught crash-course Hebrew on the human assembly line. And noted the missing: Zev Wolf, who had traveled directly from the village way out east to China—trader, smuggler, spy?—dodging the aftermath of revolution, the Civil War, reds against whites, to the "radish city," Harbin, Manchuria, whose inhabitants had to profess whatever allegiances were required at a given time—red on the outside, white inside, or vice versa, as times rippled and changed. We were all brought up on the legend, and the small sheaf of old photographs, that my dad had got at some point, before his departure, from Kolya, "Uncle's lobby cards," which Kolya said had reached him years before from Zev—pictures from South Africa of native huts and nut-brown Boers with wide-brimmed hats on the background of immense mine-work pits with hordes of half-naked black people wielding picks and baskets in the background. Pictures from Argentina of more mines, and native peasants with ponchos and giant straw hats. Or Mexico, on the Day of the Dead, with skeleton skulls and death masks wielded in the sun. Or even more enigmatically, post-marked Irkutsk, "RFSFR," with images of snowy steppes, white landscapes of beech trees, a frozen lake that seemed to stretch forever. There had been some writing on the back of some of the pictures, but it had been completely blacked out, and none of Dad's tricks with strong lighting, exposing the prints to all kinds of studio processes at the Herzliya laboratories could recover any trace of information. Both Dad and Sarah said the pictures were from Zev; they felt it in their bones. He appeared in their dreams, giving them the impish and mischievous grin that they remembered from the root, in *Der heim*...

They were convinced of this because it was common for Yakov, Vassily and Gramby to communicate in this manner, through ephemeral mist. In my father's family tales, patchy and enigmatic as they often were, he kept returning to Gramby, the professional magician who was the baby of the family even though he was two years older than Kolya, and six years older than Judit, because he was the one who seemed to have escaped most thoroughly from any vestige of the fate ordained for us, for the scattered chaff of the Pale of Settlement, lashed into place by old traditions, prised apart by new ideas, torn apart by impersonal history, battered by hatreds between others who were indifferent to their fate. But Vassily floated free into another realm entirely, beguiled by that old newspaper photograph that Boris always returned to: Houdini, the master of mystery and deception, whose image set Boris too into the realm of pictures, images of czarist ghosts and demons... Boris embraced the machine, the technological appliance of stories, whereas Yakov-Vassily returned to the oldest form of human invention, the sorcerer and his apprentice, the puffs of smoke, the crystal ball, the oracle of pure chance. And, drifting from stage to stage, from town to town, across the oceans, to even star, according to legend, at the Folies Bergere, he vanished, when the European chaos that boiled out from Berlin and Vienna rolled into Paris, on a summer of black smoke and blood... But Boris was sure, with that stubborn sense that connects brothers, that he lived on after that, and escaped as many others did, through Marseille to Spain, or Morocco, or Brazil, even to Australia, and he even made a journey once to Mexico City, to meet an old cinematographer who knew the secret organizations that smuggled both Jews and Nazis out of Europe's rubble, and who was said to have lists of passengers who left Marseille and other international ports in various intertwined guises, some Germans disguised as Jews and some Jews even disguised as escaped Nazi officers, who were often valued as the bearers of stolen loot, and there was the tale of one forger, who might have been Gramby, who packed with him a selection of counterfeits of famous paintings from museums in Paris, Berlin or Vienna to sell to gullible merchants in Rio de Janeiro and Buenos Aires. Although the search, then, was futile, Boris said that ever since, he could sometimes feel his closest brother's presence in the night, hovering over the bed, an occult "ectoplasm" like that produced by fakers and mediums, not real yet not totally unreal, accompanied by a kind of rustle of sheets that, my father said, he identified with jabs of memory of their childhood, back in the tiny room they shared, and when very little, the common bed in which they slept, listening to the rise and fall of the snoring of their gigantic baba upstairs, his breath struggling to escape through his beard...

The "vanished magician" transferred from my father's dreams to mine, and I often talked to him, in my own private agonies, in the night, when all that surrounded me was glum and hostile, and miasmas of old slights, resentments, rusty chains of past sins and disasters passed from father to son, my older brother's black hole of godliness where pleasure was pain and suffering was the greatest joy, my mother's mute acceptance of ambition stifled for the "greater family good," the mismatch between the vivacious smiling girl of her old theater pictures, the New York "scene," Greenwich Village, the clatter of dance bands, cigarette smoke and interleaved lovers, the sound of jazz that lingered in her small collection of records, from Duke Ellington to "cool jazz" Stan Getz. Then there was Miles Davis, *A Kind of Blue*, which I played so often it was scratched on every track and sounded like a ghost of something else that had once been clear and pure, but I could, by recalling it in my head, conjure up my Uncle Yakov, Vassily Gramby, carrying the crystal ball that contained my fate. "What do you see? What do you see?" I asked him, but although he kept telling me tall tales of the past, and the elephants of the Circus Medrano, the can-can girls of the Folies Bergere, the basements of Pigalle and Montmartre and the grand halls where he performed his Lazarus trick, he never performed it for me. He would always shake his head at the end and put his finger to his lips, and look around furtively as if he too was being watched, and disappear in the sweaty ooze of Tel Aviv's summer heatwave.

They were all still alive out there. Nobody died in our family; they were simply occulted to exist somewhere else in another time and space. Except Judit, whom everyone assumed had perished in Communist China, where she had disappeared after some rumored sightings in post-war Shanghai, having followed my uncle Zev to Manchuria twenty years before and was lost sight of when he vanished from there even before the war that washed over the globe. Anything out of the ambit of the Western world and the Jews was just a faint haze on our horizon.

The survivors gathered to wave me goodbye. Before our present world of electronic barriers, security checks, absolute surveillance, minute inspection of every morsel of baggage, shoes, belts, buckles, undergarments, hair, follicles, liquids, gels, toothpaste, shampoo, intentions, hidden or otherwise, unconscious desires or fears, people could walk up to the terrace balcony overlooking the tarmac and see their travelers climb up the gangplank, like ancient mariners, or the crowds besieging the great ocean liners that crossed the seas not so long ago. Perhaps, I thought—seeing their frenzied gestures, as I turned round at the plane's door, shielding my eyes against the sun, my mother waving like a crazed fan at a football game, and Aunt Sarah, still able to shake a hand in the air even in her late seventies, and Kolya, sternly pointing, strangely I thought, up in the air, towards God?— perhaps they were recalling their own epic journeys, which had seemed, at their source, an impossible quest, to destinations that could not be imagined except due to some tantalizing image or postcard that might have jolted an emerging fantasy of what might be or become something other than the origin, or simply a temporary refuge from storms that struck suddenly, or even after warnings too often unheeded, the roots clutching like ankle-chains, still moving onwards, putting the greatest distance possible from the font, deserting or chased away from the wheat fields, towards the clouds, towards the rain...

Boris—the Journey, continued:

After I shot the pogromist in the face, I was a changed man. That might seem obvious. But in men inured to violence, or who have lived it since childhood, such an event might mean little, merely a graduation. Son of a rabbi, brought up in kindness, with a gentle hand, if firm and not exactly meek, my experience was akin to that of a boy thrust into war and wrenched brutally into a different world. When Leibel Grossman delivered me back to my parents' house I sank back into the embrace of the family's calls and whispers, my mother's litany of woes that might have befallen me, my father's recital of Psalm 140, my sister's innocent cuddles and my brothers' midnight conclave to drag the full account from me in all its gory details. Yakov told me that he had dreamed of me most nights, the dreams composed of three distinct categories. In dreams of flight, I was wafted above the clouds and skimmed over the rooftops, hills and valleys, over rivers from which strange beasts beckoned, towards strange mountains whose rocks were fashioned from jade, marble and gold. In the second dream category, I was crawling underground in a tunnel, under a garden of twisted trees and strange plants, towards a mansion in which men in splendid uniforms and women in silvery gowns were dancing. In the third type of dream I was in a train, in a palatial first-class carriage, on my own not counting the major domo who was attending me and lighting my Ritmeester cigar. The train was coasting through the night, past the bright lights of a vast city that never seemed to come to an end.

Yakov was just short of twelve years old at the time, fourteen months before his own bar mitzvah. Zev had just passed his own, and Kolya was nine, still hiding behind our mother's skirts and frightened of anything unfamiliar. My father had clearly spent time with his thoughts, trying to find a way to prevent me from what he saw as destroying my life and forsaking my faith. Everyone in the village was now aware of the events that were rocking the empire. Tsvi Glitz, the new bet midrash clerk, had a subscription to the *Bessarabian Gazette*, in which we could all read of the continuing strikes and riots that were taking place everywhere, as well as small incidents closer to home that echoed like the baying of wolves. The most dangerous appeared to be the mutinies of army reservists, one of which occurred in our own region, at Bender, in which the rebel soldiers attacked civilians, both Jews and Christians, and looted shops and houses. There were pogroms at Rishkan and Sirdi. At Kishinev police fired on the funeral of a poor Jewish woman who had been killed by hooligans. A mob then attacked the Jewish quarters and our people were fleeing the city. Leibel rushed off again, though I was strictly ordered to stay behind, and reports came that the Jewish resistance forces fought the pogromists with guns in the streets. Much further away, in the Caucasus, there were battles between Armenians, Georgians and Turks. The *Gazette* printed an article by Maxim Gorky accusing the Black Hundreds and other shadowy groups of inciting Russians against Jews, Tartars against

Armenians, setting peasants against students. In no country, he wrote, has the struggle of the ruling class to keep its power been fought so basely and with such thirst for blood. In October, we read that Moscow and Saint Petersburg were on the brink of revolution: the railways were on strike and workers had thrown up barricades everywhere. The czar ceded the reformers' demand for a constituent assembly, but even that failed to stop the demonstrations. Troops were massing to "restore order."

We all knew what would happen next. In October the pogromists struck in force in Odessa, Kherson and Kiev. This time many hundreds were killed. Leibel Grossman appeared again, with a gunshot wound in his right arm, reporting that many fighters of the Jewish Bund had been captured and executed. Our friend Atom, the friendly Armenian, was shot dead in a skirmish. Leibel took me aside, to the blacksmith's shed, and told me that our names were now known to the authorities. The baker, at whose house we had gathered, had been beaten to death by the local police chief. He had divulged the whereabouts of the print shop, where old rosters of guard duties had been found. The police and Black Hundreds were working hand in glove, they were one and the same. Orders from the capital were to eliminate all local militias, and the names were being copied to every province. If the list reached Kishinev, his name would be recognized, and the trail would lead to the village.

This time we had to tell my father directly, in his study, his refuge from all the storms and deluges. It was November and winter had closed in again, its white shawl drifted over all sins, and the house warmed to the boil by the oven. I remember how the gold letters on the covers of the holy books glinted in the light of his reading lamp. He liked a strong lamp, as his eyes were failing, and he had obtained a massive pair of reading glasses from Belzi, which made him look like the sorcerer from some half-remembered tale. His jowls seemed to have sagged from worry and from his realization of the burden that he knew would fall on him in due time. My mother had fussed over Leibel's wounded arm in the kitchen, and she had spent time washing and redressing his wound while I could hear my father clump about upstairs. But he was sitting down when we came in. I realized for the first time that both Leibel and I towered above him as we stood, so that I was looking down on his sparse hair straggling under the yarmulke as he looked up at me, a symbolic loss of his unbridled authority. He motioned for us to sit in the wooden chairs that were placed for his adult supplicants.

I was well aware of his plan. My absence in Odessa the year before had thwarted his attempt to match me to the daughter of the Rabbi of Markolest, who deemed the potential groom too fickle, or already a heretic, and he had married her instead to a good scholar of Soroki who also owned a dairy business. There were of course other daughters waiting all around the region, but the fall-back plan was to appoint me as the assistant to the Russian teacher assigned to the new town gymnasium, a post that both paid well and would allow me access to the full range of secular writing, which my father knew well I had already sampled. He knew the proposal would take me off my guard, as my picture of him as the Constant Shield of Tradition would be blurred by this sudden modern twist. "The world is rushing towards us," he said. "People are said to be 'enlightened.' We await the proof. But a book is still a book. God's words, even reflected by the pen of fools, is still God's word." I am not sure what he meant by that. A year before, I would have wanted to sit down and engage in an argument, or just to listen to what he had to say on something other than a quote, or an interpretation, of the Torah and Midrash. The very idea of any limit to that all-encompassing universe would have made him frown and lower his head, as I imagined a bull might in the bullring of the foreign magazine pictures that had already infected my brain.

"Papa, we have a problem," I told him. He had already guessed it, having been informed by the network of local notables who kept their ears pricked and their noses to the ground, ever alert for disasters that might penetrate the outer perimeter of the unchanged. He would already have weighed up pros and cons, made inquiries, set up contingencies.

"I'll send you to Belzi," he said.

"Not far enough," said Leibel, perhaps on the brink of saying something that could not be said.

"Belzi first," my father bargained. "Then, if necessary, across the border, to Radautz. Our cousin Shimmel is there. There is a large community of the Sadagura. The bell is struck here and tolls there. I will talk to your mother."

He stood up, but the crown of his head, amazingly, was still lower than mine. He still needed to look slightly up, into my eyes, and pulled my head forward to kiss my brow.

"The Name will keep the righteous."

But after I left the bounds of the village, I never saw him again.

*

The trains, the trains, the trains... Once you are in Bucharest, you suddenly realize that you are linked to the world. Like a modern cathedral, the great railway station beckons in and disgorges travelers from the furthest reaches of the Austrian-Hungarian Empire and the German Reich, and places that reverberated only in legend in the sluggish vale of Celovest: Paris, France, Milan and Rome in Italy, Antwerp, Brussels, Amsterdam, down south to Madrid and Lisbon, and further on by the cross canal ferries to London, Birmingham and Glasgow. From there, the Atlantic Ocean separated us all from the New World, America, the Golden State, *der goldeneh medineh*, where so many thought the future of mankind must surely lie. There lived fabulous people who were chronicled by Karl May, whose name reached us even in Celovest, whose library held three copies of his famous Indian novels. I was able to hold them once in my hands, but though I could just about read the characters and words, my German was much too basic. But I remember the frontispiece pictures, the noble features of Old Shatterhand and Winnetou the Warrior. Nobody told us, at the time, that the famous writer had never visited the land of his tales before he had written all those stories. There was no need for him to be there, for he portrayed his own truth. I still remember the picture: Two youths of dark and naked beauty, with long flowing hair, rowing a canoe across a river towards a small group of men in Western dress. It was certainly not the Dniester...

But Bucharest was my first port of entry into this other world, a grand, princely city, even larger than Odessa, with great colonnaded mansions and palaces, tall churches with glittering spires, fine red-roofed houses and wide avenues along which electric carriages moved in a stately speed on rails, and well-dressed gentlemen and ladies passed on sledded droshkis, clad in furs, with jeweled rings on their fingers. There were parks, academies, and arched arcades of shops full of fine clothes, perfumes, tobacco, toiletries, books and journals, and so much else that came directly from Paris, Vienna, Berlin, London, all the capitals of money and culture. This country had its own czar, King Carol I, who had ruled for more than twenty years, though not as long as the enduring Austrian, Franz Josef, who had been on the throne since 1848. His real name, my new Romanian friends told me, was Karl Eitel Friedrich Zephyrinus Ludwig Hohenzollern, and he had led his people in their victorious war against the Turks, who had ruled here for many generations. He was apparently related in some way to Napoleon Bonaparte, though not, luckily, to Nikolai of Russia. Therefore he was willing to allow in the refugees fleeing in greater and greater numbers from Bessarabia and Ukraine. Not that they could be stopped; they just flowed through the forests, crossed the open fields, trudged over the central Moldovenesc mountains or walked, as Leibel and I did, into the border town of Galatz, on the banks of the Danube. From there, you could take the train southwest to the capital and arrive there within a few hours.

In our first weeks in the city, as winter closed in, we stayed in a crowded house full of students and exiles, in what passed for the Jewish quarter, south of the main King Carol Boulevard, close to the banks of the Dambovita. The community in Bucharest was divided between the European Jews of Austrian descent and the older Sephardic families, some of whom were immensely rich and were targets of envy and hatred. All the Christian Rumanians appeared

126

to believe that the Jews hoarded great wealth and oppressed the country's peasants. The king's police, however, zealously guarded the peace of the capital, and we could walk around unmolested. In any case, we, the younger newcomers, took on the simple dress and clothing of the local students and mingled with the crowds, able to walk up and gaze upon the palace and the rituals of the guards as they paraded in the square with their bright costumes and plumed helmets. We could stand at the shop windows of the bourgeois, eyeing the rich women as they entered the dress shops, gazing insolently at the fur-clad men who entered to buy a case of cigars. Carefree, we thought, only for the moment, since here too, as we believed, inevitably, revolution would arrive.

As everywhere else, Bucharest had its underworld of thieves, beggars, fraudsters, counterfeiters, smugglers, along with a host of rebel groups. As in Russia, they were illegal, though there was a party of Social Democrats that was called the Socialist Union. All the cells were buzzing with the latest news of the fate of the Russian rebellions. The revolutionary parties were in disarray everywhere. The entire Saint Petersburg soviet had been arrested, and Trotsky himself was being held for trial at the Peter and Paul fortress, along with other leaders. The czar's police and the Black Hundreds were arresting, beating and murdering people all over the empire. Pogroms were continuing in Gomel, Vasilkov, Vyatka, and in June, a terrible attack at Bialystok, where pitched battles were also fought between the army and the Jewish self-defense units. Two hundred Jews were killed in one day.

Of the active revolutionaries still at liberty, hundreds were still fleeing abroad, to countries in the West when possible, to Paris, the Netherlands, and London, even to America, and many to Austria-Hungary and Germany, where they were under strict surveillance but still able to hold meetings and organize.

In Bucharest, however, we could only find a way to make ends meet, day by day. The obvious job I could do was in a print works, and both Leibel and I found a sympathetic employer, who printed greeting cards, travel brochures, and shop leaflets, and took us on as apprentices. One of the less pleasant aspects of this work was the printing of anti-Jewish leaflets for the Rumanian Peasants' Party, which we tried to smudge, only to have to print them anew. We succeeded in inserting some ridiculous proof errors that made the authors appear gauche and illiterate, but this was only a temporary triumph.

After a few weeks, a Rumanian student, Radu, who was our chief contact with the local radical groups, came to the printing works with a new offer: he had found me a place that would be much more congenial, at a photographer's shop off the Elizabeth Boulevard, which specialized in family photographs, wedding portraits, and other "special occasions." Since he heard I had an interest in pictures, this seemed an ideal solution.

The photographer himself was a curious character. His name was Nicolae Makedonsky, and he was a minor member of an apparently illustrious aristocractic family, or one that claimed aristocratic foundations of Polish-Lithuanian origin. His uncle had been a government minister, and his cousin was a well-regarded poet, playwright, and politician of the National Liberal Party. He was apparently a "symbolist," though I had no idea what that meant. Nicolae was the black sheep of the family, who had wandered about much of Europe, photographing people and mountains. He had had great success, I was told, sitting around in cafés and convincing women he took a fancy for to sit for photographic portraits, many of which graced the walls of his studio—a fine catalog of Bucharest beauties. He was very tall, with mischievous eyes and a perfectly tended waxed moustache whose ends quivered when he laughed, which was often. His charm was evident, but it was also a mask, behind which he concealed another family legacy, that of brave and committed insurgents. Among his forefathers, he boasted Serbian rebels who had fought both against the Turks and Greek *hospodars* in the service of the Ottoman Empire. Consequently, he said, he abhorred empires, czars, kaisers and kings, and all hereditary ranks, which he said were like plague pustules upon the body of humanity. Because of his birth, he said, he could hardly count himself as a class warrior along the lines of Karl Marx, but he was an adherent of another form of revolution—that of the anarchists, veering between the opposite poles of Prince Kropotkin and the German philosopher Max Stirner. Less than a week after he had engaged me, he handed me a well-leafed book entitled *The Ego and Its Own* and said, "Read it boy, and free yourself of the cobwebs."

My German was rough-edged, but I was able to make out passages that had a profound effect on my mind. It was not a book that one could imagine in Russian, or in Yiddish, though perhaps those versions existed, beyond my limited sphere of knowledge. Stirner believed that only the individual spirit could ever be truly free, and not only the spirit but the material body had to be free of constraints. Thus he had no truck with theories that left the individual person in thrall to an external force, be it the state, a certain class, "the people," religion, or any organized party. His was a doctrine of absolute individualism. There were sentences that seared themselves into my youthful and unformed aware-ness, that I recall to this day. Writing of Christianity, but cutting the cords of my own faith, he wrote: "If it ever became clear to you that God, the commandments, do nothing but harm and ruin you, you would throw them from you as the Christians condemned Apollo or Minerva or any heathen morals..." and "Everything sacred is a tie—a chain..." I could feel, as I read these words, my father rising in a kind of paroxysm, a paralysis of rage, holding his fist over me, and I had to put the book aside. But only for a while, because then I opened it again.

Stirner caused my first rift with Leibel. When he saw me read-ing the book and struggling through the gothic type he snorted and rapped me on the head with his knuckles. "I should have warned you about that old roué," he said. "He will just fill your head with bourgeois garbage. It is a game he plays. He likes to play games." He was going to warn me of something else but held back. In any case I could not return to the print works because Leibel himself had left, and was hawking bibles in the market. This was not quite a moral example.

I went on reading the books that the photographer kept bringing me from his library, in his house up on a hill overlooking the city from the southeast. In fact, he owned a motor car, a French model, I think it was a Renault, that he drove like an infernal machine to and from his city workplace. There were few cars in Bucharest and it was a general novelty. People knew him and stopped in the road to wave as he cluttered past in his leather coat and goggles. It was as if someone in our day owned and operated his own airplane. Once he had taken me to the library and let me loose among the volumes, I was lost.

Makedonsky's advice was that if one learned German, French and English, all the rest would follow, apart from Chinese, Arabic and Hindu. He envied me that I could read the Hebrew, because he believed there were secret messages in the text of the Torah. If one was pressed for time, German and English would suffice, since most things in other languages were translated into one or other, or both. He gave me some primers and I began to study. The photography studio was not like the printworks, there were often long periods in which one could sit in the side room and read. Taking the pictures was the easy part, but the preparation of the solutions for the developing and fixing was time consuming and the vapors of the darkroom often made one's head reel. To save time, my employer suggested I should move into the room behind the darkroom. That way I could work at the developing at any hour and start devouring the books.

Leibel warned me, when I took my suitcase with my few clothes and toiletries, wagging his finger in my face, like the good elder brother I never had: Beware! The man is not after your soul, as you think. He is one of those, everybody knows it, he wants your virgin Jewish behind!

I was so green then, and had lived so protected a life, that I had no idea what he was saying. My behind was of limited use to me in any case, and I could not imagine its use for anything but defecation. Later I remember childhood hints and nods about Herschel Fruck, who had a strange way of walking and talking, and kept to himself and ran away from girls. But I thought it was probably something of the kind I was guilty of myself, failing to wash the private parts often enough. I always believed that real purity was in the heart.

Soon after I left, Leibel disappeared. I went back to the small crowded apartment one day, and our friend Radu told me he had returned to pass messages to the Jewish self-defense groups back across the border. We waited for months, but he never returned. I wrote asking about him in my letters to my father, which I sent in the mail but never knew had arrived until I received an answer, in a letter covered with markings, which had clearly been opened by the czarist censors and clumsily stuffed back in its envelope, sealed with paper tape. My father wished me well, and everyone was safe so far; my mother was in good health and my brothers missed me and my sister Judit demanded my instant return, but he understood that some time had to pass. At the end of the letter he had written baldly, "No one has seen your friend."

I immersed myself in reading. Stirner was pretty turgid when one got by the aphorisms, but I found a new friend in Nietzsche. His German was easy to read, and direct, and full of startling thoughts and stunning fables. I read *Ecce Homo: How One Becomes What One Is*, in one long night, with its strange headings: "Why I Am So Wise," "Why I Am So Clever," "Why I Write Such Excellent Books." I could never imagine the somber Russians—Turgenev, Tolstoy, Dostoyevsky—writing in such a vein, perhaps Pushkin, or Gogol. Then I plunged into *Also Sprach Zarathustra*: the astounding images, notions, ideas—"To be truthful—how few can achieve it... all that the Good call Evil must come together that one Truth can be learned..." What on earth did the man mean? I came to understand that I was standing over the rim of a gigantic soup tureen, in which a fabulous and full potage was bubbling, or the grandest of Mama's tshulents, but I was only tasting the merest morsel of an immensely complex meal, in which so many ingredients that I had never even dreamed of were mixed in a grand, vigorous stirring. I myself, without any doubt, was an idiot, a sleeper only beginning to stir from a long sleep that had lasted from the day of my birth. In fact, I had not yet been born!

German was straightforward, once one knew Yiddish, the old jargon of the communities. But English was slow; one had to learn by rote, the grammar was so complicated. The larger part of my host's books were in French, and I left that for the next stage, which had to be postponed. I could just pass my fingers over the rich spines that promised the world of Stendahl, Dumas, Hugo, Zola... In English, Makedonsky had a set of volumes by H.G. Wells, which were written in a crisp prose and were my first samples of the English-speaking mind. And what a mind! *The Time Machine*, *The Invisible Man*, *The Sleeper Wakes*, *The War of the Worlds* and *The Island of Doctor Moreau*. I was completely unprepared for these, as my lack of French had kept me from the world of Jules Verne. The only fantastic tales that I knew from childhood were those of the Name, the Creator, of Adam and Eve and the giants and Cain and Abel, and the mixing up of the tongues at Babel. Now that I could unmix them, I was spellbound by the far-off Englishman's imagination: the making of the machine that could travel into the future, the man who could not be seen and could only make himself visible by swathing himself in bandages, the most wounded man on the planet... the perils that came from Mars, and the world's devastation, a prognostication of something vast and terrible that would come to pass, not at the hands of creatures from another planet but from ourselves... The terrible doctor who made his own creatures, and played God at a fearful cost... The books had been well-thumbed by my host; they were among his favorites. "Man is not at his heart good," the Romanian said to me as he saw me struck by these stories. "He has to make himself into something. He must look to himself. The social sphere is a battleground, but the greater war is fought within." He looked at me in a way that made me think of Leibel's warnings, but there was no malice in his love. He would sometimes simply gaze, and sigh, and walk away to the darkroom, where he toiled in silence over his pictures.

One day in April, amid a gorgeous glow of spring sunshine, he motored down from his house and called me to help him unload a precious box. From a polished wood casing, he took out a camera that I had not seen before. It looked much simpler than the mounted Busch cameras that we were using in the studio. It was just a simple box, with a lens at one end and a smaller one at the back to look through. Inside was a series of cogs and wheels that drove a reel of perforated film past the lens.

"This is an original Lumière," said my host, beaming with pride, as if he had given birth to the object in question. "My friend Paul Manu first began using it nearly ten years ago, only two years after the brothers Lumière showed their first pictures in Paris. It is an ingenious device because you can use it both to take the pictures and to project them. Today of course we have more modern projectors. Mr. Manu took moving pictures of the king on parade, the gentlemen and ladies in the cafés, street fairs and matters of moment, such as the flooding of the Danube and our naval fleet on maneuvers. Unfortunately he was blighted in love and sold the camera to Professor Marinescu, of the College of Medicine, who used it to record medical pictures, 'cinematograms,' of various pathological conditions. Where Master Méliès at Paris made his voyages of the impossible, the good professor used special microscope lenses to show 'myosclerotic paralysis.' I bought the camera back from him three years ago and have been making my own moving pictures. As you know, the 'flickers' are very popular in variety theaters, but in America they have built theaters specially made to project them. In our own timid country people think it is just a novelty that has had its moment. But this is the apparatus that will discover the future."

We set up a canvas screen in the studio space, and later at night Makedonsky showed me his own modest achievements. They were short films, no more than two minutes—one could not fit larger reels into the Lumieres' box. He had used it mainly to record mountain landscapes, moving the camera around—what became known as panning—on his photographic tripod, resulting in a somewhat jerky panorama of the Transylvanian range and alpine vistas in Switzerland and Italy. In several scenes, he mounted his tripod on the observation car at the back of trains and captured the landscape receding, mountains passing by the two sides of the frame and then moving further and further. Normal things to our eye, but genuine magic at that moment. There were some scenes of city streets, but not many of people; Makedonsky said he was more comfortable with subjects who stood still before the camera, in his studio environment. But, he said, it was purely a matter of taste. There was scope for physiognomic study of anyone who passed by the camera lens, as a lasting witness for the future. People would be able to gaze for the first time on the true moving visage of their ancestors, and would inevitable understand them better. Or at least glimpse the mystery.

It would be easy to say that when I saw the Lumiere camera I saw my own future. But my host had too many enthusiasms, and this was just one of his fads. I was still more taken with the idea of the satirical prints I had worked on at the doomed baker's house in Odessa. Keeping contact with Radu in the hope of hearing news about Leibel, he showed me copies of new rebelious journals that someone had smuggled across the border. The Russian cartoonists had not stopped their work. Clandestine journals, called Zarevo ("the dawn"), Burya ("storm"), Sprut ("octopus"), Kosa ("scythe"), Gvozd ("the nail"), Leshi ("the goblin"), were still being produced with gruesome full-color plates of images of the Reaction—the massacres and slaughters. Skeletons presided over fields of corpses, hanged men on lampposts, Black Hundred vultures feeding on living flesh, government ministers as naked, tusked demons bathing in tubs of blood, cities crumbling while uniformed ogres feasted, the czar himself as a pitiless hydra. I felt the itch in my fingers to get down with inks and card, but there was no point, no such seething anger around me, except among the peasants, who were disgruntled at King and Jews alike. Ironically, the most popular graphic cartoons in Rumanian journals were those aimed at ourselves: the Jew, a demonic, bat-like figure—Mephisto, with his broomstick and fangs, gloating from rooftops over the country's dismal plight.

The cartoons brought back the days of Odessa, the reek of real blood, the moment of revolutionary hope so swiftly crushed. And Tanya. I thought of our days of summer in the Alexandrovsky park, the taste of the piroshki and the tea of the cafés, the magic night of the Frenchman's *Impossible Voyage*, our endless discussions about politics and *revolutsia*, and our naive passions, the question I answered so vividly in my inflamed certainty: Are you willing to die for the people? The question nagging me now, still unresolved: Which people? And would I ever return there? And was she dead or alive? I felt, in my youthful instinct, that I would know if she were dead, some occult bee sting would jab my flesh and I would sense the moment, but I never did. I felt she was alive, but could only hope that she had a fond remembrance of that younger village boy with muddled dreams. There were others, sharper and braver than I, who would sweep her up, and I hoped at least she might manage to survive, to fly away, to disappear safely in the rolling wheat fields of her homeland. Go forth, and multiply, I called out to her, feeling godlike, in my magnanimity, in the brightening Rumanian spring.

The big city—so many beautiful girls, walking confidently, twirling their skirts and parasols. Not as many blondes, but many as enticingly aglow, black-eyed sirens. But whenever those eyes turned in my direction, I felt they could look though my plain student garb, my coat and peaked cap, and see the gabardine-attired, side-curled, bowed-down failed graduate of the bet midrash and synagogue.

As my German reading improved, I took in more serious works of philosophy: Kant, Hegel, Schopenhauer, Feuerbach, Marx, but the journey became too heavy to bear. My host's anarchist writers attracted me more and more—Proudhon, Bakunin and back to Kropotkin, the gentle prince. Utopian thinking became more and more tempting, the world was so wracked with problems, tyrannies so unbearable, the differences between rich and poor so unbridgeable, that it made sense to think the unthinkable, to break the barriers all at once. Tolstoy's communities seemed very admirable, but I could not see myself as a peasant at heart. Among the Jews, there was another rival creed to the Social Democrats, Bolsheviks or Mensheviks, or the Bund. There had been a few in the village, who had spread the writings of the Austrian dreamer, Theodor Herzl, who advocated a "return" of the Jews to Palestine, the biblical ancestral land. Next year in Jerusalem. One repeats the prayer endlessly, it is woven inextricably into the thread. The son of a previous rabbi, Kopfernich, had pulled up stakes when I was about ten and headed off to Constantinople to take ship around the Aegean, past Cyprus to Jaffa. But what happened to him no one knew. In Bucharest, there was a party of these Zionists, who published a journal in Hebrew. It was full of news of the Jewish colonies that had been established in Palestine from the middle of the last century but were now calling for more immigration of Jews tyrannized and displaced by the Russian repression and fear of the pogroms. There was also much ado about other immigration schemes, to South America, and a big argument among the Zionists about a British offer to set up a Jewish state in Africa. But I did not see how we could look for a small haven if the entire world was lost to the Reaction.

Almost a year passed, a busy summer, a swift autumn, and another long winter, with the icy winds from Russia clutching again. Letters were few and far between across the border, largely due to the rumbling of peasant revolt among the Moldavians who bordered Bessarabia. The trains from Galatz had stopped arriving.

I stayed in place just beside the darkroom, still hoping that it would be possible to visit back home, although I decided if that happened I would only stay for a short while and then return to the city with the grand railway station. So far we had only gone as far as Ploveschi, where Makedonsky wanted to photograph, of all things, the great iron rigs of the oil fields. He had a methodical mind and had decided, after landscapes, to begin chronicling modernity. New buildings, railways, the shopping arcades, his own motor car, factories, chimneys. I went with him on these journeys, but I was allowed less and less access to the house on the hill, where other companions visited. My host seemed to have an army of cousins, all of them boys of about twenty, and all characterized by a kind of languid concealment, a false exterior that at a brief glance deemed one as either "in" or "out." I began to realize Leibel's allusions but still could not connect the ebullient, charming photographer with the type of men gossip alluded to, in coded hints, as predators with perverted desires. Only later did I realize that in his eyes I was neither friend nor potential lover, but the son he never had. But I was too stupid to understand. I accepted the hospitality, the job, the good pay, the books, the companionship, a frequent hug round the shoulders, an occasional squeeze of the waist or pat on the head, in good faith. In the end, I had to admit to myself that he was a means to an end, to a burgeoning self that my upbringing could not allow me to face. For if we were put here on Earth to do the Name's work, there was reason for every move, even if hidden from one's own senses. Fear, love, ambition, self-education, all resonated with a preset trajectory, a road, a railway, even if one puffed away at a siding for months or years till one set off again along the track.

In the event, I did not go home. The peasants rioted, burned farms, fought gendarmes and troops with pitchforks and hunting rifles, and then subsided, their leaders locked up, their wrath calmed by some new land decrees conceded by the astute king. The trains moved again, and news came to the students I still saw occasionally about Leibel, but it was bad. He had been arrested in Kishinev, hiding among the remnants of the Jewish self-defense stalwarts, who had been inevitably betrayed by a secret police informant planted among them. They were put on trial, and, I was told, sentenced to exile far in the Russian interior, beyond the Volga, in the Kazakh desert.

The comrades, however, were not downcast, consoling themselves with the news that Trotsky and several others had escaped from their chain gang on the way to Siberia, and he had made his way out of Russia to London. The revolution was once again gathering steam. I fantasized that perhaps Leibel had escaped with him, but there was no way to connect the exiles—one towards the wilderness of the Arctic Circle, the other east, towards the Caucasus. The world out there was too vast, and the only track that led that way, I realized from the train maps I bought at the station, was along the Trans-Siberian trail.

At this point, Makedonsky saw that I was becoming restless, despite the fact that I had learned the trade, both of the still and the moving-picture photography. He had bought a new moving camera, a Pathe, from France, which was much bigger than the Lumiere, which was, after all, almost ten years old. It had a much larger box, with two wooden magazines that could hold reels of more than 100 meters. As well as the double cam on the internal shaft, it had a toothed sprocket wheel over the gate aperture that pulled the film out of the feeder magazine, and drove it up to the take-up magazine as it went through the gate. Another innovation was the Latham Loop, which formed between the feed and the top of the film gate so that the continuous pull of the magazines could be converted into the intermittent movement that was necessary for each frame's exposure. This was the basis of all future movie cameras. This new toy, which came in a cargo crate that required at least five different tax stamps, displaced the boy "cousins" for several weeks.

Having unpacked it, however, the Romanian nobleman had a desire for a much wider canvas to paint his new visions than the streets and mountains of his home country. I had also misread his private leisure activities for a lessening of his old radical tendencies. Once the excitement of the Russian crisis had passed and the peasants put down, King Carol's Rumania seemed too stable to challenge. One day he came down from the house in the afternoon, having left me to deal with a large extended family that required a set of engagement portraits: father, mother, uncles, aunts, two sets of grandparents, siblings, children chafing in their festive best, brats crawling under the tripod, the couple looking somber, as if they were being groomed for the guillotine rather than the marriage bed, all the social graces I had to learn from my host to deal with the Bucharest bourgeoisie required in one fell swoop. Having serviced them and ushered them out with countless bows and little toys for the tinies, Makedonsky came in through the back door and settled down in the armchair reserved for the waiting, pressing his fingers together and nodding sagely as I finished sweeping the floor.

"Malatesta!" he said.

I continued sweeping. I knew he would come to the point eventually, when he was either in the contemplative or educational mode.

"You remember, I showed you his pamphlet," he prompted me. I did remember, since he had mentioned the name more than once, but not for some time, since the pamphlet had been in Italian, and I could only make out vague references that sounded a little like the Romanian, which was a sister language. It was called "Anarchy and the State." There were so many of these booklets, I could not get through most of them.

"Why do young people retain no memory?" he asked. "My old brain is dull and dried up, but yours should be fresh and full of room for all the best ideas." He quoted: "'What is government? A disease of the human mind, the metaphysical tendency, that causes man to be subject to hallucinations that mistake the abstract for the real thing. So many people think government is an entity, that contains attributes of reason and justice independent of the interests of the people who make up that entity. The same thing goes for the State.'

I met him at Ancona, about nine years ago. There was an uprising of the working-class movement. A veteran of many struggles, he was first arrested when he was fourteen years old for writing a letter to the King Vittorio Emmanuel about the injustice in his province. Then he joined the International and met Bakunin, Reclus, Kropotkin. Not just a man of thought but of action, he was twenty-four when he led a rebellion against the king. He was in Romania soon after that, but I was myself just a young lad then. Again and again he instigates revolts, he is imprisoned, he escapes, he spreads the anarchist cause. He goes from country to country, lighting the flame everywhere—in Egypt, in South America, in Belgium, Spain, even in England. After Ancona they exiled him to an island, Lampedusa, but he escaped again, in a small boat, in a storm. He is never still. Now my friends tell me he is going to speak at the Anarchist Congress in Amsterdam. It is an important moment. Delegates are going to arrive from many countries, even from Russia and America. We must go there! We will take the new camera and photograph the proceedings! I have a friend in Brussels who records sound on the phonograph. There is an atelier in Paris where I am told they can match the sound to the picture in perfect synchronization. It is called the Biophotophone. Are you with us or against us? Speak now!"

There was no arguing with his enthusiasm. We began to pack the same evening. He had already bought the tickets, and one of his young men, who may have been a real cousin among the impostors, drove us in the motor car to the station, where porters took care of the crate and we embarked, just the two of us, on the grand journey west.

Having gazed at the long-distance trains clattering in and out of the station, I was now on board—and in a first class carriage! That was a true opulence back then. The wood paneling was varnished and inlaid with ornate designs, the bunks well padded and soft, with a table between them laid out with white tablecloth and wine glasses in fixed metal cups. Small lamps hung from the ceiling and were fitted at the head of each bunk. The uniformed attendant came through zealously at close intervals with trays of snacks, small bottles of wine, tobacco, cigars, and napkins. Makedonsky saw my unease at this unexpected luxury and laughed, urging me to take the cigar.

"All true rebels must travel first class!" he said, tipping the waiter a full two kreutzers for special treatment. "My nephew is not a seasoned traveler," he told the attendant, "but he will soon be at home with the world! What is your name? Fritz? Be sure and keep us informed..."

It seemed that I had left a certain way of life that was not naturally mine either, but I had become used to it to a degree. Now the door had blown open and completely new vistas opened up, unimaginable and glimpsed not even in dreams. Even when my brother Yakov had dreamed of my flying, he had seen me drifting over the mountains and valleys of our province, even if gilded with gold. But now we had left the familiar far behind. The train rattled through the fields towards Ploveshi and then, after a few hours, began to climb into the mountains towards the border town of Kronstadt. It was near midnight when we reached the border, but I was still hanging out the window with the excitement of a small child.

At the border, an army of extremely officious Hungarian policemen poured through the corridors, motioning all those still standing in the corridors to get into their seats and meticulously examining papers. Passports were not a familiar sight in those days, and people drifted across the borders in the countryside without much let or hindrance, but those people who wished to travel would be wise to carry their residential permits, which were issued by provincial or municipal offices. Peasants had land certificates, or some kind of wrinkled, tattered document that might have been issued by the pharaohs. I had spent some time during the journey from Bucharest walking through the second- and third-class carriages, the second full of ebullient artisan or middle-class passengers, red-faced with beer and gobbling chicken and sausages, children clambering over the bunks and stout housewives hauling them down by their britches. The third class was like a traveling farmhouse, with the poorer workers, clerks and students crammed on wooden benches, the men with great bundles of belongings or goods, the women with baskets, here and there a tethered goat bleating as it tried to make sense of its moving and rattling quarters. One family had a massive crate of caged chickens, crammed in, squawking, and clucking, their beady, angry eyes, suggesting that deep down they knew the purpose of the journey. Bundles tied with string gave off powerful whiffs of sausage meat and cheese. I could not move from our own carriage during the guards' scrutiny, but I could imagine the confrontation of the State and the People in its rawest form, in the humid night—it was the middle of August. There had been many soldiers traveling the domestic route, crowding the corridors, but the last of them got off at Predeal, on the Rumanian side.

In first class, the officials were courteous but firm, showing no sign of deference. They seemed to have been issued, apart from the immaculately pressed uniforms, a variety of imperial moustaches ranging from the full handlebar brushes—in all shades from tar black to snowy white—to pencil-thin affairs resembling misplaced eyebrows or those tiny toothbrush snips. They examined every document with calm thoroughness, asking short, terse questions: "The herr's destination please? The purpose of travel? Any commercial goods? Tobacco or cigars?" They were matter-of-fact, purveyors of routine. The year was 1907. The empire was at peace. King Karol's Romania and Franz Joseph's Austria-Hungary were allies, each standing guard over merely local squabbles. The Bohemian question, the language question, Bosnia-Herzegovina (though the annexation that would cause so many problems was still a year away), and always the Hungarian national question, the Independence Party campaigning for the official use of Magyar rather than German. Still, unlike in Russia, there were real parliaments in both Budapest and Vienna. In the former, the Magyars were a majority, and in the Austrian parliament the socialists were a strong force, and a new universal and direct suffrage law had extended the right to vote. All except the radicals, pro-Bolsheviks, and anarchists agreed that the empire was the acme of enlightenment.

None of this meant much to me at the time, since I was not aware that my host and mentor was on several lists of dangerous subversives and had barely disconnected himself, by the skin of his teeth, from an anarchist plot to kill the king, Karol, back in 1902. Those lists, however, were not Austrian, and he was lucky his old friendship with the firebrand Malatesta was unrecorded, as the

Italian was persona non grata in many countries other than his own. Anarchists were all potential regicides, albeit that Makedonsky's class credentials covered up a multitude of sins. For my own part, he had obtained for me a resident's paper in Bucharest, under the name Boris Goureau, which sounded vaguely Romanian and identified me as student. The guard, eyeing us with customary suspicion, asked me if we had any cargo, and Makedonsky told him of the Pathe camera, which roused the policeman's interest. He said he had an Ernemann Kino, which was very portable and recommended for police work, enhancing the criminal archives with moving pictures. One must be modern in the modern world, he added. Makedonsky listened to him politely, nodding his head. "Ach zo? Ach zo?"

We crossed by night into Hungary, and in the morning I awoke to the glorious vista of the Transylvanian mountains rising on either side. As we passed by along the Muresul River, we saw countless small farming villages, the women in white billowing costume, marching out to their fields. I waved at them and they waved back to me. The air was sharp and pure. I noted how much better dressed the farmers were here, and how much better tended their fields than the raggle taggle of the Romanians, not to speak of our own hard-pressed province. Then, at one station, a name that had too many S's and Z's to be remembered, a gypsy band stood on the platform and belted out a medley that brought some of the third-class passengers out to join them till the train whistled its sharp reminder. These, too, were tunes that still echo, in ears attuned to other tones entirely but which still wail their piercing Carpathian lilt when time halts for that brief moment when the chords come keening from the depths.

The train moved slowly, as if fate decided that there was no reason to rush to the next stop. I think the average speed in those days was about 26 miles per hour. It was DeMille who looked it up for me, as usual. Put it all in, he said, set it all down, look up what you don't remember, dates, geographies, details. It's all in the invisible background. Then, when you're ready, just get up and belt it all out.

It must have taken another fourteen hours to get to Budapest, with all the stops and halts and delays that seemed to be part of the schedule, since we arrived on time. Somewhere outside Szeged, for example, somebody in the pay of the Imperial railways have walked a cow across the track for the exact twenty minutes it takes to stop the train there and restart. For much of that time I was alone in the carriage; Makedonsky spent most of that time in the dining car, having found some companions for cards, three upper-class gentlemen, two with hair that appeared to have been clamped down by a soup bowl and a third in hunting getup with knickerbocker trousers and tweeds. I think he was an Englishman, and the two others had waxed moustaches that rivaled his own. I kept away from the car, and my host appeared just an hour before arrival, with a small wad of banknotes that I had never seen before but were revealed as British five-pound sterlings. They seemed large enough to swaddle a baby.

As I looked out the window, I dreamed. I didn't have my brother Yakov's gift for flights of fancy and fabulous places that existed only in imagination and myth, but I dreamed of new streets of fresh cobbles and majestic houses where I walked tall, clean-shaven, and with fresh clothes and shining boots and a spring in my step, so that I felt not an interloper but a man of substance who could walk with confidence and owned his own fate. I couldn't tell whether the place was Vienna or Amsterdam or London or New York, but it was full of people like me, young men of enterprise, who did not answer to their parents' hogtied visions but to the beat of the engine of the New World. I saw factories and great shops, and myself idling by a large store of cameras, not only the enhanced box of Makedonsky's Pathe but even more elegant instruments, and I saw myself in my own studio, presiding over banks of workers, men and women, also smartly dressed, who rose and bowed to me as I entered. I fancied that they might be those people I had heard about who made the hand colorings for the latest moving pictures, carefully adding reds, purples, greens, and yellows to the tiny images, piece by piece. I had my own laboratory, in which

I invented new processes that would revolutionize the art. And I knew this could only be done in the cities furthest west, as far away from the Pale of Settlement and the caricatures of the czar's demons that I had thought so clever and enticing only a year or so ago. I would never return until I had amassed enough capital to pry my whole family loose from the chains of their oppression, whether they wished it or not. I knew my brothers would come, Zev for sure, and Yakov, though perhaps Kolya would cling to our mother's apron and she, I was afraid, would not tear herself from my father, who would not leave that shadowed room, the lamplight on the pages of the Books...

Makedonsky came into the carriage, waving his banknotes. "Gott min uns!" he cried, pulling his case down and sticking his winnings in a deep pocket. The train slowed down, approaching the environs of Budapest.

We left the Pathe camera at the left luggage cargo warehouse and took a fiacre into the town. Makedonsky wanted to stay for three days as he had a friend he wished to visit, a Professor Ferencszali, fellow moving picture enthusiast, who owned an original Edison. We put up at the modest Hotel Erzsebet, in the center, close by the bridge bearing the same name. The city was ablaze with lights; its night was daytime. I wandered about as in a daze. Under the vast cantilevered bridge the Danube glittered with reflections. In a vast dining room, under metal arches, the table legs were polished and immaculate, the waiters rushing to and fro as if the customer's request was an imperial command. Burnished silvery trays appeared as if by magic. Unlike the tinkling calm of Bucharest bourgeois dining, there was a buzzing roar like a racecourse. The goulash was enormous and delicious, the wine exquisite, the very air intoxicating. I slept like a baby, and in the morning the enchanted tour continued. While my mentor left to seek his friend, I wandered alone through the city. The magnificent buildings dwarfed any I had seen in Bucharest or Odessa. The great opera house, the newly built parliament, the palace across the river, the statues on high columns, even the synagogue was tall and splendid, like a Turkish monument, though I did not try to enter. And in its center, like a natural jewel, the azure waters of the river, under the perfect summer sky. Everywhere the people seemed well-dressed and elegant, bowing to each other as they passed, and even the horses pulling the fiacres seemed to preen, tossing their manes as they clacked over the cobbles, snorting at the municipal omnibuses and the trams that carried one up and down the slopes, around the gardens, along the spotless streets.

When Makedonsky returned, I realized that none of this interested him, as his principal pleasure lay in the dining and late-night taverns. He introduced me to his friend, a rotund, jocular fellow whose boots and top hat were burnished like mirrors and whose moustache seemed to reach all the way around his face. I don't remember the name of the tavern, just round the corner from the hotel on Kossuth avenue, but I recall its decorated booths and the polished floor, which I soon slumped down to. I vaguely remember their voices wafting down to me as they continued to talk while I lay there.

"The boy's too young. Can't take his liquor."

"Don't worry. I'm training him for greater things. There's more to him than meets the eye. He killed two people in Odessa."

"Young wolves shouldn't taste blood too soon."

Or maybe it was just my dream, again. They might have been speaking Magyar, which was just a tune to me, a rising-falling sheeplike stammer. They hauled me back into my seat and put another bottle before me.

After another two days we took the train to Vienna, still with the crate, a quick journey of barely five hours and more marvels, the hub of the empire itself, more palaces, mansions with statues of generals on horseback guarding grand avenues from the rooftops, wonderful ornaments, fountains, cathedrals, markets, arcades, elegant citizens walking with pride. We did not linger more than a night—just long enough for a taste of the famous Sacher torte in the café of the Sacher hotel, and then off early in the morning from the Nordbahnhof to Berlin. (Years later, DeMille asked me, clutching his head: "You went to Franz Josef's Vienna for one day? No Klimt, no Schiele, no Schoenberg, no Schnitzler, no Strauss, no Mahler, no Freud? Just a Sacher torte?" He might have mentioned Herzl, my sister's Austrian Zionist idol, who was I think dead by then.) But Makedonsky was raring to get on, to spend at least some days in Berlin before getting to Amsterdam in time for his conference, to taste at least his modicum of wine cellars and other delights before the grand flow of rhetoric, the Pathe camera in tow but never yet unpacked... another long journey across Bohemia with its rolling hills and beautiful churches into the next Empire...

Berlin. There seemed no end to this tour of escalating sensations. Grand squares, grand monuments, statues of heroes, Bismarck, the Reichstag, the Dom und Stadtschloss, the Brandenburg Gate, Hallesches Tor, Potsdammer Platz, electric omnibuses... Flaunting his winnings, Makedonsky took us to a room at the Victoria Hotel, right on the Unter den Linden. Women in silk gowns and men in shining tzilinder hats moved slinkily about the lobby. I was so used to this by now that I simply followed Makedonsky to the immense reception desk, behind which clerks stood like sentinels of the kaiser's own residence, hair pomaded, uniforms immaculate, buttons shining like beacons. One felt like saluting, but I merely signed the register with a flourish—as myself: Boris Gurevits.

Berlin was full of Jews, but one would not know it, because they dressed the same as everyone else. All around were Germans, hordes of them. I had never seen streets so full and busy. Everywhere a host of vehicles maneuvered around each other—horse-drawn carts, fiacres, omnibuses, vendors' vans, cars of a much newer vintage than Makedonsky's proud Renault, and people bustling everywhere, so that each street junction had several policemen directing the traffic, or trying to, each policeman looking like a general with his spiked helmet and moustaches. It seemed that as I advanced westward, the moustaches were getting larger, as were the women's hats, so ornate that they seemed like extra-living appendages that had landed directly from the great

147

fashion shops onto the ladies' heads. The din was fierce: horses' hooves, screaking trams, chugging carriages, and the hooting of the car horns, sounding like ships' warnings.

Despite his boasts, Makedonsky had never been here before, and he looked somewhat awed himself in the surroundings. He even bowed to the concierge at the hotel, as that ancient specimen, with immense white whiskers, told him he would arrange for the carriage of our camera from the left luggage of the train station. It arrived and was opened amid a great scrum of people who gathered to watch as we assembled the box and tripod in the lobby. The hotel volunteered two brawny porters, who carried it for us through the streets like a trophy as we set it up on various corners and vantage sights along the Unter den Linden.

For a whole day, we took shots along the city's main boulevard, photographing the traffic, the people passing, the opera house, the university, the Panopticum waxworks theater, the Kaiser Gallery, the vast Brandenburg gate at the far end, and into the Tiergarten. We filmed street vendors, walking billboards, advertisements on omnibuses and trams, car drivers, cyclists, and the policemen, who twirled their moustaches grandly for us. Once or twice we were asked if we had a license to photograph, but Makedonsky told them we were from Budapest and that seemed to tickle their fancy. The policeman who walked the beat in the gardens told us to make sure we would photograph the "maidschen" who cycled up and down the avenues. We should show the world Berlin as the most advanced and civilised city, where women were taking the lead as well as men. Everyone must play their part and benefit. The Kaiser himself insisted on it, as well as the policeman's wife, he added, giving his whiskers a mighty tweak. Everything around us conveyed the same message: this was the center, the hub of the world. London might pine, Paris might preen, but Berlin was the beating heart of modernity.

When we packed up the equipment, Makedonsky made an unusual request. He needed to have the hotel room in private that evening and asked me to find my own way around town until midnight, at the earliest. He gave me fifty marks in small notes and coins and a Baedeker map that he got from the concierge.

I ventured out, into a sea of lights. What people take for granted in our time was so incredible then. Where people back home wrapped up their prayer shawls and slunk off to the comfort of hearth and samovar, Berliners poured into the streets. The daylight bustle of work was transformed into the nighttime rush for play. Taverns, cafés, beerkellers, wine cellars, cognac rooms—there were ten thousand ways of drowning your soul in liquor, just a few blocks from the hotel, and the further one stepped into the side streets south of the boulevard, the more they proliferated. All about me there were also modes of transport that could take me anywhere else in the city, even the most newfangled of them all, the U-bahn, the underground railway, but I was too timid to try that. A variety theater enticed me with its headline acts: Marceline, the famous French clown, the Bratz Brothers, the Howling Dervishes, Paul Rota the Cannonball Juggler, Captain Spaulding, the American fire-eater and Hackenschmidt, the wrestling champion. I really wanted to see these, but I was hungry, so I went into a bustling tavern just a way along full of people having a good time, the buzz of loud voices, laughing women, the clink of glasses and cries of waiters trying to match plate to mouth. All the tables seemed to be occupied, but a fat waiter with the usual moustache waved me over and pulled up a spare chair. Within three minutes I was tucking in to a huge mound of vursts with lashings of potatoes and sauerkraut. Without my asking, the waiter also brought me an immense mug of beer almost half my height. I nodded my thanks, and, like everyone else in the establishment, I blew off the great froth on top.

Sometime later, I staggered out into the street and looked into a clockmaker's shop, which was full of dials all pointing to the precise same time: 10:45. I had more than an hour before I was due back, and knew I had to avoid catching my mentor-employer in the embrace of whoever it was he was entertaining up there, or was entertaining him. I had my suspicions, since I had seen him eyeing a bellboy, who looked somewhat rugged behind his uniform, and I was long inured to the fact that I knew very little of what adult people did with each other in their private moments, with the lights off. There were so many things I was realizing I was completely ignorant about.

But the beer had gone to my head, and my stomach, though it seemed to weaken the legs, so I felt I couldn't go far. I staggered down the street, under the tall buildings, leaning up against a street vendor's van. More sausages! I couldn't even look and moved away. I noticed a certain type of women who passed me by and seemed to throw me a quick glance, just sizing me up and moving on. I am just a fool, I thought, a raving idiot far from home, failing to pretend to be something I was not and never would be. A city sophisticate! What was I doing with this peculiar Romanian dilettante in any case? A bag carrier to his sinister whims... What had anarchism to do with all this? I missed my mother and my brothers, and the cool resolve of my big sister Sarah. I had not prayed for more than a year, and my sins and transgressions must be piling up beyond any possible redemption.

I was beginning, of all things, to miss the bet midrash, and started whispering the prayer that I began every day with: "*Blessed are you, our God, King of the World, who has sanctified us in our commandments... How precious is your mercy, God, and the Children of Adam will shelter in the shadow of your wings... They will be satisfied with your House's bounty, and the River of your delight will nourish them...*" when I came up against the window of another tavern, behind which people were gathered in a dimmer light, in a quieter mood. I needed to sit down so I entered. Someone in a chequered jacket and a collar that looked undone, with yellow shoes, pointed me towards a padded seat in a booth. I sat down and asked for a glass of wine, recognizing that another three-foot high stein of beer would finish me off for the night. They brought me a glass of dark red stuff, which was very strong and rather sour. I closed my eyes, and when I opened them, a young girl was sitting before me. She was quite petite, and pale, with blonde ringlets and bright green eyes, looking at me with a kind of amusement. She was dressed in a loose-fitting affair, almost like a dressing gown, which revealed her bare arms. She had a packet of rolling papers and a small tobacco pouch on the table between us, from which she was deftly preparing a cigarette. "Would you like a smoke?" she asked.

I shook my head. There was something terribly beautiful about her, although she was not pretty. I couldn't figure it out. She lit the cigarette and exhaled. A small halo of light showed on her hair from the dim lamp behind her seat. I thought it was a very interesting light. Perhaps my mind was trying to distract, or protect me, by drifting into the diversion of a visual idea.

"I would like to photograph you," I said.

"Ach zo?"

I felt strangely bold. I told her I was a photographer, and had a studio in Bucharest. I was traveling with my business partner, en route to Amsterdam and Paris, where we were going to buy new equipment. We were only in Berlin a few days.

"Would you like to dance?" she said.

"In here?" I asked. Looking around, it seemed the few regular patrons of this place would have difficulty making it to the door. She laughed. No, she said, there was a place she knew, only a short tram ride. I waved my sophisticated hand. "Why not?" At least, my befuddled mind told me, I had money, and it was not mine.

The dance hall was a small, packed ground-floor hall in a neighborhood that was blessed with few gas lights and poorer, more worn-down houses. A thick fog of smoke almost choked me as we went in, the cigarette smoke mixing with a stronger, sweeter odor that immediately made my head swim. Couples were moving in a kind of seething mass to a music that was completely alien to me, a rapid piano beat being played by a sweating man in white shirtsleeves whose fingers moved like lightning over the keys. There were many soldiers on the floor, with their collars undone and their jackets loose, holding fast to a welter of young ladies of all shapes and sizes. Some were rake thin, others almost grotesquely fat, but most were girls not unlike Lottie, who had

151

introduced herself to me while on the tram. She took hold of my hand and led me through the throng as I tripped and stumbled over the moving feet. Here and there someone lunged at me with their fist, but Lottie swept me out of the way. She wound her arms around my neck and I put my arms around her waist, trying to move my feet in tune with the others. A large beery face with the usual moustache tried to pull her away but she clung on to me, and before I knew it she was pulling me towards the other side of the hall into a passage that led to a stairway. From that point on I needed no encouragement, and what followed followed, as needs arise...

I was woken suddenly by a massive shaking that turned out to be the giant hand of an immense doughball of a woman standing over me and shouting in a foreign tongue. It was only slowly that I was able to make out the German words, by which time I was being dragged through the door, naked, with my clothes thrown out into the corridor. Some curious faces peeked from other doors but withdrew. Lottie was nowhere to be seen. I asked about her but was roundly cursed in several languages which all merged strangely into Yiddish, albeit a different patois from the tone I was familiar with from home. The gist of it was that there was no Lottie, there had never been any Lottie, that the girl who had brought me here had engaged the room until six in the morning, which I had exceeded for three hours, and that I owed a full day's extra fee, which came to six marks thirty-eight pfennigs. I never found out where the thirty-eight pfennigs came from, but it may have been some kind of tax. It being difficult to argue with a giant woman when one has no shred of cover, I had to pull my pants on and put on my shirt careening down the stairs. At the bottom I stopped, with enough presence of mind to check my pockets. They were empty, but the giantess handed me a paper envelope that contained the remnants of my wad of money and my card of the Victoria Hotel. With this I managed, having paid the unavoidable excess, to hail a cab, which clattered off down the cobbled alleyway, the driver nodding nonchalantly at a familiar daily fare.

I arrived back at the hotel just as the clock above the mahogany reception desk clicked to 10 a.m. Other clocks showed the times in other parts of the world: In Paris, also 10 a.m. In Vienna, eleven. In London, nine. In Moscow it was twelve noon, in Pekin it was already six in the evening and, in New York, four in the morning. What had been the hour of my crucial moment, the point of the irrevocable loss of my innocence? I was not so stupid, by then, to realize that it was not the same moment for "Lottie." Calculating the sum I think I left the dance hall floor with, and the sum left in my pocket after paying the giantess, who had extracted ten marks for her services: Oh Lottie! I would have pressed the whole wad into your hands! Had she left moments after, when I had fallen asleep after the volcanic event, or stayed with me for a few hours until the necessities of her own life required her to go? I understand now that she must have pitied me for my gauche ignorance and innocence and left without fleecing me to the skin. But whatever the hour, in Berlin, Buenos Aires or Brussels, I felt I had to find her again.

The immaculate guardians of the Victoria Hotel looked me up and down with indifferent eyes, and the duty clerk took the key of the room from its pigeonhole along with a folded note from my mentor. I took it and went to the elevator, whose flunky turned his gold-plated handle for the fourth floor and wrinkled his nose at me as I unfolded the paper. It said, in Makedonsky's familiar scrawl: "I am called away for an important meeting. Wait for me here. If you return in time, we are leaving on the 4:35 post meridian to Amsterdam, via Hamburg. Be ready. If you are not in time, *buona fortuna*."

Thus far my Berlin tragicomedy.

When Makedonsky came back, about 12 o'clock, he had a small, compact and pugnacious-looking man with him, clad in a loose suit and somewhat battered hat, with a small suitcase. The man had a prizefighter's face, with a crooked nose and small eyes set in a craggy face. His hands were muscular, and looked used to work. His every move declared "I am not a bourgeois." I had by then showered and smartened myself up with a fresh shirt and trousers, and had a coffee called up from room service. He held out his hand to me.

"Max Baginsky," he said.

"Max is coming with us to Amsterdam," said my mentor, who had simply nodded to me as he entered the room. Business was business. "Or rather, we are accompanying him. He is a delegate, if such a concept applies to the anarchists. Max is representing the American comrades. A short home visit, to his native soil."

"Berlin," said Baginsky, "is Berlin. We are not shunning life. We embrace it. Mac tells me you are from Bessarabia. And you have been in Odessa during the uprising. Are you too a photographer? I have heard such descriptions of the event. One should make a moving picture of it!"

"Max is an American now," Makedonsky explained. "They make a moving picture of everything. The shooting of President McKinley—they made a moving picture of that. I saw it in Paris."

"Did they now?" Baginsky said. "Most interesting. That was a dubious action. Many people believe the shooter, this Czolgosz, was a government agent. He told the court he knew Emma Goldman, but she only met him once, at a train station. There is great debate about these actions. He said he was following the example of Bresci, who executed King Umberto of Italy. But America is not a monarchy. One must be careful with one's targets. It has made our life very difficult."

"Perhaps so, but it certainly shakes the tree! Some schnapps?"

Makedonsky took out a bottle and three glasses. The visitor looked around the room, at the lush fittings, the fine wood paneling, the polished desk with silver inkstand.

"I am only a poor sinner," said my mentor. "We cannot all be saints, like this brave boy here, who defended his people from the Cossacks."

"I must hear this story," said Baginsky. "We will have plenty of time on the train." He accepted the schnapps. "Your health!"

"To the revolution! Damnation to all czars and kings!"

Makedonsky turned to the set of portraits above the desk, the dour visage of the dead English empress whose name graced the hotel, and two uniformed, moustached worthies on either side of her—one perhaps her German consort, Albert, the other some subsidiary member of that far-flung family, perhaps, in my remembered fancy, an Austrian archduke whose future would soon change the world.

On the train, Baginsky talked incessantly. Makedonsky was slumped against the window, asleep. His night must have been exhausting. Whatever cache of money he had on the way to Berlin, it was sufficiently depleted for him to book us seats with the general public, in the second-class coach, shared with two young businessmen who spent the journey quietly reading their newspapers and a stout, fastidious lady whose hat filled the baggage rack and who was accompanied by a boy of twelve in a sailor suit, meekly plying colored crayons on a picturing book. I think it was a version of Max und Moritz, which would have kept him suitably chastened.

Baginsky talked about Berlin, which was always about flux and turmoil. New inventions gave an illusion of progress, but advancement meant the forging of new chains, new means to keep the workers enslaved: "The era of parliaments, citizenship, political rights, is trumpeted as progress marching hand in hand with the great steamships, trains, bridges that connect us to each other. But where is the right to live? To secure the means of existence to organized society so that each can have the material basis for this new freedom?" In reality there were only greater means of control, a great machine of government, acting the same way whether it was brought to power by votes or by kings. All followed the iron rule of the sanctity of property, ever protected by the law. "Any person who is not counted among the rich and owning party," he said, "will soon find out the price of demanding equal rights—prison, the poorhouse, the grave."

He talked a great deal more, about free organization, the solidarity of working men and women, syndicalism, the ultimate weapon not of firearms but of the general strike. I was wondering about all this sedition in a crowded carriage but we were hunched close together, and at one point he motioned me to follow him as he rose and made his way along the corridor to the small lounge before the dining car, where there were a couple of seats for waiting customers. He offered me a small cigar and puffed away at his own when I declined. He asked me how long I had known Makedonsky. "Pardon my curiosity, but in our affairs one learns a certain caution. Some comrades are always suspicious of friends from the wrong side of the shop floor. I know that Malatesta vouches for him. It seems your friend saved his life once, in Amalfi. I know him as a generous funder of our European journals—*La Guerre Social* and *Die Anarchist*. Our own members always have empty pockets. His family has a history in the wars against the Turks, I understand."

I gave him a quick résumé of my time in Bucharest, omitting the more private rumors, and said that I knew Makedonsky as an enthusiastic photographer more than anything else. I told him how he had opened my mind to the world of books and ideas. My German was not good enough for emotional statements, so we found ourselves speaking Yiddish, and our talk flowed more freely. He asked me about Russia, and I tried to give him a concise account of the events in Odessa and my involvement with the Jewish self-defense forces. "Social Democrats," he sighed. "They claim to have a human science, but I am very much afraid they will end up as harsh masters as those they fight to replace. They have a controlling zeal. We fight side by side, but often like rival packs of dogs. Individuality and organization, these need not be polar opposites. I am afraid Marx has a lot to answer for."

Speaking the old language set him to reminiscing about his life in Prussia and the family hardships and conflicts that led him to leave for America. His father had been a shoemaker who supported the revolt of 1848. "Europe has had many revolutions," he said, "but the main dish is yet to be served." He was not himself a Jew, but working in anarchist and socialist communities, the Yiddish language was a necessity. He told me the anarchist movement in

America was like "a league of nations," a conglomeration of those on the bottom of the scale who worked to build the owning class's prosperity. Men and women of great energy and moral force, as were their comrades in Europe. "You will meet many good people in Amsterdam. There are some youngbloods, close to your age. Kibalchich and Vigo. I will introduce you. And you will meet Emma, Comrade Goldman. She is a great mind, a great mind."

Time passed so quickly that we were jolted by the train attendant moving through the cars calling out the terminus, Hamburg. We went to wake Makedonsky and help him transfer the Pathe box to the next train, the overnight sleeper to Holland. "Mac" had sleeper tickets for two, and Baginsky went off to the public carriage. I lay awake, thinking for the first time of what might lie in the future. I thought of "Lottie," but she was already far away and in a different world.

Of all the cities of my grand passage across Europe, Amsterdam was the most beautiful. For all the fame and fortune and splendor of the Dutch history even I had read of in my provincial corner of the world, the city was small and compact. I was charmed by the canals that curled around the city and were backed by tree-lined streets, with people strolling, riding, bicycling up and down in the shade. Further out, in the workers' quarters, I could see the tall residential houses that reached down to the canals, so that one had to enter by boat, and barges plied up and down them like cargo carts in other parts of the world. Grand buildings of wealth and commerce, but also a quiet confidence among the strollers in this small nation that had once ruled the seas. Even the poorer people were better dressed than I had noted in Budapest, Vienna, and Berlin, let alone Odessa. There seemed to be a narrower breach between classes; even the bourgeois were cycling with their black bowler hats. People were friendly, and looked at strangers not with suspicion but curiosity. Shopkeepers were open and eager, and even simple folk spoke more than their local Dutch—most knew German and English. Our own people were evident in great numbers, and not only in the bustling Jewish district, where they too were well-dressed and walked with confidence among the Dutch. They had a great market, in the Jodenbuurt, with many bookstalls with volumes in every conceivable language. I even saw books that the vendors told me were in Arabian and Chinese characters, and there were people in the city, I was assured, who could read them! From their small, low-lying portals, the Dutch had ingathered the world.

It was characteristic that the anarchist conference, which the three of us had come so far to join, took place not in some dingy, concealed basement or smoke-filled tavern but in a splendid building close to the center of the city, the Plancius Building, a venue for concerts that also housed a synagogue. As the delegates pressed in with their briefcases and sheaves of documents, up the stairs, the daily devotees were just leaving their morning prayers on the ground floor, clad in their white taliths and clutching their daily prayer book. It was the first place of worship I had been in since I left the village. Was it my imagination, or were some of the delegates unsure as to which part of the building they should show their devotion? But we were just in time, coming posthaste from the station on the Monday morning, where Baginsky introduced us to the organizers who would billet us among local sympathizers. Makedonsky made his way directly through the crowd to a small, wiry man in a gray suit, clean shaven, who was gesticulating boldly, waving his hands and greeted the newcomer with a bearhug, pointing him out to his friends. All were quickly engaged in a furious foray of handshaking, which Baginsky joined in till he broke away at the entrance into the hall of a short woman in a dark dress, with blonde bobbed hair, a strong angular face, and a pair of spectacles perched on her nose. She had the air of a house manager who had come to put everyone in order, and the crowd moved to coalesce around her in turn. I was left behind, standing at a desk piled with journals and magazines. I recognized the titles Baginsky had mentioned on the train, as well as an English magazine called *Mother Earth* and a Yiddish one called *Der Groisse Kundem* ("the big stick"—a *"zhournal fur humar, weitz un satireh"*); both were marked "Printed in New York."

As I watched these people buzz around each other, greeting and gripping their comrades' shoulders, I had no idea that I was in the presence of the bane of police forces around the globe, people wanted for various acts of rebellion against the state, attacks on police stations, sabotage of factories, manufacture of bombs, shootings of police, attempted assassination of kings... I did not know that this small, busy woman, Emma Goldman, had been arrested as a suspected accomplice of the assassin who had shot the American president McKinley six years before, that she addressed spellbound audiences around her country with her fiery rhetoric about workers' rights, women's oppression, and the destruction of nature, stirring up trouble for company bosses, stockholders and politicians alike, and trailing government and Pinkerton spies wherever she went. Nor that the flimsy newspaper I was leafing through, La Guerre Sociale, was enraging the French government with inflammatory prose and scurrilous abuse, or that the Jewish anarchists of London, represented by the mild-mannered Rudy Rocker, were condemned by the English press as a horde of seditious foreigners who polluted the heart of the British Empire. They all hated tyranny, and in the modest Dutch hall over the shul I saw them hold forth at great length with their ideas on how to end it .

The Jews had finished with *mincha*, the afternoon service, and were preparing for the evening prayers, shuffling quietly in and out. Their congenial atmosphere seemed to seep into the deliberations of the comrades as their early passion began to fade into long-winded speeches and resolutions. I missed the opening statements because Baginsky brought over a friendly Dutchman called Ruusen, who arranged my passage with Makedonsky's camera and our cases to a house on the fringes of the Jewish quarter, an old five-story dwelling full of working families whose women adorned every facade with their washing, and urchins who spilled over every stairway. Our host was a figure who could have stepped out of an old print, an old man called Mayer who wore a large black skullcap and smoked a long meerschaum pipe over vast gray whiskers that swept all the way over his broad shoulders. He had large, strong hands and told me he had spent his whole life as a stevedore on the Amsterdam docks. He had led the great seamen's strike of 1895, I was told later, but he was too modest to boast, whether in Yiddish, German, or Dutch. He showed me to the room I would share with the two young guests who were attending the sessions, whom Baginsky had recommended I meet. I was so exhausted by the journey I fell asleep on my narrow cot, which must have been made for a ten-year-old, and was awoken a few hours later by the two lads, who came to call me to supper.

Since Leibel Grossman, these were the first companions of roughly my own age, although both were older, in their early twenties. Vigo, who called himself Almereyda, was Spanish in origin, though he had lived in France as a child. Kibalchich was a Belgian, though his father was a Russian anti-czarist rebel and a cousin of one of the men executed for the assassination of Czar Alexander the Second. He had escaped across the border to Austria and then found his way west, to Brussels. Both Vigo and Kibalchich were also photographers by trade, so we had an instant bond, though neither had any interest in developing their trade into an art. I think they thought I was a sensitive innocent Jewboy from Yehupetz-land, and only half believed my Odessa tale, which Baginsky had relayed to them. Kibalchich, in particular, was clearly eager to test me at the earliest moment. He said he had been an anarchist from birth, a disobedient child, a terror to his parents, a stealer of money, a street urchin, and an early member of the Jeunes Gardes, the socialist youth group. But after traveling across mining towns in both Belgium and France he became involved with the anarchists, who attracted him with their bold strategy of all-or-nothing. He wanted action, not talk, and was very sceptical of the Amsterdam congress for that very reason. He had only come, he said, because he wanted to meet these legendary figures from abroad: Malatesta, Baginsky, Rocker, Goldman. He confessed himself a little disappointed with the latter, having expected an Amazon-like figure with an amazing bust and a mane of flying hair, rather than this dumpy little woman with glasses who looked like his schoolteacher.

Vigo was a little younger than his friend, but had already served two terms in prison. He had lived by his wits in Paris since he was about twelve, and fallen in with anarchist friends. He was obsessed with "the propaganda of the deed." At the age of sixteen, he said, he had made his own bomb, with some magnesium and sulphur, out of a shoe polish can, to blow up the judge who had sentenced him to prison for some minor theft offense, but it had failed, and he had been sentenced to a year in prison in solitary confinement, where, he said, "I honed my own mind as a weapon." He changed his name to Almereyda, to emphasize his Spanish and foreign roots. He was indeed a wild-looking youth, with untidy clothes and a great shock of hair, though his moustache was still an action in progress. Both Miguel and Victor, as I was soon calling them, had the most piercing gaze I had ever seen—they were like twin eagles who swoop from the sky and land on your shoulders, nuzzling at your ear and daring you to join them in flight, on the hunt.

My first impulse after I had spent just one evening with them was that neither would live very long. They seemed to be connected by a common fuse, which was lit and burning down rapidly. The only thing that would save them, I supposed, was that the bomb would prove to be defective again. I was amazed to hear from Kibalchich that Vigo actually had a small son, called Jean, two years old, born to his girlfriend, who was waiting for him in Paris. This was quite difficult to understand, but then, I was still a young fool.

The anarchist dinner was a raucous affair at the Cafe de Bishop (or was it "Bisschop"?) in the center of the city, just off the famous dam. It was a veritable steam of rushing waiters and beer steins, and mounds of mashed potatoes, sauerkraut, and giant "worsts." Anarchists seemed to eat as if every meal was their last, even the famous Emma was tucking in like a stevedore, Malatesta in a huddle with the older delegates, still debating some unfinished point of order. Suits were slapped on the back of chairs, shirtsleeves stained with sauce, waistcoats unbuttoned, sweating faces wiped with old handkerchiefs. I felt strangely at home, as if I had known these people all my life, sitting at our own junior table with Victor and Miguel, a Jewish lad from London called Daniel and his companion, a feisty young girl dressed in man's clothes, with a huge head of black hair, who ate like a coal miner and had a laugh that reverberated through the room and out into the docks. Her name was Yolanda, and she talked loudly in an unfamiliar Yiddish argot, full of dubious references to *tuches, schvantz* and *freie liebe* ("free love"). Vigo was looking at her with blazing eyes, and Victor nudged him under the table.

We talked a great deal when we returned to our small room that night, our host, Mayer, sitting up with us, smoking his pipe, all of us communicating in a mixture of German, Russian, French, and Yiddish. My French was limited to some of Makedonsky's phrases; Kibalchich spoke Russian and relayed Vigo's words to me; the old man had been around the world and was in his quiet way a living dictionary. Victor was chiding me at being embarrassed by Yolanda's free talk and said an anarchist must be prepared to talk about any aspect of human existence, regardless of bourgeois convention. Equality meant that all barriers had to be thrown open and all fetters broken, whether between class and class, master and servant, man and woman, or people of every race and color, be they white, Chinese or negro. The true anarchist would be a polymath who could have access to any knowledge of the past and present. Only thus could we charge into the future. Vigo went into a long tirade, which Victor relayed to me in bursts, telling me that I was a child who had been brought up on a completely fallacious view of the universe. The Jews were an ancient race of great wisdom, but we were constrained by our slavishness to the Bible and the concept of God, which promised us heaven but chained us to the earth, made us subservient to authority, and had given the Christians an opportunity to create the church, the most monstrous machine yet known to oppress all of mankind. We could never break free unless our rebellion encompassed everything, from those who claimed hegemony on the earth to those who claimed they knew heaven. When we died, all that we left behind was the memory of our deeds and the seed that gushed out of our sexual organs in ecstasy.

The old man sat on his small wooden stool and smiled at us, emitting fumes from his meerschaum. But as the other two fell asleep, exhausted by their own tirades, we could see the first light of dawn peeping through the window shutters, and Mayer gestured for me to follow him through to the modest living room, where he took from a small cabinet two cloth packages embroidered with the star of David, one of which he handed to me, nodding his head and preceding me down the quiet stairwell, the silence of the new morning only broken by loud snores from the second floor. Outside, the cobbles echoed under our shoes and we could smell the brisk salt of the sea. He led me around the corner to a smaller building with a modest door, over which the Hebrew words were etched plainly: "This Is the Gateway to the Lord, the Righteous Shall Pass Through It." Four or five other figures, already draped in their white talliths, were stepping up towards it, nodding to Mayer and me as we approached.

It was only while filing in with the other worshippers among the plain wooden benches that I noticed how tall the old stevedore was, towering above the small crowd of the local *stiebel*. We both opened our packages and unrolled the shawls, took out the phylacteries and the Book. It was strange how immediately the old rote came back. Folding, wrapping the arm, the head, the bending, the rocking, the murmur of the words of the daily repetition, the knitted brow of my father as he seemed to be contemplating the consequences of every phrase and utterance, the repetition of the covenant of a moment so far back and so intensely present—"*Into the house of God we will walk with feeling... how good are your tents, Jacob, your dwelling places Israel... magnified is living God and praised, He is present and there is no Time to his Being...*"

The Dutch were very speedy, unlike the *shtetl*, in which time was no factor, though there were rhythms of the land to tend to, the open sky, the fields, the world stretching beyond any compass far and wide beyond its tiny spot on Earth. Clearly they were busy people, with much business to attend to in the grand port, which gathered in all the bounty and commerce of the world. When we got back, Kibalchich and Vigo were only stirring, but needed little reminding that Mayer's wife, who only appeared, like a magic visitation, when required, had tea and breakfast rolls on the table, fresh from the bakery next door.

They were both eager to get back to the Congress, and probably to seek out Yolanda, but by the time we walked into the Plancius Building the meeting was in progress, a French comrade, whose name I forget, holding forth on "the question of organization," dealing with "individual action," the l'affaire Dreyfus and its effect on the anti-militarist movement, and syndicalism. Emma Goldman spoke next, and I could see why she was regarded as so great an asset to the movement. She spoke clearly and vividly, with a voice that was used to carrying across a crowd of hundreds in a busy city square. She berated the State, which was born of despotism and sustained by force, imposed on the masses by the "divine right of kings" or supine parliaments that acted only for the sake of industrial magnates and the pursuit of profit. True organization should be an organic growth, which sprang from the true needs of people and their desire for liberation and the nurturing of each person's individuality. Malatesta spoke next, and all were captivated by his passionate delivery, also in English—albeit in a mostly Italian mode, with many flourishes and waving of his hands—on the subject of the individual and the collective, and the necessity for an international organization to further the aims of a world revolution for the good of all mankind. My friend Baginsky was next, calling for the merger of Stirner and Kropotkin, and Ibsen, art and practice, a movement that would, without the blind force of authority, unite individuals in a common interest to further a new kind of humanity.

We did not see Yolanda anywhere, that day, and as there was glorious sunshine outside, and the afternoon was reserved for private discussions among the delegates to formulate their resolutions, we younger ones adjourned to the zoological gardens, whose entrance was just opposite the hall. This gave Victor and Miguel another chance to chide me for my country bumpkin status, as I had never seen a zoo before. I passed like a child before the camels and llamas, the parrots and the gorgeous plumage of the singing birds, the monkey house and the reptiles. We lingered for feeding hour of the carnivores, watching the lions and tigers grab at piles of meat flung inside the bars by the keepers, while Vigo supplied running dialogue, naming the beasts: "That one is J.P. Morgan—that one is Carnegie, that one is Frick—see how he grabs the ham hock..." The hippopotamus was of course Clemenceau, and the peacocks Franz Josef and Wilhelm. We had run out of names by the time we reached the hyenas and the wolves. We enjoyed the sea lions and the aquarium, and sat in the café in the garden as the band played marches and waltzes.

As we were sitting and joking, I noticed Makedonsky passing by at the other side of the bandstand, together with another figure, whom I thought I had noticed earlier that day at the conference, a young man who looked vaguely familiar. I had not seen my mentor and traveling companion since the day we arrived, and he had not attended the dinner. But things had moved quickly, in a swirl of events and new faces. I was not sure if he had seen me and was trying to avoid me, but he didn't join us at the café. I idly remembered his comments about the "biophotophone," the combination of sound and picture recording that might have captured the Congress for posterity, had time and opportunity allowed. In any case, I had not seen the Pathe unpacked. I was living day by day. All around me the trains ran, the trams rattled, people came from far-off places and returned to them, and Odessa was even further away. Kibalchich had already told me of his plans to foment revolution in the mines and factories of Belgium. There were vast coal mines in the Borinage region, where thousands of miners lived like animals under the whip of the mine owners, and in Liege there were armaments factories that made weapons that were used across continents, sold to potentates even in China and India. Yesterday, swords, pikes, and lances. Today, rifles, pistols, and machine guns. A strike or factory takeover there would reverberate all over Europe. Vigo-Almereyda told me I should come directly to Paris, where the comrades were braver, the cafés better, the streets full of vigorous life, and the girls the most beautiful in the entire universe. "Forget about your Yolandas," he said. "Jewish women are taught from birth to propagate the race! The Parisian woman is born and remains free!"

I did not return to the synagogue. Mayer did not wake me or make any comment, but departed and returned from his daily devotions. The third and fourth days of the Congress continued with more debates about anarchism versus syndicalism, the perfidy of the Social Democrats, the "solidarity of the workers," the general strike and "direct action." For a forum that threatened the world with revolution, the overthrow of all governments and dethroning of emperors and kings, it was a very staid affair, with lunch breaks, snacks, tea, beer and *boerenkoolstamppot* with *rookworst*, walks around the canals, and even an outing to the great Rijksmuseum, with its Romanesque and gothic halls, its Delft plaques and Rembrandts and Van this and Van that, the glories of the past that flourished while the Dutch navies were scouring the world, colonizing and plundering, Malatesta careening through the vast rooms calling out in his loud voice, "Pirate loot! Pirate loot!" And so the Congress ended, on the Friday, with the delegates' resolution for the formation of an anarchist international to supplant the Marxist model and communicate to the anarchists of all countries its support of the general strike, the syndicates and the destruction of capitalist and authoritarian society through armed insurrection and expropriation by force. And then all filed out, tired but satisfied, as the Jewish burghers of Amsterdam filed in to the hall downstairs for Eve of Shabbas prayers.

It was only when everyone had left and the attendants and cleaners moved in to clear the detritus and collect all the unsold books and magazines that the police rushed up, a phalanx of twelve officers, demanding to see the organizers and be given lists of all who had been present. We were back in Mayer's house, gathering our belongings and thoughts, when Baginsky rushed up the stairs and told us there had been an armed robbery at the Amsterdamsche Wisselbank, on the Damrak, just before closing time at 4 o'clock. Two men had entered the bank, put on masks, and held the few remaining customers at pistol point while they filled two bags with a large sum of money, mostly in foreign banknotes, as the bank was also a foreign exchange. They had taken gulders, marks, French and Swiss francs, sterling, kronen, and even American dollars. Then they had rushed out, running through the crowd, and boarded a boat by the Oude Brug, which took them out through the docks and into the open jaw of the port.

The robbers were described as a tall, middle-aged man with a clipped moustache and a young man with a sullen look and "lazy eyes." The puzzle pieces fell into place right away in my mind: I saw my mentor, Makedonsky— still with his long moustache—in the garden, and the youth beside him, whom I had recognized and now pinned down precisely as the sullen bellhop at the Victoria Hotel in Berlin. Who had been, I was now sure, the reason for my employer's desire to get me out of his room on the night I wandered the street and found Lottie. Thus did the unprincipled flourish.

The police huffed and puffed, but they could not ignore the fact that all the delegates and almost all the visitors to the Anarchist congress had been present at the Plancius at the last session and had not left until five o'clock. But I knew they would set their hands on the missing Makedonsky sooner rather than later, and if they had his name, they would have mine. For doubtless they had their spies at the meetings, probably as journalists, whom we could see scribbling in their notebooks despite the tedium of much that transpired. Everyone joked that it would be nice to see the proceedings written up in *The Times of London*, or even *L'Humanite*, rather than in the archives of the Dutch secret service, but one should not raise one's hopes to the sky.

I told Almereyda and Kibalchich of my suspicions. They were roused into instant action. Within less than half an hour, all our belongings were packed, old Mayer and his good wife were bade farewell and informed that we had never been in their rooms. The old woman simply shook her head and the old man twirled his whiskers, as if to say everything comes full circle. We walked out the door and on to the Waterlooplein, where we took a tram south, to the outskirts. We knew the police would be scouring the docks and train stations, but as yet they would be after the older man. Three young lads with suitcases making their way towards the workers' quarters and the industrial parts of town were just small specks in the landscape. I wondered, as I walked, if Makedonsky had planned the whole thing ahead of time or had run into money troubles, due to gambling, cards, or his own strange affairs. He had aided me so much, not wholly for his own purposes, that I felt guilty that I was not remaining behind to help him. But I knew that I could not, in any case. He lived a strange life, and only one part of it had opened out to me. Whatever the grand plans of world solidarity, the unity of mankind, and the solidarity of rebels, I began to understand how difficult it was in one's course in life to understand one's fellow humans. Who was I myself, who was brought up in so meek and mild a place, my family hearth, my daily religion, and had shot two men at point blank range, in rage and anger? Was it "direct action," a political deed, *Revolutsia*? Or simply the fact that someone had put the instrument of killing in my hand and my finger itched for the trigger? How many times, I thought, as I looked at the jaunty duo beside me, the two young men who embraced suffering and adversity, and were dedicated and eager to fight violence with violence, to spend their lives in the unequal battle, beggars against the vast armories and legions of empires, how many times would I be called upon to repeat that so easy gesture, that soft squeeze, so unexpected at the first instance, but which might become so banal and familiar? Was that my fate? The outcast forever? Until my own luck ran out, and another man's trigger finger ushered me into the void? What would God say?

And my father? My sisters, my brothers, the dreamer Yakov, who saw me flying over mountains, or crawling laboriously through a tunnel, poised between heaven and earth, between triumph and failure, mansions or tombs?

After about an hour we had left houses behind and were walking through open fields. The night was very clear, the stars resplendent, the trees seemed to glitter like the jeweled forests of Yakov's dream. Mayer's wife had packed us some bread rolls and jam and some cut meats. We sat and ate, mostly in silence. Then we walked some more and lay down on the banks of a stream, drowsing to its soft and constant gurgle.

In the morning, we hailed a passing cart, which took us through the next few villages. Victor said there were only another few kilometers to Utrecht. We reached there by noon, passing many mansions and landscaped gardens on the way. It was a fine town, with a tall cathedral, but we did not linger. We found our way to the station, and Victor bought us three tickets to Antwerp, across the border. No one questioned us or showed any curiosity at three young lads enjoying the summer. Along the way, my two companions were already mulling my future, the new name I would have to adopt, the new life I would have to create for myself as a world-citizen, a shipwrecked sailor adrift on the land. I would become someone else, as Vigo had become Almereyda, and Victor Kibalchich had already decided on a less foreign name and would call himself Serge. It is a truism that the future is always unknown, but there are moments when, rather than an old saw, the thought itself becomes a new instrument, a polished sword, to carry with pride.

"The Road to Utah"

Asher:

Seven years after my father's death, I found his manuscript. He had never told me about it. He kept mounds of notebooks—of his own jottings, of camera angles, lighting calculations, shot lists that he had kept from the great DeMille collection that swallowed everything up, the giant maw that consigned all the production records, correspondence, press clippings, scripts, photographs, drawings, designs, background research, studio plans, account books, logs and breakdowns to the grand archive that the master had decreed would rest in the far-off western Utah town of Provo, deep in Mormon country, in the Harold B. Lee Library of Brigham Young University. Even if I wanted to go there, I was warned by an archivist whom I met at a memorial service to my father held a year after his death, in Los Angeles, that, in keeping with the strictures of the Church of Jesus Christ of the Latter-day Saints, there was no tea nor coffee served on campus. On the other hand, he said, if you went along to their family history centers, either at Salt Lake City or the Mormon temple that towered just off Santa Monica Boulevard, at Manning, just before Overland, you might be able to find vital records of your family, those who came to America, from the moment they landed off the immigrant ships at Ellis Island, through whichever addresses they lived at in any state, their employment, if listed in the census, marriages, divorces, offspring, all sorts of stuff you'd be amazed you didn't know, or things about which you were told lies. He had been there himself, to look for his wife's grandparents, whom she had been told had been third-generation Virginians but who turned out to have been on the boat from Bremen with their parents in 1895, having been born in Kamenetz-Podolsk. The Mormons were sticklers for facts, since they were painstakingly constructing their vast census of every person who could be identified as having lived on Earth since vital records began, so they all could be baptized retrospectively and be blessed with the Saviour's grace. They had already baptized over a million dead Jews before the American Jewish Congress, the Anti-Defamation League, the State of Israel and other interested parties had intervened to persuade them to drop this controversial part of their universal plan. On the other hand, the archivist said, they held amazing seminars such as "The Genealogy of African-Americans and Non-African Americans," which had many zealous Southern white families weeping at the revelation of their own imperfect roots. "The first thing they tell you when you start searching," my friend told me, "is everything you were told of oral history in your family is sure to be untrue."

Well, that was something I never doubted about my own people, the scattered seed of Bessarabian corn. Every one of their voyages, it seemed, was preordained. Fate sent them on their way, to the Goldeneh Medineh America, to the Promised Land of Palestine, even to Manchuria. Russia's chaff, cast off to the winds. The diaspora.

Only once, I remember, my father told me that he had written some records of his own past, B.H.—before Hollywood—before the blessed marriage of commerce and celluloid with his mentor DeMille. In DeMille's autobiography, my father was only mentioned once, in a paragraph about the shooting of *Union Pacific*, with Joel McCrea and Barbara Stanwyck, in 1936. It said: "Bill Gore suggested an ingenious trestle that we rigged up for the train wreck." And that was it—not even a footnote. My dad said, "He wanted me for *The Greatest Show on Earth*, after *Samson and Delilah*, but I decided to go with Anna and come over here," to Israel. It seemed DeMille resented his betrayal and ranted at him for nearly an hour. The great director bore grudges, as well as favors, staying loyal to his old crew and actors for decades. My father took some of his notes with him, for memory's sake, and a batch of six bound screenplays, which I thumbed through over and over from when I could read. They were of *Forbidden Fruit*, *Fool's Paradise*, *The Golden Bed*, *Madam Satan*, *The Sign of the Cross* and *Cleopatra*, the first three silents, the others sound pictures, all early work. Around 1925 or '26, my father said, DeMille decided that he was going to be the world's most famous film director, and therefore he should collect his movie negatives, prints, production records, and all historical data that would preserve every trace of his oeuvre, so that the World Should Know who was great and who was trash. At the same time, he asked some of the crew that had worked with him from the start, from 1914, to write down their own memoriams and histories. Some did and some didn't; his regular writer, Jeannie McPherson, who was also his primary lover, despite the wife he had married back in 1902, told him she had written enough for his records and wanted to keep at least some of her mystery. "But I wrote him some pages," my dad said, offhand. "It's somewhere in his boxes."

He told me this in 1968, when we traveled together to California, a few weeks after I was demobilized from my three-year national service in the army. I really didn't care much for the family history, which had been drilled into my ears forever by my Aunt Sarah, and letters from Kolya, who thundered on about Our National Duty and told me how proud he was that I was wearing the uniform, as one of the warriors who had liberated Jerusalem, even in the service of the limp socialists of the so-called Labor Party, who had "suddenly dis-covered a backbone after a decade and a half of cowardice." And so I didn't question my father any further about his "few pages," and didn't look for them, or even ask where the pile of boxes of Cecil B. DeMille were stored. We went around L.A., exploring Hollywood, looking at the old barn where DeMille and Jesse Lasky had started up their business, in the winter of 1913, when there was nothing around but mountains and farmland, and meeting Dad's old friends at home and at the studios from Warner Brothers to Universal and down south to Culver City.

"Send the kid here," they said. "We'll get him started." But they had said that before, in '65, when I first visited on my own, just before the army service began. "When you get out of the khakis, just get on the plane, boy. Bill Gore is an open ticket to this town." But in 1968 I made other discoveries, and other friends, who led me to other places. I stayed behind, and Dad flew back to Tel Aviv together with another old cinematographer, whom he had known from Paramount, who was making a pilgrimage to his own son in Beersheba and could keep him company on the way. Dad was already seventy-nine years old at that time, and although he still looked like a stripling of only seventy, he wheezed a lot and would sometimes stop halfway up some Hollywood driveway that he insisted on ascending by foot instead of being driven to the door. "It's been a long time..." But I wasn't sure if he was talking about his sore legs or his life.

I had gone over to UCLA on my own, but since I couldn't drive at the time, I went around L.A. on buses. This was in the days before public transport was the exclusive province of drunk beggars, the poorest Hispanic workers, servants, street-sweepers, and various auxiliaries who kept the city in its pristine sheen before anyone else got up in the morning. At the campus I met Lauren, the granddaughter of one of my dad's "lenser" friends (she had been taken to see *To Have and Have Not* fifty times). Lauren introduced me to the Students for a Democratic Society cell, whose people roped me in as a tripod and cases carrier and then assistant camera on a film they were shooting about the Cesar Chavez grape-pickers strike at Delano, north of Bakersfield, on Route 99. It had been going on for about three years, and eventually led to the Delano grape strike, which spread all over the world. And so I got into the cause of the Chicano pickers and "the movement," such as it was then, but not, alas, into Lauren Lebowski's pants.

Those were the days that myths are made of, the Children's Crusade, the new End of Days and outlaw manifestos, the BAMN, the days of "We Are All Criminals," "internal liberation," freedom from the Man, the Future Belongs to Free Spirits—"Everything

173

they say we are, we are/And we are very proud of ourselves ... We are obcene, lawless, hideous, dangerous, dirty, violent, and young..." the Peace and Freedom Party, "the Provotariat," "Beware of Structure Freaks," "Fuck Leaders," the Vietnam War riots, Chicago, Planetary rebellion, the Black Panthers, macrobiotic food, Jerry Rubin and the Yippies, the Delaware Obscenity Group, smoke-ins, the International Werewolf Conspiracy, "Up Against the Wall, Motherfucker," "Acid-Armed Consciousness," the Outlaws of America, W.I.T.C.H. (Women Inspired to Commit Herstory), the Gay Liberation Front, the Sexual Revolution, "Rehearse for the Apocalypse," etcetera...

In the midst of our Chavez shoot, we were called up west to the great Berkeley People's Park crisis, where hippies had started to plant trees and shrubs in an area of local houses and gardens that had been demolished by the war-mongering RAND-research-funded University of California, sparking an invasion of new "whole earth" revolutionaries, who had been attacked by police in full riot gear, leading to a pitched battle on campus with thousands of students, a shotgun killing, "Bloody Thursday," shootings on Telegraph Avenue and a rebellion over the protection of "the most oppressed classes of society—animals, trees, grass, air, water and earth." By the time we got there, there was just rubble, mounds of upturned earth, torn clothing and shoes and sandals scattered all over the road.

Somehow, I kept some of my own archive, including this faded strip of paper on proposals for "Yippie Activities in Chicago 1968" during the Democratic Convention:

1. Poetry readings, mass meditation, flycasting exhibitions, demagogic yippie political arousal speeches, rock music, song concerts.
2. A dawn ass-washing ceremony to be held with tens of thousands of participants to occur each morning at 5 a.m.
3. Several hundred Yippie friends with forged press passes will gorge on 800 pounds of cocktail onions and puke in unison at the nomination of Hubert H. Pastry.

174

4. Psychedelic long-haired mutant-jissomed peace leftists will consort with known dope-fiends in porn-ape disarray on the sidewalks every afternoon.

5. Filth will be worshipped.

6. There will be public fornication whenever and wherever there is an aroused appendage and willing aperture.

7. Poets will re-write the Bill of Rights in precise language, detailing ten thousand areas of freedom in our own language to replace the confused rhetoric of two hundred years ago.

8. Total assault on sick hamburger society of automobile scheiss-poison freaks and white killer industrialists.

9. There will be 16 tons of donated fish eyes.

None of this happened, apart from the rock concert. Instead, hundreds of people had their skulls cracked open and their arms broken in the police riot that accompanied Hubert Humphrey's selection as the Democratic Party's nominee for the presidency. I was already in New York at that time, filming a short about kids in housing projects in the Bronx. My father was back in Tel Aviv, and all he said to me about the whole business of world upheaval and the revolution against the Man was one line in a letter about the new neighbors who were driving him crazy every morning by screaming for no reason at 6 a.m.:

"Whatever you shoot, don't monkey about with the frame."

I always used that when people asked me the usual questions about what I had learned from my father or what Cecil B. DeMille was like. Dad never spoke about him much, except to repeat his mantra: "He was the world's biggest son of a bitch, but screw it, that man had talent." My father didn't talk much about the past. Kolya took care of that. Dad spent the years of my childhood, since we arrived at the port of Haifa when I was three years old, trekking back and forth, by bus, to the Geva and Herzliya studios and overseeing their camera departments. That used to be my dreamland as a kid, for a while. The big studio space, with its giant lights, cat's cradles of rigging and cables. The editing room, where the editor Danny S., who had some childhood illness that had left his arms and hands twisted but pulled and cut and shaped the celluloid film with the quick dexterity of a magician. Gideon the soundman, who was slightly deaf but seemed to hear everything nevertheless. Simone the negative cutter in her white coat and white gloves, handling her ghostly strips on editing tables that were the cleanest surfaces I ever saw in the country. Sometimes when we went on location, Dad let me go by myself with the film crew down to Jerusalem to film some dramatic comedy the director Uri Zohar was shooting around Mount Zion, overlooking the Old City walls. This was always a thrill, as the valley between the old Ottoman walls and the Jewish city was still strewn with barbed wire and concrete blocks, burnt-out armored cars of the 1948 War of Independence and ruined buildings that had never been rebuilt since the "armistice"—our only peace agreement with our enemies had frozen everything in No Man's Land. In the midst of this, of course a "love story," though I can't remember its progress, and whether it had a happy or tragic ending. To sit through a single day's shoot on any film is to see a fragment, suffused with vague longing, unsatisfied desires, too many sandwiches, and mumbling banter among the crew about whatever mental itch was tingling that day.

When Dad bought me the 8-millimeter camera, his advice began to be a yoke rather than a lifeline, since there was not much to be gleaned when trying to film your schoolmates crawling around with water pistols in a Tel Aviv stairway with nothing but one's short pants and a light meter from somebody who had been used to swooping above the mass action on a Louma crane behind the giant weight of a Mitchell BNC, with its two steering handles like the controls of a B-59 bomber. The close reality of the only land we knew, growing, made this old man whom everyone assumed was my grandfather more and more of a stranger and an interloper in a country he never seemed at ease with, unable to hold his own in the stifling summer weather, spread on the sofa with the latest batch of magazines from his old friends and colleagues abroad: *Variety*, *The Hollywood Reporter* and the *American Cinematogapher* magazine, with its photo spreads of vast and intricate machines, locations, tales of magic light and the advertisements for equipment that only increased one's youthful drool. I had to study diligently the intricate details and graphs and diagrams of the *American Cinematographer Manual*, the real bible of our home.

When my brother Yitzhak, who already had sons and daughters my age, came to visit, he only stayed a short while because he could only drink tapwater and could not imbibe any beverage or take a single mouthful of food in our house because it was not glatt kosher. Eventually he took to bringing with him and leaving a standard pocket Bible, just in case one of us heretics might be moved by some miracle to start examining our real patrimony, The Truth and Meaning of our life. "Ashik," he would whisper to me, in the kitchen, leaning towards my ear and gazing at me intently. "When will you start laying tefillin? Even once, the Name is not a fanatic." Which was a novel approach, but I was too hard-assed to respond. Tel Aviv and Jerusalem, the two versions of the cities of Zion, divided between the mountain, one looking east towards Moab, the other west to the sea, towards Cyprus, Athens, Rome, London, New York and Los Angeles.

After the Yippies, a long winter in New York City, working as an assistant projectionist at Lionel Rogosin's Bleecker Street Cinema in Greenwich Village. That was a true education. Lionel Rogosin had made one of the key movies of the American documentary movement, *On the Bowery*, and then shot a feature film called *Come Back, Africa* in South Africa, under the disguise of shooting a musical, which showed the true conditions of black South Africans under the apartheid system. When he finished editing the film back in America he could find no one willing to show it, so he bought a rickety old theater on Bleecker Street that became the first stopping place for any independent, radical filmmaker, or audience interested in something different from the main. He was a big bear of a man who enjoyed talking but needed other people to keep the show going on a business basis, this being the United States. I sat for three years on those old seats watching everything from the American experimental filmmakers like Shirley Clarke and the Mekas brothers, Jonas and Adolfas, Bob Downey and all sorts of visitors who came in from abroad. I saw the whole French new wave there: Godard, Truffaut, Chabrol, Resnais, Rivette and so forth, most during that long winter' of '68, trudging through the rain and snow to the apartment I shared with three other down-and-outs on Second Avenue and Fourth. We also showed a lot of Hollywood "auteur" films that were guaranteed kosher by the Cahiers du Cinema lot and our own homegrown *Cineaste* magazine—films by John Ford, Howard Hawks, Raoul Walsh, King Vidor, William Wyler and the like, but nothing by Cecil B. DeMille. He was the enemy. All I told my friends, and my girlfriends, was that my father had worked for DeMille for forty years, to emphasize the long road I had traveled from my patrimony to the new age. It served to mark me as much of a savage as those three years of army service, my khaki credentials as a camera hand for the Man in my own right... the American left had not yet discovered the occupation of Palestinian land...

And so I advanced along the path of resistance, the camera operator and co-conspirator of the New York Granma Commune—three guys, one gal, the cutting-room cat, and the lifeline of Duplex Art Labs and the Gorilla Filmakers outlet, the unwashed, the un-waged, the unstoppable. Somehow money trickled in, from donations and a from a few professors at Brooklyn College, Columbia, even at Yeshiva University, who peeled off a percentage of their mite for the cause. We produced, on our explorations beyond the Bleecker, three films in the first two years. We made *Fragged Nation*, a movie about Vietnam deserters that we shot mainly in Canada, though there were a couple of folks who hid out in Boston, in the Roxbury district. *Mary's Hammers* was about a group of nuns who broke into nuclear bases in Arkansas and Texas and smashed up a batch of missile nose cones; and we made *Commie Sugar Brothers*, in which a group of Americans infiltrate Cuba to help the 1970 harvest. We were unclear whether we should be shooting the movie or cutting sugar cane, and Esther Brodie, our feminist member, quit because of the title, and because she was "fed up at all your macho fucking shit." My two co-defendants were Alex Foardelawder, who called himself Al Ford, and Shabtai Wasserman, another semi-Israeli, who was credited as Shad M. Waters. I called myself Asher Gurevits, which was my name, rather than Asher Gore. We had a female deficit for a while, until we were joined by Sam, who only had one name, and Cassandra Daws, a black firebrand from Brooklyn Heights. That took us into 1971, and *Amerikan Outlaws*, a Black Panther saga, and my pet project, *Palestine-Israel — The Unchosen Land*.

When I came back to Tel Aviv, in April, my parents were still in the same perch on Melchett Street, my father on the sofa by the window overlooking the rooftops that gave way to the tiny shimmer of the sea, my mother in the kitchen or in bed, reading popular novels, as if neither of them had moved since I left. My father had after all spent the previous decades dining at Canter's, Chasen's, the Kit Kat Club, Lucca's, the Brown Derby, the Trocadero, Ciro's, Perino's or the Russian Eagle, where, as he always told me, Greta and Marlene used to hang out. The blinis—ah, the blinis! It was run by Count Andrei Tolstoy. Classy days. All gone now. I remember, in '68, how I followed the old folks from the DeMille barn, down the hill towards Hollywood Boulevard where they remembered a neat little diner they used to stop at when the talkies were just starting up. Unlike every tourist in the known universe they hadn't realized how the neighborhood had mutated into a tatty row of souvenir shops and Mexican taco parlors, with strange young men in drooping pants hanging around the curbs giving passersby the glad eye. At least they identified the Roosevelt Hotel and Grauman's Chinese, but the nostalgia soon petered out. Now my mother, who had been a budding actress and playwright in Greenwich Village when the "Beat generation" were still idling at college desks, bustled about preparing my father's defrosted schnitzel.

I tried to talk to him about the way my life had changed and what I had discovered about the world, and the different America that was emerging out of the movement to end the war in Vietnam. But it only sparked a familiar rambling memory about DeMille's wartime movie of 1944, *The Story of Dr. Wassell*. My father said it was the worst film he had ever worked on and had convinced him that his own days of movie glory, the joy of the lens and the perfection of the frame, were almost over, and that Los Angeles had run its course. "Ben Hecht was sending guns to the militias in Palestine," he said, "and Kolya was writing me about it as well. We had our own war to fight." As do they still. There was no point in bending his ear about my own heretical thoughts.

Now in his mid-eighties, my father was getting more frail, less combative, beginning to lose focus, though he could still project that aura of control, if only to his closest circle. Kolya appeared, on one of his rare visits from Michigan, deigning to enter the country despite its government still being held in the socialist vice, this time of Golda Meir, for whom he had some remnant of respect and obligation due to her old friendship with Aunt Sarah. He went to a closed meeting of the cabal of grizzled elders, comrades of the 1920s who had shifted sheep dip and cow dung with his elder sister and the current prime minister in their kibbutz days. Otherwise he spent most of his time going in and out of the so-called Fortress of Ze'ev, the Herut Party's headquarters, just twenty minutes' walk up the road, settling into long-term strategic discussions with Menachem Begin and the other veterans of the Irgun—the National Military Organization with whom he had borne arms against the British, firing pistols at their patrols, laying explosives, blowing up convoys, and other matters of high patriotic valor that his elder sister disapproved of. A history that only my mother would mention, since it took place outside the frame. Kolya was five years younger than my father but looked older, his face a mass of brown wrinkles, a landscape marked by deep fissures and harsh winds. I think he had reached volume 15 of his "Jew Hatred Through the Ages" and was collecting material on the dark dreams of Egypt's

Muslim Brotherhood, a task for which he had been deepening his knowledge of the Arabic he had picked up in his terrorist days. According to one legend, he and two other fighters had disguised themselves and lived in an Arab village for six weeks waiting for the visit of the deputy commander of the British Palestine Brigade, whom they riddled with bullets before escaping on white stallions. I had not bothered to find out whether this was in any detail true.

I arrived at Lod Airport with Shad Wasserman and Sam, carrying our silvery camera boxes through customs after a long session convincing the officials they were all registered to Samantha Jacobson as a bona fide American citizen, not a putative immigrant. The political landscape was relatively quiet after the previous year's upheaval in Jordan—Black September, when King Hussein had chased the PLO guerrillas out of his kingdom to Syria, and the Israeli government was consolidating its hold on the West Bank and Gaza, holding elections for municipal seats. Travel was easy between the Israeli cities and "the areas," most smoothly through "united" Jerusalem, where one simply stood in line for a service taxi just outside the Damascus Gate in the Old City, cramming aboard with the locals en route to Bethlehem, Hebron, Ramallah, Nablus or Jenin. Most days the soldiers at the road blocks just waved everybody through, unless they encountered a dirty look that annoyed them on a long, boring day. An American passport was an automatic license for passage. The easiest way though was from west to east Jerusalem, over the old No Man's Land of only four years before, the concrete blocks and razor wire cleared, but most of the buildings still derelict around the junctions leading towards the Jaffa Gate and entry into the Other Side, the alternate universe that had floated in our youth and in my Aunt Sarah's old stories. How she used to cross over every day, in her own time in Jerusalem, when the British ruled and when the soldiers were bored Cockney kids, or dour Scotsmen, or Welsh or Irish squaddies who had no idea why they had to go so far from home to boil in the sun and be shot at both by Jews and Arabs on some unlucky day. Why she crossed over there I never knew; I had to assume it was not the same reason that Sam took us over there, apart from the filming, when she discovered the source of the immense slabs of hash that appeared on our friends' tables to be cut with a hot kitchen knife and mixed with cigarette tobacco on Rizla papers, a heady brew that shut down conversation for the rest of the day.

Our primary guides on the project were Gershon and Link, twin sons of one of my father's old acquaintances in the local movie business, Aaron Apple. He was a studio manager and one-time official at the State Information Ministry on cinematic affairs, a deep-dish Labor Zionist and confidante of the ex-chief of staff and current defense minister, Moshe Dayan. The sons were early members of the Tel Aviv branch of the small left-wing Matspen "compass") movement, otherwise known as the Israel Socialist Organization, which had formed even before the Six-Day War of 1967 but had expanded beyond its first handful of members in opposition to the occupation of the West Bank and Gaza. We met in Berkeley, as they appeared in my lens from behind a ridge, bouncing along two wheelbarrows of pot plants that they were about to insert in protest against the military-industrial complex. "The gun and the shovel," they said. "Just like the old days! Build up the homeland with asparagus!" It was never easy to remember whether Gershon or Link was speaking. They were not identical; Gershon was taller and leaner and Link a little shorter and chunkier, or maybe it was the other way around. We lost touch for a couple of years until they turned up again, at the Bleecker, at a double bill of Godard's *Les Carabiniers* and *Alphaville*. In the former, Godard's two young oafs, Michel-Ange and Ulysses, who are called up by "the king" to serve as soldiers in "the war," send batches of postcards to their wives telling of all the places they have conquered and subjects despoiled: Paris, London, Berlin, the pyramids, the Taj Mahal, the Parthenon, Ava Gardner, Elizabeth Taylor as Cleopatra. Then, in *Alphaville*, the dark journey of Eddie Constantine as Lemmy Caution across the "exterior lands" in search of the shadowy scientist Professor von Braun. Strange, what moments affect one most, for no immediately apparent reason. My father took me to see Akira Kurosawa's *Yojimbo* at the Mugrabi Theater when I was just sixteen. In the opening scene, as the samurai enters the village, a dog pads by, holding a severed hand in its mouth. I was glad we had left my mother at home because she would have dragged me out on the spot. She could not abide "modern cruelty," since, she said, her generation had had enough of the old type. Israeli films, or the few that we saw at that time, extolled the strong, silent determination of the new Hebrew youth to rebuild their lives from the embers of Europe, or at most poked fun gently at the new state's bureaucracy in settling the new Sephardic immigrants. But the Japanese director's savage images of a town rent in two by rival gangs, whom the samurai, Toshiro Mifune, goads into killing each other off, were like a visual nuclear explosion. My father shifted about in his seat at the violence and at my rapt attention, but all he would say later was he regretted not having the chance to work in Cinemascope. "Great possibilities," he said, "if one pays proper attention." Of course, we had sat through his mentor's epic, *The Ten Commandments*, to which DeMille had issued him an invitation to consult on location, but since the location shots were due to be taken in Egypt this was not exactly a practical offer. Still, my father was generous, affirming afterwards: "The man knows how to make hokum pay off."

Gershon and Link were my mentors in the Israel-Palestine film and we still skived off to the movies in between our excursions. With myself shooting, Shad arranging the journeys and the equipment, and Sam recording the sound and supplying the hash. Gershon and Link, alternating, would travel with us or drive us in their dad's jeep, which he used to go on bird-watching trips in the Negev, crisscrossing the West Bank north to south, east to west, and down the spine of the Gaza Strip, from Bet Hanun through Gaza City itself down to Rafah, where the government was building a whole new Jewish town called Yamit on the Sinai shoreline that had been taken from Egypt in the Six-Day War. Contacts with local people had often been made ahead by the twins' friends just across the political lines, members or fellow travelers of the Israeli communist party—the "Arab" segment that had split from the "Jewish" party either over Krushchev or China or something, but which also included Jewish members. We would meet for these planned trips in Jerusalem, at the Ta'amon café, a tiny hole-in-the-wall on King George Street that was the meeting place of the Left, although it was run by a charming religious gentleman called Kop, with the assistance from the waitress Carmela, who had no interest in politics, he presided over "upside down" coffees and hummus.

We filmed in Arab villages that seemed to have weathered the ebb and flux of conquerors, kingdoms, and regimes in an age-old calm of hilltop isolation, but quivered with the agitation of uncertainty and the incursions of the new Jewish settlers whose first long, portable cabins they could see unloaded off giant trucks rumbling up the next hill. We filmed in towns where young men stood on corners leaning against railings or sitting in the coffee shops looking out as the Israeli patrols rattled by in their khaki jeeps, gun barrels pointed in all directions. We went to the tent encampments of the settled Bedouin displaced by the Jewish enclaves on the Sinai coast and recorded their laments. We recorded the old man in Ramallah telling us about his birth in Turkish times and counting off on his fingers the various rulers he had seen come and go: the Turks, then the British, then the Jordanian Hashemites, then the Jews, the first invaders whose goal was transference, not rule. Other armies come and go, he said. This one wants to stay forever, which guarantees an explosion. And we drove through the Gaza refugee camps, with their open sewers and children standing aside and raising their hands in a mock—or real?—surrender when our jeep with its Israeli number plates passed.

Then I would return to Lord Melchett Street, to be told off by my Mum for not eating properly and have my father press into my hands the latest edition of *American Cinematographer*, with its in-depth analysis of the upside down sets of *The Poseidon Adventure* and articles like "A Systems Approach to Light Control Materials" and "Budget Filming 'The Candidate' on Location," which he thought would be useful for me in my current project. My mother was less enamored of my rushing "over the line," eating peasants' yogurt that lay around in courtyards to be consumed by flies. My father's essential concern was that I made sure the right stuff was "in the frame." I used to protest at this, in 8-millimeter days, shooting *Murder in Jerusalem* and *The Vanishing School* in the streets. "Dad, not everything is a Cecil B. DeMille film," I would tell him, but he would only touch his nose and respond, "Every film is a Cecil B. DeMille film." Some ideas cannot be shaken.

We shot the film, and flew back to New York to start editing at the cubbyholes in the basement of 345 West Fourth Street. We were just about finished when the October War broke out in the Middle East, as Egypt and Syria launched their surprise attack across the Suez Canal and over the Golan Heights on Yom Kippur. I scrambled to make a call home, waking my parents at three in the morning, my father making me instantly furious by asking: "When are you coming?" as my mother broke into the call and said firmly: "Don't come. If they get here, we'll have barricades. Your father never throws anything out."

Fuming at my father's political naivete, I labored on at the cutting table, all of us realizing we would have to revise the picture, having forgotten or ignored the truism about the Middle East: something happens all the time. We watched the television news with dread as tank battles raged in the Sinai; Shad's little brother was an eighteen-year-old recruit. We traveled together back to Tel Aviv in December, when the returning soldiers were beginning to rally against what they saw as blunders by Golda Meir's government. To our relief, we discovered Shad's brother was intact, but we had to thumb through the paperback book of the published list of the fallen, a tome of more than one hundred pages, to find out. More than three thousand soldiers had been killed on the southern and northern fronts, and the Israeli army was stuck deep inside Egypt, where it had broken through in a bloody counterattack. I was still fuming with my father over the phone call, but he told me I had simply woken him up, and he had forgotten all about the war for that moment. Somehow all meaningful conversation had stopped. My older brother, Yitzhak, deigned to visit the unkosher apartment, and was full of stories about Kolya's son, my cousin, Adir, who had fought as a company commander with General Ariel Sharon at the breakthrough battle in an Egyptian village known as the Chinese Farm and had been wounded twice but fought on to save his unit. Yitzhak glowered at me as if I were Heinrich Himmler in person, and I shot him glances as if he were the angel of death. Somehow we got into a political argument, about the folly of war, the occupation, the stupidity of the Labor government's ignoring of that ticking time bomb, all the warnings that anyone with half a brain had been repeating since 1967, the crazy religious settlements that had been springing up in the West Bank and Gaza Strip, and the whole self-destructive path of the state. How many more dead brothers, fathers, and sons are you going to sacrifice for this delusional, cowardly defeatism, we yelled at each other. My father just sat blinking in his chair until my mother came out with her hands over her ears and told us she was going to torch the apartment.

And so we separated in silence. More films, several aborted projects, the final split with Sam, the meeting with Claire, the London period, Queen's Park, the exiled Israel socialists, Shai Baer and Moshik, encounters with Palestinians, life with Claire, the teaching job at the London Film Academy, and the annual or biannual visits, climbing up the stairs again at Melchett, the time machine, the bright white walls, the window on the rooftops, the patch of blue, the noisy radios from downstairs and the open balcony across the way, the washing lines with Dad's old trousers, the fat piles of the *Los Angeles Times* that friends were sending him in air mail packets, news of things gone by, but keeping the calendar sections, with all the giant ads and reviews and gossip about the latest studio news. *Variety* was stuffed in there occasionally, but he was steadily losing touch, getting up late, sleeping the long afternoons away, enjoying the relative balm of the evenings, listening to the sounds. "It's a symphony," he said to me. "I should have gone into music. Learned the violin, the piano. None of us did that. We were *am-ha-aretz* ("people of the land"), ignoramuses, except Yakov. Have you looked for him, Asher? You've been in Paris, London, Berlin. Sometimes I feel he's still around there. I know the Nazis never got him. Vassily, the Great Gramby! He knew how to disappear! The Lazarus trick, I told you about that, didn't I? It was his big hit in Paris. At the Folies Bergere. Ace knew all about it. The black kid, his assistant. Have you talked to Ace? He's still alive."

"I know Dad. I sent you the clipping."

It was a *New York Times* article. The Sunday arts section. Ace Harrington. The jazz legend at home in Madison, Georgia, outside Atlanta. A smalltown bungalow and a grizzled old man, born Abraham Adams Harrington in Augusta, rode the rails in his childhood to New York City where he found work in vaudeville as a boy stooge for a magician, Vassily Gamby ("Can't even spell the name right, the idiots..." my father fumed, unfolding the page I had stuffed into an envelope.) Learned to play the saxophone in Los Angeles from the famous Red Billy Gibbs, who had begun his life playing in movie theaters, but he stuck with the magician for several years and even followed him to France in 1921, where he began playing the sax on his own. Began recording for Okeh Records in Chicago in 1924. Later moved down south, to Atlanta, settling in Augusta and then in Madison in the 1960s. Stopped playing after starting up a flourishing garage and auto-sales business. At his seventy-fifth birthday, he tells his tale to *The Times*.

"There's a subject for a documentary for you," said my father, punching the picture of the diminutive old man with the gray moustache and tight white curls, surrounded by sons, daughter, grandchildren, neighbors black and white. "Get him to talk about Yakov. I'll bet he knows where he is."

But I didn't go to Georgia, as I was still living in London. Two years later, the family gathered for Dad's ninetieth birthday. My brother hired a hall in Jerusalem where he could assemble his own growing brood, little boys with skullcaps and dangling tsitses and little girls dressed for the shtetl as if nothing had changed in the last hundred years. Tradition! Tradition! At least they didn't dance with wine bottles. Kolya didn't come, as he was still boycotting the country because of the Camp David Accords with Egypt. He was livid with his ex-comrade Menachem Begin, who had signed away Sinai and had even more heretically agreed on some principles for Palestinian self-rule. He sent my father a telegram of congratulation that read like an official communiqué of the All-Party Union of the RSFSR. The hero son, Adir, now resurnamed as Gur-Arieh (the "lion cub") came in his place; the somewhat frightened, taciturn teenager always buried in a book and glowering at all interlopers on his private space had morphed into a ramrod-backed man of action who walked into the room with his arms swinging and shoulders thrust back, his hands ready to clench at the first sign of some antagonist who might want to swing a punch in his face. He was still glowering. His war wound had left him with a slight limp. The wags said it must have been his groin, and he had not yet confounded them with his marriage and son—yet another Yitzhak for the lost Celovets child. Gone was the kid I used to slouch around with in the streets, putting our old, tattered half-pound notes together to go to a matinee Tarzan.

Most of the guests at the party were old Hollywood colleagues who had traveled from California and surrounded my father in his padded armchair. He was already walking with great difficulty and my "observant" brother had not been observant enough to realize that a third-floor venue without an elevator was a problem; it would take another year or two for him to figure out that Dad would better off at his own place in Jerusalem, where an endless stream of charitable grandsons and granddaughters could minister to his needs, before the care home beckoned. They bought crates of champagne, which my brother of course couldn't touch, and a batch of Czechoslovakian tipple, the Becherovka, which made one's eyes water after one gulp and which my mother surreptitiously sipped. She was growing tired too, I could see, and exhausted by the years of care and worry and the private thoughts that were balling tighter and tighter under her gray hair. She seemed to be growing older than her own sixty-eight years in solidarity with him. I saw for the first time that this fixture in my life was disappearing, and I had left myself no lifeline to reel it back in. My life was my own, with Claire, who watched my tippling warily, as the past gathered around my father telling uproarious stories about the old days, DeMille and his craziness, how he had come back on the set of *Union Pacific* after a prostate operation, strapped himself to the camera crane and swooped down on some crew member who was canoodling behind the wind machines with his girlfriend, shouting, "Get back to work, time wasters! There's a law in this state against taking money under false pretenses!"

Of course one never recognizes the cinematographers, the ones behind the camera, but I knew some of the greats: Ray Rennahan, who shot *For Whom the Bell Tolls* and *Unconquered* for DeMille, Burnett Guffey, who had shot *All the King's Men*, Joe Walker, who had shot *It Happened One Night* and other films for Frank Capra, Howard Hawks and everybody else, even for Orson Welles—*The Lady from Shanghai*. He got talking with Dad about some silent Western called *The Fighting Stallion* Dad had advised on, with Yakima Canutt and Boy the Wonder Horse. He had designed the wide-angle lenses for Todd-AO, thirty years later, and they got into a long technical ding-dong. I was looking at history as a cozy cabal of old codgers who had done wonderful things, once upon a time, that enthralled millions and millions of people across the world. It was the first time I felt a kind of envy at Dad's life, which I had always considered a distinguished but somehow frivolous aside from the heavy lifting of a fallen humanity. Where were they all, these happy gentlemen, when I was buzzing around the sweaty streets of Tel Aviv, waiting for a preordained doom? Lining up on the stage of the Sheinkin Street school to intone paeans for the dead heroes of Israel? Yakima Canutt, for God's sake, the stunt rider of John Ford's *Stagecoach*! What made you give all that up, you old bastard?? I finished off the Becherovka.

Then, finally, in 1984, the shiva—the ceremonial seven days sitting in the house of the deceased, still the same sunlit top floor, the old divan along the wall, more chairs and cushions borrowed from Mrs Sarfati from the floor below, the old lampshades I used to read by on nights when my parents had gone to bed, and nothing remained but the light tinkle of the late-night music way across the road, or the draggy motorcycle of the maniac insomniac of Melchett, up and down, up and down... The last ingathering, probably, of the wider reaches of the clan: the full complement of Yitzhak's brood, the eldest, black-draped and bearded, with three small ones in tow, putative Yitzhaks, suitably subdued for the occasion but reaching for the plate of rugalach on the old glass table, scuffed with coffee rings from all the mugs and cups I'd ground into it over the years. There was also a strong contingent of Aunt Sarah's offspring, one of her sons and her daughter, Tsadok and Rivka, both in their late sixties, with a van-load of their own next generation: Eliyahu, named for the missing son, her firstborn, killed in a car crash in Germany on some business trip disapproved of by Kolya; Uriel and Orna, hearty cooperative dwellers from kibbutz and moshav, carriers of the pioneer gene, despite the fact that Uri, I understood, now owned his own software business, selling his identity encryption to eager buyers as far apart as Guatemala and China. And many others I barely remembered...

Kolya turned up this time, flown in overnight directly, with Adir and his new wife, a fashion executive, dolled up in what I imagined The Woman's magazine recommended for grief—suitably dark but formfitting. Adir's swaggering walk had now morphed into a full-swung orangutan lurch, as if his legs and arms wanted to march off in their own direction but were held back by sheer willpower and the mass of his jutting shoulders and chest. My mother had told me that he had been appointed as a prospective member of the Knesset for the Likud Party in the safe portion of the list (number 35 or 36) for the elections that were due in only a few months' time. He was a rising star of the New Right. His eyes roamed the room, looking for voters, but he shook my hand politely and murmured the required condolence.

Kolya gave my mother a big hug and she sagged in his arms, small as he was, and much shrunken from the last time we'd seen him; at eighty-eight years of age, he was still standing and walking unaided, with his fierce look mitigated by a dewy aspect in the eyes. His mane of white hair was much reduced and seemed finally to be giving up its efforts to keep its scholarly grandeur, wisps straggling hopefully over the ears. He came over to me and embraced me. I felt he was reaching out to his brother through me; after all, their rivalry had lasted more than six decades, probably stretching back to the smoky room in the village, back in times we only read about in history, when the czar still ruled. All the others were gone—Zev, Sarah, Judit, Yakov, the Great Gramby, kept alive by Boris's dreams. I felt a sudden twinge that I had been so little interested in this grand saga, one that after all predated all the arguments and controversies that charged through this ravaged land. Except the first perhaps: Theodor Herzl, though he too was still alive, and had not even written "Der Judenstaat" when Kolya and Boris were kids.

I let them drape me in the talit and donned the kipa for the afternoon prayer that Kolya, the eldest, now led. A Jew is a Jew, sinking into surrender at moments of dread. But I was only glancing through the words as those present muttered their way through the verbal wedges at the usual breakneck speed, nudged occasionally by my elder brother as he pointed out to me particular passages that he considered due my absolute attention, such as Psalm 38: "O lord, do not rebuke me in your wrath, nor chasten me in the heat of your displeasure. For your arrows have sunk into me and your hand has lain upon me. There is no innocence in my flesh against your anger and no peace in my bones for my sins. For my transgressions have passed over my head as a heavy burden, weightier than I can bear. My wounds are rotted and festered from my foolishness. I writhe and bow down greatly, all the day I walk darkly... I roar through the disquiet of my heart." I nodded back at him and he seemed mollified.

We said the Kaddish for my father. Then we sat back and waited for the neighbors, friends and latecomers from the film community, the old studio executives and technicians with whom he had reminisced so much in his last years. Those for whom the old days were the 1950s, rather than the dark before the Russian Revolution.

Kolya was exhausted and fell asleep on the divan, where we stretched him out and brought blankets. I heard him snoring in the night, little gentle peeps that sounded like a baby. He got up once and cried out like someone lost in the dark. I though he cried "Zev!" But by the time I struggled awake to check him, he was back under the thin sheet.

In the early morning the religious neighbors downstairs, the Agassis, whom I didn't know, came in with the man's brothers to pray, but they gathered softly in the kitchen and Kolya and Yitzhak joined them, not to wake the less devout. My mother got up and laid out some yogurt and tomatoes and I went out for fresh rolls. When I got back Kolya motioned to me and said, "Let's go for a walk." He nodded to my mother and we stepped back out.

Tel Aviv on an April spring morning has a fresh taste all its own. You know the day is going to be hot, most probably stifling, so each breath is worthy. Sheinkin Street glistens in the sun, old houses, as old as this new, modern city provides. Nineteen-thirties art deco, leavened by 1950s bare concrete lumps. The cafés lining the east side of the street are not yet open, not even the cheap dairy breakfast. Long Friday lunches with the cascading mass of the weekend newspaper keeping its infinite time. Coffee, ice cream, more dessert. There is always a moment when one realizes one can't park one's weary tuches in this folding chair forever.

I walked Kolya down towards the beach. He was eager to stretch his legs, and the fresh breeze drew us west towards the rolling Mediterranean waves, the tarry blue, the soft rolls of the sand, the early swimmers already kicking in the water. The sun worshippers of dawn. I walked him carefully across the road, under the towers of the hotels that began their march up from Allenby, over the esplanade, and down the steps to the first beachside café that we came to, as he was beginning to tire. The large terrace under the awning would be chockfull of customers later and into the small hours, when the whole city came out to jam the shore from midnight. Now it was almost entirely empty. We sat down, and the waiters were in no hurry.

"I miss the sea," he said, after I'd hurried over to the booth to get some mineral water. "We used to meet in the cafés, here, and in Haifa, to rendezvous with the commander. He didn't like the sea, but he indulged us. The British soldiers used to sit with their Jewish girls. The Tel Aviv girls. They were fresh and different. But we were burning with zeal. There was some thrill in our hearts that we were planning to shoot their boyfriends. It was not as lavish as this, of course, but the sea is always the same."

"Dad didn't come here often, even when I was small," I said, making conversation. "He liked the buzz of the streets in the city. He used to sit at Kapulsky's."

"Yes, I remember," he said. "Very good cakes. He was always looking for a Sacher torte. He said he never tasted anything like the torte at the Hotel Sacher, the original, in Vienna. When Franz Josef was still alive." He looked out at the waves. Some small boys ran, shouting and screaming, kicking sand at each other, into the waves. He looked at them anxiously.

"Don't drown, Jewish boys," he said, softly, "we need every one of you."

I thought of saying they might be Arabs, for all we knew, but I shut up. The waitress finally glided over, in a thong, chocolate brown, amazing. I looked at the menu.

"Breakfast?"

"A little fresh salad," he said. "My stomach has become a coward. Some mint tea, if they have it."

I ordered the salad, the tea, a strong coffee and three-egg omelet for myself. The sea makes me ravenous.

"I wanted to talk to you, Asher," he said. "We never talked. I barely talked to your father. So many years, I don't even want to think. We were never close, even as children. He left when I was ten years old, you know. We never saw him. We got maybe three, four letters in so many years. He went to Romania, Austria, Germany. From France I remember a letter, from Paris, with a photograph. He is standing beside a fruit seller, on the river bank. The Seine. Together with two men, he put their names on the back. Almereyda and Kibalchich. I have a good memory, still. I looked them up, years later, in America. Kibalchich was a communist writer, he called himself Victor Serge. He wrote very strong books against the Stalin period, but he was a Leninist. They put him in a camp in the Kazakh desert but his French friends got him out. He died in Mexico, eight years after Trotsky. He had nothing in his pocket, only old dreams. He believed to the end, to the last moment, to the last drop of the ocean of blood. Almereyda, his real name was Vigo. He had a son who became a famous filmmaker, but he died young, in France. Your father met him before he died. He helped him shoot his movie, I forget its name. Something about a boat. Yes, L'Atalante. I still have some brain cells. We got another letter, from New York, two years after Paris. Then things got very difficult in our region. You know, Bessarabia. It was in Russia, then it was in Romania, then the Nazis, then the communists again. Yakov left soon after your father. Our middle brother. Vassily. Boris got him a ticket through to New York, with the Joint. That was two years before the war. The Great War, so called. Another brave rebel, Mr. Gavrilo Princip, shot the Archduke Ferdinand and his wife in Sarajevo. And so the world blows up."

The waitress brought over the salad, and said the eggs were following soon.

"History of the twentieth century," he said, "that's what we are. We carry it about with us like a stack of stones. The hump on our backs. The story of our people. What was Boris, Berl Baruch Gurevits, the son of a rabbi, doing with these anarchist assassins? Of course, some of us were there, as we always are. Following the general trends. I was also one of them, this of course you know. The war came, people hid in the village. The czar's recruiters came, looking for cannon fodder for the czar's war. Everybody in the village dug basements. They hid twenty men under the shul. Boys hid in attics. Our mother, Rivka, and my sister Sarah wanted to hide me. I told them, I am not going to hide in a hole. I don't know why I said that. It was just bravado. I can't say that I had much faith in God. Terrible to say, the son of a rabbi. But I don't think most of us believed. We were Jews, of course, we prayed, we *davened*, we performed our tasks. But deep inside, like your father, we smelled the change. The world was shaking. Our father knew it, but he thought he could hold it in check. He believed in all the 248 limbs of his body that God moved every atom, he would say that, if he knew atoms then. They were a newfangled invention, not yet known in the *paylech*, in the Pale of Settlement. I don't know what I believed. I felt strong, physically, although I was not what you call today a *jlobat*... I told my father I wouldn't hide, and I saw both the fear and the pride in his eyes. Fear and pride, that was our heritage. My whole life, I fought to tear out the fear.

"You know the story. They came for me in the morning, very early. Knocked on the door. Any boys over fourteen who are not completely crippled? I stood there. My mother cried, but they took me away. My sister stood there and I didn't see her for the next thirty years. My father I never saw again. He died in the village. A heart attack. Very strange. Most of us have managed to live so long and we are so weak; he was so strong, like a bullock, like a castle, and he just fell over, aged forty-three. So we were told. I never found his grave. I went in 1961, just before they caught Eichmann, you know the story. The Soviet Union. It was after Stalin; they gave me a visa, even though I had the word on my passport: "Born: Celovest, Russia." It was the Moldovan SSR. There is nothing there. The Nazis finished the village in the Shoah. Then the Soviets built an air base on top of the camp. Transdniestria death camp. Village, camp, runway. All concrete. Nothing left. But what could you expect?"

The eggs arrived on a massive blue plate, with a mountain of chips and more salad. Stuffing my face, I had no need to do anything other than nod.

"Chaff before the wind," he said. "As Sholem Aleichem put it: 'Tsuzeyt un tsushpreyt iber alle siebn yamen' —scattered and dispersed over the seven seas... Our other brother, Ze'ev, Wolf, he left the town just ahead of the czarists. Then he came back, then went away again. He went east, and then Judit followed. But I was far away from it all. I tried to keep in touch in 1919, but it was civil war then. Reds against whites, whites against reds. I had some power, for a short while, in the chaos. In Saint Petersburg, before they called it Leningrad. But I was too far from Bessarabia. The Romanians took over after 1917. I made some inquiries, pulled some contacts; they told me the village was still standing. Finally I met a Bessarabian communist from Belzi who gave me news of the family. Sarah and Judit were still there. Ze'ev had left, traveling east, with a businessman from Kishinev who traded in Siberia and China. That was it. Judit followed him, later, to Manchuria. Harbin. I never got there. I went to other places. I had to leave Russia. I was a Chekist, you know. I worked for Dzerzhinsky, the mass murderer. Then I decided to leave."

All those strange, incomprehensible stories, told by my mother to an Israeli schoolboy in Tel Aviv in short pants who didn't give a fuck. I thought it was something to do with checks. Then I read up on it later and was mildly interested, but Uncle Kolya was long gone, in Michigan, writing about the Jewish Hell. I told some friends in San Francisco, during campus sieges, but they were freaked out. They had never heard of the Cheka. They thought Lenin and Che Guevara were twins, except that one had more hair. They had been smoking far too much dope. Only one or two realized I was telling them that my uncle had been in the original communist CIA, and thought that was really cool.

Kolya nodded, more to himself than to me. "Sinners. Criminals. Assassins. That was our time. So much blood flowed. What would my defense be? I never shot more than five men in one day? I never shot a man unless I was convinced he was guilty? I was as guilty as he. Later they shot people wholesale. When they killed the Polish officers at Katyn they had to despatch ten thousand men, each with a shot to the head. The murderers staggered under the load. In the camps, they killed millions. They made Siberia their assassin. Nature collaborates in our crimes. It is the nature of terror. But your generation is spared because of what we had to do."

He seemed to fall asleep, leaning against the railing that divided the terrace from the sand. More people were tripping onto the beach now, carrying ping-pong rackets, surfboards, plastic pails, beachballs, babies. The youngbloods were already flexing their chests, purring, admiring their own biceps.

"Each of us has a task, Asher," he said, waking up and fixing me with his stare, not the usual angry searchlight but a softer look, something like sorrow. "I know what you are doing is against what those of us who have struggled on the national side believe is the way we must continue. I know your father never agreed with me, never understood our judgments. He was not a man of politics. He was a technician of ephemeral things. Images, movies, art. The so-called Enlightenment shackled so many who thought they were merely living their own individual lives. I will not lecture you. In any case, they pay me two thousand dollars a week to do that. After taxes. How can I complain, when you are following my own early path? I was also angry, full of the fire of destruction of a rotting, ugly order. But this is just us, is it not? Yiddischer folk, with all our foibles. We embrace confusion. I have studied our enemies for so long, sometimes I end up agreeing with their own image of our faults. We were strong only in our determination to keep our word. You know, the Promise? God promised, we had to keep the deal. Otherwise, what kind of weasel scum are we? Why not eat pork? It's delicious, when properly cooked. I have eaten it. I have eaten horse, mule, God knows what else. Like Charlie Chaplin, I even ate my boots. You know, in the civil war, in starvation, men sucked the leather of their belts? I don't want to spoil your enjoyment of those fries, they look succulent. But the stronger we were in keeping our souls we were weak in keeping ourselves alive. The national idea hemmed us all in. We had to embrace it or die. Herzl understood, but only very partially. Jabotinsky understood, but he was too humane. Begin understood for a while, but he stewed too long in politics. Who understands? The youth does, even if they think they don't." The stare was changing to that old sharp focus, like the beams that knit together in the head of the robot Gort in that old science-fiction picture *The Day the Earth Stood Still*. The death ray... I could see the waitress hanging by, just behind him, setting the next table very slowly, clearly fascinated by this old man curled up in so much energy.

"You go around the world, around America, making documentary films. I saw the brochure of your company, at the college. Black Panthers, Weathermen, Cubans, revolutionaries. Then there are the brave Arabs. Arafat, George Habash. The airplane hijackers and bomb makers. I made bombs too. Everybody else's revolution, except your own. That doesn't make sense. You think you are inventing the wheel, but you are just going in a large circle. When the wheel comes to a stop, you will be where you started."

He sensed that he had been speaking louder, and people were watching him, and relaxed, into his seat. Turning to the girl and saying: "Can I have another glass of water?" That got her out of range.

He stretched out his hand and took hold of mine. I had been slow to pull away.

"Do you know that I have never spoken like this to my son? To you, of course not. Or to my brother. I love my son, and he is well trained. He will expend all his energies for the Cause. I expect great things from him. But in politics. There'll be a price. Politics always disappoints us. It's shit, however much you coat it with honey. But you remind me, you know who you remind me of? My other brothers. Ze'ev and Yakov. Ze'ev always dreamed of far-off places, and Yakov always dreamed. It is so unsurprising that he took up magic. He received something directly from our mother, that no one understood. People talked about the sacred aura of the mother. But that is *kvatch*. I am sorry, may she forgive me in heaven. But she carried some dream from way back, before anything we could grasp or give a name to. You know, our region, it is in the plain, but it is at the lower end of the Carpathian Mountains. That is a region of old magic. Shamans, seers, mad men and women, gypsies, dark, black sabbaths. Portents. *Urim* and *tumim*. It is not just the Law. Nor the Word. There is something else. You understand me."

"We should go back, people will be coming in again."

We left, leaving the young bronzed princess to serve her usual customers. Sun lovers and easy riders. I flagged down a taxi on the Yarkon road, since there was no point dragging him all the way back up Allenby and Sheinkin in the quickening heat. What did Tel Aviv care for spring? It gave you ten minutes at the start of day and then flowed straight to summer. But in the taxi, in the traffic, Kolya grabbed my arm.

"You will make a document of us, your family," he said. "I know this. You will not do this immediately, but you will do it. I will tell you. Your father wrote his story. Of his early days. He wrote about Odessa and Paris. DeMille asked him to write it down. They were always thinking of making some film about your father's life. If there is no copy in your house, there will be something in DeMille's papers."

"I know. My mother told me about it. Somewhere in Utah."

"You must go there. I will also leave all my papers that relate to this to you. I promise you this. Adi won't do anything with it. He is a man of deeds, not words. But the world should know. We also have a story. You will be the one, you'll see."

Then he fell asleep, as the driver tried to explain to me the convoluted route he would have to take to get through the one-way streets to Melchett. It's impossible these days, he said, the traffic starts peaking at seven and then it never stops all day. At two in the morning, it's the same problem. And everybody needs the taxis, nobody can drive their own cars. You want parking, go to Petah Tikva. An honest man can't make a living anymore.

Because my crazy Uncle Kolya told me to do something, I ignored it. My mother always said about him: He loves Israel so much he can't bear living in it. He wants it pure, in his own image, like the Lord. And once she said: "He's like God's watchdog. He barks all night, you never get a moment's sleep." She was relieved when he left on the morning of the fourth day of the shiva. He had an appointment as a key speaker at a literary conference in Ann Arbor on the Spanish Inquisition. As Nathan Gurevits he was acknowledged as one of the world's three greatest experts on the tangled history of Spanish Jews, the post-expulsion legacy of hidden worshippers, Marranos, dissimulators, all the subterfuges used to keep the old flame alive. He had taken time off his grand opus to write a one-thousand-page volume on the subject. There was a copy on the shelf in my parent's bedroom, but it remained pristine. My father never opened it. I had dipped into it once or twice, but the print was too tightly packed, and no pictures.

I took it down on the fifth day of the sitting, but the small print still blurred before my eyes. By the time I came back for it, in December 1990, my mother had sold it, but she had kept all the old movie books for me, Joseph V. Mascelli's *The Five C's of Cinematography*, Wheeler's *Principles of Cinematography*, *The Focal Encyclopedia of Film and Television Techniques*, Corbett's *Motion Picture and Television Film: Image Control and Processing Techniques*, the *American Cinematographer Manual* and the stack of A.C. magazines, as well as the DeMille autobiography. I took that with me on my journey to Provo, Utah, four months later, in April 1991, to the new, all-glass edifice of the library at Brigham Young University, the campus filled with clean-cut young men and girls bright with smiley goodwill and devout Mormon welcomes, the venue to which for reasons unfathomable the great director had willed his enormous collection of 1,800 boxes containing every slip of paper in thousands of files and dossiers, personal correspondence, production records of every one of his seventy motion pictures, the fifty-two silent films and eighteen talkies, with over four hundred boxes dealing with the last alone: *The Ten Commandments*, which had run for six months at the Mugrabi Theater, gathering up on the way his hoard of subsidiary papers from and related to his collaborators, writers and crew, with that one file that the voluminous catalog revealed was tucked away among the dossiers of a 1926 film, *The Volga Boatman*. One of the master's oddest projects, it was the tale of a Bolshevik revolutionary—played by William Boyd, who was later to become Hopalong Cassidy—caught up in a romance in the midst of the life-and-death struggle between the reds and the whites, the file sandwiched between a sheaf of financial correspondence and camera notes, and misleadingly labeled "Notes for a Scenario by William B. Gore." A piece of paper fell out, in my father's handwriting, in a much firmer scrawl than I knew from later decades. Headed "To CB," it said:

> Here it is. You asked, so I did it. I can't see that it'll ever make a movie. The truth is too addled. Too many locations, too many trains. But you are right—the memories did come flooding back. Just write it down the way it was—well here it is. What happened to Kibalchich, Vigo? Paris in the flood! (And what happened to 'The Deluge'?) I thought of an opening title for V.G.: 'A STORY NOT OF A CRUSADE OR A VICTORY BUT OF PEOPLE—IT PLEADS NO CAUSE AND TAKES NO SIDES—IT IS NOT FOR US TO EXPLAIN THE FLAMES AND TERROR OF REVOLUTION—ONLY TO TELL THE TALE...'
> Use or lose.
>
> See you on payday,
> Boris

Later on I looked at the *Volga Boatman* movie on an old VHS cassette, and DeMille had used that opening title, more or less. But he had added, "Man cannot explain it." Even the Russian Revolution became, for DeMille, something like an act of God.

I sat in the pristine silence of the library and read the text. The atmosphere was calm and sterile. No distractions, no sudden surprises, no tea or coffee. Just my father's voice, telling the tale, answering the private curiosity of his omnivorous boss...

"A bas la patrie!"

Boris:

Paris—1908 etc.

My first real job in the movies was as an actor for the Gaumont Film Company. This was in January or February 1908, a rainy winter, and not much to go on in the northern suburbs, around Montmartre. My first berth when we got to Paris, the three fugitives, was in a tiny room just below the attic where Almereyda lived with his "wife," Emilie, and their two-year-old kid, Jean. No one else could get into the room, because it was infested with the cats that Miguel gathered from the strays he found in the street. He was completely crazy about them, and called them by fancy names, Loulou, Froufrou, Zazie, Cherie and so forth. They were like a biblical plague, but the kid also adored them, and Emilie gave in to his wishes. She was a deceptively quiet woman with flashing eyes who seemed to be almost religiously devoted to her wild husband and his cause. In fact, I think they were not married, but that didn't matter in those circles at that time. The landlord, an obese roll of flesh with a moustache attached, didn't mind who stayed in his property as long as they paid, which meant that as I had no money left at all, I had to leave pretty soon. In any case, Almereyda was arrested in December and sent to jail along with two other comrades from their newspaper, La Guerre Sociale, for agitating among the soldiers embarking at the train stations on their way to fight the Moorish rebels in Morocco. Emilie didn't seem terribly distressed, Kibalchich told me, because this happened every year, but usually some kind of pardon was arranged.

The French anarchists were a different lot from the excitable but talky men and women I had seen in Amsterdam. In Paris they were all for action. Kibalchich took me to stay with a group of Russians crowded into the top floor of a tenement on the Boulevard Barbes, who went in and out of their rooms with pistols tucked into their belts under their coats. None of them seemed to have ever enjoyed the service of a razor, as if they were determined to look as well as act the part. They were all called Ivan, or Petroff, or Ivan Petroff, sharing the name between them. I was very uneasy the entire time I spent with them, as I was honing my knowledge of French with the newspapers, that were full of items about "la menace anarchiste" and stories of robberies and bomb outrages around the world. In Brazil, the police had discovered an anarchist plot to blow up American warships that were docked there en route to the Far East. In Switzerland, Russian anarchists had been arrested at the Austrian frontier in charge of four trunks that contained arms and more than thirty thousand cartridges. And downtown Paree, at the Gare D'Austerlitz, my own companions were harassing troops and shouting, "A bas l'armee! A bas la patrie!"

My tenancy with the Russians came to an almost comical end when Kibalchich waylaid me on the way back from Gaumont one evening with all my meagre belongings as well as his packed in a suitcase and a warning not to enter the building, as the police had arrested "Ivan Petroff" and several others because bombs had been found in their rooms. Apparently the neighbours on the other side of the tenement wall had become suspicious because they had heard an explosion through the wall, but since they had not heard anyone scream or cry out they went back to bed. It was only in the morning that one nagging wife made her husband tell the police, and they raided the building, finding the bombs, various chemicals and heaps of anarchist pamphlets and letters.

The job with Gaumont came about after Victor Kibalchich took me to a cabaret tavern in the Montmartre area called the Lapin Agile. It was a dark dive frequented by artists who lived in the ramshackle and tumbledown streets around the butte, the steep hill crowned by the Church of the Sacred Heart, which was still being completed at that time. It was built on the site of the last battle with the Communards of Paris of the 1870s, when the poor of the city rose up at the generals who had lost the Franco-Prussian war. In the last fight the Communards had been dynamited and entombed in the old mines on the butte, and in their retreat they had executed the Archbishop of Paris, to whom the Sacred Heart was then dedicated. The rich had set it up to commemorate the defeat of the poor. But around this there was a labyrinth of old streets that looked more like a rural village than Paris, and it was then a fashionable area for impecunious artists to set up their studios. Among them I remember a group of young Spaniards, very poorly dressed, who strutted about and looked at you like knights in exile, impoverished matadors still seeking their bulls. One in particular, Pablo, much favored by the others, invited us into his studio once, a spooky hole in a warren-like wooden building, which reeked of a combination of paint, sweat, and a leaking toilet. It was full of large and small canvases, mostly grotesque images of naked women distorted in ways that made me think of the Baba Yaga and other dark fables of my Bessarabian youth. The women had vast eyes like oil lamps that were set in all the wrong places. I thought he was completely insane, but as I write this I have to note that DeMille tells me this kind of art is now all the rage in Paris. It has certainly stayed in mind, as the very antithesis of the cinema frame.

One of the young painters at the cabaret was a dynamic youth called Gaston, who was hoping to sell one of his paintings but in the meantime was earning some francs with the moving picture studios. We got talking about my adventures with Makedonsky and his Pathe camera, and how we had filmed in the streets of Bucharest and Vienna and Berlin. "Well," he said, "if you want to start as an actor, all you need to do is turn up in the morning at the gates of Pathe or Gaumont. They are not far from here, in Belleville and Vincennes. It's very easy, you don't need any skill. It is mostly comedy, running and jumping."

He was right. There was nothing to it. Pathe paid about three francs fifty a day and Gaumont was a little better, at three seventy-five. The first picture that I remember appearing in was something called "The Race of the Pumpkins," in which a pile of giant pumpkins fall out of a cart and roll down the street, with the owner and people in the street in hot pursuit. It was quite clever, because the pumpkins were rubber wheels wrapped in pumpkin-drawn cloths, which could be pulled on very thin strings as if they had their own life, jumping over walls or into bedrooms. Some of the scenes were shot indoors in the studio on ingenious sets that Gaumont used to show people crawling up steep walls and over rooftops in what seemed to be a magical fashion. I got very entranced by this, although my own task was just to run about and wave my arms, then fall over.

These movies were very short, sometimes a couple of minutes, sometimes as much as five. Pathe specialized in somewhat longer subjects, that could run a full reel, ten or twelve minutes, depending on how fast or slow the camera was cranked.

In one of the movies that I remember vividly, a dog steals some sausages, a group of policemen, waving truncheons, chase the dog, and then the dog turns and chases the policemen up and down the streets, into houses, up walls and over the rooftops. I don't remember who directed it, there was a crew of excitable young men with ideas, but I was more fascinated with the camera, and what it could achieve when unleashed. I befriended the cameraman, who was, coincidentally, a Romanian, though he had never heard of Makedonsky, as he had been living in France since childhood. His name was Corneliu Jaunescu. I asked him about the film I had seen in Odessa, the bedazzling "The Impossible Voyage" and he told me that its maker, Georges Méliès, had made hundreds of films since the 1890s and was still working in his own studio outside Paris. But I never got to go there, as I was soon pretty busy at Gaumont, particularly after Jaunescu took me on as his assistant, in April '08.

The great advantage of working in the movies as an actor then was that there were no speaking parts, so nobody could lip-read and complain that you couldn't speak the language. Most of the audience in the smaller halls were immigrants in any case, but by that time the companies were building bigger and bigger specialized movie theaters. The Omnia-Pathé was like a gigantic palace, and the Hippodrome at the Place de Clichy could seat up to five thousand people. Those great halls would cost up to four francs for a ticket, but you still got the same program of twenty or so shorts. You could see "The Beautiful Gypsy," "The Fatal Woman," "The Tempest at Sea" (shot in the studio of course), "The Spanish Vendetta," "The Fantastic Omelette" or "The Last Days of Pompeii." (Later, we saw the feature production of 1913, in New York; I think it was the longest picture made to that date. It seemed to run for hours, but was probably about eighty minutes.) I paid my two francs for the stalls at the Hippodrome to see myself briefly flashing by on the huge screen, enlarged twenty times. A rare close-up would make people gasp. I was especially interested then in the magical trick films, like "The Haunted Hotel," which was an American film, in which various objects—chairs, tables, beds—seemed to move on their own. These were stop-motion films, in which the objects were shot frame by frame, the start of what would become animations. One of the bosses at Gaumont, Émile Cohl, later became known as the inventor of the cartoons because he was the first to make moving drawings of figures and objects purely out of a chalk line. I got to know him well, because he was an older man than most in that young business, already fifty, and had been an illustrator of political magazines back in the 1880s. He showed me his own collection and other pieces, early strip cartoons and caricatures of the politicians of the day. He'd been a member of a group of satirical artists called the Hydropathes, who met in Paris to recite poetry and insult the government and the church. They had been temperamentally close to the anarchists but they were not men of action. They were very similar to the Russian artists who attacked the czar and the Black Hundreds, and I told him I had been one of those people, back in Odessa, in 1905. I was sorry then that I had left all those pictures behind; I explained that I had enough problems trying to escape with my hide. Cohl was making his first "animated" film at Gaumont when I met him. It was called "Fantasmagorie," and showed a clown figure being formed by a white line on a black background, which then becomes another man with a fat belly and an umbrella, and then various objects: a cigar, smoke, a balloon, a moving plant, a room, a bottle that captures the clown, and so forth. Then he made another film called, I think, "The Puppet's Nightmare," in the same style. It was a big hit in the theaters. He used a very simple system; he had a light box that lit paper sheets from behind, and he drew the changes frame by frame on these sheets so that the lines seemed to move. The problem was it took so long to make the few minutes of story; he worked for months on each little film.

I myself didn't have the patience or the time. I had to move from place to place to keep from being drawn in to my anarchist friends' dangerous adventures. In February 1908, just as I was starting at Gaumont, the newspapers reported the assassination of the the king and crown prince of Portugal, in Lisbon, by attackers armed with carbines who were immediately assumed to be Spanish and Italian anarchists. The incident with "Ivan Petroff" followed soon after, and Kibalchich and I found temporary beds at the Hotel Tourelle, on the Rue du Mont-Cenis, just the other side of the Sacred Heart church. The owner was a sympathizer but couldn't let us stay for long. Gaston Modot then got us beds—of a sort!—for a while in his own studio space at the "bateau lavoir," the "laundry boat," which was the artists' name for the horrible wooden building they all worked in on the Place Ravignan. It was the most dreadful hole, with strange cavities that you could fall in to your death, because the house sloped down the hill towards the next street down and was only bearable if you lived and thrived off the smell of paint and painter's filthy underwear. When the summer came, it was so hot they would work naked, particularly the demonic Pablo, whom girls were attracted to like moths to a flame. Kibalchich seemed to thrive on this hardship, but I found myself dreaming of the smell of soap and the clean kitchen odors of my mother's house, with my sisters Sarah and little Judit working so hard to make a poor house a home...

I was slowly discovering that I was not cut out for a life of outlawry, rushing from country to country, outcast and poor, living in terror and the thrill of revolution that was always just around the corner. The price of such a life was pretty evident in the roster of arrests, shootings, and bombings that seemed to be the anarchist mode around the world. In April we read that three anarchists were sentenced to death in Barcelona, and closer to home, anarchists were arrested outside Paris for trying to blow up the commissioner of police at Tourcoing. I could look even closer at the price paid by Miguel Almereyda and his long-suffering wife and small child. By the peculiar vagaries of the French prison system, we could go right up to the walls of the Santé prison, in the Montparnasse area, just beside a busy boulevard, and shout messages to the prisoners inside. Kibalchich told me prisoners could bribe the warders or get the special favor of a cell overlooking the road, through the tiny windows of which you could see their hands clutching the bars. Almereya, being a regular, rated such a cell, and his mother would bring little Jean, the three-year-old, and hold him up so he could wave to Dad. I found it a terrible sight, but Victor saw it as yet another sign of the resilience of the rebellious poor.

He had already shown me these lives, in the workers' sections of Brussels, his own hometown, in the two weeks we spent there immediately after our flight from Amsterdam: the Marolle, where people lived cheek by jowl in crumbling houses and fetid alleys, though it was always teeming with life, night merriment, and drunkenness. In Paris he again undertook my education in the true nature of the class war in the great cities of Europe which preened before the world in the grandeur of their grand buildings, state palaces, Unter-den-Lindens and Boulevard Haussmans and Champs d'Elysees and Arcs of Triumph. Montmartre may have been a slum of choice for the artists who never expected to make a living and only dreamed of suave bourgeois dealers who would lift them out of their garrets and make their fortunes. But there were other parts of Paris where majestic boulevards hid barefoot children and shrunken old men and women living hand-to-mouth in their alleyways and all over the city. He showed me the clochards, who lived under the bridges of the Seine, scavenging for leftovers, cigarette butts and coins fallen from wealthier pockets. He took me out early in the mornings, and showed me the crowds of poorly clad people going to the factories that swallowed up so many for long shifts and dismal pay, and the armies that went out to clean the streets and hover all day behind the carts and horse-drawn omnibuses to sweep up the horses' dung. He showed me all the street hawkers who seemed such a picturesque feature of the city's squares and quays, tired young girls and middle-aged women or bearded men from Armenia or my own country's people who sold matches and paper on the streets. He showed me the doorways where exhausted beggars slept, and the groups of sullen negroes and moors who trudged along the sidewalks of the Café de la Paix, looking for work, invisible to the leisured classes nibbling their croissants and enjoying their little cups of black mud.

Most of all, Victor Kibalchich had been marked by his time with the coal miners of his own Belgian land, the French-speaking workers of the Borinage, among the vast slag heaps thrown up by these strong and silent men who toiled deep below the ground so that the industries of Europe could be fueled and the pockets of the rich filled to bursting. He himself had worked and would continue to work among the printers, who spent their days cutting and setting the tiny metal blocks that made up the presses of books, journals, and daily newspapers. He took me to one such plant, beyond Clichy, a hot and stifling hell amid the constant racket of the great wheels that turned the papers out. The black print smudged the workers and poisoned their breath. It was a far cry from the small workshop where our Odessa pamphlets had been rolled out! Naturally, the workers also printed their own anarchist and socialist pamphlets behind the bosses' backs. Detection meant instant dismissal, but an unsurprising number of the printers were zealots of the anarchist cause.

Being less and less zealous myself, I never quite understood the anarchists' rejection of the larger socialist party, which was a growing force in France, led by the charismatic Monsieur Jean Jaurès. A rather small, stocky man with a large beard, he had a booming voice that could dominate an entire square of excitable French workmen, not all of whom were his natural supporters. I saw him speak on the May Day, shaking his fist and swaying like a Moses before his flock at the shores of the unparted sea. Kibalchich was contemptuous of him because he fought most of his fights in parliament, demanding reforms from the prime minister, Monsieur Clemenceau. The anarchists despised the socialists because they were willing to negotiate with a government that had sent troops to suppress the strike of French miners that had broken out two years before.

I am not sure why Kibalchich spent so much time trying to convince me about his path, but as time passed I figured that I was probably the only person close to him then who had actually wielded a gun to kill. The thing I was least proud of, and most doubtful about, was the very thing that drew him to me, although I have to point out that he was a good companion, mercurial but loyal, who one knew would die at your side if called. The only problem was, I had decided that I didn't want to die, or even smell the interior of that tiny cell high up the fortified wall of the Santé prison out of which Miguel Armereyda waved so nonchalantly to his little boy.

From the moment I arrived in Paris I began sending letters home to our family, addressing them simply to "Gurevits, Czelovest, Belzi, Bessarabia, Russia," but I had no way of knowing if they were received, as I could only use the return address of "Post Restante, Paris," and keep checking the post office box I had rented. Nothing ever landed there, apart from tradesmen's circulars inviting me to employ this or that service. By the summer, however, I was earning enough money at Gaumont to take a two-room suite above an inn on the Place du Pantheon, where Victor joined me, having left his own job in a machine tool works up at Belleville. He found the idea of earning money as an actor running after fake pumpkins incompatible with his beliefs. He was a man who practiced what he preached, but he could be tempted by a good perch at the Left Bank. From our top-floor window we could peer out rightward towards the gates of the Luxembourg Gardens and left towards the cupola under which Voltaire, Émil Zola, Rousseau and Victor Hugo lay buried, among a host of marquises, dukes and counts, and Victor's favorite, Jean-Paul Marat, the greatest revolutionary beside Danton, in his view, the true defender of the sansculottes. "Where are today's Marats?" he shouted at me as he leaned out the window, waving his arms at the street below. "Where are you, the pure souls?" He would have been livid to hear that his bête noire, Jaures, was also buried there, a few years ago. Then it dawned on me that I finally had a return address to write on the envelopes of the letters I kept sending out.

I asked Victor to find out for me what had occurred in the aftermath of the event that had made us run out of Amsterdam, and what was the fate of my Romanian mentor, Makedonsky. I was relieved to hear that he had not been caught, and had vanished from the city together with his accomplice, who was indeed the sullen bellhop from the Hotel Victoria in Berlin. The gossip was that the two men had been enjoying a pederastic relationship, which did not surprise me, but did not explain their sudden criminal action. It was only in the autumn of 1908 that Victor found more news, on the anarchist grapevine, that my eccentric mentor had returned, on his own, to Bucharest and resumed his social and professional life as if nothing had happened. There was no trace of the Berlin youth, who presumably dropped out or was discarded somewhere along the way. There was some talk that the Romanian had gambled his money away on the journey to Amsterdam, and having concealed a loaded pistol inside the camera case he had carried across Europe, used it to replenish his capital in the traditional anarchist form. I thought of writing to him, at least to express my thanks for the service he had done me out of the goodness of his strange heart, without any designs on my poor own corpus, but somehow the letter was never penned.

Despite the silence from Russia, which remained a dull ache in my stomach, those were my happiest days in Paris, stretching to almost two years, as my salary became more constant and I dedicated myself to learning the camera operator's profession. The rooms by the Pantheon were a long way from the Gaumont studios but I could get there and back by the funicular railway that took me pretty close to the gates. The atmosphere of the Left Bank was invigorating as I imagine it still must be today. Some things have the aura of the eternal, and DeMille assures me that was still so on his own visit, in the winter of '22. The Boulevard San Michel with its busy tram lines and bustling bookshops, the lazy cafés of Saint Andre des Arts, the strange shops everywhere selling everything from the latest fashions to ancient pots and statuettes that must have been brought over from Egypt by the encyclopedists of Napoleon Bonaparte. All were a delight and quickened the senses. There was romance, as well, but it was not lasting. Paris did not encourage constancy, and at least in that sense, I was still an anarchist at heart...

(Two paragraphs crossed out with thick black ink here, Ed.)

Almereyda remained in jail until the summer of 1909, and both Victor and I tried to support Emilie and their son financially throughout this period, as far as was possible. Kibalchich achieved this by giving French lessons to daughters of the Russian exiles in Paris, not all of whom were "Ivan Petroff"-like ruffians by any means. There were many reformist liberals who had opposed the czar's tyranny and had to flee the consequences, although they still tried to live gentlemen's and ladies' lives in Europe. I knew some who dressed in the same top hat and tails that frayed more and more over months and years until they were like some clown tramp's costume. Piano, ballet and language lessons for their daughters and financial studies for their sons were de rigueur. And there were many from the various social revolutionary parties whom Victor courted more and more. They were obsessed with the conviction that the Russian secret police had planted spies among them, and history proved them right, so there was always an air of conspiracy and subterfuge among them, even if they were only discussing venues for lunch. Between these cultured and literary Russians and the sansculottes he wooed under bridges, Victor was in some considerable ecstasy, although the grand passions of the anarchists were always tempting him along more dangerous routes. He would burst in, telling me excitedly of some violent outrage or other, in India, Spain, Mexico or Buenos Aires, which his fellow ideologists had braved. Even in England, the gunmen were active, robbing banks in Tottenham in London and blowing themselves up, presumably by mistake, with one of their own bombs. A true Russian in essence, he could be gentleness personified in his dealings with the Tolstoy-reading ladies of the Rue Saint-Jacques, and then rush in with praise of the assassin of one Babu Biswas, an Indian prosecutor at Alipur...

The summer of 1909 saw a resurgence of strikes that were the summer pastime of French railway, telegraph, and postal workers, with anarchists blamed for cutting telephone and telegraph lines around Paris and way out in the suburbs. Victor arrived late one night with a pair of bolt cutters, which he hid behind the sofa. I said nothing, but took them out with me to Belleville the next day and deposited them with the property department of the studio. I suppose if I had been searched on the train that morning I would have joined Almereyda in the Santé. But some weeks later he was released and rejoined Emilie and Jean in their dreadful attic, with the cats. He wasted no time, however, in risking his liberty once again, rushing out with his anti-militarist leaflets and the latest issues of La Guerre Sociale to shower the poor troops loading up at the station for their journeys of death to Algiers and Morocco. Luckily he had missed the visit of the czar himself to Cherbourg, which caused the greatest flurry and calls for action among the bloods, young and old, but passed without incident, as thousands of police and army guarded his route.

The autumn brought another major crisis and mass demonstrations over the execution in Spain of a Senor Francisco Ferrer.

He seems to have been, by all accounts, a mild-mannered educator who had founded a "modern" school in Barcelona, but he was known as a staunch Republican, opposed to the kingdom of Alfonso XIII. I had no idea there had been so many of them. The trial was a travesty; no witnesses were allowed for the defense, and the accused was promptly shot. This was all part of a general movement for the separation of Catalonia from Spain, of which I knew nothing until Kibalchich told me that all Paris was about to march for its cause. It was the last time I was to veer back from my newly chosen pathway to join the thousands that poured into the city's streets. A flood of people converged on the Spanish Embassy in the Boulevard de Courcelles, pressing against a huge cordon of police. The anarchists were out in force. I linked arms with Victor and Miguel Almereyda, and we surged forward until suddenly some shots rang out. Later the police said that the anarchists had fired upon them, but I saw no one with arms in the crowd. The shots were followed by an immediate and violent charge by the police and the mounted Republican Guards; truncheons were wielded right and left, although there were women also in the march. This infuriated the crowd even further, and before I knew it I was scrambling with the others to tear up the cobblestones, break up the ornamental protections around the trees in the boulevard, and form barricades of overturned carts. This took place in the very heart of the city, in the triangle between de Courcelle, the Avenue de Villiers, and Batignolles, which became a complete battleground as lampposts were torn down and the gas mains hacked open and set alight, darkening the surrounding buildings but illuminating the night with a gigantic bonfire. The more excitable comrades began to proclaim the night fireballs as the start of a new commune. This lasted no more than about half an hour, however, with several loudmouths climbing on smashed woodpiles declaiming the end of the republic and calling for an immediate war with Spain. Then the guards came back in a great cavalry charge from the corner of the Boulevard des Malesherbes. My immediate thought was a tinge of regret that I was not here with Makedonsky and his Pathe camera, that could be so quickly mounted to capture it all in the frame...

The police charged, with a zest reminiscent of the famous six hundred of the Crimean War, thundering into the valley not of death by cannon fire but of a shower of bricks, sticks and cobblestones, as well as abuse and curses in at least a dozen tongues, from Lett to Yiddish, via Russian, Italian and Spanish, and a few choice Yankee expletives. The riders pulled out their swords and began smashing the people with the flat of the blades—and not always the flat. I saw one man cut right through the shoulder and several spurting blood from their skulls. Almereyda, convincing himself he was the fiery Spaniard he never was, rather than the son of a good French bourgeois, wanted to rush forward and martyr himself on the cold steel of the Enemy, but Victor and I pulled him away, and, in the best tradition of those whose principles require them to live to fight another day, hightailed it up the side streets towards the phalanx of railway tracks from the Porte de Clichy to the Gare du Nord. Then we physically propeled Miguel Vigo back towards his woman, his son and his wailing colony of true Parisian feline clochards.

Thus ended my last battle against the State.

Back at Gaumont, I continued working and was expecting to graduate from assistant to camera operator at the new year of 1910. I continued to help Émile Cohl with his animations, though this work consisted merely of moving his illustrations and pressing a switch for the next exposure. I soon realized animation was not quite my field, although I enjoyed the pictures themselves. Cohl was making a series of films with animated puppet figures, expanding his ambition from the chalk drawings. He made *The Battle of Austerlitz*, a graphic movement of little armies across a map of the battlefield, and then a bedroom comedy, in which a newlywed couple's shoes played the principal parts. Then there was *Don Quichotte*, and a Méliès-like picture set in medieval times about a young man whose girlfriend tells him she will only marry him if he brings her the moon. He goes to a witches' cave where the witches agree to help him, and fly off on their broomsticks to fetch him *la lune*. It was very popular. But not everybody was happy at Gaumont, because the bosses were considered to be stingy and had lost all the big names of that era's comedy to our rival Pathe. Pathe had Zigotto, Little Moritz, Rigadin, Calino, and the most popular of all, Max—Max Linder, whose antics were clearly much more sophisticated than those of his fellow actors and whose films were becoming more and more ingenious. He made short films like "The Maniac Juggler," "Max and the Lady Doctor," "Max, the Lady Killer," and the funniest of all for me, "Contagious Nervous Twitching," in which he starts sneezing on the streets and everybody around him catches the itch until the whole city is blowing its nose. It was a simple idea that worked perfectly. Max's films were popular not only in France but all over Europe, and we were told they were selling like hotcakes in America. It began to be a kind of slogan down on the shop floor of the studios, and not only Gaumont: "I'm going to follow Max to New York." America, as the Jews called it—"der goldeneh medineh," the Golden State, where even the poorest could flourish. It began to glisten in one's dreams, the brash posters and pictures of New York City, Chicago, the skyscrapers, the life of teeming enterprise, where class and birth counted for nothing. Of course, the anarchists told us this was just our delusions, that class war existed everywhere, and their comrades across the ocean were paying just as dearly for their convictions as those of France or Spain. Victor reminded me that Alexander Berkman, the close comrade of Emma Goldman, whom we had seen speak in Amsterdam, spent fourteen years in prison for shooting Henry Frick, who had sent three hundred Pinkerton detectives to shoot down nine union strikers at the Carnegie Steel Company in 1892. But I had stopped stocking up on the roll call of anarchist martyrs.

America! It was the next big move, and I was stacking up money, enough at least to pay the passage and my time until I got started, which would not take long, since motion picture companies were springing up like weeds. The more I saw the American films, the more eager I was to try my luck there. The French-made films had tricks and gimmicks, but the American films were more exciting, more ingenious. In one picture that made a deep impression, a man leaves his home with his three little daughters inside, and burglars break in and shut themselves in the girls' bedroom. But instead of telling the story in a series of sequential tableaus, the filmmaker cut between the children inside and the rescuers rushing by car to save them. Cutting back and forth, the director created tension in the audience, who were visibly confused and then delighted as the story jumped from place to place. I wasn't aware on that day, in the small theater on the Boulevard St. Jacques, that I was watching one of the earliest films by D.W. Griffith, the wizard of our industry, who was inventing the cinema week by week, trying out audacious new ideas. Or that the little girl trying to save her sisters was Mary Pickford, later "America's sweetheart," whom I would be lighting for DeMille's *The Little American*, nine years later...

I was held back, however, by my empty letterbox, which still refused to greet me with any sign of life from home. I began to consider using my earnings to travel east instead of west. Despite the warnings from the Russian exiles in Paris, revolutionaries and liberals, the newspapers were reporting some degree of quiet in Russia. There was some tension in the Balkans, when the Austrians annexed Bosnia-Herzegovina, but that seemed just one more dreary tangle of Europe's politics. Nothing there to shake the world. In Saint Petersburg the reforms of the newly elected Prime Minister Stolypin seemed to be making progress. The zemstvo land system was being developed, order seemed to have been restored, the empire was being modernized by industry, there were no new reports of pogroms, and the revolutionaries seemed beached on my doorstep, still declaring the imminent collapse of the empires, squabbling among their divided factions, and talking themselves into the ground.

Kibalchich, although he remained friendly to me, moved out to join more militant comrades just down the road, closer to the

Seine. This meant he was caught out more than most in January 1910, when the river flooded, inundating most of Paris and turning the grand boulevards into lakes. People cruised in boats along the Rue St.-Andres-des-Arts; carriages were marooned in the midst of the Boulevard Haussmann like wrecked ships, their reflections shimmering like ghosts below them. Men with bowler hats seemed to walk on water as they trod gingerly on planks laid just below the surface or scrambled over makeshift pontoons and ramshackle wooden bridges. The entire city changed into a magical landscape that might have been dreamed up by Emile Cohl in his animations; all shops closed, and everyone joked that now they need not bother to visit Venice, since Venice had come to us.

More and more I was viewing the world through the camera lens, imagining the frame, composing the picture. I became, for the first time, a primary photographer, cranking the new studio cameras, which now came with an inverted image viewfinder, so that one had to guess what it all looked like right side up. One April evening, I came home to the Pantheon apartment to find a thick, somewhat battered envelope in the mail box, which I pulled out with trembling hands.

The front was covered with tiny, unusual stamps, some with the emblem of the imperial double eagle, others with the garlanded head of the czar, Nikolai the Second, and his frumpish wife, Yekaterina, marked with ten- and twenty-kopek values and a postal marking that I read as "Belty." The front address was painstakingly drawn in Latin capital letters by what seemed a childish hand, spelling my name as "Baris Gurovitchi" but accurately inscribing the Paris location. On the back, in a flowery cyrillic scroll, it said merely *"semlya gurevitch, celovets, rassia"*—the family Gurevits, in Russia.

There were two letters inside. Both were in Yiddish, one a three-sheet affair in the very precise and firm handwriting of my father, as if set out in the formal terms of a Talmudic argument. The other sheet was covered with a tiny scrawl that I had never seen before, but it was obvious by the little drawings of angels and stick figures that it was the work of my little brother, Yakov. The sheets enfolded a single photograph, about five by three inches, of the only tableau I had ever seen of the family. On the back it bore the stamp of the photographer: Aaron Shatz of Belzi. There they were, on a studio background of trees and fields, with some wavy mountain peaks behind them, my mother seated on a chair, my father to her right, his hands folded before his belly, wearing his best black gabardine and a proper hat, gazing stoically ahead. My brother Zev on her left, his right hand on her shoulder, looked like a young blade ready for some exploit, his nature hidden behind his somewhat drooping eyelids, as if he were looking inward,rather than out. Just behind Zev stood Kolya fourteen and on the threshold of manhood, dressed as a student, lips pursed in a serious expression. My sister Sarah, with a golden smile, wore a kind of peasant dress, her head-shawl masking what might have been in her imagination a full blonde Moldavian crown, and beside her, not-so-little Yakov, who was almost as tall as Zev, holding what looked like a small stack of playing cards in his right hand, down by his waist. He was looking out with big bright eyes, forward not so much at the photographer but at some unknown destination, far beyond him, the kind of look that made you look around as you held the picture, as if to see what the subject himself saw beyond you. Finally, at my mother's feet, ten-year-old Judit sat on a cushion on the raised studio dais. (*I enclose this for you, C.B.*)

As if primed for duty, I read my father's news first. The family was all well, he wrote. Your mother Rivka has been in good health despite a stomach ailment which was recurrent but with God's help was not crippling and she remained a tower of strength. My eldest sister Sarah was in good health too, although as yet she had not remarried. She is, as you know, he wrote, a woman of great virtues who knew her Torah as well as any man. She had been teaching for some time at the town's primary school and now was starting to teach at the new gymnasium, which the notables had now found enough funding to open. Harvests had been bad for two consecutive years but trade was brisk and regular since the "disturbances" had died down.

He was glad to hear that I was in good health and prosperous in my current place of dwelling. This was a new world, in which boys were hardly bar mitzvah before they began to think of their own fortunes and set out beyond the old boundaries. Now my brother Zev was thinking along the same lines and had set up in business with a trader from Kishinev who had a good reputation, though reputations are not, alas, these days what they were in the past. A man's word is not always his bond nowadays, and he was hoping I would bear this in mind in my own dealings, even our own. Zev has already been on two trips to Ukraine, beyond Kiev, and has begun, mercy be upon us, to look at world maps. For himself, my father wrote, he was bound to his village, though the only bonds that were of pure steel were those of the Eternal Torah and Commandments, as of course he need not tell me. Times change, and even little Judit is being sent to the primary school, to learn the language of the goyim and be prepared for whatever joys or burdens God would bring in His good time. Kolya is at his studies, and we are sure with God's help he will become an asset to his faith. (One sensed a certain distance there, but I could not interpret it; even as a child, Kolya kept his thoughts to himself.) As for Yakov, my father wrote, he is including his own letter, he already voyages far and wide in his own mind, in his imagination and his dreams. The rabbis say he has the potential to be an *illui*—a genius, should he apply himself to his proper studies, but, my father wrote, I have become soft in my old age, for what has sternness brought me? Love, and not only of God, is my only bulwark.

I was weeping as I read the letter, and my hands shook as I turned again to the picture. I had a rush of doubt as to whether my vocation as a maker of images was of any value, as I had myself set up so many of these family tableaus in Makedonsky's Bucharest studio. One posed the family in pre-ordained fashion, on whatever background took the fancy of the five or six who were available. And yet in their presence was an entire world that could not be created, for it existed in its own actuality, in the recognition of its own dreams, memories and presence. Only the present could be photographed.

Yakov—Vassily—now sixteen, wrote me of his dreams. He had seen me often, he said, in different parts of the world. Once he had seen me on a tall building, looking up at the sky with a sword, as if I were about to do battle with angels. Then he saw me riding a horse, across an immense flat field. I was approaching a gigantic river, more than ten kilometers wide, which the horse was gathering pace to leap over in one great sweep. But, as horse and I leapt in the air, we receded from his vision, and he had woken up to find the blacksmith's cat, Gussi, a fat beast of the underworld, sitting on his face. Then he had seen me entering a room filled with men in black coats and beards, but they were not Hasidim, or other Jews, because their beards were of various colors: red, blue, purple, orange, and green, and they wore strange hats, some with gigantic plumes of feathers, also multicolored, others with live animals seated on top, ferrets, river otters, and owls. Each one was talking in a different tongue, and none could understand the other, yet they were growing more and more agitated in their attempts to communicate. Eventually, I stilled them with a wave of my hand, and took from my coat pocket a small rod, which I held up and from which emanated a brilliant, blinding white light.

I could sense my father's hand on his shoulder, as he nudged him in another direction, and Yakov concluded by wishing me all the best wherever I was and saying that they all missed me terribly and hoped that one day God would grant us all a reunion in our home, under the divine wings. There was a drawing of a magical being with great goose wings and a long neck that ended in a feminine face, with long blonde hair that he had colored yellow, probably against my father's wishes. It was stamped with a kind of red blotch, Yakov's attempt at an imperial seal.

I walked the streets of the city that night like a stray dog. I walked down the Boulevard St. Michel, threading through the shop windows of St.-André des Arts with their strange souvenirs of other dreams and far-off places, secondhand poets, garish portraits of seminude women with gigantic hats made of the plumage of South American parrots, pictures of cats playing cards or dueling in the manner of Dumas' musketeers, miniature medical skeletons, ancient maps of the world before it was known, bookshops of the anarchist and socialist movements; the shop dedicated to the Paris Commune with gruesome pictures and paintings of the mass executions of the communards and ghastly dolls of executed leaders; shops selling tobacco, gloves, perfume, down the Rue Dauphine to the Pont Neuf and across the bridge to the vantage point at the tip of the Ile de la Cite. There it was before me: Paris, glittering lights, the clatter of traffic, the shouts of revelers, the rippling reflections in the river and the leisure boats and barges breaking up the lights and mooing like mechanical cows as they warned each other of their passing. Across the way, the dazzling illuminations of the Eiffel Tower, sentinel of the new century. The future! I sat down in one of the cafés on the island and took out the letters and the photograph, trying to reconcile its mute influence with the noise and bustle all around me. The hefty fellow arguing with the barman, the couple murmuring at each other over the plat du jour, I think it was the roast rabbit, the two businessmen in fine waistcoats and watch hobs agitating their whiskers and hands in animated discussion, the fat German-looking man wrestling with a plate of sausage and sauerkraut. Even as a stranger one was not a stranger here, but the mute supplication of the family oozed out from the small rectangle. Only Yakov seemed to release me from the gravitation of their gaze. At the same time, in the sound and smells of the café, the nagging question from the demon sitting on my trembling shoulder trickled: Just who are these people? Dressed in so formal a fashion redolent of times gone by, phantoms revolving slowly inside a closed drum. You escaped into the wide open world, the world of life, mirth, anger, action, open boundaries, opportunities yet unimagined, an unlimited scope...

Yakov was right to dream. From afar, I felt most powerfully the unleashing of his young mind: He was right to dream about me, perhaps not as the bringer of a magical, blinding light, but there were nevertheless beams shooting out from the hot lamps of the studios, illuminating different kinds of dreams. He was right to see me leaping over a gigantic river, willing me to take the challenge, keeping me towards the other side. The sea! The unimaginable ocean, which so many had been crossing for decades... Why not? I had the wherewithal, I had the will, I had the skill, I had the money. Like so many before me, I could go ahead, and then summon my brood. My father, I knew, would never come; he was rooted in his time and place, a great tree whose inner rings counted the longevity of his species. My mother would remain by his side. Could I deprive them of their own future? The children of their dream? What terrible guilt might lie there! Zev had his own mind; he was a question. Kolya I could not know. But Yakov would come. Little Vassily, the dreamer. He would follow the dream. We are, after all, more than we were made by our patrimony, custom, tradition, primal chains. We may not all be able to be fulcrums, like Almereyda or Victor Kibalchich, to change the world, or turn it over. We may be only travelers, fated to watch and wait, and learn and develop our own individual promise, and take things as they come.

Asher:

I turned the page, but the next page was empty. There was a note attached to the next page, which was the last in the stapled chapter, fastened with a rusted paper clip. The note was a short handwritten scrawl from an obvious source, that said only:

> "Looks like Boris doesn't want to tell us about fucking in Paris!
> File and log this. C.B."

I looked through the pages again. I reexamined the first two bound chapters, but there was no photograph attached or stuck between the pages. I went over to the curator's desk and showed him the file. An amiable man, Scott, he was just that mite more disheveled than the standard Mormon sample. He told me the photograph would be logged and filed among the 50,000 and more photographs stored in the archive boxes. The clock behind him reminded us that I had just about run out my time for the day, and the archive would close before the image could be pulled. I filled out a form and was promised that the picture would, if found, be waiting for me in the morning.

I left the library, its stark, sharp glass angles set against the Wasatch Range, which loomed over the town. I had already realized the truth of the warnings I had been given before setting out on this quest: no coffee on campus. No tea, no alcohol, no smokes, straight or bent, nothing. The name of Brigham Young was sacrosanct, apart of course from the polygamy, which was no longer practiced apart from some diehards standing over their harems of child brides with shotguns. Or so the story went. Yet another tribe of brethren who ran the gauntlet of exile from Egypt, or at least from Missouri and Illinois, to make the great trek westward to the Salt Lake in Utah. For Abraham, Joseph Smith, for Moses, Brigham Young... Scott had confided in me, however, that there was a bona fide coffee shop outside the campus, on East Bulldog Boulevard, near North. There was also a pizzeria nearby, so I pulled out the rent-a-Pontiac and drove slowly to the junction. Ever difficult to shake off the foreignness of hinterland America, not so much Midwest as Magic Mountain, despite so many good memories of the old Greyhound rides with Claire. Time passing, time passing, but somehow not here. The truths eternal of the golden tablets revealed to Joseph Smith. I had bunked out in the Cotton Tree Best Western, chosen out of the brochure, reasonably close by, reasonably quiet, trees, grass, walking paths, the Provo River, hot waffles, eggs and sausages for breakfast, but still no coffee. Passing the time at night with the Book of Mormon tucked in the bedside desk drawer. The Origin, Joseph Smith's epiphany, the testimony of the Witnesses who saw the golden plates... The First Book of Nephi, Lehi's vision of the pillar of fire: "He predicts the impending fate of Jerusalem, and foretells the coming of the Messiah—The Jews seek his life..."

As do we always. Seekers of this and that. New prophets prophesying, having visions, seeing the angels of God descending unto the face of the earth, bringing new books... all is predicted: the fall, the exile, the wandering, visions of war and new foundations... the "Doom of the mother of harlots" (the Catholics?) Lehi's sons and the daughters of Ishmael intermarry (interesting), and yet more wilderness, and manna, and a long voyage across the seas...

"But behold, Zion hath said, the Lord hath forsaken me, and my Lord hath forgotten me—but he will show that he hath not..." And "all that fight against Zion shall be destroyed, and that great whore, who hath perverted the right ways of the Lord, yea, that great and abominable church, shall tumble to the dust..." And then of course, the Messiah, as ever… and the gentiles are called upon to repent...

In the morning, I saddled up the Pontiac again and whispered my way to the campus parking lot. Scott is waiting for me at his desk as soon as I have marked out my table. He has a clean crisp envelope. "Seek, and ye shall find," he says cheerfully. He handed me a pair of white gloves and waited until I pulled them on before handing me the envelope. I opened it in front of him, and there it was, just as Boris described: the nuclear family: Rabbi Eliahu-Abba Gurevits, mother Rivka, and the children: Sarah, Zev, Kolya, Yakov and the black-eyed Judit. Only my father, of course, is missing, but we have always had a youthful image of him, a sheaf of images in fact, but from Paris and New York, the new émigré in the classic pose, at the ship's railing, with the army and the torch of Liberty just peeking into the right hand of the frame. He always hated that composition—"not mine of course," he always said.

A slightly faded picture, but as well preserved as one might expect from at least sixty years within a closed cellophane wrapper, kept by the master director's own archivists until its deposit here, some time in the late '50s or '60s.

"There is something else," said Scott, with a thin archivist's smile, denoting He Who Bears Gifts. He brought out one of his huge bound folders, the set of full and definitive catalogs of every item in the maestro's magic boxes, down to the merest scrap of undated, uncategorized flotsam floating among the dossiers. He turned the heavy book towards me. "There is an entry here for a file entitled, can you see? 'Letters, sent to William Gore as "Boris Gurevitch," language: Russian.' Then there's a reference to another volume..." He pulled the other book out, a smaller ledger, with entries both typed and handwritten. He turned the pages and ran his finger along the numbers. "Here it is—675g. It's a bit of a scribble: 'Twenty-four letters, some with envelopes, franked "Tel Aviv." Addressed to Boris Gurevitch from Sarah Gurevitch, dates from July 1920 to October 1929. Sent to Paramount Studios, Hollywood, California, USA. Returned to William Gore February 1953 by C.B. DeMille.' It doesn't say how they were returned or where the batch is. Your father was living in Tel Aviv by that time?"

"Yes, I think so." I wanted to touch, to hold the volume and look more closely at the entry myself. Turning a few pages as the curator looked at me anxiously, even with my sterile white gloves. Civilians are so clumsy. But there was nothing else.

"I pulled quite a few volumes," he said. "This is the only reference. They were originally filed with the chapters of memoir. Then they were separated out to correspondence. Then to correspondence not pertaining to DeMille. That was long before we had the materials. DeMille was collecting his own archive in preparation for the autobiography, as we discussed earlier. It was an ongoing effort. Made my predecessor's work easier, as well as mine, I can tell you."

Passing the ball back to me. There was not much else that I could do that day except to arrange for the photocopying of the memoir chapters and the photograph, both of which required special dispensation as a Special Request, on grounds of family. I had to sign away all rights in perpetuity to any claim of copyright on the materials, which were vested in the archive and its donors for all time. Any legal claims to the archive arising out of any use

I might make of the materials payable by myself and my heirs in perpetuity. Signed in blood.

I had one more night booked in the Best Western but could already feel the smiles of Provo grating on my gentile flesh. Another night with the Book! "Beloved brethren, behold, I declare unto you that except ye shall repent your houses shall be left unto you desolate...your women shall have great cause to mourn in the day that they shall give suck; for ye shall attempt to flee and there shall be no place for refuge..." the Book of Helaman, Chapter 15, verses 1 and 2... I made a long-distance call to my mother at Lord Melchett Street. She was surprised to hear my voice and seemed to be moving something around, either plates or furniture, while speaking. "Yitzhak is here," she said, "their boy Michah has had another baby. The bris is Tuesday."

"I won't make it, Mum," I said. The connection was not brilliant. "Tell him congratulations. How many does that make now? Don't tell me. This is an expensive call from a hotel. Can I ask you something quickly, about Dad's letters, the stuff he left behind? Was there a sheaf of very old letters from Aunt Sarah? You know, back in the twenties. When she was in the women's pioneers, the kibbutz, building the roads, remember she used to talk about all that stuff? I know we looked though it all, but did you ever hear him talk of such a bunch of letters? Letters she sent to him in America? They're listed in the archive here, but it says they were sent back to him by DeMille in 1953."

"Oh, you're still on DeMille. Your father's favorite subject. DeMille this and DeMille that. I didn't need to see any of those films, because he used to sit and describe them, shot by shot. You know we still have your old 8-millimeter camera? The one you made all those funny films with? What is it Yitzhak?" she went off mumbling. I heard his voice booming something.

"I don't have much time, Mum," I said. "You can't tell me anything about those letters? He never mentioned them to me."

"Aunt Sarah left her own writings to the center," she said, speaking very loudly as people of her generation did on a foreign call, perhaps figuring that you might hear them even if the bloody machine didn't work. "You know, that what's it called, Beit Berl, the socialist place. I don't know about old letters to Boris. It's way before my time. Kolya has copies of most of Sarah's stuff. You know, when he was going to write the family history? And it always got pushed back, because of the anti-Semitism? The Big Book? You're going to have to check there. Were you planning a visit? Dvorah said he was still responding. He's pretty indestructible. Ninety-eight in September, can you believe it? We're all invited to the hundredth birthday!"

"Till a hundred-and-twenty," I responded automatically. "I don't think I can get over there, to Michigan. It's not that simple."

"Nothing is simple with Kolya. Didn't he promise to leave you his papers? You remember, when Boris died."

"That was then, this is now."

"It's all about Adir now. His career, his progress. He's in the running for the ministerial places you know. He may be our prime minister in a few years."

"God help us."

We faded out on some small talk. The hotel room was air-conditioned, but I don't think that caused the shiver down my spine. What is the problem with this family, that preached so much togetherness and flew so far apart? Not much escape from Cain and Abel. I'm sure my brother Yitzhak would explain it to me, if I wanted to listen. I had a ticket back to London via New York. It could be possible, if I dug into the surplus, to change it with the airline for a stopover in Detroit. Then another rented car to Ann Arbor, or more correctly to the rest home somewhere near Ypsilanti. I had never been either at Kolya's university or in Ypsilanti, wherever that name came from. All I knew about it was an old paperback I used to have, *The Three Christs of Ypsilanti*, by a psychiatrist at an asylum there who had three patients who each thought he was Jesus Christ. Instead of treating them apart he brought them together, to see if that would rock their minds. But the three Christs all found subterfuges to explain the existence of the other two and undermine the psychiatrist. I think it was one of the books that got lost or sold in the move to London with Claire. Not enough room in the Queen's Park apartment. Something always has to give. But the idea of detouring so far off track and time to an old age refuge to sit by my ninety-eight-year-old uncle while he bent my mind about the long history of the unbending and unshakeable hatred of everyone else towards the Jews, the faith to which he had dedicated his life, made me shiver even more. Maybe if I brought him the Book of Mormon he would have some more fuel for his fire, but I could not imagine that he would have neglected that, in yet another volume of the magnum opus I had not read. I have enough holes in my head.

I decided to risk another coffee-less day and went back to Brigham Young in the morning. I asked Scott as yet another special favor to search his catalog sources for any more sightings of possible Gurevits or Gurevitch entries. In particular Yakov, Vassily, alias the Great Gramby. I told him I had tried to track down Ace Harrington, Ace Blue Note, in Tennessee and Georgia, talking to people in New York from Bleecker Street times who knew the jazz historians, but they said he had passed away in '86, and whatever archive he left was trapped in a family conflict, between different ex-wives and heirs. What to do, who owned what, whether and where to donate. It was not even clear whether there was any written material there at all, just a houseful of old knickknacks, instruments, records, photographs. The photographs might hold the key. But the experts had already frightened me about archives. Unless they were pre-sorted, like the obsessive DeMille's, they could take years for a university or other library to catalog and make public. The Mack Sennett papers in Los Angeles, I had been told, took twenty-five years. I would be an aging sage myself, jabbering in my own rest home, before I could find anything out.

But Provo held no more Gurevits ghosts.

I called Claire. She told me if I was on the trail I should keep on it while I was still over here. Why had I started in the first place if I didn't mean to carry on? "You've been obsessed with your father since you had your 8-millimeters," she said. "You're always running away from all the others. If you don't speak to your uncle now it's probably the last chance. Then he'll be dead and you'll be moaning about it for another ten years."

Has it been that long? She wasn't pining for me in any case; professional people are always busy. Trouble at pit, as she used to say. Schedules, programming, politics. Tantrums of the director of the new visiting German play and subsequent cold feet of the actors. Months of good work about to be pissed away by foolishness. What else is new?

The moving finger writes, et cetera... I called the airline and changed the ticket. Endured one more night in Mormonville and drove the car back to Salt Lake City in the golden light of promised lands. One and a half hours in a tin can to Detroit, another rent-a-car and then down the suburban glut westward. Ypsilanti, hometown of Iggy Pop and the failed Preston Tucker car. Another place like 1,0001 middle towns, historic buildings, shops, local festivals, old stuff, new stuff, university campus and derelict jungles of rusted metal and broken windows that used to make cars. Drove right through to the other end, towards Ann Arbor, the rest home just a batch of neat-looking homes with a linked garden, a little stream, a low fence with several gates, and a host of road signs warning "Slow Down—Seniors Crossing," since there were some chalets on the other side. Land of the living dead. At least the smiles were free of the religious dimension. I had not called ahead. I thought that if Kolya fell dead at the sudden sight of one of his relatives, he would have been gone long ago. There were hordes, I understood, from his wife's family, members of Temple this or that. Down unto the great-grandchildren. But I was the only one on this day.

I had to wait, as the day-manager, one of those blonde-maned ladies who stoke the engine rooms of social America, sent a minion off to check if I was receivable. "His Hawking boy is with him this week," she told me. "You know, Stephen Hawking, the scientist? We call him that because he writes down what the professor says. The professor still does work most days. He's our oldest guest at

230

the moment. We had Mrs Windleschaeffer, who made her century, but she passed a few months ago. You're his grandson?"

"Nephew."

"Gee. His siblings must be pretty young."

That sounded nice, so I dutifully spent half an hour with a three-month-old issue of *Time* magazine, from just before the Gulf War, whose cover asked, "The Recession: How Bad Is It? And What Gives on Wall Street?" Nothing gives on Wall Street; it only takes, comrades. "America Abroad: the Low Point of the Bush Presidency," "Crime: The Deadliest Year Yet," "Europe: Lurch to the Right—Politicians stir fear and loathing of dark-skinned immigrants." More déjà vu. Wagner in Israel—should he or shouldn't he be played?

"He's ready now." The minion, a young crew-cut man with an un-Mormon smile, took me along the landscaped lawns towards a small house a little separate from the other chalets. It had its own gate and driveway, with a small Toyota parked by a larger pickup. The door was opened by a compact young man with dark eyes and a standard black skullcap, who ushered me in. "You're Asher? Come on in. I'm Yonni. I told him you were here and he seems OK with it. Some days you never know. You have to speak loudly and move your lips right. He doesn't hear well, but he pretends that he doesn't lip-read. But the mind—still sound as a bell. When did you see him last?"

"My father's funeral," I said. "Nineteen eighty-four. He was walking then. We went to the beach."

"None of that any more, I'm afraid. Had a run up to the bay in the summer. Prof looked at the lake. Didn't like it. Came back. We're working on a revision of the Proskurov pogrom this week. There are some new studies from Stanford."

The joys of a spring afternoon in Michigan. I tried to think if there was any mention of this event in Boris's journal, as a talking point. "What year was that?" I asked.

"Nineteen-nineteen. Ten thousand Jews were killed in one day, on February fifteen. The whole job took about six hours, which accounts for more than one and a half thousand per hour, or twenty-six people every minute. Some revisionists claim only twelve hundred were killed. So we have been working on listings."

The old anxiety that used to seize me whenever I was in Kolya's presence. Even in his shrunken state, fitted into his armchair, the skull weighing heavily on the thin neck, the glare a little dimmed as his eyelids seemed to be sliding down to shut out the invasions of the outer world. The "Hawking boy'"s chair was thrust up against the armchair so the scribe could be closer to the quivering lips as he leaned forward over the keyboard of the beige desktop in the midst of columns of files. Far from mental retirement, the savant kept his cage lined with bookshelves, creaking under the weight of his classic hardbacks and dog-eared trade paperbacks, packed like weary immigrants on the ship from the Old World to Ellis Island. Everything brought to bear on the burden of hard information, the unbending count of corpses strewn in the valley of ghosts, each one of them a stubborn accuser whispering in my uncle's ear. It would be easier to move the Earth from its orbit around the sun than to deflect him from his purpose.

There was no point in trivial preambles. "I found my father's old manuscripts," I said, directly and loudly, "in the DeMille archive in Utah. It's what we talked about at the shiva, remember? I made a separate copy for you." I pulled out the file from my sidebag. "It covers the early years in the village to the time he left for Odessa and then later, with the anarchists in Europe."

"Anarchists? Kvatsch." Yonni, the "Hawking boy," seemed to have already flashed up a new file and began transcribing a new page on his screen. "Cogs spat from the machine thinking they could make it stop. Sun in Gibeon stand, moon the valley of Ayalon. He should have stayed in pictures. Samson and Delilah. That was DeMille. You know who wrote that story? Jabotinsky. Vladimir Ze'ev Jabotinsky. You know how he started? The Zion Mule Corps. A loyal subject and servant of His Majesty in Palestine. Under the command of Allenby. General Allenby. They named a street after him but what did they put there? Monuments? Museums?

Schools? No, just falafel shops and pornographic movie theaters. Who remembers anything?"

"It was written in 1926." I said clearly. "That's what the archivists estimate. So it was very close to the period. Dad had a good memory for people, images, things that happened."

"He was unreliable. People remember kvatch. My father was like this, my mother was like that. I went to school. My teacher was a tyrant. I stole an apple. I had my first kiss. There was a fruit stall at the end of the avenue. My mother fed me kasha. I saw the soldiers come to the house. I hid under the straw. There were twenty-four of them. They wore flat caps and galoshes. None of it matters. To defeat the criminals, you need the evidence. In flagrante delicto. Before the world of the photograph and the tape recorder and your father's camera, what do we have? But the criminal always glories in his deeds. Always the bloody fingerprint, the record kept in the butcher's own books."

"There was a photograph," I said, desperate to pry him loose, "that was with the manuscript. It was filed separately but I made two quick photocopies. I've ordered two proper copies, but they take a week to ten days. I can send one on to you. It's the family. Have you ever seen this?" I pulled out the photocopy and Yonni took it from me, shaking his head in wonderment. "Is this true?" he asked. "The Gurevitses? Do you see this, Professor? Which one is you?"

My uncle shook his head and did not look at the picture. He was seeing something far far away. Exhibit A did not interest him. He was already far advanced along the prosecutor's summing up, clearly unimpressed by any case for the defense, even of himself. Human, all too human. But I had read his book on Nietzsche—best not to open that old wound. Wounds stretched all the way back. Remember what was done to thee by Amalek.

Yonni moved the picture close to his eyes. His finger pointed.

"No doubt at all, Professor. And the rebbe himself. The rebbetzin. May their memory be blessed. This must be Sarah. This one, yes, this must be your father. The young girl, that must be

Judit. The tall one in the middle, that must be Zev. I have never seen a picture of them. So the other boy..."

"Yakov," said Kolya, "Yakov."

He finally took the picture with a slightly quivering hand. I could sense that he was annoyed by the tremor and trying to control it, as it might be evidence of some emotional turmoil occasioned by a banal sentiment. His nose twitched with an expression of distaste or just another involuntary shake. His eyes glared at the image, first with the right eye, then the left.

"Ah, yes." He handed it back to Yonni. Then he closed both his eyes, laid his head back in the chair, and shut down, only the slight rise and fall of his puny torso showing signs of lingering life.

"Shall I file this?" said Yonni, turning to me. I nodded, and he took a new document holder from one of the trays, and, holding the photocopy carefully by its edges, extending to it the privilege of a pristine witness, placed it within, writing neatly on the cover and finding it its proper niche among the myriad paper witnesses of my uncle's great saga of pain, terror, misfortune, and defiance, the burning brand of his refusal to compromise or deviate in the slightest measure from the path of absolute right against the great iniquity, recognizing at its moment of inception the first cancer cell that takes no prisoners in its march of ruin and destruction—to realise the definitive purpose: That burden that God thrust upon Abraham when He commanded the One Truth, when chaos was suddenly ended and the order of the universe began. Or maybe it was not God at all, but the indomitable certainty of his own will that came upon him long ago, in his forced exile from the certitudes of the ancestral hearth, my grandfather's shelf of The Books, my grandmother's stews and tshulent, the calm center that could not hold and flung apart, scattered in all directions. The march of war and the recruiter's inventory of lost souls that could be molded into weapons for their own primeval enemies...

And maybe there, in that moment captured by the photographer, Aaron Schatz of Belzi, nine decades ago, that brief moment of cohesion before the world split apart and disintegrated, and in the dead center of the image, Kolya could not gaze upon the source and wonder whether some other path might have materialized, if the ethereal gaze of the dreaming brother, Yakov, Vassily, the Great Gramby, hinted at a different tale...

VOLUME 2

THE NOVELTIES

"All Cohens look alike to me..."

Ace Harrington:

The next time I saw the red-haired saxophone player who had wailed at *Birth of a Nation* was in Chicago, on the New Year of 1917. We had arrived after Christmas, after playing in Cleveland, Toledo and Detroit on the Western Vaudeville wheel. It was bitter cold, with the wind howling off the lake to the Loop and under the bridges that rose to draw the ships down the river. Down the railway tracks lay the giant stockyards, where pigs and cows went to die by the millions. Poles, Germans, Italians, Greeks, the Irish marched down there by the tens of thousands to do the slaughtering and the packing. South towards Englewood and beyond, the blacks poured up from the Deep South towards the great buzz of life and industry. Even on the coldest day, the city seemed to fizz and crackle. Like bees in the hive, nothing stood still.

Gramby was booked for a two-week time at the Majestic, which was on South State Street, near Monroe, an Orpheum house that gave the usual all-day booking. Shows began at nine in the morning and went on until eleven at night. You broke for lunch while the other acts were on. The house was almost always full, especially in the winter, when your bones could turn to ice outside.

In Detroit, Gramby had already teamed up with another act, what they called a "Hebrew act" in those days, with a Yiddisher tone: Der Naaveltie Minstrels. Strange to say, they were not the only act of the kind in those days of anything goes. There were twelve of them, performing in blackface, which was useful because the audience could not see how long in the tooth most of them were. The leader of the group, who played the right-end man, was Shimmel Krauss. He was seventy-three, and he had been in shows for fifty-six years. The first twenty or so had been in Germany, where he started off as a fake ventriloquist's dummy and then sang and danced around in country fairs and small-time before getting on the boat to New York. He said he traveled with a German show family, the Schonbergs, whose young daughter later married a French-German tailor and then her name changed to Minnie Marx. "Those boys! Those boys!" he used to say. "I taught dem all dey knew!" He could probably speak American as well as anybody, but he liked to keep that Jewish spiel that made his living. He would come on stage and jig and dance like a twelve-year-old, and then go into a "sidewalk patter" with his left-end man, Percy Fiddler, who was actually an Englishman from some small village back home. They would do dialogues and jokes that would get you run out of town nowadays, like the stuff between Schwindlebaum and Pawnheimer, which went something like this:

> Schwindlebaum: Say, Pawnheimer, did your vife enchoy herself at der masquerade ball last night?
> Pawnheimer: You are mistaking, Schwindlebaum, dere vos no masquerade ball last night.
> Schwindlebaum: Oi vei! Vos dat her face?
> Pawnheimer: Ve had a vonderful dinner. At der next table a man vas eating three bowls of soup, four dizen oysters, nine kosher mutton chops, eighteen potatoes, seven puddings und two buckets of coffee. How vos dat fer an appetite?
> Schwindlebaum: Dat vos no appetite, dat vos a tapevorm. You should be taking care of yourself, Pawnheimer. Vot should happen if your store caught fire ven you had no insurance?
> Pawnheimer: Dat is foolish. Vy should my store catch fire if I haf no insurance?

It used to get big laughs. Krauss worked his way up from the medicine shows and the "dime museums," the freak shows, playing the "Seal Man" or the "Wild Man of Siam," till he joined Minnie's brother Al Shean in the Manhattan Comedy Four. They specialized in Irish songs and dances. Minnie's boys were still too young to act in those days. Then he found a group of Germans who had split off from one of the big minstrel shows, and they started their own act with four other Jews. There were so many blackface acts they decided that playing in Yiddish would give them a special angle. Later on, several other groups like them formed, but they were the first, Krauss always said.

Krauss was a great boon to me because he took me under his wing and taught me how to play both the cornet and the piano properly. I had picked up the sounds along the way and was noodling along, but he had spent a long time in New Orleans, learning from the new jazz performers, though they didn't call it jazz yet. Maybe he felt he owed something to me, the only "real negro" among the fakes. In those days it was no big deal; even the black acts would put on burnt cork and hit the stage as "Ethiopian minstrels." The great Bert Williams, who was in the front ranks with Ziegfeld, blacked up himself, but he still had to enter the swanky hotels they stayed in through the trade door, even when he was getting a thousand dollars a week.

Gramby had changed the show. Since Alma had joined us, stepping shyly forward from behind the broad backs of her uncles the Gross brothers, he had fallen in love, and he was able to live his infatuation openly once the brothers had left to set up their own show with two German acrobats as the Four Brooklyn Bouncers, in the summer of 1916. They recommended two replacements, Federico and Lutz, who were Swiss but had no separate shtick of their own. Now they were the turban-clad stage stooges who moved the magic cabinet and all the fittings and stood by with arms folded for "Sultan" Gramby's orders. I was sprouting up taller by the month, no longer a boy, but I was still the all-purpose Sambo or Mowgli. The show's new centerpiece, the Vanishing Princess, featured the dream disappearance and recapture of Alma in an assortment of exotic costumes: Indian robes, Arabian harem shifts, gypsy dress, the Spanish *infanta*, Cinderella, Rapunzel, the Sleeping Beauty, the Rajah's Bride. He had a whole raft of plans to expand the act into an extravaganza like the famous Plunging Elephants of the London Hippodrome, where Krauss had once played, but the Barnum boys had snapped up all the pachyderms in the Midwest and there was only a small baby zoo cub that we used to visit so that Alma could feed it and make friends. But the Humane Society pitched in and said the cub was too small to go on the payroll. So Gramby had to make do with the Naaveltie Minstrels setting up the show with their mock Arabian, African, Indian and Hottentot numbers, which got the crowd in the mood. Krauss put in the deal that he would not "vanish"! At my age, he said, there would be no guarantee I'll come back—I have made too many bad bets to risk rousing the "big black shmendrik down there." So he would go into his standard numbers, including his signature song, "All Cohens Look Alike to Me," which he had learned at the knee of Ernest Hogan, who billed himself as the Unbleached American back in the golden nineties. In the original, Hogan used the word "coon," but Krauss made a small change to it.

> *"All Cohens look alike to me,*
> *If they spend their mazuma free,*
> *I work in a bakery, and knead lots of dough, you see!*
> *If you stay long with me, it's mighty short you'll be—*
> *Then honey, I will shake you—all Cohens look alike to me!"*

The great climax Gramby was planning was the Flying Princess, when Alma would come swooping down from the flies and soar over the front rows before landing in the Sultan's arms. This would need a very complicated apparatus that Gramby had ordered from his regular supplier of the secret equipment, the Hungarian master Milos Vas. Vas lived in New York but was currently in Mexico manufacturing magical mirrors for the army of Pancho Villa, of whom he was a great supporter, as a member of the Anarchist League of Sorcerers, the ALS, which he had set up on his own (the only other members being his wife, Oneida, who was Spanish and had trained as a circus knife thrower at her father's knee in Barcelona. (Her father had been executed for missing a throw at

241

the King of Spain, when she was twelve.) So Vas was not easy to get hold of, because Villa was being chased by General Pershing across the border after Villa's big raid on Columbus, New Mexico, was reported in all the papers. Despite this, many people in America still saw him as a hero, especially the blacks and some show people, who were sympathetic to rebels.

Gramby therefore had to wait for his grand finale, and come on after Shimmel Krauss and his dark dozen had warmed up the crowd with their bad jokes. ("Swindelbaum was crossing Monroe this morning when a motor car comes along suddenly and knocks him down. Pawnheimer rushes over and asks him: Oi, mine heavens, how much are you hurted? I don't know, says Swindelbaum, I'll heff to esk my lawyer.") The show went down well on New Year's Eve, and Krauss suggested we take a streetcar right after the show to the negro bars and cafés on South State Street to see in the new year. There was no time to change costumes or wipe the black off the white faces, so we just packed up the props quickly and rode down through the huge crowds. At that time most of the black entertainment was between 31st and 34th streets, near the elevated railway, where Tom McCain had the old Pompeii café and the Elmwood that featured Ollie Powers, Jelly Roll Morton and Tony Jackson and a host of high flyers who brought the folks down from all over the city, and there were the Elite Clubs #1 and #2, that were set up by Teenan Jones and Lovie Joe Whitson, and these were the places all the actors hung out. We went straight down to the Elite Club #2, where Estella Harris had a real "jass" band that had once been the Pekin Trio. They did the "Happy Shout," the "New Dance" and the "Shimmie Sha Wobble," which was as near indecent as a regular show went in that spot.

When we got there, the place was packed, but people knew Shimmel Krauss, and he got us all in through the crowd, me in Mowgli turban, Gramby still in his sultan get-up and, Alma in her gypsy dress, with clanking bangles and foot-wide earrings. There was a white girl up on the platform, waggling her hips and bouncing the choicest pair of bosoms you could want on a young woman, whose arms and face were so pale they could have lit the place up with no lamps. Everybody was just about ready for the big moment, as the clock was showing three minutes to midnight and the champagne was flowing like water from a busted pipe. The girls, black and white, got up on the tables and we all counted down: nine, eight, seven, six, five, four, three, two, one— Nineteen-seventeen!

The band lit up, just two feet away from me, and there he was, the red-haired foxy kid from Los Angeles, whose strange licks had shaken me up from that time. I pulled Gramby's sleeve and pointed the boy out to him, but he didn't understand what I was on about and was too busy with his hands around Alma's waist. He was, after all, not many years over twenty himself, and in that company, with the "sage" makeup run off, he was just a man in the crowd, not a boss or a sorcerer but like a kid himself, in fancy dress. Alma was just as crazy about him, and they kissed like she was Theda Bara in *The Vampire*. I felt I was going weak at the knees. You saw a lot of girls running in and out of the dressing rooms in the shows, but they were always guarded carefully by the managers and their own boyfriends, or husbands, who hung on them like barnacles on a shipwreck. But this was the first time I was in a real crush with so much female flesh pressing on me, all colors, shapes, and creeds. Apart from the usual tumbles with chambermaids, I was pretty green at that time.

Krauss called the white girl with the big breasts over, and shouted in my ear that her name was Mae, and she was already a star performer in the vauds, sometimes with her little sister Beverly, sometimes with an Italian accordionist, Guido, and sometimes on her own, singing ragtime. There were so many of these, and most of them called Mae, too. Later I heard this was the famous Mae West, but she was no great beauty then, just another twenty-year-old dame with assets and a sassy manner, who looked you over as if she was buying prime beef at the yards. I was too young for her, so her eyes passed over to Gramby, but I guess he was too Jewish, certainly not beefy enough, and clearly taken, as Alma wound

243

herself around him like the serpent of Eden spotting a rival. So Mae fixed on the drummer, who was built like a prize-fighter and gave her the wink as he thrashed away on his skins.

I still wanted to talk to the red-haired cornetist, but I was pinned to our table and the booze was flowing. Shimmel Krauss passed some cash to a waiter, who brought over a tray of wieners and a big golden bottle of Johnny Walker, with a whole clatter of glasses. Gramby and I passed, but Alma downed her share, and pretty soon all the twelve blackface Naaveltie Minstrels were passed out, stretched either on or under the table, with Krauss conducting himself in a less than rousing chorus of "Down Honolulu Way" and "Baby, It's Because You're Irish," which gained some scattered applause.

As it turned out, there was no rush. Just as I was coming to feel that my time was up, and I was just about done with the heaving and hauling, lying cramped up in the cargo cars of every train that ever crisscrossed America, seeing the light of day only early in the morning, with the rest of God's hours climbing on and off the stage in a weird get-up pretending to be God knows what, God knows who for no reason that made sense anymore, for wages the lowest riverboat stevedore would spit on for toting a bale. I was fond of Gramby, and got to see myself as a kind of protector, a guardian of his airy dreams. Without me to be his good luck he would be left with nothing, only the cards. And the Almas. That wasn't nothing. I was lost, as well, in all those dreams. And in the end, I was not the Rajah's bootboy, the pigmy witch-doctor, the midget-king of Cipango, little Sambo, the inkblot kid. Here were all these jiving, ass-shaking black folk, the music boys, getting off the floor of the wagon and breaking free, making sounds, being themselves...

But these are the breaks: One day just before the end of the Majestic engagement, I came into the dressing room to find Gramby, Krauss and his Yiddish minstrels and a parcel of other actors rowing and shouting, with the man from the management poking his head in now and again and then rushing out. I asked

Alma, who was sitting aside doing her makeup, what it was all about and she said, "It's the strike."

I had never seen Shimmel Krauss so full of passion. Everybody was talking about "the Rats." The Rats were going to do this, the Rats were going to do that. This I knew about. The White Rats were the vaudeville union, to which most of them belonged; they used to go off to meetings and drink a lot of beer and sing songs:

"This is the emblem of our society!
Every one of our members acts with propriety!
Raise your hats, to the merry old Rats!
Rats! Rats! Rats! Rats! Rats!"

That was about it, as far as I knew, but I know they were always arguing about the terms of their deals with the bookers and managers. There was always somebody from the union coming in and out of dressing rooms, talking about a general strike of the members for better pay. I was all for it, because the pay was pretty lousy, but I wasn't a member, and couldn't be one, for obvious reasons. Those were the days. But I was not so dumb as not to know what was going on around me in the white world. Life was fast and dizzy, but also rough as it goes. Men and women were sucked into the great factories and steel mills and the Chicago railways, as well as the stockyards, and the big shots were getting so rich they let their chauffeurs drive around for themselves in their big swanky cars. The working Joes grabbed a cold piece of chicken and a handful of onions for their lunch while the masters gorged themselves on lobsters. Everywhere there were organizers, moving along the factory floor, waiting at the gates, or shooting their way into banks just to even up the score. Tales were told of strikes in coal mines and steel mills where the army was called in and mowed down the strikers with machine guns. And there were rumors that our American boys were soon going to have to go overseas and fight in the Great War out there. Nobody waved the flag so high as when some working stiffs started muttering about their wages and conditions. America was building, faster and higher, with hands that were hard and calloused so you couldn't tell the white from the black. That was the most dangerous, to those whose motto was "divide and rule."

I got this stuff on the road from lots of people, but most up-to-date from Shimmel Krauss. He was what would soon be called a Bolshevik, though none of us had heard the term then. We heard about "anarchists," who planted bombs and robbed the banks and wanted to destroy America and set up a world's workers state. There was the IWW, the Industrial Workers of the World. Gramby had told me his brother had been close to them when he was in Russia and in Europe, but that didn't square at all with the busy movie camera master we had met in Los Angeles. The only anarchists there were the crazies in the Mack Sennett studios, and all they were after was laughs, not revolution. It didn't make a lot of sense.

Shimmel Krauss told me that the White Rats had agreed to strike against the managers around the country. The strike had been started by their leader, Harry Mountford, who was in New York. He was an Englishman who had organized the Rats in England pretty successfully, and so the New York branch thought he could do the trick for them. They had the support of other unions, like the garment workers in the Lower East Side, who supplied costumes and props. But the managers had been preparing for months and had set up their own union, the National Vaudeville Association, which all the variety stage actors were being invited to join. Those who didn't join were due to be blacklisted, if and when the strike began. It was all, Krauss declared, the work of Albee, the boss of the United Booking Office, which controlled who would be hired and who was shut out.

"They got two million dollars stacked up!" Shimmel shouted. "Those bastards see us all like whipped dogs! They built us all a big kennel and we'll all troop in. Our own Hog City. Where are we? Are we in America, the Land of the Free, or are we back in Russia, with the knout?"

"It's just acting, Shmuel," said Harry Holmes, who had a double act with his girlfriend, Lili Devere, who was really Gerda

Pawlowicz, trying to mollify the old man. But he was brushed aside.

"It's all for one, and one for all, or it's nuttin' for nobody!" The other minstrels all nodded. "I don't care if everybody's signing on. I got into the business when there was no money and the theaters were fleapits and whorehouses where the girls would shtup the ventriloquist dummy for an extra dime. Everybody was treated alike—like beggars. Then we made the union: brothers and sisters of the proper art. Anybody who betrayed his brother was a Black Rat; everybody shunned them, nobody would ever play on the same bill with such a creature! Brothers we were and brothers we are. Or who are we? Answer me that?"

Gramby was quietly adjusting his turban in the mirror. The fake jewel glinted in the red light. Alma looked at him but he said nothing. Krauss turned to him. "Vot do you say, Vassily? Yakov, you are like a son to me! Tell your poor old deluded father why I am wrong?"

"Times are different," said Gramby, so quietly that Krauss had to shush the others to hear him. "Maybe we are all wrong, or all right. I don't know yet."

"He needs to look at his fucking cards," said one of the younger minstrels, Micky Meisel.

"He needs to look at his pocket," said Harry Holmes. "He'll find it needs filling up, like mine. Like all of us. This ain't the steel mills, or mining. It's not dangerous work, only stupid."

"The new world!" scoffed Shimmel Krauss. "The new century! New thinking! What it is, is that we are all machines. You crank us up, and we all march on the stage like automatics, all in line, all in step. Everybody does the same thing, makes the same moves, sings the same music, like the Ziegfelds. Pretty girls like cogs in a wheel. Men in top hat and tails. That's your new God, what's his name, Taylor, the 'Scientific Manager,' everything is an assembly line. Once the human being was first, now it's the 'system.' Vot 'system'? It's all just the same theft, exploiting the working man, capitalist accumulation. You should read Karl Marx instead of the

Katzenjammer Kids. Read Engels, not the funny pages. What are we here, Happy Hooligans? That is your labor, up there on the stage. Vot about the families on the road? The man with a wife and three babies screaming in the baggage racks, pissing down on Daddy trying to sleep upright on the midnight red-eye from Cincinnati to Dubuque? So some of us are doing okay. Vot about the others?"

"You should be with the Wobblies, in the Mesabi Range," said Holmes. "They could win double wages with all that syrup instead of clubs on the head."

"There will be victory in the Mesabi Range strike!" Krauss shouted, lifting a finger towards the sky. "Solidarity and faith!" Another finger went up. One more and we would have been with the Trinity. But the meeting broke up. The minstrels stalked out, and I sat down with Gramby as he and Alma continued their dressing.

"What are you going to do?" I asked him.

"After the show," he said, "we'll see."

It was a long night with the cards, no question. Judgement, the Hermit and the Hanged Man seemed to come up all the time, signifying delay, stagnation, lack of decision, guilt on separation. The Hermit—imprudent actions, negative decisions, foolishness and obstinacy, bad habits; the Hanged Man: inability and failure to act, lack of decision or flexibility of mind? Gramby kept hoping for more positive signals, the Heirophant, the Star, the Chariot. But they were scarce. The stubborn absence of the Lovers disturbed him, since this would have allowed him to make decisions based on insight rather than calculation, which was always his most favored mode. Eventually I was banished to my cubbyhole at the Monroe Hotel, while he went off to bed with Alma. In the morning, as we were setting up the equipment, he still said nothing about the situation, although it was clear that Krauss and most of his troupe, though not perhaps all of them, would join the strikers, threatening the combined act. In one of the intervals, Holmes came up to warn Gramby that Shimmel Krauss and six others in the group were already on the Albee blacklist, and almost everybody in Chicago was rushing to join the managers' union. Variety had published a two-page spread with all the new members on it, and one of the country's biggest headline acts, McIntyre and Heath, had also made a full-page plug for the new union, which he showed us, and made pretty sick reading, even for my own taste at the time. Even Gramby snorted at the ass-licking: "The vaudeville artist has something to sell, and the only one who can buy it is the manager. Why shouldn't they trot in harness instead of pulling in opposite directions?" The big guns were lining up.

But Gramby wasn't as lost as he looked. Five years on the stage toughen you up. On the night of the last show of the two-week booking, two big black men in sharp suits turned up at the theater and he went off with them, leaving me to see Alma home. In the morning, at breakfast, he gave me the news.

"We're staying in Chicago," he said. "We got a three-month booking at the Terrace Garden for the magic act. We are breaking with Krauss. He's standing pat. He's going to picket the Chicago theaters but there's going to be no strike in the city. It's all sewn up. We just get out of the way for a while. We ain't striking and we ain't strikebreaking. We are just someplace else. This will suit you, Ace, the cards stack up for you. Your friend, the redhead, is in the band."

His name was Jacques Souchot, and he was named for his mother's family, as nobody knew his father. He came from Baton Rouge, and then got his start in New Orleans with Tom Brown's Ragtime Band, playing alongside Ray Lopez, but when they went to Chicago he joined his mother, who had remarried a silent movie pianist who had worked in Los Angeles and got the kid his place in the downtown black theaters, where I had caught him playing. He was only three or four years older than me, and nobody thought he was a star. A few years later, Louis Armstrong would make that same wild wailing tone a massive hit in Chicago and all over the country, but I was already far away then. We were before our time, and the world caught up with us when it already had other heroes. Those are the breaks.

But I learned the licks there at the Elite #2 while Gramby did his magic act, which had to be pared down because the stage was not fixed up for any of his more extravagant numbers. The beauty of it was, he was only on nights, so the days were free for me to learn and also visit the movie theaters that Jack was sometimes playing at. From January to June, we saw all the latest releases. We saw Charlie Chaplin in *Easy Street* and *The Cure*, we saw movies like *Pride and the Devil*, *The Gates of Doom* and *The Fortunes of Fifi*, and we saw the two latest pictures that Gramby's brother Bill had photographed for Mr. DeMille: *A Romance of the Redwoods* and *The Little American*, both of which starred Mary Pickford. We were really crazy about Charlie Chaplin, like everybody else in America at that time. When he was dressed as a cop, holding the gas lamp down on the head of the giant heavy, and then feeding some poor guy's kids with chicken feed, the house would be rolling and crying. It was like somebody doing everything we all wanted to do, and then, in *The Cure*, getting stone drunk and dunking the big man in the well. The DeMille films were a Western and a story of the war that was still going on in Europe. Gramby and Alma came to see these, and I could see he was very disturbed by the war film, which opened just after the country had got into the war and things around us were changing.

I know Gramby was happy for a while at the cabaret, not only because he was away from the strike and the blacklists that made old friends enemies and killed off the White Rats union, but because he could write and get regular letters from his brother, since we had a long-term address at a boarding house close to the work. Bill couldn't come to Chicago because he was busy shooting one DeMille film after the other. They had spent most of the year before, I think, shooting the big epic about Joan of Arc—*Joan the Woman* I think they called it, with thousands of extras storming castles and throwing each other into moats. At the end of the picture, the girl, played by the same Geraldine Farrar, the opera singer, who had been Carmen, gets burned at the stake. It looked so real you could feel the flames, and the whole scene was played in a red color; they could do those things in those days. Everybody gasped in their seats, but Gramby looked so proud that his brother could do magic tricks, too. The war film was about two friends, both Americans, but one from France and the other from Germany, so that when the war broke out in 1914, they were called up on opposite sides. There was another great scene, with an ocean liner like the *Lusitania* that gets sunk by a German U-boat, and Mary Pickford escapes on a raft. It was also colored, a kind of deep blue.

Although he stopped talking about it, I knew Gramby was worried all the time about his folks back in Russia, who were close to one of the fronts where the Russians were fighting the Austrians and the Germans. I didn't know who was who, but there were movies that were shown about the war, one I remember that Jack played the piano for. It was called "The Austrian-German Front," and showed a lot of armies marching and generals with big hats and feathers prancing about on their horses. Then there were some scenes from the front and a scary shot of a huge machine that squirted out a spray of fire. Gramby came to see the film on the matinee but walked out when they showed that shot.

In early March, I remember, we were surprised one evening at the cabaret when Shimmel Krauss rushed in just after the show and came into the dressing room. He spoke to Gramby in Yiddish and was very excited. Gramby listened to him with his eyelids drooping, as he did when he wanted to put a distance between himself and any disturbing news. After Shimmel rushed out, I asked Alma what had happened, and she said "There's a revolution in Russia." I wasn't sure what a revolution was, though I heard the Naaveltie Minstrels sometimes talk about it, like, "When the revolution comes, they'll all be sorry." I figured it was another actors' business, some kind of general strike, or some other thing that wouldn't happen because everybody talked about it all the time. But Alma told me there had been a big fight in Russia, and the czar, who they always talked about, had been chased away and there was a new government that was going to be for the people, just like in America. I wondered if that meant that black people over there would get more rights, or would end up just the same as they were during slavery, like some people said would happen here, but she told me there were no black people in Russia; the slaves there were as white as the rulers. It didn't make sense to me, but I was still reading pretty slowly, and then mostly the weekly *Variety* that all the actors read like the Bible. In the strike, they were all tearing pages out, because the paper had pages that were for the White Rats, and pages that were against, so you didn't know where anything stood. But there was not much news in *Variety* about general events outside theaters, moving picture houses, burlesque, cabaret, and circuses. Some weeks later, Gramby showed me the only news that ever appeared in *Variety* about the February Revolution in Russia. It was a few lines about an Irish comic, Tim O'Donnell, who was asked what he thought about the changes in Russia and he said: "It's impressive—what the Irish have been fighting for for hundreds of years and haven't got, the Jews got overnight." But I didn't understand that gag either. I asked Gramby about it and he said: "It's just blarney. We got nothing yet. The war is still going on. The cards are not with us."

Everybody was nervous, I could see, because one thing outside showbiz that *Variety* did write about was America entering the war. Some Americans were already fighting over there: Buffalo Bill Cody's son, Frank Cody, was killed flying an airplane for the Royal Flying Corps, shot down by four German planes over France. And in March Gramby and all the other Russian-origin actors were buzzing about a report that the English government was going to declare that all the Russians living in England would have to join the English army or be sent back to Russia, where they would be drafted as well. If America entered the war, the English actors in America might face the same kind of draft. Then in April we finally got the news: America had declared war on Germany.

The next day all the cafés and the cabarets and theaters were decked out in the stars and stripes, and all the shows started adding songs that must have been written and printed practically overnight, songs like "Root for Uncle Sam" and "Let's All

Be Americans Now" and "America, Here's My Boy!" George M. Cohan weighed in with "Yankee Doodle Boy" and "You're a Grand Old Flag" and "Over There!" "Right off the griddle," the *Variety* ad boasted. "New war songs full of pep!" Pretty soon parades full of white folk marched down the streets with pipes and drums, and motor cars rushed around filled with young men who were going off to enlist. Our people were slower to put their black hides out to be shredded for the war of whites against whites over in Europe, but the flags went up in our neighbourhoods too, and young black men were saying that if we want to be seen as Americans we needed to put our lives on the line. The managers of the cabaret slung a huge red-and-white banner across the dance hall with "SUPPORT THE PRESIDENT! WE'RE ALL ROOTING FOR UNCLE SAM!" and there was a cardboard cutout of a black Uncle Sam holding a musket at the side of the stage.

The owner of the cabaret, a plush white man called Jones who lived in a nice mansion on the north side, hired one of the best shouters in the business, Estrella Harris, to belt out the Uncle Sam song. She was so powerful her voice could reach to the White House. I can still remember the words:

"Come on Chicago boys and girls,
It's time to show your nerve
It's time to give the enemy the licking they deserve!
Although at peace they sunk our ships,
As friends could never do,
They've turned their guns upon our flag,
I won't stand that, will you?"

I told Gramby I wanted to enlist, though I was only sixteen, and it was the first time he got really angry at me. He said, "Anybody who wants to join in an army is a complete schlemiel." Alma also told me not to be stupid, so I thought I'd done my duty by asking and went on tooting the horn. Red was of age, but he was less dumb than me, and just winked at me, starting to play some new notes that gave little hints of "The Star Spangled Banner" among his usual melancholy wails. The manager noticed it and told him to cut it out, but he just made the hints that bit softer, though they were always there.

People still needed to be entertained, though they had no real idea of what the boys were going to face out there. Because of Gramby's stories I had no way of knowing if France was close or far from Russia, or part of it. We saw a picture called *Darkest Russia*, in which a Jewish violin student is in love with the son of a high czarist official whose daughter is in love with a revolutionary. The violin girl gets whipped because she won't play "God Save the Czar" at a reception, and the young people all end up in Siberia. I asked Gramby if this is what it was like and he just said, "What is real and what is not real? It's all smoke and ashes." Alma cried all the way through.

In all the war panic, the White Rats had to call off their strike and their union went bankrupt. Everybody could now join up with the vaudeville managers' union without feeling bad, but Shimmel Krauss and his band never rejoined. They went off to play small time on the weakest burlesque wheels and dropped out of sight, playing town halls and saloons in the West, which was still not that different from the old days that were seen in the Westerns, the very early ones, with people like W.S. Hart, who were real cowboys with bandy legs that showed they'd grown up on a horse, and made movies like *Knights of the Trail* and *Hell's Hinges*. You could play venues out in Colorado and Texas and New Mexico, where they would shoot at a car that backfired and had tumbleweeds for an audience, and anybody over thirty years old still remembered the Wild Bunch and Butch Cassidy shooting up the town hall. That was the last stand of the Naaveltie Minstrels, though that tale was never told. Or maybe they played in Apache reservations, there were stories about that too.

Back in Chicago, there were a couple of reunions: Mae West, the little girl with the big breasts, stuck around at the Elite clubs, hiding out in the same way as Gramby from the Rats-and-managers bust-up. Red went out with her once or twice, and I asked him what was the big deal, and why she was always mobbed by admirers. She seemed to be nothing special. "The moves," he winked at me, "oh those moves..." It seemed that she could use the muscles inside her female parts to draw your cock in. I had no idea that women could do that, but I had to take it on trust at that time. I was still pretty raw. I was more excited by our discovery of where the Marx Brothers, my old blackface buddies of California, had got to, because they had pretty much vanished all the way through the run-up to war. It turned out they were near Chicago all the time, but their mother, Minnie, had got a terrible fright that, as the sons of a German family, they would be interned or called up to fight their own people in Europe, so she had pulled them out of the vaudeville game and made them into farmers, who were exempt from the army in order to grow food. She had bought them a plot of land in La Grange, southwest of the city, where they'd got themselves a stack of chickens. We drove out there one free Sunday in a car, Gramby, Alma, and me, with Red driving, since he had the kind of friends that came with Mae West, the mob that ran the South Side. We found Leonard and Milton and the kid brother, Herman—who would become Zeppo—mooching about the coops with big straw hats, looking like hillbillies, while Julius and Arthur (Groucho and Harpo) lolled about the farmhouse, even though it was noontime. Leonard (Chico) was all in his mock-Italian character:

"Great job, eh boss? Fresh air, plenty o' corn. The chickens do their stuff when they a-want." Later they told people the whole thing folded because they had bought roosters, who couldn't lay eggs, but that was a lie, because we saw plenty of eggs there, the boys were simply bored and wanted back on the stage. After the summer, most of the men who were drafted were sent off, and the brothers could sneak back into vaudeville.

A couple of times I found Gramby in the dressing room, reading a letter from his brother, and I asked him what was new in Los Angeles and what new picture "Bill Gore" was working on now. He said they were making another big war epic, like Joan of Arc, but about the Aztecs in Mexico, with the opera singer again.

At least she was getting a pretty good rest for her voice. I didn't know anything about the Aztecs, but I saw the movie later, and it was full of women and men dressed only in long feathers, making human sacrifices until they were conquered by the Spaniards, who killed everybody except the heroine, who escaped with her Spanish lover. It was very weird. But most of the letter, Gramby said, was about Bill trying to find out what had happened to their family in Russia, after the revolution. One of the actors in the Aztec movie was a Russian dancer who had contacts in Moscow, but that was very far from the village where Gramby and Bill had come from. They had both hoped the revolution meant that the Russians would pull out of the Great War, but they went on fighting, and it seemed that the war had got close to their village, because the Austrians had taken over Romania, which was just next door.

I wished I knew more about this, but then I wished I didn't, because there was nothing on Earth or in heaven that I could do about it all; all I could do was go on learning how to make the cornet do exactly what I wanted it to do, and work out my own songs. I could see that all these troubles brought Gramby and Alma closer, and suddenly one day in June Alma told me that they were going to get married.

I was surprised, because I knew she was sweet on him, but he didn't seem to me the marrying kind. Vaudeville folk used to double up without needing to tie the knot; the life was hard enough without starting families and dragging kids around, which seemed the only reason for a visit to the church, or justice of the peace. In any case he was Jew and she was Christian, and that could cause complications, as even I had figured out, who knew nothing about religion except the singing and dancing that my aunt had dragged me to at Mount Zion Tabernacle up in Harlem when I was a kid. But Gramby's god was the cards, so maybe it was the cards that told him, once again, that this was what he should do.

At least part of the story, as it turned out, was that Alma, who everybody thought was Dutch, was actually German, and there was this story in *Variety* that the government was going to intern all the German- and Austrian-origin people at a camp up near Lake Erie. Actors were a special target because they traveled all over the country and could make perfect enemy spies. Although Gramby was a Russian himself, not an American citizen, they figured marriage would make them both safer, him from being drafted as an English-man and her from being listed a spy.

They were planning a private ceremony at the Masonic lodge on Adams. Lots of actors, I knew for a long time, were members of the Fraternity, which was a home from home for those folks who wanted to be in on good deeds but didn't want God interfering with their private moments. I never attended, but Red, who poked around everywhere and knew the negro lodges, told me they had all sorts of strange ceremonies, like rolling cannonballs along the floor, sticking hoods and shackles on new members, rolling up their pants legs, writing in secret letters, and invoking all sorts of grand masters from the past: Egyptian pharaohs, Arab caliphs, Hindus, Buddhists and even more ancient beings who were half men and half animals. Practically all the magicians were members. I think it was a safe place where they could talk shop and exchange secrets, or plant fake rumors with each other to confuse the competition, or just feel the spirits of the old great magicians that surrounded them everywhere.

Gramby was planning a whole new act, which he would unveil as soon as possible after the marriage, if he could get "the fix." Now that Alma was in his mind as well as his bed, I was less involved with them, especially as he knew that I was set on carrying on with the music. I had ideas of my own of how I wanted to make my life, and where I wanted to go. I knew things, I had friends, I had a reason for getting up in the morning and working on my own thoughts, my own dreams. We were drifting apart. Alma talked to me. She said he was working on something spectacular that had never been done before. He called it "Lazarus—Return from the Grave." The curtain would open, and there would be no magician on the stage, only a backdrop of night, and an open tent, like in biblical times. A small boy, like the one I was when I first went with the act, either negro, white, or Chinese, it didn't matter, would be sitting crosslegged, playing a flute. There would be a scent in the air, something oriental, jasmine or the hint of the Bible story of frankincense and myrrh. But there was no one else there, no one to be born, no one to perform. Then, from the back of the theater, the doors would be thrown open, and four stooges would come down the aisle carrying a big wooden coffin. They would bring it up on the stage and prop it up, and then open the lid, and there would be Gramby, totally still. They would call into the audience for a doctor, and they would choose only somebody who was with friends, or family, who would swear that he was the real thing, not a plant. He would come up with his instruments, or they would give him some, which he could check, and he would examine the man in the coffin and pronounce him absolutely dead. If nobody from the audience rose up to object that this was an old trick, there would be a plant at that point, and the doctor and his wife or friends would call up his bona fides. They would lay out the dead corpse on the carpet in the center of the tent, then the doctor would be asked to stand by so he could bear witness for any more trickery. There was always going to be a doctor in the house, and if not, somebody would be sent out for a real one as close as possible, while other members of the audience were asked up to poke the body, or put a mirror by his mouth to check for breath. Meanwhile some dames would come in from the sides and sing some oriental dirges, something Turkish or even more exotic, like Albanian. When the doctor had pronounced and drawn back, the lights would change and the dead magician would begin to rise, with the carpet, up towards the flies. The doctor or audience members would be called again to pass under the carpet and feel above it for wires. Then the corpse would go up until it had disappeared above.

Alma would come in then, with the stooges and the magic cabinet. They would open the cabinet and show there was nothing there. Then she would begin to chant the magic incantations. *Oolah loolah aktashbaktash om mani shatas bastas*, all that kind of jazz. Then the magic cabinet would open, but some animal—a dog or pig or something else—would come out. Then, as everybody would be laughing and paying attention to the pig, the carpet would descend slowly from the flies, wreathed in clouds of smoke. It would stop half way down and Alma would fly up suddenly, take the magician's face in her hands, and give him the kiss of life. The carpet with the magician would then descend to the floor and the magician would stand up.

I had no idea how Gramby intended to do this trick, if it worked with substitution, or with "Hindu" methods of trance, which were known then and worked in the theosophical circles, like Madame Blavatsky and other occult mediums, or whether he had finally made contact with Milos Vas in Mexico, if he had ever gone there, for some special machinery that I assumed he would be using. Since it was not pulled off using the magic cabinet, it was like nothing he had tried before. He was going to trump Houdini, Hermann or the Great Lafayette. The trick would be performed once, on the opening night of Gramby's new tour at the Orpheum, as a safely paid-up member of the National Vaudeville Association, and the morning after he would marry Alma. Then they would go on tour again, playing the circuits, opening each week with the Lazarus trick. So Gramby would be reborn, again and again, in city after city, from Chicago to Des Moines, from Cheyenne to Reno, in Albuquerque, Phoenix, Fort Worth, Tulsa, Memphis, Atlanta and back up the road to the big cities, St. Louis, Indianapolis, Columbus, Cleveland, Pittsburgh, Baltimore and all the way back up to New York City. And when the war would end, he would do the Lazarus act one more time. Then he would stop and never have to resurrect anymore.

But the fix never came through while we were all in Chicago, and I never saw Gramby's reopening at the Orpheum with the old act. Red fell ill the night of Gramby's opening, and I had to take his place at the club, which got me noticed by the same label that was recording the Original Dixieland Band.

I saw them married, in a big hall full of strange symbols and plaques. The Compass, the Plumb, Square and Level, and the Book. The great eye in the pyramid and a floor of chessboard squares, black and white. Big framed portraits of men in old costumes wearing long white wigs, standing or sitting, with all sorts of building implements all around them, and one with an open tomb. In the middle of the floor was a blue canopy that was held up by four people I recognized as the four members of Shimmel Krauss's minstrels who had stayed behind. I was surprised that Gramby was dressed in a simple black suit that looked like it was spare from the wardrobe and Alma wore a long, chaste blue dress. She looked really nice, with a red rose in her hair. It looked like a wheat field in bloom. A man with a mask and a Turkish style of hat read some brief words about the Craft and the Fellowship, and then another man with a beard and a Hebrew skullcap said some more words and put a glass under the groom's foot, that Gramby smashed with an unusually violent stomp. Then the fake minstrels all shouted "Mazel tov, mazel tov," and clapped the groom on the back. I had brought a bag of Aunt Jemima's rice with me but there didn't seem to be any call to use it.

Right at the end of the ceremony, just as we were getting ready to leave and I was fingering my rice again, a man in a flashy suit I recognized as Bill Gore came running in, taking his hat off as he entered the hall. Looking a little flustered, he rushed up to Gramby, arms flung wide, before clasping his brother's shoulders.

"Hey, Yakov, I'm so sorry. Did you get my telegram? The train was late. I had to change at Des Moines. You dumb kid, you should have told me earlier." He leaned forward to kiss the bride. "At least you have a chuppah. We'll need a little footage for the folks. I arranged something with Essanay. I've got a car outside."

They rushed out, too quick for me to haul out the rice. There was a pretty plush rented car outside, I think it was a Locomobile, a six-seater, with a tall black driver who had the look of an Ethiopian king. At the door, Gramby gave me a handshake, along with a sigh that stood in for all that we passed through, all the things that were done, or not done, said or not said. And I got to kiss the bride, despite the frozen look of some passersby, but with a wink from the driver. Then Boris grabbed Gramby again.

"I almost forgot. I have a wedding present." He unclipped his bag and brought out an envelope. It was pretty crumpled, and covered with foreign stamps.

"It's from home," he said. "Sarah wrote it. Our sister," he said to Alma, now that she was part of the tribe. "*A brief*," he added, in their own language, fondling his brother's arm and drawing him near, as all of Chicago passed by, hooting and hustling. "*A schoene brievaleh, mein kind, fun der heim...*"

"Masters of Our Own Fate"

Sarah:

(first page of letter missing)

...about twenty days before Passover, we saw Mendel Clubfoot running down the street towards our house, shouting "Revolutsiya! Revolutsiya!" Mother was worried, because there had been rumors for days that there were meetings and disturbances in Kishinev, and any time there were disturbances there would be talk about a new pogrom, because changes always brought trouble. But he passed the house, and we thought it was just his usual madness, or his foot throbbing again. Then Shabssel Lev, the new blacksmith's boy, came running up flashing a newspaper and Zev let him in at the door. It was the latest copy of the Beletski Listok, the Belzi paper, and the news in a huge headline, saying: "PROVISIONAL GOVERNMENT IN ST. PETERSBURG—CZAR ABDICATES." My mother didn't understand the word, but Zev explained to her: "It means there is no czar." Father heard all the shouting and came down the stairs, with his prayer shawl, ready for *minheh*, and some of the other men came in from the general store and the cobbler's, crowding around, gabbling like geese. Soon afterward, a crowd of young men, and some girls as well, in school student uniform came rushing down the street and passed our house, in the direction of the *"strazhnik's"* office, which is now, or was until that day, on the outskirts of the town, near the river bridge, as close as possible to the Moldavian village. Father looked at them and said, "These people are out for trouble," but he was torn between following them to prevent a disturbance and his need to pray at the bet midrash in the other direction. Deciding that they were just letting off steam, he went off to the synagogue. But soon after, shouts and yelling came from the policeman's house, and I went out with Zev to see what was happening. A group of older people had joined the crowd around the house, and at the door, the young men had dragged out the *strazhnik*, Captain Struch, and were holding him by the arms. His hat had been snatched off and was being passed among the boys excitedly. The blacksmith's boy, Shabsel, stepped up and tore the officer's epaulets off his coat, and half the coat came with them, so he stood there with his moustache shaking and his sleeves half torn off. Behind the crowd, a group of men on horseback were crossing over the bridge. They came from the direction of the Christian church but they were wearing red armbands, and made no move to rescue the *strazhnik* or impede the Jewish boys. Mother went up straight to the boys and called them to stop, so they sheepishly let go of the policeman and Mother took him by the arm and marched him back to our house, where she made him a hot tea and brought down one of father's old suits to replace his torn uniform, and fed him some black bread with freshly churned butter, with some pastry she had made to use up the *chametz*.

That was the only violent act of the revolution in our village. The small military outpost on the other side of the church was abandoned when its three soldiers ran away, and the customs officer had packed his bags and left in a cart the previous night. The whole town was soon filled with cries of celebration as the youths paraded down the main street with their red armbands painted with the words "Revolutsoniayh Militsia" and banners scrawled with the slogans "Peace! Freedom! Democracy!" and so forth, in both Russian and Yiddish, and there was also a big Hebrew slogan with the words "For Zion We Shall Advance!" Father, watching it all from the front of the house after he returned from the prayer, shook his head and marveled, "I never knew we had so many parties in such a small village! We have become Belgium in less than one hour!"

By the evening, it seemed that we had a new "Committee for the Election of a New Duma," and Yankel Vinshell, the town treasurer who keeps all our accounts, became the "Acting Chairman of the Revolutionary Plenum." By the morning, we also had a working committee—"*ispolnitelni commitet*"—in charge of the self defense of the community, to try and rein in the "*militsia*," which was also headed by the same Yankel. This was only in the Jewish village; the Christian village had its own committee, with the priest, Father Ignat, and the carriage-maker, Andreii, at its head. We could sense that the Moldavians were getting excited at the hope of the province breaking from Russia, but it was too early to tell.

In the afternoon, the young men marched again down the main street, with a new slogan: "WE ARE MASTERS OF OUR OWN FATE!" Father and the other elders huddled in the bet midrash, trying to work out what all this excitement meant and how things were going to change, if they were going to change at all. For those with long memories, the main worry was what would happen in the East, in the Ukraine, from which Father and Mother had come after the great pogroms that took place there before we were all born. Then of course everybody remembered 1905, when the "first" revolution seemed to be happening. But of course you know all about that.

You may be surprised to find your older sister talking about all these matters supposedly reserved to the affairs of men, but so much has happened with myself too; even little Judit is becoming knowledgeable about the things that happen outside the borders of our own small world. Since my own changed circumstances I have worked a great deal with the primary school and the little ones, teaching them general knowledge, while the men took care of their spiritual and ritual needs. So I have had to learn about these secular affairs: history, geography, geometry, sums, some elementary science, and all this has expanded my world. You remember that while you and Yakov were still here, there was some activity of the Zionist movements in Bessarabia and in Odessa and these have increased, so that now we have a party branch of the Socialist Democratic Workers Party of Zion in our town, as well as the Social Democrats that you remember from your own time, the Bund. We are still a small town, but now we have as many opinions as we have inhabitants.

But you want me to get to the main reason of this letter, which we are all hoping will reach you despite the confusion and the war that still seems to be raging in the north, though it has not yet touched us here. We had our Passover, with a mixture of hope and fear that was heightened by all the uncertainty. As we have done for the last few years, we left three chairs vacant, for our three missing Eliahus—yourself, Yakov and Kolya, whom we all felt was closer to us on that evening than any other. Zev sat by Father at the top of the table, feeling the weight of his responsibility as the only son in the house, although we had the Yosefson and Birenboim families with us this year for the celebration, so there were both men and boys around. Father reclined on his huge pile of cushions, as he always did, looking more and more like a Turkish pasha, with the big black cap that we always joked we could use to cover leaks in the roof.

We sang out the old verses with a new kind of confidence, because even Father began to believe that perhaps there were footsteps of the Messiah sounding from the marches of the young people and the news that poured in from the north, how the czar had abdicated for the Archduke Michael but he had refused, accepting that Russia had chosen a republic and that the long night of the czars had ended. Everyone reported that jubilation had spread even in the remote parts of the Empire when the news reached the towns and the peasants alike. So we sang out our praises to the Name who took us out of Egypt with a strong hand and an outstretched arm, and gave a greater voice to the call of "This year we are here, the next year in the Land of Israel! This year slaves, the next year, free!" There was added vigor to the roll call of miracles that brought down Pharaoh, and Father dipped his finger in the wine and splattered the table as if the blood of the czars was spurting out.

Then, to cut a long story short, because this letter must be completed by the morning, and the lamp is beginning to burn low, it was a bright sunny morning, on the 24th of April, in Sivan, ten days after the end of Passover, when the blacksmith's other boy, Gershon, came pounding at the door, when we were all at breakfast, after *shahris*, and was so excited that he couldn't speak till Mother gave him a seeded bun. He said that there was a soldier, coming down the road from Floresti, with a small rucksack and a ragged uniform, who had called him up from the field where he was playing with the other children to ask him if the Gurevits family was still in the village. When Gershon said they were, the soldier told him to run ahead and say that Nathan was coming.

We were struck still, like one of those old paintings of a family at table that I saw once at the Kishinev museum. Then Zev rushed forward and caught the boy's hand and dragged him back out the door, and said: "Show me!" And he waved Mother and me away and ran off up the road. Father sat, continuing to eat his kasha, but I could feel his heart pounding, though he just waved us down and said, "Are we Jews or are we animals?" Motioning us back to unfinished plates. But Mother gave him the wave you must remember and we all went out after Zev, Mother, Judit, and me, walking briskly up the road. After about fifteen minutes we could see them, two dots in the landscape, coming nearer, so we waved, and soon we got a wave back, and then all of us were running.

Well, you remember Kolya. He was never the most outgoing boy. Yakov dreamed, and you were the doer, and Kolya kept to his books. He became a serious scholar after you left, though he and Zev seemed to have between them always some kind of conspiracy, whispering together, making plans, that made Father ever more suspicious, till Mother told him "You can't tether up your sons like goats and expect them to stand around bleating." Mother always spoke with silences, a glance here, a glance there, bustling about, doing everything, always in the present, so as not to tempt the future. But the future always comes. As I wrote at the beginning of this letter, the last time we received news from you—through the Joint, Moishe Glick the American—we had the first confirmation that you had got our news about Kolya, and how he was drafted when the war started, more than three years ago. But we don't know if you had the details, because all the ordinary postage had stopped, as I am sure it did everywhere. It was the most dreadful moment, because the army came upon us suddenly, in a special troop train from Kishinev, with armed guards and a whole division of recruiters with draft forms and lists of names. Nobody was really prepared, because we had been hearing for months how this and that was going on in Austria, and in Serbia, and Sarajevo. But what had that to do with Bessarabia, our sleepy Moldavian fields? Mothers began shepherding all their sons who were over sixteen years old, or were younger but didn't look young enough, out into the fields, into attics, or the cellars of the storehouses and even cubbyholes in the bet midrash. We were helped by the fact that the officers' lists were very partial and many names were misspelled, but it seemed they had a quota from each village and town. We were fortunate that Zev, who was 22 then, was away to the yeshiva at Belzi, where there were many more hiding places, and the rabbi squirreled him away into a back room. But Kolya, 18 years old, was too stubborn. "I will not hide." He went into the bet midrash and sat down, over a volume of the tract "Avot," hiding himself in the text. But the soldiers came in and took him aside. The only name they had from our family was yourself, Boris, also listed as "Berel." So Kolya told them he was you. They pulled him out to the military doctor who asked him to lift his arms and cough, and then nodded to the soldiers. So that was how Kolya was taken to fight for the czar in Poland.

Zev came home a few days later, after we were clear that the troop train had departed, taking several hundred terrified Jews and Moldavians away, no one knew till when. Everybody thought there would be some battles to sate the mad ambitions of the emperors and then they would make peace, since they were all related to each other in any case. But you know it has not turned out that way.

All the village came around to greet Kolya, once he had told Mother that we had nothing to fear from the army. We had all been told that the army was still fighting but that was a fantasy in the minds of the new government in Saint Petersburg, which was not in control of the events. They thought they were running the revolution, but the revolution was in the people's hands and not theirs. On all the fronts the soldiers were deserting, throwing their arms away and going home. Now that winter had lifted they were choking all the roads and alleyways away from Germany and Austria, swarming over the fields and crossing the mountains. Kolya was not, however, coming home for long. He was, he told us quickly, a "commissar" in the Bolshevist wing of the Social Democratic Party, and his work was to go back towards the front to spread the revolution among the troops. He had special leave for three weeks, and had already spent ten days coming over from Galicia, in the Przemysl area.

He looked very different, as if the old Kolya who had sat smoldering over his books and ideas had suddenly exploded into an intense young man with glaring eyes that had seen things we did not want to think about. He spoke in quick dramatic bursts, as if he was still addressing a crowd of soldiers who had to hear him through the roar of the battlefield and over their own officers' futile orders. Mother went into the kitchen and began making a tshulent, in the cunning calculation that the smell of the cooking would keep him at home at least for the hours till the pot was ready. Judit clung to him and I tried to measure the distance between the little brother I knew and the bursting man of action who strode through the door. All the children and most of the lads in the town came calling, the "marching masses" with their red armbands and banners. Everybody wanted to know the news from the center. The word "soviets" was on everyone's lips. For a while it seemed some of them thought that Kolya had come to organize them to replace the first "revolutionary committee," run by the same people who had run things before, but then they understood he was not going to stay.

As the afternoon approached, Father took Kolya aside and they went upstairs to the study. They must have done their own *minheh* there together because Father did not go to the synagogue for the prayer, but came down with a satisfied look, although Kolya came down in his soldier's tunic, without the trace of tallit or tefillin. They were up in the room for an hour, so they must have had a long talk. Kolya then took Zev and me aside and said he wanted us to write a letter to you and Yakov, which he could arrange to have sent from the city. He said, "Sarushka, the war is continuing and because of this the revolution will continue as well. This Winter Palace government will not last for very long. The Kadets cannot make Russia into a state like England or France. I will send you some books by Lenin that explain the way the world works. Imperialism has to continue the war. But Russia cannot go on bleeding for those bloodsuckers. Land, bread, peace, we must have all three. The real revolution is coming. Write to Berl and tell him that the hour he dreamed of in Odessa is almost here. The entire world will shake. I can get the letter sent on from Kiev to Moscow and then by rail and ship to Denmark or Sweden. From there it can reach America in less than two weeks. Tell him what happened here."

"The last word we heard," I told him, "from the American, is that Yakov is a magician in New York. He travels around America making people appear and disappear from his magic cabinet."

"There is no magic cabinet," he said, very seriously. "There is only the will and need of the people, and the party that understands the foundations. You too, Sarushka, can play a part. Women are equal to men. But don't say that to Father. He is locked in the past. You two must help him and Mother to overcome. Be very careful. Stay strong and wait for the storm."

I am giving you his exact words because I want you to understand his passion. So different from our childhood games. He spoke to me because it was clear that Zev was not very convinced by his words. He does not speak to me much about it, but when I sat down to write this letter he joined me at the table for a while and shook his head. He said: "This will only lead to more blood. The Bolsheviks can light all the fires they want but they won't be able to put them out. Kolya is like a man struck by lightning. His hair stands up and all his skin is electric. Tell Berl and Yakov to stay in America."

I can hear our family around us. Father's constant snores, the soft sound of Mother like the whistle of an old and large kettle. Judit, like the purring of a satisfied cat. And the unfamiliar snore of Kolya, cutting short in sudden abrupt snorts, a soldier's sleep, I imagined, never constant, always alert to waking danger. Zev brings with him feelings of dissatisfaction that have caused a rift with Father, who understands that sons go their own way but whose attitude to change is like a rock that stands in the ocean and is lashed by the waves. He knows the waves will always break on his shore, but the science of geology teaches us that mountains and rocks are worn down over time, and deep fissures form or break them down altogether, and even the continents shift. I will confess to you, my dear Berl, my dearest Yakov, that the ground shifts beneath my feet as well. I know everyone sees me as Sarah, the wife of the patriarch, made to endure and continue the dynasty. But I will tell you that this is not my fate. Not here, not in this village. When one's mind opens up, the world becomes so much wider. I know Zev also plans to travel. He has been talking for years, from the time he took up his quiet work in the Bet Midrash library, out of harm's way, the scholar's life that Father dreamed might take him too to the rabbi's chair, talking to Leizer Fish, the son of Kotik the merchant, about trading companies that might be set up as soon as the war is exhausted. They do not want to be minnows in a small pond, they want to be whales that coast around the world.

Father's tragedy, I fear, is that he knows about all of this. Nothing in the house, in the village, in the province, escapes his eye and ear. But he remembers that he was cast out of his own father's home by the hatred and fear of the goyim, which is whipped up whenever rebellion and uncertainty break out. All this pain lives in Mother's eyes when she looks at him, knowing that the only answer he has to offer is in the great shelf of books, and the Truth that emanates from the Torah. There is no other Truth. But we know that change is always coming, that empires have risen and fallen, that Ahasuerus has been defeated but rises again, that people quake both with fear and with courage. I wonder if, when you two went off to the west, towards the great city of the New, with its promise of life and prosperity and escape from poverty and constriction, if you thought about the other destination that our people are talking about, even in the compelling storm of the immediate uprising, to the Old, to the east, to Eretz Yisroel, to Zion, to a life that is our own, not of others. The destination that Father prays to every day, morning, afternoon, and evening, the Passover words, Next Year in Jerusalem the Rebuilt. Is it another phantom? Another magic trick to conjure out of Yakov's box? How I would love to see his performance! Do you remember when he used to collect shoeboxes, and make little puppet figures out of straw and wood, and pretend they were the Baba Yaga and Maimon the Demon, and make spells over all the people that he didn't like in the village, till Father took his little toys and burned them in the yard, and muttered his own personal prayer, which he didn't want any of us to hear, and Yakov was so proud, because he'd made Father enter into his own world? Perhaps it is not surprising how we each turn out, as if, when we were asleep as babies, the angels did come and put their stamp upon us, so that we would know, inside, who we were, and who we were going to be, and each one of these prayers was a magic charm and a map that drew our predestined futures? I know, it is not a very Marxist idea.

So. The dawn is breaking, and I must get this letter ready for Kolya to take, in the hope that his map will indeed carry it across the seas to my two brothers, whom I love beyond all comprehension. And that some word will come back, on the wings of eagles, somehow, before we are all scattered to the separate fates the new, scientific theories and creeds determine, or leave to our individual wills. If it is true, that we are "masters of our own fate," how shall we carve our own little figures of the future that we evolve from our intellect, our knowledge and our own dreams?

You remember that moment, when the first crack of sunlight enters through the knothole in the panel just beside the cupboard where Mother still keeps all her kitchen things, the spoons, the bowls, the pots, the chopping boards, the jars of herbs and stuff? It shoots through like a message from the Light, that something new is born. Excuse the flowery language, I don't know how to express something that moves me beyond the bounds of ordinary affection, to thoughts I know I was not supposed, by my patrimony, to expect or nurture.

I feel a great hope, and perhaps this too, will travel.

Nu, that's it. With the Name's help.

Your loving sister,

Sarah.

Asher, April 1992

It was difficult not to well up a little over the old letter, its fragile original pages nested in separate transparent envelopes, the translation marked briefly as "Courtesy Paramount Art Department." The blue envelope containing the letter and its translation forming the only item in a file marked "William Gore, Correspondence," accompanying the "Cinematographer's script" of the 1917 film *The Woman God Forgot*. The twenty-seventh film directed by DeMille, and his sixteenth collaboration with my uncle. Why was it there? Why was it kept without any other correspondence? Where were the other letters sent by Aunt Sarah to Boris? They were not at Beit Berl, the center named after the old Zionist socialist pioneer Berl Katznelson, where my mother had trekked out in dutiful research after my puzzled phone call from Provo. There dwelt the archive of the old Labor Party, Mapai, which had governed the State of Israel from its inception to the sudden shock of its eviction from power by Menachem Begin's Likud ("unity") party in 1977. An event that prompted one of Kolya's rare interludes away from Michigan academia to visit the Jewish state, with a quick appearance at Melchett

272

Street before striding round the corner to the Likud headquarters to be briefed about the new nationalist ascendancy and its plans to undo the Labor decades.

My mother searched the catalogs and spoke to the archivists and they brought out their file on Sarah Gorovitz, which was the spelling she used when first arriving at the port of Jaffa in the autumn of 1919. There was a sheaf of newspaper cuttings and some printed essays, position papers, pamphlets, booklets edited by, and participation in various later seminars of the early history of the socialist Zionist movement and its constituent parties, the Fourth Aliyah, pioneers of the kibbutz movement, and all the names that had floated past my head in early "homeland" lessons: Katznelson, Tabenkin, Myerson, Green, all whirling briefly before escaping to oblivion. Childhood memories of the imposing aunt who would sweep in, climbing up the stairs with the steady clank of an armored truck, the loud knock as if assuming that everyone within was deaf, the obligatory bussing, even though she seemed even in primary school years to be a strange monument off a party poster, or a stamp, preserving in the crags of her face and the hair that stubbornly sprouted from one corner of her chin some ancient monuments and memorials of those whom custom told us came and suffered so that we might frolic on the beach and munch falafel carefree on the corner of Sheinkin and Allenby.

No early letters. No private correspondence beyond the public record, which was the essential cadence of the founding pioneers, whose words were written in their deeds and whose privacy was burnt in sacrifice on the altar of the Hebrew renewal. Those stories were so often told in our own family circle that one soon forgot them, like constant background noise that is screened out, wiped clean by the whirring mind, ever alert for new experience. So one knew that Kolya had once been a communist before seeing the light and being born anew as a Hebrew zealot, that my father had been a young rebel who tore away from the religious life, that Uncle Zev and Aunt Judit had both disappeared in China well before I was born, that the magician, Vassily, Yakov, was a figure of mysterious legend last seen in Paris in the thirties, just before the Second World War and the Holocaust, which he had perhaps foreseen in one of his magical dreams, and that Aunt Sarah had carved her name as a pioneer of one of the early Ascensions, having arrived in Palestine from the village around 1920, soon after the establishment of the British Mandate, that she had worked as an ordinary laborer on the roads and risen to be a prominent organizer, trade unionist, and founder member of the union of labor movements that formed the main labor party, Mapai. That later she briefly worked with Prime Minister Golda Meir (then Myerson) in the kibbutz of Merhavia, that she campaigned for workers' and women's rights throughout the 1920s and '30s, that she had been a follower of the Socialist Zionist program of Dov Ber Borochov and had later split from the main Mapai Party to join the Marxist-Zionist Mapam in the late 1940s, just before the founding of the state. We knew that she had married one Zachariah Sasson, an Iraqi immigrant, in 1924 and had three children by him: Eli, Tsadok, and Rivka, the sons becoming bywords for boredom and conformity. Eli, the premature accident fatality, Tsadok, the business mini-mogul, and the daughter, the youngest, Rivkie, the pearl of good humor and artistic talent—dancing, jumping, play writing, stage directing—as if she sprung from a quite different family. I had a real crush on her when I was ten years old, and she must have been in her mid-thirties, with a big bust and an enormous mane of brown hair. Aunt Sarah's early marriage in the village was a vague scar left by the most ancient troubles, a teenage marriage to the other rabbi's son, Moshe Zonenson, whose lungs caved in on him, leaving her with her first child, Yitzhak, who died of illness before he was three years old, and that despite her father's desires, she refused to remarry and became a schoolteacher, before her departure to the Promised Land...

The family diverged along the inevitable fault lines of their individual fates, and though my father tried to keep up with them when he arrived as a late comer to Tel Aviv in 1952, parting my mother rather reluctantly from her life of art and the big city, he made at best perfunctory advances to Sarah's family, attending the wedding of Eliyahu's eldest son, Kobi, who was a major in the army Ordnance Corps, or an occasional birthday, or the launch of Tsadok's new bulldozer company, which I came to loathe as a primary contractor to building and demolition works in the occupied territories after 1967, and merged with the American Caterpillar company to make him a frequent flyer to all corners of the globe; he went to China while Mao Tse Tung was still alive, and according to the family lore inquired after the whereabouts of our vanished uncle and aunt but only received polite "ahs" and "ohs." He kept saying, "I am going to find Judit. I know she is alive. Blood is always blood." He knew many things, most of which were complete nonsense, like the true links between the Muslim Brotherhood and the Communist Party, the spies planted by North Korea in the Cultural Department of the Tel Aviv municipality, the fact that Einstein had destroyed evidence about the actual existence of God, the existence of a remnant of the Lost Ten Tribes in a series of caves in Mongolia that reached deep towards the center of the earth, bones of whom had been unearthed by a Caterpillar digging at a gold mine near the Russian border, and the fact that all Jews were endowed with a special "righteousness" gene that would soon be identified by science.

Rivkie was in the very opposite mode—a person so authentically open to the world that she was always bursting with discoveries. When my father bought me the 8-millimeter camera she was always around with advice about movies she had just seen and offers of actors who could play minor or major parts, subject to availability. But I was too shy to risk looking like a complete idiot with my two left feet, my amateur antics and my imitations of the little I'd seen myself. She would come in and say that she had seen a new film by a man called Jan-Luke Godard, which was just about an ordinary young guy and a girl selling newspapers in Paris, or a film called Le Bow Serge by somebody called Shablul, or something, and telling me that I had to go to the cinema club at the university that was showing another film by a young filmmaker called

True-foe, called *The 400 Blows*. But I didn't go to see those films, because I wanted to see thrillers and Westerns, like John Wayne in *Rio Bravo* and *The Man Who Shot Liberty Valance*, which held me tight in my chair though the riff-raff around me were booing the screen and cursing the projectionist because, despite being billed as a brand-new film, it was in black and white. The thrillers were in black and white anyway, so I could enjoy Bogey in *The Maltese Falcon* or *Murder Inc.* Or *Beat the Devil*, with its conglomeration of freakish villains, whose names I didn't take in at the time: Robert Morley, Peter Lorre, and some strange Italians I don't remember even today. Moviegoing at that time could be a chore, with noisy audiences, sunflower-seed spitters, and creeps who nuzzled up and reached for your balls. It was even more difficult when my father took me, because he would never stop muttering about the double subtitles that ruined the frame—every picture had them in both Hebrew and French, the French presumably for the North African immigrants mainly from Tunis and Morocco, or perhaps just because the French, who sold us Mystère jets and Super Frelon helicopters, were our only friends in the world. He kept telling me that when he had first come to the country there were still translations projected separately from the picture on a hand-scrawled celluloid reel, so that the Hebrew seldom matched the film's spoken dialogue and the whole thing would keep breaking down, to loud cries, abuse and the throwing of projectiles. Nevertheless, he said, he preferred it that way, since it preserved the purity of the Frame.

Turning back from the reverie to the cinematographer's script of *The Woman God Forgot*, another curiosity of my father's early life that begged for rediscovery:

"Opening title:
The Greatest Racial enigma in history is the riddle of the Aztecs—civilized enough to use finger bowls—barbarous enough to offer human sacrifice –
Ages ago—a certain people of White Skin—possibly Carthaginians—sailed over the seas and conquered the ancient coast tribes of Mexico...

276

Blonde and blue-eyed was their Leader—who came to be worshipped by the dark skinned Mexicans—as the Fair God. His followers refused to accompany him when he returned to his own land; and centuries later their children's children became known as the "Aztecs"—who looked ever after for the Promised Coming of the Fair God...

Close Up—GONG—"Now the hour of sacrifice is at hand!"
On the sea shore—the conquerors land on the beach –
Tezca on bed with flower frond girls and lute plucking servants, in the Court of Birds—exotic parakeets—
A messenger arrives, in a great hurry and agitation –
"From across the sea come fair skinned strangers—who burn our temples and destroy our Gods!"

As do they ever... Geraldine Farrar, DeMille's New York opera star, as Tezca, following Joan of Arc in her roster of heroines. What happened to her afterward? Did she return to the opera? Did she eke out her living in other DeMille stories that became stranger and stranger? The unknown stretched out before me in the great desert of my ignorance (this was not yet the age of open access, of every jot and tittle, worthy or otherwise, spread out in bites and symbols). I was overwhelmed by what I did not know and had not wanted to know about Boris Gurevits, a.k.a. William Gore. And here I was, in Los Angeles, at yet another archive, turning the pages of a Famous-Players-Lasky scenario, with all my father's barely readable scrawls in the margins, storyboard drawings, proposed camera angles, suggestions of individual shots, calculations of distance, question marks, exclamations marks, insertions, signs of a young man vigorously immersed in his task...

By what twist had I, of all people, become the family historian? That was Kolya's job. It was clear, from phone calls with Yonni, my uncle's "Hawking boy," that Kolya had ingathered reams of material for a project of his own that had become endlessly postponed for the grand saga of Our People's destruction. Anyone around the world who had ever harmed a Jew, or harbored a grudge, or extended a threat, or even thought ill, or conceived cruel dreams of revenge for whatever slight, mythical or otherwise—let alone the condemnation of the Messiah, the rejection of God's chosen prophet, or allegedly infecting fair-haired Aryan women with syphilis and other charges written in the books of blood—was grist for the mill of Kolya's grand chronicle of justification for his worldview. His version of Luther's "Here I stand, I can do no other." Except that Luther, as far as I remember, occupies a whole volume of the saga so far. Those were, presumably, the papers that he had promised me in our breakfast on the Tel Aviv beach back at Dad's shiva. But, in the guarded comments from Yonni hinted that some of Kolya's files might be held back on the instructions of his son Adir, the man who was set to inherit the kingdom and had already advanced to the very electable status of No. 12 on the Likud Knesset members' list. Most likely, he would want to keep any family skeletons from falling out of the cupboard and spooking his future as the flagwaver of patriotic delights...

Sarah's letter seemed a small harvest for the long trip to California from London, but there were some parallel goals: reconnecting with San Francisco, if not Berkeley, where, last seen, the old hippies lined Telegraph Avenue selling redwood dreidels and banknotes bearing the image of Frank Zappa promising "One Million Dollars." Old sights down the Castro and along 24th Street, the old music stores and Herb's Fine Foods. Blasts from the past... Los Angeles providing its own quota of "doors"—old friends, old colleagues, old comrades you could call on at short notice, escapees from the Middle Eastern knot who had somehow scored a visa combined with a previously settled relative or some other link in the chain of those who had floated forth in search of a refuge, somewhere the daily rage was lessened, consigned to those left behind, with their own sack of troubles, less able to escape their own pain.

My current bivouac being up Lookout Mountain, in a somewhat precarious house perched on stilts overlooking the twisting road down to Laurel Canyon and Ventura Boulevard—the Valley—temporary headquarters for the son of an old stalwart of the Ta'amon café in Jerusalem: Ibrahim Khouri, principled non-joiner of all political parties, left or far left, but fellow traveler of some of the old radical wings, known to all as "He Never Gets Up Before Noon." The son, Suleiman, determined to pull a better fate than shit-kicking along as a second-class citizen in the Jewish state, had won a place at the UCLA film school, courtesy of some old connection too byzantine to disentangle, weaving from Palestine to the Netherlands, from Amsterdam to Toronto via a film festival contact, and across the North American hinterland down through Portland and Seattle and to La La Land.

Leaping to the current status, Suleiman was renting this place together with his French girlfriend Julie and two other Palestinians who had squeezed through the eye of the needle, from an elderly couple whose stay in Jerusalem some years past had left them with a different perspective than the usual Zionist infatuation and spent their retirement roving around the world from Argentina to Zanzibar, having made their fortune vending the strange accessories resident Los Angelenes appeared to aquire by necessity from the tchotchkes shops of Rodeo Drive: marble basilisks, gigantic granite panthers, Pharaonic masks, mock Babylonian friezes, Tibetan thousand-armed buddhas, Greek columns for gardens too large to leave empty, Samoan timber canoes for their olympic pools, and so forth. In payment for the house, one had to water the exotic plants, hose the lawn, keep the footpath tidy, fill the refuse receptacles in front and look out for mysterious strangers who might find a nonartistic interest in the owners' private collection of objects d'art, in particular the locked cabinet of old Disney memorabilia, grotesquely hinged Mickeys, Donalds, Goofys, Clarabelle Cow and the entire original barnyard.

From here I could drive down in my rented Grand-Am, either along Lookout Mountain to Laurel Canyon, join Sunset, turn right and then left, the traffic-jam route, or I could zoot up the road a few hundred yards and take Sunset Plaza Drive all the way downhill to Sunset by Mel's Café. Ah! once upon a time...and from Sunset down the steep swath of La Cienega all the way across Wilshire to the blinding white pueblo-style Academy of Motion Picture Arts and Sciences library, passing through the looking glass doors guarded by a large and beautiful poster of Marlene Dietrich in *The Scarlet Empress*—not one of my father's, alas, but Bert Glennon for Josef von Sternberg…

And up the stairs to the quiet hush of the archive, the papers that revealed who had done what and why, the many steps in plan and paper towards the classics or the also-rans of once upon a time. The workload of the star-studded legends and the grinders who made it all happen, the clatter of roomfuls of typists preserved in the stacks, the grind behind the glamor, the alchemical marriage of imagination and commerce.

They never gave Dad an Oscar. He was nominated twice, but not for a DeMille film. The goblins and gnomes behind the Academy were loath to neglect the Moloch maw of he who had it all and always craved more. Growing up with the myth of all this entitlement, my supposed inheritance, the hallowed U.S. passport, just mention the name Gore, and the doors will open, my son, all you need is the will to power…

I sniffed around, but the doors were still politely locked. All the stories that wafted through my childhood… I had a costume of the Prince of Dagon, which was worn by George Sanders in my father's last assignment, *Samson and Delilah*. My dad was waiting for me to grow big enough to wear it at Purim, but by that time I'd lost my yearning for disguises. Just old enough to wear the last one: the khaki uniform, no choices offered. Just leap into the swamp, and wade through it…

I remember there was a gold helmet, made of tin, with scratched paint and a kind of golden buckle for the belt. And sandals. Even the prince wore sandals, among the Philistines, albeit gold ones. The Hebrews had coarse leather ones, and ragged schmattas for robes. They screened the movie at the new Cinematheque in Jerusalem, and my father was asked to give a talk. He surprised them by telling how the original story was written not by some Hollywood hack, but none other than Ze'ev Jabotinsky, founder of the Revisionist movement, who had been Uncle Kolya's commander in the Irgun. A family problem, as sister Sarah was on the other side, with the socialists of David Ben-Gurion. Jabotinsky's Samson was the perfect Irgun man, betrayed by his fellow Israelites and at war with the idol-worshipping Philistines. A patriotic suicide, the Irgun ideal. My father explained that DeMille always signed on a source novel, because crazy people were always suing him for their own copyrights on the Bible. The audience were more interested to know if it was true that DeMille had wanted Victor Mature to wrestle with a real lion, but substituted a rag dummy when the great macho hero refused. And if Hedy Lamarr, as Delilah, had a nude scene that was cut from the film.

My father said it was an easy shoot. DeMille always knew exactly what he wanted, everything was storyboarded and planned, and only the model of the Philistine temple had to be reshot when the engineers blew it up, because the statute of Dagon failed to fall over and crush the Philistines with Samson, leaving God's and DeMille's plan hanging in the air. There was no nude scene with Delilah, he said. He would have remembered if there was. That at least got a laugh.

"That Victor Mature, he was a pussy." I remember my father saying that. But he still worshipped DeMille. The voice of God himself, speaking from the mountain, intoning the whole prelude to the Ten Commandments, the moment of creation, dividing the waters, day from night, good from evil, and the swift lurch from baby Moses in the bullrushes to Charlton Heston, all flexed biceps and heaving hairy chest, set against the glistening torso of Yul Brynner as Pharaoh Ramses. "So let it be written—so let it be done." But my father was already far away on Melchett Street when they shot that.

Suleiman Khouri had shot his student film back home, in Galilee, in his home village of Jish, an ancient mountaintop site where the two halves of the village, one Christian and one Muslim, perch on either side of the narrow main road, the church and the mosque

281

facing out to the south, the minaret tolerating the spire and vice versa. I had visited there once, with his father Ibrahim, taking a rest from the jolts and traumas of Jerusalem where he was gracing the radicals' café with his presence, a gaunt phoenix peering into his "upside down coffee" while the seconds, minutes, days slid by, the traffic and the politics rumbled past the open door, and the few like-minded souls came and went, talking of Althusser and Mandel. It was the first place I heard about Victor Serge, from the bearded and shock-headed Arieh B., who pushed a copy of *Conquered City* over the table to me. The unique Serge, the believer who nevertheless worshipped the truth…

Suleiman's film was about his hometown, the Muslim section, in which a young girl, Leila, is told by her father that he has promised to marry her to a sixty-year-old merchant whose prime attraction was that he could save the family from their mounting debts. But shse is in love with a young man from Nazareth, who packs her under a tarpaulin in the back of his company truck in the flush of dawn and drives her across the mountain as she lies on a stack of watermelons, some of which roll off and shatter on the road. Not everyone at UCLA understood the movie. The feminists protested the film's narrow view of Leila's choices; apart from marriage, why shouldn't she be able to forge her own way and become a doctor, an engineer or world traveler? She might even come out as a lesbian. Suleiman tried to make the audience understand the restrictions of Upper Galilee, but to no avail. All reality was California dreaming. In keeping with the program, we drove in our separate cars down to Ventura Boulevard, to Art's Deli, where memories of past times were lost among the menu's infinite choices of corned beef, pastrami, brisket, tongue, roast beef, turkey, turkey pastrami, ham, liverwurst, salami, hard salami, meatloaf, knockwurst, chicken finger, stuffed cabbage roll, lox, sturgeon…

"The first time I was here, my Jewish girlfriend brought me," Suleiman said. "She said I should eat every item on the menu and I would understand what being Jewish meant. I told her I never knew a Jew who ate anything but hummus and falafel, and what were kasha varnishkes anyway? She pointed out an old man eating a plate of it, and it looked like the most awful slops I saw in my life. Do you know what is a bag of kichels?"

I shook my head. We settled for the pastrami sandwiches. I was unsure if this was the right moment to bring up my Aunt Sarah, but showed him the copies I had made of the letter and its English translation anyway.

"Your aunt?" he said. "Wow. Did she write in Hebrew already? In Russia?" He squinted at the Yiddish scrawl. "Oh. It reads like German."

"I can't read it either. I have to trust the rendition."

I handed him Yonni's translation and he began reading while we waited for our pastramis. Creatures of habit. He was halfway through when the gigantic sandwiches arrived and he took a break, then resumed while I continued munching away. When he reached the end, he put the typescript down.

"It's like a Palestinian story," he said.

"Well, it is a Palestinian story."

"If you read the sources," I said, "you find that when the papers refer to Palestinians, they mean Jews."

"We were not even there," he said, adding some mustard.

"Absolutely invisible," I agreed.

"So there must be more letters," he said. "You have to find them."

"They're with my Uncle Kolya," I said. "I told you about him. I'm sure about that. He's my cousin Adir's father. The new Likud member. Kolya won't come back to Israel until they cancel the Camp David peace with Egypt. He left when Ben-Gurion accepted what Kolya called 'blood money' from Germany, in the nineteen-fifties."

"A man of principle. We must respect that. At least with the Likud we know where we stand. With Labor what did we get? Refugee camps and an old key that burns a hole in your pocket and soul. I'll go for honest fanatics."

"You're welcome to them."

It's the old argument. You can't choose your oppressor. Everything cascades upon you from afar, a landslide that can't be avoided. Except by distance. Suleiman suggested a trip straight up east to Burbank, where his cousins Rashid and Ghassan dwelled just below the Verdugo Mountains, on a street called Joaquin Drive. I had been told their tale by Gershon and Link, another fable of the spiraling diaspora: They were the two sons of a famous father, Kamil, who had been reputed to be Palestine's first Trotskyist, recruited in his teens before the Second World War and eking out a life of stalwart defiance of all local and global political trends for over thirty years, when his position suddenly became fashionable and his unknown books on the pre-war conflict were published, if only in English, French, German and Hebrew—no Arabic version could survive the filters of the Communist Party.

Kamil was known as the one man who would "tell it like it is" in the days when everyone's soul was mortgaged to some zealously guarded ideology; he had tramped through every village in Palestine in his day, writing down the tales of peasants and town workers alike, including the narratives of women and children, which was unheard in those days. The Israeli mavericks had discovered him in the wake of '67. Gershon and Link classified him as the Chosen One, though who had chosen him for what was unclear. He died of a cancer, ten years later, in exile in Los Angeles of all places. He had been deported by the occupation to Jordan, where he was even less welcome, and shunning the rival Baathists of Syria and Iraq he had somehow talked his way through the U.S. immigration process as an anti-Communist, certified as such by a cabal of American fans at Harvard who had translated his work and knew some old tricks. One of the professors, an old survivor of the McCarthy purges, arranged the house in Burbank through some "Deep Throat" at Warner Brothers, or so went the tale told by his sons. They then made it a place of pilgrimage for their friends and the devoted few who knew the old man, who were famously greeted with the brothers' ploy of asking each new guest: "Have you come to see Kamil? He's in here." And they would take the puzzled visitor into the living room and point out the large brass urn that stood on the mantelpiece under an entire wall of identical portraits of the sage in negative red; they were genuine Andy Warhols, painted after the artist had met the old man in a diner just around the corner from his famous Factory on East 47th Street, back in the golden age, and been captivated by his "oriental" gaze.

"He wanted to be buried in his home village," the older brother, Rashid, explained to me, when I was shown the sacral shrine, "but it was underneath a suburb of Haifa, on the slopes of the Carmel. There is a big store there now, the Kolbo Supersol. He would be just under the home furnishings department. The owners refused us permission. We make an application every two years. We offered to buy a sofa to embed the receptacle, but they still said no."

We clinked glasses and drank some vintage Lebanese arak to the memory of the departed sage. Arab or Jew, we excel in repetition, recycled narratives, old failures, discarded ideas that yet return in ghostly fashion as if spewed out of one of Stephen Hawking's black holes. One often wondered if the brothers were only playing with us, and there was just plain dust inside the urn. Or even an ingenious method of concealing their stash? So many open questions, so many ghosts drifting along the mutually connected skeins...

We talked inevitably about the Gulf War, launched the year before after Saddam Hussein's Iraq had attacked and occupied Kuwait. Yasser Arafat, Mister Palestine, had rushed over to Baghdad to kiss Saddam for his brave achievement, the most expensive kiss in his people's history, since it led to the expulsion of hundreds of thousands of them from Kuwait when the tables were turned. What was it in the Palestine psyche that brought on such spasms of political masochism? "Ah, we hate our pain," Rashid nodded sadly. "But we love it as well. For now, it's all that we have."

Driving back to my own bed after an irrefusable wet tribute, turning down Laurel Canyon I remembered where and when I had first heard about Kamil's Urn: at Shai Baer's, at Queen's Park, London:

Nineteen-Seventy-Five... Another hub of one's story... Going nowhere, and expecting nothing... On the rebound from the parting of the ways with Samantha, swept away in the arms of the Puerto Rican Liberation Front, a.k.a. Pablo, who probably spent not one single day in Puerto Rico in his entire life, from his birth in the Bronx. I can look it up later... I have archive... A whole sheaf of newspaper cuttings kept as part of the abortive research for another lost project... The grandly titled "World History of Oil and Power, Standard Oil to Aramco..." Stillborn for lack of funds and contacts. Apart from the usual suspects—Gershon and Link, calling from London: "Start at this end, man, the whole city is jumping with Saudis. There's a guy who knows a guy who knows a guy..." But that never happened. They offered a free berth at another Israeli friend's house while we ploughed through the contacts. Yet another "door." I packed my bags and climbed aboard Pan American Airways... ah! How many things that seemed eternal have passed... A balmy autumn of sunny spells and blustery clouds, greeting Gershon at Heathrow in the bud of morning and whisked by bus and Bakerloo Line to Queen's Park... I remember running down cabbage-smelling streets in a typical London shower towards the gate of a typical semi-detached house perched between a porch filled with a row of old movie-theater seats and a garden overgrown with weeds and scrub. And a man in short pants and a loose string vest who looked dressed for the height of summer down on the kibbutz stepped lazily from the open front door and took hold of my rucksack with his left hand as he clasped my palm with his right:

"Welcome to the United Kingdom!"

Enter Shai. And with Shai and his wife, Lana—the Queen's Park battalions: old and new comrades, neighbors, Jews, Arabs, poets, pushers, punks, drifters, youths with exotic plumage, exiles of every stripe, Albanians, Iraqis, Kurds, Turks with strange musical instruments, Belgians, gypsies, horticulturists, merchant seamen, fressers, shit-kickers and passersby who drifted into the garden and sat around the long wooden table and drank beer and wine and orange juice and Black Label and gobbled summary concoctions prepared by Lana as it took her fancy, among the regular Israel-Palestine deserters who buzzed around the hive, Gershon and Link and Farajul and Moshe and Uri and Jalal and Mounir and Mustafa and Sargon and Mikado and The Goat, floating in on the lazy Sunday afternoons of a dying summer and the gathering clouds that just might stay away or scud above us without incident or precipitation.

And in the melee, the hustle and bustle of small and large talk, among all these, there was Claire...

"What Do You Seek?"

Back to the correspondence :

Sarah:
August 20, 1920

Dear Berl—and Yakov, wherever you may be!

Whenever I write to you it is as if I am addressing my words to some presence in the sky, because I have no way of knowing if you have received them, but I have hope now that this letter will reach its destination and that you will be able to write back to this address, since if there is a power on earth that can ensure delivery it surely must be the British colonial post! Even though there were days of relative peace in our Bessarabia, the New Rumanian Order was not quite as efficient, or just, as it promised to be. I will write of our family, who are still well, I hope and pray, but my hand cannot resist writing of the event that fills my lungs with a pure air and makes my temples pulse with fire: I am in Palestine! I am in Palestine! I sit below a blue sky as pure as the heavens can be, and though the wind blows hot and dusty through these tents that surround me, although I have nothing but a battered case with some clothes and a few belongings I feel as rich as any baron who ever enjoyed the earth!

True, it was a tiring, an exhausting journey. We had to travel through the regions still marked by war, west instead of south, through Serbia, where many villages still lie ruined, and past many battalions of soldiers still guarding borders that were only yesterday a rubble of mud and death. Then the sea voyage, my first, the storms battered us when we cleared the Italian coast as if to throw up more obstacles, to test our strength and our resolve. Some mothers had babies that died on the way, at the threshold of their salvation. So much that we have been spared. Then someone cried out: "Jaffa!" And we crowded around the side of the ship so quickly that the Captain had his crew push us back lest we capsized within sight of land! At first I was only confused. What we saw was a low skyline of Turkish style buildings, with a spire or minaret of a Mosque, we saw many of these destroyed and ruined in Serbia. And before we could savour the view about thirty small boats came up rowed by turbaned Arabs who pulled up to the ship and cried out in their own tongue. I had somehow expected it to sound like our own Hebrew but it was very different, I couldn't make out a single word. Everyone made ready, but a British tugboat came up and some customs officials came aboard, forcing us to process our papers in a melee of cries and complaints. Fortunately, some people from the Zionist Committee came on board with them and spoke Hebrew and English, as well as Russian and Rumanian. The British set quotas for the immigration of Jews into Palestine, but thankfully our own small group was very well organised, and our papers were soon stamped and returned.

Disembarkation was like the landing of cargo—we were physically picked up by the Arab stevedores and thrown into the boats like sacks of potatoes! We didn't care, since we were more and more excited as the boats approached the stone quays. We reached out and touched them, our first contact with the soil of the Torah's land. Then, immediately, there were more customs officials—I never understood why the British always needed two tiers of officials, I thought that was true only of Russia! But one learns that officials are all alike!

My hand trembles as I write, as so many new impressions crowded each other like visions from the world of the unreal. The committee members who met us were efficient and businesslike and we were soon parcelled into groups boarding a line of horse-drawn carriages, which took us out of the town. I have to say these

Palestine horses are no match for our sturdy Bessarabian steeds! Most looked ragged and almost emaciated, glistening with sweat as the drivers lashed them forward. We passed many stalls drawn up on the seafront selling watermelons, citrus fruit and baskets of plums. Many people sat on low stools at the shopfronts smoking the oriental "hookah" or water-pipe. I think the Arabs call it the "shisha." I wanted to talk to them for we had discussed between us before we left, and on the way, not only what we might be expected to do as pioneers—as "halutsim,"—but how we were to approach the "others" whom Herzl wrote of so eloquently in his works. But we just clattered by them, as they looked at us, neither, I thought, with any disdain or even curiosity, since many have been coming now, but with a studied disinterest. Perhaps, I fancied, they might be thinking that if they ignored us, we would suddenly disappear. Or perhaps they might even have been glad in some way that we leavened the everyday fatigue of their day. But these are afterthoughts. The blur of impressions still overwhelmed us, as we trotted along the dust covered road.

I should return to those whom we left behind, as is my first duty. I am sure you will forgive me, you can see how far I have been transported—over the seas, beyond the clouds... I wrote to you before of my intentions, but was not surprised as the weeks and months passed and there was no reply. Since the Rumanians marched into Bessarabia only some weeks after the October events in Russia there has been some calm, but also a great anxiety over the fate of our people just across the border, in the Ukraine. The mail still does not seem to reach us through Bucharest, so I will repeat news from before: Father and Mother are well, and Judit too, who is still not married yet—I think she has been watching my example, to our poor Mother's dismay! She knows the anguish of my experience, but I have tried to tell her that each person is another world, and each spirit must forge ahead on its own path. But my mother complained that I was filling her head with bad ideas about the independence of women. I cannot explain to her how times have changed even though she sees the evidence every day and hour with her own eyes. They are of a different time, my brother, as you well know. In their lives there was boundless refuge in the love of The Name. Suffering was like a piece of baggage that they carried away from place to place. From the village in the steppes that I only saw as a babe in arms, and of which I have no memory, but sustained their parents and their ancestors for several generations, I cannot know from when and where. For worldly comfort they went to the Rebbe in Sadagura, who had the light of spiritual awe and the "shekhina," and whose white clad disciples you remember Father speaking of like a host of earthly angels. All the rest was in Torah. Though you could not find a more practical man than our father—you remember how he toiled to fix the troubles and arguments and conflicts of our farmers and merchants, holding their deeds and keeping their account books, and plying the Russian strazhnik with vodka to keep the wolves from our door. I wrote to you, in one of the lost letters perhaps, how he started to print his own "Celovest" money when the second Revolution, in November, made the Kerensky scrip totally worthless, so that people could still buy and sell. And how, with the stealth that you know he was so capable of when it was necessary, he advised the self-defence groups when we readied ourselves for the assassins of Petlyura. We were all waiting in the hedges with our pitchforks and pistols for the pogromists, but the soldiers who came were dressed too neatly, and spoke in Rumanian, so we knew we were spared one fate to live another.

But I was already speaking then with the small group around Itsik Vinshel, who had reformed the old "Young Pioneers" when the first group left, before the war. We talked about so many things, our life, our ideas, our past and our future, and the old longing came back to me. Zev, who was still there then, told me that I was just translating the everyday prayer, to Next Year in Jerusalem, to a material form, taught by Marx, more than Herzl. And I couldn't disagree with him. My mother's generation lived only in the path of true obedience, to the law and to the man. Of course, she knew how to get her way, but once the mind is opened to new thoughts, you can't stay where you are, not as a woman, not as a Jew, not as a human being.

I will admit, I was thinking also of Kolya, the Revolution that was not just an idea and a word but a real presence in the family. Even in absence. More so in absence. I knew Mother had been living in terror from the day the Tsar's recruiters came down on the train to swoop him up. To the day I left she still looked on the train tracks as sinister conveyers of disaster, and all uniforms as shrouds. The miracle of Kolya's coming was followed so quickly by his leaving, and from then on we heard of him only by messenger's packet. When the Rumanians came, of course, all the Social Democrats and revolutionaries in the villages and towns went underground, hid their armbands, uniforms, books and guns, and kept their faith in secret. The Zionists were allowed some more leeway, since on the one hand the Rumanians regarded them as part of the pro-Russian party, but on the other hand they liked the message they preached that Jews should leave, they cared not whether for Palestine, to America or to China, it was all the same to them.

I have to leave the rest to another day, because the postal man is here collecting letters, and I need you to know that I am safe, and our parents are still healthy in the village, and even my mother eventually gave her blessing to my journey, because Father said finally that Aliyah to the Holy Land is a commandment, and cannot be seen as a curse. I will write you in the next letter about the fighting in Russia and the letters from Kolya that tell of his doings there. He, too, is alive, and in the thick of it. Zev is also in Russia on his trading business, despite the war that has no end... I am fearful for them but I hope and pray that they too will be with our people in our land, soon. This year in Jerusalem!

All my love, your

Sarah,

in **Eretz Israel**!

(*Note: the letter on Kolya does not seem to have survived in archive.*)

May 14, 1921

Dear Berl and Yakov,

Our joy at being in our longed for homeland is mingled with a heavy heart due to the terrible events that have occurred in our colony only a few days ago, which have left a trail of blood and cost the lives of many dozens of comrades. Some have called it a new pogrom, but I refuse to use that word that ties us to the old life that we have come here to change. A word that I have pledged to wipe out from my vocabulary, for it shall not happen here.

What took place was a shocking outbreak of violence that began in Jaffa and then spread to Tel Aviv and other Jewish areas. It seems that a small demonstration by one of our smaller parties (and I told you of this plague that has followed us from our fractious and foolish past) was broken up by the police, and some surrounding Arabs took it on themselves to join what they saw as a licence to attack the Jews. To my dismay, it seems that a group of my comrades from the Tiberias road crew joined this May Day march, which was organised by the Bolshevist Zionists. I know how strange this sounds. It was unwise and foolish to march with slogans such as "Down with the British" and "For a Soviet Palestine"! Because of the day there were other larger demonstrations of the main Labour unions that were caught up in the trouble. Gangs of local Arabs started attacking them and then broke into Jewish homes, hitting people with sticks and clubs. The British police began firing both at the Jews and Arabs. One of my friends from Tiberias, Baruch Sonderheim, was among the killed, as well as our well known Hebrew writer, Y. H. Brenner, who was living on a dairy farm close to the sea shore. It seems that more than one hundred people have been killed, both Jews and Arabs. There were disturbances, I am told, the year before I arrived here, but they were not so bloody or wide-spread.

I am telling you this not so that you should fear for me, or think our enterprise, or our spirit is broken, but so that you should understand the nature of these matters. One's thoughts, ideas and our very nature is changed very quickly in the influence of these daily events. Rather than received wisdoms, we need to remake ourselves in this place in more ways than we imagined. We imagined that we could be the same Jews who lived in one place but now live in another, only with renewed ideals. But this is not the case. I now realise that breaking stones and rocks in the burning heat of the summer sun was perhaps the easiest of these new lessons. For we are schooled, from the cradle, to be fearful of others.

The truth is we are, both sides, weak and still in the hands of imperial manoeuvres, of the "great game" of power. England is a democracy but, despite the "Balfour declaration," rules here with an iron hand. They appear lost, these English, Scottish, Irish soldiers who survived the Great War only to bake here in our sun. They despise Jew and Arab alike. Now there is talk of new restrictions on immigration to appease the Arab street. There are non-socialists among us who believe that we will have to fight both British and Arabs. That would involve us in a terrible struggle, a blood feud that could last for generations. There is a new party here, the "Revisionists", who reject Herzl's Zionism as too weak and are all too ready to bear arms.

I, however, am not a soldier, even though we have women here who are prepared to pick up weapons. I believe that our strength lies in the organisation of our needs and our objectives. The girls have urged me to stand in elections for the delegates of the new Hebrew unions and I am seriously considering this. What do you think, of your sister as a politician? I could say that I feel that I was never one for talking, but preferred doing, but others tell me that on the contrary, I am talking all the time!

I feel a great pity and a great sadness over all of this, as if the hand of God had withdrawn from the very font from which the great salvation had gone forth. You can understand why I cannot write of these things to our father. I have prepared another letter which tells him very simply of the marvellous places I have visited, and my feelings of holiness in the place of the Holy Wall in Jerusalem.

I know it will give him, and our mother, much comfort in their separation from us. For it is all for a purpose, that I am resolved more than ever. That we should find a synthesis of that old and this new. Bind together the endurance that brought us through so many centuries of exile to the place of our renewal, and the proper will of our communal strength and determination to forge our place in the modern world. For if we are not agents of the new enthusiasms of our new century what are we, but only dust?

The young ones see me as a teacher, although I see myself as a lowly student, sitting on the rude benches of the primary class. But, the more things appear strange and frightening, the more the challenges that are thrown up, all the obstacles in our path, the stronger I feel I am becoming.

I must tell you that I finally fulfilled Father's request that I visit Jerusalem, before the events of May happened, traveling there in February by motor carriage to Jaffa and from there the "kalash" to the Holy City.

If ever there was a road more fit for rebuilding it is this one, which should be a highway to one of the world's most wanted centers, but is a harsh and dolorous road indeed, narrow and covered with stones. There is a railway that was built in Ottoman times, but we wished to savour a pilgrim's way, past so many places that echo with the Bible's names, like Ayalon and Gibeah. The hills are very different though from the ridges of our old Carpathians, and even from the mountains of Galilee, which are rich with foliage and cultivated terraces. One senses that one is travelling into a distant past, and our little "havurah," myself and three of the girls, with two of the male comrades, all expressed ourselves surprised that with all the efforts of the new "third" immigration, the capital of Jewish life was so neglected. Our spirits were lifted to some degree when we approached the outskirts, for there were some fine buildings on the slopes of the hill, and the Jaffa Road became wider and less bumpy to ride. To our chagrin however our guide pointed out that the grand spired building to our left was the Protestant

German Schneller orphanage, which had been constructed after the Kaiser's visit in the same year of Herzl's visit. We passed several other Christian buildings, such as the German hospital and the French Catholic Sisters of Saint Joseph, though there is also Rothschild's hospital, built by our own people's charity.

On the Jaffa road itself there are also many modern buildings, with fine arched windows and iron balconies, and pretty red-tiled roofs. Here men and women in modern and smart garb walked alongside the traditional Hassidim, conspicuous on this showery day with their unfurled umbrellas. There are many shops of Jewish businesses, clothing stores, household goods, fabrics, even jewellery, as well as bookshops and shops selling Torah requisites, teffilin and mezuzahs. As well, there are many buildings housing the seminaries of the various "kollelim," the schools of the various religious courts of the European rabbis. The largest compound on the road, however, is that of the Russian church, including a large cathedral that towers over the city! Even here, one cannot escape being reminded of the "other side"... But as one travels further past the buttresses and towers of other foreign concessions, one can only pause to gasp at the vision of the old Turkish walls that surround the Holy City itself.

Coming through the Jaffa Gate one is overwhelmed by the thought that one is close to that place to which all our prayers turned for countless generations. I could see the solemn prayers of our father and all the devout of the Bet Midrash turned so vigorously towards the east. From here we proceeded on foot, besieged, I have to say, by small boys and various ragged persons, both male and female, begging for alms or trying to tempt us with open suitcases of souvenirs, as if we were interested in Christian trinkets, crosses or fake silver figurines, "ancient" goblets and clay pots.

We were of course eager to proceed as quickly as possible to the hallowed Western Wall, and see the place where Solomon's temple stood. This we had to do by foot, wending our way through the narrow alleys, which turned in to one another, in and out of archways, and even the ones that were supposed to be straight, through the bazaars, were constantly blocked by crowds of people passing this way and that. However hard the guide tried to bring us towards the Jewish quarter, we kept being pulled along towards the Christian center, and the church of the Sepulchre, which is the site of Golgotha. Even in the crush, I could not avoid the thought that so many of our troubles, over so many centuries, all began in this tiny area, which seemed no larger than the geographical area of our own small Celovest. Perhaps, after all, Man is larger than all this—but I could not voice this thought to our father, although, in her heart, Mother might have thought so too, had she stood in our place... But we cannot alter the past.

When we reached the Holy Wall itself, wending our way through the alleyways, I was at first terribly saddened by the narrow street that led to it, hemmed in from the south by a jumble of some of the poorest stone hovels one could imagine, crowded with families who seemed to be dressed in not much better than rags, and only some steps away from these stones of ancient majesty, themselves barren and worn down by the multitude of hands that have clutched at their mystery over many hundreds of years. The poor people on the south side, we were told, were the "Mograbeen," Arabs who had come from North Africa and were looked down on by their native brethren. They were certainly in far worse dolour than the other Muslims of the city, who were poor but maintained their haughty look as they moved about their own crowded quarter, filling the tiny coffee shops with loud talk and calling their wares from the endless warrens of their busy market stalls. The street is therefore so narrow it is always crowded with our people pressing in upon the Wall, praying, laying their heads on the hard surface and rocking with a kind of desperation that might move the stones themselves to tears. Over the wall, from the vantage point of the western entrance, one can glimpse the great domes of the two mosques that command the site of the Temple itself, which were the Muslims most holy sites for more than a thousand years.

I could see that some of my younger companions were experiencing a repulsion at these ragged figures of their brothers and sisters, swaying with such passionate simplicity in their contemplation of this sole material presence of the manifestation of The Word. This, the place where by tradition Abraham offered his son Isaac to the sacrifice, on Moriah…

I was the only one of our group who wished to touch the wall, and, among the women, those who were closest to the stones parted, and helped me through, placing an old shawl on my head. I wondered, would there be a shock, as of lightning, when my fingers found the surface? But it was smooth, and astonishingly warm, even on this bitter cold day, heated by so much pressed flesh.

Later, we walked through the quieter alleys of the external quarters, the newer courtyards along the market streets, the "Mahaneh Yehuda," which reverberated not to prayers but to the call of fruit and vegetables and sweetmeats, but which was also a jumble of small synagogues and seminaries. Somewhere there, I think, is a community of Sadagura, but I did not have time to linger, and even here, there was an oppressive air. Here, and the "Batei Ungarn" closer to the walls, the outer walls of the houses were often plastered with notices that attested, in both Hebrew and Yiddish, to a labyrinth of internal feuds, one rabbi accusing another of misleading the public, leading his followers towards abominations, errors and sacrilege against the Holy Torah, allowing foreign innovations, desecrating the Sabbath and leading women and children into perdition and sin. I could not tell if these were manifestations of the ills of poverty or of the rivalry over the "halukah" itself, the charitable donations that sustained these various sectish schools, like two butchers fighting in one village over their slaughtering rights. My father, I thought, would have sorted these rivals out in quick fashion, by cajolery and the authority of a superior mind, but here there seemed no authority, only an anarchy of small grievances probably lost in the coils of time.

What do we seek? We seek a meaning, in the chaos that descended on the world due to the sleep of reason, which is another way of saying the loss of our compact with God. Our folly, in allowing empires to usurp our true values, the worth of every human being who is made in God's image, for that is our first entrance into the domain of creation. Our catastrophe, in the descent of our own civilisation into the destruction of war, the sacrifice of so many Isaacs by Abrahams who defied the basic Laws of the Ten Commandments. Who did not understand that the whole purpose of the matter at Moriah was the staying of the hand that wields the knife. Why is our brother, Kolya, swallowed in this? I am sure there is a voice that will call to him, and summon him back to the fields.

We went our different ways, but I do not feel, despite this, that we are apart. For my part, I will wait for you here. I will build a new family, and I will nurture my will. I am sorry if this is not so womanly, but it is perhaps in a tradition that is older than our old Celovest. I am sorry that I am bubbling along like this, but perhaps I am becoming like a slow tshulent, that is better the longer it boils over the fire. There are certainly enough ingredients!

I will stop here, before I am suspected by my brothers of a long term softening of the brain. I still have to finish my letter to Father. As I told you, I am in Haifa, on the slopes of Mount Carmel. It is a cold but sweet night. And I am not tired.

All my love to you,
Your slightly funny in the head sister,
Sarah (not yet a matriarch!)

"The Hub"
or "Kamil's Urn"
A Masque in Three Acts
by Claire Mains & Asher Gore
Location: London, 1975

Characters:

Isaiah (Shai) Baer

Ilana Baer

Aliza (Ali) Baer—their daughter

Gershon, Link, Asher, Moshik, Mansur, Abed, Farida, Claire, Pablo,

Matosian, Imelda, Sargon, Farajul, The Goat, Daniel, etcetera—

passing guests.

Scene 1: The Garden: a long wooden table set on a lawn; a typical wooden fence, about five foot high, at back of stage, with flat of next door house, from which loud pop music occasionally bursts out. SHAI is seated at the top of the table, to our right, on a folding lawn chair, while the others, at this stage GERSHON, LINK, ASHER, CLAIRE, FARIDA, ABED, FARAJUL, MATOSIAN, PABLO, IMELDA, SARGON and THE GOAT are lolling about in a variety of garden and kitchen chairs. A very loud burst of pop music blasts from the neighbours and then is reduced.

SHAI (speaks in pronounced Israeli-German accent, always in a confident mode): I don't mind the level but I have a question about the choice. If it's Jimi Hendrix I would just listen to it all day. Have you tried this? It's some Irish concoction. The Dochertys were having a wake down the road. It was the grandfather. He was a nephew, apparently, of one of the men who was shot in the Easter Rebellion. I forget which one. Do you remember, Momo? Was it a Pearse or a MacBride?

ILANA: It was a Hanrahan I think. Or someone else.

SHAI: It was a very jolly affair. Did you see the news? They arrested Patty Hearst! They found her apparently in a house in San Francisco, with some other members of the group. The Symbionese Liberation Front. The F.B.I. winkled them out.

IMELDA: Well, nobody can hide forever.

SHAI: They were a good group but a little crazy. I don't know what the Symbionese stood for. It was some kind of snake symbol.

PABLO: It was a naga symbol. The seven-headed cobra. It stood for unity, self-determination, collective work, responsibility, work... Something from Ceylon, Sri Lanka...

IMELDA: It was from symbiosis.

FARAJUL: The seven principles of kwanza. Umoja, kujichagolia, ujima, ujama, nia, kumba, imani. African collectivity.

SHAI: How many blacks were in that group?

PABLO: Only one.

SHAI: I don't know them, I never studied them closely. I knew the Weathermen, in the U.S.. I met Bernardine Dohrn when she was living with her husband, Bill, somewhere in the Midwest. They were married with two kids and living a very normal life. They are still out there somewhere. It's a strange thing about the underground. Did you read the book by Bommi Baumann? He was with the Baader-Meinhof but he got fed up with the violence. He writes about how they had to disguise themselves as ordinary German citizens, dress normally and lead a routine life. So in the end to gain their ends they were living the exact kind of life that they were against in the first place. It didn't make sense to him. But when he wanted out it was too late.

FARIDA: But this Hearst girl, she didn't get involved out of ideology, did she? They kidnapped her, and then she started to take part in the robberies, didn't she? It was all to get back at her father, I can tell you. Imperialism begins in the family.

ABED: Was that a problem for you in person?

FARIDA: My father is a grocer in Nablus.

SHAI: "How it all began," that was the title of the book that Bauman wrote. *Wie Alles Anfing* in the German. I don't think there is an English edition yet...

SARGON: Most of our decisions come from deepest impulses that we are trained to ignore.

Enter Daniel, from stage left, holding a little plastic bag.

DANIEL: I see everybody got here early. It's good to find that so many people can get up in the morning. Hi Lana, Shai, comrades in grief and sorrow.

SHAI: Boker tov, Daniel. Sabah el hir. A gute sontag. Somebody taught me some greetings in Albanian but I forgot them. Did you get the mushrooms?

Daniel holds up the bag.

DANIEL: I spent four hours yesterday in Epping forest. A vintage crop. I think I found Psilocybe coprophila. The dung-loving Psilocybe. Gives quite a mellow high.

SHAI: Anything for the salad?

DANIEL: Quite a lot, but I just brought some samples. (Finds a seat.) You have to be careful in this kind of task. I always use a proper guide. Gustave and Chevening, Mushrooms and Toadstools of Great Britain. Also the book by Uberto Tosco. You have to pick them out by the smell, and also look at the base of the stem, for bagging. It's an art form. One bite of the wrong species, and you would need a liver transplant. The magic mushrooms are a completely different genre. I was taught the right stuff by an old Indian in Oregon.

SHAI: Did you do the peyote? What about the "yagé"? William Burroughs writes about the "yagé."

SARGON: He should have stuck to that instead of the heroin. Then he wouldn't have shot his wife in the head.

DANIEL (rummaging in his bag): Sometimes you need a microscope to detect the good from the bad. And sometimes it's obvious...

IMELDA: Is this the new politics, mushrooms?

SHAI: It's an entire universe.

FARIDA: But to get back to Patty Hearst. What I don't understand about these Americans, they always seem to get it all ass-backwards. I think that robbing banks was always something that she wanted to do. Instead of just spending Daddy's money. To get your own. It makes sense.

SHAI: Sometimes there is a genuine conversion. It happens to people.

DANIEL: I don't think that people change very much. They may change their politics, but that doesn't really count. The basic personality always stays the same.

ABED: Do you think so? Before I came to London, I believed that Jews were a different kind of human. They were not like us at all, but they were like devils with evil thoughts and deeds. But I came here and met all sorts of Jewish people, good and bad, clever and stupid. So I believe that I have changed.

GERSHON: Maybe you just switched the demonic aspect to some other category.

ABED: For example?

Link: Bankers, maybe, armaments manufacturers, landlords...

ABED: It's not the same.

MOSHIK: You can't make choices that way. All you're describing is denial of reality. It is an obvious first axiom that you have to discard these delusions. But it's still just emotion at that stage. There has to be some framework. What are you for, what are you against? Whether it's class, or nationalism, it's still all about power.

IMELDA: You can't deal with human beings without emotions. You might as well join the Communist Party and just follow the Moscow line.

SHAI: We tried that. But we didn't last very long. Did we, Moshik? I remember, a comrade from the Lebanese party told me that even in Beirut every meeting of the party cell had to begin with a prayer session. I think they were all sunnis though. If they were shias they had to join another cell. There were probably some Christians, too, but I don't know if they prayed. You have to fit in with the culture. Do you remember Anis? He was fifteen years with the Popular Front and then after the Japanese group killed twenty-eight people at Lod he decided to leave because he said he didn't see why foreigners should be killing civilians for the Palestinian cause, and then that led him to believe it was absurd to think that Palestinians should do it either. He went to France, and now I hear that he's become a Christian Scientist. That's a serious change.

SARGON: What's the connection?

SHAI: Everybody has an internal process. You can't divorce psychology from politics.

MANSUR: Exactly. We don't have political views, only pathologies.

SHAI: Let me ask Claire. You're the only native here among us. The only proper English person. Are we all crazy or is it just normal?

CLAIRE: From what perspective?

SHAI: Humanity, rationality, English liberalism.

LINK: Marxism, Leninism, Mao Tse Tung Thought.

CLAIRE: Well, I wanted to be an actress so I could be any of those things. It's the old chameleon theory, change your skin to fit in.

SARGON: In the Middle East it's the other way around. You put on the most gaudy colours so that you should be as different as possible. You have to wave a flag to show you think reality is unacceptable. In the mass you can only drown.

SHAI: Why did you want to be an actress?

CLAIRE: I became an actress because I saw a movie, a silent movie, called *The Passion of Joan of Arc*. It was by a Danish director, you would know, Asher—was it Dreyer? Everything was in close-up—the inquisitors, the interrogators, the woman. She had the most expressive face. All the vision and the pain was in her eyes. I felt I needed to learn that.

SHAI: So what led you to the theatre, rather than films?

CLAIRE: I got two jobs in commercials, one selling washing powder and the other a bathroom detergent. I was told I could have got on the packets.

DANIEL: Everybody has to start somewhere. I used to write recipes for Haaretz domestic supplement. People wrote me fan letters.

SHAI: If it was a part of yourself it was honest.

DANIEL: I preferred the hate mail. When I mixed the couscous with the Algerian war.

SHAI: You have to be true to yourself.

DANIEL: I only truly believe in two things: poetry and cooking.

SHAI: Did you meet Leila Khaled? Remember? She was in the nineteen-seventies hijackings, when they took four planes to land in Jordan. Her plane was diverted to London, where they arrested her. The first time she went on a hijacking the year before, they ordered the pilot to fly over Haifa so she could look down on her hometown. When she was in prison in England she made friends with the warders and the immigration officer who paid her a visit. She was made into some kind of terrorist hate figure, but she was an ordinary person, just like you or me. It was the circumstances that made her what she was. Ari Mendel met her in Paris last year and they had lunch in a Vietnamese restaurant. He was from Haifa so they talked for about two hours about the place. He told her how he liked to go out in a boat with Emile Habibi to fish in the sea. I think he fell a bit in love with her but nothing happened.

FARIDA: Wasn't she already married?

MANSUR: Habibti, this is not the point of the story.

A clutter from the left of stage precedes the entrance of Aliza, Shai and Ilana's teenage daughter, accompanied by a pale leather-clad youth with reddened spiky hair, her boyfriend Hoog.

SHAI: Hi, motek! Have you had any breakfast? Come and

join us!

Aliza gives her mother a kiss, whispers in her ear. Hoog nods to Shai and the others, with a special nod to Daniel.

SHAI: Are you going somewhere? Take a seat. Daniel brought some mushrooms.

Hoog waves his hand at Shai, who comes forward, so that the two of them stand together front of stage. They whisper in each other's ears. Aliza has already left the way she came, with Ilana.

SHAI: Did you go to the concert last night? I have a soft spot for Meat Loaf but I couldn't get to Finsbury Park. I saw them when they were Floating Circus, in San Francisco. Then he joined the cast of *Hair*. Some people thought it was a betrayal but everybody has to make a living.

HOOG: Not my kind of gig. How much do you need?

SHAI: Just enough for relaxation. We'll talk later. Ian Dury is playing in Hammersmith in two week's time. You should join us. Gershon and Link are coming. Somebody I know has a bunch of tickets right up in the front, where all the crazies are.

HOOG: I'll tell you if I can make it.

Hoog exits, following Aliza. Shai goes back to the table.

FARIDA: Your daughter is growing up, inshallah.

SHAI: It's a biological fact. Nothing stays the same. The big problem is you can't make your children have the right taste in music. It's very frustrating.

Abed (leaning over to be close to Shai's ear): The real problem is you let your daughter go out with your dealer. I only say this as a friend.

SHAI: Yes, but it's convenient... They get on well... he's not a bad sort. He's from Amsterdam.

ABED: You should become an Arab father.

SHAI: God forbid. A Jewish one is bad enough.

The pop music from the neighbors swells, drowning

out the conversation. Shai and his guests get up, clear the plates and bowls of food, and take them off screen, while some of the guests stay seated, Moshik, Matosian, Abed, Farida, Pablo, and Imelda have opened another discussion—Abed has been holding forth under the music, which dies down again.

MOSHIK: No, the point is not whether I'm against Zionism in theory. I'm against Zionism in theory because I am not a nationalist. Let alone a nationalist for a group that claims for itself an imaginary status so that it can impose a secular interpretation on a religious concept. In the War of nineteen-fifty-six I was a soldier. I was in the Sinai desert with the invading forces. We knew that the French and British were helping us to get rid of Gamal Nasser. I was at that time a kind of left-winger of the Mapam type variety. We believed in all the good things, liberation, freedom, equality, good relationships between the Arabs and the Jews. I was not doing any fighting, I was in the Ordnance Corps. We were handling equipment, mainly uniforms and accessories. But I realised that if I was fighting, the Egyptian soldier would not care about my political opinions. He would only care that I was in the opposing army. If I was a soldier in the previous war, in nineteen-forty-eight, I would most likely have been fighting inside Palestine, against Palestinians in their own villages. Of course I might have had to face the Jordanian Legion, or Iraqi forces, or whatever, but let's say that I was ordered to attack an Arab village. Do you think the person in that village, whom I was fighting to evict from his home, would care if I was a leftist or a rightist, or a member of this party or that one? I would be the Zionist in action. That's what I am basically against. I am against the act, more than I am against the theory. The theory can drive us into blind alleys, arguing about abstract concepts. The reality is eviction, occupation and terror by the state. That's the point.

FARIDA: And how many Israelis take this position?

MOSHIK: Well, it's like the old joke—who says there

are no liberals in Israel? I know both of them.

ABED: Well, if you had toppled Nasser it might have done us some good. I was in Cairo in the early sixties, just after the Syrians had pulled out of the union with Egypt. The United Arab Republic. No unity and no republic. The whole Arab world was shouting for Nasser but in Cairo university we had to act like the dumb. The communists and trade unionists were all in jail, and the regime's spies were everywhere. Meanwhile the Soviet Union was supplying Nasser with weapons. In Syria one general followed after the other, filling the jails up completely. In Iraq we had General Kassem. He was killed in nineteen-sixty-three, and the Ba'ath party took over. If you can find a way to import us some liberals, we would be very grateful. Revolutionaries we have by the bucketful, but there is no end to the pain...

MATOSIAN: I would love to go to Cairo. And Damascus. Those two. I hear Damascus is fabulous. Udi Shamir said it was a great place. He said it was a great mix of the ages.

MOSHIK: The mix-up was in his head. Those guys were crazy. They were told they were going to meet the Palestine Popular Front but instead they met the Syrian Intelligence. It was a clear provocation. The Shabak tries this all the time. You have to watch out for that kind of thing. There were five Israelis in that group and four are now in jail. The fifth simply went back to his old police job. If you cross the line, you should be prepared. You'll have to wait a bit longer for your Damascus hummus.

PABLO: It sounds like the Harrisburg Seven. They were accused of plotting to kidnap Henry Kissinger. My friend Eqbal was one of them. The others were Catholic priests and some nuns. You know, Moshik, the Berrigan brothers, Dan and Philip. They had an FBI informer at one of their meetings so they spun him some outrageous crap. The next thing they knew they were all rounded up. The trial didn't last very long. After the prosecution had presented their witness the defendants' lawyers just said: The defence rests. And they were all acquitted. Then the Berrigans went on the run because they were wanted for damaging nuclear nose cones with hammers at a base in Arizona. Or was it Maryland? I can't remember. I met Dan a year later with Stuart Schaar when we all went to see the movie *Catch-22* in Brooklyn. Berrigan wore a big red beard, but nobody noticed. I think we were all stoned.

IMELDA: That was a good movie, but not as good as the book.

FARIDA: All these exciting lives. The men, making and unmaking the world.

IMELDA: Exactly. Where is our story?

ABED: Well, if you don't tell it, whoever will know?

FARIDA: It's too exhausting, listening to all of you speak.

Aliza and Hoog, drawing a curtain across front of stage, light up their joints and smoke quietly, as behind them, the others shift out the props, and set up for the next scene...

Scene 2:

Asher's room in Shai's house. Aliza and Hoog open the curtain to reveal the small spare room, with a folded sofa-bed and two armchairs, a small desk and stool, a chest of drawers, small cupboard, a pile of document files, papers on the desk, a portable typewriter, and three or four shelves of paperback books, which are also scattered on the floor by the bed. Asher enters and clears the books away, making room as Claire comes in after him.

ASHER: Excuse the mess, this is what stands in for the kingdom.

Claire looks at the books. Ilana follows into the room.

ILANA: Are you okay in here? I put some coats and stuff on the bed before but I took them downstairs. Mind if I sit down a minute? Daniel's taken over the kitchen. Thank God.

ASHER: I don't think I'll touch the mushrooms.

ILANA: It's all right, they're making stuffed chicken.

Daniel wanted to make tshoolent but he should have started yesterday. It has to cook overnight.

CLAIRE: You don't do this every Sunday?

ILANA: It's a variable. Once a month, maybe twice. People gather in the summer. If I don't feel like dealing with it I'll take a day off for the beach. The closest sea here is Clacton. It's a friendly little place, with quite good fish and chips. About an hour and a half on the train from Liverpool street.

CLAIRE: I can see the attraction... I see you've got some of my books. From Caligari to Hitler. Good old Kracauer. And The Haunted Screen, by Lotte Eisner. That's a pretty key text. This one, about Murnau—I didn't know she wrote that.

ASHER: It's rare, it never came out in a paperback.

CLAIRE: We did a lot of work around Max Reinhart, the German stage lighting—light and shadow. De-linking the individual from the surroundings. The attack on naturalism and "verism." All very un-English. Thinking about our own gothic traditions—Mary Shelley and *Frankenstein*, going all out for social themes.

ASHER: No Boris Karloff, with the iron bolt through the neck?

CLAIRE: Afraid not. That was an American fantasy.

ASHER: My father used to talk about Reinhart. All the film designers and lighting cameramen in Hollywood in the old days knew about the German experiments. And the punch line is: My dad was a cameraman for Cecil B. DeMille.

CLAIRE: Really? You don't look that old!

ASHER: I was a latecomer. Second marriage, third child-hood. They all started pretty young. My father used to talk about a movie called The Whispering Chorus, which was all high-contrast light and shadows.

CLAIRE: I never heard of that one.

ASHER: It was shot in nineteen-seventeen.

ILANA: Not a good year. It was the year Shai's father got shot in the leg. Actually it probably was a good year, it got him out of the army. That was the German

310

army. He was seventeen. Born with the century. Shai talked about it a lot. Shai talks a lot about everything. It's quite interesting, the first time around...

CLAIRE: What do you both do? On weekdays.

ILANA: We both teach. Shai does a course on computer theory at London U. I lecture on mathematics. Probability theory.

CLAIRE: That sounds interesting. What's the gist?

ILANA: It's about random phenomena, and how you can ascribe patterns that can be studied or predicted. It's part of quantum mechanics.

CLAIRE: Has it something to do with fuzzy logic?

ILANA: In a kind of popular way. There are different ways of expressing uncertainty. Like the Israel-Palestine conflict. I wouldn't want to be teaching that. Far too many random variables...

Shai enters, looking around.

SHAI: So this is the retreat. A bit quieter here. Daniel is chopping and talking. We've lost Gershon and Link and The Goat to some other attraction.

ILANA: We were on to probability theory.

SHAI: It's abstruse, but useful. Gamblers use it to figure out card games. All the best people are in Las Vegas. Ilana works out of Bayesian methods, but she also works with maximum entropy. It's a fascinating subject if you can get your head around it. I've been suggesting a joint project. If we can apply it to computer theory we could let the machine take over. It would work out its own ideas and be far ahead of the curve. At the moment we're still in the infancy of computers but it's about to go sky-high. There are some kids in California who are going to change the world.

ILANA: This has been his mantra since the sixties.

SHAI: What you have to do is resist the sunshine. If you can shut yourself in to a room with a year's supply of pizza and just fiddle with the theorems and some old radio equipment there's no accounting where you might end up. You can laugh at all the crazy antics of the yippies and the flower people and all the chanting of mantras but a lot of things got shaken up. You were in Berkeley, I think you told us, you saw it all at first hand.

ASHER: Saving the Park. Every day we went down there it was another type of tear gas or baton. A lot of heads got cracked.

SHAI: There's nothing like a policeman's truncheon to teach you how the world really works. You remember the old Jerusalem joke, Ilana? The cop's defence to a charge of police brutality? Your honor, he assaulted my club with his head and then repeated the offence thirty-six times. Gershon picked that one up at a Black Panther demo. You know he gave them the name.

CLAIRE: What, the American Panthers?

SHAI: No, the Israeli ones. They were a group of radical kids from the oriental communities, you know, what we call Sephardic Jews. It all happened when Gershon and Link were living in Jerusalem and somebody burglarised their apartment and stole the hi-fi. Instead of going to the police the boys asked around and discovered there was a small group of kids from the Musrara neighborhood, the poorest part of the city, who were doing the houses round there. So Gershon went round and found them and went in and started a dialogue. They all said they were fed up with the whole scene, of all the poverty and the discrimination and the police actions against them and they were thinking of chucking in the crime and forming a political group. So Gershon suggested to them—why don't you call yourselves the Black Panthers, like the blacks in the U.S. That would really put the wind up the police. And that's how it all started.

ILANA: If you believe all Shai's stories.

SHAI: Well, on a count of probabilities it might not be impressive but it's not impossible. Be practical, dream the impossible. That was a very good slogan. Of course when you open up all the possibilities a lot of rubbish comes out. But who knows what's rubbish and what isn't? Restaurants throw away their surplus food in the bins and some vagrant comes along and finds the

312

night's nutritious meal. It's all in the mind.

ILANA: I'd better get back to see about tonight's offering. (She turns to go and nods back) I would stay for the stuffed chicken if I were you. Don't underestimate Daniel, he's a great chef. (She exits.)

SHAI: Yes, definitely stay for dinner. Daniel's about much more than mushrooms. We just took it up to relax the mind. Things get too pressing otherwise. You see it's starting up again in Lebanon? We could be looking at full scale civil war. More fighting in Tripoli and now another outbreak in Beirut. It's when they pro-claim a ceasefire, that's when all hell breaks loose. It's a complete mess, and the Palestinians are right in the middle. All the Israeli army has to do is sit back and let the others fight it all out. It never ends. Meanwhile things are hotting up in Spain as well. They sentenced ten political dissidents to death last week. It seems Franco goes on for ever.

CLAIRE: What do you think will happen in this country?

SHAI: The United Kingdom? It just muddles on. You have this new leader of the Conservatives—Mrs. Thatcher... She's a woman so she has to be harder than the men. But it doesn't make that much of a difference. Harold Wilson had his day. But the one thing this country has is inertia. Things don't change that quickly. This is the problem in the Middle East. Events can be blown off course by the slightest twist, by a blunder or a mistake. In any case there is no course, everything is up for grabs. Syria, Lebanon, Israel, even Egypt, Iraq. In Jordan at least there's a king. You should talk to Daniel. He's a monarchist. He believes in stable crowns. I started off with the British. Teenage years in mandate Palestine. It wasn't such a bad life, even during the war. Everywhere in the world people were being killed and murdered but in Palestine it was relatively quiet. Apart from the Irgun actions and the immigrant ships and the Arab-Jewish tension you could have a good life. The British were moderate colonis-ers, compared with the Italians or the French. They didn't go in for mass murder. Lots of people disagree, but that was my experience. It was a more egalitarian society then, in Palestine. Nobody was very rich. And everybody could hate the British so it was sort of equal. Then of course it all fell apart. As things do.

CLAIRE: That's an unusual take.

SHAI: Things that seem obvious to people have to be tested against reality. Of course if you talk to Moshik you'll get another story. He's still an orthodox Marxist. Fighting for a socialist Middle East. It would be a fine thing, if it would happen, but it's not very likely. The Nationalist virus is still too strong.

ASHER: What does Abed think?

SHAI: He's with the Fatah. They are mainstream. Whatever works. They have their work cut out in any case to keep that whole caboodle together. It's the same in every liberation movement. Unity is just a facade. It's very difficult, when the future is so uncertain, to know which way to take. So now we've got to tautologies, let's change the subject: Claire, I wanted to ask you but it was too crowded downstairs—what happened to the new play?

*

What indeed?

The Hub, an abortive experiment in realist writing that turned out too personal, was abandoned. I had arrived a little late to the no longer "Swinging London," as I had been for Californian frolics. Somehow I missed the acid tests, Ken Kesey's magic psychedelic bus, the Grateful Dead, Haight-Ashbury and the Age of Aquarius, although I had trawled the literary trail from Jack Kerouac through Hunter Thompson. As my own attorney, I advised myself always to do this and that, get off the track, abandon the straight and narrow, tune in, turn on, drop out, and waft towards inner heavens on a rainbow cloud of ethereal vapors. I was too locked in the technological challenges of the Arriflex ST, the lure of the BL, the synch-sound problem, Nagras, editing suites with their great desks and pulleys, outbins full with the strands of uncoiled shots and scenes. Mired in practicality. Shai Baer filled the gaps with his tales of Timothy Leary, the League for Spiritual Discovery, the seven levels of consciousness and the acid guru's trips to Beirut and Afghanistan, where FBI agents took him right off the tarmac as his plane landed at the mecca of all the best American stoners. He was still in Folsom Prison, a place he described as "the Black Hole of American Society" in his 1973 publication "Starseed"—a great rant about space, time, and life as an interstellar communication networ. At one of Shai's garden lunches, Daniel proposed Leary's proposition as a viable cosmic hypothesis: life, culminating in human space exploration, was simply a mechanism for DNA to contact and unite with other DNA. Shai talked of the opportunity for guided acid trips, but advised me to abstain, saying, "It's not the best thing for unreconstructed neurotics."

I didn't know if he'd ever offered tripping to Claire, who had only been to a handful of the Sunday gatherings before we met and bonded over Lotte Eisner's book on Murnau and the Stimmung of expressionist German movies. We discovered we had both been at the same Murnau retrospective at the National Film Theatre only three weeks before, but our glances did not meet across a crowded room, fixed as they were on the screen. We saw, separately but together, *The Last Laugh* and *Sunrise* and *Tartuffe* and *Faust* and *Nosferatu*, which everyone loves but I always found deeply dodgy as the vampire, played by the bizarre looking Max Schreck, exhibits more than a shade of the traditional evil hook-nosed Jew. The original bloodsucker. But she hadn't got that feeling at all. She had seen *Faust* at least three times, because she was studying Emil Jannings and his body language as an actor. Which led us to his performance in *Der Blaue Engel*, with Dietrich, and my telling her that my father had always wanted to shoot a film with *Von Sternberg* because he was a director with a proper brain, rather than a sadistic genius like DeMille. She didn't like DeMille, the biblical pomposity and all the macho posturing and Charlton Heston's heaving, hairy chest. We agreed on Heston, though he had his moments in the Westerns, of which she was not a fan.

We stayed for the stuffed chicken, which was fine, and met

again the next day, for a sandwich lunch, at a small hole-in-the-wall in Finsbury Park. We talked about movies, genres, documentaries, and the stage. She was directing a play with a small company about three women who meet at an unemployment office and talk about their lives as they wait. Various other people move in and out, depending on how many of the company crew might be roped in to play the extra parts. There was a Rhodesian woman exiled from the liberation war in her country, an Argentinian woman escaping the military regime, and a woman from Scotland who had moved to London in search of a better life. She said she was wrapped up in the voices, how people talked and how they explained their own lives. She was trying to get away from the more overtly political end of the business and confessed the heresy of becoming fed up with collectives, where clashing egos seemed to lead to the domination of the most cunning members, in the same way that so many of the political Left's splinter movements morphed into the controlled vehicles of some over-ambitious and manipulative true believer who guarded the holy grail of the infallible party line. She had come to the conclusion that a distinction of roles—back to producer, director, designer, actors—got a far better result.

We walked and talked then, down the Stroud Green Road, by the Finsbury Park railway station and the Arsenal football ground, along these busy streets and solid London houses weaving off into side road mazes. Getting lost in London was a favorite pastime, something impossible in New York or Los Angeles, or even San Francisco, where the ground tells you whether you are up or down, east or west. Telling Claire of the offer I had from the film school to fill in as tutor for a term with the documentary class—the regular tutor, a Czech refugee from the Soviets, having left for a more prized post at the BBC, and a whole host of eager faces waiting for some enlightened guidance—but feeling unsure if it could come from my own addled self. Pretty soon we were actually holding hands, very old-fashioned, but a definite tingle. Her fingers were very strong, very confident as we made our way to Highbury Corner and on down Upper Street, a normally dismal walk lifted by a sharp red sunset that glowed over the Islington rooftops. The puritan landscape of Victorian London lifted by the Screen on the Green tempting us towards *The Rocky Horror Picture Show*. We didn't go in. The next day we saw our first movie together, *One Flew Over the Cuckoo's Nest*, a memory that lingers. Again and again, Jack Nicholson loses the war for his mind, but the giant Indian breaks out of the asylum at the end.

Nineteen Seventy-Five, the year of *Nashville*, and *Tommy*, and *Dog Day Afternoon* and *The Passenger*, and Kurosawa's *Dersu Uzala*, and Arthur Penn's *Night Moves*, and Fassbinder, and *Monty Python and the Holy Grail*. Later in the year, we painted the ceiling of the Gate Cinema in Notting Hill Gate—the only project of the Israeli Left, Gershon/Link reckoned, in its entire history that was both efficient and successful. I was drawn in, and Claire was on standby, to comment on the design. The space was a former stage theater in urgent need of renovation that had been opened by two American radicals, David and Barbara Stone. Daniel vouched for us as a cheap crew that would be, he insisted, as good as any, as all we had to do was stand on ladders and patch up the old curlicues and mandalic flowers whose luster had faded over the years. The first film that opened after our efforts was Fassbinder's *Fear Eats the Soul*, in which a Moroccan worker falls in love with a middle-aged German woman who is shunned by her racist white family. She loves his body and his foreignness, but he yearns for couscous. A tale of our times.

I moved in with Claire, my cell at Shai's castle cramping after a while, a little too open to the prevailing blows of the wind. Her small apartment— hidden in the triangle in which Islington, Canonbury, and Hoxton formed a kind of first intimation of the swaths of northeast London—was cozy enough for two, with the slight whiff of a previous occupant of whom no immediate story was forthcoming. Here we discovered more matching books: the Hunter Thompsons, Mark Twain, Joseph Heller, Joyce, Beckett, alongside a slew of women writers sorely neglected by my male chauvinist self: Angela Carter, Willa Cather, Germaine Greer, Zora

317

Neale Hurston, Iris Murdoch, Edna O'Brien, Joyce Carol Oates, Grace Paley, Muriel Spark, Katharine Whitehorn, an A to Z of the virago output, as well as shelves of theatrical works, plays, theater anthologies, analyses, manuscript texts, all neatly pigeonholed, with a chronological count of their inception into the stacks, a penned number—CM-1 through about 750, though not all numbers were on the shelves, and so I presumed they were left behind, abandoned, or even sold off in previous seismic movements.

Eventually, I would meet the parents, an extremely square couple, in the south of England, in a suburb of Bath, which boasted a Roman spa and some rows of famous Georgian buildings and not much else that lit my candle. They seemed to exist in a permanent posture of neutrality between all things, adopted sometime in the late 1940s after their youth was exhausted by the war. A framed photograph of them in army uniform hung on the wall alongside another, taken some years down the line, in mufti, with three-year old Claire and a rather angry baby, apparently her errant brother Joe. She had a later portrait of him in full leather on his motorcycle, on which he had apparently departed one morning to ride through France and Germany, and then moved on by other means of transport across the Iron Curtain to Prague, Budapest, and Yugoslavia, pausing for some months on beaches in Greece and Crete before proceeding across the Mediterranean into the Arab world and Africa. For a few years Claire would receive occasional postcards from him, and then a rather sullen note appeared from the British Embassy in Canberra, announcing his arrest and imprisonment in New South Wales for trading in amphetamines and weed. On his release, two years later, he married a Lebanese girl in Sydney and opened a motorcycle accessories shop, a trade that nevertheless allowed him echoes of his previous life as he rode up and down the endless trails of the Australian outback. He had two small children now, who rode pillion with the wife, Naseen. There was a photograph of this too, though not on the walls of her parents, who had ventured, after the war, no further south than Avignon and no further north than the Shetland Islands.

Pipe, cake, tea and scones. They tried their best to be interested in my inheritance of Hollywood, Israel and Cecil B. DeMille, of whom they knew little apart from *The Ten Commandments*, which was transmitted on television regularly every year—either on Easter or Christmas; they never seemed to quite pin that down. I spent a Christmas there, but there was no peep of *The Ten Commandments*, which perhaps they had mistaken for *Ben-Hur*. All Charlton Heston movies look alike to most people.

It did occur to me then that one should look at the parents, as in a glass darkly, to see the contours of where the child is heading, inexorably, despite the cries, protests, rebellions, mutinies, and Dostoyevskian urges that Freud told us we are obliged, both by biology and the inner blurs to reprise, over and over, from the first Oedipal taboos. I took up an interrupted project of reading the Blessed Sigmund right through, methodically, from the first Pelican edition of *Introductory Lectures on Psychoanalysis* to the last available at that time, *Jokes and Their Relation to the Unconscious*, which included the old man's gruesome notation of some of the worst Jewish quips of all time, such as: "I have a bath every year, whether I need one or not." (Which was followed by an even worse one: Two Jews meet outside the bathhouse, and one of them sighs, "Another year gone by already." Freud says this demonstrates the idea that "the omission forms part of the allusion." I had to look elsewhere, in libraries, for the hardback editions of the case histories, which I devoured avidly, thinking of the entangled syndromes of my own family history. Claire had contented herself mainly with the crucial volume, *The Interpretation of Dreams*, which she said she had wanted for a long time to apply in some depth to the stage. She had a dream of an immensely long project, played over a twenty-four- or even forty-eight-hour period, of various dramas, monologues, mimes, dance, and insertions of radio sound and television images, which would develop, or oppose, Freud's theories, particularly, but not only, from a feminist angle. But this was still all in the mind.

Of course, we had the anti-psychiatrists on the shelves: Szasz, Cooper, and R.D Laing: *The Divided Self, Self and Others, The Politics of Experience, Sanity, Madness and the Family,* another bible for the age of uncertainties, and Knots, with its little circular puzzles:

> "One is inside,
> then outside what one has been inside
> one feels empty
> because there is nothing inside oneself..."

It seemed to make sense at the time... Shai, of course, claimed he knew Ronnie Laing well, but warned that you had to get beyond the drinking, although, he said, when sober, the man didn't make as much sense. If our parents have made us what we are, what are we? If nations can aspire to self determination, why not individuals? That too, was blowing in the wind. The nasal twang of the sainted Bob, and the other Dylan, my favorite, the dead Welsh boozer, whose dog-eared poems I added to Claire's shelf of female bards, beside the nest of Plaths and Dickinsons, so that I could sink into bed reciting "and followed sleep" and "death shall have no dominion" and "do not go gentle into that good night." Though as time passes I am not sure that at the end I might rage at the dying of the light or simply moo the mantra that came down from my unseen grandmother's day—*shoen, genug...*

It was a good year, despite the fact that the world spun on its indifferent way, cold to tears and rage and destruction. The Lebanese Civil War that descended to mutual slaughter, the IRA bombs that punctuated London with sudden random explosions in Leicester Square and Tottenham Court Road. But I entered into Claire's small world, the confines of the cramped Stroud Lane Theatre, an extra stage hand to move props behind the scenes, help sort the lights, and walk on now and then, glowering like a policeman or the unemployment officer. I glowered well. I was not sure, at the beginning, whether Claire was attracted to me or to my camera, as she had another project in mind, springing from the unemployed three-header to a wider set of monologues encompassing a range of women, and even perhaps some men of different backgrounds, creeds and colors, who might be recorded on film first so that their experience could be more focused and pared down for the stage setting. Looking in the mirror, I couldn't see what might attract so fine a specimen as Claire to my morose and manic glare, the black uncombed thatch badly in need of Head and Shoulders, the fuzzy growth over the lip. A face, I suppose, of the times. Perhaps she was secretly blind, and her posture a stunning subterfuge trained in absolute detail by a savant's study of phenomena—streets, faces, sounds. That calm center, around which we all could swirl, a stark contrast to Samantha, the forward charge of yiddischer Yankee vigor, all blood and guts and call to arms, and leave all doubt behind... She would have done well with Shai's rebel priests, smashing nuclear nose cones deep in Kansas...

Claire worked with three other women, Chiz, Shirl, and Afriya, and a couple of muscular Australians, both called Dave, who were called in for the heavy stuff. Shirl had a van, which she drove around London with our two-headed film crew. Sometimes we would become confused with another van, belonging to the Socialist Film Collective, which was dominated by a mature German Trotskyist, M., who was surrounded by a harem of Teutonic blondes, with whom he roamed the city, in his own parlance, "looking for class struggle." Sometimes we would pass them on the Holloway Road, or in Kilburn, as he raised his clenched fist out the window towards us in a gesture of defiance or solidarity—it was difficult to make out the difference.

The specter of the absurd hung over London. It was hard to tell if it was the beginning or the end. In the balance, there were still hopes of reviving the Great Oil Series, the tale of corporate control of the globe. Gershon and Link, who were also dabbling in movies, beavered away to find funds and received several offers: from an anonymous source in Yorkshire who had infiltrated the ranks of the northern Independent Television strand, from a Kuwaiti connected in some unspecified way with his embassy, with "independent means" that sounded too dubious to tap, and from a contact in the National Union of Mineworkers who wanted to shaft the oil companies but had no money at all and had to be bought endless pints. All faded away, particularly the Yorkshireman, who never turned up for his meeting.

"You are probably on the list already," Shai told me nonchalantly, waving a large and fresh spliff. "The services like to sniff new people around. If you were in the BBC you would have a Christmas tree attached to your file. It's their sign of subversion. You can see it as a badge of honor, like a DSO or MBE. Welcome to the British Empire. A little shrunk, but still just about breathing. After Northern Ireland, it'll all be over, but that could last another ten years. We have a friend in the Special Branch, who spies on our demos. We call him the Ulsterman, he speaks with such a thick accent. He used to spy on the IRA but then they assigned him to the Middle East. He knows us all by name, he knows our life stories, he hangs around when we gather at the Israeli embassy and shake our placards on May fifteenth, which the Palestinians mark as Nakba Day. Our independence, their disaster. Every year on High Street Kensington, outside the shopping mall, it's the closest we're allowed to the Israeli embassy. We wave our placards, we chant anti-Zionist slogans, then we sit around and swap stories. It's like a school reunion. One day the Ulsterman joins us in the café a round the corner and greets us by name. I tell him, you don't look worried about all these subversives, with kaffiyehs and so forth, attacking the State of Israel, shouting slogans. He said, "Look, you older people now have homes and mortgages, and the younger ones will either leave or have the same. They'll get married, have a family, settle down. So they shout a bit every year. The people I have to worry about don't come to these shows. They live somewhere else, in the caves. What can one say?" He certainly had our number.

But come May 15, I didn't join the demonstration. I had spent the long winter locked up with Claire in my private Eden, setting out three days a week to the London Film School in its warehouse block in Covent Garden, four steep flights of stone steps leading up the old brick walls that used to store crates of fruit and vegetables, now echoing to the clatter of long-haired scruffy students chasing the rainbow of celluloid dreams. My job was to pull their weed-blown heads out of the clouds of fiction to feast their eyes on the reality that filled the streets around them. The mantra: Forget the word "docu-mentary." Films aren't documents; films are moving pictures, no more and no less. Start from the image, then figure the sounds. Very old-fashioned, the primal shades of pre-World War I movies, DeMille in embryo. But though my brain was invested in my duties, my heart was uptown. Between bed, books, stage, and camera, despite the far-off thunder of guns and London's dour days of darkness by noon as the English winter sneaks in...

On January 18, 1976, the Christian Phalange militias in Lebanon attacked the Palestinian refugee camp-cum-town of Karantina near the Beirut harbor, killing several hundred people. We watched the news on the small, blurry TV set in Finsbury Park. Two days later we watched the news of the PLO's retaliation in the Christian village of Damour. Hundreds dead, including dozens of Phalange fighters. An even more deadly revenge was inevitable. The meeting at Shai's the next Sunday was held in the kitchen, as freezing rain deluged the garden. Shai was not his usual lively self, emptied of jokes, as the Palestinians Abed and Mansur glumly predicted more bloodshed. People of every stripe, Palestinians, Lebanese Sunnis, Shias and Christians were fleeing from endangered villages. Dire predictions of escalation and the drawing in of both Israeli and Syrian regular forces, leading to yet another Arab-Israel war, were muttered around the table. Even Daniel could offer no relief in the form of either mushrooms or stuffed chicken. The day darkened to a veritable eclipse around 2 p.m., when Claire and I left.

As weeks passed, the conflict seemed frozen, poised between disaster and cataclysm. The bloodletting appeared to dissipate into small skirmishes, and the dead were counted in dozens rather than thousands on the inner newspaper pages and BBC round-up sections. It was too cold and mean to drive around London in search of class struggle or interviews, so Claire stayed home and wrote, and I fought with the students as the rain lashed Central London.

Spring came late, my private paradise undimmed, although I wondered how long it would last. She would find me out, my moroseness, my shifting moods, the curse of the past, the shadows of Melchett. My mother called to say my father was ill, but then called two days later to say he was well again, another batch of old cinematographers had arrived from Hollywood to lift his spirits. Claire had a supplementary plan; following on our expanding stash of filmed interviews with Londoners, I would turn the camera back on myself, record my own experiences of the Middle East, the Holy Land, the minutiae of the experience of modern Israel from the fifties and sixties, and my own experience, which I had avoided like typhoid fever, of the Six-Day War. "I filmed stuff," I told her. "I went around with the Arriflex camera, a sun gun, and wet-lead batteries, filming for the army film unit. If you keep your eye stuck to the lens, you can usually tune most things out." But she didn't believe me, and kept returning to the mantra: "I want to know. I'm a magpie, I store things. You never know when it might come in useful." Later, I said. Tomorrow. Next week. It's not what you think. It's too boring…

One week, in June, when Claire had gone up to Liverpool to plan some joint feminist offensive on the northern theatrical hinterland, Shai suddenly called me on the Saturday morning, hallowed rest from film school.

"Have you heard the news?" he said. "The Syrians have invaded Lebanon, big time. The Palestinians are fighting them all over the place. The comrades here have occupied the Arab League building. Bring your camera and meet us there."

The Arab League building was a stately looking edifice amid a row of high-class office mansions off Park Lane, by Hyde Park. A crowd of demonstrators were gathered, with the usual placards and some newly scrawled cards marked "SYRIAN IMPERIALISTS OUT OF LEBANON" and the somewhat unusual "SYRIA— ISRAEL—USA—HOW MANY PALESTINIANS HAVE YOU KILLED TODAY?" Imperialism seemed to expand by the hour. There was a phalanx of policemen, but they were standing aside and making no move to challenge or evict the group sitting on the stairs leading up to the gold plaque and entranceway, whose door was ajar.

I brought the Bolex, which was both portable and windable by hand, rather than requiring battery power. Sometimes old-fashioned solutions are the best. I saw two familiar faces, Mansur and Gershon, at the door. Gershon ushered me in, past a crowd of excited people, young and old, mostly men but with an eager crew of women carrying banners and placards up the wide imperial staircase that led from the ground-floor offices, each of which were teeming with murmuring, buzzing hordes. Quite a few them were familiar as people who had drifted by Shai's garden table or kitchen, shooting the breeze about this or that, the flotsam of Palestine's thickening trail of exiles. There were young guys who had shared a toke with the Israelis, and Farida was there across the room from Abed, and Sargon, a gaunt Israeli who also taught mathematical theory somewhere, and an Iraqi or Iranian called Farajul—I couldn't tell the difference then—a couple of older Palestinians with gray hair who were also academics of some sort, two thirtysomethings called Sami, who were either Iraqis or Syrians, and Ghada from the General Union of Palestinian Students in London, which had, Gershon told me, organized the sit-in launched the previous evening in coordination with the clerks in the building. They had presented the Arab League officials with a fait-accompli, a symbolic three-day occupation that would highlight the plight of the Palestinians and Lebanese caught up in Lebanon's civil war and fulfill Yasser Arafat's call for the whole world to come to the aid of the Palestinians, who were being attacked by the very people who should have been their allies: the Syrian forces of Hafez al-Assad, who had suddenly sided with the Christian Phalange. In any case, the Arab League had been in recess and there was nobody in the building except the clerks and auxiliary staff who had volunteered to liaise with the students to ensure the whole affair would be conducted peacefully, no damage done to fixtures and fittings, and reasonable decorum observed. Since the league was totally paralyzed by the splits in its own ranks and its inability to do anything about the fighting in Lebanon except throw up its hands in horror and urge everyone involved to sign up to yet another cease-fire as soon as possible; their London envoys had nothing to lose.

Halfway up to the second floor, Shai appeared on the landing and beckoned me up. "You brought the camera? Good. Do you have a tape recorder? Never mind, we can find something up here." We pressed through into a large chamber, presumably the conference room, which had been cleared, the large round table upended at the far side and covered with beige drapes and the student occupiers sprawled on the plush gray carpet under a row of portraits of current leaders. The rogues' gallery of stunted military faces included the smiling visage of Egypt's Anwar Sadat, the Roman profile of Assad, the smiling Jordanian King Hussein, the prunish face of Iraq's President al-Bakr and his vice president, a young Saddam Hussein, the new King Khalid of Saudi Arabia, a potpourri of interchangeable Gulf emirs, President for life Habib Bourguiba of Tunisia, President Boumédiène of Algeria, the King of Morocco, the immoveable Colonel Qaddafi of Libia, and in pride of place, displacing some minor potentate, President Arafat of the Palestine Liberation Organization, smiling broadly under his signature kaffiyeh, with sashes of office drawn across the portrait and a slogan in Arabic pinned up above him: "In Blood and Fire We Shall Redeem You Palestine." Abed said the slogan was ubiquitous.

"All in shipshape and proper order," said Shai, leading me to an unoccupied niche in the corner. "The Goat and Moshik are in the main telephone office. You have to understand the ulterior motive. Everybody is queuing up to call home long distance at the expense of our hosts. Every now and then a backlog of messages to their families builds up among the comrades, and students can't afford the international calls. I'd say an occupation is probably necessary at least every six months. The Goat is on the phone to his mother in Sheinkin."

That would be just around the corner from Melchett, but I thought it better to defer to those who needed to call Beirut, Cairo, Nablus, Bethlehem, or even Baghdad. It seemed, nevertheless, strange for an Arab occupation to include so many Israelis, but it did provide an ideal opportunity to catch up on gossip and conduct a background seminar on the whole shebang. "Asher, this is Ghassan. He's from Damascus. He's volunteered to explain to us the Ba'ath party from A to zed." The balding man with the heavy stare of chronic goiter shook his head. "That would take two weeks. At least."

"Just give us the high points."

"There are no high points. There are only lows, I am afraid."

"All I understand about it," said Shai, "is that the original wing of the Iraqi Ba'ath Party is in power in Syria, and the Syrian Ba'ath is in power in Iraq. Is that correct?"

"More or less," Ghassan waved his hand politely. "It is more of a theological difference. Both are in favor of unity, liberty and socialism. But I am afraid we have none of these three. We have generals, who represent the will of the people. All of the people, you understand, of the entire Arab world. The leader is the embodiment of all the Arabs, at least until he is shot and replaced. You know the founders of the party, Michel Aflaq and Bitar, studied at the Sorbonne in Paris during the nineteen-thirties. They studied the positivism of Renan and Comte. I hope they are teaching different stuff there, these days."

"I wouldn't count on it."

The morning wound on in similarly educational fashion, with mini-seminars on the history of Syrian coups, the psychopathology of Muammar Qaddafi, the intrigues of Iraq, and the cat's cradle of sectional politics in Lebanon, with a Freudian analysis of Maronite Christianity's knotty relationship with Rome from the seventh century onwards, the Monothelite controversy and the condemnations of the Lateran council of AD 649 in the Pope's letters to the Chalcedonian churches. "Three fingers or one finger!" said Ghassan, fixing his protruding eyes on us sagely. "That's what you have to remember!" Meanwhile, the league's clerks moved among us with silver trays of tea and coffee, and some exquisite baklava and other sweets broken out of the envoy's personal larder. Sometime after the lunch hour, I wondered if I should risk exiting the building to try and call Claire in Liverpool from a phone booth, or line up in the main office like everyone else. In the end, the line had shrunk, and I took the phone for a brief moment after a very satisfied student of King's College had spoken with his grandmother in Umm-al-Fahm. I caught Claire at the theater just before a meeting and tried to explain to her that I was calling from the Arab League office, but the noise was too loud all around me and someone was waiting to call Aleppo.

As I squeezed my way back to the conference room I passed a corridor with a shelf of books behind two sliding glass doors. I peeked in curiously and spied a star of David on a book cover, so I pulled it out. It was an old copy of the Protocols of the Elders of Zion, printed in Baltimore, USA. Beside it was a slim volume: "Assassination as a Political Means," which appeared to range from Lincoln to Kennedy. The other books on the shelf were about cookery, mainly Italian and Indian. I brought the two books up to Shai, who turned them over and sighed, "It figures." He put them away in his satchel. "We'll keep it for the collection. You never know when you might need a spot of blackmail. But don't steal the silver. We still have some principles." He sighed again and shrugged. "I stole my own copy of *Mein Kampf* from Foyles."

1992, Asher:

The more I return to California the more it seems a foreign country, receding further and further from the childhood of my dreams. All the more so San Francisco, which my father never seemed to visit; everything he needed to sustain him stayed within L.A. county limits. Maybe a shunt to San Bernardino, or to Orange County or Ventura. He liked the Guadalupe sands near Pismo

Beach, north of Santa Barbara, because DeMille had shot the first silent *Ten Commandments* there and buried the Egyptian sets in the dunes rather than cart them back to Hollywood. I was too young to remember, but he told me later that when I heard his story about how all of Pharaoh's armies and horses and chariots were drowned trying to follow the Children of Israel, just out there, beyond the carousel, I rushed off to dig in the sand. But I couldn't find any helmets, buckles, or swords, or any trace of Moses' magic staff.

San Francisco, on the other hand always echoes for me with Richard Brautigan, whom I first found on the shelves of Steimatzky bookshop on Dizengoff Street in Tel Aviv, and made me hanker for the Pacific Coast again. I liked *Trout Fishing in America*, which featured what he called "an Israeli terrorist chant": "Long live our friend the revolver! Long live our friend the machine gun!" He'd probably got it from some old Irgun raconteur, perhaps some fellow traveler of Uncle Kolya. In a later collection of Brautigan's work, *The Tokyo-Montana Express* I enjoyed *The Menu*, which discusses the menu offered to Death Row prisoners at San Quentin State Prison in 1965, a cornucopia that included stewed prunes, farina, crisp bacon, hot cakes with maple syrup, split pea soup, barbecue short ribs, grilled wieners, spaghetti, frankfurter buns, oleo and peanut butter sandwiches. America! America! sometimes there is still a tug...

After paying my respects to Kamil's urn, I drove the Alamo car north, up 101, past Santa Barbara and Pismo, continuing on the freeway from San Luis Obispo rather than take the long route up the coast and Big Sur. Too much to handle driving alone, and not enough time. I stopped off near Soledad at a motel to sleep over, wondering fitfully what the menu might be at the famous prison there, which glowered unseen in the night. Echoes of George Jackson and the other two "brothers" charged with killing a white prison guard back in the days.

Off in the morning to the Bay Area. My friend Jim Silver (a.k.a. Long Jim) had a house on Diamond Street, four streets up from our traditional breakfast hole, Herb's Fine Foods, on 24th

Street. Bilious green seats, chipped formica tables, two eggs over easy, and waffles with maple syrup. There are some things you don't want to change. Jim Silver was a Berkeley student who had just missed out on the Battle of the Park but wandered in on the Chavez grape movie as a second camera. He never came to New York, as his license to travel, his excuse was, didn't allow him to cross the Rockies. He remained a West Coaster born and bred, brought up in Culver City. While I was back in the Unholy Land he joined the faculty of film at San Francisco State and bought the house on Diamond. We forged another link when he married a California girl who was a student at the London Film School when I taught the documentary class in '76—Adina, another ex-Israeli. Some time as I was glowering at the Lebanon War and passing by my father's slow deathbed she met a woman and became a born-again lesbian, though she had already borne Jim a baby daughter, Miri. She returned to live at Diamond Street after he had a stroke some time afterward, with Miri and the new woman, Elaine. This was my second visit since the Event and he now seemed in fine shape, walking, with a limp, but steadily, down the steep roads to 24th and then up again, a solid test for a fully functioning pair of legs at any time of the day or year.

He had been shooting and editing a long-term documentary project about an old lady, a Holocaust survivor, who lectured at schools all over the United States about her life. Jim became immersed in the saga, and so we fell and twisted into an Eastern European sidewind, with curious darts at my own family chronicles as I brought out copies of Aunt Sarah's letter and my father's papers from Provo, Utah. I told him I was pretty sure there were other letters, hidden away in my uncle's files in Ann Arbor, Michigan, in Kolya's archive stash. I told him my uncle was now ninety-six years old, but still working on his mammoth volumes of "Jew Hatred Through the Ages." I told him about Yonni, the "Hawking boy," his mouthpiece and general representative to the rest of mankind. His politics presumably matching Kolya's position somewhere to the right of Attila the Hun.

"Well, you'll just have to ease yourself in," Jim told me, working through his stack of molasses. "You never know. That kind of person might come in useful down the line, when you might need a little help of your own. God knows I've reconciled to a lot of strange things. Life has a habit of throwing the curveball. I shouldn't eat any of this," he said, holding the waffle. "When I started recovery, my doctor gave me a list of all the things I couldn't eat from then on. It was an exact list of everything I loved. You know something else? You'll have to go there."

"Where?"

"To your home village. What's it called, this Celovets. The hometown in Rumania, or wherever they came from, where all those folk set out from. Your father's birthplace."

"It's in Moldova. It was a Soviet republic, but now that's all finished; I don't know whether it's part of Russia or the Ukraine. I think I read that they declared their independence, like the other ex-Soviet states. Estonia, Latvia, Lithuania, Kazakhstan, Armenia, Georgia. All those dead histories we have to relearn."

"You have to stand on the spot and ask yourself, what happened here? Mrs. Orenstein always says that to her classes. You have to stand on the spot where they came and took you from, and say, I'm back. The healing process."

"It's not a Holocaust thing, Jim boy. The first lot got out before the First World War. Kolya was swallowed by the revolution and wormed his way out, we don't know how. Zev went east, towards China, and Judit followed him there."

"Lots more journeys then, Asher. Go while you can."

"I have a beautiful woman in Finsbury Park."

"I have two in the Bay Area, and an even more beautiful little one. I used to carry her up along the Castro. The gays all rushed up to ask me how I managed to do it. Everyone assumes you fit in around here."

"I just want to crack Kolya. For my dad. And to find out about Gramby."

"Man of magic and mystery. It'll make a great movie."

So many tales would, but never will. I used to ask Dad why he never tried to direct, and why not, but he just waved his hand. "Directors are born bullshitters. They have to make something from nothing. I have a camera; I can feel it, touch it, I know how it works. I know how it uses the light."

"A script, at least. Or a novel, something you can do without money. I had two students who gave up on pictures and discovered Mark Twain and Saul Bellow. You have a Tolstoy at least in front of you. The Brothers Gurevits."

"I'm not a writer. Claire takes care of that department. A play maybe. Something you can mount with a few flats, some old furniture, and a load of schmutters. We tried to write something together once, but it never got finished."

"Nothing of mine ever does," he said. "I can't seem to bear to let it go."

I told Jim how I'd made an effort to winkle out Gramby on the way to Provo the year before, in 1991, contacting Shad Wasserman in New York to check the trail of Ace Harrington, the old jazz legend, who my father once said he'd read somewhere had told the newspapers stories of his old vaudeville days. Shad was a dedicated jazz fiend, with a prized collection of 78s. He hadn't known much when I met him, but later he wrote me a long letter saying he had checked up on the Harrington heritage. In his last years, Ace had retreated to his house in Augusta, Georgia, where he died in 1986, leaving his money, music, and possessions in dispute between his wives and children. There had been four wives, two white and two black, and about a dozen children, all with claims. Shad wrote that an archive existed, allegedly consisting of tape recordings the old man had made for a ghosted autobiography that was either never written or unfinished. He suggested that I try and schmooze the wives, but his contacts couldn't tell him which one of the four was the better bet. They were scattered all over the country, in Atlanta, Cleveland, St Louis, not to speak of the offspring, some of whom were in Europe—France, Spain, who knew?

"Children of the famous," said Jim. "Tell me about it. I have a friend who tried to write a book about W.C. Fields, but the grand-sons led him a merry dance to nowhere. Lives of the great are a proper business here. Everybody's guarding the treasure chest, even if it turns out to be empty."

"Well, our Gramby was great only to a limited circle, as far as I can find. He was never a headliner. Except maybe in France. I might have to dig there."

"Happy hunting."

Jim lifted another waffle to his face. We walked back up 24th Street towards Diamond, along the row of cafés, the pizza store, the novelty toy and weird stuff shop, the secondhand music store that stocked everything from Ace Harrington and Beethoven to Tibetan chants and Tuvan throat singing. The corner of Castro, where the first time I came here there was still a mouth-watering ice cream shop, whose name I forget, which Claire nominated her favorite. It was her first, and only, trip so far with me to California. She loved San Francisco but not Los Angeles. "That empty space, filled with delusions." Yes, but if you peeked behind the veil, there be monsters of many brilliant shapes and models... Kamil's urn was more typical perhaps of Burbank than of Bethlehem... I think she found the poverty of the DeMille barn and its tiny heritage museum emblematic of the sparseness of Hollywood's original inception—a couple of old box-like cameras, some ancient arc lights, and some glass cases with a few Crusader shields and swords. Storyboard and art design drawings on the walls, the DeMille office with an old wicker chair and typewriter and some rusty film cans on the desk. This Is Where It All Began. My father would have certainly been at home there. But from Melchett you have at least a view of the sea. Or a glimpse. To think we could have had Malibu...

Past Castro there was another little store that I think has now long gone, the secondhand Crime and Mystery bookshop, which reminded me of all the dusty old paperbacks I used to buy in the nooks of Allenby in Tel Aviv, to nurture my own American fantasies rather than my father's iron rules of The Frame: Dashiell Hammett,

Chester Himes, David Goodis, Jim Thompson, Charles Williams, William P. McGivern and the evergreen Chandler. Down these mean streets a man must go... the heritage tarnished by the more lurid writers, Sax Rohmer, Edgar Wallace... *The Curse of the Yellow Snake*, *The Fourth Plague*, *The Four Just Men*, I can feel the crumbling covers in my hands. Hair standing on end from the devilish conspiracies of cigar-smoking, yellow-skinned, and dark-faced foreigners to undermine the stability of capital and of course the British Empire. The Judeo-Communist-Chinese plot, emanating not a million miles from our very own Celovest... Even the black Chester Himes couldn't resist his digs against Herbie Freiberger, the despicable union steward who thrives on his privileges. I was tempted to send that particular book to Uncle Kolya many years back, just to needle his arrogance, but I held my postage since, for all I knew, it already fueled half a volume of his compendium of global Jew hatred.

Life becomes obscured by jumble. Confusion, ambiguity, denial, and denial of denial, which leaves the floodgates open for yet more jumble. After Chester Himes, Dostoyevsky. After Dostoyevsky, Philip K. Dick. After Philip K. Dick, more Dostoyevsky, until *Catch-22*, and then, for a moment, all was clear. I carried Yossarian around with me across America, along with his gallery of grotesques: Major Major, General Dreedle, Colonel Cathcart, Milo Minderbinder, and all the toiling pilots of World War II a.k.a. Vietnam, the proper bible of our own refusal to keep flying our ordained missions. My own old battered copy of the British Corgi edition called it "the Polymesmeric bestseller," as good a catchphrase as any. I used to read it aloud to Claire until she started punching me in the back when I repeated immortal lines like, "Who can explain malaria as a consequence of fornication?" But these days that puts me in mind of my Aunt Sarah and her discoveries of the new world of Jewish renewal in the mudflats of Deganiah, in the stewing Beisan valley...

Somehow, as I stayed awake after Jim Silver—exhausted by his courageous walk up the sixty-degree slope of Diamond—went to bed, I sat upstairs on the veranda that overlooked the whole swath of the city towards Mission, downtown, the Bay Bridge and, on a really clear day, all the way to Alameda and Oakland, wondering if this was the night the racoon might slither up the ramparts to try and steal the dog's dinner, a good moment perhaps to try to figure out the stew of my life, what I was doing chasing old phantoms in this California in which my father's old phantoms had settled in the space of Cecil B. DeMille's frame...

Who was I before I started on all this? Rushing off in a frenzy from the materialization of Sarah and Kolya's own "poly-mesmeric" dreams. Trying to pin down new-old meanings with inherited tools, "In camera I," from Chavez to the Indians, from Rogosin's Bowery, from the armies of the night to the crimes of broad daylight, the bright sunlit sins of post-war occupation, the mea culpa, the new bleeding heart, the *tohu va bohu* of Shai Baer's garden, flying high, then leveling out on the good solid wood floor of Claire's stage. Someone who brings the world into her own space, rather than fly off in all directions searching for things that are no longer there. From be practical, to dream the impossible, to embrace the practical. Staying on at the London Film School after the documentary period, joining and then running the Camera Department... the domestic years, settlement and a little expansion by loft conversion in Finsbury Park, from participation to eavesdropping: revolutions unfolding on TV. In the East, old certainties challenged: a million students mass in Tiananmen Square, the tanks move in, but elsewhere they fall back: a wall tumbles, an ossified tyranny breaks, statues are pulled down and smashed, people flow through cracks, then fissures, then floods, armored police run from candlelight marches, keys rattle in Prague's Wenceslas Square, a tyrant gunned down in a Rumanian courtyard, new-old flags waved in scenes repeating those recorded when this defeated old guard was itself new. Instead of being there, cheering the Frame... What was it like for you, Kolya, long long ago, on that Saint Petersburg night?

The raccoon failed to turn up. In the morning I sat down at Jim's phone and dialed through to the direct number I had been

335

given in Ann Arbor for Yonni Stern, my uncle's faithful amanuensis. I was lucky that the man himself answered.

"Yonni? It's Asher Gore calling, Asher Gurevits, Kolya, Nathan's nephew. We met last year, in April. You remember, I brought you the family picture and my father's old manuscripts from Provo, Utah. How is my uncle doing? Is he OK?"

"*B'ezrat hashem*. He's doing well. I remember you. Are you in Tel Aviv?"

"I still live in London. But I'm calling from San Francisco. I wrote you a letter about my Aunt Sarah's letters, which she wrote from Palestine to my father? I found one of them on this trip, at the Academy of Arts and Sciences archive, in Los Angeles. It was in a subsidiary collection."

"Yes, we talked. I got your letter. I recall I answered it."

"Well, it must have gone astray. Maybe I gave you the wrong address."

"It's possible."

"I wrote to you that those letters from Sarah were not in the Israeli archives. The Labor Party archives."

"The Labor Party is an archive. Are you coming to see your uncle?"

"Do you think I should? My mother told me he's not very responsive."

"Who needs a response? *Mishpachah* is *mishpachah*. Even if he kicks you it's a blessing."

"I would love to see him," I lied, "and I would love to have a chance to look at some of the archive. It may well be you have the letters there."

There was a kind of silence, like the shuffling of thoughts in a crackling vacuum. Then he said:

"Knowing the truth is a mitzvah. If you come and give him a kiss on the forehead, I will have something to show you."

"I'll be glad to come."

"*B'ezrat hashem*. I'm here from ten till four, Monday to Thursday. Friday till one o'clock."

"I'll call you when I have my flight details."

"You do that. *Shabbat shalom.*"

I had forgotten that it was already Friday.

On the plane to Detroit, having changed my flight ticket back to the New York route, I remembered another event we watched from our sofa on the TV while the world changed: the release of Nelson Mandela after twenty-six, or was it twenty-seven years in prison on Robben Island in South Africa. I remember it as one of the first events in which one watched a live broadcast of crowds of people standing about for hours doing and seeing nothing while commentators tried to fill the time by relating the entire history of the South African struggle and anything else that could be dredged up—the brightness of the day, the clothing or shoes of those waiting, the significance of the cause of their ennui. I remembered that Kolya was supposed to have spent some time in South Africa when he left Russia, either in the 1920s or '30's; dates were very uncertain in those early family accounts, before I paid any attention. It is not known how long he spent there, probably at the time when Nelson Mandela was either a child or a teenager. One fades, another rises. Finally, Mandela walked out, a tall, steady and confident man in a gray suit and gray-white hair, holding the hand of his wife, who had waited for him so many years. "Would you wait for me for twenty-seven years?" I asked Claire. "Probably not," she said. "You're not Mandela." As indeed, no one else is.

We could sorely do with somebody like that, I remember thinking, in our sorry neck of the woods, in Israel-Palestine, in the Middle East, in the whole region. But all we have are thieves, assassins, and charlatans.

I hired a car at the airport and drove to Ann Arbor under lowering clouds that presaged a thunderstorm. The rains broke just as I passed through the city, the sheet lightning shearing the sky like an Old Testament warning. I had to pull over just short of the sanctuary and stop to let the rain wash around me. The deluge stopped suddenly, and a window of sunlight opened above the low villas like a corny message of hope. I imagined my uncle, like the sorceror's apprentice, sitting in his wheelchair and orchestrating the elements. But when I was ushered into his presence, he was sitting as if woven into his armchair, his eyes glinting, wide open and shining, in the wrinkled nut of his face. Yonni tapped him gently on the shoulder.

"This is Asher, Prof, remember? Your brother Berl's son. The younger one. Asher. He came all the way from Tel Aviv."

My uncle grunted and closed his eyes, submitting to the obligatory peck on the cheek and forehead. Yonni looked very pleased.

"Let's go into the study," he said, standing aside like a major domo as he waved me through into the inner sanctum. A vast desk with a large IBM computer and several boxes of electronic accessories crowded in by filing cabinets that filled most of the remaining space. Yonni drew up a typing chair and settled onto his own swivel throne. Three document files were laid out on the table, along with a small storage box and a long cardboard tube. "Sit," he said. "Will you have a coffee? I thought you might want to go straight to the business. Even in Michigan, all roads lead to Jerusalem. This is like a law of nature. We do have your aunt's letters, or at least some of them. You mentioned twenty-six, but we have only eight. There might be more elsewhere. Research is neverending. Prof taught me that if you can't find something, it means you are not looking hard enough, or in the right place. Seek and you will find. The Prof found so many sources that everyone else completely ignored. Why is it? Maybe the great weight of the evidence of our subject overwhelmed the researchers, or perhaps it frightened them off. Who wants to have so many enemies, stretching so far back in time? So many victims, and every one of them has a story. Of course, the perpetrators have a story too; we do not begrudge them their narrative as long as we set the record straight. There is a murderer and there is a crime. What we do not deal with here is divine justice. We only deal in the small justice of the word. We are not the prosecution, simply the compilers. I know, it's not your bag. You want to carry a lighter load in your satchel. But at least you started carrying something. You have to excuse me for speaking for your uncle. It's a fixed habit, I'm afraid. He had a minor stroke some months ago. So minor we didn't notice till he started slurring his words. The brain is still working away but the utterance has been affected. So I've become a real Hawking boy now." He gave a kind of low rumble, which I took to be a laugh.

"He has a plan. He intends to live to be one hundred, which means there are four more years to go. Then he'll make another plan. This is how your uncle has lived. Sometimes there is a continuity of stages, sometimes a rupture. This is how he's moved through life. I have something interesting for you. But first the letters. They are in this file. There are originals and copies, which Prof has said are for you. You have to make your own translation. I'll make coffee meantime."

He handed me the file and got up to go into the kitchen, moving with the slow stolidity of someone who stopped being in a hurry a long while ago. Sarah's letters were in separate cellophane folders, but without their original envelopes. I recognized that Yiddish scrawl from the Academy letter. My eyes moved over the familiar Hebrew letters forming that unfamiliar language. That old patrimony that we were brought up to dismiss and scorn in our bold upbringing as the first-generation Sabras, the new age Israelis, born from the ashes of the Jew. Scanning the crisp photocopies did not make it more comprehensible. Providing no translation was probably a deliberate act from Kolya and Yonni's point of view.

Yonni came back with two mugs of coffee adorned with flowers and colorful calligraphy marking "Ann Arbor Summer Fayre." He also held a small plate of ginger cookies.

"You had a breakfast on the plane?"

"The bistro meal."

"Commiserations. I can call them to bring lunch from the canteen. *Milchig* only, on Mondays. We had to train them for *kashrut*."

"It's not a problem. I actually ate the bistro." I didn't tell him it was a bacon sandwich.

"Ouch!" He put the mugs down on coasters he picked out from a side drawer, a safe distance from the files. "OK. I brought out two other files that Prof thought might help you in the family history researches. There are a few more items on Sarah, a couple of articles about her from Palestine journals in the thirties and forties. There was a time when she was allied with the 'Caananites,' did you know? They wanted a secular Zionism that was cut off from religion. Straight from the Bible to Eretz Yisrael without the agency of God. Quite interesting. It's all in the family. Then there are some official letters in the next file, also from Sarah, through the Jewish Agency offices to the Jewish Society in Tokyo, asking for information about your uncle Ze'ev and your aunt Judit who went to China in the twenties. Your aunt thought there might be records of the Japanese period in Manchuria, during the nineteen-thirties, when they were supposed to be living in Harbin. But there is no record of any answer. There might have been answering letters, but Nathan has not found them. He told me he also tried to find out about Ze'ev, but he has no documents for that. Now this here, this is a curiosity..." He reached out and picked up the cardboard tube, carefully pulling from its open end a rolled-up poster. The old, partly stained paper crackled in his hand as he slowly drew it out and then unrolled it on the desk, pinning down its corners with two paperweights, a stapler and a small silver candelabrum.

"Voila!" he called out, standing back and spreading his arms. It was a large, garish theatrical poster, about three feet by four, with the name of the printer, "Affice Louis Galice, 99 Rue Fr. St. Denis, Paris," upper left of frame, and below it two small images: an intense bearded face in a turban to the left, and a staring eye with large lashes to the right, each emanating bolts of lightning, overlooking, in frame center, on a red background, the head and shoulders of a young man of indeterminate racial or ethnic background. He could be white, Romanian, Turkish or Arab, with round eyes staring under a great white turban pinned at the front by a broach circled with jewels and topped with a feather in whose center an oval enclosed the image of a lyre. The man was dressed in a smart dark suit with a white bow tie, the index finger of his right hand poised, lightly touching his cheek in an in formal, pensive pose. The sleeve was pinned by a shirt cuff marked with a crescent and star. Beneath the image the legend read:

THE GREAT V. GRAMBY
MASTER OF MYSTERY WITH HIS
MUSICAL VARIETY COMPANY

Yonni wagged his head admiringly. "Have you ever seen this picture before? One of our sources on the North African volume found it in a shop in the medina of Marrakesh. He remembered Nathan speaking of his magician brother and bought it on the spot. What do you think, eh? *A shoene metsiyeh.*"

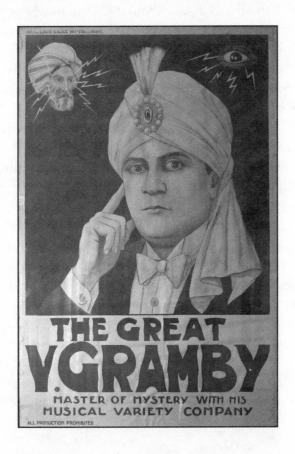

A *shoene metsiyeh* indeed. He picked it up and placed it gingerly over the filing cabinets, holding it so that I could move around, as space allowed, to observe it from different angles. It was one of those portraits where the eyes follow you around wherever you go. I looked for clues in the face, the pose, the arrangement. Was this a Gurevits face? The nose was definitely not Jewish, but neither was my father's. My own hooked Fagin look may have come down from my mother, or maybe both Gramby and my father skipped a generation, because Kolya's nose was pretty prominent. The eyes, the eyes could be anything; the portraitist had caught a certain sorrow, or was it curiosity, or a well-camouflaged mockery of the viewer, or just someone else's face, grafted in for the publicity? There must be other pictures, records, news stories... I asked Yonni if I could have another look at the ur-photograph, the one-and-only Gurevits family snap.

"I've looked at it," he said. "It's possible. A little boy's face. It could be Pinocchio, before the lies. It could be anybody. It could be a fake. Somebody heard of the name and drew the image. 'Master of Mystery,' after all."

"Nothing else? No other folders?"

He saw me looking at the box still unopened on the table and started rolling the poster back up, tight enough to insert skilfully in the tube. Then he sat back down.

"Yes, of course there are files. Yakov Gurevits is listed at Yad Vashem as missing, last known in Paris, nineteen-thirty-nine. He might have escaped to Vichy France. He might have remained until July of forty-two when the remaining Jews of Paris were rounded up. He is not on any camp lists. He might have disguised himself and reached a safe zone and, as we say, not checked back in when the war was safely over. He may have lived on as someone else. Nathan did search for him, in many places. The South American disapora, where many refugees went? No trace. Not in South Africa, not Australia. Where else? Morocco? Tunis? Algeria? All these were safety bolts, too, but people can so easily vanish. Five or six billion people on the planet. Can they all be accounted for?"

He leaned forward.

"So what's in the magic box? When you called me on Friday, I told Nathan you were coming. He seemed very excited. I have to tell you this is rare. Prof is not the excitable type. It's true, he can get furious, but that usually manifests as a kind of centripetal gathering of fury into a cold fusion, an absolute determination to turn the anger into deeds. This he was like even as a boy, eh? The letter you brought us shows it clearly. As the youth, so the sage. So many changes, but the core of personality always stays the same. This is how God made us. We are nature, not nurture. And nature is God. You want to read Marx, Engels, Lenin, Trotsky, Marcuse, Lukács? Be my guest. Lenin the cold calculating goy, Trotsky the excitable yid. In the end the cunning Georgian sticks the ice pick in his head. It's true, human nature is simple, not complicated. Prof is a kind of Trotsky, in his way, but for his own people, not for the so-called proletarian ideal. What did the proletarians get from all that? Death, hard labor, starvation, gulag...

"So I will tell you something. Your uncle loves you. He loves his son too, and his two daughters, and all the grandchildren, and the great-grandchildren, and you know about the great-great-grandchild, Ruthie? This is a tree with many boughs. But he loves you something special. You want to know why? Because he recognizes himself in you. His son, Adir, is like a bear. He follows his destiny, he prowls about the forest. He is aware of his strength. Very soon, he'll seize his prize. You know of course that he is now in the top ten places in the party for the next election. Ministerial material. Maybe even prime minister. Maybe he will save the nation from the little foxes and the squirrels who run around storing their nuts. If they have any nuts. The castrati. The Jews are a small people, and when we are bunched together in small spaces, we jostle a lot. It's learned behavior. Descendants of slaves. But God sent us Moses so that we should wake up. OK, this is boring you. But I can tell you one more annoying fact: Nathan says you are a wolf. You're the one who has the killer instinct. The only problem is, you have decided that you are a pacifist. That's bad for wolves. Nature and nurture fight within. You're restless. I'm told you have a beautiful wife in London, not Jewish. Mazel tov. You make your choices. It does not matter if you marry out of the faith, or if you run around with silly Trotskyists, or if you think you're the innocent lamb rather than the lion when Messiah comes. You feel the call of the blood. Does that sound ominous to you? A bit Nazi? Don't worry, it's just a figure of speech. It's not in the blood, it's in the spirit. Voices from the past are calling out to you. You find an old photograph, you begin to vibrate, like a tuning fork, to the tunes of the past. The old *nigun*, from the bet midrash. What, you think you're hearing something else? Negro rhythms, Hindu chants, the Rolling Stones, Bruce Springsteen? Bob Dylan? Just another Jew. You want to escape from the past? Why are you coming here? This is Past Central. What has been still is, and will be always. Repetition. That's the essence of Jewish life. You don't believe in God? Don't worry, your cells do. They're what remember the *nigun*. But you rebel, you're disobedient. This is in the cells too. You should study kabbalah, you will understand it. The loose sparks of creation. God is not perfect, so neither is man. We need each other. One day you'll learn. God made us the thinking animal for a purpose. So, end of lesson. What is the deduction? Your uncle wants to trust you with the holy of holies."

He pushed the box towards me. I opened the lid. Inside were two thick notebooks, with scuffed blue covers, pretty old and battered. The covers had simple labels, marked in blue pen "1" and "2." I carefully opened the first. Without heading or preamble, the first page of the lined paper was covered with a small, crushed but neat scrawl, which started at the top line and continued to the last, then went on, with almost no free lines, to the last page. Ditto volume two. It was in French.

"This is Prof's number four handwriting." said Yonni. "You've probably seen number five, the Hebrew he uses for letters. I have

344

to categorize everything, so that I can know his mind. Number one is Russian, of course. Number two is Yiddish, but it's not perfect. Number three is German, required at the time. So number four is French. It was to do with Serge. Victor Serge, Kibalchich—he is in your father's manuscript. Your father met Serge in Holland, when Serge was an anarchist. Nathan met Serge in Russia, when Serge was a Bolshevik. So were they both. Faithful servants of the revolution. True believers. In words and in deeds, they were Lenin's bullets. Then they both started wobbling. Nathan heard the old *nigun*. I don't know what Serge heard. Maybe it was common sense. Nathan went first, Serge followed. When they met up, years later, Serge had started publishing his novels of the failed revolution in Paris. He had friends who were communists but also French, who loved literature. Serge wanted Nathan to write his own story, which in many ways was even stranger than Serge's. Nathan wrote it, but it was never published. Serge was famous, Nathan was just chaff. He kept the notebooks. They are here. But you can relax, I'm not giving you the originals. We may be fond of you, but we're not mad." He opened one of the desk's side drawers and took out a manila envelope, from which he drew a bound sheaf of thin carbon copies in standard US letter size.

"I've translated it. There are two copies—my original and this. I should microfilm it, but the less distribution the better. I would ask you to sign a legal paper that you will not copy or distribute or publish any part until your uncle has passed. But he says what he wants is for you to warrant this orally and give him another kiss on the forehead. Sometimes I really think it's possible that he is losing his mind."

"Does...?" I was going to ask some questions but I stopped before Yonni could even throw me one of his ironic glances. If a treasure falls into your lap, just say thank you and stick it in your bag. We went back into the living room, where Kolya had just finished a meal of an orange juice and some fruit salad that had been brought by one of the attendants, a neat blonde whom his round eyes followed as she went out of the room.

"I brought Asher," Yonni annunciated clearly as I drew a chair up towards Uncle's knees. "He's seen the files we talked about and I have given him the manuscript translation. Do you still want him to have it?"

My uncle nodded vigorously, though all he seemed to say was "Urrr!"

"Say your piece to the Prof," said Yonni.

"I'm very grateful to you, Uncle Kolya, for your trust in me. I absolutely promise that I will read it but not copy it or use it for any other purpose than my own research into the family history. I won't publish it in any way, in part or whole, or any part of it, as long as you don't want me to."

"As long as you are alive." Yonni prompted.

"As long as you are alive."

"Um err um egg!"

"Until you are dead," said Yonni.

"Until you are dead, Uncle," I repeated, "till a hundred and twenty—*ad meah ve'esrim.*"

"Ug oh doo!" he responded, with a kind of wild laugh that sprayed spit around his chin, which Yonni wiped off with his handkerchief.

"That's too soon, he said," said Yonni. "Lots of jokes today, eh, Prof?"

I began to rise. "Don't forget the kiss!" said Yonni hurriedly.

I gave my uncle another, more lingering peck. His forehead was very dry, like an Egyptian papyrus.

"*Fin la visite,*" said Yonni brusquely. "Time for the afternoon nap."

He saw me out to the car, and I thanked him again profusely. As I snapped on the seat belt, I waved to him. He called out after me:

"Don't forget—the cells remember the tune!"

"If you cut the rope free, do you fall?"

Sarah: 1925

Dear Berl,

Just as I was beginning to write this letter, I received your telegram, answering mine, so quickly, as if in the blink of an eye, since I only dispatched mine yesterday! In other countries I read they can now use the telephone to call across the seas, but we have no such treasures here.

I understood with some relief that you had already heard the news of our dear father's death, which was brought to me by a comrade from Floresti whose brother remains in contact with our village. He also brought a letter from Judit, which I have copied out for you, I cannot bear to part with the original, since it is the only letter I have ever received from my beloved little sister. Our father fell to a heart attack on the final day of Passover, having complained of some pains the night before. Only our mother and Judit and a maid, Ruhaleh, who they engaged some time ago, were in the house at the time, Zev still being on his travels in the Far East, for two years now. His last letter was received four months ago, from a place called Karbeen, in Manchuria, which is in the northeast of China. Kolya, if the last dispatches received from his old friends now in exile in France are to be believed, is somewhere in South America...

It is hard to believe how far we have all drifted from each other! Judit wanted to call the doctor, but Father said it was not serious, the doctor could be called after the closing Passover meal. But in the night he had a great spasm, and apparently got up, to go into the study. He must have known his last moment had come, and wanted to be among his books. He collapsed on the floor by the table. The maid was sent to wake the doctor, but by the time he arrived Father was gone.

In keeping with the custom he was buried the next day, at noon, in the village cemetery, where it appears he had earlier obtained a plot for us all. Mother became immediately distraught, and began speaking in a strange language, that not even Judit could understand. Judit writes her letter on the third of the (seven) days of the shiva, and as you can see, she is still suffering, wandering out of the house into the streets and speaking, as if calmly and rationally, but in her own language. As Judit says, it might be an old Spanish dialect, mixed with Polish words, that have come down from some distant origins. It is clear, that we have wandered quite far...

To whom can I speak the truth, if not my brothers? I am afraid I am too cowardly to say certain things to my sister, who might in her loneliness pass them on to our mother, to whom I have already caused so much pain. But, through the tears of a daughter, I cannot say other than that I left them so long ago, five long years now, that I cannot escape blame for the choice of my own independent path in life over that they bequeathed me. Masters of our own fate! I remember the banners! And I remember my own dearest lost child who was the first to be interred in that graveyard. It was after my Yitzhak's death that our father bought the plots around that small gravestone, next to that of my husband Yosef, blessed be his memory. I must tell you the truth: I could not bear to be that Other Person that "fate" had ordained me to be. Five thousand years of Law and Commandments, tradition and continuity. This only was left for me, as woman—to be a womb, ensuring the line.

And so I chose science, and the march of history, to the words our father lived by. I chose the Deed. A redemption in this world, not in the next.

Had we not left, would we not still be gathered around the table, waiting for Mother's tshoolent, Father mumbling the prelude to his prayers, you boys kicking each other under the table or exchanging some Russian curses you had just learned in the street from who knows who, Judit in her prim child's apron, or grown up to be the prodigious seed of the Bible, like olive trees planted in our father's garden. There were no olive trees in Celovets, but there are many, here. The Arabs grow them everywhere, and soon we shall too. They have a deep wisdom, our cousins, and I am beginning to believe those pioneers who have been here longer than most, and who say that they are in fact our ancestors, who were converted by choice or force to the new religion of Mohammed thirteen hundred years ago, and who have guarded the land better than we did, in our long diaspora. This land, fallen though it was into neglect and ruin, has never been empty.

I did not stop my work when the dire news came, though of course the seven days of mourning had passed before Judit's letter arrived. But I feel more than ever that my own redemption of my father is to work the land, with renewed vigour. I can imagine the mixed up words of my mother's grief... our daily Yiddish, some Russian, some Rumanian, the Ukrainian jargon, Galician Polish, perhaps French, the Spanish of Andaluzia? The tongue of the Bible, thankfully, we never forgot, though it is revived here in strange ways. So many words that have to describe things that were never in antiquity: words for machines, science, modernity. We take them from English, Russian, German, whatever is of use. We are not shy. We are not a shy people here.

This grief of ours has come mixed with a different emotion for me, here, and I was going to write you and Yakov of this when the time came. I have met a man here, not the comrade I wrote of to you before, who is still a good and dear friend, but a pioneer of a very different background: He is a Jew from Mesopotamia, no less, born in the city of Baghdad, exotic Baghdad! His name is Zachariah Sasson. He is actually of a very old family whose ancestor was a vizier of the Caliph and others who travelled to China and India. But he is himself a man of the soil. He came here with the British army when they fought in Iraq against the Ottomans, and he heard they were raising a Jewish "mule corps" to fight for them in Palestine. He is close to the Jabotinsky tendency which is not my type of politics but politics are nothing in love. What can I say? I am of an age when women in our own world were planning their own sons and daughters' weddings but I do not feel old. In this old old country all of us feel very young. Perhaps it is a consequence of dreaming and then living your dreams. There are matters that a sister cannot write her brother, even in our "enlightened" age. Zachariah is also in the second bloom of his life, and he too lost a spouse, a young wife, to illness, when he was very young. There was no child of that marriage. I do not know what formalities might be suitable in the circumstances. Does he supplicate to my older brother for my hand? There will be of course a Jewish wedding with a Rabbi, if he can bear to travel across roads that are no roads to our new small settlement. It is called Halutsah. We are pledged to build a garden here but meanwhile it is just rocks. I look over the twin peaks on which, eight hundred years ago, the Crusaders and the Arabs fought the battle of Kittin. The Arabs, under their great general, Saladin, won that day, and the Crusaders lost Jerusalem. But we are not Crusaders. We do not come with fire and sword but with the hoe, the pick and ploughs.

I can only write of that which fills my life every day. And what of you? Is there any news of Yakov? When last you wrote of him you said he was still in Paris, but when I wrote to the address you suggested, the "Folies Bergere, Paris," there was no answer. He was never one for words. Of all the dreamers in our family he seemed to dream deepest. Where was his mind wandering? We thought he might become a wonder Rabbi, like the mystic sages of old. The Bratslav and the Baal-Shem. You wrote that he had a magic trick to resurrect a dead man on the stage. Perhaps he could perform this trick for us? What, I wonder, can his dreams be now? I cannot imagine these places that you have both been to: Paris, Berlin, Vienna, Amsterdam, London! The world is wide, and full of wonders and temptations! The "flesh pot", our father used to call it. The wiles of the goyim! Well, I see them patrolling the roads and the streets of the cities here, trying to police us unruly colonists and natives, but they do not seem very happy either. To each his own.

As I am writing this letter, one of our comrades, Leah, is cooking in the kitchen, where I am sitting writing this. Someone brought fresh fish from the lake. Do you remember when Mother fried up the fish from the river and we sat around the table devouring it with our nostrils before it arrived on our plates? But Father had to complete his prayers while it simmered in the pan.

That is past. This is future. Let us weep for what we have lost, but let us also embrace what we can gain. You wrote that you were filming history, with great sets and many actors playing Pharaoh's armies and the Children of Israel passing over the sea. I feel that I am living history. It is not at all glorious, but very tiring, and sometimes every bone in my body aches.

The fish is almost ready. *Shoen, genug.*

Your loving sister in mourning and in hope,

Sarah.

April 8, 1925 (14 Nisan 5685)

Unpublished book :

Kolya:

A SOLDIER'S JOURNAL
by "Mikhail"
1914–1924

Part 1:
The Bastion

Before I was born, when my father was yet unmarried, he told me, he undertook a great pilgrimage to the court of a famous Rabbi, who was the son of a reputed miracle worker who could cure both men's bodies and souls. He went forth by train and cart and joined a group of travelling pilgrims who were all headed to the town of Sadagure, where the Rabbi lived in a great mansion surrounded by his acolytes all clad in white robes. The Rabbi's father, the mystic saint, had lived in a small room at the back of the synagogue, where he spent his days in solitary prayer. His followers and visitors had to wait in a quiet hush for his words of wisdom to be mumbled from behind a wooden screen. But his "court" was always filled with many men and women, rich and poor, but mostly the sick and the mendicant, beggars wielding their crutches, women who were barren, men who were crippled with disease or gaunt from the long journey from their famine stricken provinces. Some rich people came supplicating for special favors in commerce to be magically conjured by the soft muttering of the holy man's prayer, and, although he never touched a kopeck coin himself, his white-clad acolytes had pockets that could be well filled. The miracle Rabbi's son was not made of the same substance as his father, and did not shun the soft sheets and deep Turkish carpets of his castle, for in his glory, like a small Tsar, he mirrored the glory of his people, who saw, in their delusions, his comforts spread over themselves, as by a magic wind, so that their thread-bare coats and patchy shirts and pants and cracked boots and empty stomachs were transformed, mended and filled by the Rabbi's grace and promise.

But my father was enticed, not by the promise of gain, or fortune, but by the odour of sanctity created by the Rabbi's stature as the "tsaddik"s son, and since the sage had died before my father was himself more than a babe in arms, he had to be content with the shadow, rather than the substance. He did not tell me this in as many words, but his tale was wistful as he spoke of the emanation that was felt by all who stood in the old synagogue, in which the old wood screen still stood.

When he approached the town, he said, with the pilgrims, they all started to dance, and waved their arms, and began singing, like a congregation that had a distant memory of some great tune but could not quite remember the music or the exact words. They wished to participate in the glory of the past, which was now more faded, and much complicated by modern features like the railways with their steam engines, and the young men who forebore to wear the old ceremonial costumes and studied books other than the holy writ. My father never spoke of those, though he knew that a new world was knocking on the creaking door of the old. The pilgrims danced down the street, like a human snake seized with unceasing spasms, till they came to the gates of the mansion, which remained closed, guarded by the gendarmes of the Empire that allowed the outpouring of their supplications as long as itself, and its already ageing white-whiskered diadem were under no obligation to cede to the people's dreams and desires.

My father broke away from the crowd, which was waiting for the gates to open and the Rabbi to emerge in his gilded carriage, to bless the throng and draw the beggars away with the promise of a shower of coins while the more thoughtful brethren were ushered through to a table in the garden at which food and wine was offered. My father made his way, with some of his younger companions who had travelled from his home province, towards the old synagogue, where they donned their prayer shawls and began to pray. Theirs was a book which never required renewal, though it was interpreted down the ages by so many who sought the secret meanings behind the gestures and inflections that had been repeated hundreds of thousands of times in the same manner, from time immemorial. For life would always continue as it always had, from one day to the next, and one season following another, down the years, through all life's trials and tribulations, against which they were completely powerless to turn the tides of misery and subjugation that had been ordained by powers that they could not challenge, turn back, or abate.

They stood before the old screen, listening to the creak of the walls that had stood, fragile but enduring, for several hundreds of years, pricking their ears for any hint of the lingering whisper of the dead saint's soothing wisdom. But, my father said, although he heard nothing, no human voice speaking from the empty preserved room behind the screen, he never the less, he said, gained sustenance from the peacefulness of the void.

(The above prologue passage was crossed out by the author, but as he did not delete or tear the pages from the manuscript, the translator has deduced that they should be preserved. Y. S.)

1.

"You sacks of mange-ridden sheep shit!" The Sergeant's voice echoed over the embankment like the howl of an artillery shell. "You pustules of horse dung! I should cut off your testicles and shoot them against the enemy! Why don't you turn the rifle around and save us all the trouble! When you first peeked out of your mother's **** you should have crawled right back in there and tossed out the afterbirth instead! What was the point of seeing the first light of day if you'll just take me with you to Jehennum?"

He stood, bandy legged, on the lip of the trench, his arms akimbo, holding his rifle over his knees, his face contorted in habitual fury. One might say spittle was hanging loose from his mouth had you been able to make it out below the massive brush-like mustaches that sprung from the great bulbous nose under bushy eyebrows, the eyes practically invisible and the whole mixture caked into a filthy mud-pie that shifted like a mound of worms. It was a familiar tirade from Sergeant Trunov, the closest thing to a declaration of love or affection that we would have until death or victory or a survivable wound might release us from the edge of the grave. He was the only human being, apart from our own comrades in the lower depths, who was keeping us alive, day by day, hour by hour, and for the last three months since we began our march, our daily trudge across the Galician plains, till we were swallowed by the Carpathian mountains, a ragged horde the hills refused to disgorge.

Trunov was a muzhik from somewhere near Zhitomir, who had risen from the ranks by his sheer effrontery in staying alive through an early engagement in which his entire platoon was wiped out by German guns and not even the officers survived. He could not be made an officer, of course, because he was an ignorant, illiterate, mud-spitting peasant who had the cunning to cry "Long live the czar!" when he saw a new platoon of fresh troops, headed by two shoulders of imperial epaulettes, arrive as he was burrowing into the Polish soil, hoping to come out the other end, he said, in Africa, where there were no winters, and men's skins, not their hearts, were black. He was as cunning as a fox, and claimed to have a close acquaintance with the Angel of Death, who often came to him at night, he said, and complained mightily about the gross overwork that he had been tasked with since the present summer. "I'll keep a few off the list," the Sergeant promised the demon, and thus our little squadron was saved.

Or at any rate, this was his tale. We were only a few small dots, a few human smudges, on an immense bloody canvas painted by the Russian, German and Austrian generals back in their headquarters, far behind the front, as they moved their vast armies of millions of insignificant chess pieces across their maps of valleys, ranges, steppes and villages which were burned, flattened, ground to ashes as the scourge passed over them, its inhabitants poured across the ground like insects fleeing from a smashed nest, left to starve in the embers, or be covered by winter's white shroud.

It was November, and we were still alive. This was a miracle beyond all that one could read of in the holy books, of whatever religion, Orthodox, Provoslav, Catholic or Jewish. For each one of us had arms, legs, a torso, a head, and other organs, intact enough to promise life, for another fleeting moment at least. It seemed a lifetime since the train of the recruiters puffed in slowly to the tiny station that served our town, causing the entire town to empty of every boy and man between the ages of ten and sixty before it had even left the previous station. The recruiters, a phalanx of grave looking officers with waxed moustaches, bearing folding tables and chairs and cases of documents, marched in to a ghost town of women only, guarded by a platoon of soldiers with fixed bayonets, ready for any trouble. Even the cats and dogs fled from their path. But I did not hide. All around me I heard the rustle of what seemed to be giant mice, scuttling in the eaves, cramped together in basements and attics, holding each other's mouths, trying to stifle cries, groans, belches or farts. But I sat with my father in his study, while my mother and elder sister trembled and bit their lips in the kitchen below, and my little sister sat with her school-books. My father held my hand, as if he could draw on the authority of his tradition and standing in the community to deflect the iron claw of the State from its task.

"Why didn't you hide?" my comrades asked me again and again, jaded Ivan who is always ready for anything with his reeking pipe, banishing the stench of our own excreta with his own vile concoctions, smoking weeds when tobacco runs out, nervous Sashka who still jumps at every shell, gentle giant Alyosha who is determined to get through the war without killing anyone and could carry us all under his arms to safety if there was any safety anywhere within a thousand miles to be had, Vassily, bearded as a priest, whose tongue is so coarse it can mould barbed wire and whose strategy is to curse the enemy to eternal plague and constipation and syphilis so that their limbs fall off before they can jump out of their own trenches, the student Vikhod, who is my own age and has no book to read, so he sits with his eyes closed and re-reads the books he recalls from his Kiev home. One night he will read Dostoyevsky, the next Goncharov, the next Pushkin, and, when idling in a snow-storm, he will recapture all of War and Peace. I am the only Jew among them, but none hold this against me, in our shared fate, even Trunov, who likes to take me by the ears and shake me and say: "Comrades—this is the only known Jew who can milk a cow properly!" Not that we have seen a live one for some weeks now, only carcases that are already picked clean. "All of us crawled into the deepest holes to escape them!" they cried at me. "They had to haul us out by the ankles." Vassily said he bit five recruiting officers, who would bear the marks of his teeth until their dying day, which he hoped had already come.

"I am not an animal," I told them. It was all I could say. I said nothing to the recruiters as they came stalking up the stairs past the women, standing with their liquid mustaches pointing at my father like loaded muskets. They had a list, naming four brothers of army age. Two of them, my father told them, were in America. The third was buying furs in Siberia. "Good!" said the leader, a small runt with the face of a weasel, laughing—"he won't need to go far when he's found!" They looked at me as if I was some kind of warped chicken that had gone mad and offered itself up to the chopping block. I gave them my name and age, eighteen. "Good," said the runt, "quick march!" He pushed me out the door and rapidly down the steps. As we passed my mother and sister he turned to them.

"We'll send him back after we've marched in to Berlin!"

2.

We were marched to the train station, five more youths from the village and myself, ushered up the steps into a carriage already crammed with young men from the other stations down the line. The guards pushed us along the seat, and one soldier sat at the end of each bench of the Third Class, to make sure we didn't bolt for it while the train made its slow chugging way across the flat fields and pastures. Now and again, they passed us morsels of food, some meat off a chicken leg, or an onion, to chase the smell of sweat and fear away. The other lads from my village were all familiar from Bet Midrash and school, including Fat Yudel, who was hardly fit for any service, let alone military, and could never control his own wind. We tried to exchange some words but were shouted at abruptly: "No talking! No talking!" and lapsed into glum looks of despair. In Floresti however we were separated into different squads and I was marched with a whole group of strangers into a room at the station which was already filled with captive recruits. I never saw or heard of my childhood friends again.

From the station our new group, about one hundred strong, was marched to an army camp on the outskirts of the town, its wood barracks surrounded by rows of tents. We marched in one entrance of a long cabin and then out of another having shed our ordinary coats, shirts, trousers and shoes for uniforms that were allocated haphazardly, blouses and pants that were either too long or too short, ill-fitting boots, the winding cloths—the army *gatkes*—to wrap round our feet, and caps that either slid over our eyes or had to be held in place with one hand. Then we were marched out again, into the open countryside, a ragtag mob of the misfortunate, the unlucky, the doomed, heading in a great shuffling convoy up towards the Dniester, where a giant barge was moored to the shore.

One week later, we were poured out, into a forest that vibrated with the thud and whistle of crashing shells, the blue sky blotted out by black acrid smoke, as if God himself were on fire, and the devil, downstairs, was pulling open all the doors to the furnaces that thundered below.

We learned the first rule of warfare very quickly: life is cheap, the cost of one bullet or fragment of steel. One moment the man next to you is a moving, breathing being, wheezing, perspiring, clutching his own rifle as a lifeline, filled with thoughts, dreams, memories, terrors, desires, the next he is a still lump of flesh, or just a pile of horrors, a body turned inside out, spilling its entrails like a slaughtered sheep, or just a pair of legs left from a soggy red mass. And you move on. You move on, till you reach the hole in the ground where you can hurl yourself, hugging the earth, licking the weeds and the worms.

Almost instantly, all that you loved and cherished has disappeared, as if it never was. All that is left are the two great extremes: the abiding, animal love for your comrades who are by your side, living the same short instant, moment by moment, and your hatred —not for the enemy, who is faceless and nameless, but for those who are propelling you on to your fate: the despised officers' class.

These fell into several categories: The first, the closest to us, were men not much older than us boys, eighteen year olds, practically cadets, who, sent by their families to add lustre to their social class and position were brought up and fed on tales of past valour, the legends of Borodino, the war against Napoleon Bonaparte, the one-eyed general Kotuzov, dashing cavalry charges, brandished swords, the great sacrifices for the Fatherland, the more recent, and more painful, battles with Japan, the Hills of Manchuria and other patriotic tunes. The idea of war filled them with fire, and they were determined to show no trace of juvenile fear as the real inferno broke upon them. They died like flies, in the first charges, and had to be replaced by older veterans.

The second category were more dangerous. These were the core of the class, young men, in the early flush of their adult lives, the younger sons who had determined to make an army career, who buckled down swiftly to the routine, so well worn and nourished by novels, of the city barracks life, the training and discipline by day, and carousing with their comrades at night, wooing the girls, seducing nursemaids, playing cards and gambling away their fathers' fortunes. Some saw themselves as Lermontov's Pechorin, deeply sensitive but hardened heroes of their time, destined for romantic adventures in the Georgian mountains, wooing exotic princesses and fighting duels on the peaks, but suddenly found themselves ground down in the mud, facing an enemy armed not with swords but with six hundred pieces of artillery hidden behind mounds of barbed steel. Those young men, strong and puissant, deeply determined not to quail or hesitate at the challenge, now lived only for the moment when they could lead the charge, across the killing grounds, towards the Austrian trenches. Something in their stance gave them a charmed life, and they would rush through the hail of shells like shining icons, as we, the foot soldiers roused in their wake, sometimes even inspired by their bravery, tore ourselves to oblivion. Among these accursed heroes, Sergeants and veteran n.c.o.s like Trunov would urge us like a faithful lead hound: "Steady! Steady! Low profile!"—showing us how to scurry like cockroaches, inches away from the ground. He could smell the shells coming, and evade them, untainted by the glow of glory. But those men were often seducers of men as well as women, and they would pass among us often in the guise of brothers, slapping us on the shoulder, asking for our tales of home life, and lapping up the older soldiers' tales of the Russian land—*ruskie zemlya*! We came to understand, we who survived, what angels of death they were in human form...

The older officers were another matter, quite another category of human being. They would drive up, in great convoys, from the rear, when they had done poring over their maps of the front lines and receiving their instructions from the higher ups, commanders-in-chief who took their orders from the highest level, the Grand Duke, brother of God himself, the Czar, in whose name all this slaughter was to be achieved. Some were older versions of the young blades, cured of their Lermontovian delusions, vigorous in their love of the battlefield, which they surveyed the way an architect oversees the construction of a grand cathedral of his own design. Some were monsters in human form, grotesque figures with beetle brows and immense grey or pure white beards, with eyes of pigs and faces pitted with the scars of a lifetime of debauchery and evil. These grand assassins were the masters of life and death over hundreds of thousands of men, in the battlegrounds that stretched hundreds of miles, from the banks of the Dniester far north to the Baltic Sea.

We, the poor boys stolen from homes in far off steppes, were the merest chaff thrown from the threshing, just splinters to be wedged in the southern flank of the Austrians, holding them down while the bulk of the Russian divisions were hurled against the

Germans in the north. The most popular of the younger officers, Captain Danilov, explained it to us in one evening lull, hoping to enthuse us for the battles ahead with our "ancestral" enemies, the new knights of the Teutonic orders. The Germans planned to attack and take over Poland, the western part of our holy patrimony, but although they enjoyed some early victories, we had thrashed them soundly from Kovno to Pynczow, as well as the Austrians between Sambor and Przemysl. These names meant nothing to us whatever, but they sounded far enough from our own homes to cause at least some relief. Two days later, Danilov was in the front line of an infantry charge two miles up the sector, and was one of three hundred who didn't return. We hoped he had at least enjoyed his duel with the cannons, although it did not take place on the peaks of Mount Gud but in the churned mud of the Galician plain. Sergeant Trunov brought out his hip flask of vodka, which was forbidden throughout the line, and we each had a small sip of libation for a genuine Russian hero. Two weeks later, we ourselves were marched out, north-west, towards the Carpathians, where the enemy was approaching the passes.

We did not toast any heroes again.

3. "The Wave"

Snow lay over the mountain, a suitable white shroud for the thousands who lay dead beneath it. A traveller might have marvelled at the picturesque landscape, but could note that the crystalline trees that covered the slopes were all stunted or reduced to bushes, though winter kindly wrapped the burnt stumps and charred branches to which they had been reduced in its familiar disguise. Sweeping his binoculars around from afar, the hardy wayfarer would also notice the sharp black stumps of the steel tangle of wire and girders that marked the trenches on either side of the defile. Now and then, a thin trail of smoke rises upwards, like an Indian smoke-signal from some strange underground tribe of gnomes.

The wayfarer arrived, a gaunt Father Christmas, dropping down a hole in the snow and landing feet first in our fetid dugout, in which all the smells and odours of seven hundred trapped men had congealed so that all of us lived, like perverse Jonahs, in the belly not of a whale, but a gigantic pig stricken by fever and filled with bile, becalmed in a sea of mud. Ventilation provided by our own belches, farts and fumes of tartar tobacco. There was some pride, never the less, in the thought that no animal, except the Russian soldier, could thrive in such conditions. And across the hill, in the Other dugouts, no doubt the Austrians were thinking in the same vein. We sat, lay, sprawled, chewing hard meat and dry biscuits, waiting for our superiors to decide when we would start killing each other again.

The newcomer was a Corporal, a messenger from the Division staff. His name was Alexei Azerov, but to the ranks he introduced himself as Volnya—the Wave. Perhaps he should call himself only "Ryabi," the Ripple, because, he said, he was only a small part part of a movement that coasted over the ocean of men and women caught in the storm that was swallowing not only Russia, but the entire world. He was a small wiry man, fit for squeezing through holes and burrows, who might have been in his early twenties but had the eyes of a fifty year old, marked with wrinkles and blinking like a man who had too many transitions between the blinding light and the dark. He was a worker's son from the Donbass region, and a recruiter for the Bolshevik party. Once he had delivered his message, which itself caused no ripples, he huddled with us over the company samovar, the officers having their own huddle with their illicit flasks.

"Dead men on leave!" he toasted us with his field-mug, the soldier's familiar battered life-saver. "And all this marvellous little warren of rat-runs dug by all these expert hands. How many have we all dug in the last five months? I'll bet you if we took a proper measure of the whole lot we'll find we could go to China and back. Do you know how long it took the labourers and convicts to lay the czar's Trans-Siberian railway? Just about twenty-three years. And you blokes have done the lot in less than half a year. What a marvel of man's engineering. And for what purpose? To carry people and trade to the far corners of the earth? To help the people communicate with each other? To make the labourer and the farmer's work easier? To increase the wealth of your country? Eh? Does it do all that? Of course not, you know very well what it's for. It's to build yourself your own tomb. But not like Pharaoh of Egypt, who left a monument for the ages, no sir! Merely to keep your bones in with the other rubbish and shame of this bloody war. And a war for whom? For Tsar and fatherland? How very noble. How much of your fatherland will you inherit if you have the good fortune to stay alive long enough to crawl out of this shit-pile? How many extra versts for your family? How many more cows for the farm? How much more bread for your little ones, for your Papa and Mama, for your dedushka and babushka? Eh? The officer returns gilded with glory! Promotions, money, business deals in the city, foreign gold to gamble away and more fucks in the whorehouses! Plenty of foreign wenches to bed, I shouldn't wonder. And the Tsar picks off someone else's country. And you, what do you do? You steal it for him!"

He was pretty good, when he got going, it was amazing how lubricated he became with our tea. He may have looked like a dog who crawled into a bunker, but his voice was sweet as honey. Land, peace, bread, he counted out these blessings on his fingers, and we noticed that in fact he only had those three—the last two digits of his right hand were stumps, and he counted the remainder off with his right forefinger, bunching the rest in a fist as if to protect that hand too from mutilation. So he began to talk about the revolution, about 1905, ten years ago, when the people of Saint Petersburg marched to demand simple justice under the sign of the cross and were slaughtered in their hundreds and thousands in the great avenues of the Imperial capital. Cut down by the same swords that every officer swaggers around with in our day. Children and babes in arms slashed with their mothers. The streets red with the blood of the innocents. But the people could not be cut down that easily. Their only weapons were the determination of the workers and peasants and the people's organisation and soviets. The elder ones among us, he knew, were familiar with all this, but had been told that the revolutionaries were all defeated and scattered, that the Black Hundreds had cut off their heads. But he was here, he said, and thousands like him, with their skulls intact—he inclined it towards us, inviting us to finger his neck. We declined, too aware of the rapacious head lice that infested even the most shaven craniums. The tobacco was often our most potent weapon to keep our bodies from being eaten alive by all the vermin that thrived in the dark. We had grown so hardened that even the gnawing of rats at our ankles could sometimes be ignored in exhaustion. Alyosha, the gentle giant, whom we nicknamed the Hindu, had added these too to the list of the living that he refused to transform into the dead: "Little animals!" he said. "If God made them, He must have had a good purpose." But what it was even he couldn't tell.

4.

"The Wave" departed with a return message from the officers in the morning, but we were fated to meet again. We could not have thought it then, when our small band of eager listeners hoisted him up and pushed him head first up the dugout, pushing his booted feet into the snow. We remained behind, with our masters. But only a few days later new orders came for our squadron, and we left the other hundreds of modern cave dwellers behind and marched behind an impatient cavalry troop of Cossacks to the Polish front near Kielce, a distance of about sixty kilometres, which took us three days to accomplish in the snow, caught up continually in massive motorised convoys that often had to be pulled by horses and men together, like landlocked Volga boatmen. Before we left, we were each given a bare postcard, and told to write home, conveying the good news of our survival, which would be scrutinised in detail by the censor. I wrote something like:

Dear Mama and Papa, brothers and sisters,
I am well, and in good health, among many good comrades. Our spirits are high, and we are all determined to make the best of our conditions so that we can do our duty. I think of you all so often and your dear faces that I see before me day and night give me untold strength. With God's help we will defeat the enemy and I shall be back soon, in time for Hanukah *(Christian soldiers had to write "Christmas")* so that we can all celebrate together. I kiss you all! Your loving son, Nathan.

I wanted to add "with the help of the Lord," but the Sergeant said "you've mentioned the Lord once already, do you think he has defective eyesight?" So I crossed it out and drew a sunflower. The Sergeant took all the cards away and swore by his mother that they would be delivered unless the entire army was wiped out by blizzards and floods. For safety he spat on each card. As we left, I embraced him as if he were my own father, but he just punched me in the gut and said: "Now boys, you've finished kindergarten. Go out there and f--k their mothers. Remember, it's the bullet you don't hear that's the bastard."

Down from the Carpathians we entered the plains of Galicia. The signs of the war were evident everywhere. The Austrians had drawn back, but where they had been the snow was banished by scorched earth and destruction. The enemy's fortifications were built in depth, one trench after another, so that the earth between them, sometimes less than two hundred meters distant from the next, was covered with the detritus of battle, thousands of empty cartridges that crunched and tinkled under one's step, torn satchels and pouches, often attached to a hand or limb, endless holes with what seemed to be discarded torn coats or discarded boots but were in fact bodies torn in shreds or decapitated, with the dried flakes of spilled inner organs. Here and there were raised mounds which were communal graves that the soldiers who passed had begun or finished raising, but then given up at the magnitude of the task and been sent on, towards the next trench. Another section was covered with the shreds of dead horses, remains of cavalry's encounter with artillery, an equally horrible sight for the muzhiks. One horse's head was even moving, still, after days, perhaps a week from the slaughter, and several of us poured bullets into the terrible vision with which the beast's eyes supplicated us. Even the officers did not stop us with the usual cry about wasting ammunition.

By the time we had crossed this valley of the shadow of death we had lost all sight of grace or redemption, and were the oldest boys on the earth.

And we were the victors, as the Russian army had pushed back the Austrians from their former strongholds and conquered vast swathes of Polish Galicia, to which their armies had laid waste as they retreated. Just beyond the trenches there had been a village, which was nothing but a heap of ruins, the houses reduced to their blackened foundations, streets and fields churned to black mud, in which torn carcasses of cows lay eviscerated, with one wall of a church left standing like a finger of stone, and before it a cross, on which the emaciated and tortured Nazarene hung from one jagged nailed arm. The Christian soldiers all stopped here and dropped to their knees in the mud, and we Jews were left standing around awkwardly, moving out of their way.

Apart from us, the village was empty of life, but as we advanced we soon caught up with the columns of people who had somehow survived or escaped the sacrifice of innocents and guilty alike, women and old men, carrying pitiful bundles, children clinging to torn skirts or borne on the shoulders of the older peasants or trundled out on carts which had given up the pretence of rescuing any material chattels or goods. When we came up to a burnt patch which might have been, some days ago, some kind of market, we found a truck with some baskets of food which our soldiers were handing out to the civilians, who were crowding around them with outstretched arms. Behind them, other soldiers were guarding a column of bedraggled Austrian soldiers, in torn blue uniforms, who were going to be marched off to the north. Their war at least was over.

In the evening, the dark chill of winter still penetrating our bones, I felt the desire for the first time in many weeks to pray, or rather a command, that seemed to pierce through the wind, from my father, and I began to remember the words of the Psalm: A song of degrees, bless the Lord all his servants who stand in God's house in the nights... let the Lord bless you from Zion, maker of heaven and earth... But I could not utter the words, because I did not feel His presence. I felt that there was no force on earth I could bless, and there was no hint of Heaven that was conceivable. I felt the dark overtake me, and I wished that I could weep. But I was hungry, and a large Cossack walked up to me and planted half a marrow in my hand that he had found miraculously growing in a piece of earth spared by the shells. He sat beside me and we shared the feast. He had immense, terrible teeth, that looked as if they could bite a man's head off with one lunge. He sensed my melancholy, and put his arm round my shoulder, saying something in a language of which I could not make out a single word. Then his comrades came up, with their huge shaggy caps, sheathed swords, and great leather boots with clanking spurs. They kindled a fire, and brought us all around it, and got up, and began to dance. They took out a framed picture of what must have been their leader, a ferocious creature with a mustache like a pickaxe, a face like Mount Gud and eyes that blazed with a strange and horrible glee. Brandishing it above their heads, they weaved and spun like dervishes, clanking their boots together and crying out a song that might have been first called out by the armies of Tamurlane as they approached from deepest Asia. They pulled us up as if we were sacks of potatoes and whirled us around with them. With no other choice, we danced along with them, swinging our arms, thumping our feet together, crying out what we thought might be accepted as the correct kind of cry. We were all one, and the officers came up and watched us, nodding and laughing, twirling their own brown and gray mustaches. Swords came out of scabbards, and were brandished above, gleaming in the firelight, ready for the next engagement, ready for blood.

5.

After the case of Sergeant Trunov, many more people saved my life in the months that followed, almost all of them by being hit by bullets or shell fragments that might otherwise have put paid to me. The hulking muzhik who pulled me aside when I almost fell on a smoking grenade and hurled it away himself towards the enemy trench remains nameless, as were most of the others. Or they were names which were a blur because they passed so fast and furious before the lectern of fate, which doled out its own lessons and scores. One I can recall here, Styopka Whirl, because he always amused us in the trenches dancing like the proverbial dervish. We had both our lives saved together, the first time, by another Sergeant, one Yakim, a dour Kazakh, who seemed to favour nobody, but would never the less settle down with his pipe, in which he smoked some extremely pungent herb he had brought from his homeland, and kept in a pouch permanently around his neck, whenever Styopka Whirl started whirling. One night, a weasel faced Major appeared out of nowhere, as these officers did, and spoke to the Kazakh, who informed us that the man was recruiting for new cadets to learn driving, since the drivers' brigade had now lost sufficient personnel to warrant a new fresh intake. He picked the two of us out, Stypopka and I, and sent us off with the Major, signing a ragged chit. When the major marched us away in the usual crawl out of the dug-outs, he winked at us and said: "The Sergeant likes you. There are more going to be lost in this quadrant than my boys, you can be sure." And sure enough, the command was ordered forward into the meat-grinder at Lemberg, and eighty per-cent of the ranks, both officers and men, were lost in the first week. In all, we discovered much later, our Russian army had lost more than four hundred thousand men in the first five months of the war, from August 1914 to January of 1915. Along the endless front line, on any single day of the catastrophe, the great apocalypse of our youth, two million soldiers were deployed on either side of the line, two million young German workers, farmers and students, thrown into the fire by the Prussian junkers, and two million Russian, Polish, Ukrainian, Cossack, Siberian, Turkman, peasants and nomad, even Buryats from far off Mongolia and Kyrghiz from the high Altai mountains, went to hell for the grand master of us all, the Holy Tsar, the Second Nikolai. My namesake! By the end of the war, more than eight million Russian soldiers had been dragooned into the world's greatest horror.

But the human soul is a strange construction. That which at one time would loom as the greatest source of terror and fear, the loss of life in a firestorm or the lingering agony of the corporeal body torn apart, limbs sheered off, inner organs spilling out no different from the entrails of a cow, the blood gushing forth onto the churned ground, becomes little more than a daily possibility, like the visit of the tax inspector, or a knock at the door from a creditor who can wait no longer to redeem his loan. The camaraderie of one's fellows becomes the one great sustenance of one's soul, whose immortality is like to be tested and revealed at any instant of day or night. So Styopka Whirl and I, having rushed out so often and returned with only small cuts and so many bruises that one ignored them completely, were neither surprised nor grateful that Sergeant Yakim had picked us to be separated from our remaining comrades and sent off to learn something new, although we were both struck almost dumb by the relative silence that enveloped the rear training base, near the intact town of Wisniewiecz, at which we were trained to drive the motorised vehicles that conveyed troops and ordnance to the front. It did not even occur to us that we were saved, we were only amazed at the appearance of normality in the town, the busy markets, the flow of ordinary people going about their business, women looking out of windows and small children playing in the street. It was springtime, after the thaw, and we rejoiced in our power over the unwieldy vehicles that were the blood-stream of our embattled troops. Only part of our training was in learning to steer the vehicles, since much of it involved the arranging of rescue and the fixing of the engine and frame of the vehicle when it broke down, as a matter of course, several times a day, the changing of the wheels, adjusting the crank and so forth.

As luck had it, Styopka and I were assigned to the same truck, a troop carrier, since it was necessary that two drivers were present, as one at least was often picked off either on the way to the front or in rushing the troops from one sector to the other. We had already vowed, when we were in the trenches, to do our best to inform each other's families of our fate if one fell and the other survived. I knew his address intimately though I had never been there: Usovo, in the steppes of the northern Ukraine, the alleyway behind Korbashev's general store, four houses down, the blue and yellow painted frontage, with the dog, Sasha, that barked as if he were a wolf, but was too gentle to bite even a cat. His father was absent, but his mother, and his sisters Sonya and Natushka would be for sure living at home. If there was any problem, Korbashev knew where everyone of the village was, even if they were hiding in the furthest corners of Sheol. And just as I knew his, he knew mine, the full panoply of the Gurevitch household, the Rebbe, my blessed mother, Sarah, little Judit, Zev—if he were around, and the full details of my absent brothers Boris and Yakov, in case for some reason of madness they had come back from the safety of America, yearning for hearth and home... "Just ask for the Rebbe," I said. "No human soul, Jew or Goy, is ever turned away from that door."

Thus we lived in each other's dreams. When we were sent out, after two weeks of intensive training, we took charge of our truck as if it was our own moving homestead, christening it—or "Jewing" it—Yasha, and anointing it with ceremonial vodka, like a ship sent out into a stormy sea. So we became observers, as well as participants in the unfolding events. Instead of being only cogs in the machine, replaceable at the moment of our destruction by a limitless supply of identical components and gears, we were also eyes that surveyed the broader sweep of the battlefield, the very process of the resupply itself, the grand visage of Moloch as the hordes of sacrificed slaves of the high priests of modern idolatry of state, empire and capital were ushered past its fangs into its maw. We saw: the courage and the camaraderie of men who were gathered from all corners of the empire, men plucked from home and hearth who kept their spirits high, who climbed on board the trucks as if on their way to a summer excursion rather than the roulette of murder, who squeezed together and exchanged their pipes, tobacco, bread, jostled like old friends and sang the melancholy songs of their disparate homelands, bringing the sound of the Ukrainian steppes, the Kazakh plains, the deserts and mountains of the Kyrghiz, the primeval forests of Siberia, the jagged peaks of Armenia and Georgia to the burnt Galician earth; we saw the people of the land, passing us by with despairing looks, the repressed anger of the local peasants etched in gnarled, fissured faces and staring, blazing eyes; we saw the hospitals, to which we transported the walking wounded, a mass of hobbling, bandaged, swathed men who threw their crutches on the truck floor and hoisted each other aboard in a silence broken by gasps, groans, wheezes, sighs perhaps of relief that they could walk out of the fire and that their shattered leg or withered arm might be their ticket out of the entire inferno, HOME! The hospitals themselves, set up in vast tents or in the interiors of churches and town halls, long rows of beds and the sickly smell of disinfectant, the nurses, the heroic army nurses shuttling to and fro, living angels bringing a touch of simple humanity to the desolation and pain. We saw even the officers waver, and stand back, their heads bowed, before the humbling weight of their impossible task. Even they too bled, had brothers, sisters, mothers, fathers back home, at their estates, who would also weep. No Prince Andrey, clutching the flag, to be admired by the overweening Bonaparte. We did not even have that, the upstart tyrant-Lieutenant, just the bloodless gaze of the feeble descendant of the Alexanders, the German Catherine and the insane assassin Ivan...

It was at one of the hospitals, in a half-wrecked church on the approaches to Brody, that I found the man I had never expected to see again—one never expected to see anyone again—since I and my comrades had lifted him by the legs out of the trenches in the Carpathian snow. "The Wave," the Bolshevik emissary and regimental messenger, literally shrunk in size, with his pinched face glaring over the sea of misery, his left thigh tucked under a coarse blanket, but unable to hide the amputation. We were carrying in stretcher cases, as the proper ambulance vehicles were in very short supply.

He looked at me without recognition, but I came up to him, and put my hand on his shoulder. I told him I was one of the soldiers he had spoken to in the Carpathians, six months before. He looked sceptical that anyone from so long ago could still be alive, and whole. I said to him, "God must be keeping us here on earth for a purpose," but he had lost none of his fire: "God is not present here," he said. "What sort of God is it who blesses both Russians and Germans when they are sent to murder each other?" And he told me the details of an atrocity that had happened further up the front, west of Warsaw, at the Bzura River, near Sochaczev, only two weeks before, of which we had heard rumours. The Germans had used a new and foul weapon against our troops—poisonous gas, which had been pumped out of steel cylinders that sent clouds of thick greenish-yellow fumes that spread like mist along the ground. The Germans had first thrown some straw upon the ground and sprinkled it with a salt-like white powder that set the straw alight and produced a billowing smoke-screen. Behind the smoke the German forces came out of their trenches, some carrying other cylinders that were later found to be tanks of oxygen. The Siberian troops in the sector stood their ground and muffled their faces with rags and handkerchiefs, but almost instantly men were falling down choking and suffocating from the gases. The rearguard elements had been forewarned, by the British and French, whose troops had been subjected to the same atrocity some days before, in France. Reserves were thrown into the battle and had prevailed because the Germans themselves lost half their men in the assault from the same fumes, and then the wind changed and blew the terrible cloud back upon their own trenches.

"The Wave" had been delivering a message at the rear, near the field hospital at Sochaszev, and had seen the casualties come in, men whose lungs had been destroyed and were fighting for every breath as if fire raged inside their chests, their faces burned and bloated, many totally blind. It was a scene of horror from the worst imagination of artists who had depicted hell in the Last Judgement. He saw gnarled old officers, who had remained stone-faced over repeated news of thousands of casualties daily and hourly, blanched with something approaching pity, if not a realisation of their own searing guilt of the past ten months.

"They tell us the Germans are cultured, civilised people," The Wave said, his head falling back on his pillow, "and our people are ignorant muzhiks. But look where learning and science brought us. Everywhere I hear that the soldiers are enraged, and want to strike back at the enemy. Why do emperors think terror will cow the people? It only makes them more determined. But this will only prolong the war. What chance have fools like me now of telling our men the Germans are just workers and peasants like us? Our message will have to wait."

I could see that he was near despair, but I told him, in a whisper, that could not be heard by the officers, that his words back in the winter had touched me, and many more like me. That I had seen the front, in so many sectors, and the suffering and destitution of the people, and was convinced that the Revolution was the only way out of disaster. I said I would take on his role as a messenger, as it corresponded, as his had, with my driver's postings. If he could trust me, I was willing to be recruited.

And thus I became a Bolshevik courier.

6.

Styopka Whirl was killed three weeks later. We were ferrying troops up the line from Halicz to Sokal, when a shell whistled over the Austrian line and hit the road just at the back of the truck. I was in the driver's seat, and Styopka was helping a platoon of reserves up to join the lads already packed in when his name was called, and the whole truck lifted, and I was almost crushed against the wheel but threw myself out on the ground, as the door was open, but when I raised my face from the dry earth I could see nothing but mangled bodies and thrashing arms. The piteous cries of the wounded and the maimed, a sound now as familiar as my siblings' cries were in the streets of our youth. The young lad, the whirling dervish, was decapitated, and I found his head in the ditch, with the mingled limbs of the others. There were several other trucks in the convoy, and we loaded up the wounded and the few survivors, and left the rest for God to gather.

There could be no lasting friendships. In time, I gained the reputation of someone who was immune to bullets, or one that had been dropped from the list of names written on each piece of shrapnel. Someone whose records had been lost by the bureaucracy of God's minions, who were toying with human fate at a moment of absence of the Almighty, perhaps tending to some other world. A moment that stretched into eternity. But many drivers wanted to be around me, until my other reputation overtook the first—the "Jonah"—the one beside whom one is shipwrecked, but rescued by neither whale nor man.

But I was rescued, in my being, by my new task, the tiny bacillus of revolution, borne on the storm winds of the war from place to place, encampment to encampment. "The Wave" had given me names, locations, persons who could be trusted, some even in the lower ranks of the officers' corps. These also managed to assign me to particular routes and duties that took me from one comrade to another, "moles" embedded in the Czarist tunnels. I travelled up and down the front, from Zamosc to Cholm, from Lomza to Osowiecz, up the line to Kovno, where there were determined Polish communists who were also dedicated to their own national cause. By mid-July, the Germans had broken through at Przanysz and were moving rapidly towards Warsaw. I was in the city, when the order came for all Russian forces to retreat. Back and forth, the line surged, like a gigantic centipede, men pushing back from one fanatically defended trench to another, and then rallying, and retaking the trench, so that, my own emissaries reported, for I was also recruiting, entire swathes of countryside were devoid of any shred of civilian life, only the rubble of homes and the carcasses of animals, mixed with the congealed blood and sinew of the muzhiks from every corner of the empire, who had come so far to die for a patch of burnt up soil. Then Warsaw fell, and was abandoned, and the battle moved back to Siedice, and to the north, to the front between the Narew and the Bug. These were the great successes of the German general Hindenburg, though we knew no names at this time, only the inexorable ebb and flow of artillery shells, explosions, fire, destruction, shredded men pulled with whatever compassion might be left onto the racks of my truck. And ever, for we oldsters, those of us who had come through, grizzled veterans, who thought ourselves as old as Methuselah even if we had yet to see the twentieth year of our lives, there were fresh rounds of human ammunition and cannon fodder trudging up from the rear, fresh faced babies, with their wind-up gattkes and new rifles, eyes aglaze with that sick look of terror and anticipation, reinforcements, from the unplumbed, unplumbable reserves of the immense hordes of misery that were the playthings of the czars.

One of our hidden comrades explained it to me. He was a field-telegraphist on General Brusilov's staff. The war could last forever, he said. The Germans were hurling forces that were technically superior to our own into the field, with better guns, better communications, vastly superior transport and railway facilities, a boundless supply of ordnance and shells. But their recruiting pool was finite. They had to commit many divisions to the western front, where the British were proving to be stubborn enemies and the French were fighting on their own soil. They had a great supply of working people and their own peasantry, but they had committed an army of students who were barely out of school age and were not an unlimited force. Among their industrial workers, socialists were legion, whose leaders may have endorsed the war but whose rank and file were no fanatics for the Kaiser, and even less admirers of the Junker military class. Revolution was knocking at their door too, though for the moment it was merely tapping out an early warning. As matters got worse in the months of winter to come, the hardships at home could prove decisive to their dwindling morale. Their armies had organization, but a low spirit. Our armies, however, had the Russian capacity for improvisation, the old Borodino spirit, an endurance which was almost beyond human understanding, and limitless reserves to absorb casualties that would drive any other nation to the depths of despair.

The generals, he said, were not worried about setbacks on this front or another, because they always had the power to recoup. Their only worry was the rotten center of Saint Petersburg itself. It was always possible that the Germans could, if not held back, bridge the short distance between the Baltic sea and Petrograd, and strike a hammer blow at the heart of the empire. The generals also knew that the heart was diseased, that the Czar was weakened by his coterie of venal and corrupt advisors, chief among them the insane monk, Rasputin, whom the Czar believed could cure the illness of the Czarevich, Alexei. Even worse, the Czaritsa herself was German, and was suspected by the Holy Synod of being the Kaiser's spy. All the royal houses of Europe were linked by their sickly and anemic blood, the English Queen Victoria was Tsar Nikolai's cousin, and her own consort was a German, like a pack of rats in a sack.

Our choice, therefore, the Telegraphist told me, was something one could not relay by any means to the ranks, at this point in the war, and that was Russia's defeat. Only in a decisive defeat would the rank and file realise the utter disaster meted out upon them by their own masters, and finally goad them to rise to kick open the door and bring down the whole rotting palace of lies. For reasons he had just told me, the Telegraphist summed up, this defeat could not be achieved on the battlefield, because the Russian soldier had no choice in his own sacred self-preservation but to kill the enemy, even if they were fellow workers and peasants, but only by dedicated comrades organising and planning the revolution at home, in the streets of Petrograd herself. Our task, along the front-line, was to prepare sufficient cadres of convinced revolutionaries that when the day came, the mass of the army would not become a leaderless rabble, turning on each other or falling to a hail of enemy bullets, but a new army, an army of the revolution, which would back up and reinforce the comrades at home. In order to achieve this, the beginning and end of this process, was that we ourselves should stay alive, and secret, and see to the survival of our own recruited comrades, above all else: "We are like healing organisms in a sick body. If we die ourselves, the body cannot survive."

Learn to be hard. It was not a difficult lesson to absorb, when any act of kindness or compassion could lead to one's own extinction. Courage and sacrifice, indeed, but for what purpose? For Czar and Country? Looking around, one could often see not a single Russian by one's side, only Siberians, Uzbeks, Kazakhs, Turkmen, Georgians, Armenians who could be fighting for their own countries but were dying for Warsaw and Petrograd. Even the Poles would rather bear arms for their own cause rather than Rasputin's. The world was turned on its head—heaven lay below, in wait for our demise, hell had surged up to the surface. Of sweet life, the daily song of one's fathers, the smell of one's mother's cooking, the bright faces of children, the daily round of the farmer gathering harvest, the rhythmic wielding of the sickle in the wheat fields, the glow of beds of sunflowers, raised to the sun, all this was gone, mortgaged to death.

Never the less, one required a cause, other than the simple animal urge of staying alive day by day. The constant fear was sufficient to dull even this will, to make one feel that the calm would come without fail if only one launched oneself out in the way of the bullets, if one offered one's corpse to the shells. Praying was impossible, I seldom found myself in the company of more than one or two Jews, and then they too were dreaming of hearths far away, one in Kiev, another in Odessa, another in Minsk, Gomel, Kharkov, Berdichev. In the first few months, I prayed alone, in my thoughts, in the trench, in the dugouts, reciting the rituals to myself. Then, one day, just suddenly, one morning, when my eyes opened, and the denseness and stench of my comrades washed over me like a wholly new sacrament, I knew there was no point in my mumbling. I made a bargain with God—end all this, and I shall return.

I still managed to write a few notes to the family, dispatched with rear messengers who might find a post service in a town still basking in peace and sunlight, and then two or three via the Telegraphist. I wrote the same story:

Dear Mama and Papa,

I am well, and I take courage and sustenance in my comrades, all brave men, and in good spirits. Our victories enable us to have faith in the final success of our enterprise. We have learned one thing above all: that Man rises above circumstances. Every day I think of you, of the sweet memories of our home, and I say my prayers for you, father, mother, Sarah, Judit and the boys. Every day I am determined to do my duty and to return to you when my duty is done, safe and ready for a new world. I kiss you all! Your loving son, Nathan.

The censor crossed out the "new world" reference. Perhaps he guessed what I was referring to. But the censors were not, at that time, too worried by subversion. When the winter snows set in, the men were even relieved, because trench warfare became less likely and the major offensives and defences of the previous winter of 1915 did not recur with equal ferocity, at least in our northern sector—though we heard of a winter offensive further south, towards Czernovitz and Bukovina. The cursed resilience of the people shone in the soldiers like a fire that still burned for its pagan sacrifice. Still, even in the snows, the drivers drove, behind great tractors with metallic shields that ploughed a way through the snow-drifts. Troops and messages were delivered, supplies came up the line, and the secret couriers could bring the latest news and connect the skeins of our far flung network. We received news of the activists of the Party who were in exile, mainly in

Switzerland—a land of snows and mountains but no war! Lenin, Trotsky, Kamenev and other Bolsheviks had prevailed over those who regarded German imperialism as the greater threat, and formulated a policy of a separate peace with the Teutonic powers which would exchange the cessation of hostilities with an abjuration by Germany and Austria of any annexations in Poland or of Russian soil. This seemed to us soldiers as the correct position, but it could not be achieved without toppling the entire edifice of the Czarist abomination, a repetition of the 1905 Revolution, but this time prosecuted to the bitter end. The war, it was considered, had weakened the Czar considerably, and it could not be imagined that the blood of workers and peasants in uniform could be spilled endlessly, like a fountain from the center of the earth.

Despite this logic, I considered another course of action—desertion. As the war lingered, more and more were gathering their bootless heels and making off, despite the snow, despite the guns and officers' tribunals, trudging the first crucial steps in thousand mile journeys towards their homes. Unlike most soldiers, my home lay to the south, rather than east, so if I cleared the last snows and picked my time I would be heading off in spring-time.

If I could watch the weather, however, so could the high commands, and the battles resumed, with full ferocity, as soon as signs of thaw set in, from Riga down towards Vilna. Fresh troops came up from the rear, and there were even new supplies, coats, rifles, boots, food, which made the troops less restive. This time it was the Germans who broke through, deploying new forms of battle from the air, with aerial planes and zeppelins dropping bombs on cloudless days. Again, we heard that the Germans were using their noxious gases, this time dropped in bombs from the sky. Once again, we were told that we were fighting incarnate evil, and could not shirk the task, even if it lasted till doomsday.

So I did not desert. By this time I was an N.C.O. myself, a Corporal, promoted through the wastage of so much life that even the meanest survivor could rise. I had managed to recruit enough fellow-survivors that someone back in Russia believed I might be a little less expendable, and I was suddenly handed a military transfer, not yet to the rear, but to Rumania, where the Russian forces had been pushing the Germans and the Austrians back well into Transylvania, and Bolshevik sentiment was very sparse in the ranks. But each victory was bought with more lakes of blood, and when the winter set in, once again, the great advances slowed down.

I bided my time. I carried out my orders. I drove trucks up and down the line. I brought young men who had just grown into the age when they could be plucked from the fields and pastures to the instant burial grounds. Ignorant children who sang the songs of their homelands as I ferried them to the banks of the Styx. Grizzled veterans climbed impassively into my moving coffin, lantern-jawed and vacant of joy. Many were so weather beaten that they were almost as black as negroes, their skin pitted by shrapnel, their movements like automatic puppets moved by some hidden hand. Those were too old and lost to reach. I had to reach the young ones, before their minds had hardened to pig-iron and their blood turned into sawdust. The smart ones, the ones who had realised before they arrived that there was only one path to survival...

February 1917 found me bogged down with a mixed detachment of Russian and Rumanian infantry in a Carpathian snowstorm that raged day after day, blessing us with more than two weeks of inactivity in our dugouts on a mountain peak near Vatra Dornei. The Germans occasionally bombarded us with their artillery but the explosions boomed in the muffled impact of the snow like a friendly giant's lullaby. Every time the ground shook around us we would lift a hand to rub our neck, feel our arms and legs to make sure we were still existing, and then dismiss the disturbance, till the next blast. No one bothered to complain. We wanted the storm to last forever, until we were lulled into the grave, quietly, with a minimum of fuss. What had I been sent to achieve? I could not remember. Why were we here? There could be no logical answer. What did we wish for tomorrow? Nothing. What did we remember about yesterday? Almost nothing. It was hardly possible that the war had lasted for two and a half years.

Thirty months, one hundred and twenty weeks, over one thousand days and nights of terror, sleeplessness, the constant threat of lethal disease, and sudden death lurking every second.

Never the less, when I arrived at this bastion, examining the map I required to have as a driver, as well as the more restricted chart of the various grids and battlefields the Telegraphist had supplied me to work out the routes of my secret task, I realised that I was no more than a hundred and fifty kilometres distant from our hometown, where, since the war had spared that side of the Prut River, my father, my mother, my brother and sisters might still be living. Who knows, they might be still pursuing the daily routine of tradition, Father's patrimony, the immemorial cycle of prayers and study, finding comfort in age-old repetition, the years passing as they had for me but perhaps touched by the glow of hope and patience for a quieter dawn. But then I would banish the thought, deleting it with the pen of my own censor, determined to keep whatever wits left to me directed to the revolutionary task...

(The above paragraph is crossed out in the notebook but still left legible, so I have translated it too. Y.A.)

February 25 *(of the Russian calendar, ed.)* passed uneventfully, still buried alive in the trench. I remember that we received a secret consignment of vodka, in our sector, which was passed from the officers to the ranks in several small flasks. Enough to wet the lips and dream of an old oblivion. The engineers had opened a road in the snow and we drivers were roused before dawn to dig our trucks out of the snowdrifts and make ready for a journey down the pass to Kimpulung for a major resupply. The sun was not expected to show its face all day but we managed to start the engines and set off in a convoy of about sixty vehicles, a familiar bone-jarring trip that usually saw at least ten vehicles slide and roll down the hill. No one could stop for casualties, as we were within range of the front line Austrian guns. Luckily we were not bombarded, something was distracting them this day. The sky was leaden grey.

We arrived in the late afternoon, when the day was almost done, in the town itself, a Rumanian resort town that had kept some vestige of normal life, the main church, a street of shops and markets, even a hotel which served as our joint head-quarters. The senior officers were being served with their dinner as we rolled up outside, by a smaller red-roofed church. I remember it well, the smell of cabbage and onions and even, or perhaps we imagined it, meat, something we had not tasted except in its dried form for it seemed half our lives. By now, however, one could not tell even the higher officers from the ranks as their uniforms were as crumpled and faded, the boots muddy, the faces as weather-beaten, with the same gaunt look as anyone else. There were two women, plump and red-cheeked, serving the platters, and we were kicked in the doorway by those after us as we lingered, gaping and gasping. It was as if we had arrived at the sanctuary of a hospital, with all our limbs somehow intact. We could tell, however, that there was a buzz of conversation among the officers that was somehow unusual. Normally we would be berated by some Sergeant or Lieutenant as we hung about the vestibule of the hotel dining room gaping at our superiors as they devoured their fatted calf. But other officers were standing about in groups, talking excitedly, and throwing us strange looks, while, from the back of the ground floor, near the kitchens, a Corporal I knew, also a telegraphist, not yet a comrade, but, I thought, a sympathiser, came out and grabbed me by the arm. I have forgotten his name. His face was flushed with excitement.

"There has been a revolution in Petrograd!" he breathed it out, half way between a gasp and a clarion-call. "The Duma has established a provisional government! The Tsar has abdicated! The Grand Duke is Regent! The war will end! The war will end!"

It was as if there was a sputtering fuse inside him, that was burning down rapidly towards an inevitable explosion, but he was straining to contain it, in the presence of the officers who were drooling with pig fat and sour cream. He held his hands up and shook all over like a leaf in the storm. His mouth opened like a cavern.

"They can't continue! They can't continue!"

But from outside, a different rumble sounded. The officers looked up, as did we all, lifting our heads and nostrils as if to sniff the prevailing wind.

The sound was still far off, but unmistakeable: The Austrian guns had finally decided to make their own comment on the day...

7.

We who came through the fire know the intoxication of the Revolution... Suddenly everything that was set in stone is liquid, and a door is thrown open, showing a hundred new roads. Sometimes, at each step down the path there is a crossing, each with more roads leading off, endless junctions, with a host of people gathered at each, gesticulating wildly and swearing by their mothers' graves that that one, and that only, is the way forward towards the hallowed goal. Other times, one knows with a kind of fearsome certainty that each road leads to the same destination: HOME!

The telegraphist who gave me the news at Kimpulung was however overwhelmed by a flood of new messages warning that the Austrians, exploiting the situation, were moving across the pass in full strength. Our first act after the great cry of Peace was to go back to war, just to preserve our lives. The Austrians occupied the road north and south and our troops battled fiercely to protect the railway that was our only route out. We took the railway, fighting for the first time not for Tsar and country but for the new Provisional Government. "Provisional Governments," however, quickly become tarnished icons, and word came down the wires, and by personal messengers, that the immediate thing to do was to organise "Army Committees," with each company electing representatives who would relay the mens' demands to regimental committees, and from them to each division, corps, army and front. The delegates could be either officers or ranks. No one was to be excluded. At first, companies and troops were cautious, electing whom the men thought were friendly officers, the younger cadres who were blooded side by side with their men, and earned their respect, despite their class origins. But then the men became bolder, and elected Sergeants, Corporals, rank and file soldiers, who were outspoken and could speak for their fellows. They could relay demands not just for better conditions, better strategies, better food and equipment, better treatment by officers, but for the core of the demands: Peace! Bread! Land!—to ask the question: When are we going home?

Where once infiltrators like The Telegraphist passed the occasional message or order down the concealed pipeline to our scattered recruits, orders now came directly from Petrograd, accompanied by boxes of printed tracts, party pamphlets, and newspapers—printed openly in Moscow, Petrograd, Kiev, the *Novoe Vremya*, the *Retch*, *Pravda*, *Volga Naroda*, the soldier's own *Soldatskaya Pravda*, the Mensheviks' *Dyen*, Kerensky's *Dyelo Naroda*, and so on, a veritable flood of words and ideas. I remembered my brother Boris bringing home his secret journals of 1905, with their bold cartoons of the blood-stained Tsar, the hydra of oppression, the hangman's noose dangling over the country, but here was a burst of utter freedom, no voice suppressed, no tongue stilled, no argument left out...

The drivers elected me their representative to the Regimental Committee, but my efforts had been noticed back at the home front, and The Telegraphist, who could now organise openly under his name, Kiril Volkov, otherwise known as "Vremya" Volkov, had authority to appoint me as the Commissar to the southern fronts, stretching from Bukovina to Galicia, with an assigned driver, Ivan "The Bull", and my own motor vehicle, to cover the vast distances. The thawing snow enabled the enemy to unleash new offensives, and our greater task had to wait on the more urgent one of organising our own defences. We, the "Red Guards," as we began to portray ourselves, had to steer a difficult path through the essential contradiction of the twin demands of loyalty and betrayal. We could not abandon the soldiers, our brothers in arms, to their fate, but we had to sow the seeds of the greater good as we saw it: to encourage them to think anew of their real loyalties: to themselves, their class, the revolution. Rather than desert one by one, they would have to desert in battalions, to leave their posts in organised groups of cadres, to become soldiers in the revolution which had not run its course in their homelands, to understand the ideals of universal brotherhood, which required that we turn our guns away from the trenches of downtrodden German and Austrian workers and peasants dragooned to war just as we had been, and, if needs be, towards our own Generals, who were determined to continue the war. We read Kerensky's call for all citizens to unite to fight the war to its victorious end, to stem the "indiscipline caused by extremist agitation and traitors in the ranks" and to save Russia and "weld her unity by iron and blood," a mirror image of the Kaiser's imperial principles. We were aware that the revolution could drown in blood on the battlefields of Poland and Rumania unless the brutal fact was faced—that we had to let our enemies win.

The harvest of our sowing was not long in coming. In June, the army command, on orders from War Minister Kerensky, launched an attack in Galicia, taking advantage of the good summer weather. A well-fortified German position, at Koniuchy, was taken, but the generals' triumph was very short-lived. Entire Russian units deserted their posts, urged by their committees, and refused to return to resist the German counter-attack. A large number of officers died heroically, defending they knew not what. The commander of the 24th division, General Dolzhenkov, perished in the cloud of poison gas. The Battalion of Death lived up to its title. The Germans broke through the lines at Bludniki and Kalusz, and crossed the Lomnica River. The whole front, right down to the Dniester, was falling apart. In response, General Kornilov, appointed personally by Kerensky, reinstated the death penalty, which the February Revolution had abolished, for desertions in the field. Men were shot in serried ranks by their officers. Others rebelled, and mowed their officers down. Some officers, even commanders of divisions, refused to order the death penalty, and were removed from their posts. In one instance at least we were informed that our troops had signalled the Germans of the approach of the hated Death Battalions. Fraternisation was spreading across the line, to the dismay not only of our own officers, but of the German command, whom, we were told, was conducting its own executions.

As if the war was not enough... It was at this stage, on my part, that I became an assassin. At the end of July the sun shone bright on the steppes north of Czernowitz. The landscape reminded me vividly of the sights of my childhood. It was just among fields like this, of rolling wheat, wild sunflowers, bright yellow under blue, that I ran about with my brothers, Yakov, Berl and Zev, playing hide and seek, or chasing a wayward goat, or just lazing away the time, and sometimes our elder sister Sarah would come out of the house and come down to the river shore and call out after us. But now whatever crops were here were wilting. The war had not scorched this earth yet, but its inhabitants, who kept it alive, had withdrawn, to the relative safety of the city, which was now finally menaced by the approaching war machine. The sky and the sun were merely mocking hope.

Down the slopes of the hill, the tents of our encampment had ploughed up whatever life was left in the soil. Nobody bothered to dig trenches here, because the ebb and flow of troop movements was so fluid. Back in Petrograd, Kerensky had formed a new government, with himself as Prime Minister, run by the Kadet Party—the "Constitutional Democrats," though what constitution they were speaking of was an open question. Kerensky had promised the Allied powers, Britain, France, and now the Americans, to continue the war, once again "Till victory!" It was reported that the Allies were—once again—about to turn the tide of the war. The Germans were being beaten back in Flanders, our forces were beating the Turks in Armenia and the British were advancing from Egypt into Palestine, pushing the Turkish army back towards Jerusalem. But for our part, the commanding General, Brusilov, had resigned, and Kornilov was now in charge of all our forces.

It was for this reason that the "Telegraphist," Vremya Volkov, approached me with new orders from the Commissariat. He had a list of stubborn Kornilov loyalists, along the front, whose personal demise would hasten the advance of revolutionary officers and sympathisers in the higher ranks, and thus save countless more lives.

The first man on the list was a Colonel Popov, who was in charge of artillery at Toproutz, just facing the Germans, and whose fanatic courage in striding out ahead of his own men and standing up in lookouts without fear or caution gave him an invulnerable reputation. I came up on him at night, snatching a rare hour of sleep in his own tent, which was as rough a bivouac as of any soldier, if at least solitary, since his adjutants, more luckless than he, were often blasted to pieces by his side. He snored as loudly as if he was blissfully at rest beside his own wife, and gave out a mere mulish snort as I put the bullet in his brain. I left quickly, as the gunshot roused the fellow officers around his tent, but there was nothing to greet them as they poked their heads into his own but the remains of my decisive act. It was not difficult to slip away, since sudden death was no stranger in any encampment, and the demise of a regimental martinet, at this time, was no loss to any person in his now loosened grasp.

After that I lost count of the names. If one were to call the roll call of the dead of the Great War one would be reading from the lists until doomsday, or well into the next century, if anyone would ever reach it. I saw myself as simply hastening the inevitable process which would see the recalcitrants who still dreamed of a return of the Autocracy dispatched by their own soldiers once they realised the choice was that one officer's life or their own. If life was cheap when I was first catapulted into the maelstrom it was not worth more than a grain of sand three full years into its satanic course. At Czernovitz, the artillery rolled back and the Germans advanced, though they did not take the city. They concentrated their force on Rumania, sweeping through our latin ally beyond the capital, Bucharest, which they had already taken the year before. We wondered if they would break through to take Iassy, where the Rumanian king was sent to, and thus be able to cross into Bessarabia. But personal considerations could no longer rule our actions. Though in a new cause, I was still a soldier—this time by choice, not by compulsion.

There is a great satisfaction in being able to strike back against those who have caused you great torment. Perhaps in other circumstances there might be another way—to write a book, for instance, or to compose some poignant music, or to express one's soul in some other artistic or productive way, but the only symphony or ode that we might have been able to produce at that stage was the only one available to us: the Revolution. Whatever was left of the soul that had been bequeathed in my father's house was this: to make the whole world new. Those I dispatched with my pistol were the obstacles, who could only lead us back into the slaughterhouse. I felt no regrets.

I was twenty-one years old.

While I was carrying out my assigned tasks at the front, crucial events were unfolding in the capital. During July, a series of demonstrations had taken place in Petrograd, with soldiers and workers rising up against the Provisional Government under the slogan of "All power to the Soviets!" As if the Tsarist days were on the brink of returning, the police dispersed the demonstrations violently, and the government ordered the arrest of the Bolsheviks. Trotsky and Lunacharsky were caught, but Lenin and several others escaped captivity and continued to organise underground. There followed the "Kornilov affair," in which the new commander of the army prepared to march on the capital in order to depose the government. The entire revolution was in peril, and Kerensky seized his chance, releasing the Bolsheviks and declaring himself Prime Minister, hoping that he could cling to power on their coat-tails. General Krimov, the commander of Kornilov's troops, shot himself, thus sparing persons like myself the trouble.

It was clear, as front-line debates reflected the civilian rear, that the revolution was fracturing into its constituent and splintered movements: Bolsheviks and Mensheviks, Left and Right Social Revolutionaries, liberal social-democrats, Kadets. Beyond the centres, other parts of the Empire were threatening secession, most significantly, in the Ukraine, where nationalists were poised to take power. Cossack regiments in the Don basin were being organised to march north, to kill off the revolution as soon as possible. And Kerensky, terrified that the Allies in the west would arm his monarchist opponents, was declaring every day Russia's "sacred duty" to continue the war on their behalf. In the first week of October, I had to dispatch five Kerenskyite officers, whom, to some extent, I pitied, since their courage in standing against the entire army's wish for peace was wasted in so doomed a cause. One man, I forget his name, stood up to face me, and said: "Shoot, soldier. Do your rotten duty." I made sure the bullet went in his forehead. Fallen, he seemed at peace, at the end. I had a sudden urge to kneel down and kiss the blooded forehead, but of course I did no such thing. Another man I marched out into the wheatfield behind his tent, he said he wanted to touch the soil. He bent down and I dispatched him in the back of the head. Some words of the Hebrew prayer for the dead flowed in my brain for a moment, then drifted off, across the steppes.

Then the word we were waiting for finally came. Lenin had seized his chance. The Party had struck the decisive blow in Petrograd, the Soviet had broken through into the Winter Palace and deposed Kerensky and his ministers. "Peace, Bread and Land" became for the first time the formal slogan of a national government. At the front, the soldiers and the officers joined in jubilant cheers, and across the lines, the day we heard the news, there was silence, as if the German and Austrian soldiers too, in their trenches, understood the momentous trait of the day. But my mentor, the Telegraphist Volkov, was strangely subdued. "Do you know," he said to me, when we broke off to boil up some tea in the regimental samovar, in a lull, "that all the while, as the guns blazed, and the warships bombarded the palace, just nearby, at the opera house, the Narodny Dom, the bourgeois audience stayed quietly in their seats, all through the evening, listening to Chaliapin?" He shook his head. "We are a strange race."

8.

I arrived in Petrograd in December 1917. What did I expect? I knew very little of cities. I had seen Kishinev for two days before my bar-mitsvah. I had seen the market towns of Belzi and Floresti. We had a picture book, among Boris' old things, that had photographs of Saint Petersburg. The Grand avenues, canals, palaces, glittering spires, cathedrals and statues... It seemed by far the most magnificent place that had ever been conceived and built by human hands. The Tsar lived there, and his evil demon, Rasputin, and there was a great prison fortress, where all those who dared to cross his path were incarcerated, before being marched off in chains to Siberia. People in rich clothes, with fur coats and cigars, moved through its streets, along which droshkies trotted, carrying ladies with immense feathered hats. All this had faded in the four years of gloom and horror in the trenches, so that I was fully prepared for the darkened mansions and avenues lying buried under a thick mantle of dirty snow, the grey steely sky bearing down like a shroud in the day, the night pressing the snow giving the whole city a ghostly glow, in which the fortress walls, the statues over the bridges, the dome of the cathedral and the Nicholas statue loomed like abandoned hulks, the rider poised to leap into the black sky but constrained, frozen in time, in a city that appeared sunk in mute rebellion against the very idea of renewal and inexplicable change that should have been convulsing its residents. Instead, they moved along its silver surfaces with a grim resilience, fighting by day to get on any of the few trams that were still working, and sliding like quick black smudges by night, rushing to escape the open spaces of the streets without trouble, as gunfire often erupted from some hidden corner, or across the rooftops of darkened buildings, in which few windows showed light, and that at most the flicker of a candle trying to brighten the sombre shade.

I arrived at one of these nights, with Volkov, after a long ride by car and train, bumping over broken and shelled roads from the front, through Zamosc and Chelm up to Brest and then in crowded troop carriages up to Minsk, Vitebsk and Novosokolniki, up further north to the capital, breathing in the same stink and mixed odour of onions, sweat and disinfectant powder that was all-too familiar, and then, suddenly, the silence, only the whine of the official car, more of a steel keg mounted over a chassis, with the protruding barrel of its machine gun, that greeted us at the station. We rushed through the drifts as if we were still in battle, spitting snow right and left like a ship cutting through the Arctic, till we reached a large imposing building which was still pock-marked with heavy bullet holes, and many windows boarded up. We went round the back, Volkov explaining to me that this was, until the last three months, Petrograd's newest bourgeois hotel, but now it played reluctant host to the leadership of the Revolution, for the time being, due to its central location. The dome of Saint Isaacs loomed down the adjacent street. We were shown to a ground level room which showed signs of having been through some turmoil—the gilded fittings were chipped, the ornate table seemed to have knife strikes carved in it, there were some bullet holes in the walls that had torn the flowery wallpaper and two round portraits of two female noble-women were tucked behind a sofa, their places on the wall taken by Lenin and Trotsky, looking, I did not like to point out, like two convicts on their way to Irkutsk. Later on the pictures would get more proper, but these were early days.

The commissar who had brought us here, G., was a bull-headed fellow who looked as if he was more used to the abattoir than high office, which turned out to be an apt intuition, whose attempt to smile was the most frightening thing about him, and who told us with an air of great importance that Lenin himself was resident in the building, but much further up, in another part of the hotel. We might be privileged to see him passing, but we need not meet, as Felix would assign our tasks and explain our new duties. There were already another two men bivouacked in the room, who were on night duties. When they returned, they turned out to be two taciturn youths, even younger than I, both former railway workers who had grown up in the city. Their names were Danilov and Grigor, and each carried two pistols, like the heroes of an old Karl May novel. They did not look as if they had used them often, except in target practice. Neither had been at the front.

Like a soldier, I of course fell asleep on the sofa, while Volkov took the spare camp bed. In the morning, at six, we were roused to a quick breakfast in what must have been the old servants' quarters, and then lined up in the courtyard for an introductory speech by the commander of our unit, Felix D..

He was a small thin man with strangely sad eyes that gave him an ascetic look, somewhat like a priest, who, we were told, had spent twelve years in Tsarist prisons and was tempered like steel by his hardships. He spoke in a high pitched voice that was curt and to the point, indicating that there was no time to waste. There were about fifty of us recruits lined up before him, and we listened raptly, as snow started falling as soon as he started, caking us with white tufts as we stood.

He didn't waste time on the niceties.

"As soon as the Revolution was born," he stated, "the stranglers moved in to choke it to death. We are at war. It is not the war some of you have been used to, against a defined enemy, with a uniform, and a trench you can charge at. It is a concealed enemy, that hides in the darkness, and comes out at night behind your back. It could even be he or she who pretends to be your trusted comrade. Behind the lines, puppets are being moved by powerful forces, set in motion from the chancelleries in Berlin or Vienna, the War Office in London, in Paris, even in New York. Their movements are not mysterious, they are declared at large, and are absolutely honest and clear. The proletarian revolution is the one thing all the imperialist powers fear, over and above each other's greed. This will not stop. This will not falter. This will not follow any cease-fire, any peace signed by Kaisers or Generals. This will continue until all of us are exterminated, to the last proletarian, to the last true Bolshevik, until the old order can be restored.

"With this in mind, the Executive Committee of the Council of People's Commissars (Sovnarkom) has decreed the recruitment of an internal police force that will serve the needs of the proletariat during this crucial period. Its activities are mandated under the rules of war. It reports solely to the Executive Committee and is not subject to any other organs of state or popular assemblies. Its purpose is to root out counter-revolutionary activities, saboteurs, spies of foreign forces, White infiltrators, agitators and anyone designated by the Executive Committee as subject to any executive order under the emergency decree. When possible, such subjects will be arrested and conveyed to the Revolutionary Tribunals. In other circumstances, emergency action is mandated and will be executed without delay."

The snow was falling down on us as if to encase his words with ice. Our feet were sinking in it to the shins, overcoming our threadbare boots. But no one moved a muscle.

"You stalwarts who stand before me now," the rasping voice continued, "are the bayonets of the Revolution. You have been chosen because you have already given proof of your abilities and your zeal. You did not hesitate to act when necessary on the front lines. We are back in the front lines now. I have no doubt you will do your duty."

He had finished his short speech, but none of us could move, since the snow was reaching up to our kneecaps, till, with a collective shudder, we all shook ourselves free, and following his wiry frame as he dashed off with his bodyguards, we retreated to the shelter of the hotel.

9.

We had all adopted the Russian infantry-man's slogan: A Bolshevik is a dead man on leave. Volkov painted the full picture for me: "Wherever you look," he said cheerfully, "you see nothing but enemies. In the west, the Germans are marching on, despite Trotsky's peace talks at Brest. The Finns and the Estonians, who are breathing down our necks, have both declared independence and the Germans, British and French together are cheering them on. In the south, the Ukrainians have done the same, the nationalists and Mensheviks merrily dance hand in hand. The Rumanians are leaning towards Bessarabia, why shouldn't they have a taste of the pie? And our good Russian generals, Kolchak and Denikin, have press-ganged every peasant and deserter they can arm with British weapons to eat away at the rest: the Don Cossacks, the Caucasian tribes from the Kazakhs to the Kyrghiz, gobbling Siberia as far as Vladivostok. Not to be left out, even the Americans are joining the British to move in on the north, on Archangel. Their newspapers are expecting our demise in days, not weeks. March on, lad, the devil awaits you with open arms!"

I had enough to think about in Petrograd, but I urged him to tell me more about Bessarabia. He leaned over and cautioned me not to think in such terms as "home" and "family." "We are the only family and home for you from now on." But then he pat- ted me on the shoulder and told me the province seemed to be escaping the worst. The Rumanians were after all allies, and we had their king, Ferdinand, in our hands, as ransom. "If they don't behave, we'll chop off his head. Just as we'll take care of our own unfinished business." He tapped his finger on his nose, but said no more.

I was beholden to him for taking me away from the front, but the task he had led me to was hardly easier. With so many enemies, the problem was how to identify any true friend. The rule was simple—no one can be trusted. As in any unit, you are attached to your comrades, even if some of them were, even if very young, little more than unthinking brutes. Some had been taken to the front at the age of sixteen, and had lost any trace of memory of any life other than hardship and terror. Our recruiters preferred those whose people, parents, brothers, sisters, had been imprisoned or killed by the autocracy, true orphans of the successions of storms. Volkov had put me on the list because of my record of dispatching his targeted officers efficiently and without fuss. "He has an old head on his shoulders," he told G., who was the direct Commissar of our squadron. "His trigger finger never trembles."

I was pleased by his words. Wherever one ends up, one wishes to be well-thought-of. More than a commander, he was an elder brother. He had come through, where so many others had disappeared like snow-flakes—The Wave, Styopka Whirl, Sergeant Trunov, so many faces that were stripped to dead bones. The great picture book city was just one more battlefield. I had to learn all its traps and its snares. The vast avenues were the greatest enemies, one was vulnerable to anyone who had good sight and a proper weapon up on the rooftops. Even at night, with not even a candle-light, one stood out stark against the snow.

I remembered the old Biblical saying—he who wakens to kill you, wake earlier to kill him. It was no commandment, but wise advice. Perhaps God was a Bolshevik after all, I embraced my new irreverent licence. Where had God been on the battlefield? Perhaps we were no longer inhabiting the realm of His creation? Perhaps we had passed through the darkest of tunnels, to a place where mercy and redemption had no place—the "other side"—the *sitra ahra*, where only chaos reigned. But we had no time for philosophy here. We had barely time even for Marxism. Our only thought was survival, once again. Day by day, hour by hour.

One of our earliest exploits, which had the bravado of an old style bandit raid, was to secure the private banks which were still operating in the city. This raid took place a few days before the New Year of 1918. We marched into the central branch of the State Bank, some of us in uniforms, others in their own civilian coats like a bunch of clerks who had suddenly struck it rich, waving the customers away and marching up the marble steps to the managers' offices, where Felix in person read out the decree of the monopoly and the rest of us hustled the directors out at pistol point to their new apartments at the Peter and Paul fortress. Since these were early days, the customers responded in an uproar, and we had to calm them down and shout that everybody's money was safe, but in the hands of the people, where it belonged. Volkov and a platoon of us was then tasked with rushing down to the vault, with the day manager, to open the combination safe and physically take as many of the steel boxes of gold bullion as we could carry out of the building onto a truck which we whisked off towards the Smolny. I was designated the driver. It was the strangest of feelings, to be a millionaire for half an hour, to transport the wealth of the country instead of a troop-load of exhausted soldiers towards a payload of German shells...

The Smolny institute was of course the seat of government at this point, the Party's headquarters since the Revolution, where Lenin and Trotsky had lived at either side of a long corridor, with many doors leading towards offices that had once been classrooms for the autocracy's daughters, a genteel girl's school that was now a hive from which the new empire was to be run. Outside it was a long imposing mansion laid back from the road, with a colonnaded entrance that was now bristling with machine gun emplacements and armoured cars, while inside sentries stood guard over those non-descript rooms, which were now ministries of this and that, the great staircase to the upper floor guarded every few steps, the steps themselves covered with cigarette butts that were ground into the old czarist carpets. It was more like a warehouse than an office of state, but it had sufficient underground basements to hold the gold safe from any attempts by internal rebels to mount some spectacular counter-attack.

Every day, in the dawn that could only be told by the hour on the clocks rather than the unchanging state of the sky, Lenin was driven from the Astoria hotel to the Smolny. Some of us were sometimes detailed to follow in our own vehicle, but sometimes he waved the detachment away. This nonchalance ceased when one day he was shot at while inspecting some red guards who were leaving for the front, but only a Swiss comrade who was riding with him in his car was hit, a slight wound in the hand. From then on, however, Felix made sure there were two vehicles that accompanied him front and rear, with men whose rifles were always at the ready. I would have been happy to join them, but Volkov and G. decided that my talents were better used elsewhere.

The situation in the city was grimmer by the day, as the ring of our enemies tightened. Coal was scarce, fuel was running out, and blizzards kept lashing the city with icy blasts that continued for days on end. The famous trams that served the city had to stop running, and the only way people could get from place to place was either on foot or by horse-drawn sleigh. If food was short for the people, it was as much so for the horses, who could barely carry their load, and one could see people stranded in the middle of the Nevsky Prospect, helpless beside the gaunt carcass. Others would creep up and then dash forward with knives to carve the spare meat off the bones before the poor nag had even breathed its last. The advances of the monarchist mutineers in the south were choking off the supply of corn from the countryside. Water was frozen, and the bad hygienic conditions were already causing epidemics, typhus, cholera, smallpox.

In the midst of this, the All-Russian Constituent Assembly was due to convene at the Taurid Palace on January 19th. Felix briefed us that this would be a great challenge. The elections to the Assembly in November had given the non-Bolshevik forces a majority, but Lenin was warning that unsolved arguments about procedures and empty declarations of human brotherhood by the Mensheviks and S-R's would bind the Revolution in chains that would leave the way open for our enemies to march in among the bombastic speeches and finish us off once and for all. There was a time for talk and a time for action. We still nominally had the majority with support of the Left S-R's and other fractions. The Right S-R's and the Mensheviks had already been marching in the streets and challenging the Council of Peoples' Commissars. A detachment of red guards had dispersed them then, but now all hands were called for the "showdown."

The assembly room was packed, and the entire convocation seemed to shake and rumble like a lion pit with rival roars. Sverdlov, chairman of the Council, opened with a rousing speech in which he declared the new Russia to be a Republic of Soviets, reading out the Council's declaration of rights of the working and exploited classes, and calling on the assembly to ratify the declaration and empower the Council to pursue all its measures, including a rapid peace at the front. I could see Lenin nodding his bald head in emphasis, and then all the Bolsheviks rose and sang the Internationale, applauding themselves loudly. The soldiers and sailors shook their rifles and waved their caps. Then the Menshevik Tseretelli rose up to speak. His own members cheered him, but the Bolsheviks roared their disapproval for an ex-Kerensky lackey. Hooting, whistles, banging of feet, catcalls, cries of "Traitor!" and "Scoundrel!" drowned out his words. Chernov, his party-fellow, another ex-Kerensky minister, who was the "Temporary Chairman" of the Assembly, tried to threaten the Bolsheviks with eviction, but he was greeted by cries of "Try it, you lickspittle!" and "Get down, your day is over!" Tseretelli went on for nearly an hour, denouncing the Bolsheviks and blaming them for the situation in which "the people" were disarmed, near starvation and deprived of all democratic rights to liberty, freedom of speech and so on. Everything he said seemed to make sense to me but I had no doubts. I had cast my lot with my comrades. We were a small unit at the back of the hall, but the hall was also filled with the soldiers and sailors who were still uttering cries against his charges. I could see Lenin whispering to Sverdlov and others. G. murmured to Volkov who told me that we would be standing down. "Lenin says let them talk themselves out. We all know what we have to do."

At one point someone stood up in the Left S-R ranks and brandished a pistol, but his comrades calmed him down, and he threw up his arms and walked out.

The talking went on and on, attempting to bore us into submission, until, in a recess close to midnight, one of the Party leaders, whose memorable name was Raskolnikov, read out a statement in the name of the Party and the entire block of Bolsheviks and Left S-R's marched out of the building. We remained behind, at a nod from Felix, and Volkov said, "we're just watching the show." The opposition droned on, until, at about four in the morning, the commander of the sailors who were guarding the hall approached the podium and told Chernov: "The guard is tired. You should close the session and let us go home." The oppositionists held their ground for a while, passing their resolutions without us, calling for further discussions on the issues of peace and land, and deferring the Bolshevik declaration of rights. Then they filed out. Our unit prepared to leave too, with an assuring squeeze on the shoulder from Felix, who said: "Hold on till they're all gone. We will have more work later." When the hall was empty, and only the stench of cigarette smoke and body odour remained, the guard came in with a large padlock and the doors of the assembly hall were locked shut. The contingent of sailors, who were in fact neither Bolshevists nor oppositionists but Anarchists, stood guard at the door, and the next day, no one was allowed to enter. The decree signed by Lenin and the Executive Council was posted on the door, declaring the Assembly annulled, as the only authority granted by the Revolution was to the Council of Soviets, and no revolutionary progress was possible without a complete rupture between the Soviets and the deceptive "democratic" organs of the liberal bourgeoisie and the remnants of the discredited Kadet government, whose leaders were now fighting openly to destroy our achievements.

Thus ended the Constituent Assembly. Three days later a Bolshevik march down the Nevsky was fired on from the surrounding rooftops. There was panic, and shooting all over the place. The list of our enemies was growing by the day.

10.

My first special assignment was some days before the Constituent Assembly debacle. *(The word used in Russian slang is "bardak" — "brothel." Trans.)* G. scrambled us at two in the morning. A strange killing had taken place just after midnight, at the Marie hospital. Two Kadet ex-ministers in the Kerensky government had been lying ill there, transferred from the Peter and Paul prison for treatment. Their names were Shingarev and Kokoshkin. When everything seemed quiet, a band of armed men pretending to be red guards broke in, and shot them both dead. Shingarev was also bayoneted in the face. Nobody might lose much sleep over dead enemies but G. told us this action was unauthorised. People acting in our own name were known to be active but this operation was designed to cause problems for the leadership during the difficult peace talks still going on at Brest. The city was full of German and Austrian prisoners who were let loose and mingling with the comrades and the atmosphere was very volatile. Felix was sure the act was also intended to fuel the opposition's suspicion of the Bolsheviks on the eve of the Assembly. They were right to be suspicious, but we did not want them forewarned. The Executive Council met the next day and formally condemned the assassinations, but meanwhile we were scouring the city.

A military orderly at the hospital had recognised one of the killers, a certain Galin, who was a member of the Left S-R's. It was a delicate situation, since we needed their support at the Assembly. We could not arrest him, or his comrades, who were probably of the same party. We tracked him down, Danilov, Grigor and I and another comrade, Sasha, to an abandoned apartment near Nikolaevski street, where six of the gang were living on the remains of some rich family that had got away a fair time before, using the plush beige curtains as blankets and burning the old armchairs and wardrobes for fuel. We waited till the whole lot had come back from whatever other exploit they had been assigned to and waited till they bedded down, among the vodka bottles. Since

Sasha and I were the sure shots, we each took two of the band, while Danilov and Grigor took one apiece. I despatched one of mine in the back of the head and shot the other straight in the face when he started up, startled. The whole affair would have taken five seconds if Danilov had not bungled his, and we had to chase the survivor onto the window sill from which he was about to splatter himself on the street. I caught him with a loose cord from one of the lamp-posts and dragged him back, so that Grigor could finish him off. The interesting thing about the whole operation was that, apart from the pistol shots, nobody uttered a sound. It was as if we were all engaged in a ritual that was already familiar to our targets but we were still only learning.

But circumstances make fast learners, in a situation that was rapidly deteriorating even from the low point at which I had started my new task. Political skirmishing and outright war apart, it was a condition rife for bandits, criminal elements who wrapped themselves in this banner or other, or none, and set out to loot whatever there was left to be looted in the already ravaged city. After the Council's decree to separate Church and State, the bishops called all Christian worshippers to protest against this challenge to their dominion. A great demonstration marched down the Nevsky, mostly composed of thousands of devout women. The march was unhindered, but later that day a crowd of several hundred hooligans broke into a church wine cellar by the Catherine Canal and began drinking themselves into a total frenzy, ransacking shops and markets and forcing out the civil militia. Since only soldiers, not police, had to deal with disorder, shooting started, with some of the drunkards hurling themselves onto the red guards with insane abandon. People were falling into the canal, drowning below the broken ice floes, and looting went on through the night. Ordinary people could hardly walk the streets even by day, and the city began to resemble a graveyard punctuated by sudden bursts of riot and gunfire. Shops were empty, the only product that was in abundance were guns, and even bandits could get hold of machine-guns. The banks were guarded closely, but any organisation that had ready cash to pay salaries could be subject to sudden raids from motor vehicles that would draw up and disgorge men armed to the teeth, ready to kill anyone who stood in their way.

In all of this, our own unit was kept apart, to deal with Special Actions, while the red guards had to act as police. We were not yet known by the name that was to become feared throughout the country—"Cheka"—although the "ve-che-ka", the special commission for counter-revolutionary struggle, was set up in December by the council members Trifonov, Ordzhonikidze, Evseyev and others, by an unpublished decree. It was not a secret, since the council wanted people to know that we were at work, and that, as in war-time, there would be no niceties in repressing our enemies. We were an administrative organ, not a judicial one, and were not to be concerned with legalities. We were not subject to the various arguments raging about the death penalty, which had been one of the triggers for the revolution at the front. We were the revolution, and we were sworn to defend it by all means necessary, and by summary action when so required.

"There will be moments," Felix told us wanly once, addressing us in an almost collegiate fashion in his own executive office, at a ground floor annexe at the south end of the Smolny, his desk piled high with files, ink jars and a large blotter with which he often toyed, with about ten of us of the Special Unit clustered round, on wooden folding chairs, "when you yourself, each one of you, will be the Revolution at some given moment, when there is no one else to whom you can turn and say: shall I perform the deed or not? It might appear, at first, to be a paradox, an individual choice, but you are not an individual. You are an arm of the Workers and Peasants' State, duly authorised by its representative Party. In the chain of command, you have been elected to make that choice. You are not cannon fodder for an autocratic figure, a Tsar, a Kaiser, a King, or a politician who can only move as a mechanical arm of Capital. This is the meaning of an emergency, that the duty of the moment is clear. It is fore-ordained. You will pull the trigger. Not from the crazed hate and greed of the criminal. But from love. The love of your own duty as a soldier. When that moment comes, you will know it."

That was the only moment I remember of any philosophical reflections from that man. The rest of the time he was dry as old timber. His eyes were always somewhat languid, as if the lids were on the brink of closing at the great fatigue of life. His jaw was slack on one side, the legacy of a strong beating in one of the Tsarist jails. He had endured so much suffering that he seemed to believe that all men could, or should, endure the same, in the service of the same iron commands of logic that had seen him through the long years of his incarceration. One endured to live, and one lived to endure.

A coldness came from him, the coldness of graveyards, that sprung up so grim in his wake. He was not the sort of man one followed as a leader, but rather in respect of that logic that appeared in our circumstances to be unassailable. We had no other choice. Lenin inspired. Even if one saw him just as a gust of wind, the strongest gust in the storm, whirling out of his office into his car, striding out towards whatever meeting or venue, in his nondescript jacket and pants that seemed to have rarely, if ever, been pressed. He was not a great speaker. He spoke decisively, with a kind of clipped authority that brooked no contradiction. He knew that every word that he uttered was right. He had thought it out, the plan and the outcome. It was concise, coherent and consistent. He expected everyone around him to be convinced, and one was swept up in that conviction. No trace of fear was ever imparted from his presence. If Lenin thought this or that was inevitable, it became so. One could bet one's life on it. I only once pressed his hand, when Felix was introducing us to him one early morning in the courtyard. He pressed each man's hand, rather languidly, and, to be honest, did not look at you. He was seeing something else, not a man, but a necessity. It was somewhat disconcerting. But one understood he had so many other concerns.

Trotsky was quite different. I experienced him only once, too, not at close quarters, but at a rally for the Red Guard detachments later in the year, a cloudy spring day. He stood on a podium and spoke for an hour. He waved his fists, he gazed down at us, from afar, but seemed to reach every heart. If Lenin spoke of the revolution as intellect, Trotsky was its passion. He held us all spellbound, speaking of the peace that was necessity, and of the war that was forced on us by those who would always be wolves. He would shout out: "I want every man to step forward!" and the entire parade would crunch towards him. Later on one could not remember with certainty anything specific that he had said, but we remembered that he had inspired us. History was on our side, there could be no other path. The darker the day, the brighter the dawn that would come.

But the day got no lighter. The peace at Brest-Litovsk kept the German armies from Petrograd but rebellions spread further: the Polish nationalists launched their own war against us, the Ukraine socialists were losing their own battle against the Petlyurists, the Cossack Whites continued their advance up the Don despite the setbacks to General Kaledin, and within the city, the Mensheviks and rightists increased their attacks on Trotsky's peace terms, which they claimed as a complete surrender of our original principles of "peace without annexations or indemnities."

Every morning we received lists of targets for arrests. We set out, in the armoured vehicles people recognised everywhere as we passed and rushed away from as if they were a return of the plague. I became a connoisseur of the city's apartments and warehouses, the seedy hide-outs where enemies on the run gathered to escape or plot the next outrage, their next ambush of our forces, armed robberies, or shooting provocations at Bolshevik marches. The old buildings, even on once commercial side-streets, were now more than often empty shells where once families had gathered, shopkeepers had retired after a hard day's earnings, merchants had relaxed amid fine fittings and furniture, intellectuals had gathered for tea and discussion about the latest books, theatre, opera, ballet, were like dusty mausoleums to a life once lived and people who had fled, some filled with assigned families who had poured in for protection from the zones of warfare, or workers from factories that had closed for want of materials or enemy action, children peeking over every staircase, women with frightened eyes, sullen men who trusted no one, other apartments having been looted and left fallow, cooking fires burned out on carpets, torn fittings, upturned beds, filthy or bloody sheets with holes from cigarette butts, bottles of liquor and the reek of spirits, vomit and caked sweat. Sometimes an old patriarch or couple, framed solemnly at some pre-war atelier, when life had aspects of normality, gazed down sternly, or uncomprehending, on the ruins, twisting from a bent nail in the wall. Some times there was an icon, which had been left there, on a broken cupboard, which, in some tic of disapproval, we removed. Anything we took was shoved in a rucksack to be piled up in the command basement, either as an item of value, or its opposite, something that no longer had any conceivable worth in tomorrow's brave world.

Here a group of men reared up, forewarned of our coming but unable to escape, guns drawn, ready to be shot down. There, a man desperately hiding under a bed was dragged out by the heels, calmed with the butt of a gun and dragged away to the van outside, his day as good as over. There, a man marked with the nodded sign of someone too dangerous to leave at large, even for trial, waited his moment, smoking a cigarette, or sitting calmly in an armchair whose stuffing reared out all around him. Once, with a teapot in his hand poised at a steaming cup, an eyebrow arched at our coming, a gentleman still in his threadbare jacket and buttonless waistcoat, his hair combed back and his moustache waxed at the tips, said "Good morning. I was expecting you earlier in the day." I shot him cleanly in the forehead. There was still the unruffled insouciance of the damned officer class.

Such a man I could dispatch calmly, with no regrets or anxiety, but with the vestige of an old whispered prayer floating, for a brief second, through my head. Those who were killers themselves, in the jungle, ready to devour us all root and branch, to tear out our entrails and hang us on the nearest nail, those too

I would shoot without faltering, the trigger finger responding to the absolute imperative of kill or be killed yourself. The war once more. Never over. Never finished. Never subject to its separate truce. Sometimes there was virtually a brigade of brigands, caught in the act, or tracked down at night, taken out in a back courtyard and shot against a wall, left to the machine-guns of our companion red guards. These I would turn my back on. Such executions in the mass I had seen at the front, when the Generals declared some debacle or mistake of their own as treason and desertion. Then the tied hands, the cliffside, the blindfolds, and the perspiration of the assigned firing squad. Sometimes, unfortunately, we had to load the bodies into the unit van, when the firing squad, with visible disgust at its task, simply walked away. This part was most distasteful. One could act, in action, but one did not wish to have to contemplate the consequences of the deed.

There were several pages missing at this point and some after, which had been clearly redacted, without comment. Yonni marked them with a red X. Then resuming:

Soon enough, the city itself was exhausted, wrung out, emptying of both amenities and people, fearful of famine, siege, defeat. People were besieging the railway stations, crowding the ticket booths for a way out, anywhere east or south, the guards were often called out to keep order among the seething masses, laiden down with bursting suitcases and bundles. In March, the situation became so dangerous that the Council decided to remove itself entirely to Moscow. The Smolny became a transit station in which crates of files were being laden into trucks and an entire special train was commandeered. Lenin, Trotsky, et al were ready to move out, to continue to run the revolution from the bastion of the old Kremlin. Felix too was going to travel with them, leaving G. in charge of our unit. This did not bode well, as he had become increasingly brutal in his pursuit of the rising tide of enemies, and his only concern became the requisition of more and more ammunition from the red guards. At one point we raided one of their depots at gunpoint, and were fired on, losing one of our own. We had been ordered to fire back but refused. G. glowered at us under his dirt-encrusted beard when we returned, although we had the goods with us, but we could see that there was no limit nor boundary as to whom could be added to the blacklist.

The news from outside continued to be dire. The Whites were becoming stronger, threatening Kharkov. The Germans were moving on Finland, threatening the city again. The Japanese had moved into Siberia, where Kolchak and the Whites were in power. The Germans were also interfering in the Ukraine, whose first nationalist government was overthrown by another, under German control. Volkov was feeding me news of Bessarabia, where the Rumanians had taken over, forestalling the Ukrainian pogromists. This was some good news, since I shuddered to think of the fear back in the home village if they were subject to the same chaos that now reigned everywhere. There was no hope, however, of getting news in or out. In May, even Moscow was in panic, with fear of a German advance from the west, and talk of evacuating the government, but where? Nowhere was safe. Our survival relied only on bayonets, and the fear that the Whites would do worse.

By June, despite the good weather, fuel and food had run out. There were no open stores to line up at. The trams were stalled once again, and did not resume working. The well-dressed women disappeared into their houses. People walked the streets with the shifting eyes of beggars, looking for anything that might have dropped in the street.

People began to mutter that the city was close to famine. Even our own enhanced bread rations were good only on paper. For the general population, bread disappeared for days on end, half a pound of potatoes per head per day, and people were rummaging through garbage and offal. Volkov told me he had seen children licking the paste off posters they had peeled off the walls. The street hawkers would appear at random, with their meagre fare snatched up quickly. In the bright sunshine, the great edifices of the winter palace, the Hermitage, the blue canals, gilded statues, bridges, cathedrals and spires now seemed to be anticipating some festival that had been postponed indefinitely. The stone rider in front of the dome of St. Isaacs was still poised to leap away, but still could not leave the ground.

The real potentates, however, were soon to be gone. As if to compensate for our hunger, late July brought the news that the Tsar and his family had been executed. The Romanovs finally met their doom in Yekaterinburg, some said in a basement, others said they were killed off in a train carrying them further on towards Perm. It was said that the Tsar of all the Russias was sent out of this world by an ordinary soldier with a bayonet thrust in the heart. We all felt a relief that the dynasty at least would not return. We had no thought for the "royal" women and the anaemic child. So many of those had lain dead before our eyes in the streets of the Imperial capital.

We continued to do our duty in the city in which everyone now seemed to be a dead person on leave. Cholera had returned, and we were all deflected from the work of finding and disposing of enemies to the vital labour of carrying casks of boiling water to streets and junctions to try and combat the infection. The people of Petrograd, however, seemed so inoculated by suffering that they sailed through even this, although, as ever, the weak, the youngest and the oldest were first to die. The hardship had now lasted so long that a resilience that had been once found only in the trenches took over the city itself. For the first time, banditry and pointless killing seemed to die down, and the long lists in our hands started to shrink. Perhaps, we thought, we were over the worst...

But this was just another delusion.

11.

Matters continued to deteriorate through the summer. Rumours reached us that the government was going to leave Moscow to set up the final stand of the Revolution further East, even in Siberia. This made no sense, as we were informed that the British had landed in Archangel and foreign forces were moving from the north in all all directions. From the east, a large detachment of Czecho troops were fighting their way through Siberia with Kolchak and the White Cossack forces. The streets of Petrograd were still full of German ex-prisoners, who had first appeared to throw in their lot with the Bolsheviks but now had become nothing more than scavengers, consuming the little food that was left us. On the brink of rebellion ourselves, we were reigned in again by the arrival of Felix in person, vouching for Kh. and approving G.'s removal.

But even our own flimsy sense of security was being sliced away, piece by piece. At the end of August, news came through of another shock, the attempt made to assassinate Lenin by another S-R terrorist, Dora Kaplan, a half-blind zealot who had, like Felix, suffered years of incarceration and torture in the Tsar's prisons, and wanted revenge for the crushing of her comrades and Lenin's "betrayal" of the Revolution's true aims. This time the shots fired hit the leader, in his back and shoulder, though he was still alive.

Once again we were plunged into a frenzy of action. All through the summer and fall we were run ragged trying to cross names off Kh.'s lists. A zealous martinet, he was relatively efficient, reviving the revolutionary tribunals which dispatched our prisoners to various prisons rather than directly to the here-after. But this policy was soon abandoned as the list grew longer and longer. In September, we arrested the British Consul and his deputy, and about a hundred other British nationals, but this was for political purposes, to put pressure on the British authorities because of their landings at Archangel. The British were also assisting the Czechs and Kolchak's Whites in Siberia. The Consul and his deputy were released soon, but the other British were being kept as hostages, since our own Bolshevik minister, Maxim Litvinov, was being held in England. It seemed that everyone, even within our own ranks, was determined to end the Revolution, if only to gain some relief from the unremitting hardships of hunger, terror and disease. Arrests apart, there was the feverish recruitment of whoever was able to bear arms for the inevitable defence of the city once the Whites reached our suburbs, or for service in the south and east. Walls all over the city were posted with calls for volunteers, who were thin on the ground, and had to be commandeered from the factory working class. The posters would cry out that:

> "The Tsarist Black Hundreds have gathered to serve the English capitalists to capture our towns and villages, slaughtering our brothers, violating our wives and sisters, destroying our crops, and sharpening their teeth for the final assault on our beloved Petrograd! Brothers! Rise and Fight for the Defence of our Socialist and Proletarian Republic!"

And in the pictures, courageous men and women flourished their guns, their faces determined, their arms and muscles flexed for the defence of our soil with rifle, scythe or bare hands.

Meanwhile, we had to commandeer the remaining bourgeois who were still clinging to their mansion apartments to clear the dead and bury them, driving them in groups to the cemeteries to wield pick and shovel on the hard ground. Doctors and nurses were becoming scarce as they too succumbed to hunger and disease. There were fewer and fewer animals still alive—no horses left to pull the winter sleighs, hacked corpses of nags rotting on the streets, and no stray dogs at all, those who were not seized for food hid crazily in alleyways and holes, their frightened eyes sometimes peeking out at night before bolting away from us as if they too were names on Kh.'s endless lists.

The situation grew so grim that orders came from above to slow down the mass arrests and executions, so that a lull stole over the dying city, and a ghostly quiet, as the first snows of the winter of 1918-1919 began to fall, like a shroud blessedly drifting to bring succour to the tormented, to ease our passing and caress our final murmurs of exhaustion. The streets were silent, there were far fewer shots and cries of anger echoing in the frozen nights, and the old buildings stood mute, great stone forebears standing vigil as the wind keened over their slaughtered children. The gold of the statues had long dimmed with grime, and the waters of the canals flowed sluggishly, weighted with sludge, garbage and filth, the occasional bloated body still knocking softly against their banks.

Still, the dying city did not die! Like a corpse picking itself up from the graveyard, having decided its day had not come yet, the people still moved, if a little sluggishly, and the factories still clattered away, albeit reluctantly, even at bayonet point, and the bayonets still stood at the ready, and few were yet ready to put up welcome signs for the Whites at our door. Slowly, sluggish myself at first, I had come to understand the Petrograd that writers wrote about and artists celebrated, holding fast like old rusty nails that held the entire edifice—Russia—from tearing off and falling apart. There were artists, playwrights and writers still clinging to the city.

An ignorant child myself, unlike my brother Boris, it was Volkov who brought this home to me, taking me one evening when he saw I was floundering, thrashing about between bouts of black depression and the brute urge of violent action, off by foot, across the Nikolai bridge to Vasilievsky island, where a number of writers had set up a "Literary House" in the apartments of an old bourgeois, Ginzburg, who had fled abroad with his money. Fedor Sologub was the chairman of this loose group, which sometimes hosted Maxim Gorky, Blok, Gumilev and Zamiatin. In the midst of all the carnage and fear, it was astonishing to see that men and women of the arts were still determined to stay in the city, and keep the intellectual life going.

The old house was a welcome diversion among the ranks of broken down, wrecked, half-burned, piss-strewn apartments I had trawled through for months, a cosy haven with some scruffy armchairs, divans, scratched but serviceable furniture, patched up walls and stuffed bookshelves… Human warmth, a hot samovar, glasses of tea, friendly faces blurring in the thick pall of cigarette smoke that sometimes required the windows to be opened even in the February frost. The buzz of loud talk, argument, greeting of old friends, a haven so far removed from the brutality of daily life that it almost cried out for arrest—I could almost hear Kh.'s sharp bark from the doorway: Seize the lot! But Volkov ushered me in, introducing so many famous names, some of which even I in my abysmal ignorance had heard of.

Chief among these, of course, was Gorky, the revolution's human voice since before anyone but a few associates had ever heard of Lenin or Trotsky, author of "On The Steppes," "An Autumn Night" and *Mother*, the conscience of the age of autocratic tyranny and the knout, who brought the simple life of Russia so vividly to light, giving voice to the voiceless, rising above the simple wretchedness of the common fate. In the flesh, he still reverberated with an intense energy, striding up and down the room, pointing, cajoling, flourishing his great black-grey moustache like a banner. He was reading out a new message he had written, which he called "An Appeal to the World," noting the end of the Great War in November, the final defeat of German imperialism, and calling for people around the world not to give up the fight for a better and more just world. He had been taken to task by the leadership for his criticism of "mistakes," "unnecessary hardships" and so forth, committed in the name of war communism, but he wished the world to know that he had not lost faith. Despite the backwardness and cultural crudeness of Russia in her current agony, he still saw no other way but to forge forward to keep the torch of the revolution alight, to continue the battle against the old order.

"For liberty and the glory of life..."

It was a stirring call, and I and some others applauded, but I could see that there were some in the room who just sat on their hands or drew on their cigarettes, blowing out smoke rings. I knew none of these people, but Volkov pointed them out to me as the argument and declamations rolled on. Later, as we walked back through the snow, he gave me a quick primer: That pale long face with the sparse hair who looked bored with everything was Sologub, the "symbolist" writer, who had written "The Petty Demon," about a vain schoolteacher who goes crazy out in the provinces, a harsh sample of the petty cruelty and perversions of the old ways. He was not a Bolshevik but supported the revolution, and was most probably on one of Kh.'s endless lists. There was Gumilev, the poet, who had travelled around the world to Paris and Italy and even to Africa before coming back to fight in the war. He was also a symbolist, but not the same type as Sologub, I couldn't make out the difference. His wife Anna was also a poet, she was a sad looking lady with dreamy eyes. He was most definitely on our lists, for monarchist leanings, but he was under Gorky's protection. There was the dapper looking Yevgeny Zamyatin, whose father had been a priest but who had been a Bolshevik since before 1905, when he had been exiled, and then lived in Finland. He was a good man, if slightly odd, and had written about his life in England, where he had worked as a naval engineer. He never said anything at any of the sessions I went to. Another odd person at the meetings was Alexander Blok, who Volkov told me was considered the best symbolist poet, though how one judged a scale of qualities in that kind of business I never could quite make out. He had eyes which were sometimes wide and glaring like a puzzled child, and at other times languid and half-closed, sitting still in his chair as if waiting for something to wake him up from some deep and hidden place. At one of the sessions he read out a poem that he had written the year before, just after the Constituent Assembly affair, which was called "*Dvanatset*"—"Twelve." It was a very strange piece, that was considered most controversial for its style as well as its content, a dreamlike description of twelve red guards who march through Petrograd's night. "Black night, white snow, the wind! the wind! blowing across God's world..." It was very strange but evoked strong images: a "hen-like" woman scrambles over a snowbank, a bourgeois stands at a crossroads, the wind "madly twists coat-hems and mows down passers-by..." the soldier rushes along with his girl-friend, he thinks of her legs, he thinks about fornication, lace underwear, breasts...

I remember Sologub at his most languid, drooping his eyes bored in his chair as the poet's voice rang out in the hushed space... "Let's sin, oh yes, let's sin! Sin is easy on the soul!" Gorky twiddled with his moustache. "Fly away, bourgeois! I will drink your blood for my sweetest love..." That rather took my fancy, and "the twelve go marching on, ready for anything, regretting nothing..." That captured my moment quite strongly... "Only the dog, beggared and hungry... only the blizzard, laughing in the snows..." Then in the end, ahead of the procession of hunger and revolution, Blok ended with "Jesus Christ, going ahead of them." Everybody told him to cut that out. But people were still, despite everything, despite the cold, the famine, the cholera, the killing, despite beady-eyed, hungry, ignorant, bloody youths like myself...

(At this point there is a missing chapter, which in early notes is referred to as "12: Petrograd women." Four pages have been torn out of the notebook, and have not been available for translation. The next chapter is numbered 13. Y.)

13. Victor.

It was at one of the literary evenings that I first met Victor Kibalchich, in one of those strange coincidences that can only be put down to fate—a very un-Marxist concept. He was a small stocky and dynamic man of sharp features and quick eyes that darted every-where, taking in everything he observed as if storing it for some future purpose. A Belgian by birth and upbringing, but both a Russian and a revolutionary by origin, as his father had been among those executed for the dispatching of the Tsar, Alexander the Second, in 1881. He had arrived in Petrograd as part of an exchange of prisoners that was negotiated among the minor provisions of the Versailles peace talks, in effect a hostage exchange of the British consular and other western detainees in Russia for the Bolshevik foreign minister Litvinov who was being held in London and imprisoned "Bolsheviks" in France. In fact, Kibalchich was hardly a Bolshevik, since he had been a renowned anarchist almost all his life, from childhood, a militant in Belgium,

France and Spain, where he had taken part in the anarchist uprising in Barcelona in 1917. Like our own anarchists—up to a point (!)—he had embraced the ideas of the February and the October revolutions, though he had a lot to learn about the differences, conflicts and deviations of our own multifold groups. Never the less, since the Bolsheviks had succeeded where all previous groups had failed, he was prepared, it appeared, to be a Bolshevik, though the entire foreign group was on one of our Cheka's lists as yet unproven human material... Kh. himself encouraged me to keep an eye on him, which turned out to be a convenient licence to meet and discourse with this extremely well-read and well-informed man. I had a very personal reason to seek him out, however, since I remembered his name, which seemed familiar, though I could not imagine at first how on earth I might have heard it. Then, when Volkov showed me his file, my memory flowed, since it contained an entire entry on Kibalchich's attendance at the well-known anarchist conference in Amsterdam in 1907. This must have been, as I recalled, the same meeting that my elder brother Boris had written us about more than ten years before, from Paris. I remembered the excitement of the letter, back in our small Bessarbian town! I especially remembered the stamps, which were stuck all along the front and back of the envelope, to make sure there was enough postage, each portraying the legend "Republique Francaise" over the famous image of Madame La France—the young woman with bare arms and long flowing hair. The symbol of Liberty—Marianne! I remembered his condensed tale of his journey across Europe from Romania, through Austria, Hungary and Germany, and all the bold people he met in Amsterdam, the Belgian-Russian and the flamboyant Spaniard whose name I forget, and how they had reached Paris together and were living among artists and actors.

Volkov cautioned me not to approach Kibalchich among the crowd at Sologub's "salon," since Kh. had a big stamp with an "A" with which he branded the files of those suspected of anarchism, his least favourite among the still legal fractions. Their peasant forces in the Ukraine were still loose, the armies of Nestor Makhno, who were neither Red nor White, but Green, a colour Kh. always scoffed at. "What is this green? Are they trees or men?" One did not argue with him in this mood, in fact, in any mood. Kh. could not however touch the newcomer, since he was highly valued by some of the intellectuals on the Executive Council, mainly Zinoviev, who recruited him for the International section and got him a room at the Astoria.

We solved the problem by giving him a lift in our car, although I am sure he had been told which office Volkov and I represented and I could see Gorky giving him a warning sign, but he was newly come at the time and still relatively naive, used to the perils of the west, but not our ravaged city. I sat with him at the back while Volkov drove across the bridge in its mantle of white, and Volkov said to him: "Kolya has something to ask you." And I said directly, "I do believe that you have met my brother." And then I told him that my brother had to flee our province in Bessarabia after he had fought in Odessa in 1905, and had written us from Paris that he had been at the Anarchist conference in Amsterdam and had met a good friend, Kibalchich, with whom he travelled to Paris.

"Boris?" he said, "Boris Gurevitch?"

He invited us to drive to his room at the Astoria but we knew it was guarded by one of our own contingents and Volkov suggested we diverge to the apartment of another intellectual friend of his, a Jewish theatrical manager, Alexander Granovsky, who had a room over his studio just across the Fontanka, and who never slept as he laboured over his designs for a production of a play by Scholem Asch. Volkov, I was discovering, had a variety of "doors" that were open to him all over the city, and where he was obviously finding refuge from the rigours of our impossible tasks. Granovsky knew me as a Jew the moment he saw me and we exchanged some words in Yiddish, the first time I had spoken the language since I arrived in Petrograd. Kibalchich was happy to meet him, as one of the city's experimental artisans of whom he had heard so much. I think he was one of those who believed that if Art flourished in the revolution then despite all setbacks, all was somehow well. He was sure to be disabused very soon...

We passed a pleasant and unexpected two hours speaking of Boris, whom I had not seen since he had been hurried out of the house on board our neighbour's cart, headed for the Romanian border, fully twelve years gone by... Since we were in trusted surroundings I told him my brother was still in America, from where we had received some letters before the war. But since that fateful day of my recruitment in 1914 I had seen or heard nothing of him, or of other members of my family. I told him of my other brother, Yakov, who had also gone to America, and become a magician, and of Zev, who wanted to trade in Siberia. He was always curious, this Kibalchich, and wanted the rounder story, so I had to tell him of my sisters and my parents, my father the Rabbi.

"I loved your brother," he said. "He was like a locomotive that lays its own tracks before it. America will be good for him, if he does not succumb to its capitalistic psychosis. America has a madness to succeed, which we could do with. We have been too addicted to failure. This is why I admire Lenin and Trotsky, and believe that we are still on the right path. But I can see so much tragedy surrounding us."

I wanted to know as much as I could of my brother's life in Europe, and he had some good stories that made us laugh about the life of the artists and film actors in Paris. He told us that he and Boris and their other friend, Mereyda (?) eked out a living hiring themselves out as comedians for the Pathe and Gaumont film companies. If we saw moving pictures here in Petrograd, we might even have caught a glimpse, unbeknown to us, of their antics in those short dramas. "Once we had to chase rounds of cheese down the boulevards," he said, "the cheeses knocked down all the passers-by and we had to weave and jump around them, knocking over bearded gentlemen and ladies with parasols..."

He himself had other work in Paris, writing and publishing for the revolutionary journals, demonstrating against the military draft to the wars in North Africa, which earned him several periods in jails. Prison life was harsh, and when the War came, he said, the socialists betrayed the cause both of peace and social change. The working class movement was full of police agents. When released, he took the train to Barcelona, and the rest we had heard about in his talk at the "salon." (Or in Kh.'s files, we didn't tell him about those.) I wanted to hear more about my brother, but he seized the opportunity of a tete-a-tete with Volkov over the latest news from the encircling fronts of our internal war. Kolchak approaching from the south, setbacks in the Ukraine, Denikin's Whites moving up from Novo-Cherkask. Offensives at the Urals, more attacks on Archangel, and, more immediate, the advances of the Finns, Letts and Estonians on our own capital city. He could see with his own eyes the stark situation: Food was terribly short, people burned their furniture for fuel, the price of tea was 380 rubles a kilo, which he said was twenty-eight pounds sterling, a fortune even for the fattest Englishman alive. Typhus was still raging, and one did not want to say the word "famine."

Yet there was Granovsky, scribbling his remarks over set designs for Asch's "God of Vengeance" at the Maly Theatre. They couldn't use the word "God" so the title was simply changed to "Sin." But the world of the mind was still alive. Clearly there was a whole world to fight for, the chances of revolution in Germany were high, their army beaten and humiliated, and hard sanctions about to be approved at Versailles would crush the militaristic spirit that had unleashed the Great War. Hungary too, was teetering on the brink. We here, at the centre of the best hope that mankind could muster, had to hold fast, despite our doubts and our fears.

Thus spoke the Belgian anarchist. After we had dropped my brother's friend off a few yards from the entrance to the hotel, but not close enough for the guards to see our faces in the car, we drove back to our own barracks quarters. Danilov and Grigor were out, on some ghastly detail, so we had the night to keep ourselves awake with some liquids and Volkov relieved his pent-up inner thoughts by entrusting me with his deepest misgivings and qualms.

For a long time, he said, he had been keeping our unit "protected" from the worst aspects of our duties by maintaining our charge as a specialist team dealing with specific threats from armed assassins and bandits. But all around us the tactics unleashed after the attempted killing of Lenin raged like the worst storms of the French Revolution's "great terror." Hoarders, dissenters, ordinary members of banned organisations, people caught stealing fuel, and striking workers were being dispatched en masse, in large numbers. Even our growing legions were sagging under the burden, and now the workers at the Putilov works and the Alexandrovsky railway workshops were out on strike and, infiltrated by the Mensheviks and S-R's, were rallying to cries of "Down with Lenin! Down with dictatorship!"

Were we going to shoot down our own workers in the streets of our city, like the Cossacks in 1905? While we were hob-nobbing with the lofty writers and artists of Gorky's "House of Literature" other specialist units, cut-throats and thugs trained by Kh. and other Lettish and mercenary enforcers were machine-gunning prisoners en-masse on the Neva banks and driving the bodies off on trucks to be dumped beyond the city in mass graveyards that were already fenced and made ready.

What did I think of that? He flourished his flask in my face, and then downed what was left in it, and, upending it, watched the few droplets ooze out and then looked at me, with all that had passed between us and that we had endured since he first spotted me hunched in the trenches of Galicia, when ice and terror had been mitigated by our unwavering knowledge of who we were then, and what had to be done, at that point.

Never the less, we returned to duty, although Volkov still managed to keep us away from the firing squads and confined to pin-point operations. The division itself was growing larger and larger. More men, and women too, often just young girls, recruited from the high schools, were needed for grand sweeps, mass arrests and interrogations. Volkov told me one day, more grim-faced than usual, that the unit sifting through the old Okhrana archive, the papers and lists of the Tsar's secret police, had unearthed the Okhrana manual of interrogations and passed it over to the thugs, some of them released and pardoned prisoners, who had been put in charge of the most "difficult" detainees, mainly the S-R's, who were pretty tempered by their own stubborn experience. "Is this what we fought for?" Volkov whispered to me, close as we were in our bunks at night. The atmosphere of fear and suspicion had penetrated my bones, too, so that I wondered once or twice whether he was testing me, or tempting me to rebellion, but then I banished the thought. If I could not trust Volkov, who plucked me out of the trenches and the lethal truck drivers' seat to bring me safe, or relatively safe, to harbour, then who could I trust? I was still, at some level, the naive youth of Celovest, who hungered for news of his brothers...

Victor Kibalchich was travelling between Petrograd and Moscow, bringing back news of the leadership there, and their confidence that despite it all we would prevail. I saw him again, at a meeting to celebrate the Soviet government of Munich, and the Red Revolution in Hungary, which had brought a Soviet government to power there. From Munich to Berlin was not a great distance, and even Kibalchich, who knew the west, was optimistic, saying that perhaps the tide was finally turning. Victory in Germany and Hungary would surely mean the collapse of the north-eastern threat from Finland and Estonia, even despite the British and French attacks, and their pressure on Kronstadt. That would leave the Whites and their allies, the Czech Legion, which was enabling them to hold Siberia. Even if the Americans would invade through Vladivostok, they would have a long way to come to Moscow.

Poor Bessarabia was not uppermost in his mind, and we just exchanged quick handshakes in the crowded meeting hall before he was borne away by his International comrades.

The Munich Soviet, however, did not last even a month, and was over-run just after May Day by the German freikorps, who shot down the communists mercilessly. The Rumanians were eating away at the Hungarian Reds, the Finns were still pressing on Kronstadt and the British and Americans were advancing down the railway from Archangel. Meanwhile, in the midst of the city, Kh. was still busy putting down strikes.

On one mission to find a German spying position that had been spotted at Staraya Novaya, and which consisted of an abandoned warehouse full of rusted carts and broken down droshkies, Volkov took me aside after we dismissed Danilov and Grigor and took out his pipe, which he stuffed with some Dutch tobacco we had found some weeks before in a hide-out. I kept to my army-issue *papirosa*.

"Kolya my friend," he said, "I have found our solution."

We sat, among the horseless and wheel-less carriages, perched on a pile of seats that provided a strange comfort in the quiet of the abandoned space, as he spun me his tale, an amazing proposal, which would have seemed, at any other time and place, a purple fantasy from a volume of Jules Verne, but which was at that moment, in that place, as logical a scheme as could be spun by two people caught in that historical swirl of events.

PART 2:
THE PASSAGE.

14.

I remember my brother Zev used to talk to me enthusiastically about the Trans-Siberian railway. He had a German book about railways that our Uncle Tuvia, who was the family "maskil", or "enlightened" one, gave him for his Bar-Mitsvah, and it had all sorts of details and photographs of the great railway lines of the world. I was nine years old at the time, but I inherited the book when he grew older and went off with Sruli "Moicher", the merchant. There were chapters on the Berlin suburban railway, Berlin to Bucharest, that my brother Boris had taken the other way back in 1907, the Orient Express, Paris to Brindisi, Paris to Madrid, London to Glasgow, the American "International Limited," the Zambezi Express, the Andes "Cog-Line," the Madras Special to Calcutta, the South Manchurian Railway from Harbin to Port Arthur, and of course the Trans-Siberian. My brother Yakov and I—he was two years older—would huddle over the book and dream about all the voyages we would make together, rejoining Boris, who had probably been on all of them, so we especially studied the American routes, New York, Chicago, San Francisco, though we were disappointed in advance because we couldn't make the ocean crossing by rail...

I couldn't remember the details of the long Russian route from Moscow to Vladivostok, which was more than ten thousand kilometres. I remember the point that at Lake Baikal in winter special rails were laid down over the ice, though the book was almost twenty years out of date, printed in 1901, if I remember correctly. I remember that the role of the current Tsar, our fallen enemy Nikolai, my namesake, who was then the Tsarevitch. was greatly lauded for his enabling of this "sacred" duty. There was also a picture of his German counterpart, Kaiser Wilhelm, with his enormous waxed moustache. He had a helmet with an eagle perched on top. Yakov and I agreed that we would like to have something like that ourselves, when we grew up. The train itself, with its great conic steam funnel, flew majestically across the pristine white tundra...

July 1919, at the Moscow station, was a very different picture: On a hot day, the smell of sweat hung over the station entrance, the hall and the train platforms that heaved with jostling, desperate humanity pressing against the locked carriages, which were guarded by armed troops, pushing the hordes back with rifle barrels and butts, as commanders stood on the carriage roofs, shouting at the crowds to calm down. Men, women and children, many dressed in heavy coats despite the heat since there was no room to store the clothes in the tight bundles or bursting suitcases cracked at the seams. The sound that rolled across the concourse was a ripple of woe, a low murmur interspersed with loud calls of names of people who had got lost, pulled away from friends and relatives by the tug of the mass.

The Russian, however, is inured to waiting. While life lingers, every-thing can be endured. At some point, the carriage doors are shoved open, and the guards stand ready as people wave their documents and torn rags of paper that they hoped would bring marvels. Despite our headlong rush from Tsarism, we cannot help but replicate its means to keep the population in check. The grand bureaucracies of Gogol, if much more thread-bare and chaotic. Inside, the carriages are already filled with soldiers who are being sent down to the front, to face Denikin's forces in the south and Kolchak's in the east. They are pressed into the seats in each compartment, four or five to a row, crushed against the windows in the corridors with their kitbags, pouches and weapons, the overflow cramming into the toilet, where three men are already installed. In the event that one cannot avoid using the toilet, the men move aside to make room, but otherwise offer no concern for the privacy of the moment. One is back at the front, where all are united in the odour of our common bestial humanity, although the foul cigarettes most people were smoking could blanket even the rankest miasma.

With all this, however, the train still did not move for a long while. Guards rushing up and down outside, shouting that the carriages were so full that a single cabbage could not be crammed in, did not signal any hint of departure. As the Russians do, we began to speak of rumours. Some said a train had departed the previous day, almost on time, another that nothing had moved for six days. One man who presented himself as well-versed but with scant evidence said that the previous train had derailed at Kosterovo, and one truck had caught fire, burning two hundred men to matchsticks. Another said we were waiting for Trotsky's personal train to come through from Perm, and yet another that a special troop train had to move before us from the next station down the line.

Volkov found us a seat, by dint of flashing his special pass which caused all but the most rough-skinned would-be travellers to move aside or even slouch off to another carriage. We pressed up by the grimy window, looking out upon the still hopeful hordes. Like those around us, we soon fell asleep, and were jolted awake by the totally unexpected but inevitable clanking of moving bogeys. We were on our way towards our great adventure.

Further and further away, from all roots and origins. The only way that Volkov could remove us from the taint and destruction of our required tasks in the city was to volunteer to take us into even greater danger. The "Telegraphist" still had his web of connections within and outside the city. He had a direct link to Felix, which bypassed Kh., and provided the brute with an appropriate reason to allow his potentially disloyal subordinate to escape his own net, rather than face the firing squad. Breaking up the original, tightly knit unit that Dzherzhinsky had personally formed in Petrograd in the months immediately following the Revolution was a positive step for Kh. in his own crawl to power.

Volkov's idea was insane, in any normal circumstance, but we were not living in normal times. Since my entire adult years had been spent in this whirlpool, another twist of the waves was no more or less likely to end in catastrophe or failure than any other. Such were our lives. We were merely part, again, of a great movement of troops, equipment, ammunition, reinforce-ments for the "civil war" that pitted Russian against Russian across the huge swathes of the country that stretched southwards to Ukraine and Kazakh lands, and east all the way to the Sea of Japan.

The Great Asian "game." In the spring of 1919, the forces of Admiral Kolchak had launched their fiercest attack on Bolshevik rule since he had established his "White" government in Omsk, in central Siberia. Armed to the teeth by the British, the French and the Americans, the Whites had swept to the Urals and taken the major city of Perm, threatening a pincer movement with the western troops in the north and General Denikin's troops in the Ukraine. With Petrograd under siege, and Moscow threatened, it seemed that Lenin's "proletarian" revolution would be a six-month innovation, a mere blip on the way to a Tsarist revival or a full-fledged military dictatorship. The enemy were not only "Whites"—there were Social-Revolutionaries, Mensheviks and others who had formed a Russian front with the Admiral. The period of leave from death granted to Bolsheviks seemed to be growing shorter by the day.

By the middle of May, however, our forces under General Frunze had rallied and pushed the Whites back. Perm was retaken, and Kolchak's army was retreating towards Viatka, having come with a hundred miles of the Volga. By the time we took our train, we had reports of a great battle in the Urals, near Yekaterinburg, in which the Whites' Seventh Division was defeated at the Chusovastkaya station, with five regiments captured and a huge amount of arms and railway equipment taken. On the other hand, on Denikin's front, Kharkov had been taken by the Whites, who were pushing up from Pskov and Orenburg.

It seemed, though, that we could count on staying on the train until Ufa, where we would be able to liaise with Volkov's contact there, Kaminsky, an old comrade of the Galician front, who would arrange our forward transport towards and across the White lines. The only problems, for us veterans of chaos, being that we could neither be sure that Kaminsky was still alive, nor where we could find him, nor if there were any "lines" that we could cross, or where they might lie on any given day. We only knew, or thought we knew, that there were comrades behind these lines, in the central city of Omsk itself, who were "Trojan horses" in the enemy's rear.

"If we want to be free," Volkov told me, "we have to find the place of maximum hazard, where the fire is hottest, around the eye of the storm." A classic "philosopher" of the trenches, he was given to metaphors and thoughts that made no sense except to all the rest of us who lived daily with talismanic and irrational hopes. Even the man who is resigned to death has the thought that at the last minute, on the brink, the clouds will part and God's hand will stretch out, or his luck, which has been so overwhelmingly foul, must be due for a fantastic and spectacular turn. The deeper the pit, the higher the leap to glory.

At any rate, he had it all worked out. He had a map, which he unfolded before me, at our warehouse meeting place at the Staraya Novaya. It was a specialist chart of Siberia, with its mineral deposits marked out in detail, that he had obtained from the Department of Mines. The vast deposits of zinc, lead, copper, coal, silver and gold that had been worked for a hundred years and those that were ripe for future exploitation. Millions of tons, thousands of millions of ounces of precious metals, lying in wait in immense areas of lode bearing mines, spread over the enormous steppes and tundras of the north-east. "You think this war is about ideology, politics, Marxism, dialectic materialism?" he asked me. "Poor deluded young man. It's about money, bullion, wealth. The Tsar's gold reserves. The government sent them out of Moscow for safe keeping in Kazan, where they were snatched by the Czechoslovak legion in league with the S-R's `komuch'. From there the whole load was transferred east to the White headquarters at Omsk. A total disaster for Lenin. Men can be inspired to fight, sacrifice, die. But guns can only be bought with money. Or, if you lack it, you need to dig it out of the ground, but that takes time, while an entire generation dies."

427

He jabbed his finger at the map, moving it around a large dotted circle in a non-descript region north of Irkutsk. "Remember this," he said, "the `Lena' goldfields. The largest deposits in this part of Siberia, and within reach of the railway. Does it belong to Russia? No, it is owned by the British, the Lena Goldfields Company Limited. The owners sit in mansions in England while our workers toil and die to extract the lode. Did they not teach you our history? The great Lena gold mine strike of nineteen-twelve? The workers rose and were shot down by the Tsar. The mines have been worked for the English since eighteen-sixty-three. The proceeds still go to the London Joint Stock Bank and the Banque de Commerce a Varsovie, in Warsaw. Do you think Capitalism goes to sleep just because we poor muzhiks run up and down forming Soviets and declaring the world upside down? The world is still the way it is and has always been. You have two choices, boy—get wise or dead."

Then he showed me another document, a telegraphic dispatch received earlier that month, in early June, from the east. A local Bolshevik commander, Muraviev, in charge of special forces in Siberia operating deep inside Kolchak's nominal territory, had raided and seized the Lena Goldfields. His army, which consisted of ten thousand men, was holding the fields against a counter-force of Cossacks commanded by Hetman Krasilnikov. Reinforce-ments had been ordered to the region by Trotsky.

"That's us," Volkov said, jabbing the map again. "Felix doesn't trust Trotsky. Who trusts who? Was he not a Menshevik? And who were we? Brave soldiers of Tsar Nikolai Dva. For three years, we fought poor German workers. We are the old guard now. We think for ourselves. Better to get us out of the way. We have a message for this Muraviev, from Felix. But who knows when we get there, if we get there, what message we might deliver? Or what path we might take? Eh, comrade? My dear Kolya, what do you say?"

I remember that I could only say yes as the logic of his impossible plan was unbreakable. Three years in the trenches induce an instinctive and fundamental urge to survive the next hour, the next night, the next day. When we joined the train we no longer had any moments in which we could talk to each other without being heard, so we became like the other two thousand men packed in the carriages, cargo carried forward at the mercy of the predictable tracks and the inevitability of unforeseen forces.

Barely an hour out we already had an obstacle at Fryazevo station, where another troop train had broken down across the junction, and guards were running up and down shouting and facing each other across the track. From there we had a straight run down to Vladimir, which we passed in the dead of night, an eerie ghost town whose cathedral dome loomed as a stubborn reminder of old times whose slumber and extinction might well be short-lived. The men in the corridor slept slumped together like slabs of meat but from some lower depths there came a low throbbing wordless song that vibrated from carriage to carriage like a witness of life that somehow never was extinguished. It seemed in our perpetual exhaustion that the train itself was singing, counterpointed by the clatter of the bogeys and the constant hooting from the engine, as if the train were driving itself, beyond any human propulsion. Every hour or so, it seemed to sag, and slow to a creaking stop, like a worn-out elephant, at some apparently abandoned station, while no-one climbed out or climbed in, until for some unknown reason it decided to resume the journey...

Dawn coming early in July, we were soon blinking at another sight that crawled by the opened windows: a train that had derailed on the junction ahead after crashing into another, for reasons that brought on the usual rash of speculation—enemy sabotage, incompetence, bad luck, fatigue. The overturned train was a series of box-cars, like our own, in which troops were billeted in long sleeping platforms warmed by a samovar in the middle. When such a train derails, the doors can jam and the stove explode, setting the entire carriage on fire. The train must have derailed the previous day as at least three cars were smouldering wrecks, the fire still burning and bodies piled up by the track, more than a hundred it appeared. Those unhurt were moving about the wreckage, trying to salvage anything of value, crossing themselves as they passed the bodies. The soldiers on our train made the same gesture, which cannot be purged from the Russian by neither revolution nor terror. Volkov however sat passive.

In all this, the train still observed meal-times, at which food was sometimes served from the restaurant car, brought to each troop by designated volunteers, who were never short. Pails of cabbage soup and kasha, and even an occasional boiled chicken, which did not last very long. Other times the train stopped at one of the more populated platforms, and the local women rushed up with bread and piroshkis. After Petrograd such fare was nothing short of miraculous, but the countryside knew how to hold its own.

Stopping and starting, lulling us to sleep and then jerking us awake, the train begins to pick up some speed across the open steppes, stretching in a golden arc under the blue sky as if to suggest that we have somehow passed into an enchanted universe, free from all the turmoil, madness and pain. Kovrov, Mstera, Vyazniki, Gorokhvetz, and approaching Nizhni-Novgorod, the old capital that gleamed in our old picture books even in far off Bessarabia... Further and further from home... Late in the evening, under a glorious sunset, we crossed the Volga at Samara, across the Alexander bridge, a feat of engineering that was never the less enabled by the fallen tyrant, that could not fail to silence even those who had so rejoiced at his fall... Like giant iron milestones, the girders of the bridge rolled by, the metal latticework transecting the great waterway, dwarfing our own homely Dniester... then the limestone cliffs and the wharfs of Samara, and another station, bristling with people, peasants and troops, surging with their kitbags, bundles, some women dressed in summer costume as if the war was far away, and the crowds merely revellers en route for some convivial fete... The train stopped here, the guards pushing through the cars and announcing that all would have to disembark and wait while the train was searched and disinfected, they wouldn't say for which purpose. Volkov showed them his

Cheka papers and the Commissar in charge told him there were suspected drug smugglers on board, who were armed, so trouble could erupt at any time. They expected a delay of three hours.

Volkov declined their offer for us to join them, and we climbed down among the muttering crowd. The platform was close to the wharfs, looking out over the great river, but we avoided the crowds between us and the vista and walked the other way, across the platform towards the main square, in the centre of which stood a bronze statue of the reforming Tsar, Alexander the Second, which had been clearly chipped away on its granite plinth by the revolutionaries, who had then given up and decided instead to drape the monument with the usual red banners and exhortations to the people's victory. The largest banner, inevitably, read: "WORKERS OF THE WORLD UNITE! YOU HAVE A WORLD TO GAIN AND ONLY YOUR CHAINS TO LOSE!"

The square was busy, with army trucks and horse-carts vying for passage, and people streaming about, enjoying the balmy night. It was not difficult to spot the Party head-quarters across the road, since it was the only building with lights in the windows among the imposing public mansions. Banners and the portraits of Lenin and Trotsky were over the entrance, and inside the main hall was plastered with posters from the propaganda division with etchings and cartoons praising the Red Army, denouncing bloated capitalists with their top hats and cigars, mincing priests hiding gold icons in their robes, the working man and woman portrayed striding together towards a brave new world and, largest of all, a kind of pasted fresco of the evils of foreign intervention and the Whites, with perfidious England as the great octopus waving her suckers with the blood-stained faces of Kolchak, Denikin, Kerensky and the rest. Other posters covered the walls with graphic presentations of the manufacture and assembly of weapons, how to put together a rifle, mortar, machine gun, how to handle grenades, and, for the peasantry, diagrams of agricultural machinery, the latest tractor, harvesters and their yield, and so forth. We passed under a giant image of White soldiers shooting down defiant women and children, the blood so vivid it almost dripped down the wall to the floor, to a small desk beneath all this weight of exhortation where a slim young girl with a red scarf slipped from her velvet black hair, and Mongol-Buryat features, gave us a rather prim smile and handed us each a booklet on whose cover the ship of capitalism teetered in the waves, with Karl Marx, undaunted on the prow, holding up a copy of "Das Kapital," emblazoned in red. Volkov thanked her and showed her his card, which froze the smile and prompted her to rise, striding before us into the inner sanctums, the usual maze of offices with even more posters, towards the telegraph office at the end of a long corridor.

Thankfully, the telegraphists' samovar was on the boil, and, though the girl declined to join us, returning hastily to her post, the two girls and two men in the office relaxed enough to break out their reserve of bread and sausage-meat. As Volkov gave the hint, there also appeared a small flask of vodka, to chase the welcome meal down.

With the telegrapher's touch, they pried out the actual departure time of our train, which would not leave, or rather could not without telegraphic confirmation, until the following morning, at six a.m., and therefore we could bed down in our own private cubbyhole behind the office, a storage space full of broken radios and coils of equipment, which had two mattresses and a pile of bedding. The boys and girls had separate quarters on the other side of the corridor while the duty comrade tended the night calls. It was a quiet moment, the train was down, the investigators were carrying out their duties, whatever they might be out of sight or hearing of those Cheka busybodies from Moscow—the drug smugglers caught, shot behind the wharfs somewhere, or shaken down for their tribute, it was not for us to interfere with the way the local comrades dealt with their problems, or their opportunities—we may in any case not have survived the consequences of any untoward curiosity. The new Russia was, after all, not all that different from the old, with its dark corners, whispered secrets, great bursts of generosity and friendship, night terrors of hidden dungeons and rivers that carried terrible burdens out of sight, beyond memory, into the unspoken realms.

We settled down, in the dark, with a guttering candle and some matches to keep it going if we so wished, but neither of us could sleep, despite our exhaustion. This was the first moment we had of some solitude since we hatched our scheme back on the banks of the Bay of Kronstadt, almost a month ago. Volkov was in a pensive mood, and suddenly, with no warning apart from a clearing of the throat, a series of coughs, and a low, unexpected sigh, he told me his story, a tale he had never offered, and had never seemed necessary, in all the years and troubles and turmoil that we had lived through, from our first encounter back in the trenches, when the bombs of General Hindenburg were landing all about us, and, as the keeper of the army staff's secrets, he gave me the first knowledge that we carried, like our own bacillus, through the disease of the times, the knowledge of Russia's inexorable fate, as the hammer of history pounded her into the ground.

"I should tell you, my friend, where it all started," he said.

And this was Kiril Volkov's story:

15. The Telegraphist's Tale

"I was born and brought up in Yekaterinburg, across the Urals, which has just been liberated from Kolchak's Whites. In my eyes it was the most beautiful city in the world, with grand buildings and a white church whose spire reached into the sky, lovely gardens with greenhouses housing lush plants, and wide boulevards down which the droshkys of the nobles clattered up and down, the men in *tsilinders* and the ladies displaying their great feathered hats. My family were of the lower gentry, the kind whose men gather in the drawing room for fevered discussions over social reforms and whose women do charitable works in orphanages, hospitals and schools. We were like Chekhov without the cherry orchard, certainly without the three sisters. I had two brothers, older than myself. One dreamed of

433

being an engineer, building railways and bridges, and the other was going to make pots of money and be the toast of Saint Petersburg, Paris, London, New York. Both are dead. One went in the war and the toast of Capital got consumption instead.

"My father went to the local medical school and was destined for good works at a hospital, after serving his Chekhovian destiny as a country doctor, when I was about eight years old. We lived for a while up near Bulanash, in a little house with ducks and a pond. I was aware that my relatives argued fiercely about the evils of autocracy and the Tsar but it all seemed pretty all right to me. My uncle was the Bolshevik, or at that point, the Social-Democrat. He revered the *narodniki*, and even sympathised with the People's Will, who blew up the Tsar Alexander the Second. But mostly he admired Plekhanov and Marx, the intellectuals. He read me Marx when I was five or six years old: Philosophers have tried to understand the world, the problem is to change it. I had no idea what he was talking about. Our life was comfortable, though I was aware that there were many people whose life was harsh in the city, and who were poor as animals or slaves in the countryside. This was bad and my parents had compassion for them too. My mother was always bringing some poor orphan boy or girl home for Sunday and telling us they were our equals. We did not think so, but there was one black eyed girl I dreamed about for a long time.

"*Nu*, time passes, and I am twelve. War breaks out somewhere far to the East—the Tsar is fighting the Emperor of Japan in Manchuria, far away in China. It is nearer to us than to the folks in the west, because our Siberian Divisions are mobilised. The army is recruiting surgeons. My father volunteers. My mother weeps, but cannot stop him. She was after all a graduate of the girls' school of the diocese of Saint Simon the miracle-worker of Verkhoturie, brought up to believe in God's grace. He leaves for noble motives, not the defence of tyranny but to help his fellow men, the poor devils in uniform who are being fed into the meat-grinder.

"Ah, Manchuria! You know the song they wrote to commemorate the fallen—The Hills of Manchuria—*tikho vokrug, sopki*

434

pakriti mgloy... the hills are quiet and dark... the moon shines through the clouds... the graves quiet under white crosses, where heroes sleep... We used to sing that in Galicia, for a few days, then there were other tunes—Big Bertha, and the hiss of the gas... It was the first Great Russian Disaster of our new century. In the battles of Telissu and Mukden our army went down to a terrible defeat. The pride of the navy, the Petropavlovsk, was sunk by Japanese mines, and the army was outflanked and destroyed. One hundred and fifty thousand men were lost, and fifty thousand prisoners taken. Perhaps we were just rehearsing for our future.

"My mother was frantic with fear and anxiety, running around, trying to get some news of my father, who was just one tiny speck in this hurricane. The official newspapers were muttering about temporary setbacks, and the iron will of the Russian army and people, but the liberal press was printing some facts about the horrible situation. My uncle and his friends would gather, white faced and grim, shaking their heads, trying to comfort my mother. I asked him: Surely nothing bad could happen to my father, he was a doctor after all, a man of peace and compassion, who was only ministering to the sick and the wounded. But even at that age I knew inside me that doctors were not immune to bullets.

"This was 1904, and the war had almost a year to run yet! My father had been posted to the Fourth East Siberian Rifle Division, Fifteenth Regiment, which was in the thick of the fighting. We prayed that he had been taken prisoner. The Japanese were a yellow race, but they also had an Emperor, so they couldn't be so bad. Certainly if they were modern enough to whip our invincible troops! I convinced my mother my father was still alive, and started keeping a scrapbook of cuttings of the war, the daily bulletins, the alarms, the proclamations.

"Then, in May, Count Tolstoy published a pamphlet, a long criticism and attack on the war. There he was, the great old man of our conscience, still living at Yasnaya Polyana, the only person in Russia who could openly attack the Tsar without being thrown into the Peter and Paul or slaughtered by the Black Hundreds. Tolstoy's words were passed from hand to hand in pamphlets, I remember the words, which were very powerful: "Again war, again suffering, again fraud, again the universal stupefaction and brutalising of men..." Tolstoy spoke from the heart of his convictions, his own Christian belief, about brotherhood and love, and the absolute prohibition on killing another human being... Strange, that I am quoting this to you, eh, comrade? But I was much affected then. I was a good child. I was not a Bible thumper, but I always remembered this verse, that Tolstoy quoted, that gave him his title: 'Jesus said, bethink yourselves, let every man interrupt the work he has begun and ask himself, who am I? From whence have I appeared, and what is my destiny? And having answered these questions, decide according to the answer to do what conforms to your destiny.'

"Well, my friend, it's easier said than done. My mother took Tolstoy's words to heart, it was as if he had lit a fire inside her, because he also quoted a letter he had been sent by two recruits for the war in Manchuria, who were being drafted in to replace all the poor dumb bastards who were lying under the calm sight of the moon, and who were asking him what they should do, as they were called to leave hearth and home, and commanded by their Tsar to kill in the name of Christianity, for the glory of God, and how the recruits had been herded together, and sent out as food for the cannons. And I remember the sage's call: 'What can measure all this vast woe that is spreading over half of the earth?'

"How can man serve God? One poor soldier asked Tolstoy. But how can we serve Man? Eh, comrade? How can we serve Man without destroying him? We should send a letter to Lenin. Ah, but Lenin is no Tolstoy, eh, my Kolya?

"My mother took all this to heart. She began knocking on doorsteps, begging for meetings with officials, petitioning ministers, although my uncle tried to dissuade her. He told her that this atrocity was not going to pass over the order of the day. The earth was being shaken. The people were rising. There was peasant unrest in almost all parts of the Empire. The king was not going to stay steady on his throne. Pretty soon even I began to notice that things were not normal in Yekaterinburg. There were more police around. People whispered. There was a meeting in the main square, under the statue of Peter, but it was broken up by the gendarmes. My uncle disappeared, sending a message with a trusted confidant that he had to make himself scarce for a while. The few Social-Democrats who remained in the city were arrested, and charged with sedition. Some were sent to jail, some to exile.

"My uncle had left a box of his books behind in our house, as he was sure his own would be raided. So I began to read these Godless volumes: Marx's Capital, Plekhanov's book Our Differences, Lenin's What is to be Done, which had just come out, and the anarchists, Proudhon and Prince Kropotkin. There were also some books by Karl May, which I confess I liked a lot better. But I was just warming up. I was still too young to set out anywhere on my own, so I went with my mother, all decked out in my Sunday best, to make a good impression on the bearded faces that always looked at us with dead fish eyes. Everything was fine, they said, our armies were winning. Our troops were doing their best with courage and bravery. We should be of good heart, and pray for victory, which in any case was inevitable.

"In the autumn, my mother calmed down, because a letter finally arrived from my father. It was post-marked from the divisional H.Q. at Port Arthur, and was a formal note, in my father's spidery writing, declaring that he was alive and well and serving his army, his people and his Tsar. My mother kissed it and covered it with such ardent tears that it became a soggy mass in less than a week, and then melted apart in my hands. My mother kept a fragment and framed it on the mantelpiece, under his graduation portrait. He was smiling, the face that I will always remember, rather than the hideous image that followed.

"Our winters were hard in Yekaterinburg, and revolutions are frozen. My uncle came out of hiding, but moved into our house, as my aunt, who was not as ardent as he for justice, stayed at their home with her sister. That winter was not Chekhov, but Dostoyevsky, with ominous rumblings, and only a trickle of news from the front. I was getting on for thirteen, and was aware of a group of schoolboys who were forming their own *narodnaya* fraction. They were two years older than me, and I was not invited to join, though I began dreaming of my own future actions. Like Dostoyevsky's dark "demons," I would be ready for violence. I needed to procure a pistol, and practice my shooting. I would start by shooting the local minister, Dukhovin, who had turned his back on my mother and had us shown out, with his pig-faced wife sneering at us from her armchair. Then I was going to shoot the magistrate, Nabukov, who persecuted the socialists and had a disgusting drool. Then I had a list of people up to the General in charge of the Siberian Fourth Division, who was in Omsk, and who was keeping my father in Manchuria. I knew I had no money to travel all the way to Saint Petersburg, to kill the Tsar, but was sure there were enough revolutionaries out there to finish the job. Then the people would rise, and overthrow all the minions, and peace and justice would reign for evermore.

"Not quite Nechayev, more like Old Shatterhand crossed with Prince Myshkin, wouldn't you say? I had not yet killed as much as a chicken. Thirteen years old, *tshorta mat*, in your world that means a `bar mitsbah,' eh? When you become a man, and finally you're allowed to toss off. I had so much to learn. But news was so slow to get through in those days, and censorship held everything back. My mother made sure I went back to school, and there was a teacher there who got me interested in engineering. His name was Mitka, `Moishe' Gul, and he was a yid like yourself. He was very clever, or they would not have employed him, they were strict on our divisions in those days. Also it was rumoured that he was an S-R, so he was particularly interesting for me. He was the one who taught me about telegraphy, and telephones, and electricity and all these exciting modern ways to shrink the distances between us all. At home, my mother was divided between times of extreme anxiety and times of what the doctors called `hysteria.'

"But she was right to feel this pain. Something connected her, more than the telegraph or electricity, with my father far away. It was only much much later that I would hear the full story of how the soldiers lived in that war, and even then I had no idea whatsoever that I would ever have the same life! Not even a chicken, eh, comrade?

"I only had the words of Tolstoy, till my father came back, a madman who could tell no story. We only knew the grim facts that the Tsar's censors couldn't hold back: how we lost the war at Mukden, when the Japanese outflanked us and shot all our grand imperial Divisions straight to hell. It was the most miserable winter. Snow and ice, and coal-black skies. As if the Angel of Death had decided to take up residence in Yekaterinburg and make the whole world to his liking. The New Year was spent in fear after we heard about the fall of Port Arthur. The loss of our only all-weather port. All the forts and ships were blown up and tens of thousands of prisoners taken. Our newspapers had to report that we had accepted terms of surrender. It was like a bolt of thunder that showed the Tsar in all his pathetic stupidity, in his abysmal nakedness, under all the medals and gold braid.

"That finally set off the explosion at home, back in Saint Petersburg. Remember, you told me even your brother was touched by this on the other side of the Empire, in your Bessarabian bolt-hole. The crowds marched on the Winter Palace, led by that silly priest, Father Gapon. The Pied Piper of Petrograd, leading all the children of Russia into the Cossack trap. Sabres and muskets. Thousands of dead. That finally woke 'em all up, eh? But we were still not organised. Every lesson learned the hard way, that's your Russian muzhik for you.

"The soldiers didn't come back for a long time. Months, close to the end of the year. The strikers had been turned back, the fleet cowed in Sebastopol, the Party leaders scattered into exile. Then one day we heard the rumour—the soldiers are coming back from China! We went to the station, this very train, the Trans-Siberian, brought them back all the way from Kharbin. They limped off, a sorry, silent bunch, our city boys, more like old men. Tired and terribly thin, emaciated, with black holes for eyes. There he was, my father, a ragged bag of bones, in a dirty, torn greatcoat. He didn't recognise us, but he allowed himself to be led off. Meek as a lamb. My father. We sent him out a proud patriot, we got him back a human shade. Human, still human, still a human being. But he barely talked. He just muttered things, phrases. He kept jumping up, shouting: What? What? And he would sometimes laugh. A kind of cackle, like a rooster woken at the wrong time. It broke my mother. She put on a brave face, tried to nurse him back to health, but there was nowhere to start. A few days after he came home a comrade from his unit called. He sat with us for a while till my mother put my father to bed—he got exhausted very quickly and was always led meekly away. Then he told me the story, I had grown up very quickly, I think. I wanted to hear it all.

"So he told me. He said he had been with my father's surgical unit in Manchuria. He told me about the conditions the men and doctors had to live in. He told me about tens of thousands of men crammed into dug-outs or trenches, in the freezing rain and mud, trapped in the same filthy holes for five months. These were the winter conditions that made the plains unbearable even for the Manchu nomads. They would strike their yurts and go elsewhere, to escape the freezing ground. But our troops could not move. There was a bug, like the bubonic plague, but unidentified, that attacked the throat and lungs, and weakened everybody, so they could not move away even if they wanted or were ordered to. There was no need for shells or bayonets to decimate the ranks. The doctors worked around the clock but then succumbed themselves. At least those units escaped the battle of Mukden that they were too sapped to join. The Japanese pressed in on General Kuropatkin's army from both flanks and the rear. The centre broke, and everything was a mad rush. A mad flight, pursued by artillery fire. Never was such a rain of metal seen before in human lives. But we saw worse, eh, comrade? Can you believe it, that when this man, this army surgeon, was telling me this terrible tale it never occurred to me in my wildest dreams that we would live through the same? And even worse, day after day, month after month, year after year? What the fuck is wrong with this world?

What can I tell you? My father died, carried off by the bug he had caught in the filthy trenches of Manchuria. My mother followed soon after, tired of life. My brothers and I lived with our uncle. He was shot one day, in the street, by a police agent. The Jewish teacher took me west, to Smolensk. We both became Bolsheviks. He disappeared in the war, like so many others. Just a fly, caught in the fire-storm.

"That is the reality of our times, my friend. We live our lives day by day. From now on, as we go further east, everything will be fluid, everything will be uncertain, all is disorder and confusion. Friends are enemies, enemies must be friends. I can tell you, there was one detail my father's comrade the surgeon told me that has stayed with me to this day. When he served in the hospital in Kharbin, they made a register of the injuries, and they found that, of the hordes of soldiers who were being treated there, twelve hundred—one thousand and two hundred men—all had the same condition: They had cut off the index finger—the trigger finger—of their own right hands."

(Translator's note: Here ends the first notebook of the Prof.'s written manuscript. There are four empty pages on which are fixed two folded full pages of photocopies from the New York Times of July 10, 1904, which contain the English text of Count Tolstoy's pamphlet "Bethink Yourselves." Prof. Has dated this insertion "July 25, 1965", which may imply that he was thinking of doing something with his text, possibly translating or transcribing sections—of which there is no known archive—or perhaps he just chanced upon the old material from another, unconnected search for "Times" material [possibly pogrom reports]. I have seen no need to add a complete translation, which exists in various forms, but I have excerpted the following segment that Kiril Volkov [if that is his true name] refers to, the letters Tolstoy is made aware of from recruits to the Manchurian war (the original translation is by Tolstoy's secretary V. Chertkov and Isabella Fyvie Mayo) :

Bethink Yourselves

Again war. Again sufferings, necessary to nobody, utterly uncalled for; again fraud; again the universal stupefaction and brutalization of men.

Men who are separated from each other by thousands of miles, hundreds of thousands of such men (on the one hand--Buddhists, whose law forbids the killing, not only of men, but of animals; on the other hand--Christians, professing the law of brotherhood and love) like wild beasts on land and on sea are seeking out each other, in order to kill, torture, and mutilate each other in the most cruel way. What can this be? Is it a dream or a reality? Something is taking place which should not, cannot be; one longs to believe that it is a dream and to awake from it. But no, it is not a dream, it is a dreadful reality!...

Yesterday I met a Reservist soldier accompanied by his mother and wife. All three were riding in a cart; he had had a drop too much; his wife's face was swollen with tears. He turned to me:--

"Good-by to thee! Lyof Nikolaevitch, off to the Far East."

"Well, art thou going to fight?"

"Well, some one has to fight!"

"No one need fight!"

He reflected for a moment. "But what is one to do; where can one escape?"

I saw that he had understood me, had understood that the work to which he was being sent was an evil work.

"Where can one escape?" That is the precise expression of that mental condition which in the official and journalistic world is translated into the words—"For the Faith, the Tsar, and the Fatherland." Those who, abandoning their hungry families, go to suffering, to death, say as they feel, "Where can one escape?" Whereas those who sit in safety in their luxurious palaces say that all Russian men are ready to sacrifice their lives for their adored Monarch, and for the glory and greatness of Russia.

Yesterday, from a peasant I know, I received two letters, one after the other. This is the first:--

"Kindest Lyof Nikolaevitch: Only one day of actual service has passed, and I have already lived through an eternity of most desperate torments. From 8 o'clock in the morning till 9 in the evening we have been crowded and knocked about to and fro in the barrack yard, like a herd of cattle. The comedy of medical examination was three times repeated, and those who had reported themselves ill did not receive even ten minutes' attention before they were marked 'Satisfactory.' When we, these two thousand satisfactory individuals, were driven from the military commander to the barracks, along the road spread out for almost a verst stood a crowd of relatives, mothers, and wives with infants in arms; and if you had only heard and seen how they clasped their fathers, husbands, sons, and hanging round their necks wailed hopelessly! ...Where is the standard that can measure all this immensity of woe now spreading itself over almost one-third of the world? And we, we are now that food for cannon, which in the near future will be offered as sacrifice to the God of vengeance and horror. I cannot manage to establish my inner balance. Oh! how I execrate myself for this double-mindedness which prevents my serving one Master and God."

This man does not yet sufficiently believe that what destroys the body is not dreadful, but that which destroys both the body and the soul, therefore he cannot refuse to go; yet while leaving his own family he promises beforehand that through him not one Japanese family shall be orphaned; he believes in the chief law of God, the law of all religions--to act toward others as one wishes others to act toward oneself. Of such men more or less consciously recognizing this law, there are in our time, not in the Christian world alone, but in the Buddhistic, Mahomedan, Confucian, and Brahminic world, not only thousands but millions.

There exist true heroes, not those who are now being feted because, having wished to kill others, they were not killed themselves, but true heroes, who are now confined in prisons and in the province of Yakoutsk for having categorically refused to enter the ranks of murderers, and who have preferred martyrdom to this departure from the law of Jesus. There are also such as he who writes to me, who go, but who will not kill. But also that majority which goes without thinking, and endeavors not to think of what it is doing, still in the depth of its soul does now already feel that it is doing an evil deed by obeying authorities who tear men from labor and from their families and send them to needless slaughter of men, repugnant to their soul and their faith; and they go only because they are so entangled on all sides that—"Where can one escape?"

Meanwhile those who remain at home not only feel this, but know and express it. Yesterday in the high road I met some peasants returning from Toula. One of them was reading a leaflet as he walked by the side of his cart.

I asked, "What is that--a telegram?"

"This is yesterday's, but here is one of today." He took another out of his pocket.

We stopped. I read it.

"You should have seen what took place yesterday at the station," he said; "it was dreadful. Wives, children, more than a thousand of them, weeping. They surrounded the train, but were allowed no further. Strangers wept, looking on. One woman from Toula gasped and fell down dead. Five children. They have since been placed in various institutions; but the father was driven away all the same.... What do we want with this Manchuria, or whatever it is called? There is sufficient land here. And what a lot of people and of property has been destroyed."

Yes, the relation of men to war is now quite different from that which formerly existed, even so lately as the year '77. That which is now taking place never took place before.

The papers set forth that, during the receptions of the Tsar, who is travelling about Russia for the purpose of hypnotizing the men who are being sent to murder, indescribable enthusiasm is manifested amongst the people. As a matter of fact, something quite different is being manifested. From all sides one hears reports that in one place three Reservists have hanged themselves; in another spot, two more; in yet another, about a woman whose husband had been taken away bringing her children to the conscription committee-room and leaving them there; while another hanged herself in the yard of the military commander. All are dissatisfied, gloomy, exasperated. The words, "For the Faith, the King, and the Fatherland," the National Anthem, and shouts of "Hurrah" no longer act upon people as they once did. Another warfare of a different kind--the struggling consciousness of the deceit and sinfulness of the work to which people are being called—is more and more taking possession of the people.

Yes, the great strife of our time is not that now taking place between the Japanese and the Russians, nor that which may blaze up between the white and yellow races, not that strife which is carried on by mines, bombs, bullets, but that spiritual strife which without ceasing has gone on and is now going on between the enlightened consciousness of mankind now waiting for manifestation and that darkness and that burden which surrounds and oppresses mankind.

In His own time Jesus yearned in expectation, and said, "I came to cast fire upon the earth, and how I wish that it were already kindled." Luke xii. 49.

That which Jesus longed for is being accomplished, the fire is being kindled. Then do not let us check it, but let us spread and serve it.

Count Leo Tolstoy,
Yasnaya Polnya,
May 21, 1904
Second Notebook (runs on from first)

16.

Luckily we awoke in time in the morning to re-board the train at the Samara station and continue our journey east. Volkov was subdued and pensive after his long night "confession," and I was also pondering his words. His mention of Kharbin brought back the memories of my brother's dreams of flight and ventures into the Far East and its magical, mysterious and endless spaces. Dreams of trading with nomadic hunters in exotic furs culled from the wild-life of the steppes, the sables, minks, the red and silver foxes. In China, he said, there were dappled bears with majestic black and white coats, which lived only on bamboos and had never been hunted by humans. He had met a man in Kishinev who had been there, and knew the trade routes. It was only a matter of waiting for wars to stop and free movement to flourish.

Dreams, dreams, dreams. Where was he now? Or Sarah, Judit, Yakov, and Berl? Maybe I was flying towards Zev, as Volkov had finally admitted he was flying back towards his childhood home, which had been ravaged by our civil war throughout the last bloody year? Who can tell where fate will lead us? It may be thought strange that we had not spoken of all this before. But this was our twisted reality in the trenches. No one had a past. Only the present. We wrote letters, if we could, into the void. Pretending to ourselves that it was all still there to be returned to, to be retrieved. But we knew, in the midst of the fire and brimstone, that nothing was there, except the dice that fell each day to determine life or death. We too, hesitated with the knife poised at our right hand finger, or the whole hand.

The train, having been reluctant to take us so far, now seemed to pick up speed. Stations glided by, I tried to memorise the various names: Smyshiliavka, across another great bridge over the Padovka River, rising up the hills, to cross another bridge, to Kinelo, the junction towards Orenburg. Turgenevka, Krotovka, Mukhanovo, Cherkasskaya, Kliuchi, Bugurusian... Everywhere signs of the war of Red and White—villages burned and abandoned, people huddled in tented encampments or in the ruins of barns, fields left fallow, remains of wrecked trucks and railway carriages either side of the track. The larger towns all bore scars of battle, bullet-pocked walls, shelled buildings and warehouses. But gangs of rail-workers along the track bore witness to the resilience and efficiency with which the Red Army labourers had been managing to fix the track ahead of us and keep the transport moving. Red to White, White to Red and back again, these areas had switched sides several times since Kolchak's advances and his headlong retreat. Never the less, the steppes, in bright summer sunlight, the glistening rivers showed the resilience of the land itself...

It took us a full day to reach Ufa, retaken by Trotsky's army back in June after the fiercest of battles. "A lot of bayonet work," one of the troops with us told us, "Russians against Russians. Nobody wants to give way."

The city was packed with troops, among whom the local population mingled, many Bashkirs, with Turkoman and Mongol-like features, rushing up to the train with baskets of produce conjured up from whatever stocks they had hoarded, abandoned or scavenged uniforms, coats, caps, belts and boots from the retreating Whites. One tall peasant type with a great mustache and turban even had a cartload of books, which I wondered about, though our carriage drew up too far from his berth, and we had other business than to push back and seek him. Was it a looted library, or an officer's hoard, or some local notable or academic's bookshelves? Were they tomes of science, encyclopedias, travel books, religious volumes, Bibles, or the novels of Tolstoy, Turgenev, Dostoyevsky? Perhaps even foreign books—Victor Hugo, Zola, Montesquieu, Goethe, Dickens? Perhaps even our own Hebrew Bible?

The Party headquarters here were housed, rather strangely, in the "Asylum for Aged Mohammedans," which had been emptied of its inhabitants by Bashkirs who took pity on the old destitutes bereft of relatives and took them into their own homes when the main fighting began. Unlike in Samara, everything had a slapdash air about it, with no organised "propaganda center" and soldiers

447

running in and out of small rooms. As there were no telephone or telegraph communications in the building, contact was made by many scribbled notes which were rushed to and fro by messengers who galloped off on droshkys. However, the man Volkov was intent on seeing was settled in one of the rooms, which had a strange tinge of incense or some intoxicating medium, perhaps a lingering scent of opium, which I recalled from one particularly violent raid in Petrograd.

The man was called Akim, and he was Armenian, about the same age as Volkov, with that same grizzled look as all the youths we knew who grew up too fast. He had an already greying mustache and an eye-patch that made him look like one of Lermontov's Caucasian bandits. He was seated behind a desk piled with papers but turned to open a cabinet from which he took a bottle of vodka and a huge round of flat-bread, with a bowl of fresh-looking butter.

"Traditional fare for guests from far away!" he called with enthusiasm. He was one of those people who shouted rather than talked, like steel-workers or battle-shocked troops who could neither hear nor utter anything quietly. The sort of man to whom it was tricky to entrust with secrets, since he might shout them out at the top of his voice. "Two kings in search of the Holy Infant of Soviet Power! He thrives, can you believe it? On gunpowder! Ah, but no virgin in sight!" He put out three battered mess-tin mugs and a tin plate. He apologised for the quarters, explaining that the administration building had been blown up by Kolchak's forces, so the commissariat was forced to improvise. The telegraphy unit was at the station, where he would take us later. For the moment we could bunk in his room, as his two room-mates there had been posted eastwards.

Akim and Volkov had served at the front, and had the trust of comrades who had looked death in the face many times and survived. Volkov vouched for me in similar terms, and set out the broad lines of his Petrograd plan. This phase having been plain sailing, from now on the coming stages were complex, and subject to unknown factors. White lines would have to be crossed somewhere, to take us further east, towards the belly of the beast, into Omsk itself. Akim wagged his head admiringly. "How on earth did you convince Felix to let you do this?" he asked. "The Cheka has its own people on the ground in this country. They have their spies everywhere, behind the lines, in Omsk, Tomsk, Irkutsk. Local experts. What did you have to offer?"

"I told him we were going to kill Kolchak," said Volkov, without batting an eye. "Comrade Kolya is our most reliable sure-shot. His trigger finger never wavers."

I was pretty astonished by that, since he had never told me of that element of his plan with Dzherzhinsky. I didn't know whether to be impressed or annoyed. A man always plays his cards close to his chest in a crooked game, but should he do this with his partner? Volkov hugged my shoulders.

"The less known, the less worried about, till it's needed," he said. "You know Felix, he trusts nobody. He would have shot us before we were able to board."

"I take it that you are not going to do it?" Akim said, looking me in the eye. I could only shrug.

"If the opportunity presents itself, who knows?" said Volkov. "But it's still the old call of the foxholes: all for one and one for all. Galician romantics. We want to tell our children about it."

"Don't forget the grand-children," Akim said, "be ambitious!"

They got down to the contours of the plan. Akim had a chart of the battlefields, with pencil lines that could be erased and re-drawn. He gave us a précis of the state of play:

"At the moment, they are fighting all over Kurgan, Yarutorovsk, and Tobolsk. Near Orenburg, our lads are pressing at Aktubinsk. Kolchak counter-attacked towards Chelyabinsk. The Whites' strategic aim is to link up with Denikin's Cossacks, who are pushing up in our direction but were chased back from Tambov. Up north, you know all about Arkhangelsk. At least the British are tied up there. Further east, as you heard, we have armies to Kolchak's rear, in Siberia, north and east of Irkutsk, at the Lena. But to reach them you have to go through the White heartland. I

449

got your message about this from the grapevine, and I have given it some careful thought. At the end of the day I have one thought for you. You need a Czech."

"What good does paper money do us?"

"Not a promissory note. A Czechoslovak soldier. They are the most reliable troops the enemy has. The Czechoslovak Legion, who were stationed here before October. They were stranded in Russia so they fought their way east, and then linked up with the Whites. Forty-thousand troops, well-armed, disciplined, no shit-takers. They should have been on our side, *chorta mat*. But they fell in love with Kolchak's gold. They're the ones who guard the train, for a fee, a carriage of bullion. They were originally going to leave from Vladivostok. But they seem to like it here. Good killing grounds, Russian women, oceans of vodka. Of course if they lose Vladivostok, they will all leave their bones on our sacred soil. Forty-thousand skeletons. The fear of death makes strange bedfellows.

"Still, not all of them are Whites. We have some sympathis-ers. One of the original Legion is with our Fifth Army. He is in Chelyabinsk right now. He is head of the International Section and keeps contacts with other secret Reds in the Legion. His name is Jaroslav. He is a perfect fixer. He can arrange supplies, transport, papers, uniforms. I worked with him here, and in Samara. He is a strange card, but smart and wily. You take a risk, but he can get you through. In Omsk there are some other Czechs, also sympathisers, if you can take his word. It's wild country, bandits, thieves, anar-chists. Personally," he turned to me, "I would take any message you have to your loved ones back home so they know where you wafted off to. I know this one," he wagged his head at Volkov, "is an orphan. Maybe he just wants to go home."

"He plays the absolute bastard," Volkov said to me, "but inside that chain-mail skin, he had a heart of pure gold."

"Let us drink to the bullion!" Akim flourished the vodka bottle. We each took a swig, and looked at the river, flowing slug-gishly under the clear blue sky.

17.

Volkov said that he had no interest in going back to Yekaterinburg. He said there was nothing for him there, no home, no kin, and no memories that served any purpose for the task we had at hand. In any case the only way there would be a heavy ride by truck or car along roads that had been already shot to hell, and would take us far off our track, though there was a rail link to there from Chelyabinsk, which was, Akim confirmed, the last major station controlled by the Reds on the Trans-Siberian heading east. At Chelyabinsk, our Czech, Pavel, would be waiting, and all after was in the hands of fate.

The train we boarded in the early morning was a full scale troop train, with no seating but dormitory bunks the length of each carriage and beds of straw on which one could lie on the floor. The troops were in good spirit, since they were a fresh contingent up from Samara, who were expecting to make short shrift of Kolchak's shrinking kingdom. They sang, unprompted by any propaganda encouragement, songs of their homelands, and made room for their star dancers to prance *kazatskis* on the straw. I wondered if Kolchak's battalions sang these very same songs, both sides making full use of the Russian's peculiar tendency to carve determination from suffering.

The track curved up from the river towards forested hills of fir and silver birch that stretched on for hundreds of miles. It cut through the Dergach mountain straining up and up towards picturesque landscapes of cliffs and rocks, among which abandoned iron works lay idle. These were the prime Ural mine-working sites, but there seemed precious little activity apart from villagers still trudging fatefully along the roads or drifting ghostlike through the trees. At Zlatoust, a pretty town perched at the foot of mountains, a whole school of children in white smocks with red armbands came out along the station and sang patriotic songs. Then they broke seamlessly into some religious hymn, which the soldiers greatly appreciated, but their teacher emerged suddenly and ushered them quickly into the station shed. The soldiers laughed uproariously as he ran around, smacking heads, upbraiding them loudly at their confusion over which band of ragged armed ruffians they were expecting to serenade.

In many places, smoke rose in the distance, and at one station stop, the rattle of gunfire sounded from the forest and men began to cock their guns. But the station commander rushed forward and got the train moving again. Several times, though, we had to halt along the way, since gangs of Red Labour were still patching up the track that had been damaged, sabotaged or shelled, and the train would slow to a crawl, as it manoeuvred over potholes around and between the rails.

There was little time, on the journey, to ponder over Volkov and the Armenian's mad scheme that had unfolded on the Ufa River. One could not think, one could only react to each momentary interruption or shout or call of alarm at the intervention of another man's elbow into one's side or stomach, feet crunching on one's own, a hand clutching one's shoulder for balance or two hundred strangers' bad breath in one's face. Spittle seemed to hang in the air like glue. A man would casually drop his machine gun on your lap while he took out and plucked an old cabbage. Soup was passed in mugs from hand to hand like pails passed to quench a fire. There was no possibility that I could turn to Volkov and ask: "Did you really tell Felix D. that we would shoot Kolchak? And did you suggest how this could be done?" The night was spent either standing up propped by one's fellows, or leaning against the stomach, legs or buttocks of someone lucky enough to have grabbed one of the carriage bunks. Although the train was climbing towards bracing air, at the cusp of summer turning into autumn, the air inside the train was hot and fetid.

It was the following day, at noon, before the train of sorrows limped into the station at Chelyabinsk, after a slow descent from the mountains past Cherbakul and Bishkil. Another bridge, another river, and the sight of the old town from the window, with its tall church spires and rows of wooden houses stretching beyond the banks. Here again, there were definite signs of fires that had raged, gutting entire streets. The train stopped some way short of the town, and commanders rushed up and down the platform, shouting for every-one to get off, as this was the end of the line.

The troops formed up, and marched into the city, like an invading army. But the city had already surrendered. There were some street markets, but it was mainly inhabited by soldiers, marching up and down, manning check-posts guarding the few stone buildings in the center of the town. It was not difficult to locate the International Section, which was billeted at the town hall, garlanded by the usual brave red banners and filled with the desks of young women handing out political leaflets and manning the telephones.

"Ah, Jaroslav Osipovitch!" They all seemed to know our man well and pointed up the stairs with barely suppressed giggles and a certain rolling of the eyes. "Fourth floor!" We climbed up, past the usual melee of soldiers carrying papers and satchels. Once the revolution settled down it always seemed to produce this vast blizzard of paperwork, reports, forms, publications in a dozen languages, pamphlets in Russian, German, Yiddish, Buryat and even Chinese. In the service, it often seemed that Felix's sole purpose in life was to compile a paper record of every single man woman and child that lived within the sphere of Soviet influence, expanding as it too expanded, till it could encompass the whole world. Paper was power, the bullet merely an inevitable adjunct to its necessary application.

The fourth floor seemed to be full of printing machines which clattered from a row of rooms. The man we were looking for was standing over one of these, clutching some fresh galleys. At first sight we thought he was the messenger, because he was a quite small dumpy figure, with a fat face like a lump of dough in which the eyes, nose and mouth were a hasty decoration. The eyes, in particular, looked out with a certain sadness, though, as we discovered they were often unfocused due to the influence of vodka, which Jarda Gasek drank as if it was tea.

When he heard Akim had sent us to him his face lit up and he ushered us into his office, introducing us to the rather shy girl

453

behind the desk, whom he addressed as Shusha, and was obviously his woman. They were very unlike a normal Russian couple, as they snuggled up and touched and pinched each other continually, like two mischievous children.

Even when we showed him our papers, identifying us as Cheka, he did not lose his friendly attitude, putting his finger to his nose, as if to say, we know all about this. There was something very different about him than the normal Red commissar type we were used to throughout the last two years. Volkov played up to his manner, leaning forward and nodding to indicate that we too had a concealed program that was not denoted by our documents, we had ideas, that floated in the air between us, that could not be defined or described in leaflets.

Our new friend filled out forms billeting us in the building, on the fifth floor, a row of attics that were filled with old publications and newspapers that formed a reasonable mattress and bedding. The print-workers slept there, and there were two cubbyholes, one for himself and his girl-friend and another for us, once we cleared it of old print machinery. We had not yet discussed the purpose of our journey here, since the usual bustle and overcrowding meant we had to wait for the right time and a proper moment of privacy.

The Czech barely slept, since he was up all night at a small desk in his room writing a book, in his own language, that he called "jokes of war and tyranny." It was a series of stories about a clownish character in Prague, "the idiot of the regiment," who gets up to all sorts of scrapes and then gets drafted into the Austrian army in the war. He had apparently already published some of these stories before the war, in his home country, until life overtook his art and he was drafted himself, serving in the trenches for some months before he was taken prisoner by our forces in Galicia. Volkov wanted to know the exact place he was taken, to see if they had met before, since he remembered some Slavic prisoners that had been ushered away from the battle of Ciezkovice, but it turned out that was a different sector. After those events the captured Czech soldiers, who were anti-Austrians, and supporters of their own national independence movement, formed their own units inside the Tsarist army, and were posted to the Ukraine, where they were fighting when the February Revolution took place. From one thing to another, some of them became Bolshevists and others sided with the Ukrainian Rada, and after that with the Whites. Jaroslav (or Jarda as he liked to be called), joined the Reds, and was subsequently denounced by his ex-comrades, those who had devised the scheme of fighting their way back home through the east, to Vladivostok, from where they planned to be evacuated by the Interventionist forces to America, and then back to Europe.

"It is a very Czech idea," he told us, "everything ass-backwards. The original plan was to get home through Persia, but the English didn't agree."

Never the less, he was still in contact with certain comrades in the ranks of the Czech Legion, who had no liking for Kolchak, Denikin, Yudenitch or Wrangel or any of the brutes who wanted to bring back Tsarism, and who somehow believed that butchering the peasants wherever they set foot would cause the people to rise up to support them. "Even a Czech would not be so dumb," he said, sadly, "but my old comrades spun a coin, and off they march in the wrong direction, like marionettes.

"Just tell me where you want to go, and I'll arrange it," he said. "Nothing surprises me."

In the night, he would keep us awake, through the thin wall, reading his latest chapters to the young Shusha, who didn't understand Czech, but laughed uproariously. One night we joined them, and he read out some stories he had written that had been translated to Russian and printed in Soviet presses about the time he had been appointed Deputy Commander of Bugulma, a small town between Samara and Ufa, for the Fifth Army, which, even in his rough accent, left us in stitches. He had a real gift for comic writing and the absurdity of our lives. It was a boon to laugh, in the midst of all the turmoil and slaughter, the sheer exhaustion of our long ordeals and the horror of our own actions in the time of constant madness. Like a human telegraph station, Jarda Gasek was a center for information flowing from the battlefields. The Whites were still pressing our forces to the north-east, in the Tiumen and Tobolsk areas, along the railway near Ishim. Under General Sakharov they threw in another force, the "Turkestan" army, which was moving on Troitsk. Our troops were counter-attacking and took Aktubinsk. Every day Jarda also had secret dispatches from Omsk. There was panic at Kolchak's defeats. There was jubilation at his successes. The city was on the brink of chaos. The Whites insisted all was calm. Kolchak's forces made effective use of re-inforced armoured trains, whose flanks were impervious even to shellfire, though they could of course be stopped by blowing up the tracks.

"What you have to understand," said Jarda, when we were sifting through these contradictory reports, late at night, after the laughter, and before the vodka ran out, "is that if the place where we are living is purgatory, and Omsk is the pit of hell itself. Which is not to say that people are not having a good time there: There is dancing, there is whiskey, there is caviar, there are women of every shade and colour, round or slanted-eyed, Finnish or Mongol, Jewish or gentile—in women at least you can't tell the difference in the light or in the dark—there is money, there are lots of gold bars that disappear softly off the guarded bullion train like feathers wafted by a soft breeze, there is opium galore, there are sweet and sour dreams, there are cafes and restaurants and bars. All the stuff that is left out of the Last Judgement after the censors have been at it. But everywhere, in the corner of every tavern, behind the doorways, lurking out in the street, the demons of disorder and torment are waiting with their pitchforks honed to the shpitz. All of Siberia is a great whirlpool of confusion and unrest, mutinies and uprisings of peasants and tribesmen of every colour and stripe: Bashkirs, Turkmen, Kyrghiz, Dungan, Taranchis, Buryats, Mongols, Chinese. Muslims, nominal Christians, Animists, Idolators. Everyone is seizing their chance. The Whites have stirred a stew that will swallow them whole. Regular Chinese troops have moved up from Manchuria, to see what they can bite off, and the old enemy, the Japanese, have scouts all over the place. If you want to get killed there is no better place on earth to get satisfaction. If you want to murder people it is a happy hunting ground. All against all. East of Omsk the winter is already set in, and if the blizzards are tardy you can enjoy torrential rains and churning mud. And if you shun the gun, the sword and the cannon the typhus will be more than happy to carry you off, retching and bleeding into the ground. This is the paradise my countrymen have chosen to rule over while they make their slow march east, into the white heart of Dante's Inferno. I can see that you two are extremely determined gentlemen. But can you be louche for a while, and just keep me company here? I love people who laugh at my jokes. Shusha has to. She is infected by love."

I might have been tempted, particularly by the bright faces of the typists downstairs, but there was something suspect about Jarda's presence in this hub of Soviet propaganda, as if he had been placed there specifically to test one's loyalties. One learned this dubious stance at Felix's knee, like a child eager for treats from an unbending father. Although it struck me that, at this point, I had not shot anyone for about two months, there was still danger in this apparent place of safety, with a person of influence who seemed to have no fixed position at all, a straw that bent with the prevailing wind. Was Jarda a Bolshevik? A converted Menshevik? A Czech nationalist biding his time? An anarchist, which he admitted cheerfully was his belief back in the days of easy tavern life in Prague, or simply someone who believed in nothing at all, but survival? There were many of these, on the road...

Volkov was equally tempted to stick around, drawing rations from Jarda's copious stack of coupons and permits, as well as his access to unlimited supplies of liquor in a situation that was supposed to be dry as the first instance of Party discipline, with stern sanctions for transgressors. In Petrograd, this meant the Cheka stockpiling warehouses of confiscated booze, ranging from the simple rotgut to Scottish whiskey brands smuggled over the killing grounds from Estonia and Finland. Even in the starving city, we had seen untouchable officials prancing about in fur coats, flaunting glittering rings on their fattened fingers. Not all the reek of bodies swollen in the Neva could drown the stink of corruption. Lenin could rail in the Kremlin in Moscow, Trotsky could threaten with firing squads, but the heartless would always find ways to flourish in the worst bed of weeds.

Something of this, certainly, made us wary of the Czech, who seemed so amiable, good company, a treasure chest of intellectual stimulation and so many hilarious stories. I particularly liked the one about his hero, Schveik, getting arrested for commenting that the flies had made their mark on the portrait of the Emperor Franz Josef in his local tavern. Or the stories of his fanatic officer, Lieutenant Lukas, who read books with titles like "Self Education in Dying for the Emperor." He would always interrupt to recall recipes of his favourite Czech stews, particularly anything involving blood-sausage. We would sit together, cradling our bowls of cabbage soup, while he conjured up the most mouth-watering aromas simply by his powers of description. "We would feed our dogs on stuff only Kamenev and Zinoviev can dine on now," he said, sighing.

"Well," he would shake himself and say, "what's the use of crying. We'll all meet up, at The Chalice at Na Bojisti, at six o'clock after the war. Make it six-thirty, in case I'm held up!" So we made the pledge, and off he went, to his bunk, with the lovely Shusha, and his make-believe schnapps.

As the days passed, we continued to waver, since one of his points of advice made some sense, in the circumstances of the tug and push of events. As the reports kept coming in of Kolchak's retreats, our successes, the victories of the Turkestan Army, the transfer of Petrograd factory facilities over the Urals to speed up the manufacture and supply of arms and equipment, the reinforcements arriving at Tiumen, Shadrinsk and Kurgan, and the occupation of Tomsk, far in Kolchak's rear, it seemed that if we bided our time we could sweep forward with our own troops towards Omsk, and link up with the second line of Volkov's contacts, in Irkutsk itself. The entire cover story for Felix of dispatching Kolchak, might be made superfluous by the events. But then Kolchak launched another "counter-offensive," and the first signs of a hard winter set in.

"Kirgiz," the best forger in the Propaganda Department, prepared for us a perfect new set of documents, which identified us as "Ivan Grigorevitch Dolgushov" and "Alexei Danilovitch Radomski," to cover my western accent and get rid of the Jewish taint. Anywhere near the White centers was deadly for any Jew, and we were well aware of the murders and pogroms that swept the regions that either Denikin or Kolchak had conquered, even for a few days. At that time, they did not resonate in my mind in any particular fashion, as we all knew the Whites were fanatical assassins, who spared their opponents nothing. Tortures, flaying, burning villagers alive in their barns or synagogues or even churches was the order of the day. The Cossacks loved bloodshed. That was our normal judgement. It helped us cast our own killings in a better light. One day in Chelyabinsk there was an execution of a small group of White sympathisers in Yekaterinburg who had taken the opportunity of the chaos of Kolchak's flight from that city to settle scores with the Jews of their neighbourhood. They ran away to Chelyabinsk and were caught there. Five of them were sentenced by the Revolutionary Tribunal and hanged immediately after outside the Commercial Hotel—in which the Tribunal had met. A small crowd watched impassively, but some soldiers cheered.

Three days later we departed the city, on the rail line which had just reopened towards the Kurgan station.

18.

The distance from Moscow to Chelyabinsk is about 1,800 kilometers. The distance onwards to Irkutsk is another 3,300 kilometers. From our second start Omsk was more than 900 kilometers away. And the entire trail to Irkutsk had to go through a patch-work of Red and White sections that were constantly shifting in the thrust and push of war and conquest. It was a full chessboard of misery, in which the king had already been chopped down, the queens raped and slaughtered, the bishops and knights soiled, and the entire board crowded by the impoverished pawns, who could only stagger around, driven by sclerotic and blooded hands.

As we puzzled over our plans with Jarda Gasek he brought forward another scheme he had dreamt up, perhaps from the shreds of one of his own bizarre stories. It stemmed from the "Kirgiz," the forger who had prepared our fake documents. This man, it appeared, had two cousins, who had drifted with him from the east with the Bolshevik regiments, but were aching to go home. Their main motive, apart from home-sickness, was to take revenge on the White bands which had ravaged their region, south of Krasnoyarsk, along the Yenisei River, killed their families and raped their sisters. They did not care if the original murderers had moved on, they would take blood-vengeance on whoever of Kolchak's or the local leader Ataman Semenov's gangs were within reach. If we took these two men along, "Kirgiz" swore they would serve us as loyal bodyguards, without whom we were unlikely to survive the long journey, even if we were well-armed ourselves.

I was less than happy at taking on these two cut-throats, but Volkov was shrewd enough to understand that we had no choice, since this would ensure the silence of the "Kirgiz" over our fake identities. Gasek was right that we required more fire-power once we entered the uncertain zone, and the Kirgiz brothers, who were called Azmat and Sabeer, would be most likely to pass as White guards once we crossed over to the other side. Gasek assured us that the Muslim code of honour ensured their loyalty when impressed by the family sanction, and they would most likely stick with us as far as we progressed towards their homeland, which was in our direction of travel in any case. "And if you want someone to kill Kolchak in Omsk," he said, with his impish Czech smile, "you couldn't chance on a nicer pair."

They were both youths in their early twenties, with fresh mustaches, both sure shots and born horse-riders, we were assured, though we did not expect any cavalry charges. Their indoctrination in Marxism was perfectly simple: "The Reds want to kill the rich people," Azmat said, "and the Whites want to kill the poor." Azmat was the elder by a year. Sabeer was younger, and quieter, a boy who liked to brood and sharpen his sabre. I was glad he was not sharpening it for us. They were a new version of the two youths, Grigor and Danilov, whom we had left behind to climb up the Chekist ladder in Petrograd. They too were certainly seasoned assassins by now, if they were still alive. I wondered aloud to Volkov, the night before we left, if it was the right thing to have others do our killing if we ourselves were reluctant, but he just said I should let go of my old Talmudic sophistry. "We left our morals behind when we shot our first Austrian," he said.

I couldn't tell him that something had happened to me when I saw Jarda and his girl-friend Shusha cuddling. We had been so long on this cruel path that I had completely forgotten what some normal, unspoiled human contact looked like. There was something about those two that set them apart from anyone else we had met along this terrible journey of murder, destruction, pretence and dissimulation that characterised my life ever since I was torn from Celovest so long ago I could hardly remember the contours of my father or mother's face. I conjured them up, and my siblings, too, but they had lost the semblance of ordinary people, and glowed like holy Russian icons in my sleep. The Torah and the Cross had merged in my dreams, twin glowing objects in a far-away star, populated by strange golden-skinned creatures who flowed across a landscape of rolling corn and wheat fields that were harvested by mingled groups of women, buxom young girls whose blonde and black hair gleamed at the hem of their head-scarves, as their beautiful hands harvested the sheaves onto wooden carts. There a river flowed, of gentle ripples, clear as glass, the heavenly opposite of the harsh rolling cascades of the Russian Volgas and Ufas branded by great iron bridges and the thunder of armoured trains...

Our transport was the first troop train to depart towards Kurgan since our forces had cleaned out this area of the remaining Whites, though there were said to be still stragglers stuck between the lines, unwilling to surrender, and mounting ambushes along the track. We crawled therefore, very slowly, past Chernavskaya, Chumilak and Shumikha, mere ghost stations, eerily silent in the first drifts of winter snow. Out of the hills, the country was level and dry, with scattered copses of silver birch, the ubiquitous inhabitant of Siberia. Several settlements, which the local commander named for us as Mishkino, Yurgamish and Ziryanka, passed by solemnly, empty, burned, ruined. In this sector we saw few people, just glimpses, here and there, of small hunched bands of figures, running away from us through the trees.

We stopped short of Kurgan and everyone disembarked, because the track had been destroyed by shelling right ahead. We trudged with the troops into the city, under increasingly heavier drifts of snow. Volkov, ever curious, was eager to see the town, which was apparently famous as the original exile of the Decembrists, among them the famous Prince Shepin-Rostovsky, of whom I had never heard. Veterans of rebellion against the Tsar, one hundred years before we trod in their steps, conquerors rather than prisoners, but of a devastated waste. The town, through sprawling and teeming with soldiers, was almost empty of civilians, the population having fled somewhere, though there seemed few if any safe havens. To the south, north and east, other regiments were fighting large pockets of White resistance, while yet others had moved to outflank the remnants and pressed on to Petropavlovsk, the next main station on the line and half way again to Omsk. The stone churches of Kurgan stood vigil over this khaki multitude, the wide streets churned to mud by the constant passage of armoured vehicles that looked like tin cans mounted on iron frames.

At this point the sense of following the troops station by station eastwards became more and more dubious, as progress seemed so slow that winter would close in with full force before we moved half way to Omsk. Our genuine Cheka documents gained us billets in an old and ransacked flour warehouse, and so we hunkered down with Azmat and Sabeer to review our next move. The two Kirgiz had been thoughtfully supplied by their cousin with their own set of "Chekist" papers.

They too were impatient, but their suggestion, that we simply grab four good horses and ride up north to outflank the main battlefield and rush through the no-man's-land of shifting guerrilla groups way up the flat steppes north of Ishim to gallop down on Omsk in the old Mongol fashion, a non-stop ten-day whirlwind, had to be turned down by Volkov and myself, both inveterate vehicular and foot sloggers. Volkov had some experience in riding but my memories of being on a horse did not outlast my fifteenth birthday, and that a mere amble by the village river. War hardened as we may have been, we were babes in the domain of cavalry. Volkov had a more modern idea. Gasek had proposed it himself, in a moment that seemed simply another drunk lunacy at the time but now had a bizarre logic: We could commandeer a train of our own.

"I've done it often," the Czech insisted, waving his vodka flask. "Just sign out a chit for a locomotive, hitch a couple of carriages, load up the print-shop, a few muzhiks to ride shotgun on the front bumpers and away we go, hooting like ghosts. The further you go from the center, the more the madder options make sense."

The solution was to combine the two: To take our own train, and to load up four horses, so that we could ride off if and when the need arose. Apart from ourselves and the steeds, we requisitioned a small gang of rail-workers with spare track and mending equipment, a type of unit that was always standing by. In the event, we marshalled a small army, a squad of ten riflemen, four "engineers" and a driver, six horses and ourselves, four liars bent on our own secret path.

Nothing seemed impossible, in a world in which Trotsky had declared that not only was total and absolute victory inevitable, but also its spread to the other nations of the world—Germany was still tottering on the brink, strikes were spreading in France and Belgium and even England was on the verge of revolution, with its working class doubly oppressed, its wages cut and its own long-suffering proletariat forced to pay the price of war. The British, French, the Czechs, the Americans, were hurling their forces at us on every front, north, south, west and east, and still we were prevailing. One only needs to conquer death.

Our train was not armoured, since the armoured carriages were sorely needed up the line. But we buckled together four sturdy carriages, piled on enough food and fodder to last for two weeks, and set off on a rainy dawn across the Tobolsk bridge towards Vargasht and Lebyazhe. The bridge was somewhat damaged by the fighting, with some girders charred and mangled, but it held, as we passed the first hurdle. The country past the river was supposedly in our hands, and the line was clear, but in fact there was no sign of life in the villages as we puffed cautiously forward, passing through what seemed a zone of the dead. The only sound was the slow clatter of the train and the rain rattling on the carriages. Both Vargasht and Lebyazhe were abandoned, and the troops had obviously moved on down the line. The next twenty kilometres were also clear, half way to Makushino, until we reached our first section of damaged track. Our labourers got down and set to with their tools, while the riflemen stood by with guns ready. We took the opportunity to munch on our black bread and flasks of vegetable soup. The Kirgiz let go with one of their eerie homeland wails, which echoed strangely across the empty steppe. No one else felt like singing.

After a couple of hours, the "engineers" pronounced the track fixed and we rolled on, inching forward. I sat with Volkov, on the roof of the first carriage, a hooded cape keeping off the rain. The train moved into glades of birch, and in one of these, we suddenly spotted groups of men rushing through the trees. We levelled our guns but the engine driver popped his head up and shouted: "They're ours!" The platoon spread across the track, and we stopped again. A Red commissar strode up and we climbed down to meet him. Volkov showed him our fake orders, beautifully aged by Gasek.

"We are ordered on Special Duty to the Thirteenth Regiment at Petropavlovsk," Volkov told the man, a heavily bearded fighter festooned with ammunition belts.

"Good luck if you can find `em," he said laconically. "Petropavlovsk is still held by the Whites. There's fighting at Petukhovo, but if you take us with you, we might get you past that, then we can take the bastards right up the arse."

"Come aboard."

We trundled on, looking like a bristling hedgehog, with thirty more men crowded on the engine and carriage roofs, heavy boots dangling over the side and two machine guns mounted fore and aft. The driver, imbued with renewed confidence, pushed his throttle forward a little harder. But this optimism on his part was short lived. Just as we felt we were set for an easier passage we were all jolted as the brake was pulled, hard. The train squealed like an injured elephant and we were all thrown forward against each other, barely managing to stay on the roof. Volkov and I, together with Azmat and two of the riflemen, jumped onto the fuel carriage, peering round to the broken track right ahead.

After that moment, it is difficult to recall the exact process of the events. At the familiar rattle of machine-gun fire our old instinct threw us down on the wood-pile. I could see the soldiers jumping or falling off the carriage and firing back into the woods. I think the Kirgiz, Azman, sat on top of me, holding me down, but I shook him off. I peeked over the rim of the fuel carriage and saw blurred images of figures rushing up through the trees. I could feel the bullets ripping into the flank of the train. Volkov shouted something about checking the other flank. I rolled the Kirgiz off me and pulled over to the left. There were soldiers running up from there too. One of our men fell on the wood pile, shot in the head. The men were shouting and firing back. I cocked my rifle and took aim at one of the enemy soldiers rushing up from the left, but from the corner of my eye saw another rushing forward very quickly and tossing something, most likely a grenade. I dropped my man, and shouted at Volkov, but for some reason he stayed standing up, trying to get his balance on the wood chips. The grenade fell on the wood at his feet. I heard him swear, and then the stick exploded. I instinctively flattened my head to the pile, and rolled over. As my face came up again I saw Volkov lying prone on the smouldering wood.

The grenade had ripped into him, tearing his stomach open. Azman was beside him, cradling his head. We both looked at the open wound. I had seen this so many times before. One saw men fall, like flies, in the charge from the trench. Or just caught, trying to figure out whether it was safer to run forward or back. Even with a platoon of medics, rushing forward with their satchels and bandages and scissors and salves, there was nothing that could be done. A part of his intestine was spilling out, slimy and red. The bastard stretched his own hands down and piled it back in. The Kirgiz tried to help him, but I shook my head. I scrabbled forward to grab his arm. He was swearing like mad, spitting out every Russian curse in the book.

"My boot!" he shouted at me, "in my boot!"

"What? What?" I wasn't sure what he was saying. "It's not your leg!" I shouted.

"My left boot!" he shouted. "Take it off!"

I thought I understood what he meant, so I began unravelling his leg-swaddles, to get at the cracked army issue leather. He continued to curse—

"**!!**!!* Fuck the bastards! They cancelled my leave!" He looked furious, as Azman held his head, looking helpless. I pulled the boot off, eliciting another string of abuse. "The Englishman!" he shouted out, "the Englishman! Irkutsk! The Hotel Moderne!"

I thought he was raving, but I scrabbled inside the boot and pulled out the sheaf of papers wrapped in a thin gauze, caked in sweat.

"Do it Kolya!" he shouted, "do it! Get the fuck out of here!"

I looked around. The shooting seemed to have moved from the train, down the copse, where the riflemen had rushed forward, firing at the enemy. Then another face peered over the flank of the fuel carriage. Sabeer, the other Kirgiz. He called to his brother in their own language. Azman grabbed Volkov's shoulders. "Help me get him down!" he shouted at me. I took Volkov's legs, despite the yelling and the cursing.

Sabeer was straining at the left side of the halted train, holding the reins of three of our horses in his hands. A fourth horse had run off, clambering up the slope on that side. The grenadier had been dropped, presumably by Sabeer, on the track. The slope up into the trees on the left was clear.

We manoeuvred Volkov off the carriage onto the ground. I looked around, peeking up to the engine. The driver had been shot, and lay across his throttle. The track ahead was smashed. I peeked between the fuel-pile and the engine, I knew there was at least one medic among the riflemen, but they had all rushed off the other side. And then, another unmistakeable sound, the whining whistle of a shell, in the air, followed instantly by the loud crump of artillery cannon-fire. The shell exploded, ahead of the break in the track. But another, without even a whistle, fell just behind the rear carriage, lifting it bodily up in the air and twisting it off the fuel-pile. The horses reared up in terror.

Azman shouted at me and we lifted Volkov, guts and all, onto one of the horses, which bucked and reared, but Azman leapt on its bare back. Sabeer shouted at me. He lifted me as if I was a sack of potatoes and threw me on the back of the second horse, leaping effortlessly onto the third.

"Hold the reins!" he shouted at me, "hold the reins!"

Sheer terror is the best teacher. I don't know how, but I hung on. The two Kirgiz galloped up the slope, and my horse followed theirs, in close order. No one, horse nor man, waited for more shells to fall. I think I felt one, slamming into the fallen carriage.

We flew up, like startled birds, through the trees. I could not feel the ground, only the heaving flesh of the animal between my thighs, the flecking of its mane, a glimpse of popping eyes, the thick hair around its coarse brown ears. I held on, hugging its strong neck, one hand holding the reins like magic tendrils, dragging me forward, out of danger.

Silver birches throbbing past us. Somehow the sound had died completely, or I had gone deaf. I have no idea how long that wild ride lasted. Somewhere the two Kirgiz stopped, and Sabeer's hand grabbed my steed's reins and brought it to a halt. I tumbled off the back, onto wet muddy grass. The ground was very black. The rain had stopped, and there was a great silence.

Volkov was lying on the ground. He was completely still, then began twitching, uncontrollably. His insides had completely come out, and were spilled all over his groin. His face was rocking, mouth filled with red spittle, eyes rolling, not quite sightlessly, as they fixed upon me. He was uttering something.

"What is he saying?" asked Sameer. Azman brought his face down to the twitching mouth. He looked up at me.

"He wants something from you," he said to me.

I shook my head. "No." I said.

"This man is finished," Azman said. "He is your brother. Help him."

What happens at times like this? Does time stop? Does his, or my entire life flash before the eyes?

No. Only the necessity remains. I took my pistol from my holster.

Azman said something in another language I did not know. I think, on reflection, it was Arabic. Something with the name of Allah. He nodded at me, and looked away. He and his brother stared off into the trees.

I said nothing else. I did my duty.

I do not remember if my trigger finger trembled or not.

*

(*Translator's note: The next three chapters have been omitted from the second notebook. The omission covers the events after the death of Volkov and the abandonment of his remains in the frozen soil in the nomads' manner of leaving the dead for the natural predators of the field and sky. The subsequent events comprised the continued journey to Omsk with the two Kirgiz companions and the entrance of Admiral Kolchak into the city, requiring the secret travellers to move on. These events comprised*

468

the first weeks of November, 1919. When asked about the omission, Prof. Gore would only say that it contained "nivzuyot"—i.e. "outrages", the connotation being of salacious material, or more disturbing witness of bloodshed. There was also apparently some description of the narrator's access to the "Kolchak Gold" train that remained parked outside the Omsk station until the Czechoslovak Legion decided to force the Admiral's hand by shipping the booty out to the east. The two Kirgiz brothers, Azmat and Sabeer, have disappeared from the narrative, and one can only assume that they did not wish to join the Czech train and decided to make their own way home to the Altai region. One wonders if they had resumed their acts of revenge in Omsk during the prolonged stay, and whether that has any bearing on the gap in the account. I cannot comment further on the motives of the exclusion, which is at the author's request. Suffice to say that it covered Kolya's introduction to the Czech Legion and his embar-kation on the onward track of its commandeered train to the east.

Y. S.)

22 :

The Czech train gathered speed as it pulled out of Omsk station, rattling as fast as it could past the town, and ignoring the pleas of groups of soldiers who ran along the line shouting and cursing and shaking their fists. Some lifted their rifles and fired shots but the bullets bounced harmlessly off the armoured plating. The Czech soldiers hunched behind the plates kept their heads down and merely watched out for any more desperate act such as an attempt to board the train at high speed. The great steel beast was, however, pretty invulnerable, and the one or two brave or mad souls who made the effort failed to find a grip and were mangled under the wheels.

The atmosphere among the Legionnaires was buoyant, and many were puffing on the clay pipes they cherished as the closest mementos of their origin, filling the carriages with their thick pungent smoke. Someone had sent over a cargo of these precious objects from Vladivostok, cheering the men up immensely in Omsk, since if pipes could find their way across the world from Europe, then men could find their way home the same way. More valuable, of course, was the ammunition and the British Lee-Enfield rifles that ensured their superiority, as well as the American Springfields which had recently been added to their arsenals. The coats, fresh uniforms and brand new boots they were all wearing, as well as their cohesive discipline, explained why the Czech Legion had been the most efficient force in Siberia since it began moving east in 1918. This key enabled Kolchak to keep our own forces at bay for more than a year, and now that the key was withdrawn back to its owners, the game was up, only the last moves remained to be played.

I sat, cocooned in the packed officer's coach, with Vaclav Cerny and his "Three Musketeers," Jan, Miroslav and Popicka, almost roasting in my stolen White Colonel's outfit, the blood on the lapel long dried and covered by other stains. My hand wrapped around my mug of hot tea, while the windows were almost frosted over by the weather outside, the landscape pure white rippled by the thin remaining dark lines of the passing trees, Russia's eternal birches. The stations we passed were buried in snow, the cartographic expert, Miroslav, counting them out from his memory of the railway chart: "Kormilovka... Kalachinskaya... Tatarskaya..."

"Sound like ballerinas in Diaghilev's Russe," Popicka said—he was the oldest of the three, pushing forty, practically a Methuselah in our short-lived generation. "Tamara Karsavina, in the `Orientales...' I saw the premiere in Paris, before the war. Nijinsky. How that boy could jump." (The narrator misspells these names in the original; Y.S.)

"Put a firecracker up your arse and you'll be sure to match him," said Cerny. They were speaking Russian for my benefit. They had enough practice by now.

"Ah, what do you know..." Popicka puffed away, lost in thought.

Despite the air of disinterest, everyone aboard was acutely aware that trouble could erupt at any point along the line. The

Czech commanders' deal with Kolchak left them the task of safe-guarding the track in order that his own train could follow closely after, and be enabled to withdraw his staff at least to Novosibirsk, if not Krasnoyarsk. In areas further from the track, north and south, the White armies were losing, with news that at least six regiments had been taken prisoner by the Red Army. Officers and divisional staff who refused to surrender had been shot by their own troops. Cerny was reporting every hour on the hour, news fresh from the communications coach, which was conveniently shared with the buffet, so that everyone could listen in. By the time we had passed Kayinsk we heard that Omsk itself had been taken, as the deep-frozen Irtysh enabled the Bolsheviks to cross over in great numbers. Kolchak had escaped just in time. The White Russian government was now transferred to Irkutsk, to which we were all heading.

Lulled by pipe smoke and the heat of the peat fires that the Czechs tended in each carriage, I thought of Volkov and the satisfaction he would have shown at the route now taken. "The simplest plan," he always said, "is the best, even when it seems the most complicated or dangerous." The eye of the storm, that was the phrase I best remembered. Where the fire is hottest. "Your best chance," he would say, "is to play the reckless fool. That way no one wants to tangle with you. They all want to get out of your way."

This was clearly the motto the Czechs themselves had adopted. From their first rebellion against Trotsky's orders, when he had ordered them to disband and submit to Party control, they simply seized hold of their trains and decamped eastward. Their air of comradeship was clear and unshakeable. I could see that it was born not of any ideological belief or prerogative, but purely out of national pride. As strangers in a strange land, the Czechs had seized their moment, at the price of supporting a movement and an army that were dedicated to return Russia to barbarism. The question was, whether Russia was in barbarism never the less, and could ever escape the legacy of tyrannical thought that was burned into the soul...

In any case, it was clear that the Czechs had never been happy with Kolchak, Denikin or Yudenitch, the Tsar's blood-thirsty avengers, as Gasek's defection and his network of sympathisers within the Legion confirmed. Their sympathies were more commonly with the S-R's, the Social-Revolutionaries who had been cast out by Lenin, and who, with Mensheviks, "Greens" and others, had support among the peasants and small-holders particularly in western Siberia, along the path that we were travelling. They were strong in Tomsk, Krasnoyarsk and Irkutsk, as I was to find out, and the Red Army, on the ground in these regions, could not afford to ignore that.

Eventually, as the time passed and the train slowed and halted, and started again, and rolled forward, the talk turned to my own origins, and I found myself talking about my father's house in the village, in Celovest, and my mother and brothers and sisters, and the life we had lived before. The main argument this sparked off in our little group was whether Jews were good drinkers or not. Cerny expressed the opinon that Jews, having been brought up on sips of the "kiddush" wine on Friday nights as small children, became immune to the harder tipple and so were relatively sober as a nation, if crazy in the head on other accounts, while Popicka pooh-poohed this theory as nonsense, saying he had several Jewish partners in the brewery trade in Pilzen who became as bug-eyed as frogs in the taverns on a Saturday night and could join the best of them under the tables. "I knew a man called Sonderberg from the Allianz Reassurance bank who could empty a barrel of Budjovice in less than an hour," he said, "and still sell you a dud policy on a sick dog that you couldn't collect if hell froze over." In the same vein, he said he knew two Rabbis who sneaked into his tavern late at night close to closing time and "devoured two full plates of blood-sausage."

"All men of religions are shams," agreed Cerny. "They'll sell their God for a flagon and a c**t..."

"Rasputin!" offered Miroslav.

"I rather liked him," said Popicka, "he took a long time and effort to kill."

It was instructive to see the Czechs' thoughtful method of securing the passage of the railway. At each station along the way, there were detachments which both reinforced the personnel on the trains and received reinforcements in turn, in a kind of rotation. In this way, with the support of some English troops and a few Polish units, which arrived from God knows where, and some detachments from their S-R comrades, the Czech Legion was able to hold the line without relying on the Whites, whose ostensibly vast armies were fading into the trackless snow, defecting to the "Greens," surrendering to the Bolsheviks, or just throwing away their arms and starting the long walk home, or riding off on their own steeds in the case of the tribal Siberian units.

All along the line, in the snow, we could see the old Russian churches standing out like lone sentinels over settlements that were either completely deserted or ruined stumps, sombre witnesses of stern shepherds who had failed to protect their flocks. Here and there one also saw carcases of livestock, cows, goats, horses, gaping jaws protruding from the drifts. The human bodies did not long linger but sunk into the white oblivion, until the thaw might lift them to the surface, bare bones that once had names and souls. The vast expanse and endless waste imposed a grim reflection even on the most jaded or sceptical cast of mind, and reduced even the ebullient Czechs to murmurs. Popicka stuffing his pipe and puffing, Cerny drumming his fingers on his knee, the two young men sadder and sadder. I sensed that we had all the same thought: how far we are from home. Not only as a place, but as a sanctuary from the great bleakness of existence. To perish here was to be lost forever, and fall away from all memory, from history and the whole repository of human knowledge, all compassion, all possibility of love...

Maudlin thoughts, unfitting of a Chekist, if common to the many millions of foot soldiers who had seen no rest since the lone gunman of Bosnia had caught the Austrian Emperor's nephew on the road at Sarajevo. A handful of bullets, and the world changes...

It took four days and nights before we clattered softly, in the winter darkness, into the station at Krasnoyarsk. A city with no night, even in winter because of the pallid light spread everywhere by the snow, and galvanised by the legion of newcomers marching in mass on the footmarked roads. Disembarkation and bivouack in the warehouses of the station railway works, filled with broken up carriages, loose and rusted bogeys and hanging rail equipment dangling down from the roofs. A Russian town transformed suddenly into a make-believe Prague. Beer-songs rising up from a thousand throats who would be lucky to see the worst kind of rotgut vodka. In the day, the townscape stretched out towards the great Yenisei River that wound up into the Siberian depths.

In this atmosphere of strange beauty, preserved "white" in body as well as spirit, still far from the defeats of their high command four hundred kilometres up the line, and slow as our progress seemed, we had still travelled so fast that the news from the west had not quite struck here, and yet were still less than midway between Moscow and Vladivostok.

Here came my first encounter with the American Siberian expedition-naries: a medical team of officer doctors and nurses that had established their own hospital in an empty granary. It was my first encounter with friendly faces that seemed fixed in a perpetual smile. I did not know what they had to smile about. Here they were, men and women who travelled from across the world to minister to a remote, fate-cursed people, as bright-eyed as if they were witnessing the dawn of an unexpected hope, rather than the midnight of disaster. The women were dazzling, in their pure white smocks and little white caps. We thought they were genuine angels, and gathered en masse to gawp at them as if they were a visitation from heaven. Every soldier's dream. The men spoke no Russian, apart from one interpreter whose Russian was almost incomprehensible but who shook hands with every single person, as if every soul was his friend. I had to route my secret thoughts through my head to reconcile this jovial apparition with the devils who had come to help the Whites to wipe out our Revolution and put the Tsar back on the throne.

They were also in charge of a train-full of orphans, and we were all drafted in to carry the sicker children from their carriages to the children's ward of the hospital. It was the first time I had handled a child since a similar encounter in Galicia with some emaciated Polish kids. But then we handled them like bundles, passing them from one broken down transport to another. In Petrograd one looked at children as one looked at dogs, desperate scavengers, who ran from hole to hole. We did not live in any ordinary atmosphere of families, fathers, mothers, siblings, but in the brutal adult world of grown-up predators, trained to kill or be killed, a nation of hyenas. Hope was just a slogan on a poster.

Here I was almost tempted by Cerny's comradely proposal: To strip myself completely of both Red and White identities and become an honorary Czech. I would then join them in their final journey to Vladivostok to embark to the United States and finally taste the air of freedom. For some reason I had not told him that I had two brothers in America, and the idea of making landfall in California made the blood rush to my head.

Never the less I held back, and told him I would think about it as we drew nearer to Irkutsk. Above all, I had it fixed in my mind that I owed my first loyalty to Kiril Volkov, my surrogate but real life brother, who had kept me alive for so long and shepherded me across so many shadowed valleys. I owed it to him to pursue his possibly phantom Englishman, the gold trail of his own fondest dreams...

Yonni's note: Missing page.

23.

From Krasnoyarsk, it took us six more days to reach Irkutsk. After the Yenisei, the land became more mountainous, with forests of crystalline branches. For hours, one seemed to rattle past a landscape of peaceful winter, where one could imagine games of snow-sleighs and sledded droshkies sliding through the drifts. But it was all empty—more villages abandoned, houses derelict, no signs of moving livestock, and groups of people wrapped like mummies watching impassively from the local stations as our armoured beast clattered by. Eventually the white outside became blinding, one only saw the train interior, choking on the increasingly fetid odour of two thousand men slouched upon each other, like sleeping cats in a vast overcrowded cage.

If Krasnoyarsk was a picturesque illusion, Irkutsk was like a frosted ghost. We entered in a mist, which I would learn to find familiar, the icy fog that floated from the great inland sea, Baikal. When I arrived, there was no water, only that endless stretch of ice across which, the old books told us, the Tsars had laid their onward tracks.

They told me the city was beautiful, but all I saw were stone shapes looming in the frozen dream. The cold was not alike anything previous experience had prepared me for. It overpowered one, seized and squeezed the lungs, bringing one's breath out in gasps.

"You'll get used to it!" Cerny was as ever cheerful. So many hundreds of kilometres closer to the Legion's goal, those troop ships moored in Vladivostok. Japanese ships, they were told. Yet another two or three weeks onward in the same purgatory, hoping for the great light at the end. What, I wondered in my growing delirium, if the old medieval believers were right, and the earth was flat? Just a giant ice cap at the end of the continent, a great ledge, looming over nothingness?

The Czechs were worried that I was falling ill, prey to the miasmas that afflicted the human microbes in the stifling air of the train. Thought was jumbled, and I was trembling with a fever. Even the strongest men, we knew, could suddenly slump and stumble, and swiftly fade away. There was a hospital carriage on the train itself, but its air was the foulest of all.

"Just breathe, however freezing it seems," said Popicka, who had some medical training. "The Baikal is life. You wouldn't know it, but in the summer it's paradise. Blue and clear as the Danube, with some pretty deadly saloons."

There was an American clinic here too, near the municipal garden, another patch of ten foot drifts. The nurses were far more homely than the angels of Krasnoyarsk but I didn't care. Just lying down straight, with a blanket, brought an unbelievable balm. I just surrendered to the inevitable. If this was the end, at least it was rest. The journey itself was pointless. I was sure it had no end.

I had many dreams, hallucinations, some of rising and flying, others of crawling along the ground. In one I was an eagle, soaring above snowy mountains, that gave way suddenly to glorious sunshine over peaks of magnificent forests, green as life, with a great river curling through it, that I knew was the Dniester, just on the way to home. But for some reason I remained on my trajectory, and flew over the pure waters, towards the endless steppes beyond. A voice was calling me. Volkov, standing below, on a mountain-top, waving his cap. But as I came close enough to brush him with my wing-tip, I saw the small black hole in his temple, close to the right ear, and I veered off, back into the trackless blue sky. I was looking for the sea, but the steppes just continued, endless, endlessly rolling, fields of wheat, fields of corn, waiting for the harvesters to come. But there were none below.

Another dream, I was vermin, a beetle or a cockroach of sorts, crawling on stone, flailing over the snow. I would grab hold of the individual crystals with my terrible thin feet, leaping from one to the other. There was no reason for my scrabbling, I knew, with a horrible certainty, and no end, and I was doomed, in my uncrushable character, to endure and survive.

Eventually I woke, not to a red-cheeked American girl singing Thanksgiving songs, but to a stern Russian woman, whose glare grabbed me into consciousness, who waved a thermometer and pressed it between my lips, saying with a grunt and a shrug: "I'm going to need this bed."

I still felt I couldn't move, but some time later I saw the friendly faces of Popicka, Miroslav and Jan, my travelling companions, and they pulled me to my feet. They clapped a cap on my head and threw a coat around me and helped me get into some pretty old looking boots and carried me bodily out, into an armoured van that might have been authorised or commandeered, it was impossible to tell, at that point, where any authority lay in the city. They took me to Cerny, who seemed to have a whole floor of a proper house, in one of the avenues, close to the Angara River, yet another stark sheet of ice. Like his twin fixer, Gashek, he had a couple of printing machines, and a small harem of women who worked at them, piling papers, amassing their news-sheets, setting and checking the press. He had an office with a good stove and a steaming samovar and the ubiquitous tea-bricks, his soldier's tin mug and two ready camp beds.

"We'll billet you here," he said. "You can't go back to the regiment. Things have got complicated." I was still too tired, and fell asleep despite the clanking of the machine. I must have lain around there for at least three days, while the girls brought me hot tea and soup. Eventually Cerny entered with a dead and plucked chicken, and this revived both our spirits as the company chef, Ondricek, turned up to ensure a proper roast.

While we ate, Cerny regaled me with the latest news, which he related very much in Gasek's style, as a tale of ructions in a tavern, or a street brawl between several drunk opponents: Kolchak and his staff, it seemed, had retreated further and further down the line, from Novo-Nikolayevsk to Taiga, from Taiga to Marinsk, and further to Krasnoyarsk. At Krasnoyarsk there were so many trains piled up that no one could proceed further, and Kolchak became very nervous about his main special gold-train, which contained all the money the Tsar ever had, over sixty million pounds sterling's worth. This could buy fifteen more armies if there were any soldiers left willing to die for a clearly lost cause. Kolchak blamed the Czechs for holding up the train and stealing about fifteen million before-hand, which were already on the way to Vladivostok. Things got so furious that General Kappel, Kolchak's chief-of-staff, called up the Czech commander, Syrovy, on the telephone, and challenged him to a duel. General Syrovy told him he was an idiot and went on eating his dinner. The General's staff informed the excited Russians that the Czechs would simply take matters into their own hands and cease all co-operation if the Russians did not calm down. While all this was going on twenty-five high-up British officers got lost south of Tomsk and a Czech brigade was sent out to rescue them.

Kolchak's command was in complete disarray, and his own generals were plotting to remove him. General Sakharov, who had screwed up the retreat from Omsk, barely escaped an attempt by lower ranks to arrest him, and General Dietrichs, the most able of a bad bunch, refused to resume the command he had resigned from. Meanwhile, down the line, beyond Irkutsk, at Chita, the insane General, Ataman Semenov of the eastern Cossacks, was manoeuvring to take over the general command, with the support of the Japanese army in Manchuria. He was said to be a slavering beast who shot his own men for minor insurrections and imposed medieval tortures as punishments, which were carried out by his adjutant, a Baron Ungern.

Meanwhile the situation in Irkutsk was volatile. The city's own municipal council was not solidly White, but composed of a mixture of ex-Kerenskyites, Social-Democrat (Mensheviks) and Social-Revolutionaries—S-R's—of both the "Right" and the "Left" tendencies. They were opposed to the Bolsheviks as one gang of bandits to another, said Cerny. Here, he said, we are very far from Moscow, and no one is interested in their distant orders. All the talk is about setting up an independent Siberian Authority, or even a separate Republic, opposed to dictatorship whether of left or right. All this was well and good, except that no-one was able to decide what to do about all the warring factions closing in on the city—Reds from the north and west, Whites from the south, "Greens" from every point of the compass. Inside the city, the civilian working force was in fact solidly Red. Since Irkutsk was the hub through which the vast areas of the gold and other mineral mines were administered and exploited, this was the frozen life-blood of Russia.

Cerny called on me one morning, while I lay dazed at my fate, unable to understand how I had got here. He had some good news, among the usual dross of chaos. My Czechs had located Volkov's "Englishman." Just as I had found Cerny at the Hotel Rossia in Omsk, so the good Briton was consuming his precious whiskey at the Hotel Moderne in Irkutsk, presumably waiting for his instructions from London. The only persons who seemed to have visited him so far were two of Irkutsk's most alluring whores.

"I would get in there quick if I were you," Cerny summed up. "Everybody needs protection in this city, and we are getting out as soon as the Generals are ready. This town is ready to blow."

"We'll still take you if we can," said Popicka. "America, my boy!" He turned to Cerny, "we can stick a moustache on him and give him a new name. Remember sapper Vodicka? We left him in the ground at Zlatoust. I still have his papers."

We drank some vodka and Cerny turned to attend to his job churning out the regimental newspaper, "The Fighting Fifteenth."

The street outside was somehow less freezing, or perhaps I had acclimatised to the place. The human heat coming off the large market that led up from the river probably mitigated the fog off the lake. Visibility was better, and I could find my way up to the main and very wide Bolshaya avenue. On one side, the snow covered park, some children were playing, amid the usual encampment of refugee yurts. Before us, another grand cathedral, the church of Our Lady of Karsk. On the right side of the avenue, the big commercial buildings and the hotels. I had discarded the battered White regimental coat and ranks, and donned the simpler covering of a Czechoslovak Lieutenant. I had all but forgotten who I had been before, or why I had embarked on the journey, and even the memory of Volkov was fading. He had fallen, as had so many, countless others. Siberia, I thought, in the end would cover us all. Memory itself had frozen here to a brittle shard of ice, that would when the thaw came simply melt and merge into the flow of endless rivers.

Never the less, the trained messenger delivers his message, even if he has forgotten what it was. The lobby was, as lobbies of these hotels were, cavernous and incongruous, like an implanta-tion from a bad dream. Dour, dark wooden surfaces. The inevitable chandelier dully lighting the row of strange portraits on the walls, groups of sallow men in European suits, with black beards and yellowing, almost Chinese complexions. Evidently grandees of the city of some sort. There was a strange pair of melancholy young people, a young girl in a black dress, and a doleful young man, each holding a violin, poised to start playing a piece. Another painting, over the reception desk, more rich in execution but with equally sombre colours, showed "the Tsarevitch Grand Duke Nikolai ar-riving in Irkutsk on 23 June 1891," The then heir to the accursed throen standing upright on the prow of a steamer drawing up to a triumphal arch over the Angara River, saluting the crowd of citizens in long coats raising their top hats and cheering, while, on the quay, more ordinary folk gazed in wonder at the demigod, the Tsar-to-be gracing their world with his presence. Festooned with medals, he looked young and puissant, the messenger of progress and wealth...

The Good Englishman, whose name was Stanley Tompson (*Thompson, Y.S.*), had left for an early commercial meeting, but was expected back for lunch. I walked the frozen streets for an hour, gazing at the ornate buildings of the "Siberian Paris," looking in the almost empty and frosted up windows of the apothecary's shop, the closed book shop, Abramoff the couturier, the locked offices of the Kuznetsov Brothers' Travel Company, but returned to wait in warmer premises. I dozed off, but was jerked awake by the hand of a large gentleman in an immense fur coat, whose young but already craggy face loomed over me, with a wry smile. He spoke Russian with a clipped but fluent style. He invited me to dine with him, and we walked into the large and ornate din-ing room, at which one table among the many was set. I gazed at a fine borscht that lured me like a dark pool in which the cream was swimming like minuscule ice-bergs. After the soup—roast partridge, a delicacy I had not even dreamed existed, nor imagined in this remote lair.

The Englishman, I could see, was used to command. Under the furs, he was wearing a dark suit with white shirt, immaculate collar and tie as if he were in the best of company rather than in a metropolis of bandits and thugs. He was very direct, telling me immediately that he had fully expected that Volkov and the "young man" who was accompanying him would turn up sooner or later, and had left instructions at the hotel to refer us onward and arrange our transport if he were, as he put it, "upstream." He had met Volkov in Petrograd under the personal aegis of Felix D. and had immediately formed a good impression of him. "I know a good man when I see him," was a recurring theme. He expressed great regret when I told him Volkov had fallen in a skirmish on the track out from Kurgan, when we had been ambushed by the Whites. I explained that my companions, the two Kirgiz brothers, had ridden with me to Omsk where we obtained our "disguises," before my rendezvous with Cerny.

"Ah, the Czechs!" he said, "they are what we call `the fly in the ointment'"—it sounded odd in Russian, like a vermin in cream—"Trotsky should have kept them close to his side. I tried to tell him about them but he was always fearful of nationalists. A strategic miscalculation. Without them your friends would have been in Irkutsk long ago. As it is they have had to come from the rear. As you must have heard, Murayev's troops are securing the Lena. They are under Lenin's orders. That man understands business. Men of the world build, dreamers destroy. I need good men. My business has its own share of dreamers. Men who dream of the `Siberian Klondike.' I have had Americans who come across the Baring Straits with huskies and a gang of Eskimos who know the ice but couldn't find gold if you took them to a jeweller's shop. They go through places that even the Tsar's worst prisoners couldn't last a week in and turn up on my doorstep, asking for a `stake.' As if we were a bunch of prospectors with a couple of picks and a pan. I have twenty thousand men working over fields of fifteen thousand versts. Whole townships and tribes dependent on our business. We have been working these seams since eighteen sixty-three."

There was a different kind of strength flowing from this man, not the desperate and reckless bravado of the revolutionary or the professional soldier but a somewhat deeper understanding of the hands that moved behind the scenes, the seemingly blind but inexorable forces that had seized the world and kept shaking it until entire peoples were thrown about and plundered, empires dislodged, armies hurled against each other, cities destroyed and nations displaced, classes flung at each other's throats and blood shed like oceans, human beings thrown like millions of living skittles into a bottomless pit. He talked in a strange language, throwing about English words like "shares," "flotations," "subscriptions" and "dividends," and annual and "extraordinary" meetings in London at which the lives and fortunes of millions of people were discussed in terms of flows of capital, investments and the unfortunate flux of events that disrupted the steady accumulation of wealth that enriched the few but also determined the fates of nations whose very supply of food, shelter and the absolute necessities of life could vanish at the drop of a political coin. He laughed at Kolchak's gold train, which the Admiral had thought carried the very keys of the kingdom, but in the aggregate was just a bunch of crates of heavy metal that did as much good to him as pig-iron.

"False gods," he said, "so many false gods."

As he continued speaking, ordering one bottle after another of fine wine that I thought had perished from the earth, but never getting drunk like a Czech or a Russian, let alone a Moldavian, merely more ebullient and talkative, it struck me that, confident as he sounded, he seemed not to have many, or perhaps any companions out in the northern reaches of the Lena River to confide his thoughts to, or any real fraternal companionship, though he could obviously obtain release for his desires. But one could not buy friendship. He wanted to know my own convoluted story, and I told him about Bessarabia and my father's house, and my scattered siblings, the two brothers who seemed to have found refuge in America, Zev who dreamed of the Trans-Siberian journey, my

sisters and mother who remained at home. And I spoke emotion-
ally of Kiril Volkov, my surrogate brother, who had carried me
through fear and danger, through thick and thin, through the Great
War and that first terrible year of the Revolution, which seemed to
devour everything it touched. I stopped short at telling him that it
was I who had dispatched Volkov. What's done cannot be undone.
One lives with the consequences of the storm.

In return, he told me about himself. Although he had been
born in England, the son of a manager in the coal business, his
father had taken him as a small boy to South Africa, where gold
had been discovered in the Johannesburg area, leading to what he
called "The Great Rand Rush." Thousands of English would-be-
miners took ship to the southern tip of Africa, and his father was
fortunate in joining a group which flourished and was soon part of
a great conglomerate of entrepreneurs. "I grew up with gold," he
said, the casting of shafts, the creak of the wagons coming up from
beneath the ground, the clatter of the belts, the shouts and songs
of the labourers who broke the rocks and hewed out the nuggets,
the great piles of slag that soon marked the landscape of the fields.

"When I first came to Russia," he said, "I thought that all
mine workers sang, those tribal songs that came deep from the
heart, and expressed their own roots and their longings. But if you
want to hear a Buryat singing you'd better pile on the vodka. Or
the kumiss. I miss those black chants, even if they were also war
songs longing for the end of the white man. And the light, Kolya!
the light..."

Then came the Boer war and the rebellion of the Dutch settlers whose patrimony the English had threatened. Production was
disrupted, and the Boers fought a stubborn war of attrition, which
the Russian Reds would have done well to study. Never the less,
the might of the British Empire prevailed. Production resumed at
a greater pace, and the Tompsons, father and son, prospered even
more. "I was recruited," he said, "by a big man with mutton-chop
whiskers, named Alfredson, to the Lena Goldfields company, as
their man in South Africa, even though I was barely twenty-two

at the time." He was first sent to Siberia after the great goldfields' strike of nineteen-twelve, which the Tsar's troops had bloodily suppressed. "This had a bad effect on profits. Even though the company did not pay wages during the strike, they still had to house and clothe the men, who had no money to pay their company bills. London was not very happy." He had come as a conciliator, promising better conditions and wages. The whole affair made the company directors wary of the Tsar's heavy handed tactics, and, when the war and revolution broke out two years later, he was sent to Petrograd to form a link with the new government.

"South Africa!" he enthused, "Kolya, you can't imagine it! The sun so hot the sky and earth are burning! Great deserts, mountains, velds... So much left undone... So much yet to explore!"

I became warmed by his enthusiasm. It was a rare boon to be able to talk—and dream—of something other than the unremitting agony of this Russia, this cursed land, frozen not only by the elements but by its peoples' implacable struggles. Whoever was to win, Reds, Whites, Greens, Tsars or Commissars, I could not feel any longer that it was any of my own concern. If I had been Czech, I too would have longed for home, but my home lay the other way, back along the terrible trail that I had already travelled. And there was no way back for me along that road.

America was, for me, a false hope. By the time our long dinner and drinking session was over, I had already agreed to be Tompson's apprentice in the goldfield business. I would come under his protection and the wide cloak of the London company's responsibility, a surrogate subject of the British Empire. A most peculiar fate.

In earnest of his confidence, he immediately procured me a room in the Moderne Hotel, two weeks paid in advance, while he ventured out along Lake Baikal, with a retinue of bodyguards from the Municipal Council, to some more discreet councils with "interested parties."

A few days later, Cerny, Popicka and the young lads departed with the advance guard of the Czechs heading on Chita, and from

485

there to Khabarovsk and their embarkation quays at Vladivostok. I never saw them again.

Six months later, Gasek himself turned up at Irkutsk, with his Red Army printing press and his newly wedded Shusha, bedding down at the very house that Cerny had made ready... But more ruptures and clashes occurred before then... Late in December, while I was still waiting for Tompson's call, the whole situation in Irkutsk erupted when the municipal council's "Political Centre," controlled by the S-R's, was overthrown by the Whites, and their leaders taken hostage, which led to a Bolshevik rebellion. Shooting broke out all over the city, and even in the hotel we few guests had to hide in the basement. I drank half a bottle of vodka with an American who said he had arrived to liaise with the council but had no idea who was firing on whom. I ventured out carefully in a lull and came across a Czech, Jasny, who had been left behind for the second tranche of withdrawals. He told me Semenov's Cossacks had advanced from the railway station but their own troops had rebelled and shot their officers. Kolchak was confined some way up the line but the Czechs had refused to protect him.

When I got back to the hotel Tompson was waiting for me, with his own armoured car parked outside. He had several safe passages signed by various commanders, but we opted instead for his regular bodyguards and rode shotgun out of the city.

Two weeks later, all the foreign missions left Irkutsk, and a "Revolutionary Committee" of Left S-R's and the Bolsheviks had control of the city. Kolchak's armies had continued to fall apart and by the middle of January he had surrendered to the S-R "Political Centre," who in turn handed him over to the Red Army. The Czechs by now had washed their hands of the whole business, and, early in February, Kolchak and his "prime minister," Pepelayev, were shot by the Cheka in Irkutsk.

But by then I was 800 kilometers away north-east, in Bodaybo, learning my new trade as a gold-mine manager, once again under the red flag, but in alliance with the class enemy, the red-white-and-blue ensign of His Majesty King George the Fifth, of Great

Britain. His portrait looked down at me, beside that of Lenin, in my administrative office, overlooking the trackless wastes of Siberia, and dreaming of the African sun.

*

<u>Translator's note:</u>

At this point, the main narrative of the "Soldier's Journal" ends, and the rest of the notebook consists of segments that are more notations than drafts of a Third Part, that was intended as a chronological continuation to the gold fields of the Lena River in Siberia and then the narrator's voyage and experiences in South Africa from the early months of 1922. From discussions with Prof it appears that at one point he was considering expanding the story, and utilising the particular details of the Siberian gold mines into a kind of "Moby Dick," a vast compendium, part fiction and part fact, utilising the extreme conditions and circumstances of the mining operations he had witnessed as a metaphor of humanity's ability to endure the most dangerous and difficult life imaginable for the most questionable material gain. There is one more passage on Irkutsk, concerning the Czech author of Svejk, and further talk with the Englishman...

Irkutsk, June, 1920:

In June, after the Czechoslovak Legion had embarked at Vladivostok and begun their long journey home through Canada, Jaroslav Gasek (Hasek) became the last original member of the Legion left in Siberia, staying at Cerny's old office in Irkutsk. He had become a member of the city Soviet and shared his house with his new wife Shusha and a Chinese comrade, who spoke neither Czech nor Russian. They were publishing a news-sheet together in Mongolian, which neither of them could either speak or read. The journal was written entirely by a Buryat teacher who was a prisoner-of-war captured from Semenov's army. Hasek wrote a play about the Hungarian Revolution and continued working in secret on his long book about the "regimental idiot." We met for the last time in September, just before the next winter's freeze, with Thompson, who took us for a four course meal at the Moderne Hotel. Hasek disappeared into the kitchen to teach the chef to cook blood sausages "a-la-Praha." He tippled heavily on the vodka, sang several old Czech songs and passed out under the table. We took him home in Thompson's droshky and the Buryat teacher slung him over his shoulder and waved us goodbye in his stead. I never saw him again but heard he was recalled to Moscow in October, and left for his home soon afterwards. Perhaps he completed his book and published it. *(An ironic comment? Y.S.)*

When the Reds took Vladivostok and the last remnants of the White stragglers vanished into Manchuria and Mongolia I sat with Thompson and the Red commander Murayev and toasted Lenin and the King of England. Their portraits were both profiles, facing each other over a grand map of the gold fields. Thompson said Lenin had the markings of a good monarch, alert, decisive, bold and cautious, with a keen understanding of financial affairs which he was afraid had been lacking in the British monarchy since the Old Queen had died. The only problem, he thought, was Trotsky, who could be a Dimitri to his Fyodor, if one follows Boris Godunov. Murayev said that Lenin was merely an avatar of the People's unshakeable will. The Tsars would never return to Russia, and all the destruction of the Civil War would be put right in five years. They drank a toast to it, which I joined. But the entire affair seemed hollow to me. Once again, I thought, I am a stranger at someone else's celebration of a tarnished and debased triumph. I seemed to suffer from something akin to the monk Grigory's dream, in Pushkin's play, in which he climbs a turret to look down on all the city, where the multitudes jeer and point at him, so that he falls into the depths. "The People," in their great march to power, seemed to know something I did not, since I could not join them in their march, but had taken refuge in this remote wasteland of the earth, where any return to home or homeland was almost unthinkable. Where could I go from here? How could I stay? I cared nothing about power or money. I could not join my strange companions, let alone the masses of the impoverished Siberian mine-workers in their vodka soaked refuge. The entire enterprise seemed meaningless, and yet, under Thompson's aegis, I was at least learning a trade, other than survival or killing.

Once again, we talked of Africa. The way home, Thompson was hinting, was on the heels of the Czechs. Moscow no longer has need of you, young man. Continue east, to go west...

Note: From here-on the pages of the notebook are affixed with news cuttings from the South-African and the British press (notably the "Times" of London) relating the curious events of what was termed the "Rand Rebellion" of March 1922. Prof. did not write directly of his time in South Africa, as he followed the Englishman's invitation to travel there, a very long sea-voyage we can surmise. But he enclosed some daily newspaper cuttings, which he does not wish to forward, apart from two indicative items. These concern the famous strike of white miners caused by the mine-owners' decision to remove the "colour-bar" that favoured white — mainly Boer Afrikaaner — workers and to replace 2,000 white unskilled men with cheaper black labour. The strike became extremely violent and developed quickly into an armed rebellion supported by "Bolshevik" elements within the white workers' union. The British army was called in to crush the armed revolt. The miners marched and fought under the unusual slogan of "WORKERS OF THE WORLD UNITE AND FIGHT FOR A WHITE SOUTH AFRICA."

Johannesburg, January 28, 1922:
EXPLOSIONS ON THE RAND:
The town was startled last night, just after midnight, by two loud explosions.
These proved to be the dynamiting of the coloured people's Bioscope. The damage done is not great, but the incident is regarded as an indication of the serious state of affairs into which the miners' strike has deteriorated. The police have already quietly arrested a number of men who are alleged to have been plotting to cause disorder. It is rumoured that

some strikers intend to take food from farms, in which case trouble with the Boers is certain.

The Active Citizen Force in the rural districts around the Rand has been warned and is ready for action...

March 9, 1922:

JOHANNESBURG MOB LAW: STRIKERS FIGHTING THE NATIVES.

Mob law prevails on the Rand this morning. Reports of all kinds of outrages along the Reef are pouring in. Intimidation has reached such a pitch that some mines have been compelled to cease work entirely... Mobs are parading the suburbs wrecking shops and destroying supplies. A grave aspect of the trouble is the growing conflict between the natives, coloured men and strikers, owing to the brutal treatment of the natives. The natives are also forming commandos for self-protection.. Fighting in the suburbs of Brixton between coloured men and whites, which started last night, is continuing. Several people have been killed and a large number wounded...

March 11, 1922:

FIERCE FIGHT ON RAND: POLICE SHOT IN COLD BLOOD.

AEROPLANES AND GUNS IN ACTION.

After martial law was declared this morning the police occupied the Town Hall of Johannesburg, where they hauled down the red flag, and the Trades Hall, and offices of the Industrial Federation, the men's headquarters.

It is clear that the Council of Action at the back of the strike aimed at Bolshevist rule. A great effort to capture the Post office, telephones and railway seems to be part of a widespread Bolshevist plot. General Smuts, the Prime Minister, has wired to the police to take any steps they regard as necessary to break up the strong commandos and organised gangs. It is reported that the police are using aeroplanes at Benoni, where an officer and five policemen have been killed... The sound of artillery fire is distinctly heard in Johannesburg. Bolshevism is supreme in the strikers' ranks; all moderating influences which have held the revolutionary development in some check since the strike began have been thrust ruthlessly aside. At its outset the Rand movement was a protest against the proposed reduction of wages and the scheme which the Chamber of Mines brought forward for the employment of fewer whites and more natives in order to restore some prosperity to the mines; to-day it is sheer Bolshevist terrorism and murder.

March 15, 1922:
A COMMUNIST PLOT:
Pretoria, March 15—In the official summary of operations on the Rand issued here to-day acknowledgement is made of the loyal assistance of citizens and the help offered to the Authorities from every quarter in the Union. People of all shades of political conviction came forward to help the government put down what there is no doubt was to have been a social revolution by Bolshevists, International Socialists, and Communists. Except for a few who managed to escape, all the revolutionaries have been taken prisoner, the total being upwards of 6,000. Those responsible for murder and rapine will now have to be dealt with.

COMMUNISM FOR THE KAFFIRS: RED MISSIONARIES TO SOUTH AFRICA:
Johannesburg, December 11, 1922:
A Russian Jewish merchant who has just arrived from Moscow states that at a conference held there in November the Soviet decided to send Bolshevist missionaries to foment revolution among the negroes of America and the native races of South Africa... A number of American negroes and South African natives are receiving training at the Oriental University at Moscow, the intention being to send them to the United States, South Africa, and Egypt to urge the negroes

and the natives to make impossible demands, and thus lead to a world revolution—which is now the Bolshevists' last hope...

End of Kolya's book.

VOLUME 3

THE CONSEQUENCES

"In the law of averages..."

Asher:

My Uncle Kolya died on June 15, 1995, the day of the "bloody glove" scene at the O. J. Simpson trial in California, when the defendant tried on a bloodstained glove found at the scene of the double murder he was accused of committing, displaying it proudly as it failed to fit on his hand. Claire and I were in London on that day, watching the show on the Channel Four News, when my mother called from Tel Aviv with the news she had just heard from Ann Arbor.

Yonni, the "Hawking boy," told me Kolya had intended to live to his centennial, but as it happened he missed it by just under a year, passing in his sleep at his hospice at 99 years and nine months old. I called Yonni's number in Michigan.

"Yes, the Prof has gone," he said quietly. "In the law of averages, if you calculate years like taxes, he just made it. The heart just stopped. The great heart. He said something yesterday to me for the last time. Do you want to know what he said? Is he still your subject of study?"

"Yes, Yonni. What did he say?"

"He said to me, 'I had a dream last night.'"

"'Yes, Prof,' I said, 'what did you dream?'"

"'I won't tell you,' he said. Then he shut his eyes again, but he seemed to be just sleeping. He slept a lot this last year. But without crying in between. This was a man who never complained. He took whatever life threw at him and made it his work."

In keeping with custom, he was going to be buried quickly, not quite the same day, as the rule would be in Israel, but the next, in the small Jewish section of the Arborcrest cemetery. It was not far from the home where he had spent his last years, among fellow academics who had also fallen in the line of scholarship.

"The Prof is the Prof," said Yonni. "His friends are already arranging a special memorial back in Israel. Adir was in New York, so he's flying over with Nitsah." I had met my cousin's wife once or twice, at the few family gatherings that floated since my own father's funeral. She seemed a normal person, well-dressed and quiet, clearly an excellent keeper of secrets.

"May you be consoled with God," Yonni told me, annunciating the formula in Hebrew. But it seemed he was the one to be consoled. What should one say of a person who almost lived out the century? There is nothing to mourn; the sheer fact is a triumph, whatever one thinks of the path.

In the morning I called my mother again. She was still at the old apartment on Melchett with my brother Yitzhak's older daughter, Sarah, performing her familial and religious duties by seeing to my frail mother three days a week. Mother walked very slowly. It took her half an hour to walk down the stairs and back up again, but she could still do it, and her mind was relatively clear, apart from the expected journeys into the past. Sarah told me that in two weeks there would be a memorial for Kolya by his old comrades in the "movement," at the iconic Tel Hai, where the Revisionist movement's most famous martyr, Yosef Trumpeldor, fell fighting "the Arabs" in the northern Galilee. and whose last words were, according to myth, "It's good to die for our country." Though subversive historians have suggested a string of Russian oaths would have been more likely as the guts spilled out of his abdomen.

"We should go," said Claire. "It's part of the project."

The project, in Claire's count, dated back to the Hub, when she realized the intricate skein of circumstances, events, memories and cascading stories that swam around the juddering stop-and-start progress of my own scattered Gurevits searches. Everything pointed to something else that was never resolved, and led to some other set of confusing accounts, tall tales, speculations, disconnections and false trails. It then gelled in her mind some time further on, I was never quite sure, perhaps after the Gulf War of 1991, which dragged her own country once again into the Middle East. We both watched, in those cold snowy January and February days as the US and Britain, with their allies—Bangladesh, Saudi Arabia, Egypt, Syria, Morocco, Oman, Pakistan, Qatar, Niger, Sweden, Italy, Holland, Australia, France, Argentina, Senegal, Greece, Czechoslovakia (not yet sundered), Denmark, Norway, New Zealand and Hungary—launched the counterinvasion of occupied Kuwait and Iraq itself, with the major partners bombarding Baghdad. We sat in Finsbury Park as the brave correspondents of CNN crawled from one corner of their Baghdad hotel room to the other to film the smart bombs pounding the city. In Tel Aviv and Jerusalem, they reported behind the plate glass of their offices, wearing gas masks that mutated their instant analyses to gaunt, incomprehensible moos. The Israeli prime minister, "Bibi" Netanyahu, my cousin Adir's boss, also wore his gas mask to address the nation about the imminent danger of Iraqi missiles hitting Israeli cities with poison gas payloads. The air raid sirens, the dreaded wail of childhood, ushering the people into their bunkers.

"We have to do something," said Claire. Still the English liberal. Watching on television, gauging, waiting, was insufficient. She had words and a stage. I still had the old Arri 16 camera, though it was becoming more and more obsolete. The world was turning again.

One year and a few months before, in the more hopeful winter of '89, we had sat and watched with the same impassivity the last acts of the play that had been launched eighty-four years before in Saint Petersburg unfolding in the echo not of tanks or air raids but of statues crashing down in town squares. As Eisenstein's *October* had begun with pulleys and ropes tearing down the granite Czar Alexander, so the people from East Berlin to Vladivostok were tearing down the stone icons of Lenin, Stalin and Kolya's former commander, Felix Dzerzhinsky. Sometimes reality comes as close to full circle as the messy pull and push of history might allow.

Claire was busy then with a new play she was producing with an American troupe who called themselves the Sudden Theatre. They took a given text—a play by Chekhov, Ibsen, or Durrenmatt, for example—and stripped it to its essential moments, in the process rearranging scenes, themes and "deconstructive" dialogues. Sometimes language would be replaced entirely, with wordless movements, animal or mechanical sounds or long silences in which words were exchanged by the actors on cards or blackboards.

The play would be punctuated by dance, acrobatic tumbling, magic tricks and images that appeared at random on TV screens perched on chairs or tables or suspended from the flies: home movies or documentary footage of historical events, sometimes distantly connected, often totally unconnected to the setting of the play. In this instance, they were giving the treatment to Gogol's old satire "The Nose," to the flicker of footage not of Imperial Russia but of Depression-era hunger marches and the miners' strike of 1984.

While the play was still running, the poll tax riots, which became the death knell of Thatcher's Britain, broke out on March 31, 1990. I was at the film school, locking away the equipment at the end of the term when an excitable Chilean student named Raoul rushed up the stairs to tell me that the revolution had broken out just down the road and was closing in on Trafalgar Square. I took the old Arri out and rushed off with Raoul and two other students who happened to be hanging around, heading for the square. We arrived just in time to catch several police vans driving into the crowd right outside the National Gallery. Hundreds of young men rushed forward and smashed the van windows with the poles of their placards, the cops leaping out of their vans. Running fights broke out everywhere, with the give-and-take of sticks and police clubs. Mounted police made cavalry charges, but the crowd melted around them and flowed on, up towards Leicester Square.

Memories of Jerusalem, "Black Panther" demos, or once upon a time in other spheres... Is anything new under the sun?

I gave my footage to Raoul, who edited it into his third-term documentary project, titled "Maggie's Saturday." It was a great hit at the next end-of-term screenings. Eight months later Margaret Thatcher resigned and her party selected a new, gray conservative prime minister, John Major, who shelved the offending tax. Three months later, it fell to him to lead Britain into war in the Gulf.

The Gulf War ended on February 28, 1991, one day after American and Saudi troops entered Kuwait City. Iraq's army lay dead or scattered over hundreds of miles on the road to Baghdad. Terrible pictures emerged, although most were censored, and only the more sanitized appeared on our screens. Once again, Claire asked me about war, about memory, about what my eyes had seen rather than the camera lens. I told her she needed to study the technology of firepower, of weaponry, "flesh penetration," cluster munitions and target impact. The science of death, not its sociology. She told me I would one day have to crawl out of my protective shell if I wanted to face the facts of the past.

One month later, as another film school term ended, I set out on my journey to the archive in Provo, Utah, leading me on to Kolya and Yonni in Michigan. We absorbed the lode of my father's tales from DeMille's boxes, but most of the jigsaw stayed unsolved.

The next year, I was back for the second tranche and Kolya's gifts, Aunt Sarah's letters, the poster of the Great Gramby and Kolya's "Soldier's Journal." We read it in turns, as I passed each page to Claire in our cozy nook in Finsbury Park on sunny-late April days and balmy spring nights.

I had a nagging feeling, at the first reading, that there was something, somewhere on our bookshelves that could bear witness to Kolya's strange connections. Sure enough, in a stack on one of the top shelves, there it was: *The Bad Bohemian*, Cecil Parrott's biography of the creator of *The Good Soldier Švejk*, which verified Kolya's most outlandish claims: The feasibility of an encounter with Švejk's author in Siberia, in Chelyabinsk, then Irkutsk, at the cusp of the Civil War... his bigamous marriage to the Russian girl, Shura, despite having left his first wife undivorced in Prague... It was something of a shock, finding the creator of our beloved Švejk, "the regimental idiot," as a Red Army commissar, a traitor to his fellow Czechs who fought and bled their way across the continent, guarding, and partly stealing, the White Admiral Kolchak's stolen gold...

And if that were true, what of all the rest?

Back to the Homeland, with Claire, flying over to attend Kolya's memorial. My mother declined her invitation, pleading bad legs and general decrepitude, though she seemed in good spirits at Melchett Street.

"I want to see out the millennium," she said. "Only five years to go. I'm told it will be a big show. The Christian Messiah will turn up, the world's climate will change, and all our cities will flow out into the sea. Your father will be sorry to miss it, with his old friend Cecil. They'd have a jamboree."

She was in one of her flighty moods, better than the black nights, when she phones abroad and tells anyone who answers the phone that we have all left her completely alone. "What about Matilda from downstairs, who visits you every day?" I asked. But she waved her hand in a familiar gesture. "She's nice, but she only has one story." The one about her dead husband, who was always constant but couldn't earn enough to provide. "I had no future," I remember her saying, "only the day. The past is gone, so what's the point?" It was a sad mantra one grew tired of hearing.

My brother Yitzhak and his wife, Aliza, would sometimes drive up from Jerusalem to see if she needed special attention, but they drove Mother crazy with their religious attentions and their complaints about the complete impossibility of parking anywhere in the vicinity of Rothschild and Allenby. A carer from the municipality turned up on Mondays and made sure she had enough groceries. She was getting more forgetful, though the oldest slights were still hewn in stone. The old family irritation about things that don't fit around the preconceived ideas of necessity.

"You should go and visit them in Jerusalem," my mother tells me.

"Jerusalem gives me a rash," I reply.

But the Project will still force me there, eventually, towards my brother, and his ever-growing number of grandchildren. As of Kolya's passing, my brother Yitzhak has three sons and two daughters, all past their eighteenth year, and I think seventeen grandchildren. And this before I, the rarefied unbeliever, have produced a single child. The bloodline stops here. We all came together just once, since my father's death, at my mother's seventieth birthday. It took place two months after the Oslo Accords of September 1993, when Prime Minister Yitzhak Rabin and the PLO Chairman Yasser Arafat shook hands on the White House lawn under the beaming smile of Bill Clinton to the applause of international notables.

My brother did not exactly mourn this event, which some of us hoped might lead to a genuine peace between Israel and Palestine, and then to cascading agreements with the Arab states, to reconciliation and smiles and kisses and all good things—if not utopia, at least a break in the wall of fear. My brother was among the sceptics who had yet to consult God about His views on current developments, rather than a fanatic of the Whole Land of Israel movement, the settlers and zealots who saw this as a moment of sackcloth and ashes, the secular Left's heresy, an insult to God's covenant with Abraham.

The brotherly brood gathered at Melchett after navigating, with their pre-prepared kosher lunches in sealed plastic containers, past the shameless hippies of Sheinkin Street. They smiled at Claire shyly, having been informed of her status, and she sat smiling at them, having forgotten my advice that she should not try to offer her hand to the boys, who would always draw back in alarm. Cross-gender hugging was out, except between parents and offspring, and then only to a certain age. I had instructed Claire on the plane, but she thought I was mad. Now she knew it was a general condition. Yitzhak's children were very polite and kind, having raised in a well structured compound. One could no more discuss with them the PLO, Yasser Arafat or the background and causes of the Israel-Palestine conflict, than one could discuss James Joyce, John Ford or Pink Floyd. They had heard that Grandpa

Boris had been a photographer of films with an American called Cecil DeMille, and the older ones knew that he had made *The Ten Commandments*, but they had never seen it because they never watched films. My brother had a television set in his house, but they only watched the news and current events, though I am sure Aliza sneaked a peak at fashion programs. They could not be cut off completely, but they spent most of their spare time with holy books. They read the Torah incessantly, they studied the Talmud, the Mishnah and an entire library of works of which I was totally ignorant. I had a glancing knowledge of titles like the Shulchan Aruch, the "set table" of religious exegesis, but I had never looked at a single page of these volumes. We were—nephews, nieces and uncle—strangers, ignorant of each other, citizens of separate worlds.

My mother told me this was my only chance to see my brother and family, as neither he nor his tribe would be traveling to Kolya's memorial. It had been planned and intended as a special tribute from his old Irgun comrades with whom he had fought the long underground war of the revisionist right against the British occupation of Palestine. Only a few of the most senior veterans of the Struggle were present, men and women in their middle eighties, some marching up, some wheeled by proud descendants or nurses onto the stone compound surrounding the stone lion that roared to the sky in the pure blue of a June summer Galilee sky.

Like an old school reunion, they stood bunched together and sang the old songs of battle, led by a small choir of young boys and girls in blue uniforms. They sang "On the Barricades" and the Betar hymn and the anthem that most enraged their rivals in the Zionist left: "Two Banks has the River Jordan—one is ours and so is the other." Then they sang the song that I remember Kolya liked to listen to on his old 1950s gramophone on the rare occasion when I visited him with my father. Since the 1940s, they had lived in a small apartment in an old stone house in the Bukharan quarter of Jerusalem, three tiny rooms in which he and his wife, Magda, had brought up two kids, Adir and Nehama. It was some kind of memorial day, then, for the hanging of some of the old Irgun martyrs. But since one or two of them had also been members of the even more extreme Lehi group, the old "Stern Gang," he put on their own party anthem, a most doleful and somewhat sinister tune that was never played on the state radio. In fact, all the revisionist songs were banned in those days, which was probably why my uncle kept playing them over and over on his crackling turntable, so that even I would remember the words:

> "Anonymous soldiers are we, in no uniforms clad,
> And around us just fear and death's darkness;
> We have all been recruited for all of our lives,
> From the ranks only death can release us.
>
> In the days that are red with pogroms and bloodshed
> In the days that are dark with despair,
> In the cities and towns we shall lift up our flag
> That declares our defence and our conquest.
>
> We have not been enlisted by whips like massed slaves,
> To shed our blood in lands foreign to us,
> Our wish is to live for all time as free souls,
> Our dream—to die for our own land.
> In the days that are red..." (continued anon...)

It had a doom-laden cadence that always impressed me, conjuring an image of a small group of men with masked faces crouched low, hugging the ground, moving through fields from hayrack to hayrack, or creeping around buildings with their hands in their pockets in pouring rain, under glowering skies. When I asked my father about it he just said, "Uncle Kolya had a hard life. Maybe he'll recover some time."

But he just seemed to get angrier and angrier, until, one year after the Sinai war, he sold the house and left with Mattia and my two cousins for America, to become a university teacher. As I was only ten at the time, I couldn't make out at all what the fuss was about. My father said he was upset about the government. He said they were unreconciled "socialists" and he could not live under their tyrannical yoke. I couldn't figure it out, because at school they taught us that we were all both Zionists and socialists, and that this was our particular strength—we took the best from these two great movements.

The zealous socialists were, of course, on the kibbutz, like my Aunt Sarah, whom we would visit quite often. But I did not like the kibbutz; people got up to work there too early. Even though we were always there on vacation days, everyone was expected to be up and out by about 5 o'clock, an idea that filled me with horror. Aunt Sarah lectured me, with quiet firmness, about the great hardship the early pioneers had endured in wresting the land from its malarial slumber, building roads and breaking stones with their bare hands. I could believe it about her, but was pretty glad that I had managed to miss the experience.

I never understood why my father plucked me as a child from paradise, from those rolling Hollywood hills that still beckoned in dreams, images from a baby's stroller of men dressed in clanking silver armor, eating hot dogs, and an image of a man wrestling with a toy lion… "That was Victor Mature," my father told me later. "He wouldn't take on the tame studio cat. *Samson and Delilah*. DeMille still rolling strong at the time."

Once the ancient veterans finished their singing, Kolya's son and daughter, Adir and Nehama, mounted the makeshift podium alongside the leader of the opposition and would-be prime minister, Adir's party boss. He was an unannounced guest, inexplicably sacrificing the television cameras and the pack of journalists that followed him everywhere in this pre-election year. Adir and his leader were a pair, both in formal suits, their bodies propelled by the heft of broad shoulders up the short flight of steps.

He didn't say much, prompted Adir to speak first. I kept the program, which contained Adir's speech. It seemed to go on forever, so here are excerpts:

"The passing of a great man who lived a full and long life is not an occasion for mourning but for celebration. A great son of a great people, Natan ben Avraham Gur-Arieh, my beloved and adored father, lived the struggles, the sorrows, the resurrection and the triumph of his people in all his limbs, in every part of his body, with the full measure of his absolute faith, and in the full knowledge and understanding of the destiny that lay in store for him, and for the nation for whom he was ever willing, at every moment, to lay down his life, and to toil incessantly, for the achievement of our sacred endeavour, for the fulfilment of our ancient promise, for victory in the long and repeated battles that he knew could not be shunned.

"A loyal son of his father, born to a long line of rabbis and scholars, a stalwart comrade to his many brothers and sisters, both of his own family and of the family of fighters that he joined in unceasing struggle, a good and honoured father to my sister Nehama and myself, a beloved grandfather to our children and a lesson to all those who might falter before the magnitude of the task that yet remains to be fully and absolutely fulfilled…"

And so forth, the whole caboodle: The birth village of proud scholars of the Torah, suffering under the yoke of the czarist empire. A time of pogroms and revolutions, learning the endurance and resilience of our people from the wisdom of his father, my grandfather, a scholar and leader, a living reminder of our history and the unquenchable spirit of our faith… torn from his family by the czar's armies, becoming a trained soldier but ever planning to deploy his experience in the interest of his own people… how after many wanderings he reached the shores of his own country and immediately set to searching out those stalwarts who shared his understanding and his ability to rise to the challenges of those fateful times, etcetera etcetera…

I moved the camera off my cousin to film the audience: students of the Tel-Hai College, fresh-faced young boys and girls with rapt expressions bunched up in the sun. There were also some residents

504

of the nearby guesthouse, European and American tourists pricking their ears and trying to read the body language, wondering why the old men in wheelchairs were wiping their eyes and those who could still stand stood as stiff as their bones could allow, on parade, at attention...

Only one of Aunt Sarah's offspring turned up—the middle son, Tsadok—half an hour late. A spry sixty-five-year-old, he came up from the car park, waving as he spotted me in the crowd. I had my camera turned on again, to film the prime minister in waiting as he followed Adir on the podium. Netanyahu gave me a gimlet look as I pointed my lens toward him, but Adir whispered to him, presumably to say that I was family rather than press. I didn't stay on him long, as he ground out the usual plaudits for the deceased: a pillar of faith, determination and courage. His later work as a scholar, his massive project on the subject of "Jew hatred," of which he had become the world's leading authority. This segued smoothly into an election speech, recounting the hazards still faced by our people now steadfast in our own land, but still under attack from all the age-old forces of evil. He counted off the latest outrages: so-called suicide bombers, the double bombing at Beit Lid in January, the terrorists who killed innocent settlers in Judea and Gaza, the continued determination of our enemies to wipe us off the face of the earth. Tsadok shook his head admiringly.

"That man can sell central heating in the Kalahari," he stated, "but can he do anything else? My mother," he said, "your aunt, would turn in her grave. Nobody else wanted to come, but I always had a place in my heart for your uncle. He took a position and he stuck to it, just like my mother. They were two of a kind. So strange, how the same blood flows in opposite streams. That cousin of ours, though, he is a real worm. Give him a good juicy apple and he'll ruin it in five minutes."

He lifted his eyes at Kolya's eldest, Adir. Another party faithful. I used to play with him in the backstreets of downtown Tel Aviv. We would run around the Jaffa docks shooting at seabirds with slingshots. One time an Arab restaurant owner came out of his seafood place and chased us down the quay with a stick. I put it down to experience, but for Adir the moment grew into a policy. Tsadok was not a fan. I had not seen him in years, but had marked his bulldozer deals that cashed in the Occupation and settlements. But he was clearly impatient with the dirge…

"If you and your good woman want to escape from all this, I know a place on the lake in Tiberias," he said. "The fish is better than Jaffa or Acco. Yemeni owners. Let's say our condolence and get the fuck out of here!"

We proceeded in convoy down the Beit She'an valley, he in his Audi and we in our rented Renault, after lingering long enough to pay our respects to Adir and give a brief hug to Nehama, who seemed lost in her own world. I realized that I knew very little about her true self, which was hidden behind the cloak of hostility that enveloped our later years. Adir was hemmed in by his cohorts, strange young men with stern faces who might have been police-men or minor party enforcers. After he went down the row of the elders, pressing hands and whispering in ears, the Candidate's official bodyguards shooed him away to his car.

One forgets the beauty of one's country when enmeshed in its political horrors. We drove past the lush green hillsides, the open fields, the neat houses and fences of roadside settlements, green lawns on which water sprinklers revolved on the grass. To the right, I pointed out to Claire the two gaunt peaks of the Horns of Hittin, where the Muslim general Saladin trounced the Christian king of Jerusalem, Guy of Lusignan, and destroyed the Crusader army in AD 1187, so that Saladin could retake the Holy City.

"What about Richard the Lionheart?" she asked.

"He came later," I said. "He took Acre, but failed to reconquer Jerusalem, and so he went back, to fight the French in their own country."

"Just keep your eyes on the road," she replied.

Pretty soon, the expanse of the lake shimmered ahead. Light blue and quiet, and looking like someone's private fishpond rather than a subject of legend. At Tiberias, along the lake's northwest shore, we found Tsadok's favored fish place. It was like an old shack, one that might have stood on the shore in the days before modernity and all its discontents took the place of rosy dreams. The walls were wood-covered with aged panels, the log-lined roof was flat and flew the blue-and-white flag and a large sign said "Cafe Yehezkel." We ate on wood tables set out on a porch overlooking the lakes' languid ripples, with the long day's dipping sun etching out the Golan mountains on the far side...

Memories of almost three decades past, the sunny spring leading to the hot, burning days of the 1967 war, when those hills were still part of Syria, and now the enemy was pushed further back, out of sight. I looked at Claire but said nothing of this to Tsadok, to avoid an unwanted diatribe. He gave forth in any case, over the large plate of Greek salad as we waited for our fish to be ready, speaking in a mixture of Hebrew and English for Claire, venting his spleen on the veterans' memorial, the blood-curdling songs, the evocation of barricades, blood and fire, the crown and scepter of greatness and all the other high-flying language.

"My mother built this country with her bare hands, right? We all know that. She believed in something more than slogans. You know me, Asher, you can't suspect me of being some kind of Marxist or leftist, whatever. I am a businessman. I work with money to make things work in this country..." He waved his fork, pointing up to the heavens. "She was of her own time, you know what I'm saying? She came to this place when there was no Jewish presence here except a few houses on the sand and a lot of hungry Shnipishoker Polish and Romanians who didn't know their ass from a hole in the field. And the Arabs who didn't want our sorry ass anywhere here. She wrote a lot of high-flown BS in her time, God keep her soul, like all those kibbutz people did in those days. Boy, they could talk! I used to hear the old people going on in our salon from five o'clock in the afternoon until five in the morning. The theories! The collective principle, the 'stychian' processes, spiritual materialization, yada, yada! But they were also doers, makers, agronomists, engineers; they made things happen, they set the foundations! No? Am I wrong? Am I completely crazy? So tell me, have I gone completely insane in my old age?"

The answer was obvious but one had to let him rant on: "OK, so those people of Kolya's backed up the system with some firepower against the Arabs and shot some British soldiers, poor fucking bastards who were sent from London or Liverpool to keep the Jews and the Arabs screwed down. Colonizers! So? Who wasn't a colonizer? Even your father, the smartest guy I ever met, Asher, smart and bright, a real artist, who left a great and well-paid career to come to this country, for what? Did you ask him, Asher? I never did. I just accepted that he had come home. Why? It's written in the Bible? OK. I'm not a religious or a spiritual person. I do business, for the state, for my profit. We are not a Soviet Socialist Republic, thank God. They sent me to M.I.T. to learn how to do it the American way. Make the market work and everybody profits eventually. Despite all the screaming and yelling. But today? Look at those people there on the stand! All that talk of struggle, sacrifice, selflessness and devotion! Those people have made business in this country into the biggest racket since Al Capone."

Then he really flew on, even through the fish course, which he gobbled between mouthfuls of bile. How everything nowadays is all about who you know at the top, and the bastards up there who take their cut off everything and have the country sewn up. Mafiosi from Russia who bled their own country dry after the fall of communism and lived in the pockets of Yeltsin and Putin. Portioning out the big cake, oil, diamonds, gold, gas. How they needed to get to the hub, in the West, and found our state a convenient stepping stone. How all the politicians got their snouts in the trough and gobbled up everything they could find. Military industries, construction, real estate.

"I deal with bulldozers, right? Small potatoes. The real money is in construction. You can build a hotel in Jerusalem that nobody needs, Never mind, you can build it, somebody will come sooner or later! Why not build three? Why not build six, eight, twelve?

You just have to grease a few palms. Then you can diversify out of the state, right? You can build in Greece, in Rhodes, in Turkey, even maybe, who knows, in Saudi Arabia one day? Money has no color, no race, no creed. Money doesn't care who you are, Jew, Christian, Moslem, your ethnic group, your party, your politics. Who do you think builds the settlements here? The Arabs, your Palestinian friends. They are the workers, along with a few Thais or Koreans. Who supplies the cement? Your friends in the PLO, your great heroes. One hand washes the other. All your idealistic talk and protests and demonstrations and marching in the streets won't stop it. It's a law of nature. You know their latest plan? They're going to build a casino, in Jericho. You don't believe me? Just wait, it'll take two or three years. Everybody's in it, our ministers, their chairman, their revolutionary committees, our security people. Everybody's just ziggy-ziggy together. Just where the old refugee camp stands, there will rise a magnificent building, with tables and halls right out of Las Vegas. And all the Israelis will come down to the West Bank to gamble, and play roulette and go crazy on the gaming machines. The future is bright, my friend. The future is shekels, Jordanian dinars, dollars, sterling, yen, rubles, and soon the new European notes, whatever they're called."

"And justice?" asked Claire. "Human rights? Some honesty? The occupation, armies, fences, checkpoints, freedom of movement? Freedom of speech?"

"Ah!" Tsadok rolled his eyes to the heavens and picked the last morsels from the bones of his fish. "Dream on, comrades. Dream on."

We passed on dessert and sat for a while in the sun, watching a group of toddlers chivvied down to the shore by their young mothers in their skimpy beach gear. Wearing wraparound sunglasses, Tsadok threw his head back and raised his face to the sky.

He insisted on paying, and Claire submitted to a Middle East farewell, a brush of his lips on both cheeks. Just before he climbed back into his Audi he turned and said, "That Uncle Kolya of ours. He had lots of secrets."

"I know," I said, keeping some of my own.

"Did you ever find any clues about the others?" he asked. "Our uncle Yakov, the magician? Uncle Ze'ev, Aunt Judit? I asked about her in China, you know. But nobody had a clue. You should keep digging. There might be a book there somewhere. Or one of those big Hollywood films, like that Schindler thing, but not so heavy on Shoah business."

"I am on the case," I told him.

But I was not so sure.

*

Back in London, Claire's experimental theater group was making plans for a possible show based on the life and travels of her globetrotting uncle, Maurice. The family war hero, he had flown in Lancaster bombers and then toured the world in the postwar recovery. He had seen India, Malaya, Mesopotamia-Iraq, Trans-Jordan and Palestine during the time that my Uncle Kolya was busy planning to blow up as many British soldiers as he could manage. Tales of perfidy of the ungrateful Jews, which Claire had sometimes heard at home, back in the day... Maurice had spent the war years squinting through his bomb sights in the bubble stuck in the back of "the crate," siting his bombs onto German targets. In later years he turned his mechanical expertise to designing scenery and props for West End theaters, where he had worked in peacetime during his boyhood. Maurice was Claire's link to the stage; meanwhile, her parents remained happy in Avon, in their perfect English inertia, cultivating the family and giving afternoon teas. He commuted to his work from a neat little bachelor home out in Wimbledon, attended a few reunions at the RAF club in Piccadilly but never watched the glut of post-war movies on the TV. The only movie he would ever watch, Claire said, was *Reach for the Sky*, starring Kenneth More as the war pilot Douglas Bader, who lost his legs but still recovered to fly. "He was a foul-mouthed bastard," she said of the legend in real life, "but he had a reason to be."

"You had the 'good war,'" I used to tell her, "but we got the wreckage. We took in the myth but screwed the reality." Claire said her uncle had not seen it that way. She had asked him, as she grew up, what he had thought of as he sat above the German cities and factories, over his deadly payload. "All he said was, 'I just looked down and checked the crosshairs and gave the pilot the signal. And then I said, Bombs away.'After that he would clam up. He never liked to talk about it at all."

Claire's uncle Maurice died just before we two met. All I told her was "He did the right thing." But all I had was 1967. The six days, rather than six years, when everything passed in a flash, the state's unquestioned military triumph, the sudden crushing of enemies, an ancient promise redeemed, the sons of Abraham raised up, the sons of Ishmael brought down, the skinny borders of 1948 suddenly puffed out like the wings of a peacock, stretching across the hills, valleys, mountains and deserts that encompassed so many sites of ancient myth, from the Hermon to Mount Sinai itself and the treasure chest of old Jerusalem, the invisible city behind the wall... not quite as far as Kolya's promise, but at least to the full length of the Jordan. And the cameraman, hefting his own weapon: Arriflex 16mm ST...

"What did you see in your sights, Asher? What did you see?"

I was not quite as reticent as her uncle, but I had pictures, moving black-and-white images, the shreds of the reels of film footage put together at the Army Spokesman Office in Tel Aviv, courtesy of my father's old friends at the Geva Studios, who dutifully snipped off shots discarded by the censor and prepared three-minute edits that were copied and sent off to television and newsreel companies whose own cameramen were kept away from the battlefields. As I had neglected to keep any of these reels for myself, I could only show Claire the compilation put together after the war by the government information office, the commercial video of the official war "documentary" called "The Six Day War" in Hebrew but given the sonorous title of "Follow Me" for the VHS English version. We had to purchase a player, so that we could follow the trail. The Maurice show never materialized.

"Bear in mind," I told Claire, "what you're watching is between eighty and ninety percent fake. It's film shot after the war when the various units were recalled for special reserve duties to restage the battles so that they could present the authorized version. There were only two of us and the driver in the original unit, so we had to recruit about a dozen extra camera operators and equip them with semi-professional sixteen-mil cameras that we requisitioned from camera shops. In the end, the generals didn't like what we filmed: too many dead bodies, burnt vehicles, blurry shots of explosions too far away—you don't see much. Before Vietnam, there wasn't so much competition to get the blood and guts in close-up. So they preferred to reshoot the war, and get the tanks firing, the infantry rushing to battle, the command-cars crashing through the gates of the Old City. 'Real war,' not the concoction of wimps."

So there I was, giving Claire my running commentary for each shot: "Authentic prewar newsreel... Mimish Herbst—Reuters... Joe Shmo, ABC News... That early dawn stuff—fake... Hilik Ne'eman shooting in the Sinai, David Gurfinkel, Jerusalem, genuine... Sinai, fake... hey, that's one of mine!" Mortars firing across the lines at Gaza... Cut to tanks wobbling ahead of the lens, firing—"Fake, fake, fake... The dead bodies, that's another of ours... maybe Yachin Hirsch, or Mimish Herbst..."

"What do all these names mean to me?" she asked. "How could I know these people?"

"You asked for facts," I told her. "That's what there is. That's another one of mine," I added, at a clip showing more soldiers cheering, cut in from another vantage entirely.

She sighed, and gave me the look that meant that whatever I had set out on my stall, she wasn't buying.

"I see what you shot," she said, "but what did you see?"

"Somebody said 'Bombs away!' And I pressed the trigger..."

We ordered pizza and watched the news: "Hijacked Lufthansa jet leaves Aden in surprise flight... Germany still refuses to free jailed terrorists... Fighting resumes in South Lebanon, PLO shelling

Christian positions... Student riots in Swaziland... Japanese police storm a hijacked bus in Nagasaki, killing one hijacker, wounding seven passengers... assistant chaplain at Brixton prison resigns after exposure as member of the National Front..." The world as ever mired in its confusions. Can one be forever culpable?

Those were the days of the Women's Theatre Co-op, in which Claire was a mere equal member, although she was ipso facto the director. Back to peacetime affairs, the new era of gender awareness, lesbian and sexual politics, work with the "Monstrous Regiment" and other provocatively titled assemblies. I remember a play called "Is Dennis the Menace?," in which the performers wore Beano costumes and made hay with male and female roles, though I became confused, I think, with Korky the Cat. Claire's suggestion that I should play the role of Beryl the Peril was scotched by my insistence on turning up with a Groucho moustache, a notion vetoed by the majority sisterhood.

So we passed our time, recoiling at the enduring buzz of London on the cusp of the collapse of the long years of Labour and the shrill baying of a very different kind of feminism: Thatcher's Britain. Returning at irregular intervals to Shai Baer's Hub in Queen's Park, where the stubborn group of Israelo-Palestinians gathered around Shai's garden table discussing new mushroom phases and the never-ending disorders of Middle East politics as the rumbles of more conflict north of the Litani River presaged yet another outbreak of war. But my father's illness called me back to Tel Aviv, to Melchett Street, and the need to move him to the refuge of more professional help, as the crawl of time caught up with his dreams...

In May 1982 I called Claire from Melchett Street to say my father had been moved from Tel Aviv to Jerusalem to be closer to my brother Yitzhak and his carers, with my mother in tow, and was now in a hospice overlooking the Hill of Rest, Jerusalem's big graveyard for civilians and soldiers. "He's obsessed with Yakov and my other missing uncles and aunts," I told her. "He wants me to find them all."

"How many more are there?" she asked.

"I told you about them all," I said. "The four brothers and the two sisters. I told you about Sarah, who came to Palestine to break stones and create the Jewish state. And about Uncle Kolya, who used to be a Bolshevik and then an Irgun terrorist and is now the world's greatest expert on 'Jew hatred through the ages.'"

"You ticked them off, like items in a box," she said, "but you never told me much about them."

"What's to say? Wandering Jews. I told you about the Great Gramby, Yakov, the magician. Dad used to talk about him a lot. He was his favorite. We all agreed Kolya was a shmuck."

"What about the two who went to China? You should talk to him about them." She was going to say "before it's too late," but didn't.

"They went," I said. "Nobody found them."

"That's not a story," she said.

"I need to get out of here," I said, "before the war starts and I have trouble getting the army exit permit."

"Is there really going to be a war?"

"There's always going to be a war."

I came back. The war took place. We watched on television. The tanks rolled in, the people streamed out of cities, villages, towns, filling the roads and fields like replays of well-worn tragedies. The censor's cut could not prevail in the Age of CNN and global reach. Too many cameras clustered, turned on each hammer blow, each moment of terror, each blunder, each war crime, each new atrocity tumbling across the other. Fresh news for every stale day. Back in a fine London summer, we marched uselessly around Trafalgar Square. Down with this, down with that. Protest, denounce, repudiate. Familiar slogans and familiar faces, all the class reunion from Shai's garden. Shouting in the square below Nelson's stone-blind eye, pecked by pigeons.

"What did you see, Asher? What did you see?"

The tired intensity of war, the gaudy repetition, the metal hunks firing, the smoke of buildings burned out, the cries of the cast out, the corpses of the fallen. The women screaming, waving their hands. The shrieks of running kids. Nothing new under the sun. All has been recorded elsewhere. Those who do not witness, watch.

I see a rectangular screen, with moving images and an immense crowd of "news gatherers" converging on each node of pain, waving their microphones and speaking earnestly of this or that strategic move. I see newscasts recorded from the attacking side, talking, I can hear, in Hebrew about "light precipitation on targets of firing," as if the artillery shells are harbingers of early autumn. I take my camera out to film protesters, but it is all too late. As luck will have it, my wisdom teeth begin erupting on September 16, 1982, as the first news comes through of a mass killing taking place in the Palestinian refugee camps of Sabra and Shatila, on the outskirts of Beirut. The Israeli army had moved into the capital despite the cease-fire that the Americans and their Lebanese-born emissary, Philip Habib, had brokered to allow the PLO's fighters to embark en masse from the city's port, leaving their own people undefended as the slaughterers of the Christian Phalange militia moved in to serve out another long-awaited revenge. Shortly after being elected president of Lebanon, in a rigged ballot under our auspices, their clan leader, Bashir Gemayel, was blown up in his own headquarters, probably by a Syrian bomb. According to the Israeli army, all that had happened in the camps was a routine sweep for straggling militants. The film cameramen who were on hand to record the results, however, captured bodies piled on bodies, men, women and children cut down and mutilated in the streets, under our soldiers' own blind eyes. If I were a writer, I could attempt a description.

"What did you see?"

I saw nothing. My teeth exploded in a volcanic thrust up the gums, searing me into the bedroom. But still there was the BBC foreign service, dribbling the facts into my ear.

The massacres went on through the nights, with Israeli paratroops lighting flares for the Phalangists. If they did not light the flares, said the official army "explainer," how could the militia troops distinguish between the innocent and the guilty?

"I don't understand," said Claire. "I don't understand."

"There's nothing to understand," I told her desperately. "I need to register with a dentist."

But she could only hold my hand, as far away others died, and killed, for a cause that had once been mine, in the age of conformity and the eternal blind eye...

"A whole people to get moving out of bondage"

Boris:

*(Draft in Professor Gurevits papers, Box 312, folder "Personal";
hold for Archive only. [Y.S.])*

It was *The Ten Commandments* that prevented me seeing my brother
Yakov in Paris after he wrote to me in 1923. DeMille had the bit between his teeth ever since he set up his fake competition for people
to write in to the studio and choose their own theme for his next
picture after *Adam's Rib*. That was another of his tall tales about
a Jazz Age flapper whose father is a Chicago business magnate
and her mother is a neglected wife who jumps into the arms of
an exotic foreigner, Jaromir, the exiled king of Morania, played of
course by Teddy Kosloff. The girl falls for an old anthropologist
who thinks she's a flibbertigibbet, the "new woman," full of gas
and gaiters. Kosloff got to do his ballet stuff in "Ancient Arcadia,"
leaping about in a leopard skin with a flute, while the cave-age
professor knits his brows and makes the first bow and arrow. At
the end of the picture, the young girl goes all the way to Honduras
to prove her true love to the prof.

The picture did all right, but DeMille was treading water.
He really wanted to stretch his wings this time around. He hadn't
done a period epic since the Aztec film, back in '17, and that
scraped the bottom of the box office barrel. Lasky just wanted him
to go on making Jazz Age pictures, like *The Affairs of Anatol*, which
was a smash hit. But the old man was ruminating. You would find
him in his office reading the Bible, and whatever bit of business
you wanted to deal with, whether it was cameras, new lenses or

your salary, which could get mislaid in the cracks sometimes, he would slam the book shut and say: "Moses! Now that's one hell of a story! A whole people to get moving out of bondage! Now isn't that worth spending some dough?"

The only answers DeMille wanted to hear in this mood were either "Yes, C.B." or "Absolutely, C.B." One could see the glint in his eyes whenever a certain battle loomed on the horizon, the flash of Pharaoh's spears just glinting off the top of the hill. I knew that he had already put forth a budget of nearly a million dollars, but the buzz around the studio was that Lasky, who made the final decision, was being squeezed by the Wall Street bankers, who didn't see where all this Bible hoopla was leading. After all, DeMille had never made a biblical picture before, and even his best historical, the Joan of Arc epic from 1916, had barely broke even after all the costs and promos were factored in. It was only those who watched his pictures closely—for content, not just for profits, like the smart critics or us spear carriers in the front ranks—who knew how much he was worrying about life in general, and things like moral codes, values and God.

Moses, the babe in the bullrushes, the desperate mother, the enslaved Israelites, the human story of Pharaoh's wife, the arrogance of the tyrant, the dogged courage and perseverance of the prophet, and that great breakout: "the greatest jailbreak in history, Boris! What do you think of that?" The great crowd, families, their cattle, their sheep, their chattels, the pursuit by Pharaoh's massed armies, the confrontation by the Red Sea, and then the miracle by the flourishing of Moses' staff: "Behold, his mighty hand!"

He would stand there, in the office that he'd kitted out like a room in a baronial hall, with roof beams and panels of stained wood, fixed with hunting trophies, caribou heads, fish in glass cases, leopard and bear skins over the soft chairs and divans and endless props hung on the walls: coats of mail from Joan of Arc, "Aztec" feather dresses and ornamental headgear, old Bulgarian rifles, a crocodile skin that seemed to have crawled over from *Fool's Paradise* and even a few dinosaur bones from his latest picture.

Pride of place, however, was a huge artist's impression of the soon-to-be-built palace of Pharaoh, an enormous gaunt room with Egyptian columns and a vast eagle whose stone wings formed the Pharaoh's grand throne. It stood right over DeMille's own plush chair, in which he sat behind his desk, drumming his fingers together as he waited for his supplicants to stumble over the huge bearskin rug that stretched from the door.

"Are you ready for this, Boris? Now this is your own story, isn't it? The people crying out for succor, the arrival of the savior, the man of courage, the hero, to tear off the chains and lead the way? You would think it was obvious, wouldn't you? But not to the front office, no, that'd be too much to hope for, too much sense to cram into their tiny skulls!"

He was in his most ambitious mode, planning to shoot at least part of the picture in the new Technicolor system, which was at that time still a two-color, rather than the later three-color process. The test runs were still far from perfect, as the colors would run very strange; reds and greens and purples were ample, but it was still difficult to get a blue sky and real-looking sands. One of the early ideas was to take the whole crew and cast out to Egypt and shoot the mass scenes of the Israelite exodus in its ancient location, with Mount Sinai standing in for Mount Sinai. But even DeMille was wary of trying this on with the front office, in case they pulled the plug on the whole project and had the boss carted off to the sanatorium in the hills of Los Feliz.

"The Parting of the Sea! That's going to be the real zinger!" he said. "That has to be the best scene in the entire history of motion pictures. Forget all these shivering glass shots. The whole thing has to be completely believable. If we can't believe that the hand of God parts the waters, what the fuck are we in this business for? Everything has to be absolutely true. From the smallest buckle on the soldier's shoe to the multitudes that walk through on dry land. Behold the mighty power of the Lord!"

He waved the script in our faces like the rod of Moses. We all had to go with the current or be dashed on the rocks and perish with Pharaoh's armies. DeMille lashed everyone to the wheel and then went off for a winter cruise down to Mexico as we toiled up the coast on the Guadalupe sands, south of Pismo, where the great walls of Pitom and Rameses were being raised by hundreds of Italian laborers. It was at least closer to civilization than Death Valley, where DeMille's rival, Erich von Stroheim, was shooting his own saga, *McTeague*.

It was one hell of a scene. Like an exodus from Los Angeles itself, about two and a half thousand people headed up the coast in a huge convoy of trucks, carrying building materials, wood, plaster, sheet metal and thousands of animals, sheep, goats, camels, horses, oxen, dogs, cats—and these for the movie crew alone! Apart from the builders and carpenters there were telephone linesmen, electricians, architects, dressmakers, musicians, caterers, cooks, doctors, all surging into "Camp DeMille," with its five hundred sleeping tents and massive mess tents, each of which could hold up to one thousand diners. And that was before the cast of extras turned up. DeMille's obsession with authenticity had no limits; he had sent off to the Jewish parts of the city and as far north as San Francisco for a whole host of "genuine Hebrews," many of them new immigrants who had flooded over during the Great War, whose English was pretty basic but were fluent in Yiddish, German, Polish and Russian. There was a whole contingent of Hasidic Jews in Eastern European religious regalia, with side curls, black hats and thick coats in the stifling heat of the desert, who gave the camp authorities a hard time when the usual ham sandwich lunches were doled out.

DeMille called me up and asked, "What do I do? What do I do?" I suggested he hire a few genuine rabbis who could advise on daily issues. They set up a synagogue, and three times a day they swayed and genuflected and prayed for "next year in Jerusalem." There was no point telling DeMille that the ancient Israelites didn't look like this, as he had all the costumes ready: the old robes, the torn garments, the Arab-style head coverings and crates of false beards for those who didn't have their own whiskers. All this was costing him more than thirty thousand dollars a day, and we were never sure when we got up in the morning if this would be the day the men from Wall Street would turn up and shut the whole show down.

Amid all this, the studio post brought me Yakov's letter, which had been mailed in Paris in the middle of April. Inside were several pages in a handwriting that I did not recognize as my brother's, but I soon realized was written by Alma in his name. The only letters I had from Yakov in the last two years, since he embarked across the Atlantic, were very brief. Even in the best of times, he was not much good at putting words on paper or keeping in touch by verbal means. Communicating in dreams, that was more his style. Sometimes I felt he was calling me at night, over some occult wire, perhaps by tarot card whispers or Masonic signs. This was a longer letter, which I filed away, but it got lost in the house move Bella and I made from Silver Lake to Franklin. It was a sore loss, since it was the letter in which Alma broke the news in Yakov's name of our mother's death back "at home."

We had not uttered those words—*Der heim*—in a long time. My head has been crammed so full of DeMille's movies, so many sets and locations framed through the camera lens, that it is becoming more and more difficult to conjure up those vanished days. Some day I must set time aside and sit down to write, perhaps as a script, or a lengthy treatment, the annals of those early years. I am sure they can be retrieved, if only one sets one's mind to it. Nothing is totally lost; one simply requires the time and the will…

I remember the letter paper, five or six pages, was marked with the letterhead of the Hotel Jacob, in the Rue Jacob, I think it was number 44, an address that would have taken my brother's fancy as well as luring him by providential accident. After I read the letter I looked up the address in the Baedeker guide I had kept from some years back and found it was in the 6th Arrondissement, not far from the Left Bank of the Seine.

Alma wrote, in Yakov's name, that they had heard from Sarah, out east working the land in Palestine, and she had heard from our little sister Judit that our mother had passed away in January, soon after the Christian new year. It had been a cold and bleak winter, but she had adequate shelter at the house of our cousins Barenboim, who were the senior rabbinical family in the village since my father passed away five years before, soon after the October Revolution. Since then she lived in the hope of her son's and daughter's return, but Kolya was lost, out in the storm of nations, and sent curt messages of his existence, in Galicia, in Saint Petersburg and even one strange missive, Sarah had reported, from Irkutsk in Siberia. Then silence. Zev resumed his traveling, about two years before the current letter, with his Odessa trading partner. Judit was at school, then enrolled at the gymnasium opened by the learned teachers soon after the region was recaptured by Romania.

When the war ended, I made certain efforts to persuade our mother and Judit to leave the village for the United States. Once the Romanians were firmly in charge, the old activities of the American Jewish Joint Distribution Committee—known simply as the Joint—resumed, distributing aid money from the US and helping to set up schools and agriculture. It also supported the Jews in Palestine, and Sarah pleaded with Judit to join her there. But our mother always refused. I received one letter, delivered by the Joint, in her handwriting, in Yiddish, but it was strange and garbled, like the wanderings of a troubled and lost mind. She wrote that the souls of both the dead and the living converged at night on their birthplace and gathered to protect the living. But if the living were not present, the dead souls would fly away to seek them, so they could all be reconciled. The dead souls could only rest among the graves of their forefathers, and even those who died in the Land of Israel would be cut off and alone.

These were very strange utterances from the wife of a rabbi, whom I remember as well versed in the scriptures and laws as our dear and revered father on whom be peace. But it was clear she was determined to be buried at his side, and so it had come to be. Judit refused to leave her mother, and was always waiting for the irregular visits of the traveler Ze'ev, who appeared in the village at least once a year and then vanished again, west and east. He never wrote a word, and even his image began to fade before my eyes. Was he tall, short, sturdy, fragile? I could hardly remember. He seemed like a flying avatar of our brother Yakov's fancy, a living wraith flitting in and out of the magician's wide sleeve. I asked the Joint representative who came to Los Angeles to convey a letter to him, but there was no reply, and the emissary himself, one Elstein, wrote me that he could not locate him, and had passed the letter to Judit.

I tried to imagine myself in our mother's place, like a matriarch in one of those Yiddish melodramas, in which everyone is scattered and lost in the nooks and crannies of the wide world. That was her truth: I had left, then Yakov, then Kolya had been brutally snatched away, and changed utterly, and then Ze'ev had flown, and then Sarah. And only the girl child remained.

What was my truth? After the great war's armistice, travel to *Der heim* was, in practice, feasible, since Romania was an ally of the Entente powers, friendly to both England and France. The borderline of the chaos and terror of the civil war in Bolshevik Russia was not far, across the Dniester, but far enough to be safe. The fault was mine, marooned in America, the Land of Plenty, a busy man, always at work, always active, pursuing my business, my craft and my art. Hitched to a tireless, unflagging tyrant, film followed film, unending enterprise, new frontiers to capture in the frame. Beyond each horizon was another, and time was swallowed as if the days simply galloped past like the frenzied human puppets of the Keystones, slapping each other down, emptying reservoirs, crashing motor vehicles over cliffs and hanging on to the wingtips of airplanes.

And so our mother died without seeing the return of her sons and her eldest daughter, but in the comfort of knowing she would spend eternity at our father's side. Services were conducted by the Rabbi Barenboim, but of the immediate family, only the younger daughter was present, so a proper Kaddish had not been said.

Alma's letter, on Yakov's behalf, said Sarah had written that Judit was not too concerned for these rituals, since she too had drifted away from the customs and shared her sister's socialist convictions, though not her abiding passion for Zion. Perhaps she had become a Bolshevik too, or some kind of "vik," though this could not be stated in her letter from Romania, which guarded against Bolshevism as against the bubonic plague. Having missed out on her schooling during the years of war turmoil, she had been accepted as an older student at the gymnasium and had graduated in the fall of 1922. Her ambition, said Sarah, was to study philosophy at the university of Bucharest, but this seemed an unlikely ambition for a Jewess from a provincial village. Once again, Yakov hinted, we should make some new effort to bring her out from that peasant sinkhole, to Paris, or New York, or California. I had written Yakov, in his previous address in the Rue Clichy, that I still occasionally crossed paths with Chaplin, who was always busy on his own account, and Yakov wrote to me once, like a child, that I should kiss the great man on both cheeks on his behalf. But I did not bother to explain to him that one did not do those things in America.

"I am riding around," I remember he (or Alma) wrote: "I am like a trained monkey in the circus arena. I pretend to so much power that I do not have. I am a puff of smoke, that evaporates to leave nothing but a slightly pungent smell. I have a new act, a bit like those old movies I remember seeing when I first came to New York, in the old fleapits, those magic movies about the trip to the moon. Every evening now I cut off my own head and show it to the crowd, and then I reattach it. It's called 'the Execution of Landru.'"

I remember that because I read about the case in the Examiner. A French bourgeois clerk married some twelve women, one by one, and murdered them for their money. The strangest thing about it, I recall, was that none of the bodies was ever found. (That did not save the ghoul, however, from the guillotine.) But Alma wrote, on her own behalf, in the letter, that as a couple, they were doing well. They were thinking of moving out of the hotel on the Rue

Jacob for a proper apartment, but Vassily—as she always called Yakov—wanted to stay on the same street. She did not have to tell me about his superstitions. I should come and visit. My brother dreamed of me often, and always conjured me up in the cards. She did not say which of the mythical creatures I was in the dealt hand: the Emperor, the Heirophant, the Hermit, the Hanged Man, the Angel or Devil, or perhaps the Moon or the Sun. Paris is a great city, she wrote, the center of the world. Everyone came here, everyone could have a place here, life was hard, but people were equal. Black and white, Jew and gentile, even Mohammedans. America spoke freedom, but Paris lived it. They were content. She was so sorry about our mother. It is a pain that is part of life.

I did not know her well, Alma. She was an assistant, someone who stood by the magician's cabinet, dressed scantily or in Arabian robes, flourishing his weave of colored handkerchiefs. The Maharajah's little princess. And what had become of the little negro sultan? The shimmy-player of Chicago? He too, I had heard, went to Paris, with his Creole Dixie Band.

Perhaps they were converging there, all the free spirits. But I was in Egypt, south of Pismo, perspiring in DeMille's bondage. Hammering and sawing all around me as Pharaoh's walls grew higher. Not much chance of breaking off from this to travel off to Paris, let alone to the graveyard in the distant fields of Celovest.

Once again, the old forsaking. Once again, one turns one's back. I went down the main thoroughfare of the great camp, heading to the cluster of tents of the hired Children of Israel. Men with beards sitting on benches trying on their rough garments, their chipped sandals and hairy shirts. Women sat on folding chairs sewing sleeves and skirts. The eagle eye of the dress mistress made the rounds, ensuring that no modern hairpins were visible in the camera's unblinking gaze. I asked one old lag to show me the way to the "synagogue." He showed me to a tent just at the back of one of the dining areas, where I found the rabbi—not a Moses but an authentic Aaron, Aaron Markovitz, who was a tall, modern conservative in a simple suit.

"Thank God I am behind the camera!" he said. I told him I needed to say a Kaddish for my mother, who had passed away abroad. He expressed his condolences and told me I could say the prayer alone, or, if I wished to follow the tradition, I could wait half an hour for the late-afternoon prayer, which would provide a quorum. He sat and spoke to me about grief and guilt and distance, like an old friend, while all around us the full measure of fantasy ravaged the clean coastal air. An overseer passed, waving his whip, as a driver tried to marshal a dozen camels to proceed in a straight row. One of the assistant directors rushed by, shouting in a loud voice: "Where's the Ark? Where's the Ark?"

The rabbi shrugged. "Madness," he said, "but still somehow sublime."

The half hour passed. The tent filled up with the devout, a round dozen. Sufficiently over the ten for a minyan. The rabbi spoke with them and the men all pressed my hand. The few women were huddled in a separate corner of the tent. They too murmured their condolences. The rabbi helped me adjust the prayer shawl, but I did not don the phylacteries, the tefillin, and shook my head when the rabbi offered them to me.

I intoned the prayer for the dead, as prompted by the rabbi, reading the old letters from the prayer book, which appeared worn and delicate from much usage:

"*Yisgadal veyishtabach shmei rabbah...*" I said the words, but somehow they did not move me. I saw only the tent, and the sandy floor covered with infinite grains that could never be cleared away, and the awkwardly shifting extras, already drawing their ten dollars a day. Time is money. I could hear my watch ticking.

A camera conference at 6 p.m… DeMille had already heard of my loss. He instantly proclaimed a moment's silent prayer on my behalf. Everyone sat with clasped hands and had to wait for their dinner. He was an old ham, and could never resist a dramatic moment, but he was massively generous with both the crew and actors he employed time after time. At the end of the meal he called me over and told me that our mutual friend Kosloff, the ballet dancer, and his regular foreign character type, was due to leave for Paris very soon with two relatives from Russia on a rare tour by the Moscow Modern Theatre. He had turned down a good role as a pharaonic overseer for this opportunity, and DeMille gave him his blessing.

We trucked Teddy Kosloff up, at DeMille's expense, just to meet me. I gave him my brother's address and a hastily written letter, with a special request to Alma to write me a longer piece on her life with Yakov in the luminous city. I also wrote a quick letter to Judit in the hope it would travel easier from France to Romania than all the way from California.

Kosloff embraced me in the old-fashioned way and got back in DeMille's chauffeur-driven car for the long haul back. He was a soft-spoken Russian with piercing eyes that could suddenly blaze, and that cat's grace of the born dancer. DeMille had plucked him from the Ballets Russes of Serge Diaghilev at the troupe's premiere in Los Angeles in 1916. I had seen their advertisements in Paris back in 1909, when they had first left their homeland. But I was an anarchist then, and a daily drudge with Victor Kibalchich and Almereyda at the Gaumont studios in Belleville. Those tiny comedies of five and ten minutes, chasing escaped cheeses down cobbled alleys. Now I returned to the stormy whirlwind of DeMille's circus, the camera tests with the new Technicolor giants, mounted on their enormous cranes, able to rise up and observe the whole multitude: the tents, the walls, the gathering extras milling about and awaiting instructions, hanging together in clumps talking and gesticulating, scratching their coarse costumes or trying out mock sword-fights with their flat mock-Egyptian blades. Children chasing goats around the tents, pursued by furious wardens trying to coax the animals back in their pens. I remembered the words of the Haggadah, the ritual intonation that we all spoke in unison, once a year, at the feast, that "in each generation, every one must see himself as if he had come out of Egypt..."

And in a flash, I remembered the table of my father, and all of us crammed against the best tablecloth that my mother and sisters had laid out with the special Passover bowls and cruets and wineglasses and cutlery, and all of us gazing forward towards the great bulky figure at the apex, propped against his pile of our best cushions, his beard on his chest, his lips moving sonorously, leading the invocation, under his great big black fez-like cap that was only used for special occasion and made him look like an oriental pasha, presiding over his unruly subjects...But I looked down, and actors were all I saw.

Theodore Kosloff's report:
July, 1923, Paris, Los Angeles

My arrival in Paris coincided with two events which were causing turmoil in the impulsive world of Parisian theater. For the first, the music halls were up in arms over a new decree by the French government that sought to suppress all stage performances that offended against the public morals. Apparently music halls were featuring not only women so scantily dressed that their fig leaf loincloths were virtually transparent but men were appearing in the nude too! At the Palace music hall in the Boulevard Montmartre, a summons was issued to Harry Pilcer and two ladies, Mlles. Rahna and Zouliaka, who were the first to be charged by the public prosecutor. M. Pilcer, the American, was accused of playing the leading part in Debussy's "L'Apres-midi d'un Faune," with the two ladies as his attendant nymphs. The good Harry protested, quite correctly, that when Nijinski appeared in the Russian Ballet at no less august a venue than the Champs Elysees Theatre, he danced naked to the waist, whereas he, Harry, was covered up to the neck in a dappled animal skin. Everyone thinks this whole new "law" is a thinly masked revenge by certain cabinet ministers who are routinely lampooned and satirised at the Montmartre and Pigalle halls. Much cheerful mayhem is expected to result.

On a sadder note, the entire theatrical milieu of the city were holding their breath at the critical illness of Mme. Sarah Bernhardt, who was suddenly stricken with uremic poisoning while preparing to appear in a moving picture that was to be shot at her home. She seemed to be at death's door, then recovered, then fell ill again, and crowds were gathering outside her house in the Boulevard Pereire, looking up at the windows, with many newspapermen clamouring to be let in. On March 26, she died. The funeral was held four days later, with an immense crowd, the largest that I have ever seen, lining the route from the church near her home in Neuilly right across Paris, down the Boulevard Malsherbe, the rue Royale, St-Honore and the Rivoli, towards the Pere Lachaise cemetery. The newspapers wrote that more than six hundred thousand people turned out for the greatest actress of the age. I stood at the place Madeleine and watched the cortege pass, a great car followed by five wagons laden with wreaths and flowers, roses and violets, lilac and lilies, with a phalanx of top-hats following after a poignant group of orphan girls walking on either side of the catafalque, each carrying a single palm-leaf. Everywhere there were masses of people, sombre and tearful, watching the end of an epochal era. All of Paris was marking the day.

It was a glorious Easter weekend, and sunshine that only Paris could provide, to light up her sights in the full glow of costume and colour. As for this year's fashions—the men as usual provide only a busy uniformity, with the possible exception of a colourful cravat or the flash of a brilliant waistcoat, but the women parade in the latest plumage that the spring vogue requires: black, brown and navy blue appear to have been decreed, but the ladies will turn to softer hues as the sun requires, a fresh apple-green dress with a soft lingerie collar and cuffs, or a pale georgette dress; coats and jackets may be copies of Renaissance tapestry material, and hats are cloche in shape, trimmed in various ways, with a narrow band of plain ribbon or a rosette at the back. Artificial blooms of muslin are worn as a finish to the dress rather than a simple buckle or bow. Brighter colors will run to apricot yellow and spring green rather than tango or jade, which I am told are very much of the last year.

Mindful of Mr. Gore's request, I set out to inquire about Yakov or Vasilly Gurevitch, whom I was more likely to locate under his stage name of "The Great Gramby." As chance would have it, I came upon a large poster of his show pasted upon a typical Parisian circular billboard, among the music hall and theatrical attractions. It stood out, by virtue of the remarkable gaze of the central figure poised in pensive thought at its centre, the large piercing eyes staring out at the spectator from whichever angle one faced him, beneath the white turban: "LE GRANDE V. GRAMBY—MAITRE DE MYSTERE," with the lightning shafts of the "magic eye" over-looking his suave, bow-tied image. I could not see the resemblance to William Gore, Hollywood cinematographer, but perhaps it was the pale smoothness of the face that was deceptive, a mask, rather than a true visage. The poster promised a new attraction: "LA GUILLOTINE! LA MORT E LA VIE!" Performances at the Casino de Paris, which I knew was one of the city's great burlesque venues.

I was relieved that I would certainly not miss the showman, and it might perhaps be better to find him backstage, rather than at his hotel address. In France as anywhere, I am sure, show people cannot abide being sought by strangers at their personal residence, in case of unwanted attentions by some creditor, or a persistent fan. My immediate priority, however, was to locate my cousin, Alexandre, who was travelling with M. Tairoff's Moscow Kamerny company, appearing at the Theatre Marigny. The troupe was performing "The Princess Brambilla", a "Phantasmagoric cappricio" which had been developed by the Russian maitre Tairoff as the very latest concept of stage art. The idea is of a "synthetic theatre" in which all the elements, such as speech, movement, gesture, music, scenery, costumes and lighting, are merged into a harmonious whole, a single unifying rhythm. This production, my cousin Alexandre informed me, was first presented in Moscow three years ago, in 1920, in the midst of the turmoil of the internal fighting between the Bolsheviks and the Democrats, whom some have termed the "Whites." My cousin, something of a "Red" himself, wrote me that it was a refutation of the image we in the civilised world have of the Revolution, which has allowed the arts to flourish despite the hardships and the general chaos that spread throughout Russia. As I did not know what strictures he and his fellow artists were subject to, the fear and threats of violence, imprisonment, and censorship, I set this aside as conjecture rather than fact. But when he wrote me that the Tairoff troupe was actually allowed out of the country to perform in Paris I was delighted, and made my arrangements immediately.

It was a great joy to greet my cousin and the other members of his troupe that evening at the Marigny. A magnificent theatre in an elegant Place just off the Champs Elysee, a rotunda with a grand auditorium that could seat one thousand persons. My cousin was waiting for me at the lobby and it was an emotional moment, as two Russians who had not seen each other for fourteen years embraced and marvelled at each other's presence. He was my childhood friend, and we had played with wooden swords together on the Moscow streets and then attended the Moscow Imperial Theatre school, back in the days when the Tsar ruled supreme.

We had much to catch up on, but the performance was imminent, and he had to get into his strange costume, befitting the cross between the Hoffman tale on which the play was based and a Venetian masquerade. The show was marked with odd electrical effects and a constant movement of the stage scenery. Characters appeared and disappeared through trapdoors, sometimes in the midst of a sentence or song, and the whole piece sought to dissolve from any semblance of a continuous structure into a series of disjointed moments, which somehow rejoined in another sphere entirely, something between ballet and circus. Much use was made of ghostly footlights and the "magical" shifting of colour which I understand is the characteristic of some of the old Chinese theatre, when a character's mask shifts instantly by a mere flick of the head.

I found it very stimulating in fact, and in the interval I caught a glimpse, as the lights came on, of a man seated some way to my right, two rows behind, who seemed to have a startling resemblance to the image of the poster magician, Gramby, although he was dressed in a normal suit and bow tie, and had a close mass of black curly hair, possibly a wig. I tried to press through to the lobby in time to get a second sight of this man, but I could not spot him anywhere among the milling crowd, who were pressing towards the wine waiters, arguing robustly about the play. Some were smiling broadly and nodding in delight, others throwing their hands up in despair, or holding their nose and rolling their eyes. The ladies seemed more sombre and subdued. I knew there was little time for me to explore, perhaps the man had gone to the restrooms, or some other corner. In any case I had arranged to meet my friend and the actors after the show for a bite to eat and, I hoped, a long chat, but perhaps one could kill two birds with one stone, as it were, and add Gramby, if it was he, to the company. It would be a strange coincidence if both the persons I had come to meet in Paris turned up at the same venue, though, given the nature of the show, perhaps not too unlikely. However, the man did not seem to be there. The bell soon rang and I took my seat again, and looked around, but there was no sign of the familiar face, and, where the man had sat before, a gaunt lady with extremely thick spectacles had taken his place, with a tight weave of grey hair. Or, could it be...? But the lights dimmed swiftly, and the conductor took up his baton.

The play was mesmerising, and when the curtain came down, to loud applause, my eyes were still subject to the unrest and dispersion of effects that the whole performance produced. I looked to my side, and the gaunt woman was gone too, and in her place a dark saturnine man with a thick black beard and a bulbous nose that seemed stuck on his face stood up, and, disturbingly, looked directly into my eyes. Then, when I looked away in confusion and looked back, he was gone, his seat empty, and not a sign of him again in the crowd.

We passed a genial evening after the performance at the Cafe de Paris, by the Opera, the players and I, although even through the fog of good wine it was clear that Tairoff himself, and his troupe, were taking care not to answer certain questions or to be drawn into certain discussions which some of the Parisian hosts wished to press upon them—conditions back at home, the situation in Moscow, the fate of certain friends who had dropped out of sight, relations missing, parents and siblings silent for many years. One assumed there would be at least one member of the troupe who would report back to the authorities on the good behaviour of the rest, but who could tell? We were not yet fully swaddled in fear.

There was another peculiar moment, when I noticed in the café another customer, alone at a booth in a corner, peeking at us, dressed in full evening clothes, frak, white waistcoat, bow tie, top hat, with a set of large ginger whiskers which looked blatantly fake. One eye, which was staring at me, was artificially enlarged by a thick eyeglass, and the other seemed to be looking in another direction, as if surveying some path of escape. But a waiter slid swiftly between us with a tray of hors d'oeuvres, and when he had delivered, the apparition had gone.

Later that night, when the Cafe finally closed, I accompanied the actors back towards their accommodations at the Grand Hotel des Capucines, falling back a little from the others with my arm round Alexandre's shoulders, and he told me hurriedly in a low voice some of what I needed to know: how the theatre had survived by the skin of its teeth through the harsh winter of Petrograd in the first year after the Revolution, how everybody had to eat scavenged potatoes and cabbage among the flats and artwork of fragile dreams, held together by the camaraderie of the artists, writers, poets and playwrights who had to cut their cloth to the new coat of red patches, how Gorki, above all, had sustained them, when Lenin had so many other matters to handle that would have sunk any lesser mortal.

"Do not let your imagination run away with you," he said in my ear, "this system is here to stay. Forget your romantic notions. The game is survival, pure and simple. We are the vanguard of a beautiful illusion, that all is well in the new iron world. We have to return, we all have loved ones back home. This," he gestured around to the great boulevard, the ornate mansions, the gleaming lights of the hotels that shone even after midnight, the hustle and bustle that still filled the street, "this is just a magnificent mirage, like one of Tairoff's sets—always moving, dazzling, but made of paper. Reality awaits us back there."

I thought this might be of interest to you, my friend, coming, as you have, from the same vast laboratory of human souls in turmoil, the great vats of the revolution. For we could still feel its tendrils, chill and grasping at our necks even in the warm spring of France. I was aware that my cousin Alexandre and I might never meet again, and he was the sole link that I knew to my own dear sister, who still abides in Moscow. What can be said is said, and what cannot can be said is imagined, beyond art, perhaps beyond hope.

But I was mindful of my other mission, that I had promised you. The night was done with, and we all retired to our rooms, but in the morning I decided to waste no time and repair to the address you had supplied, at the "Left Bank". I had been thinking of observing the "Great Gramby"'s act, but decided it might be better for me to visit Yakov Gorevitch at his hotel residence rather than beard the showman in the white heat of his own act on stage. A good walk across the river in the gorgeous sunshine was most attractive, and the Kamerny troupe were, I was told, booked by their guides for a tour around the museums. I had nursed thoughts of catching our sister company, maestro Diaghilev's Ballet Russe in France, but I was told they were performing in Monaco, and would not appear in Paris before June.

So I crossed the bridge over to the Isle de France, with its enticing buildings and alleyways, leading to the great Cathedral of Notre Dame, where I could not avoid lingering with the crowds, looking up at the superb gothic spires and gargoyles upon which Quasimodo had once perched... Musing how literature, art, was often so much more real than reality, even when reality shone with such blessed vigour. Inside, in the cavernous interior, the hunch-back bell ringer had leaped, tolling his warning to the people. Sanctuary! Sanctuary! I paused to say a prayer for my brothers, and my sister, Red or Slav as they may be... The waters of the river glittered in their glory, with the pleasure boats gliding serenely by. One approached, jangling from afar with the familiar cadences of a jazz band. It struck me how many Americans were in town, pouring over from the other side of the Atlantic, seeking a freedom we have promised so often, but still seem to strive to achieve...

I am sorry, I will get to my point. I thought it right to give a proper description of the circumstances and location in which your younger brother lives, in his Parisian setting. Describe the scenery around the stage, as it were. I walked across the river, up the left bank by the "bouquinistes," the quay-side stalls packed with old books, pamphlets, postcards, drawings and engravings of the last century, posters and cartoons. There is not a work of commercial design or advertising that is published in Paris that is not instantly copied by these quick-witted vendors for the tourists who throng their booths. I noticed similar caricatures to those hung in the Café the night before on the front pages of old journals that were displayed at one of the stalls, on the corner of the Ponte St. Michel—"La Nouvelle Lune," and "La Libre Parole," the former dated back to 1881. Among them was a set labelled "Les Hommes d'Aujourd'hui," with cartoons of famous artists such as Toulouse-Lautrec and Vincent Van Gogh. I paused by one dated 1886 that portrayed Emile Cohl, whom I remembered you mentioned during the filming of one of our joint DeMille ventures as the first moving picture director you had ever worked with, at Gaumont, in 1909—or was it 1910? You will remember better than I. I bought the copy for you, it shows the young man with a large head and elegant moustache—I recall you said he had been a graphic artist for the "Incoherents," the gilded age satirists, some of whose works I had just seen in the Cafe de Paris, and had been drawing animated figures on film when you were performing your droll roles for his company. The vendor charged me two francs, but it was worth it, I enjoy these proofs of old connections. The destruction of the past, the insistence only on the "new," however gross and horrific, chills my blood. I wonder how long the Tairoffs will last...

535

Turning up the Place St. Michel I made my way up the rue St.-Andres-des-Arts, a delightful street of countless shops and cafés, bookstores, coiffeurs, cake-shops, bakeries, antique and curio stores with windows full of strange items from the city and around the world—African statues, Dutch-Indies shadow-puppets, "hottentot" skulls, American-Indian feathered bonnets, wired skeletons of exotic birds, good luck charms of crocodile and shark's teeth (or so they looked) and even a couple of shrunken heads from the "Solomon Isles," which may even have been genuine, gruesome as they appeared. Another shop window was crammed full of exquisite sets of toy soldiers, Napoleonic hussars and grenadiers, that took me back to my childhood with a pang that almost stopped my heart. I could have lingered forever, but consulting my watch, quickened my pace, to keep the time of eleven o'clock that I thought might be best to rouse a working vaudevillian from his late slumber to the offer of an early lunch...

The rue Jacob is a long narrow street that parallels the Seine between the quays and the grand Boulevard St.-Germain. To the right it abuts on the Ecole des Beaux Arts, and to its left is the Hospital de la Charite, some of whose patients were by the gate, leaning against the walls and enjoying the sun. The Hotel Jacob is a modest building on the way, three storeys high, which had a small sign and a placard in the front lobby window announcing "Complet."

I rang the bell and entered. The lady at the front desk was a typical Parisian concierge, chubby faced and neat, with a demeanour that seemed ready for the opposite poles of response—a warm welcome or assault by broomstick. On realising that I was not looking for a room but for a guest she relaxed, and informed me that Monsieur Gramby—I drew a blank with "Gorevitch"—and his wife were both in, but she was not sure they had risen, as they were on the third floor. She would call, on the internal telephone. She dialled, and I heard a man's voice at the other end. The concierge was explaining who I was. "*Il parlera avec vous,*" she said.

I climbed up to the third floor, around a winding staircase, for the house seemed to get narrower as it climbed, although

536

from outside it seemed in line with all the other buildings in its terrace. I knocked at number 37, as I was bade, and a voice rang out: "Come in!"

I opened the door to a short hallway, which opened out like a funnel to a small kitchen with table and chairs that led to a larger room, at the open door of which my host stood poised. It was more of an apartment than a suite. The man was slightly bent forward, inclining his head, rather than his hand, towards me, which still rested on the knob of the inner door, so he could still decide to dart behind it and shut me in the kitchen, among the pots and pans. There was a large framed picture on the kitchen wall, but it was not of the man himself, or his act, but the image of a great snow-bound mountain, upon which a large oriental palace loomed proudly, a magnificent edifice of walls and terraces. I recognised it as the Temple of the Buddhist Lama King in Tibet. Its effect was to make one pause, and turn in wonder, unsure what realm had just been entered. Then I turned to the man, whose hand was now extended, as if I had passed his test.

I froze for a moment, for it was plain that this was the same man that I had glimpsed the night before, at the Marigny, when he had got up from his seat and looked me in the eye. The second surprise was his handshake, which was a firm clasp of my right hand with his thumb pressing clearly on my second knuckle, to which I instinctively responded likewise, as we looked each other in the eye. Then he stood back, cupping his hand over his left breast and drawing it across his chest, dropping it clearly to his side.

"Ah, Fellow Craft," he said. "Jachin."

"Jachin," I answered, doing likewise.

"Which Lodge?" he asked.

"North Hollywood," I answered, "Five Four Two. Friend to Friend."

"I knew it," he said. "We have met before. Or rather passed by."

A woman came out of the other kitchen doorway, from what was presumably the bedroom. She was short and blonde, clearly pregnant by three or four months, with high cheek bones and somewhat narrow eyes, probably also Slavic in origin.

"I'm Alma," she said, "please to meet you." Her handshake was brief and normal. "How is Bill? I haven't seen him for so long."

"Mr Gore is working," I said, with a shrug. "Mr Gore is always working. For the usual task-master, now on his biggest task."

"I read it in the Trades," he said. "The parting of the seas. Moses and Pharaoh. Snakes out of staffs. It is my brother who is the real magician."

"Where did we meet?" I asked, wondering if he was alluding to the Marigny, and might explain at least part of the mystery. He laughed and waved his hand.

"Long time ago. At the DeMille location. The Lasky ranch. The Aztec picture. What was it called—'The Woman Time Forgot'— with the opera singer who couldn't sing. You were the king of the Indians—Montezuma! I remember, you were all adorned in feathers, but not much else! It was an amazing scene. You were too busy, getting ready for the shot, but you were pointed out to me."

"Oh yes, I would have noticed nothing," I said, wincing, "it was a most awkward get up. There was a wire clasp, it was all very heavy, to look so light. There was amazing decor. All those palm fronds and tropical trees and flower bushes and parrots. Great pity was there was no colour. Now DeMille is trying a new process. But if we could have done that then… at least people would have been diverted from that crazy plot!"

"All that money to spend!" he said, "la grande spectacle! That's my brother. Parting the Red Sea! The trick is to start with nothing, and then work with the spectator's mind..." He waved me through into the interior room. I started as I entered, as anyone might. The walls were covered with images spread across two and three tiers. "The Great Gramby" poster was directly ahead, in the midst of a row of mystical pictures that stretched above a long mahogany working desk. A great Zodiac circle, with lettering in Greek, Latin and Hebrew, a cross section of the Great Pyramid of Egypt, showing its inner passages leading to the "King's Chamber." The Masonic table of the ineffable letters and signs, with the Skull and Crossbones in centre. The "Hand of Mysteries," which I also recognised, the outstretched palm with the Fish of Christ in the centre, the fingers tipped with the Key, the Lantern, the Sun and the Star, the Crown over the thumb, with the Moon in balance. The Tree of Noah, with the Ark at its base and Jerusalem at its apex. The Kabbalistic Tree of the Sephiroth, and above all these a long scroll of Pharaonic images surrounded by the ancient hieroglyphs.

"The Bembine Table of Isis," Gramby explained, "Plato was initiated into The Mysteries by these forms. If you gaze at them long enough, you will begin to hear a certain music."

I nodded, saying nothing, not knowing what to say. One had seen these images a number of times, in white haciendas up the mountains of Hollywood, among some pretty strange people. But I did not expect it in a Paris hotel.

"Madame Lefkowski doesn't like being in this room," he said, "we have to clean it ourselves, poor Alma." She had followed us but said nothing. His garrulousness was matched by her reticence. But there was a gaze between them, as if they were used to communicating along some kind of telepathic waves. He ushered me to an armchair in the nearer corner of the room, by the door, while he settled in a large wicker chair padded with scarlet cushions. Alma asked me if I would take tea or coffee. I was grateful for the thought of tea. "Russian style, strong and black," he said. She went out, with a slight moue of resignation, or perhaps pique. There were too many runes to read, in the cluttered space. He had two of those African statuettes on the desk and even one of the shrunken heads, I noticed, in a glass cylinder.

"Intimations of mortality," he said. "It is not real. In America they worship fakery, but they are happy with it. In Paris one has to go much further. There are so many charlatans. Show business is larger, louder, faster. And more beautiful. In America they worship the machine. Ziegfeld, Wayburn and their neat rows of ladies all stepping out in unison. So horrible. Here they just flash their underwear and glorify the natural. It is more true. People rush, but they are not in a hurry. In America they worship the immediate, but the French can understand allusions." He noticed my eye roving over a large cork billboard, to his left on the wall adjacent to the bedroom, on which were pinned images of a very different kind, eleven photographs of women, with one of a young man, arranged in a circle around two startling portraits of a bearded man in the centre of the board. The man was middle aged, with immense eyebrows and intense staring eyes under a bald head, standing in a booth of some kind, dressed in an ill-fitting suit and gesticulating and pointing forward.

"Henri Desire Landru," said Gramby, following my gaze. "You may have heard of his case even in America, I believe. He was a common fraudster and dealer in used furniture, until one day the police accused him of murdering eleven women after marrying them all for their money. The curious point was that none of the bodies was ever found. There was an oven, in his house, in which there were some powdered bones, that may or may not have been human. But the jury was convinced by circumstantial evidence of his dealings with these women, that he was guilty, and he had burned them all up in that tiny kitchen stove. He was executed just one year ago, in February, by Madame la Guillotine. It was the great cause célèbre after the War. People were so tired of the death of millions that they seized with a great relish on this story of a small man and his private personal crimes. It is the basis of my new act."

"I saw some of your posters, in the streets," I told him. "many people were paying attention. Cutting off your own head, I must say, it does sound like a challenge."

"Oh, that part is easy," he said, "La Voisin used to do it at the court of Louis the Fourteenth, the Sun King. *Le roi de soleil*. Little did they know it would be enacted in real life some eighty years after. Life always follows art. Robert Houdin used to vanish everything with great precision. People are used to seeing miracles in the moving pictures, since the tricks of Méliès and Velle. They are used to smoke and mirrors. Houdini performed behind a screen. Even an elephant could be magicked away if it was behind a curtain! He is a magician of the physical moment. All his best moments are pure gymnastics. I cannot tell you his tricks, any more than I would explain my own. There is the sacred code of the Craft."

Alma came in, manoeuvring a little awkwardly in her nascent state, with a tray of tea and some pastries, which were succulent and fresh. She sat down at a smaller chair at the other side of the desk, and poured. It was good tea, a genuine taste of the old days. A Russian remains a Russian.

I thought it might be the right moment to change the course of the conversation, and refer to the family events that prompted you to entrust me with this visit. "Your brother is very sad about the news from your home town," I said. "Your mother's demise. He thought you might know more details. I am very sorry for your loss."

"Thank you," he said. His flow of thought had been interrupted, and the flow of talk ceased. He looked at Alma, who leaned over her side of the desk and took a thin envelope from a drawer. "This is Judit's letter," she said. "We had a copy made. But it is in Yiddish which we are not sure Boris reads easily nowadays. So we kept it here. You can take it back with you. I wrote out what she said."

"My mother was not well since our father died," said Gramby. "To tell the truth, she went crazy, and wandered round the village, talking to trees and animals, and standing all day on the river-bank. Then she stayed in the other Rabbi's house night and day. She lost the use of her legs and was bedridden. So we were told. What could I do?" He spread his hands at his surroundings, the strange cluttered room, the overwhelming pictures, the occult signs and murdered women, with their murderer glaring angrily from his dock.

"Every magician is a fake," he said, fixing those limpid eyes on me, as if I had suddenly become a judge who needed to be appeased, just before sentence was passed. "He cannot wield the power when it is really required. When the call comes, he is finally helpless. It is too late. I can raise myself from the dead every night. If needed, also in matinees. You, I understand, are a Christian. You have family back there?"

541

"I have a sister. She cannot leave. My cousin is here now. With the Kamerny. Have you seen their show? It is at the Marigny."

Once again he did not rise to the bait, but it was the wrong moment.

"I don't know if you are a religious man," he said. "I have never met a magician who was a Believer. Not in the bones. From the dawn of man, ju ju men appeared to talk of God. God is in his place, but he is not a magician. This is a misunderstanding. He is a Creator who Creates. The magician creates nothing. The only thing I have created is waiting there, in my wife's belly. It is a thing of wonderment. But it is nature. It is not artifice. It is not art. Anyone can do it. Only the magician is a fool. I will tell you something. Because you are one of us, you are an artist. Who cares about Christian, Mohammedan, Jew? You saw my picture of Lhassa, outside there. It is called the Potlala. The palace of the Dalai Lama. Every generation he is chosen from a child who is sought by occult means. He is the incarnation of Buddha. It is not hereditary. The priests send out around the mountains for the birth of a magic child. Every time he is found and every time he is the right one. How does this work? We do not understand. It is another place, another people. They have kept wisdom alive because they do not believe in a God, but in a Man. They believe every man, and woman, can become holy. Everyone can be the Buddha. But they must follow a path. We are fools, we have no patience. My father prayed every day, like a good Jew, three times a day, *shachris*, *minheh* and *maariv*. Every time he said the same words. They were set words, only varying slightly. He could not change them, they are set down in the book. The book is holy, the human being is not. I have books too. I read my share of them. Tolstoy, Dostoyevsky, Dickens, also the modern psychologists, you know, the Vienna doctor, Freud. They are beginning to see the truth, that sacredness is within us, it does not come from outside. We are only part of the universe. Our brain is a chemical thing. I believe I understand this because I know how people can be fooled. Every night I trick an audience into believing something that is not so. Simple tricks, even complicated ones, we can do them better or worse. But we are not Plato, Socrates, Aristotle, even Moses. We are just fools. We cannot save those who have to be saved."

I did not stay long, and left soon after that, as I could see he was prone to sudden depressions, and his wife was impatient for me to leave.

In the evening I went to see his performance, at the Casino de Paris, in the rue de Clichy. In fact it was in the Nouveau Theatre, which was one of two venues there, not the enormous open space of the main hall, where crowds thronged the columned space of the promenoir with an open view of the main stage, which was featuring Nini and her "Elevated Angels." The Nouveau Theatre had been especially draped in black, to reduce the light in the circle and stalls, so that only the stage was illuminated, like a garish mouth steaming with coloured smoke. Then the smoke was wafted away by fans and the magician's act was performed, as he had stated, in the clearest visibility, without apparent obfuscations.

I have no idea how the effects were created, they seemed to me of an incandescent brilliance. I know that magicians are almost always no better than the stage arrangements and the ingenious machines that are built for them by specialist sources, meticulous engineers who put together engines of gossamer but steely threads and paper-thin glass which levitate the principals and produce astounding flying and vanishing illusions, rendered invisible by the placing of the lights. I remember seeing in New York the famous Carter the Great, who sawed a woman in half and played his famous trick of "cheating the gallows" by appearing to hang himself from a rope and then disappear at the plunge. His illusions were created by the Martinka brothers, purveyors of magic paraphernalia. Sometimes I wonder whether Nijinsky is not availing himself of such masters...

The centrepiece of the show was of course the Landru Act: Gramby appeared as the eponymous murderer, made up in his shabby coat and a scrubby beard and moustaches, although he had a black wig, rather than the bald pate of his model, and once again

543

bore a startling resemblance to one of the avatars I'd glimpsed the night before, the one watching us in the Café de Paris. But one might well believe, watching the masterful performance, that this prodigy could be in two places at once, if not three or four. At the start, Gramby appeared in a set of the farmhouse kitchen of the killer Landru, flanked by shelves of pots and pans, a workshop table with a lathe and circular saw and the famous oven in the centre. A maid, played by Alma, who had covered up her pregnancy by appearing as a grossly obese charwoman with double chins and a padded stomach covered by an old grey smock, came in with coals, which they both shovelled into the oven, and set it aflame. Smoke came out of a chimney stack towards the unseen flies. The audience was already uneasy, as fire on stage always unsettles all those who have read tales of past theatrical disasters.

The entire play was made in pantomime. A plumpish, sturdy woman entered and was brusquely bussed on the cheek by the principal. The charwoman left, and "Landru" motioned to the woman, who took a great wad of banknotes from her handbag, which the magician counted in a bank clerk's manner by riffling through them at great speed. Then he placed the wad in his pocket and motioned the woman to sit at the kitchen table, as he reached for some utensil upon the shelf of pans. She sat primly, facing the audience, and began knitting, while the man behind her produced a wicked looking kitchen knife. Some in the audience cried out, but the magician stilled them, and the woman took not notice. Without further ado, the magician stepped forward and slit the woman's face from ear to ear.

There was a great gasp, and some women in the audience cried out, and at least one fainted, perhaps two. What appeared to be blood gushed out, which the killer deftly caught in a tin bowl. Then he dragged the woman quickly, and pulled her over to the stove door, which he kicked open. The flames were clearly seen, and their heat felt in the auditorium. As the deed was done, I noticed that the lights on stage had dimmed to a blood red, but that was the only noticeable transition from victim to dummy, if that was indeed the case—one could not see how such a switch could be done. The killer swiftly fed the corpse into the oven, head first, where it sizzled and crackled, the feet only protruding at the last. Taking a saw, the magician swiftly sawed off the feet and moved to put them in a cupboard, but the cupboard door opened to show another woman's head inside. The head was alive, and its eyes rolled, the mouth opened and the tongue protruded. Before the head could speak the killer slammed the doors shut, and opened another cupboard, where another head grimaced and groaned. This continued five or six more times—one lost count—as the killer sought a hiding place for the severed feet. But before he could do so there was a fierce rapping from below the stage, and a trapdoor was flung open, through which a row of policemen rushed up, followed by the charwoman, who pointed to the magician in an accusing pose. The policemen seized the killer and handcuffed him, and then began opening the cupboards, which now contained nothing more terrifying than the usual household implements, pots, pans, saucers, cups, utensils, which were showered on the floor. Swiftly it was shown that the cupboards were then bare, the policemen running their fingers along the sealed panels.

The policemen opened the oven, which was still flaming, and began poking about in it with pokers and pincers, pulling out nothing but piles of ash. They brought up a large tin can and shovelled the ash in, showing it full to the brim before covering it up. They searched the killer's pockets, and began pulling out more and more wads of cash, that were piled up on the kitchen table till the hoard was almost three feet high, and still the policemen were pulling more items out of the magician's jacket and pants—copper coins, which they tossed about everywhere, giant keys, hammers, screwdrivers, monkey wrenches, circular saws, knives, hatchets, a flat-iron, pincers, a bellows and, finally, a magnificent hunting hawk with its head cowled, which soared into the flies as soon as it cowl was removed. This brought forth massive applause.

But the trick wasn't ended, as two policemen dragged the can of ashes forward and, lifting its lid, stood back in surprise as Alma, clad in a form-fitting leopard-skin, that exposed her pregnancy, stood up and climbed out—it took me a moment to realise the charwoman had exited stage left during the melee—and crossed her arms and bowed to the crowd. As the policemen held "Landru", transfixed, the curtain came down, with Alma before it, as she proceeded to juggle with four, five and then six balls which also miraculously appeared in her hands.

I found myself, like so many others, leaning forward, perspiring, shaking my head, and trying to disentangle the images that surged in my head. The orchestra had struck up as soon as the curtain came down, and then switched from a traditional circus air to the funeral dirge, as the curtain rose again, to a completely different setting. We were in a bare yard, with white flats either side, and an open arched gate, on the left, at which two armed guards in military uniforms and helmets stood to attention. From the right, the massive bulk of the vehicle of execution, the Guillotine, was pushed forward on a platform moving on rollers. A high light glinted off the sharp steel of the blade, which seemed, from the stalls, sharp as a razor. Two guards swiftly came forward, with a dummy, which they placed on the truss with its head on the lower part of the vice. The upper part was then locked in place and a woman, dressed all in black, with a mask over her eyes, who might or might not have been Alma, came forward and pulled the switch at the side of the frame. The blade came down, with a terrifying rumble, and severed the dummy's head, which was held up by a guard and then tossed into the audience. Men and women in the front row ducked and moved away, and the man who caught the head, possibly a plant, rose up and tossed it behind him, where it was thrown from hand to hand in some panic until an usher took it away.

A drumroll began, and two more guards moved forward, with "Landru" held by the arms between them, dressed in a loose white shirt and black ordinary pants, the collar released, and his hands bound behind his back. The eyes of the magician glinted like lamps into the audience—I am sure there were some tiny spotlights deployed. He was brought up to the front of stage, and spoke for the first and last time, in the words some had reported apparently from the trial:

"If I am guilty," he said, loudly and clearly, "then all are guilty. If absence of proof is proof, then all is proven. But I do not bid you goodbye." The guards then seized the condemned man and pushed him down onto the platform. The Guillotine had now been moved so that the frame and the blade were immediately facing the audience. One could see clearly how "Landru's" head was placed in the vice, the vice locked, and his face moved, looking forward, the eyes staring clearly out, and moving. Then the woman strode forward. A voice cried out, over the void, from somewhere behind the stage, but clearly amplified, a female cry:

"LA JUSTICE!"

Then again that terrible rumble. Every person in the audience gasped and cried out as the blade came down. The noise was clearly heard, like the chopping of a melon, and the head rolled off, into the basket. The chief guard seized it, and holding it by the hair, flourished it at the foot of the stage, showing it to all sides of the house. It was undoubtedly the same head, the eyes staring, but lifeless. Two other guards lifted the headless body off the platform.

There was a clap of thunder, and what seemed to be a lightning bolt came down from the flies, apparently hitting the body. The body jerked, and at the same time, the head held in the guard's hand came out a great cry, uttering the clear word:

"NON!"

The eyes opened, clearly moving right and left, but by now the lights had changed, to the red glow. One's eyes moved from the head to the body, which seemed to be propelling itself forward, in the guard's hands, but whether they were carrying it or it was carrying them was not obvious. It, or they, placed itself under the severed head, which the senior guard thrust onto the body. Then the guards stood back, and the body moved, trembled, moved its hands and then stood of its own accord, with the head attached, the red ring of blood around the neck, squeezing, with some effort, testing its perch, but then, finding its balance, turning to the audience, and making its concluding, tumultuous bow.

As they say in show business—just follow that... The curtain, of course, came down for the interval. The audience was so shaken that it could not move, and then broke open with a burst of jabbering. In the left aisle, a contingent of medical attendants with red armbands, clearly ready on the spot, carried away one lady on a white stretcher. Several more were still screaming at the back, and there was some kind of commotion in the circle.

I do not remember who was on next. There was a dog act, I think, and three unicyclists, and a woman who sang songs of spring. I left before the end, as I found the air stifling, and the proscenium of the stage and the packed hall, high with sweat and a strong aura of fear, not easily calmed, too oppressive. I was not sure I wanted to face the man backstage, at that moment. Only that morning he had opened his heart to me, a total stranger, albeit another lost countryman and an emissary of his older brother, expressing his doubts, baring his soul. Now suddenly he had closed in again, like one of those carnivorous plants one reads about in the science journals, demonstrating this phantasmagorical skill at evoking extreme terror. To be killed on stage, decapitated, and arise to life, this was not something that one expected as part of an every-day entertainment. There are horrors on film but everyone knows they are subterfuge, and easy tricks. Of course, there was tradition in France of the "grand-guignol" theatre, the spectacle of eye-gouging, tongue-cutting horror evoking the ghost train of the tumbrils. But Gramby did not comfort one with the cathartic release of make-believe. He literally made one believe in what was occurring on the stage, instead of making one simply marvel at the magician's skill.

I walked a long time in the city that night. People thronged the streets, couples embraced, sailors were clutching their lucky finds, young girls pranced by in groups of fours or fives, calling out to me as I walked. Cafés and shops and patisseries were open. From a basement club there came a blast of pure jazz. I felt myself lucky to be alive, but the city was not the same, somehow, as its darker dreams were slow to disperse…

In the morning, Paris resumed its gaity, alive with sounds and laughter, clattering feet. There was some kind of fete for students, who were out on the streets in great groups, girls and boys dressed in gaudy costumes, playing animals, pixies and elves, and other extravagances, with painted faces and whiskers, waving wands and pelting passersby with tinsel and candies. All of Paris was awash with youth. I called on my cousin Alexandre and we walked through the streets, free of the Kamerny "spy," who had overslept. We walked across the Place Vendome to the Tuileries gardens, stopping by the bandstand, which was being informally used by a group of young jazz musicians, a combination of white French and negro American players. It was incomparably refreshing to see such an easy rapport between black and white, a picture which as we know is so unlikely back in the land of the brave and the free. They played the latest Dixieland tunes very well, and the crowd was delighted, urging them to encore after encore. We walked through the Place de Carrousel, past the Gambetta monument, towards the Louvre, since despite the glorious day this was the best opportunity for the two of us lost cousins to survey this grandest display of the world's artistic heritage. The collected memory of ancient Greece, Egypt, North Africa, the Orient, and even exquisite artefacts from our own Americas, and the Pacific cultures. In the breathtaking Egyptian galleries, there is already one dedicated to photographs of the recent Carter expedition which opened the hidden marvels of the burial chamber of the Pharaoh Tutankhamun, which may have occurred too late for inclusion in your own Ten Commandments art department! But it has set the world abuzz with interest for the glories of antiquity. I was amazed by the grace and beauty of some of the Pharaonic statues, and the exquisite carvings on the sarcophagi, the runes of power and the sorcery of conquest over the domain of Death. We both paused at the long gallery, tucked away at the end of a labyrinth, of the mummies of birds, fish and mammals—cormorants, cranes, foxes and particularly cats, that showed the touching faith those ancient people had in the transference of their pets with them to the extra-terrestrial domains. It reminded me a bit of those Los Angeles séances in which old ladies tried to restore communication with their deceased dogs.

But I am diverging too far. I am mindful of the fact that you wished me to give you a rounded picture of the circumstances of your brother's life in Paris, his possible contacts with the home village, the nature of his work and state of health, his thoughts and plans for the future, and so forth. But I was unable to engage him on this. I tried to call Alma by the telephone the next day, but the concierge answered that "the magician" was not in.

My friends of the Kamerny introduced me to the meeting places of the city's artists, painters, would-be playwrights, writers and poets south of the Seine, in the Vavin district, in the Boulevard Montparnasse. There are several large cafes, the Dome, La Rotonde, the Select and La Coupole, I met some fascinating people there of all nations, French, Spaniards, Catalans, Poles, Rumanians, Bulgarians, Russians of course, even Japanese. There is a full stock of Americans, of every stripe and ambition: painters, poets, writers, variety artistes, dancers and singers, though they do not mingle as well. Famous people have their own crowds, and the black jazz musicians prefer the deeper haunts of the Butte Montmartre.

I remembered your tale of the young saxophone player who once was Gramby's boy assistant, but whose name I un-fortunately did not write down, whom I think you told me had followed Gramby to Paris, but there was no sign of him in the show. Perhaps I am confusing two stories. Among the Americans at the Select was a very intense young man who writes news stories for the Toronto Star and is about to publish a book of short stories. He was an ambulance driver in the war, and two typical poets, called Ezra and Tom, who are always arguing over verses they both believe will revolutionise the poetry world. The cafes are full of artistic revolutionaries. There are entire new art movements here that are reminiscent of the "Incoherents" of the last century but are even wilder, taking their cue from the "Cubists" and other artists like our own Russian "symbolists". They talk about dethroning language and making an art which is "surrealist" and expresses the hidden chaos of the human mind. This follows "Da Da", another strange movement that mixes up incoherent pictures with a kind of senseless scribble. You and Mr. DeMille would find them most interesting in your researches into new art forms and extraordinary images of the world. Many of them are becoming quite well-known, and their exhibitions attract prominent dealers. The new trends in the decorative arts, which DeMille used so well in "The Affairs of Anatol," are also in full blast. Over here they are now calling it "Deco." Another place you would find interesting is a bookshop at the rue l'Odéon called Shakespeare and Co., where all the English speaking writers and poets congregate, and is run by an American lady from New Jersey. The bookshop itself has just published a huge volume by an Irish writer which is apparently full of sexual language but which nobody can understand.

My friends of the Kamerny were about to move on to Berlin, before their passage back east. My cousin and I embraced, silently, as the spy was wide awake and on full guard for any messages that might be passed on...

I did succeed in meeting one more time with Alma, in a café in the rue de Saints Peres, without Gramby, whom she said was resting with a head-cold, and sent his apologies and his best wishes. He had prepared a gift, suitably Pharaonic, a certified authentic "ushabti" figure, in blue faience, with headdress and crossed hands, of the kind that were placed in Egyptian tombs, as servants for the deceased in their journey through the Land of the Dead.

Alma unwrapped it to show me, and the package contained another small artefact, but of exquisite moulding, a "toilet-spoon" in the shape of a young girl standing in a boat and holding lotuses. "For your brother," she said, "Vassily says—to show that bondage may have many faces." I wasn't sure I understood that but

I thanked her profusely. She also handed me a sealed envelope with the letter she had promised, impressing on me that it was strictly private, for Boris Gore only, she apologised for making this distinction. I told her I understood her very well, and expressed my own best wishes for Gramby in his work and life, making her a formal bow and telling her that "I am sure your husband will be well whenever you are with him. The life of a true artist is always a test."

"Every life is a test," she said. "And most of us fail it." But she hugged me close, and I could feel the life shifting inside her body.

"All my best wishes for the child. I am sure Boris will come here as soon as the overseer stops cracking his whip."

She thanked me again and hurried off, around the corner, into the rue Jacob, towards their hotel. All around me life surged, people came and went, men leaned against the bar and argued with the waiter, two girls were chatting closely at the next table, the odour of fresh croissants and coffee fought against the tobacco fumes, and I closed my eyes, hoping I could gather it all in, and preserve it, as the best gift I could bear across the sea.

(Edited from original transcript corrected with Mr. Kosloff's authorization by Agnes Pepperday, Famous-Players-Lasky copy department.)

Alma "Gramby"'s Letter:

(*Gurevtich papers, Box 312, sub-folder A-2*)

Dear Mr. Boris Gore,

I trust I find you in good health, and well advanced towards the achievement of your latest production with Mr. DeMille. Vassily and I have been very happy with the visit of your friend Mr. Theodor Kosloff and we hope we can continue to be in contact with his family, as we are scattered all over the lands. Vassily is working very hard, and our new act is still popular, but it puts a great strain on him. Vassily hopes that the report which you asked Mr. Kosloff to write will give you a picture of the situation here in Paris. We are very happy but busy. You know that Vassily has never liked putting his thoughts down on paper and so I am speaking for him. He wants me to tell you that he has a suggestion for expressing his thoughts that is connected to the time when you were both young in the village, and when you shared speaking about your dreams. He remembered that you used to try to write stories that came from the dreams he used to have when he was very small. He wants you to know that he continues to have dreams, and that these dreams play a very important part in our life, because he has to act in some way to fit the "message" that he thinks the dream is giving to him. The dreams of the magician are, he wants to say, often the only free thing about his life. The magician has a very practical life, he has to see to his performance, and we have to prepare the stage very carefully, like engineers who construct a building or a bridge and have to make sure it is safe for the people to cross over it or use it. It is a very precise business. Every performance is a dream that has been made into a reality by careful planning and the exact nature and timing of the magician's movements. In particular the Landru act is, Vassily says, a game that is played between the performer and the angel of death. He remembers the example of Chung Ling Soo who was demised some years ago in London while performing his standard act that was called "Condemned to Death by the Boxers," and in which he caught between his teeth the bullet that was fired on stage by his assistant, playing the Executioner. Something went wrong with the equipment and the bullet passed through his mouth to the back of the head and killed him. It is the magician's risk. I do not like to think of such things but Vassily says: write, tell him all about it. We are both entertainers, he says, my brother and I, we are slaves to the audience and to circumstance, to Fate. I remember the first time—and this I am writing for myself—that I was with Vassily when he stopped his heart in the performance of the "Lazarus" act at Keith's Orpheum in Kansas City Missouri. My heart almost stopped too. There was always a doctor on hand who would come up, and certify the subject as dead. Sometimes I saw them pass me by in the wings and shake their head in wonderment, looking at me with a terrible sympathy but I knew after the first performance, that it was just temporary. Vassily had learned this technique from a Hindu performer, Lal Shastri, who used to use it in séances. But he knew that in the long run there was a price to pay with the body so he decided to drop the act and then we found the Landru story. So that is one of our secrets.

Another one which I have now put together is that Vassily asks me to write down the dreams he has which he believes are most significant and which he says give him clues about his act and about his readings of the "alternative" worlds. Vassily has a great interest in the teachings of the Russian Armenian Mr. G. Gurdjieff and we have visited his "Institute for the Harmonious Development of Man" at Fontainbleau-Avon which is some forty kilometres outside Paris. There are various exercises of mind and body that we have both found very fruitful in our sometimes difficult lives. Mr. Gurdjieff valued Vassily's dreams most highly, and encouraged Vassily to write them down, which has become my task. "Stories of the soul," he used to call them. Some he told to Mr. Gurdjieff, and some only to myself. But he has picked out seven dreams that he says I should send to you as you were the first person and the only person until these recent times for whom he recounted these stories.

So I am sending to you as he has told them to me by dictation, word after word. This what Vassily dreamed:

Dream Number One:
(Note: I do not understand this dream, but I have written it as Vassily told it. Alma G.)

I am walking down the open road. It is a gravel path, winding around the steppe hills. All around are fields of rape, corn and sunflowers stretching as far as the eye can see. There is no sign of humanity. There are no animals. There are no hayracks, huts, farms, carts, churches or synagogues. All is at peace. I feel I can walk this way forever. There is a spring in my step. I experience total freedom. There are no signs, no notices, no billboards, no chains across the road, no borders, no checkpoints, no soldiers or police to say You shall not pass.

I walk eagerly forward towards the top of a rolling hill, so that I might see if the road continues in this same way over the other side, rolling down and rising again and rolling down ad infinitum. I am not thinking of any goal for my walk, of any destination. I do not carry with me any instrument, like a compass, that can tell me the direction. The sun must be somewhere in the sky but I have somehow missed it, although the sky is blue, with a few drifting white threads of clouds, and I feel its invisible warmth upon me. I am wearing a light jacket and pants, with an old pair of sandals, and I am carrying a light birch-wood staff.

I am happy, that the road ahead seems still clear, but there is, at the apex of the next hill, an object, which, as I walk closer, resolves itself into a red cow, which is standing on its own in a field of wheat, which is rocking gently in a wind that I cannot feel. Somehow I have, my mind tells me, neglected to fill in certain details of the way ahead. This is, I suddenly realise, absolutely up to me, alone. I suddenly realise that there is no God to create this landscape for me, no divine wind, no finger poised to write commandments on a stone mountain. There is no mountain, but, as I advance, I can see some stones, cropping out of the earth amid the fields, between myself and the cow. The cow looks up as I draw nearer, and I wave towards it, but my foot comes up against the nearest stone in the ground. As I hit it with my toe I look down, and notice that it is moving very slowly. It seems to be thrusting out from the ground, displacing earth and, I can see, a number of worms that are emerging from its base. These are of various sizes, some small and harmless, but one or two which look large, and somewhat menacing, more like slugs. I look up but the cow has vanished.

I look down at the leading slug, which seems to be carrying a crushed up envelope in its tiny frontal antennas. I reach down, reluctantly, feeling the cold slimy skin of the slug for an instant, as I pull up the paper. It is indeed crushed up into a ball, dirty with damp earth, which I labour to unpick. By the time I unfold the envelope the light in the sky has faded, and I am left in a deep blue twilight, in which I painstakingly pull out the letter that is folded inside the envelope, but as I try to extract it, it becomes a soggy mash in the envelope. I am convinced that this is a letter from my parents, lying dead under this ground, particularly from my father, whom I now remember I left without an explanation or a goodbye. But I am unable to unfold the letter, and it falls to pieces in my hands. In any case, it is now too dark to read it.

This is intensely frustrating, and I become convinced that the cow has something to do with it, or can at least explain the situation to me. There must be a way back to the village, where I can at least ask my brothers and my sisters to explain to me what has happened, and what message my parents have left me for my voyage. In any case I cannot see the road ahead, apart from an extremely dim line in the gloom.

The slug has climbed onto my foot, and I shake it off, trying to stamp it and the growing number of worms back into the ground. But they keep coming out. I have no fear of worms and slugs, I recall that I used to keep them, as a child, inside a jar. There had also been a spider, and several large ants, which I was convinced, once again, could explain the situation to me, if they had the power of speech. I began to curse my rashness at setting off on the road without a compass or a map to show me the way. I felt around in my jacket, as the night was becoming cold, and found a sharp and large knife, of the kind the ritual slaughterer routinely uses. I feel that if I can catch the cow I can threaten it with the knife to divulge its secret. I am convinced that the red cow understands the situation and is the key to its mystery. I can sense that more and more stones, clearly gravestones, have pushed out of the ground.

I pick my way between the stones. It is too dark to read them but I am not afraid of them. The dead have no power to harm me and, in any case, they are dead, it is only the living who can be my enemies, able and willing to do harm. I clutch the knife.

Looking up, I now see a portent in the sky, a thin tendril of light, drizzling down in the dark, illuminating some shapes up ahead. Here, finally are the hayracks, the cart, some moving objects, probably chickens and geese, and a one-storeyed farmhouse. There is a light in one window.

I am absolutely sure that if I climb forward and look through the window, I will see my father there, leaning over the kitchen table, praying in his prayer-shawl, and my mother with a cooking pot, at the stove. I think they are alone there, for all the other children, I am sure, have fled. There is an Enemy, who is lurking in the woods, with axes and armour, which is ready to move forward, and pounce.

It is no longer sane to remain in the open. I move forward through the grass, but my feet have become very slow. There is an obstacle in front of me. It is the carcase of the cow, which has been slaughtered, eviscerated, and its bones left stark jutting up to the sky. Its dead eyes look up at me, with indifference.

I step around the corpse of the cow and manage to steal up to the window. But when I look inside the room is empty. It is the kitchen of my youth, but the table is completely bare, the chairs are empty, the stove is cold, the pots are rusted on the shelves, yet, there is a Sabbath candlestick, with a pair of tall candles, still burning, with half their length left. Someone, I was convinced, was still in the house. But how to get in? The window was covered with a strong pane of glass, and, though I crept around the building, I could not, at first, find the door. By the time I found it, there was a rustling in the fields outside, but I could not see the marauders who were hiding there, although I could hear their groans. All that was required, I recalled, was to wave my magic wand, and they would all disappear. The magic wand, however, was in my bedroom, on the upper floor of the house, in the attic that I had shared with my brother Boris. I was sure it was Boris and not Kolya or Zev, who shared another room.

There was a vine, crawling up the side of the house, which I grabbed hold of to climb. But it kept coming apart in my hands. Eventually, though, by dint of sheer determination, I climbed up, and pulled myself through the small open window of the attic. There was a stirring inside, although the night was still dark. There was, I realised no moon, not even a sliver. It was the dead heart of "rosh-hodesh"—the new month. There was an appropriate prayer, but I had forgotten it. I could sense, rather than see, the contours of the bed. I crawled right into it, pulling up the bedclothes. There was a closer stirring beside me, but I was not sure if it was Boris, or someone else. I was somehow suddenly convinced it was the local policeman, Grisha Shtrach, who used to chase us after stealing the goys' apples. But before I could find out, I was suddenly awake, in Paris.

(Note: there should be no difficulty in understanding this dream. Alma G.)

Archive note: This is the only Dream that survives in the folder. Some selfish and reckless seeker must have stolen or redacted the rest from the file.

The Casino at the End of Time:

Asher:

On November 5, 1995, the prime minister of Israel, Yitzhak Rabin, was assassinated by a right-wing zealot just as he was leaving the podium at a massive peace rally in the center of Tel Aviv. He had addressed the crowd about the Oslo Accords with the Palestine Liberation Organization, and had somewhat reluctantly joined the crowd in singing their signature "Peace Song." He didn't know the words, so someone had written it for him on a piece of paper. When the assassin shot him, pumping three bullets at point blank range into his back, one of the bullets passed through the paper, which he had folded into his pocket. The prime minister was bundled away by his stunned bodyguards in his own car, insisting to them that "it hurts, but it's not serious." Most of the crowd had not realized, in the milling noise of dispersal, that the event had happened until they heard it minutes later over the radio.

It hurt, and it was serious. My cousin Rivkie, Sarah's daughter, called me from Israel to London, where I got the call that Saturday evening, while Claire was out rehearsing, and I had turned the TV off for a read. Her voice was tearful and broken, as she told me that everyone in the country was in deep shock, and young people in Tel Aviv were gathering in thousands at the site of the event, lighting candles and singing songs.

"Nobody expected this," she said. "Jews shooting Jews!"

As opposed to the others. It seemed a ferocious climax to a year of bombs and rhetoric. Claire had logged the details of each attack: January 22, two suicide bombers kill 21 Israelis at the Beit Lid junction not far from Hadera: claimed by Islamic Jihad. March

19, Palestinian gunmen open fire in the West Bank on a bus carrying settlers, two killed and many wounded. On April 9, two Palestinians blew themselves up outside two Jewish settlements in the Gaza Strip, killing seven Israeli soldiers and an American citizen: claimed by the Islamic movement Hamas. July 24, while we were still in the country, six Israeli civilians killed in a suicide attack on a bus in Ramat Gan. Claimed by Hamas. After we left, on August 21: three Israelis and one American killed in a suicide bombing of a Jerusalem bus. Hamas claimed responsibility.

The Rabin killing struck me as merely a seam in the braid, which continued to coil in 1996. February 25, suicide bombing of the number 18 bus in Jerusalem, twenty-six killed, Hamas claimed "martyrdom action." The same day, another suicide bomber killed one Israeli at a soldiers' hitchhiking post outside Ashkelon. March 3, the number 18 bombed again on the Jaffa Road in Jerusalem, nineteen killed, sixteen civilians and three soldiers. March 4, outside the Dizengoff Center in Tel Aviv, a 20-kilogram nail bomb wrapped round a suicide bomber kills twelve civilians and one soldier.

Despite the bombings, which were clearly aimed at destroying the Oslo Accords, the Israeli government and the PLO had continued implementing the written agreements, which were clarified in a "second phase" blueprint for redeployment of Israeli forces from the urban centers of the West Bank. As a result, a patchwork of zones marked A, B and C would be controlled in different degrees by each side or by both, in lieu of a "final agreement," which would follow in due course. It was his signature on this legislation, in September 1995, that sealed Rabin's fate. Despite the killing, Rabin's deputy prime minister and successor, Shimon Peres, completed the redeployment that Rabin had begun, in October. By December, the last Palestinian town in the current schedule, Bethlehem, passed to nominal Palestinian control.

In January, elections for a Palestine Authority, the leadership and an Assembly were held in the West Bank and Gaza. Claire wanted us to go and film the event, as a bonafide part of the Project, but we were both tied up, Claire with her own redeployment and me starting the winter-spring term at film school. Once again we were spectators from afar, watching the TV news as more trouble erupted on the "northern front" in April, when Hezbollah rockets fired into Israel from Lebanon sparked an artillery battle that ended in a massacre of more than one hundred Arab civilians sheltering at a U.N. base inside Lebanon hit by a "rogue" Israeli shell.

On May 29, 1996, elections took place in Israel, with Rabin's legacy opposed by the Right. On a knife's edge, my cousin Adir's boss, the Likud Party's Binyamin Netanyahu, won the election, by a thin margin of 29,000 votes. The "peace" party was out, the party of Struggle, Nation and Grandeur was in. The "Anonymous Soldiers" had finally marched to the hilltop.

On May 30, I received the package from Yonni, Uncle Kolya's "Hawking boy," sent by Federal Express from New York. Some months before, he had sent me a formal letter, informing me of documents that could now be released by the clauses of Professor Gurevits's will to "parties whose ownership had been ceded to the deceased but reverted upon his demise." Among these were various legal papers, but one file pertained to "William Gore alias Boris Gorevitch, of Los Angeles, California." This would normally have reverted to my mother, but a note by Uncle Koya authorized his executors—a panel of academics from Michigan and Chicago, with Yonni in a secretarial capacity—to release this file directly to me. "Better late than never," Yonni wrote. None of his correspondence mentioned the "Soldier's Journal," which still smoldered in one of the boxes I had tucked in the storage niche over the kitchen cupboard.

As these releases drifted in at such irregular intervals, it had become a ritual for me to wait until Claire came home, usually late in the evening, to read them with her, passing the fragile thin paper, page by page, between us, once we had carefully removed the rusty paper clips. It was these paper clips, oddly, that resonated with the feeling of that touch of history, secured by my father's hand, one assumed, back in DeMille's studio, or in one of his Hollywood homes... Why had he sent it to Kolya, instead of attaching it to the DeMille files I had already recovered? But I had ceased to be surprised by the archives. What you sought was either there or not. Or sometimes it was there even if you were told it wasn't. You just had to know where to look. Or you just waited, and little angels appeared with FedEx wings and floated it down to your hand.

"What do you think?"

The quiet hours after midnight, when traffic is low outside, and even the neighbors have stopped shrieking at each other routinely through the fragile partition wall, and one can blend one's thoughts and try and make sense of the new hoard. Undressed in bed, facing the bookshelf that has stared at us for fifteen years, it strikes me suddenly strange that we were coming up to our twenty-first anniversary together. Life swept us along without blowing us apart. We had intended to celebrate on our twentieth, but Claire was away in Liverpool, rehearsing again. And still the waves ripple on...

"I think Gramby made up his dream, to suit your Dad," said Claire. "Everything comes back to the family. Why did the other dreams vanish? Or was there only the one, in the first place?"

"Who knows. Sometimes I think Yonni's playing a game with us."

There was also a note in the package, on paper marked "Dr. Yonatan Stern, 259 West End Avenue, N.Y.C. 10026," and the telephone number. Yonni wrote: "This, per will, see attached. There is some other stuff. Call me." I looked at the alarm clock by the bed.

"If it's about 8 p.m. in New York, I can call him now."

"You might as well."

Sometimes happenstance works. He was at home. We rushed through the courtesies.

"What other stuff?" I asked him. "You remember Uncle Kolya said he would leave me papers when he would finally let go. Is this all there is?"

"This is all," he said. "The rest is a labyrinth. I'm just a curator, as you know. I don't know what he said to you, but most of the material is Adir's property. He is the estate. There are three more academics who are appointed as editors. Tons of work, well beyond the millennium. Just the materials from Boris, or William Gore, go to your mother and you. I assumed you would be the interested party. Whatever Boris wrote to the Prof is the property of the receiving party. That's the way it works."

"So there are letters?"

"Some, but not a lot. Business stuff, secretarial. Nothing more revealing in the text. I can tell you something that Prof once said to me, but as far as I know there's no documentary evidence. Do you want to hear it?"

"I do."

"Category: gossip, as far as I am concerned. You know your father's first wife, Bella? Your brother's mother. Prof told me once she was not the first."

"You're joking."

"You have met me. I'm not the ribald type. He told me Boris was married for a short while to a young actress in Hollywood, in the early years of DeMille. I figured it must have been nineteen-fifteen or sixteen."

"Did he tell you her name?"

"I don't remember. Jane Doe, who knows. Prof used to let out bursts of information and then clam up, and get you involved in something else. He said they broke up pretty quickly."

"Was there a child? Son? Daughter?"

"I don't know."

"Was her name Zuleika?"

"I don't think so. It was more like a Jane, or a Mary. Gentile girl."

"That's it? Did he tell anyone else?"

"Who, Prof or your father?"

"Either of them."

"I have no idea. But I have another clue for you."

"All right. I'm listening."

"This is more solid. You know you were chasing the black kid, the saxophonist who was your Uncle Yakov's magic assistant?

563

Well, I hear they finally settled his archive. The family battle, between his ex-wives. How many were they—four, five? There were boxes sent to the New York Public Library, the music and dance collection at Lincoln Center. You should visit. It's nice in June, before it gets too hot."

"OK. That sounds interesting. You're sure about that?"

"About the heat? You can never tell. But on archives, I'm an archivist, so I hear things."

"Well, thanks for that."

"For gurnischt. You're welcome."

It was a good summer, though I could not go to New York in June, as the term at the film school ended in late July, and I was then committed to the July-August holiday that Claire and I had planned while passing around the Vacanza in Italia brochures. Car hire at Pisa Airport and the long drive east to Florence, on past Arezzo and Perugia until the great "boat" of Assisi rises like a beached ark on the mountain, up the range of Mount Subasio, on narrow twisting roads with ever more magnificent views towards the turn-off; down and up parched white gravel paths, across cattle grids, following minuscule signposts to invisible holiday chalets, until the road petered out in a tiny cluster of renovated farmouse-barns. And almost absolute quiet: no television, no telephones, a grassy backyard overlooking the valley of green fields and farmhouses leading on towards Nocera Umbra, where the only distractions were a few other discreet guests and the bull that used to wander into the enclosure, pushing open the thin pole across the path to deposit its doings on the grass.

This, too, is life—mundane as it comes, lying back in a garden chair, reading Fernand Braudel's *Civilization and Capitalism* on everyday life in the fifteenth to eighteenth centuries. How the Italian city-states and others functioned at the kick-starting of our present system, the story from the ground up, from the experience of people, not only the machinations of the ruling class. The third volume, *The Perspective of the World*, finally revealed to me, as we mildly shooed the bull away for the sixth time, that the fortunes of the British economy were built on the the stability of the pound sterling since the sixteenth century until 1931, which meant that everyone was eager to lend money to the Bank of England. The foundation of England's financial success was "the security of long term or perpetual debt," something that may have been clear to bankers but had not trickled down to mere fools like myself. This completely changed my attitude towards my own piddling bank account, and the attraction of holding on to my meager stash, rather than spending it to good purpose—such as foreign travel, regardless of the accumulating deficit—diminished by the page. It seemed illogical, but so did the world, plunging on obliviously towards disaster, without the old Marxist dichotomy of civilization or barbarism, but rather maintaining a precarious balance of both.

Summing up, we could count the good fortune that got us here, after a solid twenty-one years of joint survival, in a world where circumstances, conflict, jealousy, ennui and despair drove so many people apart. Even Shai Baer, patriarch of the Hub, keeper of the garden divan of lost souls, and his soul mate, Ilana, had separated, and he had galavanted off to the unholy land with a younger woman, Tsiporah, who had been on the rebound after a love affair with an Israeli-Arab policeman from Haifa. Shai's old comrade Moshik had cut off all contact and followed his own path as an anti-Zionist essayist and full-time mathematics professor. He and Farajul had collaborated on a book proving Marxism by mathematical logic, which appeared shortly before the entire Communist empire collapsed, though this only strengthened his thesis. Our friend Mansur had engendered a child with an Israeli comrade, Nehama, and now worked as taxi driver in Manchester. Gershon and Link had delinked, Gershon taking up a post as a prison psychologist in Santa Ana, not far from Disneyland, and Link remaining loyal to the "underground cinema" movement, experimenting with image and language in a series of short films shot around the United Kingdom, France, Italy, Morocco, Tunis and Israel. He wanted to demonstrate that nurture trumped nature. The book was translated into Polish and Hindi. He toured the festivals, and an avant-garde writer in Paris published a volume on his work and ideas.

The Goat had disappeared, no one knew whether on a long worldwide ramble or into the bourgeois life in Tel Aviv. Abed was picking his way carefully through the Arab League states, launched on a twenty-year project compiling statistics about stateless persons, refugees and human rights in the Middle East. He was making slow but sure progress in most areas, but in Syria no one was willing to be interviewed on the issue, until a good friend of his in Damascus gave him the name of an old Armenian professor who was stricken by cancer and was not expected to last more than six months: "He'll speak to you." Farida was now a regular speaker on British television about Palestinian rights and was on the guest list of Channel 4 News and Newsnight. She told us, "If I say the same things to them over and over at least six hundred times, there is a possibility that they might pay attention. It works for Chomsky." An argument that one could not refute.

Others had faded away. Imelda went back to Argentina and split from Pablo, who lectured on "peace studies" somewhere north of Yorkshire. Sargon raised a family in the far east of London and labored in servitude for a Saudi journal in London to put his two sons through law and art school.

I remained in the Camera Department, tending the flock of eager, wide-eyed faces raised to the promise of the silver screen, the celluloid dream and the magic lens. Technologies changed, but the same strategic obstacles persist: how to make thought into substance, the inchoate wanderings of the mind into images and sound organized onto film, or onto the pictureless tape or future media looming in the burgeoning digital age. The Internet, the worldwide web, the encyclopedic world at our fingertips, instant bridges across space and time. New primers for the instructor to read, new techniques to absorb if the master wants to keep ahead of the students. Sometimes I felt I should just lean back and let the kids tell me what needs to be done. Where once I stood brash and arrogant, with the wind of change whipping through my uncut hair, a multitude of infants now stream resolutely through the door. The mirror becoming as great an enemy for Asher Gurevits as for any light-shunning vampire...

Claire continued to be the consummate observer, still mulling the Project, the long-term idea of constructing some sense out of the tangled web of our communal story. She had become a disciple of Robert Lepage, whose extremely long play, *The Seven Streams of the River Ota*, had been staged a couple of years before in London, as a work in progress. A complicated saga in seven parts formed around the Hiroshima bomb, it rippled through themes of death and destruction, the concentration camp of Terezin, the AIDS crisis, a convoluted love affair and much more that sometimes escaped Claire's often-slumbering spouse. We had also just seen *Le Confessional*, in which Lepage juxtaposed a present-day mystery with the story of Alfred Hitchcock's filming of *I Confess*, in Quebec City in 1952.

The idea of a "long piece," which would be neither play nor film, neither fiction nor document, but a combination, a stage that opens up not to the old saw of audience participation but to a multitude of images, voices, stories. Most of all, it would raise questions that have no answers. The obvious slogans—peace, brotherhood, sisterhood, fairness, justice for all—were becoming tarnished in the clutter of clashing ambitions, desires, ideologies, faux-certainties and angry demands. The opening stage might be Shai's old garden, or somebody's bedroom, or the bare stage itself, with bits and pieces of unfinished scenery, film school flats, Dada-esque backgrounds of stereotypical capital cities, Bolshevik, Zionist banners, and so forth, or even just barren, with large screens or TV sets to show the shards from the old Asherite material, the Palestine film of the '70s, the images of occupation, interviews, Kolya's memorial, the landscape itself, newsreel shots of the Six Day War, Yom Kippur, etcetera, gleaned from the available networks, television archives, the jumbled footage of reality and reconstruction captured by faked reality... time recalled, time twisted and reinvented, clashing truths of states and states of mind... We have no unblemished fathers anymore, no unshorn heroes, gold-tipped dreams.

I informed Claire of the news, gleaned from the one weekend Hebrew paper that could still be bought at the Finchley Road tube station, that Adir had been made Deputy Minister of Transport in the new Likud government. Now he was actually in charge of something, empowered to fuck up the bus service, the trains, cargo, shipping and the airport—not that the national air carrier, El Al, needed any help to that end. Inside the old Umbrian farm-house, we could sit in our rustic retreat, under the wooden beams set in the whitewashed ceiling, and the colony of feral cats who can get through the slightest crack into the house and curl up under the supper table mewing piteously or pretending to cough themselves to death by starvation as we try to eat our precious salamis and cheese, chewing over our plans and trying to figure the equation between culture and history, the structures of art against the confusion of evidence, the Seven Streams of the River Ota, six, eight or more, if you factor in the descendants, sons, daughters, grandchildren, even, in my brother Yitzhak's case, two great-grandchildren already, and all returned to the root, bona fide "black hats," destined for the yeshiva and shul. God may have the last laugh after all, behind the curtain, in his imaginary realm.

Midterm at the film school, I had to take time off in October to rush to Tel Aviv, as my brother phoned me to say my mother was ill. Something to do with her legs, which were failing to carry her up and down the four flights of stairs at Melchett Street. She had been moved, once again, as in the time of my father's care home twilight, to my brother's home in Jerusalem. Despite the growth of his own family, there was still room in his large apartment in the ever-growing outer suburb of Giloh, the mass of concrete housing blocks gouged out of the hills north of the city that had been the West Bank of the Jordan, annexed in the great hubris of conquest in 1967. I never was a frequent guest, apart from the visits necessitated by my father's long journey into the final, unpremiered movie.

Then as now, there was my brother's large anteroom, with its shelves full of sacred and religious books, all the great gold-embossed volumes of the Talmud, the smaller Mishnah, the countless commentaries and explications poured out from the printing presses of the devout. Sets of present-day texts of daily life and ritual, biographies and discourses of famous rabbis, from the Mishneh Torah of Maimonides, the Kuzari of Judah Halevi, the *Sefer Avoda Tama* ("the book of innocent work") by Benvenisti, Ezer Hayim (the "guide of life") by Hayim Siton, *The Mishnah of Rabbi Eliezer, Sha'ar Shamayim* (the "gate of heaven") by Rabbi Gershon ben-Shlomo of Arles, *Ha'kuntres Ha-Yehieli* ("the discourse of Yehieli") by Yitzhak Alfiyah, *Torah Im Derech Eretz* ("Torah in civilized discourse") of Samson Raphael Hirsch, Mintz's Sefer Meir Be'ahava ("enlightens in love") about Rabbi Shapira of the Agudat Yisrael movement and dozens more. I listed a selection one morning just for Claire's education, so she could glimpse a corner of the "other life" and complicate the Project even further, while Yitzhak's wife, Aliza, brought me mounds of biscuits, cake, coffee and tea.

In the smaller guest bedroom, where I used to kip on a hardboard single bed, there were some English-language books, mostly Penguin classics, the usual Russians, some H.G. Wells, some Galsworthy and a bunch of books on film technique, brought over from Melchett, led by Joseph V. Mascelli's *Five C's of Cinematography, The Focal Encyclopedia of Film and Television Techniques, Principles of Cinematography* by Leslie J. Wheeler and *The Film Till Now* by Paul Rotha, which my father had given me on my fifteenth birthday without realizing that the "now" of the title referred to 1929. My mother had these brought over to cover the days, weeks and months leading up to my father's passing. One set of framed photographs, which Yitzhak had moved to the big guestroom where my mother was now staying, showed my parents in Hollywood, and in early times at Melchett, on the beach, in the park, at the Caesaria ruins, and older portraits of my father with DeMille, with the two Laskys, Father and the screenwriter son, with Victor Mature as Samson, with John Wayne in *Reap the Wild Wind*, Gary Cooper in *North West Mounted Police*, Charles Laughton as Nero and so forth… The one I liked most was of my father alone, sitting behind the great old Mitchell BNC camera, mounted on the giant Louma crane. Just him and the camera, soaring into the sky.

Apart from her legs, my mother's chief problem was that she was displaying the symptoms of what the doctors now called Alzheimer's, once classified as senile dementia. Her memory was drifting away. The neighbors directly downstairs at Melchett, the Arielis, had gone, the husband dead and the wife moved to an old age home, and the couple that moved in were Sheinkin bourgeois, a polite couple in business—banking (the wife) and lingerie (the husband), so they were useless as auxiliary staff. My cousin Rivkie was in some kind of post-neurotic rehab in the Galilee, Yitzhak had a vast pool of able and willing support among the sons, daughters and even the tiny religious tots who were taught from an early age to respect their elders, help the sick and minister to the needy. They crowded around my mother, bringing sweets and flowers and bombing her with love, playing with their toys in her room or spending time there on their new computer gadgets, which were loaded with supposedly God-friendly games.

A peculiar experience, to walk among these little strangers, with their bright eyes and sidelocks, flesh of my flesh, blood of my blood, immersed in a world that would have been so familiar to my father's house, when he was a child, apart from so much that would have been alien, or a dream, to the residents of Celovest in the wheat fields of the Ukrainian-Bessarabian steppes, among the goyim. At least compared to the raucous urban reality of the split city that my brother inhabited, the ground floor of this huge complex of housing blocks perched on the side of the hill where there were still gaps, where past the spiderweb of cranes over yet more

570

housing blocks rising day by day, girder by girder, lay the Arab villages just across the valley, barely three hundred meters distant, where cars and vans moved like mobile toys and people passed like tiny ants, registering not a dot on the retinas of the hundreds of new or recent occupants of the Jewish blocks, to whom they seemed invisible. Every night, I would be jerked awake by the call of the muezzin from the mosque on the other side, reverberating more or less according to the direction of the breeze, a sound that no one else in the house noticed. Or perhaps they found it convenient, since they too had to wake to early prayer in any case. I tried this theory on Yitzhak, who simply said "Could be." There was no point in starting up a political discussion destined to end in tense annoyance, with his fingers drumming on his chair.

My mother was still at the early phase of the onset of the illness, usually recognizing the people around her, though obviously confused in Yitzhak's busy household. She knew me, despite my absences, but often confused Yitzhak with characters she had seen in films we used to go to without my father, who often disapproved of popular but vulgar fare, so that she sometimes called him Kuni Lemel or Rabbi Jacob, after a long faded Louis de Funès film. The women and girls she could name fairly easily, but she was lost among the beards.

Mornings I would take her out on her stick, out the door to the street and around the corner, moving very slowly. There was not much to see but for a flurry of black-hats and headscarved women moving to and fro. It was too far for her to walk beyond the block itself, to the Mini-Market, the electrical and kitchen appliance shops, the dry-cleaners and children's toy store. Buses were not too frequent, as most of the residents had a vehicle, a necessity in this urban outpost. Yitzhak had a typical "people carrier," a Volvo, into which he could cram four adults and four children at a time, or one adult and at least eight children.

Once, when Sari had driven my mother to the local clinic, Yitzhak sat me down and said his piece, which was, put succinctly, that he knew I did not live in Israel by choice, and he didn't expect

571

me to move back now that my mother was ailing and required total care; he knew the doctors said the condition was terminal. No one knew how long it would take, but deterioration was certain; there was no cure nor practical treatment apart from family care that he could provide. The fact that she was my mother, not his, made no difference. She was his father's wife, and this was his obligation. If I wanted to feel guilty I was welcome to do so, but my life was mine, and his own existence was mapped out.

All his life, he said, he had to deal with the fact that his father, our father, had lived a very different life from the life he had chosen, as a matter of faith and conscience, but his respect for him was never diminished. My brother Yitzhak could be very pompous when he wished, but he also knew me, and knew his good conscience bound me in bonds of overwhelming convenience. Any time I could fly over and see my mother I was welcome, without any notice. He would give me the keys to the house, the apartment, the front of the block, and the security codes to the gate. I had access to Sari's car, the old battered Fiat, when I needed it. *Shoen, genug.*

I had been put in my place. Wastrel, apostate, ungrateful son, traitor, it was all written in my own dour discomfort at the state decreed by blood and history. Needless to say, I was not to dredge up the foreign codes that mandated such matters as Arab Palestinian rights, or the division of the land, or "occupation," or issues of politics that might or might not turn out this way or that, but were not, in his eyes, fundamental. What was fundamental had been mandated by God, and my disputing that would not concern him one bit; that was purely for my conscience, not his.

On the fourth day of my visit, my cousin Tsadok, Aunt Sarah's middle son, last met at Kolya's memorial, motored up and sat with my mother for a while, till his own estranged son, Yerachmiel, turned up. I had last seen Yeri as a little boy with a speech impediment, who did badly at school and was subjected to endless tests and quack therapies to loosen his tongue. But now he was a grown man, with his own family, including the eldest, Yakir, who accompanied him on his visit, a surly young clone of his father's own somber black hat reserve. Father, son and grandson looked at each other awkwardly, as if the generations were improperly gathered, given the compartments they each had to inhabit. Tsadok, the hard-skinned urban Israeli, self-made provider and citizen, the forty-year-old son who lived in the Old City of Jerusalem, among the true believers, and the boy, who seemed to inhabit a world of his own. Tsadok told me all about it as he drove me back up the main road to Tel Aviv to check out the locked apartment at Melchett.

"My poor mother," he said. "Your aunt, the pioneer—she thought she had escaped the chains of religious reaction when she came out here to dig roads and plant trees. Scientific socialism, Zionist Achievement, doing, not brooding on God. My poor son was always a brooder. It was our fault, we expected too much of him. Today we know what a bunch of confused idiots we were in our time. They expected us to live up to them, our parents. Not yours. I always envied you so much, Asher. Your dad and mum, they met in Hollywood and fell in love, just like Hedy-Ledy-what's-her-name and Samson—except that your mum let your dad keep his hair. You grew up with cameras and movies and California, while we grew up with Berl Katsnelson and Borochov and 'stychian processes' and cowshit in the kibbutz. I couldn't wait to get out to Tel Aviv. My mother and Golda Meir, you should have seen them together, it was enough to shrivel your pee-pee to a pod. We all had to be the golden generation, the first proper Sabras, Israelis, not Celovest Jews. Muscles, you know, human tractors. So we had a son who was a bit slow and clumsy. Shoshana told me he would turn out all right, but I was brainwashed. I pushed him too hard. It's no wonder he stuttered. Couldn't do his home-work, had to have a special tutor. A woman called Chechik, she probably neutered him to the foundations. They turned him down for the army, we sent him to a technical school. The next thing I know he turns up with all this paraphernalia, the black coat, the beard, the *tsitses*, the kippa, the hat, won't take a bite or drink a cup of tea in the house. Unclean, unclean. Won't give a kiss to his sister, not even a caress or a poke. The rebbe mandates absolute purity. And who is this rebbe? Some insane degenerate who lives in the West Bank and passes decrees that the state is an emanation of Satan. Apparently we were set up by the Communists to stop the real Jews from declaring the proper kingdom of Israel. Salvation will only come when we tear down the Muslim mosques, breed the red heifer, rebuild the Temple and prepare the people for the Messiah, who is just around the corner, parked somewhere between Bnei Brak and Geulah. I'm not surprised, with this traffic, you might expect him in the twenty-third century, at the earliest. But what can I tell you, Asher, he's still my son, and that poor boy, another branch of the tree. God knows what his father is teaching him. And that's the literal truth."

Tsadok had flung his car back into the mainstream traffic to avoid using the settler route as a shortcut towards Tel Aviv. Every driver seemed to be in an extreme state of road rage. As they say in this country: "*Ze ma yesh*"—"This is what there is."

Once in Tel Aviv, of course, the traffic became even worse, and the familiar lecture ensued about the complete impossibility of parking, which Tsadok had partly solved by obtaining a fake badge designating him as "disabled." "Sometimes it works and sometimes it doesn't." he said, "If there's a cop around, just limp." Nevertheless, we made it safely to the apartment. Inside, everything looked tidy, though a little dusty, and very hot. We opened the windows to the sea breeze.

One can never avoid feeling a pang at the memory of the space in which you grew up. I had long ago got used to the fact that what had once seemed large and spacious was now tiny and cramped. But its abandonment gave a strong pang in the heart. As long as my mother was still here, the past still existed somewhere, as a refuge, illusory as it might be. In one of her few lucid moments, in Jerusalem, I talked to my mother about Claire and myself, and what we were up to in London. I mentioned the ongoing search for family documents and information about all the siblings of Celovest, hoping it might jog some memory, at least of our talking about all this before. But she became fixated on a set of photo albums that she said were still in the house at Melchett, and I promised to bring them back to her. They were, of course, the old childhood albums of baby and schooltime snapshots, and pictures of herself and my father from their Los Angeles days. I had carried some of those with me to London, but some of the albums should still be where I had left them in the apartment, in the chest of drawers of old papers and magazines, folders of letters and mounds of municipal and utility bills. The albums were not there, but Tsadok, like an angel from heaven, scooped up the bills and said, "I'll deal with these. You're just a foreigner—you wouldn't have a clue in this jungle. These people only know the language of force. I'll tie them in legal knots until the coming of the Messiah. They'll never collect a single worn agora."

I forged on, finding the key in one of the kitchen drawers to open the big windows onto the balcony. Someone had hastily spread a white tablecloth on the old garden table and chairs, and the unfolded deck chair, which lay dusty on the tiled floor, held down by a couple of mementoes of Dad's old days: some prop Philistine pottery and a helmet from the sets of *Samson and Delilah*, like leftovers from some museum case. I remembered the niche over the storage cupboard where the ironing board and other paraphernalia were kept. There was a big cardboard box there that we took down and wiped with an old rag and carried back into the flat.

Old stuff: most of it my father's correspondence, legal papers, house documents, car documents, insurance papers, scripts from Herzliya and Geva studios, letters from old friends, from California, New York, Chicago, Paris, Singapore, holiday brochures, school reports—complaints of average scores for yours truly—copies of *Variety* and *The Hollywood Reporter*, some old joke cards I'd sent from American stops on the Greyhound circuit—giant pumpkins and marrows from Texas, crazy San Francisco stuff from old freak shows: "The Man Who Puts Eighteen Inch Nails Through His Nose," the bearded woman of Terre Haute, Indiana, Benjamin Franklin being electrocuted at a wall socket and so forth. A set of exercise books on chemistry and algebra from my school years, with faded logarithmic tables that were complete gobbledegook to me now... a menu from the Frishman Café, and an old set of camera sheets from *Reap the Wild Wind*...

And then, with all hope almost lost, right at the back: the old photograph albums, three of which looked familiar and another, a cracked tortoiseshell binding I was sure I had not seen before, enclosed by a dry rubber band that broke when I touched it, and containing a torn cardboard folder sealed with a red plastic ribbon that had to be cut with the kitchen scissors.

Banzai! Two albums of regular family snapshots, the first wholly dedicated to my inglorious self, from babyhood in pram and parental embrace through toddling and the familiar calvary of school, primary and high, and then the inevitable gawky recruit in khaki, vanishing on the last page into the amorphous basic training mass. Various faces that I remembered vaguely, with the leering faces of the aged looking down upon the miracle of new life. Then, in the second book, more school stuff, the streets of Tel Aviv of then, my first bicycle, my first camera, the costumed faces of my early casts, small boys drowning in adult raincoats, with painted and false moustaches and an array of plastic guns. I had forgotten the rubber water tap we had fitted onto the pretend Luger in lieu of a proper silencer. Those were the days.

The third book, dedicated to my parents, included their wedding photo in Los Angeles, the pristine lanes and lawns of West Hollywood, the perpendicular streets of Silver Lake, the happy couple posing by the famous "Laurel and Hardy steps," the Lasky ranch museum, the DeMille lot and Dad with a whole host of familiar faces: George Sanders, Victor Mature, Gary Cooper, Fredric March, Paulette Goddard, John Wayne, Raymond Massey, Susan Hayward. Dad with DeMille and his crew, Jesse Lasky Jr, Hans Dreier the art director, Ann Bauchens the editor who had been with him since the silent days, Victor Milner, the other cinematographer. Dad behind the camera, beside the camera, mounted on the camera, hugging the camera, practically blended with the camera…

"Life with the stars!" Tsadok sat beside me, shaking his head. "He had it made, your dad. But he came here in the end. What can you do, blood is blood. In America the whole point was to make yourself something out of what you weren't. So Siggy Michaelovitch makes himself Michael Stone, or, who was it, Kirk Douglas, who started out as Izzy Yankele, or whatever. Your John Wayne, didn't he have a girl's name—Marion? I bet you even Marilyn Monroe was born Feigeh Leibovich. But here everybody is exactly who they are. Yosske Zichmich. Even if they change it to Zrubavel Yoked, or, pardon me, Adir Gur-Arieh."

I was picking my way through the old brown manila envelopes in the folder that I didn't remember having seen before. They had my mother's scrawl in ballpoint: "Sarah, 1930," "Sarah, 1931," "Sarah, 1932," "Sarah, Zionist Congress," etcetera. Each was sealed with a rusty metal clamp strengthened by cellotape.

"You remember I told you about the casino?" Tsadok prattled on while I labored. "The one in Jericho? Well, it's definitely on. The plans are all drawn up. The money's coming from all sides. There's an Austrian millionaire, who was chums with both Rabin and Peres, who's in the casino business in Vienna. There's that guy who used to be the ex-deputy of the head of the security service, and his equivalent in the PLO, some Gibril something, and a whole lot of other Palestinian bigwigs. Arafat himself is a shareholder. There'll be a big hotel next door and thousands of people will come from all over the state to play roulette in the West Bank. One-arm bandits in all the suites, just like Las Vegas. And the Walls of Jericho will fall again. You hear me, cousin? When money talks, all the barriers break down. What do the Italians say? One hand washes the other."

I opened the envelopes carefully, one by one. Each one of the first four contained a sheaf of folded photocopies of newspaper cuttings from the old Labor Zionist daily Davar. Inked lines indicated the articles that Sarah Gurevits had written for the paper in the early 1930s. The fourth contained one item with a typed cover letter paperclipped on the attached leaves covered with Aunt Sarah's orderly writing I recognized from the Los Angeles letters to Boris. The whole thing was puzzling, since when I had called my mother in '91 from Provo about Sarah's letters she had mentioned none of this stuff. Perhaps I asked the wrong questions.

The cover letter was from one Anat Bergson, curator, at the Beit Berl Archive of the Workers' Party of Eretz-Yisrael, Mapai."

The Daughter of Noah

Dear Mrs Henrietta Gurevits-Gore,

I am enclosing the original text of the letter marked "Gorovitz-Gur, Sarah, 456/3-SG-456332" in our archival system, Founders' Collection—Ahdut Ha'Avoda-Mapai 1923-1939, at your request submitted by Dr. Nahum Goldblatt. This article is being sent to you by personal courier. At your request we have not stored a copy. We fully understand the nature of your request, despite the letters signed by your late husband, Mr. William Baruch Gore, on the 23rd and 26th of September, 1972, regarding the private corre-spondence of Mrs. Sarah Gur (Gurevits), that was included in the original bequest to our collection, but restricted from public use and not included in our catalogue. I also include three envelopes of photocopies of the original cuttings of "Davar" of Mrs. Gur's article series "Nation and Origin," as published between 6 April 1930 and 1 September 1933. These remain both as original clip-pings and on microfilm in our collection and are always available for public viewing. The collection of Mrs. Gur's writings continues to be a valuable resource in our archive of the Founders and inspir-ers of the Zionist Labour movement from its inception in Eretz-Yisrael, to illuminate and educate new generations in the thoughts, philosophies and deeds of those who made our existence here a reality.

All of us here at the archive wish you good health and a long life, and appreciate the contribution your illustrious family has made to the Zionist project in our land.

Yours in great honour,

Anat Bergson,

Senior Curator

The Cuttings:

6 April, 1930:
(Headlines of the day:
CIVIL REBELLION IN INDIA, THOUSANDS VISIT GANDHI,
30 RAILWAY STRIKERS WOUNDED BY RIFLE FIRE. JAPAN
ACCEPTS BRITISH AND AMERICAN PROPOSALS ON NAVAL
QUOTAS. REACTIONS TO COMMITTEE OF INQUIRY ON ARAB
RIOTS. ANNUAL MEETING OF THE NATIONAL KIBBUTZ
"HASHOMER HA'TSAIR" ["The Young Guards"].)

Nation and Origin (*"Leum u'Mekhorah"*) by Sarah Gurevits.

I am, like many of the ranks of our movement of national renewal,
the daughter of a traditional family, born among the masses of
Jewish workers, artisans and agricultural workers of the eastern
European Pale of Settlement. Until the last generation, our forefathers and our mothers were devoted both to Torah and to work,
to structuring their daily lives according to the precepts of holy
law, subject to the secular strictures of the kingdoms and empires
in which we lived. Our existence was punctuated by the pogroms
which came like sudden but expected plagues that devastated
but did not destroy us. We hewed to the rock of our beliefs. If we
were divided among ourselves by classes, by wealth and poverty,
we were united by the powerful bonds of faith and common circumstances. My father was the Rabbi of his community, a small
town in the flatlands of Bessarabia, which was a part of the Tsar's
dominions when I was born, and is now a province of Rumania.
We were a large family, four brothers and two sisters. Today my
parents, blessed be their memory, are departed, and we are scattered among the nations. Only my brother Nathan is with us here
in Eretz Yisrael.

Before my father passed away, he too became open to the
ideas that were expressed by Theodor Herzl and the first Zionist
Congresses. But I am not sure that he believed, as many others

did, that Herzl was a new prophet, whose mission was, despite his secular life and ideas, ordained by a higher power. My father believed that if his first duty was towards God, his second was to his community. Nationality was not a matter of importance to him. He would simply say: "I am a Jew." In class terms, as the Marxists would define it, he was a "bourgeois." He owned some property, a house near the Bet Midrash, and a field which he rented out to another family, that had been granted by the Russian "zemtsvo" (the civil authority). But he was, in his small circle, a leader, to whom people came with their questions, their grievances, their daily and important requirements, such as weddings, circumcisions, funerals, as well as business matters. In all these issues he found that the scriptures, Torah and Talmud, answered all that was necessary. When Revolution came, he ministered to the needs of his community. Affairs of state were not his concern.

Those of us who were of the next generation, however, were deeply affected by the tides of both Socialism and Zionism that washed over our village. The Great War that mercifully spared us, apart from my brother, who was recruited but survived the conflagration, reshuffled all the cards of world affairs, and laid the class struggle bare throughout Europe. The barbarity of war made our choices very plain. If my birth occurred during the reign of the Tsar Alexander the Third, my adult life was marked by the example of Lenin, Trotsky, Herzl and Borochov. The first two inherited a fallen empire, the other two looked out, from modest quarters, towards a more specific solution to our own situation.

I remember the slogan that was carried through our town on that day of February 1917 which proclaimed that "We are masters of our own fate." Those of us who saw our own dedication to Zion as a part of our international Socialism have a duty to define the synthesis of these two ideas which some proclaim as incompatible. Our "*Mechorah*"—our origin—is not only a matter of circumstance, like the contours of a physical landscape, or even of language, vital though that is in our revival of the Hebrew tongue. The psychologists of our time have shown us that our deepest instincts and

desires are formed in us in earliest childhood, and these matters too, are a science, a human science that is as significant as that of class formation and struggle. Perhaps, I venture to speculate, these matters are more apparent to women than to men, for whom mastery of both nature and nurture appear more apparent, and differentiate not only classes but genders. But we are struggling here for a new equality, a new philosophical and practical dispensation that is also, I would argue, a necessary ingredient of renewal in what was always, for our forebears, our own old-new land.
(This polemic will continue in future issues.)

8 April, 1930:
(Headlines of the day: CALLS TO BOYCOTT ENGLISH TEXTILES IN INDIA. HIGH COMMISSIONER'S VISIT TO CO-OPERATIVE SETTLEMENTS. REVISIONISTS DISRUPT ORGANISED WORKERS IN KFAR-SABA. "TARBUSH MAN" SENTENCED TO 18 YEARS.

Nation and Origin, Part 2, by Sarah Gurevits.

The special report of the Investigating Committee on the "Events" of last August have concentrated our minds on the relationship between our colonists and the Arabs of Palestine, with the Committee's provocative comments that Zionist settlements have been responsible for a justified anxiety on the part of the Arabs which led to the violence, riots and killings. While the committee states that Jewish immigration and enterprise, "when not in excess of the absorbtive capacity of the country, have conferred material benefits upon Palestine in which the Arab people share" it also states that "the claims and demands advanced from the Zionist side in regard to the future of Jewish immigration into Palestine have been such as to arouse apprehensions among the Arabs that they will in time be deprived of their livelihood and pass under the political domination of the Jews." While our representatives have been quick to reject these findings, we would be wise, in light of the disturbances that have shaken the peace of the country to reflect on our own responses, in the light of the Imperial power's contentions.

While the Balfour Declaration of a Jewish home in Palestine encouraged our efforts, we must not forget that we did not come here as agents of a foreign colonial interest, but in advance of our own goals and ideals. Nevertheless, there are some among us who came wearing rosy spectacles, imagining that we have come to a desolate and empty country, the Biblical lands laid waste by wars and the profligacy of tyrants, and the neglect of the old Ottoman regime. But if we are, in a true sense, socialists, then we should also broaden our encounter to encompass the human landscape as well. For in the more fertile places of the country we can see with our own eyes the evidence of settlement of the other custodians of the land, the Muslim and the Christian Arabs, with their mosques, churches, villages and fields. They too, have their own religious authorities, and their nationalists, who are touched by the same turmoil of war and the postwar entrenchment of the world powers, their own psychology and their own "Mechorah"—their origin tales.

It does not take much ordinary intelligence to realise that the British colonial administration sees the Arabs as much as an obstacle as they often see our pioneers in pursuing their Mandate of Versailles. Just as the French have incubated rebellion in Syria, so the British face unrest and insurrection in their own allocated portions, as is apparent in Mesopotamian Iraq. Our challenge must be, if we are true to our principles and values, not to become completely identified with the colonial needs of the European empires, despite what political expediency may guide the overall Zionist Committees of Weizmann and our brothers and sisters in Europe and in America.

The future of the Zionist movement may well be lived in an environment that is harsher even than the one we found when we disembarked, battered and often confused, if exhilarated, on the stony quays of Jaffa, despite the apparent modern comforts of our new Tel Aviv, with its cafes, its cinema-palaces, its fashion stores and tall buildings. We should march towards it, with confidence in our capacities, but also with wide open eyes.

The second envelope sent by the Labour movement archive contained only three clippings of "Davar," from May 1932, including headlines pages covering—

> HITLER'S PLANS FOR PROSPERITY AND HAPPINESS: REPRESENTATIVE STRASSER PRESENTS PARTY PLAN TO REICHSTAG—Strasser's speech surprised the Reichstag with its moderation; the ideology was mostly taken from the Swedish sociologist, Kessel... Reichstag approves new law empowering the government to take steps to reduce unemployment...

> BRITAIN: FINANCE MINISTER ELIOT ASSURES PARLIAMENT—declares British credit still better than European competitors: "We have not yet been saved from the fall of western civilization, but we are advancing in a responsible way."

There were no articles by Aunt Sarah in this batch, but one poem, in the Friday Children's Supplement section of 20th May, and a commentary note, in an unattributed column, which has been marked and annotated in writing on the margin: "This is too much!" The comment goes:

> "Davar" last week published a news item under the heading "Mufti's assistant preaches support for Fascism," rightly castigating the Arab leadership that is caught out in dubious and harmful views, but what is this? On the other hand, Advocate Cohen, who has just been elected to the central committee of the Revisionists, has declared before the Jerusalem district court that "If the Hitlerists had taken out of their platform their hatred for the Jews, we too would stand (i.e. we too, the Revisionists) with the Hitlerists, for if the Hitlerists had not

risen in Germany, Germany would have been lost. Yes, Hitler has saved Germany." So the mufti's assistant is not alone in his views in this country, and he has supporters for his political views, albeit not on the expected side. (Aunt Sarah added several exclamation marks.)

Her poem was entitled: "Noah's Daughter"—

If I am the daughter of Noah,
Who is my bridegroom?
Forty days and forty nights I looked out from my window,
Searching the sea for sight of fertile land,
While the doves sheltered meekly from the rain.
But on the fortieth day when the mountain tops
Rose finally on the horizon,
My father first sent the raven out upon his quest.
My brothers and their wives waited below
While I climbed slowly up to the crow's nest
And cast my gaze across the waters.
There were forests of tall pines, cedar and cypresses
That stood calm amid receding waves.
But when the raven first returned
He was not sure the land was ready.
Only when the dove was sent out
Did she return with the olive branch
To deliver to my father's hand,
And only then could we descend from the Ark.
But my brothers were not sure
That the days ahead showed the sun's rising promise
And the animals that descended, two by two, from the Ark,
First saw the sacrificial fire
That was readied for our father's hope.
And yet I walked down with a light step,
Onto the shore, that welcomed me
With the sigh of the swaying trees
And the song of the birds
Who first made their home upon the land.

Sitting at my mother's kitchen table, with my cousin Tsadok dipping through the cuttings, his eyelids drooping at the familiar wedges of verbiage that covered "Davar"s inner pages, I finally took up the nine leaves of the letter Ms. Bergson of the Labour archive had sent my mother, according to the typed date, in September 1986. It was written in the form I was already familiar with from Aunt Sarah's other archive letters, if a little more agitated, as befitted the content. The letter was written soon after Aunt Sarah's final article in the previous envelope, on 28 August, 1933, and addressed to "Yocheved." This was a female name I had never come across before from Sarah's writings or from any memory of her conversations in old age. Nor was she anyone my mother had ever mentioned, as far as I could recall.

My aunt wrote:

Dear Yocheved,

I was writing this letter to Boris, in America, when I realised that I found impossible to confide in him in matters like this. Since he has never been here, and never seen how we live, it is impossible to explain these matters to him. There he stays, in California, working without a stop in that shining factory of dreams made to comfort the masses who go to the cinema houses to escape from the reality of their own lives. This is his life's work, but I do not think he sees it that way. Rather he is like a machinist, who is so much in love with his machine that it is sufficient for all his moral and material needs. He is a happy man, I think, and how can I disturb a brother's happiness with a tale of woe that he can't possibly understand?

So as we used to whisper together, in the tent off Migdal, so I am whispering to you now. I know it is difficult for us to meet at this crucial time. I must say that family life, despite it all, is placid. Yoav is a good man, in the widest sense of the word, and Eli is becoming a true and strong pioneer, and little Tsadok is a true tatar, and now the third, warming up and moving inside. The future, an indescribably feeling. But I could not let my brother's hand feel it. Something has come between us that has broken the unbreakable tie that has connected us since childhood, even in the long absence...

Then Sarah spoke of Kolya, her brother Natan, who had brought his long voyage from the battlefields of Russia to a close in Europe, at Trieste, from which he finally travelled to Palestine, joining the debaters at one of the many lecture-fests the Zionist left were besotted with, as she described the scene:

> ... I can't forget the day that he came, striding across the field towards me, in the Ramah, when we were settled there, the very image of the "returning soldier," dressed in the black jacket and cap of a true Bolshevik commissar who had somehow taken a different turning on the Ukrainian steppes and come through a magic door into Palestine. Suddenly, without a warning, he was before me, and we were embracing, in the sweat of travel and time.
>
> ...He told me the whole tale—from Celovest, the war, the Revolution, and the terrible years that followed... His long hard journey from Siberia, through the gold fields, to the other end of the earth, in South Africa... I could not imagine him there, my little Kolya, always an earnest child, but never bold, I thought, so often afraid of the dark, and so cautious—branching out to such adventures. It was there, he said, that he began to doubt the world theories that had flung him out so far. Even there, among the black labourers, who worked as little more than slaves for their white overseers, he found that Jews were despised. I think it was the workers' uprising that changed him, when he saw the white labourers denouncing their "Jewish" employers. It is difficult for us to imagine the strange world that exists out there. We are such a small corner, and he too realised that we need to look to our own. But, unlike us, he decided that Socialism was a false pathway, and that a narrow, Hebrew identity was the only end to our trials...
>
> I hope I am becoming less naive now, in my middle-age, than when I arrived. Things seem less clear-cut, because of world affairs, the great divisions of nations and societies

becoming more perilous and stark. But Kolya's vision was much darker than minet. He had no faith whatever in Russia, that "great experiment," which we see in the balance, but which he sees as a complete failure... At that time he was alone, and now he has Magda, but I have only met her once, and she is very much the silent spouse. I don't think we exchanged more than a few words. She keeps her peace when his volcano erupts. He suddenly burst out and told us we were deluded if we believed the so-called Soviet Federation was anything more than a charnel house. We were on a ship of fools, if we thought peaceful collective organisation would keep us alive in this country.

We are surrounded by wolves, he said. The British are hypocrites, the Americans are the most naive idealists until it comes to their own interests, and all the smaller nations are discovering the same thing: fight or die. Yoav tried to get him to agree that we did have our own defence forces, our own Guards. But he said that if we did not awake soon, it would be too late.

We argued, but he is still my brother, so we shared our dinner quietly and Kolya told Eli a story, a little awkwardly and abruptly, about a Siberian bear who found a pot of gold in the mountains. But the bear had no-one to share it with, and Eli was very sad that the bear had no cubs, so Yoav tried to explain that there would have to be a mummy bear and a daddy bear for that, but Kolya just left the story as it was. It sounded to me like a very barren story of capitalist accumulation. But he stayed over to the next morning, then shouldered his rucksack and left.

I did not see him for a while, and heard from others that he had become a military trainer for the young bloods of "Beitar." There were already rumours that some of our own Haganah youngsters were thinking of leaving to join the Revisionists in a new underground movement, but until the murder of Arlozorov we had no idea they would run so far from the house.

Our final meeting then, for a long while, was in Jerusalem, where he lives in a rented room in a house owned by an older couple, the Greenspans, who are old comrades of Jabotinsky. The house is almost exactly opposite the old Ethiopian church, which has a large and beautiful garden that we went into to have some privacy from the landlords. It was Sunday, and the priests in the church were conducting their mass, we could hear their sonorous voices all across the garden. They are quite a sight, these very tall black men in their ornamented robes, with their particular crosses and religious icons. They reminded me a little of the "True Slavs" of our Ukrainian neighbours, back in "the home."

Kolya pointed at them, saying that these "Copts" were the oldest Christian community in the world, and that they had kept their faith, deep in Africa, for nearly two thousand years, they were the oldest religion apart from the Jews. He said we should learn from them to survive in dignity, but we did not have the luxury of just continuing our old liturgy and following the Rabbis, because our enemies were gaining power by the day. I tried to soften him by talking about our childhood, by saying how I missed our family, feeling that however much we were at home here, we were so incomplete... That we are the vanguard, but we cannot force our way by violence. We have to prevail by defence, not offence.

He waved this away. His eyes were flashing, like someone who has seen a light that he cannot let go of, the light of a fire, not of human warmth and kindness. I tried to turn the talk from politics, and asked him straight out: Kolya, what has so soured your spirit? And he looked me in the eye, in that placid garden, with the black priests singing, and told me terrible things. He said he had killed a lot of people, both in the war, and after it, when all life turned into perpetual battle. He said he had served the forces of Satan, and had been an executioner, despatching the enemies of the State without mercy with single shots of his gun. He had shot men and women, and even a child, though this was a boy who had pulled out a gun to fire on him. Then he had made a long long journey through a nightmare which did not seem to end, an icy war in which men murdered each other in great masses.

I walked in the valley of the shadow of death, he said, and God was not with me. God had deserted the battlefield... He held my hand and spoke to me with a frightening intensity. He said that he had learned that men were wolves, and the idea that they could become placid and kind, and tolerant of each other's differences, was a mirage, an illusion of well-meaning idealists who would always run away from the consequences of their own dreams. He said Herzl's "If you will it, it is no fairy tale," was a bourgeois fantasy, because the will was only a beginning, an intention, which to be carried out could not avoid the use of force. He said he had seen too many people who called themselves socialists who in reality were only butchers who lashed out in impotent fury against all and sundry, murdering their own sons, daughters, fathers, brothers, mothers.

I tried to talk of our parents' house, of the loving kindness of our father, our mother, who taught us by their own example that all are at heart one family, even our destroyers, whom God cursed, but the truth of the great light of Torah was that all were part of the Creation. He said he had learned this from our parents too, but that his own life had shown him how the Good were always swallowed by the Bad. You 'socialists', he said, will learn in time, if you survive at all, that you can only survive by acting with a violence that will match or probably surpass that of the so-called "revisionists" and "terrorists" whom we are now denouncing from the height of our superior morality. "If you go on living here," he said, and I remember this vividly, "it will only be because you have drenched this land in blood."

His words struck fear into my heart, because it was my brother speaking, not some wild-eyed demagogue standing on an old fruit crate in the market. It was my flesh and blood, speaking out as if from some deep gash in my own heart. I tried to embrace him, but he pulled away from me, as if any human warmth was a move that threatened his life. Then, seeing that I was startled, he leaned forward and pressed my hand. "Let us have a bite to eat before you go," he said, "it's not every day you come to Jerusalem." We had a shnitsel in a restaurant in King George street, and he talked a little, in a much more human way, about some adventures in Argentina, when he had been involved in selling horses. Then he suggested that we see a movie, that was showing in a matinee just around the corner, at the Eden Hall. He said he had got into the habit in South Africa, whenever he needed to escape from his worries. I had never seen a talking picture before, so we went together. It was called "Frankenstein," and was a terrible tale of a human monster who is created by an insane scientist. The monster escapes and begins killing people, because it lacks a human soul. Kolya sat transfixed all the way through. I wondered whether this was the kind of moving picture that my brother Boris photographed, but I have to say I have never seen anything of his work. It made me think about our dreams and our nightmares. To some, obviously, they are entertaining. But to me, they are too close to the truth, as I recalled the sound of Herr Hitler raving in Berlin, on the radio.

My brother put me on the bus and waved me goodbye. For a brief moment, we were really brother and sister, two siblings, who took joy in meeting each other. But, as the bus rattled down through the hills back towards the plain, the feeling of dread that I had felt at our meeting returned. I am terribly afraid of the future rift between us. If we too take up the gun to attack, not to defend, where will we end? Every day we hear and read of more disturbances among the Arabs. I fear for my brother, and for all our brothers and sisters both here and abroad. Terrible times are coming. I miss our close and intimate talks. I hope so much you are well, with your family. Perhaps we can meet soon, and renew old ties. I need a wiser head than my own to advise me. So many of the younger people come to me for advice, and I feel so clumsy, and lost.

With you, in heartfelt friendship,
"Auntie Sarah."

The Dead Tell So Many Tales

One of Claire's plans for the "Seven Streams of the River Asher" was for me, or some actor representing a replica of me, to appear alone on stage, tied in a straitjacket on a chair with only my mouth free, like Billie Whitelaw in that Samuel Beckett play where nothing is seen on the stage except those continually jabbering lips. Or what was that other Beckett play, *Embers*, which we saw together at the Royal Court with Paul Scofield, or was it Leo McKern? The character, Henry, walks on the beach, you hear his boots on the shingle and the soft waves on the shore. He stops. How does it go?—"Who is beside me now?... An old man, blind and foolish... my father, back from the dead, to be with me..." Except that it was not my father who was blind and foolish, but me. I am the anti-Godot—instead of standing around, waiting for the impossible, I rush about, opening doors this way and that, peering in, shouting out, Who's there? Is that you, Dad, Uncle Kolya? Yakov? Zev? Sarah? Judit? But there are only echoes, which mumble away and then vanish into the crowd that keeps moving, running through rush hour, hurrying to the nearest underground station...

I took Sarah's returned letter back to my mother, in Jerusalem, but she just looked at it vaguely and passed it back. She had no idea whatever about it and shook her head when I mentioned Aunt Sarah. Any questions about Sarah's letters, or Kolya's archive, or anything apart from the immediate location of the canes she needed to get on her feet at that exact moment, were useless, just straws on the wind. Tsadok suggested driving me up to the Labor Party archive, in Kfar Saba, not far up the road from Tel Aviv, but I had to get back to Jerusalem to say goodbye to my mother and then rush to my flight back to London. Catching up on work, the cold English autumn, daylight non-saving time, darkness at noon, Claire's unbending schedules.

We returned together to the unholy land in late December, with Claire's taciturn but obliging parents and a giant goose—serves eight, but only four attending, the World War II pilot being too infirm to travel. The Queen's speech, Christmas pudding, winter rain at the windows. Even Tel Aviv, on the 28th, was wearing its gray umbrella, the pinpoints of rain playing on the colorless waves, only the hardiest chancing the beach or trying to windsurf without wind or sky. At Yitzhak's apartment in Jerusalem, the mountains frowning and freezing, my mother was the same. We might have just left the day before, or not returned till the following spring.

We spent the New Year, "Saint Sylvester's Day," at a party around the corner from Melchett, with a crowd of arts and theater people Claire was connected to by her own network. There was a woman called Elisheva and her man called Avishai and others called Motti and Moshe and Judd, and some French people, some Americans, two very strange Russians and an assortment of bright youngsters who were whooping it up in one of the rooms. The smell of some old-fashioned hash wafted across somewhere but Claire's gaze held me on a tight leash. I was supposed to be her host but became her guest. The wines were not bad, and there was whiskey, and Stolichnaya.

Avishai, who was in computers, cornered me and told me the coming year would be the beginning of a countdown to "an earthshaking event" that would occur on the night of the millennium, in three years' time, at the end of 1999, when all the world's computers would seize up and stop working because of some inherent "millennial bug." The computer clocks would fail to recognize the number 2000, and the entire Western world would grind to a halt: electric grids would go down, aircraft would fail in mid-flight, military systems would crash, and were it not for the collapse of the Soviet Union six years ago, a nuclear war would have been a near certainty. He and his colleagues had been trying to warn the world about this. They had got the Microsoft company busy at work on a solution but had not yet found a reliable fix. The best way to combat this was to remain staunchly stoned…

The next day, the first of 1997, I introduced Claire to the Tel Aviv central bus station, where chaos was already rampant, with its rapid-action bag searches and shawarma cafés and stalls selling cassettes by popular singers. Grinding off to Jerusalem to see my brother Yitzhak, the soul of Godly devotion. Follow-on taxi around the concrete tangle of new-built districts towards the serried blocks of Gilo. I thought I had mistaken the house because a large, official-looking brown Audi was drawn up in the driveway, a bald-headed brute in a suit standing by it, wearing the plugged in earpiece of an official security driver and surveying us from behind wraparound sunglasses. The house number checked out, but there was another bald thug in the stairway, who gave us the evil eye till Yitzhak appeared in the doorway and ushered us in to his living room.

"Just in time! Just in time!" he said. "We have visitors!"

Two familiar but unexpected faces looked at us from my brother's divans. One was Yonni, my uncle's assistant, blending in with his white shirt, black suit and soft skullcap, rising to shake hands. And the second surprise, sitting back and nodding at me with the heavy-lidded stare of my cousin: Kolya's son, Member of Knesset Adir Gur-Arieh, the new Deputy Trade Minister. Beside them, my mother, sipping a cup of tea. I looked hard at Adir, who had so successfully mutated into the model Israeli man of authority, a rigid block in his regimental suit, albeit tieless, the open-necked shirt still designating a "man of the people," still representing the properly nationalistic poor against the improperly heretic leftists of the urban bourgeoisie. He had learned to wear an earnest and serious look, as befitted the serious and dedicated nature of his task to keep the nation's transport going; I was tempted to chide him with the chaos of the central bus station, but in fact the bus had been on time and efficient. Even the airport was not on strike at the moment.

"Finally we all meet in Jerusalem!" said Yonni, looking very satisfied. He explained the miracle: "Adir and I took the opportunity to visit your mother and talk to Yitzhak and the family about Kolya's legacy. Michigan is donating the entire archive to a special foundation that will be set up here, in the city. Yitzhak has agreed to be on the steering committee and we hope you can be on the wider circle of patrons, in an honorary role, if you're interested. Seeing as you have become a sort of family historian, as things have turned out. I hear you've been following Sarah. And you have your father's own archive, and you're chasing Yakov as well. The family magician. Remember we mentioned the jazz musician's records in New York. His interview cassettes. Have you been there?"

I told him I couldn't go before the next break, which would be Easter. They all nodded, as if being apprised of some pagan festival that was of no particular interest. "Not joining us for Pesach here?" asked Yitzhak. I said I didn't know at the moment.

"Well, we have an idea for you," Yonni said, "if you're interested. Visiting the old village, the origin, Celovest. In Moldova, since it's now an independent republic. Things were unstable there in the first years, when their eastern sector split away, the so-called Transdniestrian Republic. That part is just a Russian satellite, but the village is in the Moldovan part. Adir has been telling us of plans to set up a monument to the death camp the Nazis set up there in the war. We thought, since you've been collating material, you would like to add this part and share it with the archive."

Adir's lids were particularly hooded, like a hawk just coming out of the cowl. "My father's work is the biggest existing record of Jewish life and struggle in the diaspora. He has some background records on the Bessarabian region, the pogroms of Kishinev, Odessa and so forth. But the family story would be a valuable asset. A human face on the statistics."

"People still go there to pray over the burial grounds," Yonni said, leaning forward to look me in the eye. "The entire area is thick with our bones."

"Aside from the monument," said Yonni, "you have your father's writings. And we have your uncle's memoir. I was thinking of going there myself, sometime this year. But I have to finish the last volumes first. The Prof managed to complete the first draft, but as usual there is a massive editorial structure. The final section covers the Arab world, the anti-Semitism in Egypt, Syria and Saudi Arabia. Checking sources is going to be complicated, but we'll get it done. Chicago will publish we hope, in ninety-eight. By the millennium we'll have the entire project in twenty-eight volumes, hardback and paper."

I could sense Adir's sluggish brain going through the gears as he looked at me, trying to appear neutral. Eventually, as my mother was handed another mug of tea and a biscuit, he came out with it:

"You have my father's journal of the war, and in Russia," he said, "the original notebooks. They would be a great asset to the new archive. Of course, you still have the translation."

I knew what he wanted me to say: "Don't worry, I'm not going to publish it. It's just part of the puzzle. Your father wanted me to have it. But you can have the original, as long as it gets preserved."

I felt I was jousting with a fox or a jackal over an abandoned carcass, which was still alive with swirling maggots. I couldn't tell what the impact might be on Adir's political career if his father was "outed" as a Chekist assassin, in such searing detail. A tricky past was part of the legend, but rewriting and modifying history is the very essence of our inheritance, the air we breathe, the clutching roots. It might simply make him more interesting, and boost his scramble up the pole. I couldn't work out whether he was disturbed or disappointed at my promise. I had assumed, from the moment of Uncle Kolya's "bequest," that he had given me the manuscript to keep Adir from destroying it. Whatever the new mythology he had built as a national patriot, fearless fighter for Jewish freedom and mentor of the Zionist Right, Kolya had become a zealous hoarder of background, historical materials and methodical facts, both personal and public, which swirled around his busy head. The historian had clearly trumped the political animal that had scrabbled up through life's battlefields, shifting and remaking the personas he had adopted like so many shedded skins. Adir was the battering ram shaped by his father to crash his way through the obstacles of the new State of Israel towards the essential goal. "Socialism" finally vanquished, the true patriots triumphant, ready to complete the project that the Labor milquetoasts had so abysmally fudged. And where was I? Completely outside the camp, but still a dangling twig of the old tree, not quite played out and ready for the revolution's bonfire of all the old vanities and illusions.

We said goodbye to Yonni, and to Adir, who rushed away, called by the driver to his formal duties to keep the country ticking over, the roads safe, shipping shipshape, the planes on time if humanly possible. A couple of days later, we parted from my mother, who seemed as unmoved to see us go as she had been to see us come, coddled by my brother's ever devoted brood. We left in a dark, rainy dawn to the airport's normal chaos, Claire braving the usual security questions about her reasons for visiting and her ties to me. The fact that she used her own family name on her passport and her light-colored hair led to formal suspicion of being a Christian missionary on the prowl. We had forgotten as usual to coordinate our memories, and gave differing accounts of the years we had been together, extending the security quiz until I told the young woman who was sure she had caught us in transgressions that I had not fought in the Six-Day War to face this kind of nonsense, and she reluctantly stood down, still casting a suspicious eye on the blonde.

Returned to base, to an even grayer, rainier and much colder London, the monochrome of routine at the film school, the new January intake... Camera Introduction, lenses, light meters, the infusion of dreams through the machine, and Claire's renewed rehearsals for yet another saga of women and the working class in Thatcher's ruled Brittania, the endgame of the Minor successor, the brooding dawn of a revived opposition, the Dawn of Blair, glad cheering springtime, postponing the further dive into the oceanic depths of Aunt Sarah's Zionist contemplations...

Yonni called again, in June, the sun shining yet on the good cheer of New Labor, new initiatives, promise and hope, with Claire booked for a long summer tour of the northlands, the Midlands Triangle, Birmingham, Leicester and Sheffield, further feminist frolics in which I would be a wasted third wheel.

"Hey, searcher's nephew: Seek and ye shall find: The magical mother-lode! Kiss my hand! We have found the tape cassettes of Ace Harrington! Remember? The file has been waiting for you all along, available for study at the New York Public Library for the Performing Arts, at Lincoln Center. Accessible at all opening hours. New York, New York! You got to hand it to them! The beacon of memory still glows in the stacks!"

It was Gramby time, once again. Keeping my rendezvous with the magician, after weeks, months, now more than five years gazing at the poster tacked on our bedroom wall, and he, the disguised Yakov, gazing steadily back, the limpid eyes following wherever one was in the room. Yearning? Imploring? Mocking? The hand with the crescent cuff link, the white bow tie, the elegant turban with its most likely pasteboard jewel, the lightning bolts emanating from the fakir's eyes on the left, the eye staring from the top right luring me on: To Istanbul! To Cairo! To Isfahan!

Instead I boom my way again across the Atlantic, investing in a discount week at the Lincoln Empire Hotel, Broadway and 65th, joining the buzzing crowd of young and old students, rising in the lift to the Music and Dance collection. Third floor. Polite curators point me towards the card index at the back of the reading hall. Pulling out the H's—Hagen, Uta, to Hepburn, riffling through the stacks of dog-eared cards, not too difficult to find the alphabetic entry: H for Harrington, Ace... handwritten, old style.

Pull out and fill in call form, take your number and wait at a vacant space at the tables amid the rustle of papers and the tick-tack of keyboards... My number finally called, the small pile of precious cassettes collected. Slotted into the machine in the booths. Headphones adjusted. Listening to the opening hum, the background crackle, the creak of a chair, the clearing of a throat, a hacking cough, a mumbled "sorry"… And then the cracked voice of mellow old age:

"Where are we? Yeah… yeah, yeah. Keith's Orpheum, Columbus, what was it, January, nineteen-fifteen…" *(clearing of throat again, pause, and then)* "…You can tell that Bill Fields was nervous because he never had to share the stage with the Four Marx Brothers before…"

*

Cassette No. 5:
Recorded June 12, 1981

"You got it man? O-kaay… Where did we stop last time?"

"1925, Paris. You were talking about the magician."

"Oh yeah. Nineteeen twenty-five… That was some year. Josephine Baker was setting 'em all on fire at the Folies Bergeres. She was hot. She had the moves! Man, if she had taken anything else off you would have seen her insides. I can tell you. You see, that was the whole thing about the French audience. When a black person appeared on stage they were a performer, not black, not white. That was why we kept going back there. We talked about this last time, didn't we? I'd already been there for six months back in nineteen-twenty-two it was, with Louis Mitchell's Jazz Kings. He had a five year run at the Casino de Paris, which was the hottest venue in town, and I was with them for a while. Then his lead player came back and I was getting cables from Chicago to come back with Carol Dickerson's Sunset Cafe band. Stayed with them for a year. But the heat was on in Chicago and the mayor was cracking down on the black and tan clubs over there and I had that job in New York. Louis Armstrong came after me with Carol and they set the town alight. But I was moving around. We talked about that last time, the Onyx down on Fifty-Second street and the Savoy Ballroom up on Lenox Avenue… the 'Battle of Jazz,' with

King Oliver and Chick Webb, the Harlem Stompers, the Roseland, that was a hot summer. Then I went back and played regular at the Onyx, we talked about that. So the next time I got to Paris wasn't till nineteen-thirty-four... Was that it, thirty-four, or... right honey... Linda says it's thirty-four. I got in for New Year, I remember. Louis Mitchell had stayed in Paris and he had his own club in town and a restaurant up in Montmartre. He also had the Grand Duc in the rue Pigalle and I was booked to play there for a while with Frenchie Shaw and "Jiminy Cricket" Purdue. That was the time I found out that Gramby was playing one of the magic clubs, L'Enfer, on the Boulevard Clichy. That was a pretty rough dive, at that time, a long ways from the Casino de Paris, where I had last seen him, when was that? In 'twenty-two. That was the first time we met up since Chicago. He was already working on the guillotine act, which he was still doing four years later, but in 'thirty-four he was back to the old basic bag of tricks, cabaret style, with a kind of Egyptian sarcophagus, into which he would put Alma, as the Queen Nefertiti, and then whisk her from one place to the other. He was dressed in a golden King Tut style, with a huge pharaoh's head-dress and a rod of office which he turned into snakes, beetles and birds. It was still a class act, but it was lost on that mob, who were hopped up and falling about in their chairs. The whole place had a terrible smell, like someone had poured ether into the air, mixed with incense and a kick of bad weed. I think he wasn't even calling himself Gramby at that point, he was billed as Imhotep the Terrible.

He looked pretty much older, which we all did I suppose, as if the greasepaint had got into his pores, and Alma looked really whacked, she looked coked out, I have to say. I wondered at that time whether he was on the hop, but I remembered he was always intense. He looked like he had really been seeing through walls to another world. His eyes seemed to burn right into me, as if I'd been touched with a cigarette end. But he looked pretty pleased to see me at the end of the show, and we went around the corner to another club, which had no name at all that I could see, and was so dark I thought it might be for the blind. The only lights were from ten or twelve candles that were set in the walls—it looked like the Phantom of the Opera sewer. But the dinginess of the place seemed to make him happy, I figured maybe because nobody could see him, so there was no-one to please. They were drinking coffee tipped with absinthe. You know that stuff? It kills off your brain.

What did he tell me then? Yeah, this was the point. He said his brother was in town. Old Boris, Bill Gore, the movie photographer, that we had been with in Los Angeles when I was a kid, and then met again in Chicago. When he married Alma. I told you that story, how we went to see D.W. Griffith's Birth of a Nation, that piece of shit, downtown on Fifth Street. Or was it Seventh? It'll be on the other tape. He had come to Europe to see his brother but also to check out the place they had all come from, which was somewhere out East, in Arabia. Or that's what it sounded like. It made me think of Haji Ali, that old act, and Gramby's first old flame, what was her name, Zuleika. Boy, that takes us back... But meanwhile, brother Boris was helping out another guy he had known when he first passed through when he came out, before the war—that's the first world war, we had 'em in series you know. In fact, he had known this guy's father, who had been a big radical, back in the day, even before the Bolsheviks. He had some kind of Spanish name. The son, who was now making this film, was called Jean. Jean Vigo. He is a big name in movie history now, they show his films at the Thalia. But when Boris first met him he was a baby stuck with his mother and this Spanish anarchist in a filthy room in Montmartre, only a few streets from where we were recalling this story. It's funny how things come together. The son had made this movie, about a revolution in a boarding school, where the kids rise up against the teachers. I didn't see it at the time, but later on, in the sixties, when they brought this kind of stuff out, and it was rough, but there were some funky scenes. You've seen the picture? I forget the title, I remember the kids throwing over all the plates of baked beans and shouting at the poor cook: Madame Haricot! Madame

Haricot! The headmaster was a midget, I remember. It was one hell of a crazy piece...

Anyway, the kid was making another movie, on the river, and Boris was in town, helping him out. There was another cameraman on the picture and Gore was only advising, I think. It was something about an old barge, that goes up and down the river. I didn't think much of it at the time. Then it turned up in double bills with the school movie, and is in all the movie history books. There was this old guy in it who was a famous French star at the time, Michel Simon, right? He's a crazy old sailor who's been all around the world but has ended up on the barge. Most of it seemed to be in the fog. It was no Cecil B. DeMille picture, I can tell you, it must have cost about fifty francs. I think the kid, the director, died soon after the movie. He had some kind of wasting disease. Maybe it was TB, I don't know. Life is about one thing, I can tell you—survival. You have to live to tell the tale.

It was a pretty cold winter, and there were all sorts of troubles, Depression troubles, I suppose you would call them. There were strikes, and riots, from the right and the left. A bunch of royalists, and some group called the Action Francaise, who were fascists you know, had running battles with the police just outside that café, the Deux Magots, right in the Boulevard Saint Germain. They pulled up trees and iron grilles and benches and threw them at the police. Then of course the communists had to come out, and there was a taxicab strike, that lasted about a month. The strikers set fire to the buses and blockaded the metro stations.

You got fit, because you walked around everywhere if you were like me, and didn't like to spend too much time underground. The workers come down from Belleville and the east side and fought a big battle with the royalists in the Place de Concorde. I was trying to cross the bridge to the left bank when I got caught up in it. There were thousands of people waving the red flag and the mounted police charged them with batons. I rushed to get out of the way, it was not a good idea to be a black man at that exact time and place. The royalists were shouting "Vive Chiappe! Vive

Chiappe!"—I never found out who he was—and the communists were singing the Red Flag. The whole situation was complicated by some huge scandal that was shaking the government, something about stolen stocks and bonds and some dead Jewish banker, I forget his name. Stanislavsky? No, but something Russian, or Polish. Both sides were stirring things up.

I was walking across the bridge because that was the time that I met Nadine, and she was working a club down there, the Cabaret Grillon, on the Boulevard Saint-Michel. It was a kind of supper club, and she sang with the dinner. But she had a matinee, on Tuesdays and Thursdays, for the business folk and the tourists, so I could meet her just before she went on, and then I had to walk all the way back uptown.

But that's another story. Now the magician, he was not in good shape at that time. I remembered the old days, in which he sat in his hotel room, poring over the tarot cards, looking for clues in the Hermit, the Lover, the Sun... Now he seemed to have moved on to much weirder stuff. Since the last time we met, he had moved from the hotel apartment on the left bank to an old tenement house in one of the older Montmartre streets around the Sacre Coeur that wasn't yet torn down for some new housing block. I went up there one time, it was just up the road from the big artists' house that Picasso had lived in. It was on a slope so everything was leaning, the floor, the walls, the doors, you thought you were drunk just trying to hold on to the table, that seemed just about to slide off. He had a lot of bookshelves, which were stacked with old books about magic, ancient myths, occult stuff that was pretty much in vogue at the time. He had a book out on the table, which was open when we came in, it was about that Greek guy, with the theorem, you know, Pythagoras, I remember because it was called "The Philosophy of Music." It was open at a chapter about the "Mundane Monochord." I'm still not sure what a mundane monochord is. It looked interesting so I read a page while Gramby went into the kitchen to make some coffee. Alma was too whacked to do anything and she just went to bed. We stayed up in this strange house that was full of noises. It was creaking as if it was just about to tear off its moorings and carry on down the street. It was like one of those movies about the haunted house, and I think Gramby felt quite easy living in a house that seemed to be full of ghosts...

What Gramby was trying to do, he told me, while he served out the absinthe, was to apply this to his act, so that the musical background would lull the audience into a kind of hallucinatory state, where he could make them believe things were happening that they would get wise to if they were properly sober. I guess that as he was working the smaller and dingy halls he didn't have the dough to pay for the complicated machines that the Spanish engineer who supplied him during the fancy years made for the more spectacular acts. The guillotine piece alone cost him a fortune. All the magicians relied on this precision gear with fine mirrors and invisible wires. So he was thinking of a kind of hypnotic effect, with what we call today ultrasound chords. Having them drunk was just not enough. He also wanted to put himself into this state in which he was totally aware of his surroundings and moves but also "connected" to the other spheres. He also talked a lot about magnetism, and how to make it work without magnets, by the power of the mind by itself.

I never met Gramby's brother, Bill Gore, that time. He seemed to be busy on the film with his old friend's son and then Gramby told me he'd already left to go east, or maybe he was called back to Hollywood for a new movie, I can't quite remember which. But I caught up with Gramby a few weeks later, in March. He came to the club and was very excited because he said there was some news from Tibet that he wanted to talk to me about. He said that out there, in China, in Tibet, the Dalai Lama, who was the head of their religion, had died, after being poisoned by his rival. He seemed to know all these names, I don't know, Lama Rimpoch and Ten Zin and whatever. He said that when the Dalai Lama died, the priests would go looking for a little child, a baby boy, who was going to be the new Dalai Lama. He said they had to find this boy and then bring him up and teach him the whole religion and how to be their leader. He said they had been doing this for thousands of years and each time the choice had been the right one. The reason he was telling me this was that, the night before this news was in the newspaper, he saw the death of the old Lama while he was on stage, and also had a vision of the new high priest, the baby. He had opened the mummy of Imhotep or whatever it was and saw, instead of the usual guy they used to switch cabinets, this corpse of a very old Chinese man, whose finger was stretched out, pointing to him. He slammed the mummy shut, before the audience could see the dead man, and opened the other one, and there was the child, wrapped up in a yellow cloth in a sort of bamboo cradle, and also pointing its tiny finger towards him. Then he tried again, and both the cabinets were empty. He did his usual bow to the audience and walked away.

I have to say, I thought he was really going nuts at this point, but he seemed pretty much as usual in our club. He suggested a walk, since the night was clear and a bit warmer, up the hill towards the new cathedral. We walked in silence and he held on to my arm, like he was remembering how it was in the old days, when I helped him get calm before the shows. We stood at the top in front of the big white dome and looked down over the city. It was beautiful. Paris at night, it's something you never forget. A million lights and they're all winking at you. A million friends, just waiting out there. That's real magic, even when you know it's a fake. I loved this man, he had taken me in hand when I was a lost crazy fucked up kid and showed me the road could be a home. Without him I would never have trusted myself to survive. I could forgive any crazy shit and ideas that he had but I was really worried about him.

I told him straight out. I said, you can really go crazy, with this stuff. You keep shoving it in you and then it's in control, I've seen it happen to so many friends. He said, like they all say, that it wasn't a problem, that the main thing was to train the brain to see things that were not apparent to the ordinary eye. It was what the mystics called a "kandaloni" force [*"kundalini"* ed.] that the

Buddhists called a third eye, which the Buddha had in his forehead. He said he had tried séances, to communicate with the dead, but like Houdini had figured, they were all fake. Paris was full, he said, of all kind of charlatans, Rama Das this and that, Hindu mystics and fraudsters who latched onto rich stupid women and told them they had the secret of life, fucking anything that moved and had a good bank account, pardon my French, and all sorts of shenanigans that they were learning from the old Marquis de Sade. I knew there were places here where people did stuff that would make New York blush, let alone Los Angeles. But he told me that if you read the right books, and talked to people who had really traveled out east, and seen all sorts of things that we couldn't imagine, you would find that there were methods that could make it possible to see across huge distances and make contact with people who were far far away or who seemed to be missing. The goal, he told me, was to communicate with his brother and sister who had gone out there, the one called Zev and their youngest sister, Judith, who had gone to China. He said that he was not sure if Zev was alive or dead, but he was pretty sure the girl, Judith, was alive and well, and still somewhere out there. He said they had gone out to a place called Karbin [*Harbin, Ed.*] in Manchuria, where Zev had set up a trading company, about ten years before, and his sister had followed five years after that when their mother had died in their village. Then a war broke out when the Japanese army invaded China, and the place where they were living became a military center for the Japanese forces. Boris had got a letter, from the two of them, when they first lived in the city, but then they lost all contact.

I asked Gramby how he was contacting them now and he said he knew I wouldn't believe him, but there was a child, a small boy, with Chinese features, who was part of another act at the club, beckoning to him and who painted "pictures with light." He saw his brother's face, and his sister's, but that after about two years ago his brother's face vanished, but the sister was still there. When he saw the news about the Dalai Lama and the new holy child he realised that this was what he was seeing. "Time works differently in the other spheres," he said, looking over at the city lights. He said he thought his brother had vanished in the war, he had read about in the newspapers, it was a big story. The Japanese had tricked the Chinese and made up a pretext to invade. They took over all of Manchuria and would probably march on into other parts of China. Now they had taken the last Chinese Emperor, who had been a small boy himself when the old Empire had been thrown over, and they were making him the "Emperor of Manchuko." He said his name was Mister Poo. The last messages he got from Judith was that she had left Karbin, and had moved further south in China.

I didn't know what to say about that, so we talked a bit about what was happening here in Paree. We knew there were a lot of the same problems in France that had made the government change in Germany, and there were going to be dark days ahead. He said I should be careful, I might be having a good time in Paris, but all those royalists and fascists who had been fighting in the streets were dead set on getting rid of everyone who was not properly French, in particular black people and Jews. "We are polluting their precious French blood," he said, "the purity of the virgin, Joan of Arc. But they burned her at the stake, untouched vagina and all." I remember he used the word, that nobody said at that time. "We are all thieves, we're stealing their soul."

We walked back, pretty silent after that, and I went home, I was pretty whacked out myself. I didn't see him for a while after that. Mr Mitchell was putting together a new band, with some of the old boys, to play at the Alcazar in Bordeaux. Josephine Baker had opened up there, and there were some great singers, and comic acts. We played with a girl called Shellee Prideaux, who was a young ingénue from New Orleans, but you probably never heard of her because she died about a year later, she was burned to death in a car, with her lover, who was a mobster of some sort in the city. She was a kind of black Marilyn Monroe you might say, diamonds were her best friend. All of us were sweet on her, but we were poor. Too damn poor, all the way...

Then when I saw Gramby again... What? Oh, you want to stop the tape here? You got to the..."

(Cut. End of tape.)

Cassette No. 6:
Recorded June 13, 1981

Where did we stop last time? We were still in Paris, with Gramby, right? Round about 1925... lots of strikes and marches, the concierges were on strike, can you imagine that? It was a good time to sneak up to your girlfriend through the courtyards, all those old biddies had shut up shop, and stopped minding everybody else's business. That was the year Gramby's brother Boris was in town but we didn't meet. He was helping that kid make his movie about the barge, the one who died young, in the same year. Movie people in Paris were mostly like us those days, small time, like other artists. There was a crazy guy called Gaston who was a great jazz fan, and hung around the Montmartre painters. He mostly did bit parts for Gaumont, but he invited us once to see the only movie he starred in. It was a crazy picture made by Dali, the surrealist painter, and another Spanish guy who later also got famous. He had to leave Paris after that and made a lot of movies in Mexico. Luis Bunuel. He broke up with Dali. There were lots of fights between the surrealists because they could never agree who was a real surrealist and who wasn't. Hell, we were surrealists in music before any of them was even born...

Anyway, the reason I remembered this Gaston's film was that there was a scene in it in which he runs across the street and kicks a blind man. Then he's making love to this woman who was kissing his toes and the toes turn into a statue. Most of the time he was rushing around throwing giraffes and stuff out of the windows. It was really weird. The fascist hooligans raided the theatre once and smashed it up, he had to move to some private venue. I didn't have much time for the pictures those days in any case. The only ones I remember, apart from that crazy shit, was the Charlie Chaplin picture, *City Lights,* and *King Kong.* Everybody saw that. Somebody told me once it was a veiled racist riff on big black men going for small blonde women. Veiled by heck! That was a discussion in UCLA, in the sixties, I was there with Dizzy and Ray Charles, it was in nineteen-sixty-eight I think. I don't know how we got around to that...

There sure was a lot going on in Paris in those days. The society of war amputees had a riot at the Place de Opera. Imagine, hundreds of veterans with legs and arms missing rushing the cops on their wheelchairs, waving their crutches, down the Boulevard Capucines. I was talking to some guys who were starting up a new band, the Hot Club Quintet. That was Django Reinhardt. He was a gypsy, and he had a way of playing the guitar that was traditional with the Romany people, but it was a completely new sound in swing. They were thinking of having a sax player so I played a few gigs with them and then they decided they would be all strings, with that violin fellow, Grappelli. They were young and hot. I kept in touch with them later on, when I went back there in thirty-nine, just before the war.

To pick up on Gramby, he was still at the club L'Enfer, being Imhotep the Great, making mummies come to life and disappear. There was a new girl who was assisting, I forget her name, she was just temporary, when Alma was in the clinic. She was being treated down south, in the suburbs, at the Bicetre hospital, which had a psychiatric unit. That was also famous, you know, the Marquis de Sade did time there, back in the revolution... It was a pretty dingy place, but they had a big garden, with trees and benches, and the lunatics walked around there. Alma was in a room with three other women, who didn't do much but sit and glare. But she seemed not too bad, just very shaky on her pins, and she slept a lot. I guess they kept her drugged up, but they didn't do all those experiments they used to do on mental patients, you know, all the lobotomies and electric shocks. They were into hydrotherapy big time. Patients spent half their time in baths. The area around there was very poor, and there was a big gypsy camp across the way. Gramby had made friends with the gypsy king down there, and when I mentioned Django he invited me into his caravan and said I should be his brother and we should cut ourselves in the gypsy blood oath, but I said maybe another time... I was surprised because Gramby was talking to the guy in his own language. I'm not sure if it was the Romany dialect, I think it was maybe Romanian, which Gramby remembered from childhood. Suddenly he became another person, sitting there chatting among all the pots and pans, ornamental carpets, Saracen swords, pictures of folk in strange costumes. I guess he was a gypsy at heart.

As I think you know our band went back to the States after that, and after we left the whole Spanish Civil War thing blew up, and all the crap that was coming from Hitler and Mussolini. Our last tour was in thirty-nine, things were pretty dodgy in Europe but we liked being back in our wonderful Paree, the bustling streets and all the noise and hoopla, we were just in time for the big parade of the Quatorze Juilette, the fourteenth of July, with the President of the Republic. We didn't know it was the last one for a long time. A bunch of generals driving in an open motorcar down Champs-Élysées, and then thousands of soldiers, army, navy, marine, Foreign Legionnaires with their butcher-like aprons, the zouaves and all sorts of north African troops with coloured turbans and fezes, black Senegalese, little Indo-Chinese troops, all the glory of the French empire, that looked so strong and powerful on that day. Then the crowd cheered for the English soldiers, who were out there with the French, and the sudden roar of airplane engines made us all look up, at the squadrons of French and English war planes came by, with those red and white roundels of the Spitfires.

It was just a spectacle for us, but it turned into a grey cold rainy day. We snuck off to Nadine's favorite cafes on the Boul-Mich. We were just glad to be back. All the little streets on the left bank were just as they always were, the cafés and bistros, the famous places where the artists hung out. But you could feel the tension in the air. People were reading the newspapers more intently. Nadine tried to tell me what was going on, since my French had got pretty rusty. The Nazis had taken over Austria and were now making threats against Poland. It was all about a place called Danzig, which they were claiming for Germany. The Italians had taken chunks of Africa and threatened to bite off more close to home. The Japanese were fighting in China.

I went into a big hotel and heard Mister Winston Churchill on the radio, warning against America being neutral between the dictatorships and democracy. He was talking about "the hush of fear hanging over Europe." I remember that phrase. It got into my head, and I thought about a special blues number that would express that, something very quiet that had slow hints of trouble that kept tailing away and then emerging again, and it was a very unfamiliar sound at that time, because those were the days when swing was moving into be-bop, and we were like kinda years ahead of Miles Davis. It was what later came to be our Summer Cloud Blues. But people in Paris cafés and the music halls and clubs wanted to be happy, and dance, and drink, and pretend there weren't no blues, no real blues at all. They wanted music to forget. So I really couldn't sell this sound to the band, not at the Casino de Paris, or even at Mitchell's.

August was a lot warmer, so people enjoyed themselves in the parks. Nadine was happy, and she was singing with the band, so we were together all the time. I didn't have that much free time, but I did try a few times to find out about Gramby, where he was at, what had happened with Alma, I still felt responsible, just like I was back on the road in vaudeville, making sure he was kept from floating off on his clouds. But he was not in town. I made contact with the club impresario, Monsieur Eluard, who told me that Gramby and Alma were still in business, but they had been touring small clubs in the provinces, mostly in the west and the south, in places like Nantes, and Limoges and Toulouse, and all the way down to the Riviera, in Nice and Avignon and Marseille. The magic act was now much less noir, he told me, they had a group of four, a black Senegalese boy who was an acrobat-contortionist and a little Japanese girl of fourteen, Soo-Kie, who danced, and they both could fit, I guess, into the old magic cabinet, but the whole thing was much more family oriented, and was back to the old banner of the Great Gramby. Part of their tour they were linked up to a family circus, the Monteneros, who were exiles from the war in Spain.

I wondered what had happened to all that keen stuff about the harmonies of the spheres, and Pythagoras, and the mad mathematician's numbers and all that flying across time and space. But I was relieved they seemed to be O.K., and back on the road instead of being stuck in that heavy atmosphere of the club L'Enfer and the boozy streets of Clichy. But, no mind how much we mooched about the cafés and hung over the bridges of the Seine looking into the sunny ripples and listening to the gabble of the tourists cruising along on the bateau-mouches we couldn't ignore the storm clouds that were coming our way.

It was the third week of August, I think, when all the political people around us were jumping about and arguing over the latest news that was headlined all over the newspapers. The Nazis and the Russian communists had signed a peace treaty in Moscow, and the French communists were running about like chickens with their heads cut off. The deal was the Russians would let the Nazis do whatever they wanted in the east, and everybody said war was just around the corner. Since the communists and the fascists had been at each other's throats all those years it was a pretty colossal magic trick for them to pretend they were all suddenly friends. People who used to call each other devils from hell were now supposed to be partners. Old friends beat each other up, husbands and wives threw plates at each other, lovers split up, party headquarters were trashed. The government was rounding up the communists, and all sorts of mayhem was going on while we were playing our licks in the casino and hoping the fights wouldn't start in the audience before we got to the second set. Then the call-up began, and the school kids were being evacuated from the city into the countryside. Trains were going to transfer the sick from the hospitals. They even moved the animals from the zoo! Nadine was getting really scared because she had an elder brother, Maurice, who had three small kids who were also supposed to be bussed out of the city.

Then, on the Friday, I remember, the beginning of September, we were hearing that the war had already started in Poland. The first set at the casino was interrupted by the patron, a little fat fellow called Monsieur Gerard, announcing that the Germans had bombed Warsaw, and that France would be at war by the next day. Then we all put down our instruments and the whole audience sang the Marseillaise. Us too. We were all suddenly Frenchmen at that pretty solemn moment.

Things began to shut down. The army mobilized. The English declared war on Germany. The next day, we heard the first air raid sirens in Paris. People in the north of the city said they heard explosions. All the theatres and clubs were closed. Foreigners who had been in Paris a long time began lining up to join the army. I thought about it and decided I wasn't really French, and Nadine told me she would stab me with the kitchen knife before I could get out the door. But the French seemed pretty confident. They had the Maginot Line, all those heavy forts and bunkers, that they had worked on for years and they were sure would hold back the German army.

After the first day or two, nobody heard any more explosions. Then they allowed some movie houses, theatres and clubs to open, but only till ten o'clock. We had to play only matinees and early evenings, then shut up shop. We wondered what we should do, but the management said people needed to know life was continuing. The people of France were not afraid. The show goes on.

It was about that time, I think the end of September, when we heard the news on the radio that Warsaw had been taken by the Germans, that Nadine told me that Gramby and Alma were back in town. They were playing, as The Great Gramby and La

Belle Alma at Au Camelion, on the left bank across the river, on the Boulevard Raspail. She didn't know where they were staying. I thought... Okay, you want to change the tape. Right...

(End of tape cassette 6)

There was no cassette number 7. I checked the box the tapes had come in, took it back to the library counter, and waited till the one of the supervisers came back to say that was all of that request number that had been in the stacks. Of that call number, I had been provided with cassette available. I still had cassettes 8 and 9, but closing time, 5:45, was upon us.

The inevitable virtue of patience. And photocopying, if I wished to preserve anything, was limited to twenty-five pages a day. I had to come back the next day to absorb the remaining cassettes, 8 and 9. There was a date sheet attached. Harrington, 1945–1965, "recordings for the Columbia label." The later life. His first wife, Nadine, had disappeared from the narrative, and instead there was another woman, Gilda, a ballroom singer-dancer whom he married in 1948. Then came a succession of great names with whom he shared the limelight: Charlie Parker, Thelonious Monk, Miles Davis, Clifford Brown, Sonny Rollins, Oscar Peterson, big bands, small bands, country-wide tours... A slowdown in the fifties, then a third wife, and more names: Ornette Coleman, John Coltrane, Sun Ra... Then a long lament about the sixties, rock and roll, the youth culture, big business and, perking up just before the end of the last tape, the revival of the old-style blues. By then his voice was drying out, bouts of coughing taking over, and then an abrupt cut. The transcript noted: "Paused for summing up session." But that seemed to be the last word, rolling in my ears right bang on forty minutes past five, when the library shut down.

I tried to call Claire from the library paybooth, at 11:30 p.m., London time, but she was not home. Perhaps I'd got the dates wrong. I was coasting perplexedly between Ohio, Chicago and

615

Clichy. The missing tape, Paris, 1940. The last vanishing trick. Or was Gramby's fate as just another Holocaust victim? Calm down and take it in methodically. Relax. Go see a movie. Enjoy New York. My eyes were dragging. I thought of calling Yonni, but not yet. I staggered up Broadway to a very old haunt: Big Nick's between 76th and 77th streets. The "original charcoal grilled," the clutter and steam, the cramped booths, the counter seats built for old time skinnies, the heat and sizzle and ginormous menu of carnivorous delights: the American Cheeseburger, the Bacon Burger, the BBQ Burger, the Chili Burger, the Hawaiian Burger with an aloha lei of grilled pineapple, or the "simple classic, cooked to your taste." The classic American cheeseburger would do fine, with a Greek salad—a giant bowl of feta. Claire had come with me here once but would never enter again, after she spotted two tiny red roaches chasing each other merrily down the wall.

"It's New York, honey." Some culture shocks are too much to assimilate. Jetlagged, I turned in early after a bit of local TV. Something about the mayor, refuse and drains. In the morning, I reread my first transcripts and walked some old haunts, across Amsterdam, Columbus on the west side of the park. The daily joggers, the earplugged skaters, dog walkers, shitkickers, benchers.

Twelve-thirty sharp, back at the library, I took my "missing" slip to the lady at the main desk, who said she would consult the curator. Meanwhile she suggested I check the other cards under the Harrington name in the card index. There were six of them, three listing photograph folders and two of documents, biography and clipping files. One of the photograph files was named "Scrapbook." I called all the four files I was allowed at any one time and spent the wait having the second tranche of the transcripts photocopied by the girls in the back room.

The clippings were a mass of yellowing, fragile newspaper cuttings tossed together in a folder, shedding tiny bits of frayed paper all over the table and the floor. I picked them up carefully and shoveled them back into the mass. The clippings were grouped loosely into chronological periods: 1920–1940, 1940–1950,

1950–1970. The two later parts were the most detailed, full of information about programs at New York clubs like the Vanguard in Greenwich Village, Birdland, the 55 Bar, the Royal Roost, the Five Spot, the Lennox Lounge and other Harlem venues, record notices, gossip. And plenty about the big scandal of 1955, when Ace was busted in connection with a dope ring at the Shabadaba further up Lennox Avenue that involved his second wife, Gilda, and led to a headline-grabbing divorce epic involving black and Cuban gangsters trying to muscle in on the Sicilian mobs. Divorce, an all-American tale. A third wife, Zambezi Goldberg, reputed princess of a then "Rhodesian" tribe, though according to one columnist she was the daughter of a poor drugstore owner from the Bronx called Ebenezer Lincoln Barnes. They split in 1962. The gigs moved back to Chicago, Kansas, St. Louis and the Midwest circuit, with shorter and shorter notices, and little scraps of scissored paper briefly laying out the long decline. In the end, fame was a past story, with some reminiscences in daily paper supplements and weekly music journals, in the "Where Are They Now?" genre.

There were no French-language cuttings, and no mention of Gramby or anything but brief comments on the player's vaudeville days. A couple of the later articles caught up with the old period, and in one reminiscence in the Augusta Chronicle Ace talked about his early wandering childhood and his vaudeville life, mentioning famous acts like McIntyre and Heath, Williams and Walker, Haji Ali's Arabian Acrobats, the Marx Brothers and "a couple of magic acts, where I played the Happy Indian Prince."

I called Yonni from the hotel. He was not far away, on West End and 98th, thirty blocks of a brisk walk up Broadway. He met me in the lobby of his apartment and we walked around the corner to a Broadway bagel joint filled with older people munching through the soft fare and sipping coffee carefully from paper cups. He apologized for the simplicity.

"Even in New York, kosher is not that easy," he said, queuing at the counter. "Not for us fanatics. We can go up to the apartment later, but its messy. I'm indulging in untidiness now that Prof is not watching. Or at least not watching from the next room."

He did look a little more disheveled than the neat amanuensis of Ann Arbor, the black jacket a little frayed, the beard a little straggly, but still the same enigma. Apart from his ongoing dialogue with God, I was still not sure which part of the argument that had consumed the Gurevits clan in Palestine he was trying to illuminate. Or maybe he was just an inveterate collector of facts, the archivist's Sisyphian labors, endlessly rolling the rock up the hill. He sat down over the coffee and all-purpose bagels and flicked through my archival transcripts. "Nice, nice, nice," he kept saying. He read with blinding speed, devouring each page at a glance. I could see he had trained over the long haul to eat and work at the same time.

"Life in another *mishegas*," he said. "Show business. I know nothing about it, but the Prof used to like watching war movies. John Wayne, and all those fifties movies. *Hell in the Pacific*, stuff like that, on TV He liked that guy, what was his name, Audie Murphy, he made a film about himself?"

"To Hell and Back," I said.

"Exactly. You are the right man for this conversation. It was quite realistic, Prof thought, but all the films about communists were pretty stupid, he always said. 'They don't get it,' he said, 'they don't understand.' He gave some talks, on Radio Free Europe. But it was more than enough to deal with the Jews." He looked at the gap between transcript 6 and 8. "Information, information. We call out for answers, and get just more questions. I know the syndrome very well."

"In the segment from the other archive, that Koslov, my father's messenger, wrote about Gramby in Paris," I reminded him, "his wife, Alma, was pregnant, but two years later she's in this hospital, having a breakdown, and no mention of a child. So what happened? Is there a Son of Gramby? The Gurevitses seem to be disappearing even before they're born."

"You never can tell. You just have to keep looking. Missing pieces might be really missing, or mislaid. If you persist, and nudge in the right places, they can be found, more often than not. Prof did all the work that needed to be done. Dug out Celovest from mud to sky. But he was more concerned with the period previous, when your grandparents came from the Ukraine. Most probably escaping the pogroms which broke out after the Narodnaya Volya killed Czar Alexander the second. There was a pogrom in Elizabetgrad in April, then pogroms in Kherson, Taurida, Ekaterinoslav, Kiev and Odessa in May and through the summer. Many Jews fled across the Dniester, seeking safety in Bessarabia, although things were not very stable there either, because of the Russian-Turkish war. That had ended with the province still under Russian rule. But there were reforms, which gave some land for Jews to settle under the zemstvo protection. Celovest became a Jewish commune beside the Moldavians. The Jews and the gentiles did not love each other, of course, but things were quiet for the next twenty years.

"In nineteen-three, all of the Gurevits children were present, from the eldest, Sarah, who was sixteen years old then, to the youngest, Judit, who was three. Kolya, Nathan, was seven, and your father was fourteen. We don't know whether your grandfather and grandmother married before they reached Celovest or when they were there. Records were lost, too many wars and massacres. Jewish Celovest lasted till July nineteen-forty-two, when the Germans came, with their Romanian troops, and began clearing out all of Moldavia. Between the seventeenth and the twenty-first, most of the region around Floresti was wiped out. Before Auschwitz it was bullets, not gas. You know the story. We were killed in our thousands, and the Transdniestria *lager* was set up on what was the Jewish part of Markolest, just across the creek. The survivors of Celovest perished there. But the sons and daughters of Rabbi Avraham Gurevits had already left way before.

"It's all in the work, volume fifteen. He didn't include Ziv and Judit because a package from Shanghai was lost in the post. Ziv went to Harbin, China, and Judit followed in nineteen-twenty-eight. I didn't tell you all this because you didn't ask. You were fixated on your father, some sidelines on Sarah, and Yakov. So this story you have stops just at the war. Paris, nineteen-forty. We all assumed Yakov was taken, first to the camps that held French and other stateless Jews in the jurisdiction of Vichy. We know that mass transports out of these camps took place in August forty-two. It's all in the work, volume fifteen. We did search for the name of Yakov Gurevits, Gurevitch and Gore. When you reach Gur, there are too many. But under Gramby we didn't look. He was a man of tricks and artifices, he could have been registered under any name. Or none. Or escaped. But there is no trace. Your Mr Harrington, too, may have missed our material. Could he have remained in France, as a black band player? There were Nazi jazz lovers, you know— they liked to keep human pets. Shame and guilt. Tell me about it. I nearly drowned in this material. Your uncle was indefatigable. You know that word? Unrelenting. Remorseless. Unfaltering. He wanted to know everything. But the family was just a drop in the ocean. He let go of you. There was too much at stake. Even his son was neglected. Adir, the one whose shoulder doesn't bear a chip but a log. A redwood, carried around from childhood. I am sorry for that boy, I can tell you. You think he's a fanatic. You have no idea. The Prof trained him like a circus trains lions. By the time I came on the scene, he was fully grown and ready for the kill. He had already been through the IDF special unit, what do they call it, it had a number, two-six-nine. He never talked about his exploits. A modern Jewish hero, but too fucking hard."

"We used to go around together, when we were kids," I told him, wondering if I should get a third bagel, to have something to do with my hands and teeth while the spiel unreeled. "We ran around the neighbourhood, peeking in windows. Looking at girls undressing, making up fantasies of people's secret lives."

"Is that right?" he said. "He sure hardened later. Maybe it was not just Prof, but the situation. I can tell you now, I was glad he was not my father. Even when I devoted my life to him. Perhaps it wasn't him, but the project."

"Is that why you gave me the Journal?" I asked. "To keep it away from Adir?"

"No, that was Prof's idea, for real," he said. "He thought Adir would burn it. With a lot more from the back stacks. He knew he had made a rod for his own back. He was a completely honest man. If we were Catholics, we'd call it confession. But we don't confess, we beg forgiveness from our maker. He is the judge, not human beings. You believe we should all be brothers and sisters. That would be nice, but it's not history. Our history is a pit of ravenous wolves. I don't need to lecture you about this. I respect your path, even if I believe you're wrong. I see Kolya in you, every time we meet. You ran around, trying to save mankind. Making movies, for humanity, not like your father, blessed be his memory; he was a kind man, but lost in Hollywood. You will forgive me in saying this."

"He wasn't lost," I said, "simply busy. He loved his work, his craft."

"Cecil B. DeMille," he said. "He was an anti-Semite. And a Jew. His mother was Jewish. *Shoen, genug.*"

"My mother used to say that," I mused. "*Shoen, genug.*"

"But it never ends. There is no *genug*. It just goes on. That was your uncle's message. If we believe in the eternity of Israel we have to accept the burden. It's not fun. It's only natural that people try to escape it. Movies, politics, art, fornication, lies. Magic. Dreams. Your uncle Yakov was the consummate dreamer. He thought he could save you all with his dreams. Then he covered his disappointments with more and more layers of gaudy costumes. Pretending to cheat death: the guillotine, the 'Lazarus' act. What happened in nineteen-forty, when Yakov came back to Paris when the war started? It was the 'phony' war, till May, when the Germans invaded Belgium and Holland. Then they crashed through the Maginot line after Dunkirk. France collapsed in two weeks. The Nazis were in Paris on June fourteen. Was Gramby there? And his jazz friend, the Ace? Don't you feel you need to know?"

"Where do you think I can look?"

"*Cherchez la femme.* It's always the case. The jazzman had a girl-friend, the first wife, Nadine, in Paris. Did they stay or leave? The archive was donated by the fourth wife, the survivor, was it not? I'll phone the curator tomorrow. Who was it, Rod Bladel? I know him well; he is thorough. There'll be an address, a phone number. We'll make a call. It shouldn't be difficult. It's not like asking an eighty-year-old widow what did your husband do in Treblinka. They have no stake in you. You're looking for Gramby, not for Ace Harrington. Maybe they're evangelicals. We'll tell them you're from Jerusalem. Tel Aviv doesn't score. Trust Yonni, I've done this a lot."

Takeaway dinner from Empire Szechuan on 97th, then back to the hotel. A message from Claire, with a Birmingham number, saying "call any time." Waking her up at four in the morning, a drowsy selection of "ah ha," and "oh ho," to my tales. The busy lady of modern arts. Too weird, that I am the one that ends up buried in the past. But as I told Yonni, "I can't put this together. The story has more holes than Emmenthal cheese." "You have to keep prodding," he said. "Don't let the files fool you. Keep scratching the surface, you'll finally get to what lies underneath."

The next evening I got to visit Yonni's, after he told me on the phone he had news. It seems strange that this was less than fifteen years ago, in a world in which there were few mobile phones, no text messaging, and the World Wide Web was a strange novelty available only via telephone sockets that would disgorge webpages onto one's screen with the speed of a turtle squeezing through a bent pipe. Yonni was the only person I knew who made much use of this "internet," on the bulky machine on his desk almost buried amid piles of paper and document folders. He lived alone in an old Upper West Side block in a small and compact apartment somehow filled with his creaking cabinets, cupboards and bookshelves. The place was a one-stop Holocaust museum. Every book that had ever been published on the subject was packed in along the walls. He waved at it all dismissively.

"This is nothing. Less than four thousand items. The stacks at Prof's library in Michigan held twelve thousand and six hundred and seventy-two volumes. Not counting the manuscripts. The man taught us all to be zealots."

I didn't tell him that it felt like a tomb. The weight of all the horrors, the killings, the camps, deportations, the mechanisms of death and mass slaughter, the vast acreage of witness accounts, the endless drumbeat of misery, agony and grief gave the house an air of Pharaonic doom, a modern scroll of the dead, of the impossible journey to a place where the sun could not rise. It was too much.

"How do you live with all the dead people?" I had to ask him.

"I'm used to it," he said. "They're all my friends. The dead tell so many tales."

"I thought you had your own family?" I asked him, pressing the wound.

"Oh, I do," he said. "But they can't really take it all either. I visit them, but they don't like to come here. My life was your uncle, Nathan Gurevits. He was my teacher. I was just happy to be his student."

He pulled out a paperback book from an upper shelf and handed it to me. It was *The Vietnam Primer, 1968 — A Guide to Folly*. It was a thick book, about 800 pages.

"My father edited this," he told me, showing me the author's photograph on the back, which showed a solemn, gray-haired man with a white beard, who looked pretty familiar.

"Shaul Stern," he said. "He was very famous. He marched with Norman Mailer and the Berrigan brothers and Noam Chomsky and Dr. Spock—the baby man, not the one with the ears. He was a faculty chairman at Harvard. Then he got sacked for punching a colonel. He was bludgeoned at Berkeley and in Chicago, and was in the same cell with Abbie Hoffman and all the yippies. We had draft resisters hiding in our attic. And one of the Weathermen, can you believe it? This book sold a million copies. It put me through college, I can tell you."

"So what happened?" I asked, nodding at his black skullcap.

"Oh," he said, "I was brought up to be contrary, so I suppose I conformed to that." He paused and put the book back carefully in its proper slot. "I just thought that God might have the answer rather than Jane Fonda."

Finding a seat for me among the piles, he gave me the news from his friend the curator. The Ace Harrington donation was made by a Mrs. Luella Legrange, of Augusta, Georgia, the site of Ace's passing in 1983. She was his last wife, and had reverted to her original name some time after. There had been, as I knew, several years of dispute over the jazzman's inheritance: money, property—he apparently owned several houses in Augusta, in the "historic district"—artefacts, instruments, his collection of rare records, his papers, and the cassette recordings, which had been made by a local journalist, Washington B. Slope, but, for reasons unknown, never published.

Ace had died after a lingering illness, and two of his previous wives were present at his funeral. His first wife, Nadine, who had traveled from Geneva, Switzerland, and his second wife, Gilda. The inevitable wrangle between the three wives, aided by their legal advisers—Nadine's then-husband was a retired lawyer—froze the deceased's assets until last year, 1996. The curator had given Yonni the address and phone number of Mrs Legrange in Augusta and he had taken the liberty of calling her. He had told her he was the literary executor of the brother of the magician whom her ex-husband had spoken of so fondly in his recorded memories, and that since this brother's nephew was in New York, on a short visit from Israel, he would be happy to make a trip to Georgia, to talk to her about her famous ex-husband and his memories of the Great Gramby. We were writing a book together, he had said, about our own family history.

"Mrs Legrange is a member of an evangelist church in Augusta," Yonni told me. "Their members are regular pilgrims to the Holy Land, visiting Jerusalem and all the other sites where Jesus walked. Mrs Legrange has already made four such trips and she's on the organizing committee. So a meeting with an authentic citizen of the Holy Land was enthusiastically approved."

He was as thorough as ever, having printed out a fax with flight details to Atlanta and discount prices from his travel agent. Nine flights per day from La Guardia.

He had sent the ball soaring; all I had to do was make the catch.

*

And so I flew to Atlanta, drove around tangled freeways and Route 20 east, booked into an old Southern-style inn just on the white side of the tracks, quite literally, as the train passed honking by several times. Crossed over to the other side, which was James Brown territory, a short tour to 38 Summer Street to see Mrs. Luella Lagrange. She was delighted to see me, and most helpful and obliging, allowing me to marvel at Ace Harrington's piano, his sax, cornets, and framed photographs of Ace with every jazz personality—Dizzy, Buster, Fletcher, Bird, Jelly Roll... the golden disks, the framed testimonials, the Wall of Fame of Mrs LaGrange's Holy Land pilgrimages to Lake Tiberias, Cana, the Basilica of the Annunciation Church in Nazareth, the Stations of the Cross in Jerusalem, the Church of the Holy Sepulchre, the Church of the Nativity in Bethlehem. On another wall, images of Mrs. LaGrange and her fellow pilgrims from an earlier age: marching in Alabama with Martin Luther King, Mrs. LaGrange with Rosa Parks, participating in a sit-in at a Woolworths store, on a sidewalk, with a German shepherd straining on the leash towards her during a march, in a forest of placards proclaiming VOTING RIGHTS NOW! END SEGREGATION! JOBS FOR ALL! Over tea and cakes she told me of how her faith was fortified by her tours of the Holy Land, and how she had made friends among the religious Jews. I told her that my brother was religious but I was not, that I marched down the other path... She said she understood there were many different views, and the Holy Land should be shared among all its people, and we drank more tea and managed to get onto the subject of Gramby. She told more tales of Ace's story, how he had come to New York as a motherless child, riding the rails, and the Jewish magician had taken him in and given him a job, and how he played so many roles, as the Little Rajah, and Mowgli the Jungle Boy, and all sorts of stuff that ignorant people expected of black folk at that time. And then he had met some movie people, mainly my father, whose name she knew from the tapes. But she didn't know he had ended up in the Holy Land too, and she said she would be glad to pay her respects to his grave. She asked about my mother and was sorry to hear of her plight, but surely for such a great soul, rooted in the Holy Land, the Lord would surely provide. She didn't want to speak so much about the missing tape and other items she didn't know about so clearly, as some of that stuff had been taken by the "the First, that woman Nadine," whom she said was still alive.

We had lunch together at a local place, Fannie's Kitchen, traditional Southern fare, on Laney-Walker, the main drag of the old historic district. I wanted the old pan-fried chicken and black-eyed peas but they didn't serve it, and we had something more fancy. She sipped orange juice, which seemed to loosen her tongue a little; she volunteered that Ace had stayed in Paris for a while during the war, with Django Reinhardt, who despite being a gypsy had some German colonel who was crazy for jazz protecting him, as far as she knew, right through the war, though the band had to live in cellars and such-like. She said it was all down to Nadine, whose father was a club owner who had deals with the Germans, and so she stayed in France all through the war, though they moved out of Paris, after the first year, and lay low in a small village in the south, in "the provinces." Ace was stuck there when the US entered the war, but he did some work for the resistance, in the last years. He was back in New York by 1945. Mrs. LaGrange had no news of the magician during those years, and clearly did not wish to speak of previous wives.

To cap the visit, I agreed to attend Sunday services with. Mrs. LaGrange at her local church, whose preacher, a very handsome old gentleman in a golden robe, gave a rousing account of the Lord leading the children of Israel out of the land of Egypt, drowning the armies of Pharaoh, and how the pillar of fire led the chosen people through the desert into the Promised Land. He reminded the congregation that in less than three years they would see ushered in the new millennium, the two-thousandth year of the

Savior, Jesus, and millions of people would be gathering at the site to await His Second Coming. He neither endorsed nor denied this expectation. If faith was strong enough, he declared rousingly, it would shake the foundations of the Earth...

In the fullness of time, when that day came, the last evening of 1999, in Jerusalem, as elsewhere, the millennium moment passed peacefully, with no Second Coming, no computer cataclysm or major incident, just a quiet night at my brother Yitzhak's apartment with Claire, observing my mother in her inexorable slide from awareness; she had no inkling whether the day was portentous or not, or which city or country or century she was in. It was a Friday night, so Claire could have the full experience of my brother's house on Eve of Shabbas, candles, blessings, bread and salt and kiddush wine. The apartment was too far from the city center for us to wander out for the spontaneous celebrations that some wall posters had promised, so we just walked out on the moment and looked over the valley separating the suburb of Gilo from the Arab villages beyond. The lights were off, and the cold night was silent, except for some late traffic on the road. Out of sight, on the Mount of Olives, groups of apocalyptic Christians were gathered, waiting for the white light from the sky.

"I am history, and I should investigate myself..."

My mother deteriorated slowly, and then much faster, in the first year of the new century, the new dispensation. Yitzhak had already booked her into the Dementia Center of the same hostel at which our father had spent his last days. It was a separate ward, further down the hill, staffed with a team of young nurses with down syndrome whose patience and compassion was boundless. She was transferred there when her bodily functions began to fail, and my visits became less frequent. Yitzhak himself was not in good health. He had been hospitalized after falling down in the kitchen, and diagnosed as having survived a minor stroke. He was told to walk, not run, the kilometer to his synagogue. There was a closer one, but it was not extreme enough for his taste. I did not delve into the gradations. Tsadok's son, Eli, had attended the severe synagogue too, but left for an even more hard-line shul. The awkward grandson, Yakir, became even more zealous, living in a settlement deep within the West Bank with a group of fanatical followers of Meir Kahane, the so-called rabbi who was assassinated in New York in 1990. Thus Jerusalem takes her toll on her children...

*

Back in London, Claire and I resumed our own routine as she was offered the post of artistic director at the RiverWharf Theatre in southwest London. A prestigious venue perched by the Thames, just by the iconic Hammersmith Bridge, which shoots out frail as a butterfly over the water to touch base on the southern bank, at Barnes. We take walks along the green verges, dodging bicyclists, as amateur canoeists glide past from the boating clubs, amid the cluck of ducks and dog-walkers, joggers and pub lunches of fish and chips and mushy peas. Here, Claire can at last reach out and touch the multiple streams of the River, the crème de la crème of experimenta and latest tropes, eager minds from all over the world: the Synaesthetic Theatre of Liege, the Berliner Soap Factory, the Budapest Crocodile Group, the Irish Republican Drums, the Xianfeng Xiju of Shenzen, Oto Shogo's Tokyo Water Station Numbers 1, 2 and 3, the Grotowski Society, Theatre Complicite, the Welfare State, Bread and Puppet Theatre, La Mama's latest tour, and other novelties coming down the line... In parallel, retrospective seasons of the "Pioneers of Documentary" began turning up around the city. People I remember dragging their sad sacks around the lobby of the Bleecker Cinema or cavorting around Berkeley in pursuit of revolution are now honored as artists of bygone eras. Lionel Rogosin couldn't raise five dollars to finish some hard-fought project, and now they're gaping at the rawness of *On the Bowery* and the triumph of *Come Back Africa*. D.A. Pennebaker is still alive and kicking and making movies but now you look at the Bob Dylan movie *Don't Look Back* and gasp at the fans' haircuts in 1965...

I am history, and I should investigate myself. This has long been Claire's mantra. All the answers, she became convinced, lie in modern Moldova, just west of the Transdniestrian rebel line. She had bonded with a feisty Romanian, Dorotea M., director of the Laughing Ceausescus of Cluj, who had heard Claire's account of my rambling and interrupted quest for origins and offered to take us to the sod itself, driving west and across the lines into the remains of what was once the Soviet Union and was now independently destitute. She was a large black-maned woman who looked like a character from an old Jules Feiffer cartoon of Greenwich Village life of the golden age.

"You must seize the moment!" she cried, making a hard fist, as if there were a real person of that name, some French aristocratic fop, whom I might grab by the neck and shake. "It is your story! You must stand on the soil! You must breeze the air! You will understand things!"

But we didn't go to Celovest that first millennial year, nor the second, in 2001. It was a busy year both at the RiverWharf and the film school, which seemed to increase its intake year by year. Everybody wants to make films. As the screens get smaller and smaller, the Big Screen becomes more and more tantalising—the king of beasts, DeMille's last laugh...

At the tail end of summer, on the 8th of September, Claire flew off to New York to check out a new Off-Off-Broadway show, somewhere in my old haunts south of Houston. She was only going for a few days, and I had some preparation work for the new term, so I stayed behind. On the afternoon of Tuesday the 11th, I had gone back to Finsbury Park to get some groceries and was trying to figure out whether to eat in or out and take in an early movie when her colleague at work, Arlene, called me in a state of panic. "Are you watching?" she asked. "Are you watching?"

I soon was, for the duration. Thick black smoke billowed out from the two tallest buildings in New York City. I tried to phone Claire's contact number, rapidly trying to map out in my head the exact location of her host's address. The lines were down. People kept calling me and I screamed at them to get off the phone. Hordes of people, caked with a gray dust, were running up from the cloud, up Church and West Broadway. I thought I recognized the Tribeca buildings, still standing. I tried to figure the distance to Lafayette and East Houston, or Prince, or at the southernmost, Kenmare or Delancey. We used to go to Katz's Deli for breakfast, but that was further east, on East Houston and Ludlow. The planes had struck the Twin Towers at around nine a.m., a time when Claire is rarely up unless for something work-related, and that was unlikely if New York actors were involved. Everything comes down to the immediate risk. General compassion becomes a luxury. I set up a network of seven friends who would all try her number, or contacts, and meanwhile I had to stay put, by the phone, with Zen breathing, the old army emergency mode. At about five, the phone rang and she was on the line, sounding amazingly calm. She said,

"Asher, I know you're panicking, but calm down. I'm OK. I was nowhere near the buildings. We're staying at home because you can't breathe out there. We can taste ashes even inside. They say it's a terrorist attack. I just hope it's not Muslims. The Americans will burn down the world if it is. Are you safe?"

It was the strangest question. "I'm here," I said. "You phoned me, where else would I be? Do you want me to fly in?"

"They've closed the air space. No one flies in, no one flies out, except the assassins. There were two, maybe three more planes. Nobody knows. You're breaking up, I'll have to phone later. I love you."

"Don't say that!" We have a pact on this. It's what people say when they're about to fall from the sky. "Call me when you can." The line was lost then. I stayed in and had spaghetti and grated cheese. It also tasted like sulphur and ashes.

My mother died the following March. She dropped away in her sleep at the Jerusalem mountainside hospice. It seemed that her body could no longer take the toll of the collapse of her cognitive functions. She was seventy-eight years old. I missed the funeral because the religious authorities in Jerusalem insisted on burial within a day of death, and, as she died in the small hours of a Thursday night, there was no way I could arrive in time. Interment had to take place on Friday, before the Sabbath, and the body had to be transported by van to the resting place beside my father in the cemetery in Tel Aviv. The earliest I could arrive was Saturday morning, breaking rules by flying during holy time.

This was Yitzhak's show. He was not her son, but he oversaw the procedure from the morgue all the way to the grave. When I arrived at his house, back in Jerusalem, we looked into each other's eyes and understood our particular compact.

The problem had loomed throughout her decline. My mother was a Christian; she had converted to marry my father, as a matter of course in keeping with the bare fact of his being the son of a rabbi. She always told me it was not a big deal. No one was dressed in funny clothes, and while the skullcap on my father's head looked a bit odd, it fit him snugly.

The conversion was by a Conservative rabbi, and was not recognized by the Orthodox rabbis in Israel. The approaching problem, as my mother's condition worsened, was therefore a knot that had to be cut. The last time I saw her at the hospice, in December, she had recognized none of us, and gazed vaguely at the wall. When I entered Yitzhak's apartment, he took me aside and held on to my arm.

"I want you to understand that I have dealt with the problem," he said. "I didn't tell you before because I know you, and because the deed had to be done. Your mother underwent a second conversion, some weeks after we moved her here. Everything was carried out and documented *kadat-ukadin*— by the law. She was aware enough to answer the questions. Curse me as much as you want. This is the way things are here. May you be consoled in God's blessing."

I wanted to kill him, but he was ill too, and his grip was quite feeble, for the powerful shvantz he once was. In his house, overlooking the subjugation of Palestine, there was a sitting to endure. Old friends of my mother came and told tales about her, how she had played amateur dramatics in Tel Aviv in the early fifties and even played the trumpet in an amateur jazz group in a beach club down towards Jaffa, how she had been the life and soul of parties among the movie crews in the Herzliya studios, how she had worked with Aunt Sarah to help new immigrants in the old tent camps and ma'abarot that still lingered in those years, and started a class to teach the Moroccan kids music, and so forth. An old gentleman I had never met came in and told me he had been a player of traditional oriental music in a café on the north beach that my mother had dragged my father and me to once, and how I had slipped away and got lost on the beach and everybody went to look for me in the dark. I had never heard that story before...

Beside this trickle of Tel Aviv friends and acquaintances, Yitzhak's living room was filled with the offspring and cousins on his wife's side, a stream of black hats and headscarfed women who came to observe the condolences, with a certain amount of bizarre debate over the height of the chairs they should be sitting on. Apart from the ceremonial tearing of one the few clean shirts I hurriedly packed for the trip, which Yitzhak performed with zeal, I was supposed to sit on a lower chair than the guests, with my brother, the closest relation. In point of fact, Yitzhak's wife Aliza mumbled, as the only son, I should have been sitting directly on the floor, on a cushion if needs be, but I rebelled and sat on a more comfortable armchair. Of such matters were the rudiments made.

My brother knew better though than to enfold me in the prayers, the encompassing shawl, the book, the phylacteries. I did it once, minus the winding leather strap and box upon the forehead, mumbling my way with the stalwarts, swaying and reading. I said the Kaddish, once, and then desisted. They all knew my mother was not observant. She did some Friday night shtick at our Sheinkin home when Yitzhak was present, but eventually, as he hardened, he decided that he could not eat in our unkosher home. My mother kept a little corner in the kitchen with separate meat and milk dishes just for him, but he was not fooled. He had found a properly kosher dairy café down Sheinkin that he would grab a bite in. But in his own home he was strictly zealous.

Within a day I was driven quite mad, and found a way to walk out just before the prayers began. I told them I only had this week to pass in the country and had some old friends to look up. I took the first bus towards the town center, winding round the newly paved streets and new buildings of the suburb, itself a mini-city, crossing down what seemed to be a permanent traffic jam into the narrower confines of the old Jerusalem, not the Arab heart but the Jewish lungs of the city, the once buzzing districts of Geulah and the Jaffa Road, the once crowded central triangle now pretty sparse, the once busy clothes shops forlorn, the cafés half empty, tourists loping by, musing at the apparent small-town nature of this supposed hub of global consequence, the Ding an sich of three religions, tempered by a few shoe shops and the department store of Hamashbir.

I looked at my mother so often in Yitzhak's home, and every time I wondered what was she doing in this place. Sometimes, when my brain was really muddled from the mixture of jet lag, airport fatigue, culture shock and my brother's neo-medieval surroundings, I felt that the force leeching her memories and her self from her was external, rather than from within. What was she doing here? Her life should have been lived in the vibrations of another refuge, larger, grander, more diverse, more exotic, more magnificent, more entertaining, New York City, or even Los Angeles, the kingdom of illusions and make-believe. There she would have flourished, enjoyed life, danced, shimmered, pressed my father towards his well-earned awards. Why should not both of them live their fancies for real rather than vicariously, in Art Deco's last gasp? What was wrong with Hollywood?

Or are there no tears simply because in the end I'm only mourning for myself? Am I, the failed escapee from Zion's triumphs, like Them, the sole subject, the shining fake diamond in the mirror, the grand object of my own admiration?

On the last morning of the sitting, the close family members climbed in Yitzhak's people van and he drove us back to Tel Aviv, to the cemetery where my mother and father now lie together. Leastaway, the remains. The body material. The day was fair and sunny with a trace of a breeze, a rare balm in the humid metropolis. It was a hilltop, overlooking the Reading Power Station, a massive pimple by the military airfield. There were bushes and lawns and chugging sprinklers, as if the souls would regrow from the ground. My father's stone was in place, with his Hebrew name: Baruch Ben Avraham Gurevits, and the dates in the Hebraic calendar: 5649–5744. The inscription read: "Righteous and Brilliant in his Craft"—*Tsaddik ve'gaon be'melachto*. My mother had a patted-down mound of earth and a small board marked with her name, according to Yitzhak: Hannah Bat Herman Gurevits, and the dates: 5684–5762. In that light, they both seemed like Methuselah. There was no inscription yet; Yitzhak was waiting for my lead. He had suggested "Woman of Courage and Grace"—*Eshet Hayil ve'Hesed*, the last word of which would also translate as "righteousness." I was not sure if I was ready to go there. We stood on the hill, myself, Aliza and their three eldest males, all pale and black-clad, somber and swaying, as he read out the sealing prayer. Thus my mother was consigned properly to the afterlife, her soul assigned to its ascendance, to be with God and her husband. I only saw the two-shot in frame.

Finally there was a modicum of tears and some hugging, my brother's arm pressing around my shoulders. We linked arms for a few seconds. His three sons swayed, shook and rocked, their lips moving. Talking to God, expecting some answers. I knew that whatever conversations I might have wanted to have with Father and Mother, I could not have them now. The devout ceased their mumbling. At my brother's prompting, handing me the book with the page open, I recited again the prayer for the dead. Then we all moved off, down the hillside.

VOLUME 4

THE CONCLUSIONS

Boris:

When DeMille was in one of his moods, he used to sashay through the set with his Bible, waving it around to show people that he wasn't impressed or inspired by mere mortals. He would climb up on the crane, where I was trying to find a distance from all the razzle-dazzle behind me and concentrate on the image in the lens, and wave his preferred passage in my face.

"See this!" he would shout, his bald pate gleaming like a boiled radish, "you come from a noble lineage, Boris. These were the words of God to your father Abraham as he moped about in Ur of the Chaldees: Get thee out of thy country, and from thy kindred, and from thy father's house, unto a land that I will show thee! And I will make of thee a great nation, and I will bless thee, and make thy name great, and thou shalt be a blessing!"

You could never be sure with DeMille if he was sacking you or trying to egg you on to better things. I would just say, "That's great, C.B., an Oscar nomination will do fine." He always thought that when he hired somebody, he should trust that person to do their best professionally and not expect to be told how to do their job, but he wanted to control them all, regardless.

Now that I am lying here, in the Holy Land, reunited with my beloved Hanna, you could say I have squared the deal with DeMille, if not with my rebellious son. The compact with the other one seems to be holding, though he seems to be further away, in spirit, if not in distance. I don't understand all the praying, but at least somebody turns up, on occasion.

I followed DeMille's strictures, at least in part. I got up and got out, though not from reasons of great piety or stern commandment. The ties that encircled my father's house did not extend that far. Beyond the river, all was mystery. There were no blessings to be sought, only a great vista of things that could not be dreamed or imagined. I remember the great swath of fields, the tall wheat swaying in the wind, the narrow endless path along, the cart wheels bucking and squealing. I remember the city, the great building with its majestic rotunda that was neither cathedral nor synagogue but opera house, the white-columned mansions, the wide cobbled avenues, the tall spires and domes of churches, the stone robes of the Imperatrixe, her crown raised above the pediments, her hand stretched across the city of her own imperial dreams. Odessa! You saw the steps, you saw the steps, DeMille would rag me—you were there, you saw the blood flow! The slashing sword, the pince-nez and the baby carriage!

Nothing happened on the steps, I told him. That way to the harbor was locked off; all the action happened in the avenues. The marching students in their peaked caps, the soldiers firing from street corners, doorways, rooftops, why should they march forward, we had pistols too...

I lost her in the crowd... Lena... Tanya... I never saw her again...

Apologies to my wife. You can't help with memories. They come, they go, they ebb and flow. Nothing is properly connected. Somewhere, in the warp, it's all there, but it floats away on the wind.

Trams, I remember trams in all the cities, rattling along on the rails... Odessa, Kishinev, Bucharest, Vienna, Budapest, Berlin... I earned a living there for a while, walking down the Unter den Linden with a sandwich board. I was advertising for the Cafe Schiller, in the Markgrafenstrasse—nach Mittagstisch, quite pricey; I could never afford even breakfast there. All the policemen were dressed and walked like generals. Chin up, moustaches erect, buttons shining, masters of the world...

Amsterdam, also trams... canals, waterways, pastries... so much talking... Red Emma, Malatesta, Rocker, Baginski, pounding the podium: the destruction of capitalist, authoritarian society can only come about by armed insurrection... ah, my son could wholly approve... There were good comrades then, Kibalchich, "the Spaniard," with his baby son in the garret, with cats. Little Jean. The bargees of Paris... Such an intense lad, cursed with a short life. Helped him set up the fog in the night shots, as the "patron" staggers along the length of his barge, searching desperately for his missing wife... if you put your head in a pail of water, you will see your beloved—I remember that line. Such a good dreamer...

One remembers the individual shot of life: My father, hunched over his books, enormous as a whale, his face illuminated by the oil lamp in classic Rembrandt lighting, the eyes seemingly lit from within. My mother at the stove, waiting for him to climb down the stairs, an ascending line from her gaze. The drooping tree by the river, the errant youth crouched in the rushes, a lark swooping through the sky. The little kids bunched up in the *haider*, bent over their books as the teacher looms with his stick—light modeling on every tiny face (a good Gregg Toland shot). Color changed all that, killed off the poetry... The open road along the steppes, low angle, the sky empty except for light clouds. Hayracks break the horizon line. The harbor with its docking warships, great funnels and the bristling guns, grim bearded sailors, the living witness of a far-off war. Eisenstein would put them in a curving line, to meet the bridge above. I would put them in a straight march, crunching off towards the unknown...

So my boy chose documentary. He wanted to expose the real. He thought if you just pointed a camera in the street you would tie it down, as if the essence of the shot was the actuality of what the lens is pointing towards. But that is not the case. Who was that new philosopher, Wittgenstein, who said "the world is everything that is the case"? Even he discovered later that he was wrong. The world is not just the case. The world is everything that it conceals. Otherwise you'd think the audience really believes Victor Mature is Samson, let alone that he really wrestles with the lion, rather than a stuffed dummy in the close shots. But they know he's just another cheesy ham.

At least the younger son has found true love. It's hard to find the constant nowadays. Back in the day, it was only Hollywood that married and divorced on the turn of a dime, now everybody's at it. It's good that Anna and I lasted the course. The English girl, she keeps him steady. It's better when it's internal. A free choice...

We tried to do our best. I'm sorry I didn't discuss this before with you. I tried to talk to you, remember, on your bar mitzvah? Uncle Kolya and Aunt Sarah were there and we talked about the others, and about our parents. But you were young, boychik, you were a kind of sabra, a Tel Aviv brat—you liked the sun, the streets, the movies, the sea. What could we tell you about those old days, in the stetl, and the bet midrash, and the old Reb Avraham-Abba, and why he was different from all those Hasidim who wandered around the shuls here mumbling and moaning... It was not the same. It was *Der heim*. But all you could see was ashes, and then they caught Eichmann, and put him on trial, and all you saw every day was victims, victims, poor people, mounds and mounds of slaughtered bodies, and Auschwitz, and gas chambers, and horrors... Why would we even talk about that? It was so shameful, as if we had willed it ourselves, because we were too weak, and stupid, and sunk in superstition and madness, and all our past was dust and ashes.

So all I could bequeath you was my own eye, the movies. I could gift you Hollywood, the movies, the silver screen, the old lobby cards: Marilyn Monroe, Greta Garbo, Bogie, Gary Cooper, John Wayne, Victor Mature with his big man-tits, Groucho Marx, Laurel and Hardy... and I suppose all those crazy Greek soft core porno films you used to sneak off to see near the Central Bus Station... The eight milimeter camera, so you could find your own way into a great medium. But you know what? When you took hold of that lens, you went back to your mother, not to me. You went back for the underdog, the people screwed by McCarthy, the Bolsheviks, the blacks, the Mexican farmworkers, the Bowery bums. I was proud of you, do you know that, boychik? But I still had all my own vices.

Fathers and sons. What a catastrophe...

You hear me boy? I never ate a falafel. I never liked the sea. I didn't like those cafés where they played that oriental music night

641

and day, those jolly Jews from Tunis and Morocco and Iraq, with strange instruments that sounded like a cat tortured. They were my brothers too, and sisters, and I embraced them, because we were all in this together and we had lost too much, too many… And Hannah found her friends. This was a good place for her, Melchett, Sheinkin, the blue sky and the trees, at least these kept L.A. for her… And Kolya and Sarah were here, and although we were not together that often, and fought like cats and dogs when we did meet, or would have, if we didn't know to keep out of each other's gardens, it was good that they were near, within reach. Because that's all we come into the world with, and we sure don't carry nothing with us when we leave, except for what we were, and how we lived, and whether we dredged something up, from the mess…

OK, boychik? So run along, and just keep your eye on the frame…

Asher:

I had watched it all on television—from the Soviet spring, and the marked scalp of Gorbachev, the marches in East Berlin, the breaching of the Wall, the hordes pouring through, the hammers breaking it down, the waving keys of Prague, the return of Dubcek from the political grave, the triumphs of Poland and Hungary, the fall of Ceausescu, the handheld execution, the waving national banners, even unto Moldova and Mongolia… the Moscow coup against Gorbachev, the Soviet Union's end, the ascendance of Yeltsin, his tanks bombarding the "white house," while housewives wandered with their shopping bags under the rows of tank cannons, twenty-four hour news… Nine-eleven, with Claire's personal witness, the American backlash, the invasion of Afghanistan, the first shock and awe, bunker-busting bombs without bunkers, the triumphant march of the BBC into Kabul, Israel suicide bombings and retaliation attacks in Ramallah, Gaza, et cetera, siege of Bethlehem Church of the Nativity, hostages taken in Moscow theatre by Chechens, U.N. sends arms inspectors into Iraq, Bush threatens war with Saddam Hussein, elections in Israel, Ariel Sharon elected, new ascendancy of Uncle Kolya's hard right, protests against impending war in global capitals, one million set to march through London...

So there we all were again, Shai Baer, Gershon, Link, Mansur, Moshik, Abed, Pablo and Imelda back from Buenos Aires, Claire and Asher, packed in among the vast phalanx that poured through the funnel of Piccadilly towards the park, a cold but bright February day, everybody astonished at the size of the crowd, far outnumbering the usual suspects, the stay-at-homes surprising themselves, with their own banners, the English finally outraged: "MAKE TEA NOT WAR!" and "DOWN WITH THIS SORT OF THING!"

Who's here? Who's not here? Some missing faces, the Goat, Sargon, Matosian, long gone, and other old warhorses nobbled somehow, either exhausted or simply grown too old to stand or even dead and departed, Shai Baer tries to keep us up with the gossip, but the crowd roar overwhelms. The usual stare at faces that look familiar, but have grown grey hair, white wisps of beard, wrinkled cheeks, tired eyes, shrunken or fattened, dark beauties of old become determined gray panthers, some sprouting the next generation, the young faces exceeding the old, some carrying old mothballed banners that seem preserved for posterity: the old DOWN WITH THE OCCUPATION, FREE PALESTINE, ALL HUMANS ARE HUMAN, and so forth.

Twenty-five days later, the United States, Britain and the rest of the "coalition of the willing" invaded Iraq. Once again, shock and awe. Repeats, always repeats. We met with Shai Baer, Abed and an Iraqi communist called Tariq in a Turkish restaurant up a way from Finsbury Park, in Green Lanes. The skewers were excellent. Tariq, another gray-haired veteran, argued that even a hundred thousand dead were a fair price to pay to get rid of Saddam Hussein, whose victims, he said, ran into millions. Claire, arguing the English liberal position, could not understand this at all. She set out the full Noam Chomsky agenda: the systemic nature of the

American empire, the greed for oil, the need to control the Middle East, the perfidy of foreign policy, the first commandment of any reaction—above all, do no harm.

Tariq said that Chomsky was a liberal and didn't understand the Middle East at all. I said that Chomsky always called himself an anarchist who believed that human rights were indivisible. Shai said he had had an interesting discussion with the professor sometime around 1970 about the links between the Soviet Union, South Africa, the Pentagon and the Mossad. Chomsky said you had to know the facts behind the facts, which were not as impenetrable as you might think, all you had to do was pay attention and not get diverted by all the flak and falsehoods put about by those in power. He said Chomsky had no illusions about the Arab regimes or the flaws and corruption endemic in many liberation movements. Tariq said he would have to choose Bush over Chomsky, when the blood was set to flow. Claire put her hands over her ears...

All the years we had scratched away at the wall to talk up the many sins and grievances of the Middle East, the police states, the corruption, the festering sore of Israel-Palestine, and suddenly millions are marching around the globe because America had fallen out with Saddam Hussein. Iraqi exiles like Tariq, and the more acceptable faces of the nationalist opposition, used to hang around the Montmartre café in Bayswater, sipping coffee mournfully and wondering if they could afford the suits they needed to press their long lost cause with the clerks of the Foreign Office or the State Department. Now, people I remembered vaguely slumped at the plastic-topped tables appear in company with Tony Blair and George Bush as candidates for a new government to be parachuted in a blaze of star-striped glory into the wreckage of Saddam's Baghdad. Abed, looking on in our flat one evening at the Channel Four news, pointed to one of them, standing awkwardly between the two masters of the universe, and said: "That man still owes me a fiver. He ran out of money for a profiterole."

Time passes, things change... we watch it all on television. Blast bombs, Ba'athists found and routed, Saddam's sons located and killed, bodies laid out for the camera, explosions seen in real time. In my day, it was a rarity to catch some act of violence or terror in the frame—the Vietnamese officer shooting the bound Viet Cong in the street became an icon for the times; now there is no time for icons, only for the twenty-four-hour roll. Cameras everywhere, in helicopters, on armored cars, on steel helmets, in the street, in the sky. Drones fly above the battlefield, capturing everything, making no sense, chronicling madness and confusion. Victory calls still proliferate: Saddam is caught, hiding in a hole in the ground on the bank of the Tigris River, close by his hometown. He has a long beard and disheveled hair, and an American army dentist opens his mouth and pokes a light in his teeth.

Happy Christmas 2003…

Early in 2004, while the Mission Accomplished war was still raging, I got a package from Yonni Stern in New York. It consisted of three slim folders of photocopies from originals unearthed in the continuing trawl through the dregs of Uncle Kolya's Michigan archive. Yonni wrote:

Dear Asher,

Still cleaning up—after more than five years, there are still boxes mislaid in storage. Three stragglers you might find interesting. Shows you every life is a mystery. A couple of cuttings from the *Rand Daily Mail*, in South Africa, from 1922, about the white workers' gold mines strike. Some material from Palestine 1939–44. Some stuff from Argentina, in 1925. We knew that Prof had traveled there, but he was always vague about what he did there. I suspect this is important because he met some people who took him into the Beitar movement. Buenos Aires was strange as it had both a large group of Jewish immigrants from the Russian fallout of 1905, as well as a new group of German Nazis. Prof sometimes said he worked in Argentina as a gaucho but I always took that with a pinch of salt. The Prof's clips are a bit strange but it's a known fact of research that not everything can be neatly bundled. Loose ends, God save us all…

Missing links, but not much enlightenment: handwritten letters, an advertisement in English for the "Primitiva Gas Co. of Buenos Aires Ltd—Founded in 1885—The Largest Gas Undertaking in South America." Capital £2,339,644, H.Q. at 1169, Calle Alsina, and at 10 and 11, Austin Friars, E.C.2, London. No mention of the name "Gurevits." News of "NEW OIL GUSHER AT PLAZA HUINCUL, BEST STRIKE SINCE 1918." Go figure.

The third folder contained some photocopied front pages from the *Palestine Post* of Jerusalem, dated 1939. The first, from May 30 that year, headlined: "EIGHTEEN INJURED BY BOMBS IN JERUSALEM CINEMA HOUSE," reporting a bombing at the Rex Cinema, Princess Mary Avenue, Jerusalem, at 8.10 p.m., "during a crowded performance." Three British, thirteen Arabs and two Jews were hit. This I knew about, another part of our heritage. An early Irgun operation in the campaign to chase the British out of Palestine... No new items of correspondence, no letters from Sarah, no clue to the lost cassette of Gramby's last stand, no vapor trail to Zev or Judit. I wrote back to Yonni, thanking him for the clips and mentioning nothing about current wars or political arguments. In the age of email, he was rigorously old-fashioned, and about six weeks later he called by phone, on a weekday evening.

"Happy Purim," he said. I had no idea when that was anymore, so now I was properly informed. "Are you dressing up?" I asked.

"I disguise myself as a Jew in New York," he said, "it always works like a dream. Have you heard from your brother?"

"Not for a while," I said, "I think he's OK. We can email now."

"I don't like it," he said, "I have to use it, but it means everybody's at your door all the time. I have something for you. A big surprise. You'll like it. Blessings come to him who waits."

"I thought blessings came with good deeds?"

"Good deeds can be covert. Or even unconscious. Good thoughts can also be a category."

"Have you found something new?"

"I think we've found your Aunt Judit."

And so it had come to pass. After I had left New York the last time, on my return from Atlanta, Yonni had spent some time contacting film archives and asking for any correspondence or material that connected my father with Kolya, items I might have missed in my own searches. Nothing had turned up, until he received a call from the archivist at Brigham Young in Provo, who had helped my own search of DeMille's boxes. A letter had only recently come in, forwarded from the Paramount public affairs department, sent by a woman in Shanghai whose name was Go Yuan. A friend of hers at UCLA in Los Angeles had sent her a link to a *New York Times* article about Cecil B. DeMille's cinematographers, which mentioned my father's original name and his Russian-Bessarabian origins. Go Yuan wrote that her grandmother was a Russian woman of that name, Gurevits, who had come to Shanghai through Manchuria. The grandmother had always said she had a brother in America who worked in the movies. Her name was Judit. Go Yuan, it appears, was a writer, who had already published, in a local Shanghai magazine, two chapters of an ongoing book about her grandmother's life and fate.

"Have you been praying?" asked Yonni. "You must have been praying. This kind of thing doesn't happen just like that."

"No," I told him, "I haven't been praying."

"It doesn't matter," he said, "God hears your silence anyway. I have the lady's address, though not her email. You can write to her, she can send you the text. There might be a translation, or we can arrange one. Or better still, you can go out there and meet her. It's only a twelve-hour flight to Shanghai."

I clicked off the phone. Claire came in a while later, exhausted after the usual slog on the Piccadilly Line. The usual frustration over some financial glitch that threatens everything she has been trying to put in place for three years. The funding shortfall, the shrinking Arts Council grant—an overdose of ideas but no quick path to attainment...

We watched Newsnight, observing the malefactions of Bush and Blair and their minions embroiled in the Middle East.

We turned the sound down and watched the American soldiers yomping over the debris-strewn streets of Baghdad. We talked about Yonni's news, about deus ex machinas, about old thoughts brought to life:

"What do you think, Clarikins? Remember—the Project? The long haul: the Trans-Siberian railway, Moscow-Beijing and all onward connections... It's a sign. You can't ignore a sign."

But she was busy. She was always busy. I'll have your people speak to my people, we'll do lunch sometime, maybe the first Tuesday in March, 2030...

We looked at Bush. We looked at Blair. We looked at the ragged presenter, who looked as if the white cliffs of Dover had collapsed into his face. She sighed.

"I'm getting a replacement. I'm due a break anyway. We're not getting any younger."

"Do the trip while we can still walk without creaking. This summer, coming to a screen in your galaxy. Escape from Alcatraz."

We clinched the deal over Sainsbury's Assam tea bags.

Four months later, we flew to Saint Petersburg.

"Far away from here..."

Now the war has wandered
Far away from here,
We in quietness settle
To our evening beer.

Night now falls so gently,
Darkness shrouds the sky,
No more fires are blazing
Planes don't fly up high.

There hasn't been an air-raid
Since the last full moon,
By the rules of warfare
We should have one soon.

Whangpoo still looks gloomy,
Curfew's yet imposed.
Half an hour to midnight,
Cabarets are closed.

So now all good children
Early go to bed,
Fighting's done a mizzle,
"Peace" is here instead.

   – R.T. Peyton-Griffin ("In Parenthesis")
    from "Shanghai Schemozzle," *North China Daily News,*
1937

Judit's Story
by Go Yuan

(Translated by D.Kelly)

Preamble

Shanghai, my city, is an awakened giant spread out over a once sunken shoreline that has been raised up to a forest of majestic towers, standing guard over a seething army of vehicles, almost as many cars as citizens, gliding over the spider's web of motorways, screaming their lust of power by day and cascading lights by night, celebrating their new-found festival of life. They are an insatiable machine that has discovered the secret of perpetual motion. The people flow by them constantly, drawing their energy from this collective process as from a colossal battery, that sustains as well as draws their collective and their individual warmth and vigour and feeds it back into the city itself.

We are told that everything has changed in our country. But the impression my grandmother might have had when she arrived in Shanghai more than seventy years ago may have been not that different from our own, as it was a city seized by a frenzy of building, not by its own teeming population in their own interests and desires but by the privileged foreigners, who had adopted it as a monument to their power and dominance over the people they perceived as passive, indolent and essentially unable to exercise control over their own lives and fate.

My grandmother arrived, as did so many in those days, as a stranger, escaping the tumult of the north, which was suffering from the ravages of competing generals and from the first blows of the Japanese invaders, who had already overrun the place of her first refuge, in Manchuria, and imposed their own mock-empire with its tinsel crown adorning the head of their puppet, the surviving grandson of the last Empress of China, the dissolute drug addict Pu Yi.

She arrived, I was told, by train, on a sixty-hour voyage from what was then Peking, the imperial city that had lost its empire and was hard-pressed by the Japanese army that was marching ever closer from the northeast.

My grandmother had certain skills, that enabled her to find her way through the chaos that was about to engulf the country. She was an actress, skilled in subterfuges and disguises, although she herself, as the tale went, was a person without guile, who only sought her way back to a certain innocence that she remembered, through the years that followed, in a time before the world had descended into madness, destruction and war. She was learned in many fields of study, theatre, literature, poetry and song, but also in the sciences, mathematics, physics and chemistry, which had been her first aspirations. She had dreamed of travel, and she was part of a large family that had lived at a slow and deliberate pace, before the great sundering of the twentieth century had scattered them all to the four winds. But she lived as she could, when the old orders fell apart, and what remained could only be her own sense of a life that had to be lived in dignity, rather than slavery, in small victories, rather than one great defeat.

My father told me these tales, because he was sheltered by this great spirit, that had been present to guide him when all seemed dark and opaque, when the glass between one's own self and reality seemed to be misted up, filthy and cracked, with strange shapes gesticulating and screaming beyond it, crying out in a cacophony of voices that demanded obedience and surrender. We were all lost in the abyss, he said, wandering about in the halls of the dead that had risen up and invaded the living, and all paths were barren and circular, and only led us back to the broken mirror that reflected our own helplessness and despair. But then, he said, my mother would suddenly sing, one of those old songs she used to sing in the jazz clubs of my own city, in the very midst of its troubles, crooning—Autumn Memories, or Sunset on Suzhou River, or the Song of Fishing Boat Lights. And then a magic would descend, and the harshness of the surrounding life, its terrors, and the bleakness of the rooms in which they were crowded with their broken furniture and rusted pots and kettles, and the few old mementoes that could no longer be tacked on the walls, or displayed on tables and bedsides, but had to be squirreled away in nooks in the kitchen, or under the floorboards, could vibrate with a strange, vibrant tone, that made him see, as if in a sudden apparition, the smooth shining floors of the old dancehalls, the ballrooms oozing with floating figures clutching each other in the smoky space of dreams, the languid call of the band at the back of the hall on its podium, wailing their melancholy but defiant sound over the swaying couples, far away airs that drifted on opium fumes, capturing a strange moment that stretched out beyond its faint origin to swirl into a sweet oblivion that defied both its time and place.

My grandfather met my grandmother at the Paramount dance hall, in the summer of 1934, my father told me. He saw and heard her singing a melancholy song and fell in love with her on the spot, her air of sadness and bravery, standing up in a strange place and expressing her inner emotions, so foreign an idea to the manners of his own country and people. My grandfather was a commercial artist. He was trained as a boy in the Tushanwan Arts School in the city, which Jesuit missionaries founded in the first flowering of Shanghai's development several decades before. The first students trained with the models of western religious art, the portraits of Jesus Christ and the saints, and then, after the first European great war, in the light of more experimental art. They copied their designs from Monet and Van Gogh, and then, in the twenties, some of our Chinese students went to Paris and came back with an entirely new art, that became the model for the city's transformation in architecture and in design. My great-grandfather had been an illustrator for a magazine called the Dianshizhai Pictorial, which featured many comical drawings of life in the city at the end of the nineteenth century. He specialised in portraying the awkward encounter between the traditional Chinese and the foreigners, with their constricting clothes and strange customs. His son followed him into the same trade, and designed illustrated covers for cigarette packs and matchboxes, pictures for shop displays, postcards and advertisements. By the nineteen-thirties he had his own business, but he identified himself more with the avant-garde artists and students than with the merchant class of the city. As a youth, he had taken part in the demonstrations against the foreign concessions granted at the Versailles conference, that grew into the May Fourth Movement of 1919, the same movement that sparked the young radicals who two years later founded the Chinese Communist Party, led by Chen Duxiu and Li Dazhao. He was not himself a communist, since he shunned political parties, but he was an eager participant in the cultural rebirth that marked that era.

Shanghai, at that time, was full of enthusiastic young people, painters, writers, poets, cultural figures like Lu Xun and Cai Yuanpei. My grandfather's easygoing temperament led him to the coffee shops and taverns rather than the streets and intellectual circles. He had a friend who played the trombone in the band that opened the new Paramount hall, a tower of glass and "moderne" construction that glittered with light and contained two dance halls, the larger one having enough space for a thousand dancers, who could whirl away in all seasons, as the ultra-modern apparatus of air-conditioning cooled the rapt sweating couples.

It was one of these July nights, so my father told me, that my grandfather saw and heard my grandmother sing, and when she finished her set to great applause and sat down at her table, and the jazz band struck up their mellow dance tunes, he approached her, ignoring the scowls of the male companions who attended her on either side, and asked her to join him on the floor.

This was a time and a place, one must remember, in which entertainment and prostitution went hand in hand in Shanghai, and many of the White Russian women who had poured into the city after the civil wars were reduced to making a living by selling themselves. The "singsong" girls of Shanghai had a longer tradition, alongside the cabals and empires of crime that creamed off the pickings of every new prosperity. Yu Qi, as my grandmother was then called, was of another category entirely, as her reputation had preceded her from Peking and Tianjin, but she too had to make her way carefully in the opium-soaked world of the gangs who ruled the night life of the city and the militia officers who ruled by day.

My grandfather knew nothing of her life before he saw her that evening in the smoky light of the dancehall. He had no idea if any of the men at her table were her companions, or owners, nor of the extent of their power. He only knew that he had met the woman he wished to spend his life with from that moment onwards. It was a very western thought, with a very eastern certainty.

As they danced, they could sense that many eyes were watching them, although they tried to be lost in the crowd. My father told me his father had told him the tune the band was playing was called: "Please don't forget this night in Shanghai."

My father never spoke to me about my grandmother's early days in her village. I don't know if she never told him, or if he forgot, in the burden of events and memories that fell upon his generation like a mountain falling from the sky. My grandfather had died before I was born, worn out by his own troubles, and the family's experience in the "Great Cultural Revolution," which had also come to an end before I arrived. When I was sixteen, at school, we were asked to write an assignment, a literary exercise, about our families and their experiences. I could not write about my parents, who had lived their lives in that period, but would not speak of their own pain and their thoughts. I know my father had been a Red Guard, who was himself purged by his high school comrades because he was the son of a marriage to a foreign devil who was tainted by her "decadent" life in the old days, before Liberation. He was forced to denounce his parents in writing and sent off to a far-off village in Shanxi province to labour five years in a steel plant. He often said, with the wry look that I always recall as his signature, that it was the great blessing of his life, for it was there that he met my mother, who had been sent away from her own home city of Zhezhiang, for the same reason: her father was suspect, because he was of the small merchant class. Neither spoke of other common humiliations. My father just said: I went deaf from the noise. He always walked and moved with his head cocked to one side, and relished saying to people, when life became better: "Speak up! Chairman Mao is still in my ear!" My mother spoke very very softly, as if even in the terrible din of the steel works, your innermost thoughts might be heard.

What they kept, from all the searches and marches, and self-criticism meetings and purges, was a small collection, images of my grandmother from old cigarette packets, the Nanyang Brothers Tobacco Company, Hatamen Cigarettes, advertisements of bath soap, matchbox covers, and some folded up calendar posters, all except one, the bath soap, showing her with characteristic Chinese eyes, although her fair skin and oval Russian face fail to disguise her real origins. There used to be an old movie poster, my mother told me, but it became torn after being folded too many times to fit into its tiny hiding place under the kitchen floorboards.

Where was she from? Far far away, said my father. The other side of Russia, closer to Europe, a small village, he said, by the river. I had no idea whether this was one of Russia's great waterways, the Volga or the Dnieper, the furthest west being the Dniester, which ran into the Black Sea. She came from a large Jewish family. She had four brothers, my father said, and he thought two sisters, or maybe it was only one. She had come east to follow her older brother, who had been a travelling merchant, probably a trader in furs. He and another brother were caught up in the civil wars in Russia, after Lenin's Revolution. The other brother had been a soldier, and then a Bolshevik commissar. But he did not remember his name. He also worked on the gold-fields, in the great wastes of Siberia, north of Irkutsk. But what had become of him later no-one knew. Two other brothers had gone to America while she was still a child. The trading brother was called Zhiv, and he found his way, after the civil wars died down, to the Manchurian city of Harbin. When he was settled there, and had a trading company, he wrote to her in her village and asked her to join him, since matters were not well in their home province, and there was great hardship, and even famine, in the surrounding countryside. Brother Zhiv had reached Manchuria by the Trans-Siberian railway, but he did not advise this for a young woman who would have to travel alone. He sent her money, or a ticket, my father was not sure which, to embark on the long land and sea journey, taking ship at the French port of Marseille, for Tianjin, in northern China, where he could meet her and convey her on to Harbin.

This much I know. The rest is an adventure that the writer has to imagine from the patchwork of tales and following the frail woven thread…

I will speak in my grandmother's voice, which I never heard. Or at least try to see things through her eyes. For a long time, I sought her recordings, with the jazz bands of lost Shanghai. But I could find nothing. In our country, in which vendors sell millions of pirated cassettes, c.d.s, movies, recordings, there is no trace of the singer, Yu Qi. I found the jazz bands preserved, in memorial sessions, played by the survivors of those hazy days still blowing their horns past eighty years young. But not the voice, not the trembling song. When I was preparing my essay for my senior class I had a teacher, Peng, who was very encouraging in my search for historical truth. I was already planning to study our history at university, and although our most recent years were still a painful and difficult subject, teacher Peng was determined to steer me towards a true understanding of those decades of chaos before Liberation. He kept urging me to nag my parents for exact dates, rather than vague assertions, for the small details, for any vivid memory that might have survived the great levelling.

"When did she arrive in Tianjin?" I asked my father. "She must have told you. Arriving after a long voyage in a strange place, she must have remembered that moment…"

"Yes," my father eventually admitted, to be rid of my questions at least for the day. "She did tell me. It was summer, nineteen-twenty-eight.

"Yes, I'm sure," he said. "It was wartime." He gave me that look, cocking his head, as if the furnaces were still thundering in there.

"It was always wartime."

I took that date to my teacher. He sent me to the "morgues" of the north China newspapers of that time. So much memory denied, buried, deleted. But it's amazing what still survived...

1928. June. Tianjin. Tientsin, as the foreigners called it. The northern port city. The entrance gate towards Peking. Like Shanghai, another foreigners' market and playground: a series of "bunds," though not as spectacular as our own, divided between the British, French, the Germans, the Italians and the Japanese. The German concession is dominated by a bronze statue of the legendary knight Roland, erected in memory of the German soldiers who died in the Boxer Rebellion of 1900 defending the sacred rights of Berlin. The British take pride in the wide Gordon Road—named after their hero of the Taiping Rebellion who died far away in Sudan in defence of the British empire in Africa—along which are strung the great commercial houses and banks: the Chartered Bank of India, Australia and China, the Hongkong and Shanghai Banking Corporation, with its branches and agencies already present in all the continents of the earth. In the Japanese concession, in the "Quiet Garden" hotel, an unusual guest, Pu Yi, the last emperor of China, with his entourage of servants, eunuchs and concubines, has abided since 1925, after the Republic's decrees forced him out of the Forbidden City. He can be seen often in the other districts, at garden parties, sporting events, polo games, cabarets, an exotic, gaunt figure in dark spectacles, watched over by the Japanese officers and bodyguards, who have their own plans for his future.

At this point in time, the foreign commandants are mustering their forces for the defence of the city, which is at the center of a bloody struggle for the control of Peking and the surrounding regions. Tianjin, the railway hub of south, east, west and north, is crucial for the northern Manchurian warlord, Zhang Zuolin, who controls Peking and Manchuria, and the Kuomintang forces of General Jiang Je-si—Chiang Kai-Shek—who have marched up from the south on their campaign to lay claim to all of China. More than a hundred thousand soldiers are converging on the city, and tens of thousands are already bivouacked within it, menacing the exposed Chinese quarters, and protecting the foreign concessions.

Could Yu Qi have arrived at this time? After a month's journey from Marseilles, on a ship that would have docked in Shanghai, then switched to a local steamer, pressing on, up the China sea, to draw in alongside the cruisers and battleships disgorging fresh European and Japanese troops to keep their own hold on this industrial and commercial hub of China. The Japanese, in particular, want neither Generals Jiang nor Zhiang to have any lasting control on these assets, that they consider theirs for the taking.

Could she have arrived some weeks later? Perhaps she was spared the nights of terror, in mid-June, when the Kuomintang and allied troops from Shanxi entered the city and occupied it, and the Chinese quarters were looted by troops of both armies as well as the retreating northerners, deserters and bandits, who went on an orgy of pillage and killing, causing hordes of refugees to crowd into the foreign concessions, amid confusing clashes between Chinese nationalists and the Japanese, who retreated into their own district. None of the competing forces recognises the other, police buildings are set on fire, and all lights cut off. Meanwhile, Peking itself has fallen to the Kuomintang and Shanxi armies, and the Manchu warlord has been chased out. Some days later, General Zhang himself, travelling in his armoured train towards Manchuria, is blown up by a mine placed on the tracks, the Japanese having seized their moment to rid themselves of at least one of their foes. A strange quiet has descended upon Tianjin, and Peking itself lies denuded, the nationalists preferring to declare their own southern base, Nanjing, as their new Chinese capital.

What does Judit, the pale student girl from western Russia, make of this chaotic moment, when she steps down the gangway of the passenger ship onto the quay? The busy wharfs, the brick customs house, the storage buildings, the moored steamships, all these would look familiar, though she would also see the old sailing boats, the famous Chinese junks, the crowds cramming the jetties, the shouting rickshaw-men, the vendors and greeters, a raucous, bewildering world. Perhaps she had her baptism of this in Shanghai. Battalions of soldiers would also be here, forming a cocoon of safety around the foreigners while the porters rushed to carry their bags. Where is the familiar face? Is he here? Was there a telegram, directing her to a meeting place? Why is she here? Above all, the heat would envelop her, like a constricting shroud. The summer heat of China, this humid oven, the actuality of our country long before our own period's fierce industrial furnaces added their choking clouds of smoke to our sky. The reality of constant perspiration, clothes sticking to one's body, as the vast noise of the crowd blares out…

Let's assume that her brother is there to meet her: A dapper man, one might think, in his western suit, perhaps even a tie for the occasion, with his own conveyance, a rickshaw "boy" and two or three servants for the baggage, perhaps he is one of those tall Russian traders, adventurers in leather jackets—deep furs in winter—with a cap of animal skins, or in the heat of summer, who knows, even "gone native," with the long Chinese gown that allows the limbs to breathe. The European suit, though, might be more appropriate. Perhaps, too, he has his own protection, an armed guard or two, Harbinski Russians, veterans perhaps of sorely lost battles, alert for any trouble in a land that has known very little but troubles for the past three decades…

They embrace, as brothers and sisters do. I cannot know for sure, as I am an only child, an early product of more organised times. My father was the only child of my grandparents, not from any ideological reasons, but because their years together were spent in the midst of hardship, terror and war...

They talk, in the lobby of the hotel, or in one of the cafes of the city, on the rue de France, in the French concession, or perhaps they ventured out to the Chinese city, if the arrival had taken place later in July, after Peking had fallen, and the northern troops of the assassinated "Old Marshall" had left the city, and the Kuomintang had left their Shanxi minions in charge when they decamped to Nanjing, so they could stroll around the old Temples of Heaven, or the Confucian temple or Drum Tower, relaxing in the local tea rooms in shaded gardens, in the soft tinkle of ornamental pools.

What did they talk about? What tales did he tell her, of his far-flung travels across Siberia, the days of civil war, hardship and flight, the life filled in since they parted eight, nine or seven years before? What did she tell him of the remaining family affairs, back in the village in the Ukrainian steppes, amid a landscape so different, and so sparse of people, in comparison with the crowds that engulfed them here? Did she have news of the other missing siblings, the brothers who had gone to the west, perhaps to America? Did he have news of the other brother who had gone to the Siberian gold-fields? He must have spoken of his plans for her, since we know, from my father's tales, that she would later enroll at the University in Harbin, to continue her scientific studies in the Faculty of Engineering, where she must have learned skills that in the disorders of time she would never put to work. But she could dream, of a new life and new hopes.

Most probably, they would not have lingered long in Tianjin. I have a fancy that, perhaps, in one encounter, they might have brushed past the dark-shaded figure of the last emperor of China, Pu Yi, as he enters the lobby of the Astor House Hotel, for a rendez-vous with one of his mistresses or one of the local sing-song girls. Perhaps his concealed glance passed over the pale-faced beauty of the young Russian girl, who might have seemed so demure in this world of snatched pleasures and dissolute passions before the world slid inexorably towards disaster. The glance born of his own constriction and imprisonment in the fetid luxuries of the descent of a great and once inevitable power towards oblivion. Even the blink of the eye cannot be seen behind the opaque lenses. And then they have passed, beyond imagination.

They took the train, from the Tianjin central station, up the line, into Manchuria. Or, if the line was still disrupted by rival militias and bandits, they might have taken a car, with an armed and reliable driver, up to the next station along the line. In whichever case, a journey of at least twenty hours, in an armour plated coach, or longer, if the dangerous roads had to be taken, before they reached their destination of Harbin.

When Zhiv had first arrived in Harbin, in 1921, the town was already full of Russian civilians and soldiers who had fled across the border from Siberia. Entire battalions of defeated Whites were bivouacked in tents set up along the banks of the Sungari River, all the way to the docks, and in the wide streets that divided the Old Town from the New, across the railway. The railway was the mother and father of Harbin, which was until the last years of the previous century just a small village, but the new Russian Tsar, Nikolai the Second, was determined to hew the empire's way east towards the mineral treasures of Siberia, and south towards Mongolia and Manchuria, the Chinese Empire's northern frontiers. In 1896, Harbin was chosen as the hub of the linking branch towards Peking. First came the surveyors, then the Russian engineers and overseers and the Chinese labourers who laid the track, just as they had the great American railroads, linking a more alien continent. They settled along the Sungari River, the Chinese in a sprawling maze of courtyards and alleyways and the Russians in the new grid of Pristan, raising a new European-style town, with stone houses and paved avenues that were soon lined with shops, trading posts, entertainment halls and cafés. A patchwork of other nationalities were also drawn to the town: Germans, Poles, Tatars, Japanese, Armenians, Georgians, even Latvians and Lithuanians, who together with the new Chinese working force, composed almost ninety percent of the inhabitants, leaving the native Manchurians as minor hands.

In 1904, during the Russian war with Japan, Harbin became a forward headquarters of the Russian army, midway between Irkutsk and Port Arthur, as hundreds of thousands of Russian and Japanese troops slaughtered each other in the kaoliang fields. As Russia went down to defeat, her soldiers passed in their hordes through the sombre town, forward towards the unmarked graves of Manchuria, or back to the hospital trains carrying them home mutilated and scarred, many carrying with them a terrible fury that would convulse the empire in years to come.

In 1914, war supplies passed again along the Manchurian railroad to feed the killing machines of the west, and the town thrived as a major depot for commerce between China and Russia. The railroad officials built themselves homes beyond the already teeming old Harbin in a New Town, with modern offices, trading centers, schools and hospitals away from the alleys of Chinese Fuchatien. A hub which then expanded to accomodate the new flow of foreigners who were themselves often destitute when they arrived in the wake of revolution and war...

But this was still a haven. If Zhiv survived the years of absolute uncertainty all the way from the streets of Moscow to the gate of this unlikely sanctuary, he was well-placed to thrive. Money was God in Harbin, and almost all the people who flocked here saw themselves as passersby, transients, temporary sojourners, far from home. The city was built of their memories, a living tapestry of all that they had lost: The shape of their houses, the furniture, the carpets and tapestries, the pictures on the walls, the drapes and curtains, the windows, the roofs, the signs on the stores, the horse-drawn droshkys that clip-clopped through old sights and sounds, the poetry, the writing, the music, the string quartets and sweet chords of shattered homelands, alongside all the rowdier business of the dancehalls and cabarets. Plenty of desperate white flesh here... And alongside all this brash noise, the drumroll of the old politics that might have been trampled in the bloody battlefields but rose here again, a ghostly resurrection of the same faiths and fears that propelled most of the inhabitants to this crowded sanctuary in the first place.

They are all here: the Tsarist faithful, the monarchists, the Ka-dets remnants, the Old Believers, the survivors of Kolchak, Kornilov and Denikin, a smattering of right S-R's, even Bolsheviks who fell foul of the prevailing Leninist wind, Siberian separatists, Polish nationalists, remnants of no-one could tell how many private armies, the most dangerous being the deranged followers of the Bloody Baron von Ungern who had proclaimed himself the new Khan of Mongolia and terrorised the whole of that country until he was caught and shot by the Reds in Irkutsk. Another feared ex-white commander, General Semenov, the Ataman of the Trans-Baikalian Cossacks, still in charge of several hundred ragged soldiers, was also lingering in the taverns and brothels of the town.

Here, my father told me, Judit's brother Zhiv, the trader, kept his wits about him, while he established his new base with his partner, another Russian Jew who may have been called Isaac, making new contacts and finding new routes in which to seek, buy and recruit new representatives, new agents to send out into the dangerous hinterland where bandits still roamed the vast and lawless wastes. Fur was their main business, coats and hats, as well as the heavy duty leather boots and gloves that everyone had to have to get through the harsh Manchurian winter. And who knows what else besides.

In Harbin, at least, they were better served as Jews, since among the Poles and Russians there were many thousands of their faith who had been present from the very earliest settlement of the "Chinese Eastern Railway." The Tsar encouraged Jews to move eastwards, away from the Orthodox Christian centers, and provided various inducements, grants, promises of unrestricted movement and rights. After the attacks of 1905, many hazarded the long journey along the Trans-Siberian railway on these pledges, and the war drove more and more in their wake. Zhiv would have known there was a large and supportive community, with their own schools, synagogues, mutual societies and their own numerous political parties: liberals, socialists, zionists, with their own organisations, offices, and schisms, for they too were Russians, and no party could remain for long without dissolving into their respective splits. It was of no concern to Zhiv: everyone needed a hat and coat for the winter, the warmest gloves and best-fitting and warmest boots.

Go Yuan's tale continued:

When I flew from Shanghai to Harbin in 2003, I was met at the airport by the woman I had been communicating with by email, Huang Li, who was a journalist working on the local newspaper and specialising in the city's Russian history. She guided me through the city's new transition into yet another of our urban miracles, a sprawl of residential blocks and high towers, the hub of Heilojiang province, with shopping malls and cranes looming everywhere, billboards along the main road proclaiming: "ADD SPEED TO THE ECONOMIC DEVELOPMENT! ADVANCE TOGETHER FOR A PROSPEROUS FUTURE!" Bigger, better, faster! How much further can we go, when we've already scraped the sky? But Huang Li has made sure I am brought down to my own archaeological level by booking me into the Hotel Moderne, Harbin's oldest stopping place, built in 1906 by a group of Jewish entrepreneurs in impeccable Art Nouveau style, with its vast chandelier presiding over columns and corridors lined with paintings of the city's heyday, the droshkys in the street, a Russian village, a sad musician looming over a piano, a strong quartet, a portrait of the founders—a Chinese painter's image of Jews, all sallow and somewhat mysterious, with a great lobby canvas of a mass dinner of Harbin worthies seated at three long tables. The long gone staring wistfully at us, as I stared back, puzzled and intrigued.

"It's not the best hotel in town," my host said, "but it will get you in the mood."

Huang Li has spent her energies writing and lobbying for the preservation of the city's few remaining Russian-style houses that are still dotted about the districts marked for demolition and renewal. The common theme of our time: Out with the old! Up with the new! Memories are superfluous, left to the academics. History best preserved in great dioramas covering entire walls in vast new museums, to which all the curious should go. We all have other priorities, people to serve, one billion two hundred million mouths to feed, hordes of those still left behind in the mammoth rush into the middle class. No one can afford nostalgia, no one wants to replicate the past. We march inexorably forward, we can't afford to look back.

Quick—before there's nothing left! There is a society for the preservation of the Jewish past, a project of the university, a way to please new allies and interested American parties, the ex-Harbinskis, who are scattered, mostly in the United States, in Israel and Australia. Delegations visit annually, poring over the old photographs hung in the Russian orthodox Church, no longer used for worship, as the last Russian believers faded away soon after Liberation. Now under the grand cupola and the sad icons left over from the old presence, we can peek at the old way of life: the musicians, the ballet dancers, the Russian shops, Cyrillic signs, the women in Russian garb, the blonde bearded faces bundled in furs, the young girls in bathing suits laughing on the banks of the summer river, beauty long faded, and the sombre look of the Chinese, servants in their own habitat, the original "coolies" crowding behind the railway moguls posing as they open the line, in 1903.

Nothing of course of Manchukuo, the Japanese occupied empire of the puppet Pu Yi, the most shameful episode of Heilonjiang's murky past. In the preservationists' offices, there is a big portrait of a foreign man whom I cannot place, but Huang Li explains to me he is Mister Olmert, a Minister in the government of Israel, who has the distinction of being the son of a prominent Harbin citizen, who founded the Jewish community's largest Zionist movement, the "Betar," in the 1930's. The period when, Huang Li noted, my grandmother would have been here, either studying at the Polytechnic or already pursuing her new career as a performer in the Russian theatre scene. There were, she explained, many venues for actors to shine on Harbin stages: the Palace, the Atlantic, the Moderne itself, which was both stage and cinema. After the Russian Revolution, Harbin usurped Irkutsk's old title as "Paris of the East," a domain of culture, where the "Moulin-Rouge" cabaret vied with the ballets of "Coppelia" and "Faust."

The man from the preservation society, Hu, brought me books of photographs of Jewish Harbin, working in shops, praying in the synagogue, in renovation, shaking hands with officials, visiting the Jewish cemetery outside the town. I was offered the grand tour, but Huang moved in to rescue me, saying we were on our own quest. She was going to show me what was left of the districts in which the old residents had lived and worked.

Not much to see. A small clump of three or four storey Russian houses, an ex-mansion in an overgrown and neglected garden, still standing in the midst of the new high rise buildings and the older Mao period ageing blocks. with weeds growing in its cracked stairs, that used to be the Soviet consulate before the Great Scare of 1969 chased even them back across the border. There were some Russians in town, mainly to buy and sell. Now that we are the Communists and they are, we are not quite clear what, democrats, nationalists, roving vagrants? "You know how it is," Huang sighed as she drove me back to the Moderne, "money talks, everything else is silent."

The rooms at the Moderne are large and seedy, the fittings renewed some time during the seventies' but not recently, the wallpaper barely covering the vestiges of older, dank layers. Two small cockroaches scurry away behind the bathtub. In one of these rooms, Madame Soong, Sun Yat-Sen's wife, had once stayed, I think in number 213. The brochure by the bed, in both Chinese and very strangely translated English, sings the praises of the hotel, stating that it was "not only own European style luxury and elegance, but also has denses modern mushy." (*English in original, D.K.*) I did not know what that was, but the description was apt. The old endured somewhere amidst the new, but I could not fit the one inside the other. They neither meshed, nor contradicted each other. I had brought the CD of the Shanghai jazz band with me, and slid it into my laptop's disk drive. The melancholy tunes surrounded me: "By the side of Suzhou river," "autumn memories," "this crazy world," "spring on Zhong mountain" and "when will you come again?"

I moved the flimsy curtain and looked out the window on the street. The lights of the shops and restaurants flashed in their yellows, reds and golds. A large display of Harbin Beer tipped its green light into a large gleaming mug. The crowds were moving and murmuring below. It was a pedestrian precinct, probably Central Street, which was once the Kitaiskaya, the main thoroughfare of the Pristan quarter sixty years before. I tried to imagine my grandmother and her brother Zhiv strolling by, or perhaps her alone, or with her arm entwined with some unknown lover, or holding hands with a friend, as we do here in our land.

There are two small framed photographs on my room's wall: One shows a man mounted on a small horse-drawn cart which has stopped by a store, marked in Russian "Molochno-Bakaleinaya"— Dairy-Grocery. Looking out at the camera, a cheerful moustached fellow with a peaked cap and a typical Russian peasant-style blouse. The other picture depicts a social gathering of some sort in a room backed by a large lace curtain. Four men, five women, bunched together, the men in jackets and bow ties, the ladies also in evening dress, the group smiling, laughing, looking at each other rather than at the camera, except for one younger woman, frail and blonde, who looks out at me with a quizzical look. I am not sure if she wants to ask me something, or whether she is ready to tell her own tale.

Those were my grandmother's happy years, my father told me. Zhiv enrolled her in the Polytechnic, which was full of eager Russian students, many of them Jews. He had a large apartment in a house owned by a rich Jewish family in the "Novi Gorod," the New Town of Harbin, on the other side of the railway, where there was more space away from the now crowded Pristan. She remembered that first summer, when the sons and daughters of the host families went boating on the Sungari River. There were pleasure gardens across the water, with shady cafés from which they went down to the water to bathe. In the evenings, they could stroll along the Kitaiskaya and linger in the crowded street.

Zhiv's trading business was, however, becoming affected by the growing crisis in Manchuria. This was drawing in not only the Japanese and the Chinese Nationalist government but the newly named Soviet Union and even Mongolia, which the Soviets now controlled. Bandits were a major problem both east and west, frequently attacking the trains, robbing passengers, kidnapping merchants and demanding ransom money. The mail train to Harbin was attacked in July 1928, four passengers were killed and forty kidnapped. In August five thousand Mongolian troops invaded the province, under the command of Soviet officers. The Soviets were making ready to preempt any new attempts by the Japanese to send their own troops into Manchuria, the prize goal being the Railway itself. Many cooks were stirring the broth: the old Chinese warlords under their own "Young Marshall," another army of the "Noble General" Feng Yuxiang, the Nationalists still trying to rule China from Nanjing, and various independent militias.

As a trader, Zhiv was more aware than others of the pressure building in the city, the greatest shock coming in the following year, 1929 when, in October, at the onset of winter, Russian troops invaded Manchuria.

The Harbinskis still lived in their bubble. At the Polytechnic, Judit was involved in its amateur theatre society, putting on plays by Chekhov and Gogol. In Chekhov's "Three Sisters," she played the youngest sister, Irina, who dreams of going back to find her true love in Moscow, but ends up marrying the luckless Baron Tuzenbach, and in Gogol's "Grand Inquisitor" she played the Governor's wife, Anna Andreyevna, with much makeup to make her look middle-aged. My father thought she had said they also put on some Shakespeare, Romeo and Juliet, but this might have been a false memory. The Harbinskis discovered that she had a fine singing voice, and sang many old romantic Russian songs, as well as modern western tunes.

During this period, she also learned Chinese, making her proficient enough to make her way down to Peking later, when the tragedy struck. It was most probable that Zhiv taught her the language, since he had learned it for his own travels and trade. How far and wide he travelled south, however, we never found out, as there were neither written nor oral records. In modern Harbin, when my host Huang Li and I searched through the existing records of the Preservation Society, there was no trace of either of them. The surest identification, we were told, would be from the graves in the Jewish cemetery, where the names were hewn in stone. All other records, municipal or police archives, were locked up by Beijing's fiat, unobtainable until further notice. "Too many secrets," Huang Li told me later, "local collaboration with the Manchukuo government. The Japanese occupation kept all names and records—everything is sealed."

What was Zhiv's role? What has vanished has vanished. One may search long, and never discover. Or one might get lucky some day, in some forgotten archive, a locked basement, some treasure of lost souls, perhaps even in Tokyo, in a hoard of Kempetai records, the old Russian, Chinese, Romanian, Polish, Jewish names transcribed strangely into Japanese. How would one look up Gurevits in Japanese, when I have only Yu Qi to start with?

The grand politics of China made their mark on Harbin. Once Chiang Ka-Shek made his break with the Communists, and massacred them in Shanghai, his relationship with the Soviets became more strained. The big break came in Harbin, when the Chinese authorities swooped down on the Russian managers of the Chinese Eastern Railway offices in the New Town and deported them on the train back to Russia, seizing control of the railway company and all its assets. Other Russians designated as "Red" were arrested. This happened in July 1929, and caused great confusion among the émigrés in the city. In August martial law was declared after a train was derailed west of Harbin. Chinese newsreels shown in

Harbin projected scenes of Russian Soviet soldiers driving Chinese peasants into the Amur River, at the border, and massing to attack and occupy Manchuria. At the same time the Soviets broadcast propaganda about the Chinese arming Russian "White Guards" to attack the loyal Reds in their communities.

Even the ballrooms of Pristan seethed with discomfort. Since the great migration of the civil war Russians in Harbin were regarded as "radishes"—Red outside and White inside, trying to steer a safe course in the storm. Once the Soviets and Chinese became lethal rivals, with the Japanese ogre poised to sweep down on both, the rose-tinted spectacles became blackened and fogged. The Jews were doubly fearful of Reds and Whites alike, Reds because they might be suspected of treachery, and Whites who were openly anti-Jewish, now fortified by a new breed of Russian Fascist black-shirts who had established themselves among the remnants of Semenov's armies and openly attacked Jews in the streets, smashing shop windows, burning down trade depots, and committing murders and robberies. The old safe haven was safe no longer.

Zhiv's trade with Russia was abruptly cut. Where in the old days he could hew trails to and from Siberia along the chaos of post-war confusion, there were now armies deployed at all the major and minor routes into the province. There were rumours that Russian gunboats were about to sail down the Sungari to take Harbin. The émigrés were under no illusions about their fate if the Soviets took the city—there were too many old scores to settle. The skin of the radish would be swiftly stripped. China was pressing in—Pristan and New Town facing two enemies from north and east. And other foreign elements in the city were also threatened, by official and by criminal forces: Three British citizens, commercial agents in Harbin, were kidnapped and held for ransom in August, although they were released a week later for a sum of 150,000 pounds sterling. In September the train was bombed again, near Hailar. In October the Russians began firing across the border, and on November 21, 1929, the Red Army finally invaded Manchuria.

Winter in Harbin is always brutal. The northern winds close in like a vise, paralysing body and mind. Snow and ice cover every exposed surface. But people were hardier in those days, and the hardships that brought them to this place fortified their spirits, and taught them to live day by day, and await the next time, far off as it might be, in which the sun's rays would bring some warmth, rather than just at best a frozen blue sky.

The bubble of life continued indoors, drinking, dancing, playing music, studying, making a living. Outdoors, like human yaks, people trudged across the white landscape, from shelter to shelter. In this world, war was slow, like an invasion of giant slugs crawling across a blank shroud. But it was, at this point, a false alarm. The war stuttered along for two or three weeks, shedding its needless blood, and then stopped, the whole machine halted by a ceasefire cobbled together by tired generals and the cabal of railway officials meeting at Harbin and Khabarovsk. A Chinese-Soviet conference was to be called to talk through the commercial issues. The Japanese sat on their hands, happy to allow their two giant rivals to bleed each other, and bide their own time.

"What happened to Zhiv?" I asked my father. "Where does his story go, when Judit leaves for China?"

"He disappeared," said my father.

When exactly, and it what circumstances?

"My father didn't say," said my father.

One peers through the old news stories. Newspapers tell tales devoid of hindsight. Unlike historians, they do not begin from a point at which consequences are evident. They do not know on November 23 what November 24 will bring. One looks into the past with a blank future. The Japanese bided their time. The Chinese Eastern Railway was reopened to traffic between Harbin and Moscow on January 22, 1930. People, officials, families, traders could then communicate again with the Siberian hinterland, or even escape completely, if they had the need, the funds, the will or any chance of life and security elsewhere. But Judit did not leave Harbin, my ancestral story suggested, until two years later.

Let us assume Zhiv resumes his trading. Let us assume Judit is still studying. My father said he thought she had graduated, with an engineering degree. Hoping that there would be work available, in a new age of modernity, when science would overtake emotion and greed for land, and want, and the gathering storm whipped up in far off capitals, where strange financial crises were erupting, stock markets plunging and crashing, economies slumping, and new plots being hatched in conclaves of Generals whose armies were preparing for decisive battles that were to consume the world.

The fuse, as history tells us, was lit at Mukden, along the track to Peking, on the night of September 18, 1931, when the Japanese army detonated a bomb on the track of the South Manchuria rail branch, and then declared it an act of sabotage by the Chinese. Moving swiftly in "retaliation," their troops occupied Mukden and other towns along the railroad, and moved towards Harbin.

The Manchukuo period had begun. On November 12, the Last Emperor, Pu Yi, secretly left Tianjin and travelled to Mukden, to head the new "provisional government" and give the occupation an old legitimacy.

But in Harbin, even in this great crisis, life continued its sluggish winter affairs. The ballrooms remained open, the cinemas projected their old films, the restaurants served lunch and dinner, the cafe waiters scurried along, the Polytechnic was still open for classes, family life continued, indoors. For the émigré communities, the change of title from Manchuria to Manchukuo meant very little to some. But for two categories, the Redder than White Harbin Russians, and the Jews, the new system was ominous. Hated by the Chinese, and mistrusted by others, the new regime could rely most firmly on the White Guards, the old Russian monarchists, dreamers of Restoration, and most of all, the new Fascist Party, whose members now openly paraded in their black uniforms. The Jews, in response, strengthened their own growing youth movements, the Zionist "Young Guards," and the more zealous "Betar." The Japanese, not yet German allies, had no particular hostility to the Jews, as long as they rejected the Reds. They had no hostility to businessmen, restaurant owners, merchants and traders as such.

But Zhiv disappeared, and Judit left. Did he head off back to Russia, and fail to return? Was he along the way by suspicious Soviet commissars, who held him as a spy? From this time on, but on a vast scale, years later, when the Harbinskis began leaving in droves, hoping to be received back in Russia, they were arrested and condemned as "Japanese spies." Stalin's purge of fifteen thousand Harbin Russians was the first of many, so well known to history. Their records, the lethal roll-call of arrests and murders, were found sixty years later, by the daughter of one such family, an Australian writer (Mara Moustafine), in the NKVD archives in Nizhny-Novgorod. Thousands of handwritten transcriptions of prisoner interviews, that always began with the bald and harsh assertion: "When were you recruited as an agent of foreign intelligence?" No denial of any kind was accepted. Interrogations would invariably continue with "we have evidence that you are an agent of Japanese intelligence and that you returned to the USSR with the intention of gathering information and recruiting more spies. Please supply all their names and their details." Each file would end with the transfer of the prisoner to the state "organs" and the final act of the executioner's bullet in the back of head.

Was Zhiv one of these fifteen thousand accused?

We know only that Judit, his sister and ward in Harbin, was no longer in the city in the autumn of 1932, when, my grandmother told my father, she had first arrived in Peking.

Why would my father ask her about painful memories? There were so many of these, tragedies without end. The plots hatched in Tokyo, warlord rivalries, the harsh ascendancy of Chiang Kai-Shek, all cascaded down upon the Chinese people like a rain of fire, a storm of pain, agony and dispossession without precedent in our entire history. To our north, in Joseph Stalin's Russia, more hammer blows rained down on a population that had no way of proving its absolute loyalty amid the hunger for mass human sacrifice. What was one individual among these millions?

We surmise this: Zhiv vanished, and my grandmother waited, week after week, for some months, until, my father said, a Chinese friend advised her that she too could be targeted, and offered her help in finding a refuge, beyond the lines of new Manchukuo, among her own family, to the south.

(End of Part 1: G.Y.)

Asher:

Saint Petersburg, white nights of mid-July, the grand canals, onion dome cathedrals, the Hermitage, Nevsky Prospect, Peter and Paul's, the old Smolny. The streets and avenues that Uncle Kolya trod in bleaker days, and nights of terror and frost, with his assassin's pistol, hunting the revolution's many enemies. The bronze horses still rear above the Fontanka Canal, the griffins' gold-burnished wings still guard the bridges, the palaces still preening in the sunlight as if nothing had ever happened. Tourists flowing by thousands through the gold doors that Eisenstein opened for Kerensky so the montage could feed the pretender into the peacock on his way to ephemeral glory. An exquisite clock stands on the mantelpiece of a small room somewhere in the golden labyrinth of the Winter Palace, mounted on a small black rhinoceros hunched on a gold stand and capped with a tiny gold cherub, marking the exact time, 2:20 a.m, at which, on the night of the 25th to the 26th of October 1917, the Bolshevik revolutionaries burst in to arrest the members of the provisional government, the moment that shook the world. All around us, Matisse, Picasso, Gauguin, Degas, Van Gogh, Raphael, Leonardo and all their essence triumph, while in the Malachite Room, and the hundreds of other grand chambers, with their high-chandeliered gold ceilings, one is lost in the great game of surfaces, the improbable and inevitable twists and turns of history.

If Kolya saw these imperial palaces, once upon a time in the city, it must have increased his rage and made his trigger finger itch all the more. In the streets, it is impossible to see or feel the biting cold of those starvation winters, the foggy moonlit nights that Victor Serge described as filled with "an intense, gray, diffuse phosphorescence." Where the statue of Peter the Great reared up in a terrible threat of vengeance as it now rears to a storm of clicking cameras. I remember Kolya's image of children licking the glue off the back of the proletarian posters ripped off the walls for some nourishment, and Alexander Blok's poem "The Twelve"—the Red Guards marching through the ice and frost of a bitter black night, passing by a woman keening and weeping under the banner of "All Power to the Constituent Assembly." Two degrees from the poet, I can reach none of it; there are only cars, buses, hooting taxis hoping for a sucker who can be enticed to pay five hundred rubles to rush five minutes down the road to the Winter Palace. Where is the contact? The meaning? "In the dead-end alleys where only the snowstorm swirls its dust..." But the sun beats down, cheerfully, out of a clear blue sky...

"What are you thinking, Asher? A kopek for your thoughts!"

"Well overpriced, my dear."

Saint Petersburg to Moscow. From the Hotel Dostoevsky to the Hotel Ukraine. Post-Stalin extravagance, booked by Claire via Rough-Route Travel Agents. The vast Christmas cake palace I had always imagined as State Security headquarters turns out to be a thousand-room lodging. A vast lobby with a huge ceiling mural of the Train of Revolution, all red flags and bayonet-wielding troops. Six empty restaurants offer the same bland cuisine out of the same central kitchen system, along with a panoramic view from the 30th floor of the gray city stretching across the Moscow River down the Novy Arbat, the "White House" that Yeltsin shelled in 1992 and the walls and spires of Red Square. No time to take it all in, beyond the vision, the imprinted specter of false expectations, the imagery of so many illusions and fears.

On a steely-skied morning, even Red Square was empty, the

grit of the city stuck in throat and nostrils, the long battlement wall, the domes and towers and flags, the ugly lump of Lenin's Tomb like a nuclear bunker that has thrust its way above ground, all set against Saint Basil's licorice domes. Below the statue of Marshal Zhukov at the northern gate of the square stand the last vestiges of the Communist Party in Moscow: two old ladies and a white-haired veteran, his jacket festooned with World War medals, the stubborn babushkas holding aloft the red hammer-and-sickle standard and lecturing a few bemused local youths on their discarded history while the Marshal's horse rears in alarm and the tourists stumble by.

Claire wants to go to the Novodevichy Cemetery, where so many famous Russians are buried. She wants to visit Gogol, Bulgakov, Chekhov, Mayakovsky, Stanislavski, Andrei Bely and Shostakovich, to name a few, but I am graveyard shy—until she reads out that Sergei Eisenstein and Dziga Vertov, Lev Kuleshov and Sergei Bondarchuk, who made the immense and excellent *War and Peace* of 1964, are also tucked in there, alongside my father's old favorite, Count Kropotkin. That is, if one can scurry by Nikita Khrushchev, Andrei Gromyko, Molotov, Mikoyan, Boris Yeltsin (freshly embalmed in vodka), and, God help us, Lazar Kaganovich, Stalin's evil henchman of the gulags.

I leave her to commiserate with the soul of Chekhov and old comrades of the pen and stage while I wander among the strange sculptures and monuments: Khrushchev's head peering from two stone zig-zags, Mayakovsky glaring angrily from his plinth, Gogol rising in triumph, the grave strewn with fresh flowers, Eisenstein defiant in profile on a jagged slab, Nadezhda Stalin, the monster's long-suffering wife, looking blindly, with her nose chipped, out of a white stone in which her body seems to be imprisoned, only the hand and head escaping. Nodding to forgotten and obscure luminaries such as Gleb Kotelnikov, inventor of the knapsack parachute, Lyudmila Pavlichenko, female sniper, Zoya Kosmodemyanskaya, heroic partisan, and Sergei Obraztsov, puppeteer. And here is David Oistrakh, the violinist, and Ilya

Ehrenburg, the consummate survivor, the cellist Rostropovitch, whom my father used to listen to with great rapture, Rubinstein, on the piano, and Mikhail Romm—did he not direct *Quiet Flows the Don*? So many sounds and sights of my youth, trickled down from far-off podiums... I joined Claire and Bulgakov, 1891–1940, a simple granite stone, interred with his wife, Elena Sergeevna Bulgakova, who lasted till 1970. Seventy-seven years old. The old incantation from Tod Browning's *Freaks* that we always intoned: "Gooble-gobble, gooble-gobble, one of us, one of us...."

Shoen, genug. The train for Irkutsk leaves from the Yaroslavsky station at eleven p.m. Stocking up on Moscow sausage and plastic-wrapped cheeses and teabags at the hotel-side supermarket, rushed by taxi at a breakneck and reckless speed across the city center to the station, mercifully met by the Intourist guide who shoos us up the platform to the designated carriage, having advised us to stick a 500-ruble note in the hand of the "prodvonitsa" who will rule our berths for the next four days. Rucksacks stowed in what appears to be a very snug berth compartment morphed into first class for our benefit, the grimy window looking out on the streaking lights of the station, the tangle of criss-crossing rails, the strobing eyes of rows of apartment blocks, the doleful sound of the clattering points as the long haul begins.

In the bag I have copies of Kolya's "Soldier's Journal" and the two segments of Go Yuan's story, as well as two meaty volumes of Dostoyevsky, *Demons* and *The House of the Dead*, the first long due for a reread and the second somehow left out in spasms past. My memory of *Demons*, which was called *The Devils* in the old Penguin translation, was that most of the rebellious nihilist characters reminded me of people I had met not long ago, at Shai Baer's garden table at Queens Park or among the eager marchers in Berkeley and London, at gatherings of the IMG, the CPGB (Marxist-Leninist), the Socialist Workers Party and its rival twin, the Workers Revolutionary Party. I particularly liked Shigalyov, whose intense study of the future society that would replace the current failed systems had led him to the inevitable deduction that "starting from unlimited freedom, I conclude with unlimited despotism." The full explication of this, he states to the group, would take at least ten evenings, but, "apart from my solution of the social formula, there can be no other." Here Uncle Kolya comes full circle. How Dostoyevsky would have loved him. The old devil himself carved his way deep into each sinning soul. The pitiless dissector of hope, he foresaw the trajectory of Russia's long uprising, the desire for freedom colliding with the ascendancy of the true Shigalyov, the master of prisons and death. The author's ultimate wisdom, that he himself will never arrive at the good deeds he is impelled to preach.

Trying to follow Kolya's trajectory of 1919 by the Trans-Siberian handbook, we have to note that the main route has shifted. Instead of heading down the track to Samara, Zlatoust and on to Chelyabinsk, the train now goes from Nizhny-Novgorod, at kilometer 442, to Semyonov, Kotelnich, Glazov and Perm, at kilometer 1436, then proceeds to Yekaterinburg, Tyumen and only links up to the old Siberian route at Omsk—kilometer 2712—leaving us without any opportunity to imagine the armored trains chugging past Kurgan, Petukhovo and Petropavlovsk, where the Reds and Whites shed each other's blood for each ragged mile. Kurgan, the original exile of the Decembrists, where Kolya, following the advice of the real-life Svejk, Hasek, had, if his account was true in any detail, commandeered a train for the fatal run in which his comrade, Volkov, was killed on the way…

There he is, somewhere. One presses one's nose to the window, which has become grimier and grimier as the miles pile up, and short of the foresight applied by the German tourists in the next carriage to bring along a long pole with a squeegee sponge to clean the glass from the outside, as it is too high to reach by hand from the platform, one sees more and more "through a glass, darkly," mostly the endless blur of the tall silver birch trees that seem to cover half of Russia. "If you've seen ten million silver birch trees, you've seen them all," becomes a mantra Claire refuses to hear anymore.

At Omsk, Dostoyevsky was imprisoned for four years for his involvement in the so-called Petrashevist conspiracy. This was the experience that would spark the intensity of *Crime and Punishment*, *The Brothers Karamazov*, *Demons* and all that followed. I tried to complete *The House of the Dead* before we arrived there, but only got as far as the page in which the author describes how he learned to take his prisoner's smock on and off around the shackles that bound prisoners' wrists and legs when they left the fortress on work duty. There is apparently a wall of the old fort that still stands in Omsk, but all we saw of the city was the neatly restored buildings of the station, with the unfettered passengers stretching their arms and legs on the platform and the headscarfed women marching up with their baskets of piroshki and fruit. If I got off, and wandered down the avenue of dreams towards the Rossiya Hotel, might I find Hasek's friend Vaclav Cerny still waiting for my uncle, in his disguise of White Captain Kovalov's greatcoat? And if we sat for a while drinking tea in front of the clocks that told the time in Moscow, Saint Petersburg, Paris, London and Peking, would we too witness the sudden entrance of Admiral Kolchak and his gray retinue, the failed saviors of Holy Russia? But the train only stops in Omsk for twenty minutes.

We are in a mechanical womb, rocking body and mind in the two narrow bunks of the enclosed compartment, day after night. The tiny headlamp shines just enough light for the page, but one eventually gives up on the words and sinks into the rhythm of the rails, the soothing clatter of something constant and old-fashioned, the way trains were once, crossing the wastelands, the great plains, the forests, the unfettered land mass. Borders lie ahead, but they are rare interruptions, unlike the jagged chessboard of Europe or the abrupt ends of warring statelets, where checkpoints signify stop and turn back. If we had so booked, we could have gone on another seven days from Irkutsk, until the sea off Vladivostok sealed the end of the Eurasian mass...

Inside the chugging iron worm ploughing the murk, the

human cargo shifts and sways in its confined spaces, the elites in their minuscule luxury, the middle classes in their jumbled four-somes and the plebeians, in their dormitory carriages, sprawled up against each other in a jumble of opened food packets, tossed pants and shirts half on half off, some leery faces flushed with booze slouching towards the toilet, where one has to endure the screeching of the metal plates that seem to mesh right at the pissing posture…

This too is a world, a social space, an intimate gathering, where thoughts collide, and destinations are not imminent, and time endures its own displacement. The train always follows Moscow time, and so, after each zone changes, reality and the train diverge by yet another hour, until, at Irkutsk, one is five hours ahead, and the *prodvonitsa's* unbending cleaning schedule creeps from an afternoon program to an evening slot and then closes in on midnight as we approach Ulan Bator, when all but she have adjusted to the rotation of the Earth.

And on to Beijing, Harbin, Shanghai…

*

Go Yuan's tale of Judit, continued.

My father kept only a few artefacts of my grandmother's life in Shanghai—those few pictures and posters he had hidden under the kitchen floorboards during the cultural revolution, the bath-soap poster, the cigarette pack and tiny matchstick covers, Ruby Queen Cigarettes lady, dressed in pearls with an imperial crown. She also featured in cigarette cards, which I only found when I was an adolescent, looking for her image in the new picture books of old and forgotten Shanghai. There she is seen as herself, in pale beauty, with her glossy black hair, her hand softly caressing her own cheek and chin. The round face is essentially Russian, but there is still a slight slant to the eyes. Did Grandfather paint this, to conform to the obligatory style?

Grandfather did not speak of this period, before he died,

when my father was eighteen years old, having been born only a few weeks before the Japanese surrender in August 15, 1945. He was two weeks late emerging, he used to say, because he was waiting to be born in a China free of foreign occupation, but his mother couldn't wait any more, and pushed him out. He was just in time for the Soviet invasion of Manchuria, the American atomic bombs on Hiroshima and Nagasaki, and the Japanese Emperor's declaration that his country was a defeated nation. He was just over four years old at Liberation, and said he remembered being held above the crowds on May 27, 1949, when the Peoples' Liberation Army marched into Shanghai, holding and waving the new red flag. "Mother was happy," he said. "Grandfather would be able to enter his home as a free man, instead of a fugitive, hiding from the Japanese secret police."

Grandmother and Grandfather lived together as husband and wife for only three years, from the autumn of 1934 until the autumn of 1937, when the Japanese devils came to blanket the sky. After that, my father said, she wrote him letters that could not be delivered, and that she kept hidden in the different places where she lived in the city. Once they were written, she could not bear to destroy them, but it was too dangerous to even try to contact him, and the few times when he appeared, in the night, they had no need for words set down on paper. But they were careful, evidently to avoid pregnancy. It was no time for a child.

The letters were lost. Grandmother told Father about them, when he was an adult, and the first winds began blowing in the universities that were to become raging storms. When he returned, she said, they were not needed, and words were better kept in their ephemeral form. He did not know if this meant that she had destroyed them, or whether they had been mislaid.

Often I have closed my eyes at night, and wondered about them, these records of a time when all seemed lost, when the dangers she had faced and then fled from more than a thousand miles northwards rushed south, and engulfed the city of her second adopted refuge. If I get up, and wander out, onto the Wulumuqi road,

I am surrounded by lights, of the hotels, the shops, the nonstop traffic, the blast of life in the streets that were so familiar to her, that have their Chinese names now, but then were called the Avenue de Roi Albert, Route Pichon, de la Tour, Vallon, Pere Robert and the Avenue Joffre, around the Cathay Mansions and the Cercle Sportif Francais, which is now, ironically, the Japanese owned Okura Garden hotel. I can imagine the refuge of these foreign enclaves, carved out of the vastness of the China that was then so divided, fought over and devoured by its rival suitors, criminal consortiums and the greed of conquerors congregating like locusts over a vast fertile field, and I can feel the fear of a woman who is also a stranger, but has adopted this place of perplexing beauty as her own, committed her spirit and flesh to it, in which her own image has been absorbed...

And I wonder if I can dare to retrieve these lost words, echoing in my own mind, down the ages, and whether I have the right or the presumption to enter into her mind, look out through her own eyes, and rescue those memories and sights from their void— ?

August 11, 1937,
Judit:

My dearest,
I pray to God that you are well. I am well and healthy here in the city, but everyone is anxious since the news came this morning that a whole fleet of Japanese ships has steamed up the river and moored at the city wharfs. Two days ago two Japanese and two Chinese citizens were killed in a shoot-out near the airport and the Japanese are blaming this on our army. The people up in Chapei have been crowding into the Concession areas since they heard the news of the Japanese advances in the north, in Tianjin. From Monday the whole population started streaming across the Suzhou creek bridge, and they crowded across the Peking road, down to the shopping streets, overflowing into the Recreation Ground *(the*

then Shanghai Race Club, today's "People's Square", D.K.). The French and British troops began erecting huge fences south of the creek, but the people became even more agitated, and pushed through them, men, women and children, carrying bags, sacks, pushing bicycles, or just with the clothes on their backs.

The life that you thought would protect me here in this enclave became more fragile by the hour, but somehow I felt relieved, as if a great painful boil was being lanced, and my skin was being cleansed. While the refugees streamed, what passes for normal life in our "protected" zone continued to stream the other way, into its contented dreamland. On the night of the airport incident the dance halls were packed. Louis from the Paramount band told me the dancers were not just cheek to cheek, they were pressed together "like cows in an abattoir," in his expression, their feet did not even have to touch the floor, as they were carrying each other slowly squeezing in a packed mass. The guards still march up and down outside the Consulates and the fashion shops are still open along the Bubbling Well Road. The members are still sunning themselves on the lawns of the Country Club, playing tennis or sipping their daiquiris at the bar. Tiffin is still served daily at the Rotary, and I was invited to sing at the German Women's Benevolent Society at the Deutsche Garten Club for next Saturday, as if nothing untoward might happen to prevent our ordinary life continuing till then.

You need not fear for me, though, Louis and Millie are seeing to it that I am not left alone for a minute, and Madame San is still a generous protector, in the usual manner. It is strange, I know, to be guarded by the very people who have been bleeding this city of its life blood for the last four years—and longer—but as we have both known, life is what it is. I feel I should have come with you, but I know this would just have dragged you down. You need not worry for me, I can do enough worrying for the two of us.

I have decided, nevertheless, to volunteer, with two of the German women, Natalie and Gertrude (we met them at the last annual Orphan's Charity), at one of the new nursing and social aid centres set up for the refugees of Chapei and surroundings. We have set up a new office at the Y.M.C.A. just across from the racecourse. I still remember something of my nursing course back at the gymnasium of my hometown—so long ago now, so distant, a completely other world! The doctor in charge, Schmidt, is a German martinet, complete with long waxed whiskers, whose chief activity seems to be to go around terrifying everybody out of their wits by saying: "It's wartime! No place here for sissies!" We're glad he doesn't just put us in a row and examine our hands.

To be truthful with you, the odour of fear is everywhere. Louis says it oozes off the dance floor, but here at the nursing centre it is tangible, a physical reality. The faces of the working men and women are grim, skin taut over sweating faces, whole families crowded together, man, wife, ageing parents, uncles, aunts, children, bewildered and scared by all the others. They do not need to read newspapers or hear the squawking voices on the radio to know that some dire event is near. These are the same faces I saw in Harbin in the months after the Japanese marched in there to impose Manchukuo, people whom an imminent disaster had reduced to one impulse—the absolute need to stay alive. The disappearance of choice is, I suppose, the most terrifying thing. Suddenly the safety and isolation of the Concessions seems even more of an affront to the great Chinese ocean in which we outsiders have established our island than it ever was, or perhaps I am simply being stripped of the last traces of makeup that is required to be able to get up on the stage and sing about autumn and rivers and blossoms and romance under the stars...

I have taken to staying overnight at the hostel, because the apartment on the Fuzhou road is too close to the Bund and the grim hulks of the enemy troop ships who are disgorging their marching ranks of soldiers on the northern banks of the creek. I miss you all the time, I miss the way you would turn even the worst moments or fears into a joke, and the little drawings you used to slip under the covers when you thought I needed reminding of what world and country I am living in. Believe me, I am very aware of it now.

They say the post is still working, but without an address to put on the envelope, these ramblings can wait with me for the right time...

August 16

The terrible moment came with sickening suddenness. It is difficult for me to write, and I hesitate to set out these details for you, but you have always said one ought to grasp the essence of a given picture. This is what happened. This is what I have seen with my own eyes. First came the sound. Those were the guns, the Japanese ships' cannons opening up from the waterfront. That was on Friday afternoon. It was like a massive thunderstorm coming out of a hot summer's day. Then the Chinese guns answered, from the north. The walls of the hostel where we were working shook, and children started crying. Rashly, we went outside, to see if there were people who had been hit, but the shells were aimed across the creek, at Chapei. I knew that whoever had not already pressed across the creek to our shelter would be rushing down now. The Settlement guards were already hurrying to reinforce the barbed wire fences that were strung up along the Peking road. There was much shouting, and the thunder of the shells continued, but then all was strangely quiet, apart from a military truck, clattering through the streets with a loudspeaker that announced a complete curfew from ten p.m..

Once again, I stayed at the hostel, with Natalie, Gertrude, and Millie, who came up to help us. No dancing that night at the Paramount! But as you know, there are the basement nightclubs, where life always continues, and where anything goes...

There was sporadic shelling during the night, but somehow we slept a few hours, exhausted, in our cots. Natalie and Gertrude have some lotions, which they surreptitiously put on their arms and faces, out of Millie's sight, to mitigate the "smell" of so many tightly packed Chinese. It is so strange that even when dedicated to help others we are still slaves to stupid ideas. Perhaps it is just German thoroughness. I don't think either of them know that I am Jewish, or they might have packed even stronger lotions, but perhaps I am wrong, and they don't care, as long as our skin is the same. There are too many of us strangers in the Settlements to set up fences inside, at times like these. (Sometimes those who know us well have asked me what is it like to sleep with a Chinese in close quarters, in real intimacy—only the women dare to ask this—and I tell them there is a distinct and pleasant lemony tang. Or I might quip that you are the olive in my martini. But those days of banter are now gone. I stopped caring about that a long time ago...)

I am trying to avoid the moment. But it came, the next day. We were woken by the droning sound of airplanes coming from somewhere in the south. We were sleeping near the door to the courtyard, to get some air, and I went out, but could see nothing. A strong wind was blowing, and the air was gritty with a steel-grey sky. I heard the drone again, and saw three aircraft pass overhead, followed a minute later by a series of explosions from the direction of the Bund. Then other guns opened up, and flashes of explosions in the sky. Everybody rushed for shelter, as we saw Japanese planes coming over from the river, whizzing angrily over our heads. The refugees who were still streaming down the Nanking road, who had somehow managed to break through the fence, ducked and rushed to shelter in shop fronts and doorways. The doctors called for us to get inside. There was a blockage close by the Garden bridge, and more and more refugees were apparently trying to scramble across. More people would be heading our way.

There was more firing, but then things seemed to quieten down, as if the city still imposed its summer ritual of noon. Someone came and said the planes had missed their target, and some of our own people had been killed by the wharfs. Maybe there was some kind of cease-fire. We thought this would be a good moment to replenish our medical supplies before the shooting restarted. As I had made some arrangements for extra supplies from a clinic close to the Swedish embassy, I volunteered to go down the road. I went with the rickshaw boy, Hu Lin. As he was pedalling down the Tibet road we could see refugees trudging through the French Concession streets, who must have broken through the fences. Hu Lin manoeuvred around and through them, and we were just approaching the Boulevard Edward VII when a whole squadron of airplanes came over above us, clearly heading for the Japanese ships. They passed very low, and then I could see the bombs falling, out of their metal bellies. I remember thinking, why are they dropping the bombs here, we are still two kilometers short of the river, when there was a tremendous explosion, and our rickshaw was blown over as if it was physically picked up and thrown onto the kerb.

I remember Hu Lin thrusting his hand to pick me up, and shaking my head, because I thought I had gone deaf. The bombs had fallen across the Boulevard, and suddenly what had been a familiar sight of houses, trees, lampposts, trams and pedestrians was turned into a scene from hell: An entire part of the road had been blown away and replaced by a gigantic crater, and bodies were strewn across the area as if they had been dropped from a jagged hole torn in the sky, rather than being the mass of humanity that had been moving there only one moment before. I can barely describe their condition. Some were recognisable as persons, others mere stumps of people, or worse, things fallen out of an abattoir. As I turned my head I saw a completely naked man, sitting on the ground, his arms raised up, his torso white, every shred of clothing torn off, his face untouched but bewildered, opening and closing his mouth. Behind him, all the way towards the crater, there were clumps of the dead, some moving underneath those who were not. Hu Lin was intact, but trying to disentangle himself from a bicycle wheel that seemed to have slammed into his side. There were smaller bodies, that the mind refused to contemplate, so that I looked up with some relief at the buildings, whose windows and facades had been blown out, but were merely masonry displaced, just objects. A tram had been stopped, its side shredded, and the electric cables drooped all over it like the fallen corpse of spiders.

One could not think, but I staggered forwards, as did many who came running from the surrounding streets, passersby, policemen, a group of Concession guards, people just streaming out of buildings, picking through the wreckage and pulling people out of piles. There was still a terrible silence, until suddenly the senses all came flooding back, the sounds of cries, screams, supplications, crying children, shouts, a terrible smell of burning, something beyond the putrid, as if from an open wound gashed in the earth itself.

Later we heard that more bombs had dropped from our own airplanes, which may have been hit by the Japanese firing from their positions and from the attacked ships. They fell, again, on refugees, who were pushing down along the Nanking road between the Cathay and the Palace hotels. Both the hotels were hit too, but the toll on the people was unbearable. The Japanese ships, which were the objects of the raids, were not hit at all.

I cannot understand how such things happen. I have been a fool. I have lived and listened to the tale of events that were unfolding around the corner of my sight but I could not see them. We saw the wounded and the casualties in hospitals in Harbin. We saw the soldiers, packed into their constricting uniforms, weighed down by pouches, helmets, guns, kitbags, marching like automatons in the service of the unseen pitiless powers that move people like pieces upon a gigantic chessboard. But I have not seen the battlefields, the places of carnage, and could not imagine them dropped from the sky onto the streets where I live, eking out my own imaginings that I could be of some help. As I crumpled into my cot at the hostel, I do not know how many hours later, I had a dream, which was midway between waking and dozing, not able to find the proper escape of sleep—I saw myself in the dressing room of one of our old shows, the "Jade Princess" I think it was, plying my makeup, trying to slant up my eyebrows and sharpen my Russian cheekbones, trying to transform myself into the slender but determined aspirant to an inheritance of which I had been shamefully robbed, but no matter how vigorously I applied the makeup, it never stayed on. As I looked into the mirror the gossamer lines rubbed out, the paint vanished, and I was left with my naked shame absolutely displayed, the complete inability to be anyone other than the one I was, a stranger in a strange land. Then I looked deeper, but I could not quite make out who else might be hiding under the skin...

Go Yuan:

What did she write to him? I asked my father. "She wrote to him about Shanghai," he said to me, "she described what she saw, in the war, in the occupation. He was on another front then, with the Party." I don't know whether my grandfather was in the Party when he married my grandmother, or whether he told her so at the time. My father said they were married in a "Buddhist" ceremony and then celebrated with all their friends at the Huxinting Teahouse at the Jade Garden, quaffing tea and other stronger libations, and singing patriotic songs. My grandfather was part of the "Modern" movement of writers and artists who published in the movie and art magazines and who were influenced by the European Dadaists and Surrealists, particularly Grosz and Dix, and also by the English war cartoonist Low. He began drawing cartoons for the Communist party, though my father did not think he was a member until he was "called out" in 1936. By 1937, with the Japanese closing in again and the Kuomintang mobilising, it was too dangerous for him to stay in Shanghai. But he could not anticipate the terror Judit would be engulfed in, or his inability to return to the city to help her. My father would be often silent about that. But he did say that my grandfather told him they used to talk together about their dreams. They had both read translations of Sigmund Freud, for whom dreams revealed the deeper thoughts and impulses, and knew that Grosz, Dix and the Surrealists were deeply influenced by those ideas...

The battle of Shanghai, as history tells us, lasted for three months, with the Chinese forces holding their own on the barricades of Chapei against the full onslaught of the Japanese troops and the daily bombing of the city. Hundreds of thousands of civilians overwhelmed the fences of the International Settlement and flooded further into the French Concession area. Grandmother Judit remained in the city, although thousands of foreigners were evacuated by ship along the coast to Hong Kong. Although registered as a Russian national, her contacts with high-ranking British officials, many of whom were fans of her theatrical appearances and the local Chinese radio shows—which continued broadcasting during the occupation, using entertainment to conceal the national message—could have enabled her to escape. My father said she would sing some of the songs that she had sung at the time she met my grandfather, and he had heard them, in his refuge in the outlying villages where the Fourth Northern Army was stationed, until they had to retreat out of range. He said he had heard her voice as if coming through a storm and a crackling hail of atmospheric shrapnel. But as her letters could not be sent at that time, she told him later that she spoke in them as if he were in the same room...

Judit:

My dearest,

Life in the Settlements and the Concession is suposed to continue "as usual," if one is deaf to the continual bombing and shelling, and the sight of the many thousands of refugees who are camped in the parks, squares and avenues. They sleep, entire families piled together, in open lanes, the corridors of office buildings, warehouses, temples and churches, wherever there might be a space. A whole group has occupied the lobby of the Cathay cinema, under the posters advertising the Hollywood movie "Alibi for Murder" (with William Gargan and Marguerite Churchill—I know you would want to know!). The cinema stayed open for a while, but there were few customers. The English and French, in particular, try to keep up appearances, sitting in the cafés while the bombers drone overhead and the bombs scream down outside the fences. The most nonchalant still hang out in the Cercle Sportif, where your old friend Sapajou sits drawing his cartoons "under fire." The old boy still limps around with his dapper jacket and cane, and the drawings appear every day in the British newspaper, together with Bob Peyton-G.'s column. I don't find it very funny, but the British seem to think jokes about war are the best response in a crisis. People send in little "limericks" like "There is a young Welsh fusilier, who has a great liking for beer..." Or "there is a young man in the Loyals, who is badly afflicted with boils..." (*English in original, Ed.*) I still spend some time with them, as you requested, but they are often too drunk to discuss anything serious. They all hate the Japanese, but are supposed to be "neutral," despite the air attack on the British ambassador on August 26th, when his car was strafed by a Jap plane. So far however, no more bombs, of either side, have fallen inside the settlements. But the horrors of the war stare us in the face, and even if people close their eyes, they can't escape the sounds, and the smell of the war, that all-pervasive odour of fear.

I am still working with the German ladies, even though we know the German and the Japanese government have their "Anti-Comintern" pact. It's quite crazy, because the ladies now wear their swastika armbands, which protect them when they have to go through the lines, across the creek to Hongkew, past the guards. They asked me to wear one myself, but I couldn't do it, so I was stopped once by the Japanese and had to show my Russian document. Fortunately, I also had my Japanese pass from Harbin, which was enough, at that point to get me through.

I am also doing work with the Jewish refugees, the families who came from Germany while we were here. It seems that some-one over there has been issuing Chinese visas to thousands of Jews, and the community has taken them in. The Fiaker Cafe-Restaurant on Avenue Joffre is still open and serving sachertorte! Pepi still entertains on the piano but I don't sing there any more. I have been asked to sing on the radio station, which is still broadcasting Chinese speeches and defiance of the Japanese from Hongkew, but they might be shut down any day. I don't know if I can perform, in this atmosphere. How can one keep up the pretence?

We hear the news of Japanese advances and bombing further inland, in Canton and Nanjing, and I can only pray that you remember our promise—to stay alive, at all cost, to see matters through... I know you have other considerations, and it is selfish, in the face of so much sacrifice, and so much courage shown by our defenders, and the harsh, impossible choices that have to be faced. But you are my "quiet one"—you can slip between the noise and the barrages... I wake in the night and feel your touch, and know that you are still there.

September 20, Judit:

Shells are now falling regularly in the foreign areas, and outside them the Japanese have been bombing refugees still heading out of the city. There seems no limit to their cruelty. And the violence begets violence. Crime has not stopped in Shanghai even when people are fighting an invader, and, as you might expect, shadows are moving in the shadows. The gangs are as strong as they ever were, and Louis has reported to me that the old master Du, of the Green Gang, has returned to his mansion on the rue Doumer, with a deal from the Kuomintang to set up his own guerrilla brigade. This is apparently called the "Loyal and Patriotic National Salvation Army," and will combine attacks on the Japanese with the continuation of his opium business between and across the lines.

Smuggling is the only way at the moment that we can get goods in and out. For both medicines and food, we have no choice. Louis has trekked down to the rue Doumer and made the deal on our behalf with Du's men. The quid-pro-quo is a contact, through Gertrude, with the German consul, who represents the Nazi government here, although he is at heart a humane man, left over from the Weimar regime. We had coffee with him once at the Fiaker and he showed us a whole list of race-conscious measures he was supposed to implement in his jurisdiction. Since the vast majority of Germans around, with whom he can speak his language and share his taste in pastries, are Jews, he ignores it all and waits to be relieved, upon which, he told me, smiling faintly, "I will follow in your footsteps, *gnadige frau*, disguise myself as a Chinese and join the resistance. *Morituri te salutant.*"

Nevertheless, we are all just working to survive... On Saturday, the 18th, the air raids resumed, and the Japanese bombed Pudong and Chapei. Chinese airplanes counter-attacked the Japanese positions and the troop-ships on the wharves. It was the fifth anniversary of the occupation of Mukden in Manchuria. Shells fell on the Concession area as well and we could see the tracer fires shoot through the sky and the flames of fires nearby. When Gertude and I ventured out after the raids died down, to reach the refugee families in the lane we lived in off the Avenue Joffre, the fires were still lighting up the night and fire engines were still racing to put out new fires. On the corner of the Swedish consulate we saw a large unexploded shell, softly revolving as if by its own force. It must have fallen not long before. It was in our way, so we had to step around it, and its blunt point seemed to swivel after us as we passed. In the midst of the noise, the crackling fires, the firemen's bell and shouts from afar, it was a strangely silent moment. Just ourselves and death, dancing. We skipped away, and lived another night...

November 4

The planes have become more random these days, the pilots more ruthless, bombs falling on clear columns of refugees, or civilian crowds in streets and squares, so that the sight that so horrified me on that "Black Saturday" that began it all are now an everyday matter. It becomes a routine: the bombs fall, the explosions mushroom out, the fires burn, the honking of carhorns as their drivers push through the crowds loaded with the wounded, the Russian, German, Chinese, and volunteers of all nations rush down to the hospitals, hastily arranging their stained medical smocks. The corpses are collected and transported to the lanes outside the hospitals, counted and arranged in makeshift coffins as quickly as possible, though we are very short of wood and now have to make do with sheets.

Cholera haunts us now, the contaminated water from the river swollen with bodies, the broken pumping systems for the treatment of the water. Sapajou drew the cholera as a rabid dog, haunting the ruined houses as the God of War swings his bloody sword. We do not need to read Bibles to learn of the Apocalypse because we live it every day. The old cartoonist still provides some relief! The other day he limped into the Central Hospital with a grey smock over his jaunty pinstripe country club pants, and his jotting pad, greeting me with his usual *"nazdrovya, molodoy zhena!"* and showing us a cutting from the English newspaper, which still carries a "personal" column, in which someone who seems to be living in a different universe advertises as a "Lonely Briton seeks companionship of lady, any nationality, of independent means, seeking to travel and assist financially in profitable business; strictly confidential."

Shanghai lives! But it is a strange existence, always on the edge of failure and disaster. The Chinese resistance, outside the International sectors, is heroic, the soldiers do not care that they are dressed in the uniforms of Kuomintang or any other force as long as they are defending China. The line is held, day after day, somehow, and the Chinese planes are still flying to attack the Japanese in their own base. Shanghai has seen this before, in 1932, before I arrived, a raw naive, I must say, though I was hardly a spring bird even then. I thought Harbin had hardened me to these realities, but it was just an introduction... As the winter set in, the cold and the rain increased, turning the city for days on end into a shivering sea of mud, churned up by the bombs. This seems to be our existence now. Nobody speaks of either victory or defeat, only of endurance, the slogan I have learned to know—"eat bitterness and endure hardship," that has completely transformed my image of this country. It is beyond logic...

I have been asked to sing again, on the resistance radio, and have learned new Chinese songs, which I hope you have heard, wherever you are: I sang "The Song of Youth," and "The National Flag" and "Chinese Women Resisting the Enemy" ("*zhongguo fu kangdi ge*"), as well as one or two of my old favourites, to keep up the morale. You will be pleased to know that I have, in any spare time—though that has been rare these days—began again to study the Chinese characters, so that I may read and not only speak the language. This is so very hard. One needs to be a child, with a mind malleable rather than hardened and rigid. We have a small circle, Gertrude, Natalie, two Russians and a new German immigrant called Kreutzer ("I am not the sonata," is always part of his introduction), who labour on this when we can.

One of these days I had time to read the local German news-paper, the "Shanghaier Tagblatt", and find out what was going on in the rest of the world, which seems no less troubled than ours: "Terrorism in Palestine," war against the Fascists in Spain, the French are fighting in Morocco, the Italians fighting a war in Lybia—even Africa has been drawn into the cycle of destruction. Hitler talks revenge and war in Berlin. Many of our new friends are certain that war will engulf Europe again. The world seems to be turning very dark.

Sapajou came over another day and told me morosely that a bomb had gone through the roof of the Country Club, though for-tunately after the hour of curfew, so that only a couple of drunks who couldn't master their legs to go home were in the premises, and both, as is the case with drunks, were unhurt. "There is soon not going to be any refuge," he said, "even for the haute-bourgeoisie."

There are slogans everywhere on the buildings: "China Cannot be Lost!" Enormous sense of defiance in the city. Yesterday there was another lull in the shelling when the whole city was shrouded in mist. One had the sense of a ghost town, eerie silences punctuated by rifle fire from across the lines, and people looming suddenly out of the fog. By now, one takes things in one's stride, nothing is unusual, nothing unexpected. I had the strange feeling, in the afternoon, that I would come close to one of the figures in the mist and discover your face, smiling at me with that shy look. For an hour or so I thought I saw you in every face that passed, even in the women. It was a strange feeling, but also not unexpected. It was comforting, because it made me certain that you are somewhere close, rather than far, and that our spirits are united. We are all somehow the same. Gertrude told me another Chinese saying that people are using, to describe the times that we are living: "A family with only four walls, all possessions gone." It is in these times that one discovers one's strength.

But it was all over, very soon. Japan's military machine finally told on Shanghai one week later, and the Chinese army was forced back from its positions, followed by an immense stream of refugees. Those who could pressed into the International Settlement and the French Concession, swelling the ranks of those already crowded in what was to become the "isolated island" ("*gudao*") of Shanghai. Both the British and the French soldiers held the barriers open for a while to let through the desperate hordes, entire families with what remained of their belongings, or an animal, pig, goat or cow, and thousands more from the villages beyond Chapei fled west, in the wake of the retreating army, towards Najiang. The Japanese continued to bombard the "die hards" remaining in Nandao, along the river, whose people had nowhere to go but west into the French Concession, whose police shut down the barriers and used their truncheons freely. By November 13 all was silent, as the war stopped in Shanghai, but continued westwards along the Yangtse, towards the Nationalist capital at Nanjing. When they reached Nanjing, on December 13th, and breached the city walls, the Imperial Japanese army wreaked its revenge on the long months of Chinese resistance by massacre, torture and rape, as history records...

Ten days before, on December 3rd, 1937, the Japanese army marched in victory down the Nanjing road in Shanghai, six thousand infantry soldiers, cavalry and tanks, with the Japanese naval band playing, and the troops shouting their victory cries. At the corner of the Guanxi road, a 23-year-old patriot, Sun Jinghao, ran forward and threw a bomb at the march. Three Japanese soldiers were hit, along with two Chinese bystanders. This was the first act of resistance in a campaign that lasted for the next seven years. The Japanese never rested easily in Shanghai, but the city entered into its next uncertain phase.

Go Yuan, continued:

My grandmother remained in the city through its next two stages: *gudao* Shanghai, and total occupation, when the Japanese moved in to occupy the foreign sectors after the attack on the Americans at Pearl Harbor. The British International Settlement was abolished, and the French remained on sufferance by agreement with "Vichy" France. More than one hundred years of western rule over China's largest city was coming to an end.

Why did my grandmother stay in Shanghai under occupation?

My father said: "Where would she go?" She had many friends in the city, her own network of "family," the theatrical performers, musicians, the radio entertainers, contacts that connected the various groups in the city, the foreigners, the British, French, the Russians, Germans and the Chinese. Conditions at the front made it impossible for her to join my grandfather, who was then in charge of the Fourth Army's propaganda section, printing and preparing pamphlets and documents, and even, later on, books, on printing presses hidden in caves. This was the legend, that I had always heard, in the family: She received a message, in the first year of the war, to stay behind, and act for my grandfather and the Party in her own circles. There was much to do—information to be gathered, messages to pass on, other contacts to be made. In short, my grandmother was a Communist spy, and lived in daily danger of discovery, in a city which was full of spies of every description, serving every conceivable master: the Japanese, the western governments, the Kuomintang, the puppet forces of Wang Jingwei, the Japanese themselves, the criminal gangs, the opium smugglers, and the various fixers who made their commerce and money on the misery of the trapped masses.

"What did she do?"

My father was always vague: "Small things, that were important—passing on messages to Party agents, getting information from the foreign officials, helping in morale—she used to have messages in songs transmitted on the radio, code words that she was given, or just using the song to make comments that the Japanese didn't understand. To show that Shanghai wasn't beaten, that despite everything it was still ours..."

This was Shanghai under occupation: A city of pretence and denial, a city of want, a city of many masks and deceptions, a city of hidden defiance, a city of opportunities that were absent in the rest of ravaged China. A city of an enforced peace, wracked by violence—the violence of the gangs, killings by the police, assassinations of Nationalists by the Japanese, of Japanese and their paid Chinese puppets by Nationalist groups and guerrilla fighters, and also killings that seemed to take place not from any discernable reason but from the general cheapness of life. Gangsters fought gun battles with the police on a regular basis, banks were robbed, ordinary citizens were accosted and killed for a few crumpled dollars... On the surface, the city recovered from war, its factories reopening, with cheap labour from the pool of three million displaced workers desperate to earn any pittance. The old capitalists reached their accommodations with the invaders, with a few exceptions, but the fixers could make sure that good relations were kept with both sides, when the right palms were greased...

As the war erupted in Europe, the flow of German and

other Jewish refugees also increased, and signs proclaiming Cafe-Konditorien—spezialitet Deutsche Schwarzbrot, Chemische produkte, Damenmoden, Drukerein, Friziere, Fotographen, Glaser, Krankenpfleger, Optik, Reklame, Schneider, Schokoladen, Teppiche and Unterricht, sprung up in the strangest places, including new premises in half destroyed streets across the creek in Hongkou. There was a strange multiple life, even stranger than Shanghai of before—a life of luxury still lived at the top, with top-hatted gentlemen and soft-gowned ladies gliding from their well-guarded villas in chauffeur-driven beautifully polished cars to the night spots and the upper class stores; a life of desperation and near starvation at the bottom, heaving with humanity, with rice riots and mob action held back by phalanxes of police with batons and rifles; and the middle, increasingly populated with foreigners who lived a precarious and isolated life, islands within the island, speaking their own languages, frequenting their own shops, publishing and reading their own newspapers, dreaming of their own places far far away. The Russians dreamed of Moscow, the Germans dreamed of Berlin or Vienna, the Jews dreamed of Palestine, which they had never seen, but argued about with great ferocity, in their own Yiddish language, attending their Zionist clubs and meetings, at which flowery speeches were made about outrages perpetrated half the way across the globe.

In 1943, the Japanese, responding to the pressure of their German government allies, decreed that all the Jews who were now stateless should move into a ghetto area, which was carved out in the eastern area of Hongkou, the more crowded sector of the now defunct British settlement, from which so many Chinese citizens had fled. This became in itself a little Palestine, lined with shops, makeshift cafés and restaurants, small workshops, soup kitchens for the indigent and a variety of political clubs. Here my grandmother eventually found herself, when her protectors could no longer shield her from the fact that her documents proclaimed her as an ex-resident of Harbin, of Russian origin, but no assigned nationality other than that consigned by Japanese stamps.

"She could have protected herself," said my father, "if she had chosen to be close to the Japanese, rather than her French protectors. But when they asked her to reconfirm her Russian identity, she refused, and said, `I am a Chinese Jew.'"

As the Japanese recognised no such category, she was assigned to the Hongkou ghetto. From there, on 12 November, 1943, she wrote the only letter that reached my grandfather, or the only letter that he kept. He kept it and treasured it, my father said, because it was written in Chinese, which she had continued diligently to study, character after character, piece by piece, throughout occupation Shanghai. This was the only letter from Judit to my grandfather that has since been preserved:

Judit's Letter (undated)

(Note: Foreign words are included in German in the text.)

I can only write simple sentences. I am very aware that I am like a schoolgirl who writes a test for a beloved teacher. Through all my lessons, caught in odd moments, I always heard your voice beside me. You were saying—slowly, slowly, nothing worth doing is done fast. Keep the picture simple. So I will write what I see from my window. I am staying in a first floor apartment in a long terrace of houses between two narrow alleys. The street is also narrow and the houses are leaning forward. I can almost touch my neighbours on the other side. But somehow cars and rickshaws and carts can pass below. The street is always very busy. The street level is full of small workshops where the refugees are learning new trades. There are too many doctors, teachers, professors of philosophy, orchestra musicians, tailors and chemical engineers. That is very fine in a society that is different to ours. The doctors have their hands full but even some of them must train for other things. So they are learning woodwork and carpentry and fixing bicycles and rickshaw wheels. Bespoke tailoring is fine but few people can afford a new suit. Some of them are learning agriculture but I am not sure why. I think perhaps they are dreaming of being farmers in Palestine. But meanwhile they are stuck here, in Hongkou. Everyone who wants to leave even to the Chinese section needs a special permit from the Stateless Association, a Japanese office that is run by a Mister Goya-San. He is the king of the "ghetto." This is all by agreement of the German Gestapo officer Meisinger, who insisted on this move that he called "The final solution for Shanghai's Jews."

So I have very strangely returned to my first roots. I grew up in the Jewish village of my fathers and mothers and here I am back with them again. But with the Chinese manner. There are still many Chinese who stayed in Hongkou and live among us, as we live among them. Many parents bring their children to our schools, because we have so many, and some of them have learned to speak our language. So we have invented the Yiddish Chinese. There is a boy called Hseng who is twelve years old and has learned all the Hebrew letters. He has learned the right blessings for every weekday and Shabbes meal. Naturally he is getting fatter and fatter, and has been adopted by the synagogue to be the holy days' "goy."

I remember when you first saw the synagogue you said the Jews were stranger than Buddhists. You liked the black-and-white uniforms rather than the saffron robes of the priests. You said they made you understand George Grosz and I said that you did not understand them at all. But I was very far from all that. Now we have an entire "Talmud" school that has moved from Poland to Shanghai. The Chinese look in on them nodding and shaking and calling out in loud voices. It is difficult to explain to the Chinese that these people are talking directly to God.

Most of the refugees are as poor as the Chinese, and have nothing but their clothes and their ideas. I am now teaching them Chinese. We set up a school for adults in an old bathhouse, where there is no water. That is my daily bread now. We are talking about setting up a new radio station in the "ghetto" which will broadcast in Yiddish and Chinese. This way I can sing again on the airwaves, and people might hear my voice south of the Suzhou creek. The British are still there but some of them are in prisons. Bob Peyton-G. is in a prison somewhere. My old friend Sapajou is still drawing cartoons. He is working for a German newspaper, that is owned by the Nazis. I hear he is very sad and sick. But everybody has to work for rice.

One time I got a pass to go to the "French Concession." It was still looking like the past. Cars and trams rush by. Factories are belching out smoke. People are walking. Couples arm in arm down the Avenue Joffre, but they walk with their heads down, talking quietly. The Cathay cinema is open, showing Japanese movies. I was allowed to go to see my old friend in the French police, Sarly. All the officials now have to swear their loyalty to Marshall Petain in Vichy. But the police are always the police. He said he could sign a new document that would allow me back to the district, but I refused. He asked me about you but I said I knew nothing and had heard nothing for some years. I think he is sweet on me but do not worry, my dearest, because you are the only one. I am a tough old boot now and I can take it. We are as we are.

Yesterday morning, Saturday, I looked out of my window and saw a group of children playing in the street. They were Chinese and Jews, jumping in their chalk squares as if they didn't have a care in the world. A big group of our "Hassids" came up, dressed in their black hats and prayer shawls. After morning prayers. They parted into two streams and walked around the children, leaving them like an island in the sea. I thought of you again, and what you would make of this strange picture. I could imagine you drawing it, for your magazine: The Chinese surrounded by the Jews, the Jews surrounded by the Chinese. Am I writing this correctly? The bicycle mender in our doorway, Old Ling, checks my Chinese writing, so I do not fall into the worst errors. I want to state what is really important, but I am not skilled enough yet. The words do not translate from mind to page. I should go down and hop about with the children. Not to think about the future. But I cannot, because you are not in the present. I have to wait, until the present must change. I can only say that, when tomorrow –

(The letter terminates here.)

Go Yuan wrote:

The present changed for my grandmother in the fall of 1944, when the Japanese were still in full control of the city, but the war had entered its last stage in Europe, after the Americans and the British invaded France and liberated Paris. The news invigorated both the Kuomintang nationalists and the Communist armies. After that time, there was no need for letters, because my grandfather was sent into Shanghai by the Party, to help to organise the internal resistance. She must have been able to leave the Hongkou ghetto then, because my father told me they were living in the French area again, close to the Swedish consulate, whose deputy consul spied for the Americans. The Americans at that time were secretly helping Mao Zedong's guerrilla army in the north, through their military envoy General Joseph ("Vinegar Joe") Stilwell. Rivalries with the Kuomintang continued till the Japanese surrender. But meanwhile my grandfather and grandmother conceived my father, who was born late in July, 1945. It was not only the creation of their love for each other, but also an act of their faith in the rebirth of a free China. Therefore they named him Jiayi—the auspicious one, and my parents named me Yuan—the original... My grandfather had taken the family name Guo, to conceal his own, the common Zhang, which came closest to matching grandma's "Gurevits."

After 1945, when the Kuomintang tightened its grip on Shanghai, they escaped and lived for a while in the mountains of Shaanxi, which my father remembered fondly. He remembered the rocky slopes, the snow, the flowers in springtime, and even toddling about in a tiny uniform with a red star on his cap. Grandfather fell ill, in the bad winter of 1947, and his lungs were in poor condition from then on. But they lived to see Liberation, and were in Shanghai a few weeks ahead of the triumphant entry of the Red Army in May 1949.

New Shanghai, old Shanghai. Now that the old is gone, Shanghai of the "international" settlements and foreign concessions, leaving us with its stone memoria to the Sassoons and Jardine Mathieson, the loot of the opium wars that raised up the Bund and the city's first skyline, we are beguiled by the next, the tall towers of Chinese capital, the forest of skyscrapers across the river in Pudong, the flashing multi-coloured lights of the Nanjing road and the shopping malls, the concrete maze of freeways that snakes around what was once the old city, now disappearing block by block, street by street, under the thunder and creak of giant cranes, a solid mass of cars rushing east and west over the Yanan overpass that runs over the old Bubbling Well Road. The British Racecourse has become People's Square, the opium headquarters of Du Yuesheng is now the Donghu Hotel, the French Park still has the old residence of Sun Yat Sen, and the dumpling teahouse still serves locals and tourists beside the Yu Garden at the end of the Nine Turnings Bridge.

Money is Shanghai's new religion, nationalism and faith. Youth is its high priesthood, garbed in the latest fashions, hairdos and accessories. The old foreigners left, and new foreigners flood in, temporary sojourners, no longer looking down on our poverty, but looking up at our new visage of wealth strobing on giant screens high on the new temples of China Rising. The British straggled home, worn and emaciated from the Japanese prison camps, defeated by another Asian country which proved more ruthless than their own. The French returned to France, or moved onwards to other exotic lands they still held, in Vietnam, from which they soon had to run away too. The Russians and the Jews left, most to western refuges in America, Canada, or Australia, which took in many of the "Harbinskis." In Hongkou, the Jews left some traces: the synagogue, a museum, and a recent plaque in the Huoshan park, commemorating their presence in Hebrew.

My grandmother was among the few who remained. Her story continued, which will be related in Part Three of this account of a woman who chose China, and despite the rigours and challenges that followed, continued to bind her fate to its own.

"Through a glass, murkily..."

Asher:

Day 5, Irkutsk to Ulan Bator (Ulaanbaatar): A different train, but the window in the compartment is even grimier, though some of the windows in the corridor can be prised open, to whir away at the sight of Lake Baikal, glimpsed through the trees, as the train spends several hours skirting its shores before turning directly south, cutting away from the Vladivostok leg of the Czech Legion's homeward route. A change of landscape as we head towards the Mongolian border, from lush forested hillsides to barren desert hills, all jagged rocks and bare slopes, as the night closes in. Here the camera has to be shut off to accommodate the infamous Russia-Mongolia border scam. Armed soldiers with dogs shut down the train, searching the carriages for contraband. The Mongolian traders who boarded at Irkutsk sit calmly, as their sackfuls of purchased goods, clothing, electronics and gadgetry had all mysteriously vanished in the coach interstices, niches, hidden compartments and the roofing over the toilets. Four hours later, the train is reluctantly released to rumble on the short stretch to the Mongolian post, where less aggressive guards appear, briskly revisiting passports and stamping the visa pages with a friendly shrug and a wave.

Welcome to Mongolia! As we rattled on through the night, I managed to jimmy open the window at dawn to let in the cold air of the northern Gobi, providing a great shot of the nimbus-rayed sun rising into the deep blue, scarlet, gold sky as Claire, tossing and turning, protested the early hour. In the domains of Genghis Khan, the desert opening out to a serene plane, featureless apart from line-side electricity poles and the track itself, ploughing on and on. Here and there were small clumps of Mongolian gers, the rounded all-purpose tents... A tiny fleck on the flatland grows into a motorcycle, bearing two passengers behind the driver, all three waving at the train as they draw parallel and then diverge again, on no discernable path. The sky deepest blue, not a trace of cloud...

And then, a few hours later, out of the desert, the first concrete blocks of Soviet style housing presage the city suburbs come into view: Ulaanbaatar! Industrial plant, gunmetal-colored sky, the trace of a stagnant river, more blocks and, abruptly, the station itself and the lingering metallic squeal of arrival. The young dressed as the young always are, older men and women in traditional "deels."

Guided tour, Ulaanbaatar in three hours: Gandan monastery-temple, central Suhkbaatar Square with statue of Chingiz Khan on parliament steps... Natural History museum, relics and costumes of old Mongolia, armor and armaments, Tibetan Buddhist era, photographs of the Bogd Khan, last priest-king of Mongolia, ancient and modern scripts, a special exhibit of the Stalinist purges of Mongolia's national leaders of the 1920s and '30s, photographs of founders of the revolutionary Mongolian Communist Party purged in Stalin's day... Bunched together in their fur hats and peaked caps, army uniforms or the long Mongolia *deels*... partisans and lost leaders who rode with the red banner to free the country from China and Japan... Buddhist lamas, targets of Stalin's anti-cultural revolution, killed in their tens of thousands, and almost all of their temples and monasteries destroyed. This too was part of Russia's revolution. Even here, most of all here, in East Asia, one cannot escape the same tendrils of history, the crashing echoes of the old collapsed kingdoms and empires long gone but still remembered. And in other rooms of the musuem, Tibetan-style figures, old gods and demons, masks garlanded with circles of skulls... Life before Stalin: portraits of alongside, in the Fine Arts Museum—Zanabazar—artists' panoramas of real life in the period of Chinese subjugation Mongolian celebrants of "airag" feasts, gathering in the old trading center of "Ikh Khuree" from which Ulaanbaatar emerged… Clusters of gers, people cooking, cleaning, talking, making love, amid their animals—goats, sheep and hosts of horses, some of whom lustily coupling as well…

On a morning of dazzling sunshine, a jeep driver and a young guide, Sarangerel, takes us out of the city towards the Terelj National Park, jerking lustily over potholed roads, the countryside opening up across the trickling river: a range of conical mountains blue and distant, twisting trails invisible to any but the trained driver's eyes. Bucking over rocks and dried-out gullies, towards a destination that Sarangerel tells us is "not far away."

Night and the stars. There would be silence, were it not for the cicadas in the glade of trees below. The whinny of a lightly sleeping horse downhill. Sleeping in nomad style, with central fireplace boiling away, lying on narrow beds… This tranquil range once the leisure refuge of the Communist Party elite, set among jagged mountains, forested slopes, strange-shaped rocks and empty grassland stretching off towards the next range of mountains, and the next…

Close up inside the *ger*—Claire lying on the tourist bed, reading our copy of Turgenev's *Virgin Soil* in the light of an electric bulb hanging on a wire: A young man of the aristocracy, Nejdanov, becomes involved in a revolutionary group that preaches a return to the roots, a descent from the city to the country, eager to persuade the peasants to understand the roots of their poverty and rise up against the tyranny of the czar. Claire reads me Turgenev's description, for the record:

> "He was highly strung, frightfully conceited, very susceptible, and even capricious. The false position he had been placed in from childhood had made him sensitive and irritable, but his natural generosity had kept him from becoming suspicious and mistrustful. This same false position was the cause of an utter inconsistency, which permeated his whole being. He was fastidiously accurate and horribly squeamish, tried to

be cynical and coarse in his speech, but was an idealist by nature. He was passionate and pure-minded, bold and timid at the same time, and, like a repentant sinner, ashamed of his sins; he was ashamed alike of his timidity and his purity, and considered it his duty to scoff at all idealism... He was furious with his father for having made him take up "aesthetics," openly interested himself in politics and social questions, professed the most extreme views (which meant more to him than mere words), but secretly took a delight in art, poetry, beauty in all its manifestations, and in his inspired moments wrote verses. It is true that he carefully hid the copy-book in which they were written, and none of his St. Petersburg friends, with the exception of Paklin, and he only by his peculiar intuitiveness, suspected its existence. Nothing hurt or offended Nejdanov more than the smallest allusion to his poetry, which he regarded as an unpardonable weakness in himself..."

Nejdanov goes to the muzhiks, but in the end they betray him to the czar's authorities. What goes round comes round. The purpose of this journey has become deflected by the detours. The calm of the *ger*, the balm of the morning when, opening the little red door and stepping out in the open red slippers provided one looks out, down the hill and up across the vale towards the mountains, and the realization that this pristine landscape continues on for at least a thousand miles... One cups one's ear—one hears... nothing! No engine sound, no loud puttering, no airplanes flying overhead, no city buzz—a goat, emitting a sour bleat on the far slope, where the small dots move slowly? Sarangerel emerges from the ger with the two assistants, all waving at us with girlish smiles. No anxious thoughts, no disturbance of memory, no allusions to things that were or might have been. Only the moment...

And on to Reel 16: Back in the iron womb. The final stage: Ulaanbaatar to Beijing. No longer Moscow time, but on the Chinese train—better, newer, different, more organized.

Eighteen hours to the border, eighteen more to Beijing. At the border stop the train's most famous ritual unfolds: the bogie change, in which the entire train is shunted into a vast warehouse, uncoupled into two separate sections, each hoisted on massive hydraulic hoists, to switch the wheels from the Russian gauge to the Chinese. Dozens of blue-overalled workers close in on the raised carriages, unbolt the bogies, roll them out, roll in the new, all in the space of one hour. China's new efficiency... Reconnected, the train then winds into the Chinese station, ready to board new passengers and roll on to its new dawn...

WE ARE IN CHINA! the platform signs no longer in Cyrillic, the landscape changed, desert gives way to fields, villages, towns, mineworks, factories, crowds. A chemical plant belches orange fire. A large industrial town of gray tenements squats in the shadow of an immense mound of black slag. As platforms zing by, a uniformed policeman stands rigid on a boxlike stand, not even turning his head as the train passes. The traveling Mongolians, hanging half out the windows, wave at him, but he does not wave back.

Morning wind rushing in, bringing the whiff of soot, then more hills and open fields. Walls, cities, temples, a cathedral. At some point the train stops for a half hour, to be shunted backward and forward. The German passengers, who know it all, say it is a change of engine, we need a more powerful thrust to rise into the mountains. And so we do, making a slow ascent, creaking and hissing into a new landscape entirely: a range of forested mountains, higher and higher, the summer sun replaced by dank mist. Passengers point and shout. You can make out the contours as we continue to rise—up, up on the crest of the mountains, something jagged and man-made comes into view: the Wall, snaking up and down the ridges, its crenellations and watchtowers edged in the mist at the extremity of the camcorder's zoom.

The train pulls into a tunnel, right under the Great Wall of China, the battlements rearing only a few hundred yards away... I am reminded of the puffing train in *Dumbo*... "I think I can, I think

I can…" Almost visibly relieved, the train now plunges downhill, emerging into another different backdrop—a suburban vista of clustered towns, houses, modern buildings, billboards, roads, trucks, buses and cars. A large billboard of a cow rushes towards my lens and recedes, and then another, a jumbo jet taking off. Bursts of activity all along the carriages—people rushing back into the compartments, calling, shouting, climbing on bunks for the luggage racks. Claire checks her watch. Nearly there.

Beijing arrives! Suddenly, after eleven days, the city announces itself with a rising tempo of high-rise buildings crowned with giant cranes, residential fortresses already cast up, or yet unfinished, the cranes hanging over them like metal storks. Then, with a blast, a bridge over an eight-lane motorway crammed with cars, as if dropped from the sky with a howl of machine rage to signal that a new world is here. Beijing! End of the road. Terminus. Claire fumbling for the notebook in which she has jotted Go Yuan's mobile phone number and contact address. I point the camera at her:

"Comments, feelings, conclusions, on arrival at destination?"

"Fuck off, Asher. I can't find the bloody paper."

But she always does. Clipped together with the identifying photograph the girl had emailed, a smiling woman with long, flowing black hair. I remember we both examined it, searching for that Gurevitch look or any trace of her part-Russian heritage. But the pert smile just looked back at us: our Shanghai Gioconda…

Off the train at Beijing North, a run of cooped up travelers flowing down the platform, we join with countless other streams like tributaries of a continental river bursting its banks as it opens into the great terminal hall, a vast, colossal crowd pouring past the gates into the grand concourse outside. Blinking in the sun, besieged by ever more thousands rushing up to meet and greet, Claire clutches our own personal enigma, peering about in the mass.

One face among one million Chinese. Not an insurmountable problem, for those familiar with the globe. One simply needs to relax and stand one's ground, close your eyes and let the inevitable happen…

"Mister Asher! Miss Claire!"

A determined figure thrusts forward, holding a makeshift sign aloft with the two photographs we sent her tacked on together, looking like the ultimate mug shot of unwanted foreign devils. Lest we do not know ourselves, our names are printed, in large font, below the snaps: ASHAR—CLARE—LONDON—ENGLAND.

As she pushed her way forward vigorously through the crowd, I could identify the unmistakeable Gurevits gene. It's not in the face. It's not in the eyes, or the widening smile, which is not at all Gioconda, but warm, welcoming and happy. It's not in the jet black, straight and velvety hair. It's in the walk, the thrust itself, my father's gait, the Kolya swagger, Aunt Sarah's determined stride as she elbowed her way to the counter of the Tnuva dairy canteen that was once upon a time on Melchett Street. A walk that says, I know what I want and I will have my way. She came forward for the big hug, gathering up Claire. Another clue: her unusual height, among her own people. She shook my hand and we touched cheeks.

"You have all your luggage?" she said. "We have to go quickly. I have taxi waiting. We need to go and see the old lady."

There was not a moment to lose. The Old Lady had asked to see me, and she was sinking fast at the approaching end of her 95 years. She wanted to tell me something about my Aunt Judit. They had known each other in the old days, when Judit had just come down from Harbin. The Old Lady had been relatively alert the day before, Go Yuan explained, but her granddaughter had called early this morning to say we had better come right away. Go Yuan said she had not mentioned the Old Lady to us before because she had been unsure we could see her. She had been in and out of hospital, and only recently moved down from another city, a new township closer to the Great Wall, to live her last days with her granddaughter, who lived in one of the only surviving old Hutong districts in Beijing. Now a preserved area, the alleys lay alongside the three small inland lakes created as long ago as the Yuan Dynasty north of the Forbidden City. According to Go Yuan, few long-term residents lived here anymore, among the hordes of tourists and the babble of flag-wielding guides and the constant bells of the rickshaw tour tricycles. We would see.

First, the taxi had to take us to dump our bags at the apartment Go Yuan had arranged for us with friends, a writer couple, Eric and Aymee. who lived "near the second ring road," which could only be reached via the first ring road, which could only be penetrated through a total immersion in the city's monumental traffic jams. We plunged in, pulling out of the North Beijing station's slip-road into the crush, inching forward between tall rows of grand hotels and tower malls and glowering blocks of residential housing, looming in the haze under the yellow grit of the polluted sky.

The couple were called Eric and Amy, he an Australian-Norwegian academic who wrote erudite studies on the new Chinese economy, and she an old friend from Shanghai who wrote short stories and painted, and worked part-time in a gallery uptown, "near the fourth ring road." We had to rush through introductions, handshakes and a quick brunch of bread, yogurt and cornflakes from the western food store around the corner and then rush again out of the apartment block to hail another taxi on the main road ("Gongrentiyuchangbei Lu") to the Houhai lake district.

Back in the jam, the taxi driver reported on the endemic traffic problems, the inevitable choke points of the journey, the one-way systems and regulations that destroyed the cabbies' peace of mind and livelihood. Go Yuan commiserated with him while, between the rants, laying out the essential facts we needed to know to appreciate the Old Lady's tale:

Her name was Fang Ling. She had been, from the age of seven, an apprentice and then a performer with the Beijing Opera, versed in the traditional art of song, movement and drama that was often passed down the generations, but in her case was the result of a rich benefactor who frequented her father's antiquities store in the days just before the republic, who spotted her talent. When she was born, the Qing Dynasty was in its last years of existence.

After three centuries of absolute rule, foreign intervention and internal revolt had caused fatal damage, culminating in the Boxer Rebellion and the foreigners' sack of Peking. In the year before her birth, 1908, both the Dowager Empress Cixi and her nephew, the last reigning Guangxu emperor, died, leaving only the two-year-old successor, Puyi. When she was three years old, the Chinese Republic was declared under its first president, Sun Yat Sen. When she was six years old, Sun died, with China riven by the ambition of rival generals who ushered in the "warlord" period. When she was ten, the students of Peking marched to protest the Versailles Peace Conference's accession to Japanese demands on Chinese territory and launched the May 4th movement. But by then she was a veteran apprentice, under the tutelage of a senior master, learning all the forms, details, dance movements, tones of song, costume, makeup and masks of the art. The training was arduous and harsh, endless repetition, long hours starting daily at dawn, with every mistake corrected immediately by a stinging flick of the cane.

By the time she reached fourteen, she was performing both female and male roles of the younger characters in the traditional plays: *The Peach Blossom Fan*, *The Peony Pavilion*, *The Romance of the Three Kingdoms* and *The Journey to the West*, the legendary tale of Monkey and his companions. She played the lead role of Monkey for the first time, at age fifteen, in 1924, the year, Go Yuan reminded us, that Mao Zedong and his comrades founded the Communist Party of China in Shanghai.

At this point, a cry of triumph came from the cage up front, as the taxi driver spotted a gap in the left lane of the ring road that enabled him to break out and bypass the blocked junction and maneuver onto a side road that skirted the lake and headed straight into the Hutong complex. Go Yuan paused her narration in order to help guide the driver through the maze while he leaned out and yelled at the rickshaws. The cab had to stop when the road was blocked by a phalanx of Chinese pensioners in white T-shirts and red slacks and caps. We all got out, the fare was paid and we continued by foot.

714

The day was abominably hot. We crept on like beetles in the dust. Go Yuan soon recognized a familiar wall, with a black column rising behind it, and the crowns of garden trees. "Not very far!" she called. It had been pretty far already, but we lumbered on, past several souvenir shops, a small grocery and a CD-DVD shop with an arresting sign: The Punk Store. The jingle jangle of the Grateful Dead playing "Mountains of the Moon" diverted us in. "This is not punk," Claire told the boy behind the counter, but he just shrugged and told us everything was half-price today. There were piles of new releases, hotly copied from Hollywood, and among the classic DVDs I spotted an obviously pirated cover of the 1956 *The Ten Commandments*, the one that got away from my dad. So let it be written—so let it be done." Yul Brynner's Pharaoh gazed out at me with amused contempt...

Go Yuan called us out to say she had found the house. It was only a few doors down in the alley wall, the entrance inset under a typical Chinese angled roof, leading to an inner courtyard from which a maze of smaller alleyways branched off. A whole panoply of household objects lay around, pots and pans, potted plants, brooms, washbowls, buckets, bamboo poles, a couple of birdcages with tweeting birds, a small white dog sprawling in the shade, too hot to bark, worktables, bicycles, a wheelbarrow, chairs, footstools and a large white banner slung across one of the inner lanes, in Chinese and English, proclaiming: "NO TO HOOTONG DEMOLITION! DEFEND OUR HOMES!"

Behind the sign, under an open window, two men were seated on small stools in the shade, hunched over a low table, playing mah-jongg. They looked up at us warily, but Go Yuan stepped forward and addressed them. They nodded quickly and waved us forward.

"It's this way," she said. "I can never remember the direction to the house... It's a big red door."

And there it was, wide and imposing, with an official look, as if stamped with an imperial seal. The handle, however, let us in easily, and a small, earnest-looking woman who looked neither young nor too old was standing there, in front of a neat inner quadrangle, with a landscaped porch leading to a short flight of stone stairs capped by two white squatting lions. She bowed slightly and extended her hand.

"Good morning," she said. "I am Fang Li."

Her English was obviously limited, so she turned and spoke to Go Yuan in Chinese, and the two chatted as she led us up the stairs and into the main room. It was a cluttered space, filled with two sofas, soft chairs, cupboards and low chests of drawers and a thick ornamental carpet. The walls were covered with an array of framed photographs and posters of the Chinese opera, each featuring a performer in splendid costume and mask: kings, queens, demons, princesses, generals, in magnificent headdress, multicolored beards, twirling swords, pennants, staffs and wands. As one looked closer, the truth became clear, as Claire exclaimed, "These are all the same person!"

"Yes," said Go Yuan. "It is all Fang Li."

A bamboo-curtained doorway leading to an inner room was flanked by a giant poster featuring a beautiful youth, man or woman, the features exquisitely brought out by a white-painted face, in a golden robe and brandishing a richly ornamented sword. It was a garish poster in the old style, festooned with curves, curls and ornate characters.

"This is her famous role, as Monkey, in the nineteen-thirties," Go Yuan explained. "Fang Li says her grandmother is not well, but she wants to see us very much. She has something for you."

"We can always come back another time," said Claire, ever the Englishwoman.

"No, no," said Go Yuan. "She has been waiting. Since I told her about you. She is very commanding."

Fang Li went out to the kitchen across the yard to get tea, while we sat on the main sofa and looked around at the amazing display. Aficionados, no doubt, would recognize all the characters of the traditional plays. Unable to contain herself, Claire got up and walked around.

"I've read so much about it," she told Go Yuan, "but I never saw a performance, except on TV. The Chinese groups always brought us new shows."

"The young people are not very interested nowadays," said Go Yuan. "It is an entertainment for the tourists and old people. The tourists get the short versions, but for tradition, the play is very long, maybe seven, eight hours. Sometimes three days for the most famous versions."

"We must do it without fail," said Claire."

My heart sank. Fang Li came in with tea and Chinese buns and then went in through the curtain to see if her grandmother was ready to see us. Claire got up again to examine a more modern poster, one in the familiar Mao style, a tableau interior of a simple hut with three figures in peasant dress: a heavily made-up man, a young girl with long plaits in a red smock and a white-haired old woman, striking a heroic pose between them.

"Is this also her?"

"That one is the modern opera-play, *The Red Lantern*. It was one of the twelve revolutionary operas that Mao's wife, Chiang Ching decided were the only proper plays that Chinese people were allowed to see in the Cultural Revolution. It is Fang Ling. She played the role on the stage, but in the movie it was another actress, who was more politically reliable. But she had to do this to keep working, at that time. I heard about her, but I didn't know there was any connection with our own life."

Fang Li came back through the curtain. "Grandmother says please come in," she said. We went into the bedroom. Curtains were drawn over two small windows that filtered in the dull midday sun in pools of heat rather than light. It was a bit like Von Sternberg with heavier diffusion. Some light fell on the face of the Old Lady in the bed, propped up on a pile of pale cushions. The bed was narrow but set very high, on one thick or several thinner mattresses, so that when we sat down around her on low chairs she was almost looking down at us. She seemed a very small person, or had shrunk with age, so that her oval face was almost a miniature, her head, which was probably hairless, covered with a thin white cap. But her eyes were open as we came in. A thin hand in a white pajama sleeve slunk out of the bedclothes and pointed at us. Her granddaughter came forward and leaned down towards her, talking quietly in Chinese. Go Yuan drew up her chair, and Fang Li's thin fingers took her hand. Fang Ling nodded at us, took in Claire, and looked me in the eye.

"Yu," she said, in a clear voice. "Youtai –Yudit brodder."

I was confused, but Go Yuan nudged me.

"She can speak some English," she said. "Youtai means Jew. She thinks you are Judit's brother. "Nephew," she said to the Old Lady, "*Zhizi*. Son of brother."

She beckoned me closer and took my hand. Her grip was amazingly firm. She seemed to have exhausted her English however, or wanted to make sure she was understood. She spoke Chinese to Go Yuan, who translated for me.

"She says your auntie was a great friend to her. When she was young. She was performing in the opera—*The Peony Pavilion*. She played Du Liniang. She had a girlfriend who took her to a bar in the foreigner's area. This was in [query and answer] "nineteen thirty two. She was not allowed to go there, but her girlfriend was naughty. There was a Russian singer there, who came from Harbin. She was not so young for the foreign sailors and soldiers, so she was sitting alone. She and her friend went to speak to her, because they thought she sang so well. She sang Russian songs and also Chinese. They invited her to the opera. She came the next day. Then they met every day after that. Judit told her she had many troubles in Harbin and she had a brother who was disappeared. She had trouble with the Japanese. She came to Beijing but the Japanese were soon here too. The two girls were very interested in her story because they were Communists. Judit was a Communist also. The best place to go at that time was in the south. But the Japanese were there also. When they were beaten that time, Judit went to Shanghai. There was opera there also, in the Shanghai style. They call it Huju opera."

The Old Lady called for her granddaughter to step up and she propped up her cushions. Then the Old Lady began to sing, or quaver. Her voice rang out for a few bars until she started coughing, and Fang Li patted her back and made her take a sip of tea. Then the grandmother waved her back. She had let go of my hand to sing but took hold of it again.

"I sang every evening for fifty-five years," Go Yuan translated. "Sometimes there was war, sometimes there was peace. We kept our traditions. But we are not fools. We know the world is wide and full of other songs, other traditions. They are not all savages. We heard Russians sing opera. We heard *The Snow Maiden*, *The Golden Cock*, from Pushkin, also *Boris Godunov*, but it was condemned. We had Verdi. *Nabucco*. That was about the Jews. Also *Tosca*. She always wanted to play Tosca but it was just a dream. She says, something that—our voice became the voice that always was China. Then there were political problems." The Old Lady fell silent, mumbling for a while. Then she took hold of my hand again. "Your aunt was a great friend of China. Her husband was a great patriot. Later the government shamed us all. But I helped your auntie. She was still in Shanghai. I was very famous then, they couldn't touch me. I worked with that awful woman. She died in prison—she is talking about Mao Zedong's wife, Chiang Ching. Yes? She says: I went to see your aunt in Shanghai." Go Yuan asked something in Chinese, and was answered. "This was the time she was working in the printing works, during the Cultural Revolution. After my grandfather was shamed. He was an old guard Communist, and they took him down the streets, in a big hat, what do you call it, the dunce cap. But he got her a job as a printer, so she was proletarian. She says: She gave me something." Go Yuan glanced at us, puzzled, "I don't know anything about this..."

The Old Lady beckoned to her granddaughter. Fang Li went over to a lacquer cabinet and opened a drawer. She took a small cloth bundle out of it and showed it to Fang Ling. The Old Lady nodded vigorously and beckoned again. The granddaughter handed her the bundle. The Old Lady tried to unwind the red plastic string that bound it. The two women leaned forward to help her but she brushed them away and placed the bundle in my hand. I could feel a very small package inside. The red plastic was tied with a bow that I managed slowly to pull open.

Inside was a familiar object, though I had never touched one before. A small plastic-covered book. The Book, in fact, the Little Red Book of Chairman Mao's quotations. The red front had a tiny inlaid yellow circle with the head of the young Mao. The pages were somewhat faded and crinkled, as if they had been damp and dried out. The Old Lady gestured to me.

"Open it, she says," said Go Yuan. "It is for you. Judit gave it to me in Shanghai. She said to keep it for her. Look inside."

Two hundred and seventy pages of tightly packed Chinese print. Another portrait of Chairman Mao in cap and red star as frontispiece. But that was not all. From the first chapter, there were annotations on many of the pages, handwritten in the tiniest, most minuscule writing I had ever seen. Tightly packed in the narrow margins of the pages, and at chapter breaks. The room was so dim I had to take off my glasses, curse of middle age, and bring the pages right up to my nose. I had to move over to the window and pull the curtain aside to make the writing out. It was in Hebrew letters.

"Jesus Christ!" I said.

They crowded around me—Claire, Go Yuan and the grand-daughter, but I could hardly read it myself. In fact, I could not read the writing at all.

It was in Yiddish. Written in the Hebrew characters, but as foreign to me as Russian or Greek. My eyes blurred, and I had to sit down again. The Old Lady said something softly. The grand-daughter bent her ear to her and then spoke to Go Yuan. Go Yuan said:

"She promised to hold it till it was safe, or till she could find her brothers. The ones who were far away, and still alive. She knew they were there, somewhere. But when the politics had changed, Fang Ling found my grandmother had died. She died in nineteen seventy-four, two years before Chairman Mao died. She was together with my grandfather then. My father married four years later. He was in the countryside, and my grandfather was in another region. I never knew about this book. My father never said anything. He probably didn't know also."

We looked back at the Old Lady, but she had fallen asleep. For a moment we thought she had left us there and then, but she was snoring softly.

We walked around the lake, in the late afternoon sun, treading the pathways that only the imperial courtiers could have taken in dynastic times, a rare oasis of peace and tranquillity in the new empire of money and steel. At the end of the hutong courtyards, a more crowded space heralded the glut of restaurants corralling the small lower lake, approached along a line of stalls selling more DVDs, CDs, T-shirts, children's shoes, toys, souvenir nicknacks and a stall of old Maoist posters, which interrupted our stroll. Were there more messages hidden in the interstices of these bold postures—the Red Book-wielding masses pushing towards the radiant sun of the chairman, waving to them from the mountaintop? Workers, peasants, men, women, Chinese, Africans, Arabs, Latinos, flourishing the red flag, holding up hoes, sickles, guns, soldiers of the Red Army crushing under their feet the cowardly minnows of Uncle Sam, John Bull, perfidious France et al., proclaiming the Word. Mao leading the smiling peasants in simple slacks and white shirts, peasant girls in flaring skirts dancing towards the hammer and sickle, children in white shirts and red neckerchiefs looking up to Mao in the sky, Mao with Stalin, Lenin and Marx ("Very rare," said Go Yuan), and one Claire nearly bought, of a beaming family: a father with a pipe, three children and a wife wearing an apron, bringing in a bowl of soup to a neat table overseen by wall portrait of Mao. Go Yuan translated the heading: "The happy life Chairman Mao gave us."

"We can put it up instead of 'The Great Gramby,'" Claire suggested, but I just held my peace. I threatened in return to buy another arresting image, two stalwart women holding the red flag aloft together, one dark-haired and Chinese, the other blonde and clearly Russian, from another proscribed age. It could be Granny Fang and our own Judit. But Go Yuan didn't find this very funny.

My new Chinese cousin. Or second, third cousin? This was not my forte. My brother Yitzhak and Yonni were the ones who delighted in the genealogies, putting together the family tree, adding branches, lopping others off as the spirit and their searches led them. The Six Gurevitses were enough for me. Either Yitzhak or Yonni could have read the messages on Judit's red bible, but it was difficult to explain to Go Yuan why I could not.

"I know the Yiddish is a special Jewish language," she said, as we settled down at one of the lakeside eateries for a cold beer and Go Yuan's recommended Hakka cuisine. "But I thought it was written in German. My research is not good enough."

Bloody amateurs, all of us. I squinted at the book again. I looked at the first entry, at the top of part 2, which I could just make out began with "Liebe Yakov..." Then the writing got smaller. How had she managed it at all? "What does it say in the Chinese text?" I asked her.

"Chapter Two," she read out, "'Classes and Class Struggle'— Classes struggle, some classes are victorious, and others are wiped out. This is the history of civilization for thousands of years...' This is from the essay 'Cast Away Illusions, Prepare for Struggle.' Every schoolchild still learns this."

"Liebe Yakov..." What is the past telling us? More threads unfold along the way. The more I gaze at my Chinese cousin, the more I see the traces of the old genetic strain. The way she holds a beer glass, making sure it doesn't spill. The careful glance, that was my father, but I had always assumed it was a cinematographer's tic. It was not characteristic of Kolya, whose gestures seemed always reckless to me. He would wave his hands, but somehow not knock things over. Only ideologies, principles, states. She reminded me of Aunt Sarah, or is that the socialist strain? Or am I imagining things here that have long been discarded? Everything here is buy, buy, buy, like a Parisian bazaar on the Seine. Claire interrogating as usual, trying to get the full picture. I have long come to the conclusion that this objective is a delusion.

Go Yuan unfolds her own background: did well at school, won a grant to study abroad in America, at San Francisco State. She studied law, but it was difficult to practice law in China. She went to Melbourne for two years met some people there whose parents had come from Harbin. They swapped tales. Go Yuan recalled her old school project. That was the spark that led her back into the story, and started her writing her own two chapters. An Australian academic in Shanghai helped her translate the segments for us. She had made plans for us to visit Harbin. We could get there in an hour, internal flights were cheap, we could stay at the famous Hotel Moderne, where Judit had performed. She had already been there twice and talked with the local Jewish Preservation Society, who were renovating the old synagogue. They were always eager to meet old Harbinskis, even if their connection was tenuous. We could see the Jewish cemetery, but she had looked and there were no Gurevitses there. She found no trace of Zhiv or Zev, as she now understood he should be called. All the municipal records were still closed by the state. Too many old secrets of collaboration and compromise. Travel around and understand much more of China. The endless quest par excellence... We should see the Forbidden City before it is all renovated, the beautiful old tiles, faded and cracked, were going to be completely replaced, not repaired. The new China was up and coming, the whole city sparkling and shining bright for the Olympic Games in 2008. New districts, roads, subway lines, bigger, richer shopping malls, new triumphs for the party and the nation. Build the Harmonious Society. Capitalism is the new Communism. Money is the new red sun glaring over Tiananmen Square.

Then we would visit Shanghai. She would proudly show us her city and its amazing high-rise skyline, mercifully leaving intact some quieter nooks and corners, the preserved avenues and streets along which Judit walked and worked. The Paramount Ballroom, where she sang of her longings, now a karaoke hall. The corner by the Old World show center where the bombs fell. The old Hongkou ghetto was all renovated, the only relic still left the synagogue, which runs regular tours, and a Hebrew plaque in the park. And we could visit Lu Xun's house and see the garden where the only photograph of Judit and Go Yuan's grandfather was taken. She would show us these few remaining mementos when we visited, she had rushed back up to Beijing to make sure the Old Lady was still "awake" before she picked us up at the station.

When we were ready and had the inclination, she also wanted to hear our tale. She knew it was a lot to ask, but my emails summarizing some of my own trips and searches had whetted her appetite. She wanted to know as much as possible about the siblings. Were there more? What about the parents, in the village, Judit's birthplace? Had I been there and what had I found? Were there any traces of the past? I could see she did not understand how I could have spent all this time digging and searching without bothering to go to the source, since it was not that far distant from my own location, if one figured in Chinese geographical terms. So I began telling her of some of her missing history, starting with my father, whom she could appreciate, stuck in Hollywood, making films, fame and fortune, though his skill was known only to his own profession and film buffs. I drew on a napkin a brief family tree, starting with the rabbi and his wife, in Celovest, and the six offspring: Sarah, Boris, Zev, Yakov the Magician, Nathan-Kolya, and Judit. The other child, Isaac, died aged two, when Judit was a baby. She seemed very interested in that one, a pure soul who must be present in all the others. We must go to a temple and pray for him. The others lived their life, but he missed everything—the sun, the dew, the view of fields, of mountains, forests, roads that could be traveled, destinations that could be dreamed and achieved. Love. Pain. Anguish and recovery. She believed in the immortality of the soul. What about us? I passed, but Claire agreed with her. I was surprised. I had never heard that before. You live and learn something new every day, even about your closest and dearest.

I told Go Yuan that I had brought her some material to fill in her own writings: data CDs with scans that I had made of my father's segments, Sarah's letters and the copy of Kolya's "Soldier's Journal," if she could bear the revelations of our uncle's journey from rabid Bolshevik Chekist to the Irgun, which might or might not blow up her brain. She said she had done some reading on Israel, some books by Amos Oz and some nonfiction, but the Chinese found the whole conflict between us and the Palestinians peculiar, involving such small populations. I told her the old joke about Mao saying to Yasser Arafat, "What's your problem with these Israelis? I hear there are only thirty million." She said that question rang true for most Chinese people. Three or four million was a population that could be easily moved somewhere else, like the more than a million people displaced by the construction of the Three Gorges Dam.

The whole burden of the journey was suddenly weighing down on us, the realization that we had been on and off a train for nearly two weeks, our sleeping cycle wavering between reality and Moscow time. Go Yuan became terribly apologetic about calling us down for this difficult experience without proper warning, subjecting us to Beijing's atmospheric catastrophe. It was the same in Shanghai, she warned: the heat, the dust, the pollution of China's industrial revolution accelerated beyond human tolerance. She offered to show us other places, if we had time. We could go to the canals of Suzhou, or Hangzhou's beautiful West Lake, a respite from the hustle and tumult and noise from before the Southern Song Dynasty. I had no idea when that was, but it certainly pre-dated Celovest, czarist Russia, Franz Josef's Austria-Hungary, the Plantagenets, the Pilgrim fathers, George Washington, Theodor Herzl and all our current wars, conflicts and tsuris...

We dozed our way back in another taxi plunge through the maelstrom back to the apartment, where we discussed our discoveries with our gracious hosts, Eric and Amy, Australians well versed in China's marvels.

We unpacked a little, and I put Judit's Little Red Book in a mylar envelope and stashed it in the accessories pocket of the camcorder pouch so that it would be safe with the essentials. I tried to look at it again in the bed-light lamp but still couldn't make out the writing, beyond those first scrawled words: *"Liebe Yakov, dos ist..."* or is it *"vus ist...?"* This is, or What is... What are the chances of finding a Yiddish reader among the expats in Dongzhimen district in the summer of 2004? Eric had suggested the Israeili Embassy, but I threw my hands up. No way. This is our family heirloom...

Go Yuan had supplied us with an English-language version of the Mao bible so that I could read the text of the pages equivalent to those whose margins were filled with my lost aunt's microscopic lines. How did Judit manage it? What uniquely shaped calligraphic tool could she have used to achieve such a miracle?

"Liebe Yakov..." He's not here, Auntie. But I'm here, Boris/Berl's son. Come morning, ask Eric and Amy about a magnifying glass. And a Chinese Yiddishist. In a city of fifteen, maybe twenty million, there must be one. Maybe ten, a full minyan. The world is full of miracles—not the spectacular ones that resurrect Messiahs, save nations, raise the dead, part the seas, but tiny ones that tell steadily, against all odds, in strange places...

I fell into fitful sleep, to the familiar beat of some nightclub across the alley, somewhere close in the district. It was not the Grateful Dead, but some undistinguished, neutral, aggravating current pop. Disco's greatest hits, for the young in body and heart. Doomp doomp doomp doomp. Voices chattering outside, coming out of the restaurants. The sing-song Mandarin tones, oddly comforting. We all wander. We all emit messages, one way or another. Some shout, some sing, some turn up the sound system. Some whisper, some ease out their last words. Some even write. But only a Gurevitch could try to write something that nobody can fucking damn read!

I had a dream. There was something stirring in the room. In a cupboard. Ghost or bedbug, who could tell, but somehow I felt it was Uncle Yakov, the Great Gramby, stuck in his magic cabinet, knocking on the inside, expecting me to rise from my age-old stupor and set him free. But I was just too exhausted... When I woke up, I felt there had been more, a continuation, but I could not remember the details. Claire was still fast asleep. The room was unfamiliar, and there were still voices outside in a language I could not fathom. I tried to return to the dream, but there was nothing in the frame. And, within seconds, the frame itself had vanished into the musty, sticky air...

"On the correct handling of contradictions among the people..."

Judit's letter (translated):

Dear Yakov,

You remember when I was a little child and you were my closest brother that you told me that we would both fly away some day? It was the dream you told everyone: How you would climb on top of the roof, over Father's study, and jump, and rise up, over the fields and the mountains? You said you had a book that showed you the way over the mountains and the rivers to immense cities that were full of people who did nothing all day but ride about in omnibuses and sit in s and read newspapers about all the news of the day, and they travelled between these cities by railway, and by aero-planes that could cross over the seas? You had a book by Jules Verne that told you how people could even fly to the moon, but they would have to come back, because there was a fierce tribe there that could not stand any strangers?

Well, I live in that strange place now. It is full of people, but they don't hang around in cafes, and the only news in the news-papers that they are allowed to read is news about themselves. The people are filling the streets every day, demonstrating, shout-ing, praising their leader and denouncing everybody else. It is a cacophony that they keep up day and night. They don't go to bed. They are on fire, they must make Revolution every moment, with every fibre in their soul. I am not sure if they are allowed to have souls. That kind of thing is never discussed. If you are found out talking of such things you are dragged out into the streets and marched along to be spat at and kicked and have a million angry fists shaken and often hitting your face. This happened to persons near and dear to me. But I have learned to be armoured with steel.

I know about the newspapers because I print them. I work with the printing blocks in the plant. There are many many small blocks, in this country's writing. You would say it looked like Chinese to you and you would be right. It is a very repetitive labour but it suits me fine. In this strange country it is a fine thing to be a manual labourer, even if you have only scraps to eat. Your head is filled with words that make sentences and paragraphs and whole pages of slogans that contain the only truth that is allowed to be. Where are your flights of fancy, Yakov? Where are Berl's brave words of freedom? Where are all the great books we used to read? After you left I read all of them. I read Tolstoy and Dostoyevsky and Pushkin and Herzen and Lenin and Gorky and Victor Hugo and Mendele and Peretz. I filled my soul with new companions after you all climbed on the roof and flew. I was too little to fly, and I was too timid, afraid to climb up so high. The only time I tried Mother admonished me so heavily, telling me that girls were not boys. So I stayed behind, and fulfilled my tasks, till there was nothing left to be done.

Dear Yakov,

After Father died, our mother became very odd in the head. She started going around in the streets, asking people where they were going. They told her that they were going to the store, or to the blacksmith, or to the Bet-Midrash, or to the school, but she didn't believe them. She believed they were all going to the railway station to leave for Bucharest and Vienna. She knew once people reached these places they never came back. Soon after that she became ill and was taken in by our uncle Mordechai the new Rabbi. Then even Sarah left, because there was nothing else for her in the village after both the child and her husband had died. She went to the Holy Land. I wrote letters to her there, and to Berl, in the place where they make the moving pictures. He wrote me back that you were in Paris, and become a great magician, with a new name. I was so glad, that you were fulfilling your destiny.

I remember you told me once this *psak*, as if you were quoting from the Holy writ in its sanctity: You said that one has to become something different to the thing one is, but to stay yourself. I did not understand it then, but I understand it well now. I have become so many different things to the thing I was, I remember my own life as if it were lived by a completely different person. You and the others called me Little Judit, but here I am Mama Chi, the *alter kakeh* who lives at the print-works, who has no children and whose man was killed fighting for Mao, the leader, the Great Helmsman who navigates the ship of life. They do not know that my man and my son are still living, but live far away from me, in a quieter place, where they are not so well known. It is true that my man was a hero, but a hero is too difficult a profession to have and to hold in this world. He did not fly away from the rooftop, but he did take the train, but not to Bucharest or Vienna. We promised each other that we would meet again. We are old now, and cannot fly, even my son, because the rooftops in the place he lives are too low, and the wind is too dusty, and holds men down.

You can't believe the ruckus and the noise the people make outside my little window. I am a little below ground, in a base-ment, so I just see feet, thousands of feet, marching, marching, going to the end of the streets, and the square, and then marching back again.

What do they want? To smash all their enemies. Who are their enemies? Their mothers and fathers, their brothers who unfurl the wrong slogan, the municipal leaders whom someone wants to get rid of, any group that has got on the wrong side of the Helmsman, whose majesty, like the Lord Blessed Be He, lies in his infallible truth. The only difference is, we had but six-hundred and thirteen commandments, whereas he has many more, possibly thousands, and each and every one must be obeyed.

The strange thing about it is that I know exactly what all these millions of people are going to say the next day, because I have set up the blocks of words and sentences they have to utter as they march about, gather in the square, and rush to attack their opponents. "Take firm hold of the revolution, oppose economism and promote production and utterly smash the bourgeois reactionary line." I have to be very careful. If I set the wrong character in the wrong order who knows what instructions I might be giving. Sometimes I wonder if I am the one who is making all these millions of people dance to these peculiar tunes. The Great Helmsman speaks through me, but he does not know it. So there must be limits to his truth. Does this make any sense in our own *mameh-loshen* (our mother tongue)? Perhaps only the grand magician can know.

My mother never understood, Yakov, why you all left her. She said it was the curse of the unravelling world. The world used to be tied together in the Lord's plan, and then everyone forgot the truth and marched off in pursuit of their dreams and illusions. If one argued with her that the dreams might be true, she would say, only the *maggid* would know. Only our father, who was all-wise in her eyes, and had been taken by the Name for reasons we could not be allowed to question. And so she went about questioning everyone on every move she thought strange. Time had stood still, after his departure, for her, and so everyone should stand still, from then. Only after she died, and was laid to rest beside him, I could follow Zev myself into the world.

I have no room to tell you my story. I have only the space above and beside and in-between the sayings of the Great Sage who rules this world. "On the correct handling of contradictions among the people." And yet their contradictions keep multiplying, until all the people are at war with themselves. I built a life here, which was strange and terrifying, but also enticing and full of wonders and marvels. I followed your advice, to become something else, but I am not sure if I remained myself. In the reaches of the night, when the shouting dies down—I believe for lack of nutrition and sheer exhaustion rather than from choice, because no one dares to be the one who chooses to fall silent first. I go back along the trail and try and find the forks in the road and the other paths that might have been taken. But I always find that I have taken the same fork I took at first. I do not know why. My man, who is adept at many things, and also knows the stage well, told me when I spoke about my magician brother that the basic point about magic was that no magician could ever take a pigeon out of a hat unless there was a pigeon in the hat in the first place. In other words, we make our own luck. He was also a communist, you see, but of a different sort from these, he would never repeat words for no reason. He is a good man and I would like you to meet him.

I had a strange dream, a few nights ago, that I was standing in the middle of the crowd in front of the podium of the leaders in Peking, in the great square where the Great Helmsman's face looks down on us from the giant gate of the Emperors who came before him. Everyone was cheering and waving their little red books. I was quite close up, before the podium. I looked up as the leaders climbed the steps to the dais where they were going to speak, but instead of the leaders I saw all five of you, Berl, Sarah, Kolya, Zev and you, clapping the crowd and waving back. Berl was in the long black coat that he wore when he came back from Odessa, Kolya was in a soldier's uniform, handsome and grave, with medals on his chest. Zev was in his fur trader's coat, with the sable hat, the wide smile under his great moustache, a little like comrade Stalin on the posters. You were as you always were, a mischievous sprite, dressed in your striped pyjamas, because you never liked to get up, but would rather stay in bed and dream. You looked straight forward and winked at me. I waved, calling out, loud as possible—"Hurrah! Hurrah!" and the crowd was following, until they suddenly started to fall silent, clumps of people, lowering their hands and mumbling, the loud cries tailing off, till there was a great silence in the square. You winked at me, and brought out, from behind your back, a great shimmering scarlet cape, like the one in the pictures you once showed me about the bull-fighters in the great ring in Madrid. You twirled the cape, and it blossomed out, right over the entire square, covering everyone. I rushed forward to take hold of its fringe, to catch a corner and bring it towards me, to press it to my lips, to draw myself forward, into its depths.

That was it. A dream. *Fata morgana*. The thirsty see it in the desert. *Shoen genug*, as Mother used to say. What has been has been. I lived my life, and went into the whirlwind. I chose my path. I do not know yours. I hope there were many joys in it, that you could snatch as they came by. Like catching a wind with your teeth. We seem to have fulfilled some ancient curse, to be scattered among the nations, but we made this choice on our own. Our father would have told us different, but we moved away perhaps because in our hearts we believed that we knew better than he. That was his dream, and this is ours. In our father's house it was the will of the Name. In the place I am now it is the will of the Face, that smiles out from the cover of this book. This tiny volume in which I write. In so many ways it reminds me of the tiny *humash* (the five books of the Torah) that we used to have as children. Kolya used to read in it a lot. The letters were so small you could go blind reading it. Father had his giant volume which had been passed down the ages from the founding village, in Podolia. I remember it was called Murachwa. There they sat, generation after generation, bowing and scraping and learning the *midrash*. From where they came we cannot know. Was it ancient Palestine? The gulags of Egypt? Or from exile further east, along the paths Zev and I have trod? The lost tribes. But we are only mortal. Memory lives in our brains, and when we are gone, it has decayed and been snuffed out. What we leave behind abides in others. What they recall, what they record, what they seek out, what they desire.

I have reached the end of this section. The next is called "Correcting Mistaken Ideas." I think I will just leave that to itself…

*

Asher:

We did not find a Yiddish speaker in Beijing, but read Judit's secret scrawl in Shanghai, where the curator of the Jewish museum in the old synagogue found us an interpreter, a Lubavitcher from

Jerusalem who was the advance guard for a full-scale invasion of the Chabad group, those people who accost you on the streets of New York and press you to don the phylacteries, say your prayers and return to your faith. His name was Gershon, and his Yiddish was not much better than mine, but he found an old Chinese gentleman who had learned the language from the Jews he had worked with as a doctor back in the ghetto days. He bent his wrinkled visage right down to the paper and deciphered the minuscule letters without a magnifying glass or even spectacles. His name was Yin Chun. Even Go Yuan found him difficult to understand, as his Chinese and his Yiddish seemed to have merged. She had limited time, as she was pressed by then to return to her legal work with her advice bureau, dealing with divorces and other entanglements. The Chabadnik Gershon insisted on showing us around all the old sites, the other synagogue, the plaque in the park, the old preserved Jewish house hidden behind washing lines. He said the little book was a God-given treasure and should be donated to the museum's store of mementos, but I said it was a family heirloom. He gave me the look my brother Yitzhak has thrown me all my life. I just left him with a handshake and we moved on.

Time runs out. Brief tours of the West Lake, Hangzhou, back to Shanghai, Judit's old haunts of the French Concession, excellent food, new normalities: Starbucks, museums, art galleries, a local play for Claire, unfortunately sans translation... Her time off work run out, no time for Harbin, no longer cosmopolitan, just another industrial city on the go... Settle for a book of photographs: "Jews of China,"—with somewhat familiar faces, but no recognition. The empire has moved on, heading for times yet to come...

Our return to London is an instant immersion in the curse of the new: scandals of the Blair government, the Iraq war crunching on. American soldiers' death toll passes one thousand. Bush dismisses fears of civil war. CIA report finds no signs of Iraqi weapons of mass destruction. U.N. Secretary-General Kofi Annan declares war illegal. US forces battle insurgents in Fallujah. Nine billion dollars of American aid to Iraq stolen somewhere along the line.

Suicide bombings continue in Israel, Prime Minister Ariel Sharon plans unilateral withdrawal from Gaza, opposing talks with Palestinian Authority. In Palestine, Yasser Arafat lies close to death. Yasser Arafat dies. Yasser Arafat is buried with full national honors. Nondescript deputy Mahmoud Abbas takes over his thankless task. Tony Blair proposes an Israel-Palestine peace conference in London for 2005.

Selah.

*

Claire returns to the RiverWharf, and I climb up the four flights of stairs at the film school towards my cubbyhole in the Camera Department. As the fresh faces of the new intake of the autumn term buzz in, I realize that I have spent twenty years in this place, hiding comfortably inside the Frame, observing it rather than trying to become its master. Where had all the time gone? The shallowness of the search, the shabby dragging of feet, the slapdash method, all the exact polar opposite of what I preach here.

Thus Spake Zarathustra, in the eternal recurrence: "I am unsettled in every city and I depart from every gate..." One should know one's Nietzsche from one's negligence. The inability to fit it all together, to find all the missing links...

Yonni emailed me when I returned, to ask what I had found out about Judit. I told him about the Little Red Book and I could practically hear him wetting his lips. Then he called and asked, "When can I see it?" I said I would scan the pages and send them, but he said he had to see the Thing Itself. "Originals, originals, the Prof always said. Never rely on copies. You want to feel the breath of Eichmann on the stamp." I said it was not quite the same thing, but that Claire was talking about a theater trip to New York in December, just before Christmas, and he would have to make do with the ersatz until then. He said, "I am a patient man." I told him about Shanghai, Harbin, the remnants and the old Chinese man who could read shrunken

735

Yiddish with the naked eye. He said: "I love him! I want to marry him!" I thought he sounded pretty unhinged.

Time tells on us all. Emails flying back and forth between London and Shanghai, Go Yuan searching the Internet, now that she knew the name of the origin village, for any data on "Celovesti." Sending me links to amateur videos on a new site called YouTube, on which people could post any clips that they wanted, showing some crazy Moldovan kids bashing on drums and guitars in a backyard among chickens and goats. There were "social networking" sites called MySpace and Facebook, which she recommended to me, where people could meet virtually and exchange ideas, information or chatter. We could communicate in "real time," on Yahoo Messenger, or even speak directly, on something called Skype, which was apparently invented by Estonians and Swedes. The system was still not very common in China, which censored and blocked all these networks, but there were ways to get through, on "proxies."

The entire world is connected, except myself; I feel the threads slipping day after day. Old age, the dreaded round 60 coming up in two years, the symptoms examined in the bathroom mirror at home. What is this sagging puss, those bleary eyes, the crow's feet, the hair receding as if in accelerating shock? Once we were young, facing the unknown. Now do we "know" far too much?

Letters from Go Yuan, who was parsing the third book of Judit but still wanting to know more. She was ploughing through Holocaust sites, weeping at the fate of the origin village—the Transdniestria camp, exile and dispersion... Surfing through Zionist and anti-Zionist sites that confuse her even more than before. Ye shall know the truth and the lies, but ye shall not know how to separate them, and ye shall be perplexed and fettered for evermore...

She wrote:

"I want to follow Judit all the way from 1940's to the time she stayed here in Shanghai with Grandfather after Liberation.

We have more and more information about the early cam-
paigns, and the 'hundred flowers' period, and the 'great leap
forward' and all the problems, when people were having a
really hard time, and then the cultural revolution. It was impossible to be a foreigner at that time, you would be arrested,
put in prison or worse, so she had to become completely
Chinese. This is what she is writing about in the book. And
did you find more stuff about Yakov?"

Claire left for New York at the beginning of December, and I followed her when the school wrapped on the 10th. It was not too
cold when I arrived, but the temperature dipped a few days later
and was on course for an icy Christmas-New Year's. Claire had
friends up on 110th Street and Amsterdam, in a apartmentt full
of theater books, published plays, pamphlet scripts running the
gamut from Aeschylus to Zindel. As Yonni's apartment was only
a few blocks downwind, I called on him the day after we landed
while Claire stayed in with the motherlode. The doorman seemed
to remember me from the last time, and shooed me up, but when
I buzzed the door of the apartment I was sure for a moment I had
gotten off on the wrong floor. The man before me was clean-shaven,
without a hair on his chin, and something missing on his head
as well. No kippa. Behind him another man, whom I had never
seen, fair-haired and blue-eyed, though also past the last bloom of
youth, peeped behind him and said hi.

"This is Bob," Yonni said, as if there was nothing noteworthy
about a lapsed Hassid who had cast off the signs and accoutre-
ments and become the man no one else knew he would be. I
shook hands with Bob. The apartment was the same, blocked with
books, filing cabinets, shelves of document folders. It was just the
habitant, transformed from a dedicated and godly scholar of the
incessant pain and calamities of the Jewish people into the aging
half of a typical Upper West Side gay couple.

"Ah, Asher," he said, half to me, half to Bob, "ever the perfect
dissimulator. You are your uncle's true nephew, the ex-Chekist
who blinks not an eye when he sees the bodies dumped into the

Neva. I remember you, you used to be an American. Now he is an English liberal. Bob used to be a rabbi in New Jersey. You wouldn't know it, would you? It's amazing what a beard does for a man. I always thought women should try it too. But alas, vanity wins over prudence. You brought the book?"

For a moment I thought he'd dropped his guard, but he'd only exchanged one pose for another. Still the fanatic archivist, he took the wrapped object carefully over to the huge desk, brushed away some papers and pushed back the flat screen, pulling an angular lamp over for light. He handled the tiny artefact as if it were diamonds, and brought over a large magnifying glass.

"Check out the dedication," he murmured over the Chinese frontispiece. "The Great Leader's handwriting... Note the flow of the characters. Quick and decisive. No pissing about for our Chairman Mao." Then he got to the first annotated page and leaned forward carefully.

"*Liebe Yakov... gedenken die ven az mir kleine kinder...*" He bent, with Bob's face close to his, over the glass, losing himself in the minute flow, breathing heavily, interjecting every now and then a deep sigh, an "ah" or an "oh," shaking his head, scratching at his eye, trying to catch the tear before it even started,

"A *nayches*," he murmured, "a *nayches*... a real treasure, can you believe this...? Looking up at Bob, at me. "*A yid is tomid a yid...*" He took his time, and eventually Bob straightened up and said, "I'll go and make us a coffee." I sat with Yonni as he turned the pages meticulously, with the unexpected light touch in his fingers of a man used to fragile materials.

"The Prof would have absolutely loved this. He would have wanted to add a new volume. We had very little on China. What could we do? They didn't persecute Jews. A little trouble, after the Tang Dynasty. In the auto-da-fé of the Buddhist books, they added the Koran and the Torah. They just thought it was all the same. Wipe the old system to bring back Confucian truths. Even the Japanese were not Jew-haters. They bought into the Protocols and the entire Jewish plot, but that just convinced them the Jews were super smart and should be brought on board their own project. It was only after their Nazi friends told them Jews were nichts-gut that they reverted to Plan A—kill everybody. But their 'Jews' were of course the Chinese. There was a Doctor Ho in Vienna, the Chinese consul, who signed thousands of visas from nineteen-thirty-eight, on the assembly line. So they could get to Shanghai. Maybe we need a companion volume, Jew-Lovers. It would be a slim publication, I can tell you."

Not much change here, after all. I asked him about Gramby and the archive. He said the Lincoln Center library had been reor-ganized during the year, and it might be worth my while checking again for the missing Ace Harrington tape. Some of that material had gone online, but so far only music recordings. You could listen to all the scratchy old 78 recordings on your computer; it was like hearing Ma Rainey singing from Mars. I was surprised that he knew about Ma Rainey, but I suppose nothing about my uncle's chosen guardian should surprise me any more. I turned down dinner at the local bagel noshery and rejoined Claire at Empire Szechuan. When I told her Yonni was now gay and living with a rabbi from New Jersey, she simply said, "Honey, this is New York."

There was nothing new at the archive. I had squeezed it dry, Gramby-wise. There was endless DeMille, but that led nowhere but to my father's grave.

We stayed in New York through Christmas Day and New Year's. In memory zone, Times Square—42nd Street—was no longer the shabby sleazebag alley of our youth, but a new dream of a coming gilded century, beset by new facades and multivision screens, the old whore decked out in new sequins, Disneyfied from top to tail. Temperatures dropped duly to freezing, but the people stood packed like sardines, cheering the countdown to the third millennium blues. And the band played on.

Go Yuan continued to email me with more information gleaned, the past receding and more memories loosened in the new China, more stories and outspoken witness of the years her grandfather had never talked about—his years of rejection and humiliation, his betrayal by the cause for which he had risked all. The rehabilitation, which her father was granted in his own father's name, but never elaborated on, as it too was a further humiliation, the moment when so many people were told that their suffering and their rejection was canceled and all the years of fear and terror were for naught, merely a mistake that the state had made and then simply unmade, blaming it all on the old Gang of Four. She was still working on the third section of the story, but had been slowed down by overwork due to the proliferating legal troubles of so many ordinary folk falling short of the new social skills required in the dispensation of capital...

Fang Ling died in early January, soon after we returned from New York. She had simply drifted away, among her old portraits and posters, the glories of old, the Monkey King lifted to heaven, the rebelious Red Lantern flying over enemy lines. There had been a big feature in the Beijing dailies, and a memorial performance of *The Peony Pavilion* was planned for the summer in the Opera House, in her honor. China was reconnecting to her past.

February was dire that year in England. The winter clock, mandating the usual darkness at noon, was unusually onerous, given that the short days were consistently gloomy, and the usual sunlit days that sometimes lifted the spirit in that month did not arrive. One morning, at 6 o'clock, still pitch dark in Finsbury Park, the phone rang, and I struggled to adjust to the familiar but unfamiliar voice of Tsadok, my Aunt Sarah's second son. I listened to him for a while and then turned over and croaked at Claire, "They want me to go to Jerusalem."

"What is it?"

I have been pondering the answer to that question all my life. I have tried thinking of it, looking at it, photographing it, listening to it, copying it. But the one who had the easy answers had succumbed to the inevitable before me.

"My brother had a stroke. A big one. It looks like he won't last the day."

Finally it comes home to the heart. My brother died while I was in flight, on the British Airways overnight schedule that heretics like me use on Friday nights to travel free of the black hats, who will not travel on the Sabbath. This was a Tuesday night, but on the Wednesday, at five in the morning, when the plane touched down at what once was Lod Airport, but was later named after my Aunt Sarah's idol in the Labor Zionist movement, David Ben-Gurion, I turned on my mobile phone to catch a text from Tsadok: "Yitzhak passed two pm. Call me on landing."

I was just rising from my seat, all the passengers around me shifting about, emptying the overhead lockers and girding up for the exit, when I read the call. I felt the air expelled from my mouth in a cross between a grunt and a sigh, after a direct punch to the stomach. The new airport terminal had just opened, a massive ornate construction, with direct through gates and an interminably long walkway between the plane and the entrance hall, a complete change from the previous provincial gateway where armed guards ushered one onto buses that drove travelers two hundred yards to the entry point. Now it was a prestigious, ultra-modern cavern, on a Chinese scale, designed so that Israel could be, when peace dawned by some miraculous dispensation, a vast hub for all the nations east and west, north and south. At 5 a.m., the arrivals hall was a gigantic open space with Karnak-sized columns, a drizzling fountain and a few airport seats, with a small cafeteria marooned in the center.

Everything seemed intensely tactile: the ugly green plastic chairs of the café stall, the banter of the taxi drivers waiting for customers, the array of yesterday's pastries in the plastic counters and the giant lit panels showing a row of grinning youngsters, advertising the Cell-com mobile company, the names of the youths emblazoned on their T-shirts: Bobi, Roni, Dudu, Baby and Ruti. Their slogan was *"Ha-ahava shelkha khozeret"*—"Your love is returning." I felt a strange surge of affinity with these strange creatures, since however synthetic their commercial joy, the images themselves were vibrant, against the void into which my brother had disappeared. A beautiful and commanding woman's voice boomed out: "Attention please, carrying weapons is prohibited in all the terminal halls, thank you for your cooperation."

You're welcome. I called my ever-efficient cousin and Tsadok told me nothing could be done. "The blow was massive. The funeral will be around noon. You know the drill. Jerusalem, no mucking about. Take the taxi direct to the house. I'll be there. Dina and the rest are in shock. I saw him last week and he was OK. The usual kvetchting but nothing abnormal. They'll be glad you came. A brother is a brother. You have only one and that's it."

The service taxi ride around the city, which drops each passenger or batch at their exact destination, provided a somber tour of half a dozen of the new neighborhoods that sprung up in the last three and a half decades, east and west of the original city. Great conurbations of stone and concrete, entire districts that seemed nothing but new seminaries, yeshivas of the courts of so many competing rabbis. Where is the Sadagura, whom my grandfather worshipped, in the chapter Kolya cut from his own journal? A city in which the past, not the present, let alone the future abides.

I was the third to be dropped off, after a long diversion around the center of town, along the first districts to be thrown up after the Six-Day War, and on to a six-lane freeway, across the bridge that now hid the Arab village of Shuafat behind a slatted fence, then snaked up the hill towards Gilo, now twice the size it was when I had last come here, after my mother's passing. We continued up the hill with the separation wall, now a complete enclosure, locking out the unseen neighbors.

An instant immersion in the extended family. The Gurevits name, now set to last for generations of genuflecting lads, bending and swaying, calling out the words of comfort from the words that never change or waver, unequivocal in their foundation and meaning:

"Our father our king, open the gates of heaven to our prayer...

Our father our king, do not turn us back empty-handed from your presence...

Our father our king, remember that we are dust...

...for the sake of those who were slain in your Holy Name...

...for the sake of those who walked through fire and water to sanctify your Name...

...avenge before our eyes the blood of your servants that has been shed...

...for your sake, if not for ours...

...for the sake of your abundant mercies..."

How to explain to all my secular brethren out there, the cut and the uncut, to Claire, to Amanda, to the playwrights and protestors and companions and friends of the oppressed and the disinherited, that all this had very little to do with their mantras of state and nation, with armies and money and colonial ambitions and projects, not even with the pioneer dreams and aspirations of Sarah or even the sectarian nationalist fervor, the blood and fire of Kolya, but with these age-old lines, the unshakeable commandments spun off from the finger of fire on Mount Sinai, and all that followed, not in the ersatz voice of Cecil B. DeMille but the unchangeable Truth of the Name...? All in the interior, not the exterior...

Wish you were here, Claire, wish you were here. One needs to learn the lesson.... "It's not business, only personal...."

We climbed into a set of cars to get to the funeral. Tsadok drove me, with his wife, Aliza, and his sister Rivka, looking old and drawn, no longer the flighty cousin of old times. Everybody looking shocked and tired on a pure blue, early spring Jerusalem day. Visibility for miles, clear across the Wall, the Arab villages, the Judean hills, across the dip of the Jordan, full on to the distant mountains of Moab. The entire crucible. All converging on the mortal hub, the vast cemetery of the Hill of Rest, across the valley from the military section. Not for him the alien plains of Tel Aviv, the final destination of our father and my mother; theirs was a new family plot in the heartland, the City of God, the altar of Abraham. I let Tsadok talk, which was his default mode, the solution to all his problems. It tamped down his emotions, so that they sunk deep, where he could not be harassed. He gave me the blow-by-blow—of the sudden failure, the fall in the house over dinner, the rush to the hospital, the call to his office. The traffic jams, even at night, to Jerusalem. "Nine o'clock in the evening, can you believe it?" He told me to pay no attention if his son, the fanatic Eli, and his even more fanatic grandson, Yakir, glared at me throughout the ceremony, as they had at the morning prayer, where I had sat aside, watching. "To them, you are the worst of the worst," he explained. "An absolute traitor. No *kipa*, no flag, no faith, married to a Christian, no children—that's at least in your favor... You're one notch down from Adir, whom Eli now hates as much as he hated Rabin and Peres. Adir is now the government delegate to the talks with Abu Mazen, on the side of course, officially they're still not negotiating. Sharon needed a reliable stooge to do the stuff the Americans wanted him to do, but he doesn't. Very dicey after the Gaza withdrawal. It all continues the same way with Bibi. Adir was in Ramallah last week, eating shawarma with them all and drinking arak. It's all bullshit, you know. They all know each other. If they wanted to do a deal they could do it in three hours. But our lot up there," waving back towards Gilo, "they would scream and shout and pull down the house. Still, be nice to Eli, he's my son. The young one's from another planet. You're not wearing your only shirt, are you?"

He glanced at me, but I reassured him that I'd remembered the drill, the gashing of the lapel, the stern sign of the mourning. We headed up the hill, past the gravestones. There was little time to lose. Whoever could be gathered was gathered. Some faces were familiar, if drooping with a few more lines, others were Yitzhak's fellow congregants at his *stiebel*. The rabbi of the Hevra Kadisha, the burial society, came up to me and asked, "You are the brother?" He gathered myself and the three sons, and we went up the path into a small unadorned structure. There was space for a few benches and a small podium, with an alcove behind it. He said, "Who is identifying the body?" I stepped up with the elder son, Yosef, already a heavily bearded "black," almost my age. He was pretty much a stranger to me, but we hugged, and he pressed my shoulder with sympathy. "This is the most difficult moment," he said. We stepped into the alcove. My brother Yitzhak was laid out in a simple cloth, on a stone slab. Two "guardians" who were sitting in the alcove left when we came in. The rabbi drew down the cloth over the face. It was very white, as if the man had not spent his entire adult life living in the Middle East sun. His eyes were closed. He was very still.

We both certified that this was Rabbi Yitzhak Ben Baruch Gurevits, my brother, his father, may his memory be blessed. Then the rabbi covered the face again. He explained the procedure, the gathering, the obsequies, the family and friends' comments, then the transfer to the grave, a short carriage in the van, with the mourners following by foot for about three hundred meters. He took a knife and slit both our lapels, then pulled the tear down to the bare chest. "You keep it this way," he said. "Seven days of the sitting. Then on the seventh day the gathering again at the graveside, completion of service. The Lord will console you with the mourners of Zion and Jerusalem."

The body was brought into the small hall and laid out before us, naked under the cloth. Yosef spoke about my brother's godly attributes, his adherence to the faith, his great knowledge of Torah and scriptures, his mediations between disputants and his calm conduct in resolving problems and helping any person in need or distress, his great love for his family, his loyalty to his country and the purity of his soul. I told Yosef I would not speak, and he did not press me to. He said, "It's good that you came."

People I had never seen came up to comfort me. The rabbi and others transferred the body into the blue van marked with the words "Righteousness shall walk before him," and took the body up the hill, towards an open mound, with another empty slot beside it. Two spaces ready, one hole dug, the other for the wife Aliza. The proliferating children would have to be accommodated elsewhere. Space was at a premium in the Holy City. The more the living, the more the dead.

The final moves were quick and rigorous. The burial rabbi said the last prayer, the apology to the deceased in case during the cleansing and preparation of the body the attendants had offended inadvertently, presumably by contact with his forbidden parts. Then, as her children held Dina fast, the bearers tipped the body swiftly into the hole and then lifted away the covering shroud. They then filled in the grave at great speed, as some mourners came up to add their spade-full. Dust to dust, earth to earth. The sky was radiant. But somewhere not far down the hill, a bulldozer never ceased from work, turning over new ground and creating more spaces for those who would inevitably follow.

The world is not a global village after all. Back in London, Claire shows me more emails from Go Yuan, telling of her plans to apply for a visa to visit the U.K. and Europe in the summer, and that we should all travel together to Celovest. She had faith that the Source would tell us something. Who knows what we might find? I told Claire it must be a Buddhist or Taoist hangover, that the spirits still stay in place. How could I explain to her by email about Jerusalem, New York, Los Angeles or Moscow, let alone the kibbutz at Deganiah? But Claire said my time was running out. This time I would not be able to sidestep...

Claire returned to the RiverWharf cycle of plays by women, including playwrights from Senegal, Sri Lanka, Bolivia, Japan, Shanghai and New Zealand, as well as two of Amanda P.'s own alluvial voices from the Deep South, Detroit and New York.

Yours, back to work at the film school. Back to the frame. The new generation, elbowing up from the ground floor, climbing to my booth, hungry for skills. The generation of images, floods of data, information overload, the sky's the limit. But what are they so eager to say? I talk to them about cinematographers, about Gregg Toland, Russell Metty, James Wong Howe, Gabriel Figueroa, Vittorio Storaro, Otello Martelli, who shot *La Dolce Vita* for Fellini. I even talk about William "Boris" Gore, and all the advice he used to give me when I was swinging out of Melchett Street to the beaches with my old three-lens eight-millimeter. "Hold the camera steady and don't bullshit." Not as easy a maxim to follow as one thought, and nowadays operators seem to be expected to shake the camera around to make the image more "real." Even Hollywood blockbusters do it, because they want the audience to think them "authentic" and disguise their zillion-dollar budgets in fudge. The only one who could have done this handholding the old Technicolor camera would have been Hercules, on one of his better days.

Even in this shelter, Celovest beckoned. A second-term student from Romania, Andrei, to whom I had let slip my Moldovan origin and some of the coils of the family tale, proposed using our quest as a subject for his third-term documentary movie. He volunteered to drive me, along with Claire and Go Yuan, if she turned up, from Romania into Moldova, in late July or August, during the term break. His home city, Iasi, was close to the border, a mere hop across the river Prut. We could do the whole trip there and back in two days, and even extend it, if I wished, into Ukraine, to search for the mythical Gurevits source, wielding his own camera on the way.

Fate was closing in on me, from every direction. Claire was bullish on coming around. She would probably have enough time for a short break during the summer, but no more than a week. The studio's finances were shaky, but not yet desperate. There was a trip to Hamburg to be carried out, and to Munster, a university town whose main attractions were the Anabaptist cages that still swung over the town hall, although devoid of heretical villains. Ego te absolvo. We spent the Easter break mulling over our sins. All that might have been achieved, if we had achieved it. The Gurevits Project, festering in disuse. Write it down, Asher, write it all down. We can adapt it. A series of plays, rather than one. One part for each Gurevits sibling: Boris's long haul from east to west, Sarah's pilgrimage, Kolya's savage voyage to the Lena goldfields. Judit's story, in all its glory. The missing Zev, and overall— Gramby, the magician whose last trick was his most effective: to vanish into thin air. And if we're doing it, it's showtime for you too, Asher, all the parts you failed to tell: the missing links, your own early immersion, the military years, the Six-Day War. The "secret book," my own cut-down diary. She threatened to take it away one day and have it translated by her Israeli friend Dalia, who was preparing a feminist Palestine performance in song, poetry, witness readings and dance. I had to hide the file deep in the "outtakes" cupboard…

In June, Go Yuan wrote that her trip was on: She had received both her U.K. and Schengen visas and would be flying direct from Shanghai to London in mid-July.

On July 12, war broke out again over Lebanon. The Israelis claimed a cross-border raid by Hezbollah had killed and captured Israeli soldiers. The Hezbollah leaders claimed the Israelis had crossed the border into their side. Their militia forces began firing rockets from southern Lebanon into Israeli border towns and further south, hitting Haifa. The Israeli Air Force launched bombing raids deep into Lebanon, hitting the airport and blasting the villages of southern Lebanon and the residential parts of Beirut. But the rockets continued to fall in their hundreds, day after day. The entire population of northern Israel descended into shelters.

Cluster bombs rained down on Lebanon like confetti. As in Lebanon I, in 1982, their effect was horrific, each shell opening to hundreds of bomblets that would often lie unexploded in fields and hillsides and streets, where children would pick them up and be killed. Hezbollah killed dozens, the Israeli Air Force killed hundreds. The usual multiple eyes for an eye.

Once again, we marched. The usual route in the West End. Gather at the Thameside Embankment down from Charing Cross station and stride up Whitehall, pause to shout at Downing Street, continue past Trafalgar Square, down Piccadilly towards Hyde Park, trying to avoid marching side by side with politicians and persons you do not wish to be seen dead with. Mingling with large clumps of Muslim protesters in full flow, veiled women pushing prams with bloodied dolls to represent dead Lebanese babies, and idiots with fake plastic bombs strapped to their chests with the label "Martyrdom Bomber." Sidestepping all these, Claire and I spied more familiar faces: Shai Baer was there with his daughter Aliza, and Gershon of Gershon and Link, Moshik, Mansur, Farida and even Sargon, who was said to have decamped to the Philippines over the past ten years, and all looking as if, like the young Orson Welles, they had just emerged from the makeup studio having been transformed into the aged Charles Foster Kane. All the sagging jowls, crow's feet, white hair. Shai's bald head itself was like a wrinkled map of a new earthquake zone. Holding aloft the same old banners.

"We meet again, in the same situation," said Moshik, squinting to see if we were really the same. "It doesn't change," said Mansur. "Only the facade slips. The teeth, the lungs, the polyps. Only the situation is mummified."

"You're not in L.A. anymore?" I asked Gershon. "Where's Link?"

"He divorced," he said. "He's a child psychologist in Tel Aviv. Alma kept the kids."

Farida introduced a fresh-faced, dark-eyed girl to us, who was holding a card commanding "ISRAEL OUT OF LEBANON!"

"My granddaughter, Amina."

It goes on… "I saw the two plays you put on about Iraq," Shai told Claire. "They were good stories. The one about the Iraqi volunteer who went to fight in Palestine, and the one about going off to eat magic mushrooms in the Philippines. Sargon can tell you all about that."

"I flew away and I came back to Earth," said Sargon, who now resembled an old elf who had tasted immortality but had decided it was too much of a burden. "They're promising to increase the old-age pension."

"He's a Labor voter," explained Farida.

"The revolution abandoned me before I abandoned it," said Sargon.

"I hear your brother died," Shai said to me. "I'm sorry to hear it. Is that the religious one?"

"The only one I have," I said. "Or had. A stroke took him."

"A brother is a brother," said Farida. She gave me a hug and took Claire's hand. The crowd pressed us on, down past Hatchards, the Royal Academy and the Ritz Hotel. Shuffling on, the mortal remains of the Hub. Merging with the crowd calling around the roundabout, swallowed in the vast greenness of Hyde Park. Filing through the gate past the age-old booths of the vendors of all possible political causes, the British Left in all its misglory of bent and ashen figures thrusting forward the latest edition of The Socialist Worker, The Weekly Worker, The Socialist, The New Worker, The Socialist Standard, Workers' Power, The Proletarian, Class Struggle, Marxism Today, the Socialist Resistance, Challenge, Fightback, The Red Flag and countless flash-sheets from whatever minuscule fraction might still survive in the heart and soul of some stubborn militant who will never give up the fight! On the other side of the gate, the red-shirted stalwarts of the Islamic ginger groups, the Muhajiroun, the Hizb ut-Tahrir, dreaming of caliphates. The yellow flag of Hezbollah flying proudly not far from Shai Baer's head. For a moment, it flutters just adjacent to his Hebrew banner reading "Time to Wake Up From Tyranny!" But then it is whisked away again, as another group forms to break away from the main march and stride down past Knightsbridge and the Albert Hall towards the Israeli Embassy off High Street Kensington.

"You have to accept the confusion," said Shai, shrugging at the receding vanguard of God's army, addressing Farida's young inheritor. "The Israelis didn't want to make peace with King Hussein, so they got Yasser Arafat; they decided that didn't want to make peace with Yasser Arafat so they got Hamas; they didn't want to talk to Hamas so they get Hezbollah, who don't need to talk to anybody. The cycle continues."

"Lecture number twenty-one," said his daughter Aliza.

"But it doesn't have to be like that!" said Amina.

"Ah!" said Shai with a shrug, as the march of the elder veterans stalled by the hot dog stand, where a long line had already formed.

"This is where we face the serious choices," said Gershon. "Either an early bite or go up to listen to George Galloway and the guys on the podium shouting 'Takfir'!"

"It goes with the territory," said Shai.

"There's a place across the road," Mansur said, "near the Curzon, which is cheaper than the posh Lebanese spots around it. It's the Saudi Embassy there, they drive up the prices. They do an excellent pigeon, and stuffed chicken. Remember the Arab League occupation? We had a lunch there when the thing began to run down..."

Thirty years ago! We had more energy then, running up and down the stairs twelve times a day, and much greater reserves of righteous anger. The civil war in Lebanon. The Syrian invasion of Beirut. Then 1982. Are we ever doomed to repeats?

"We're going to march on to the embassy," said Farida. "Let the police stop us if they want to."

From the podium, one could already hear the drone of the speeches, the claque's responsive cry of "Allah hu akbar!" and the polite clapping of the English section.

"Well, Asher," Claire asked, "what is it going to be—police clubs or pigeon?"

We stood, treading the well-worn grass, at the accustomed fork in the road...

Celovest and Beyond the Infinite...

Asher:

The road from Iasi curls northeastward along a green plateau to-wards the border, a comfortable, modern, freshly asphalted way. The busy city of culture, cathedrals, museums, languid lunches on shady terraces, the acceptable past preserved and the unac-ceptable years scrubbed clean, slips behind, the last bastion of the European Union before the border post that guards the old world. Within half an hour, no more, a shaded glade approaches where a handful of cars are drawn up at the Romanian side of the border. At a small whitewashed booth, the languid officer is in no great hurry to peruse Andrei's sheaf of documents, his driver's license, vehicle registration, insurance, student papers, passport. The purpose of the journey is half evident in the bland, smiling faces of the three tourist passengers, Claire and I on our best cus-toms post behavior, Go Yuan, unused to crossing from one nation to another except over the semi-hostile parameters that divide Taiwan from China, or the whole wash of the Pacific further east. But she is nevertheless inured to long pauses, poring over the Freytag und Berndt combined map book, the full version, with all its semi-paved trails.

"I have so often wondered how my grandmother could have so easily become Chinese," she said, "but I am beginning to un-derstand. This is before modernity. One can change cultures, if the economics are the same. How many Jews do you think we will find today in this country?"

"One," I told her, "once we manage to cross the border. I sup-pose you can still find some remainers in Kishinev. Not counting the Israeli Embassy. You have to fast-forward a few decades for the denouement."

"Don't listen to him," Claire said. "The nearer he gets to what he regards as 'home,' the more Mister Pessimisto takes over. You have to keep an open mind."

Not when the sliding doors are closing. The Romanian customs agent, having rummaged through the back of the Peugeot, finally decides there is no point dissuading us from the futility of our journey. We inch forward, the fresh asphalt giving way almost immediately to a torn, potholed road. Two hundred meters to the Moldovan border post and another halt behind two German cars and a van. The van has been pulled over, and three military types have unleashed two skinny dogs upon it, sniffing the tires, the chassis and inside, while the burly, bald driver stands by calmly smoking under a tree.

Andrei is very nervous, since he has heard so many tales of Moldovan police harassment, extortion and general petty malfeasance in Europe's poorest country. He is nervously fingering a fifty-lei note, but I have advised him to allow the natural course of events to unfold. Eventually, the Moldovan dogs give up on the suspect van, and the hulk, flicking his last butt in the gravel, climbs aboard and rattles off, allowing us to be waved through next.

No welcomes and no rejections. The landscape alters, as if flicked by the magician's cape, and we are bucking over the road up from Скулень. The world is instantly Cyrillisized, the road bumpy, the verges rough and ragged, the fields gaunt to the horizon, the cars few and far between, maneuvering around ramshackle horse-drawn carts whose drivers peer out of brown-faced stubble. The effect is immediate, rather like those old cartoons in which the Road Runner runs out of Technicolor into a black-and-white world just before the Coyote spirals out of frame entirely, into the abyss.

Go Yuan, a quicker Cyrillic reader than I, shakes her head at the post-border signs, matching the locations to her maps and mark of the lost village that has been for her a zone of myth for so long:

"I can't believe it—only four-hour drive from here to Celovest. In China that's a visit to a friend."

She had already mapped out the entire area along the arterial road from Balti to Floresti, following the parallel railway line that Holocaust websites revealed as the route along which the Wermacht and the SS moved their troops. We stopped at the precise station at which, a generation earlier, Uncle Kolya had been shipped on to the Dniester to start his journey to the Galician front of World War I. She had found an ex-Soviet, now Moldovan airfield featured in the United Nations program of minefield clearance of the debris of the Moldovan civil war of 1992, alongside the nearby village of Marculest, site of the Transdiniestria camp. Celovest no longer featured, having been incorporated into the small region between the twin villages of Marculesti-Baltinesti and the larger town of Floresti.

There was an empty space on the map, detailed as it was. One could see the blue line of the river that my father described in the earliest chapter of his remembrance, which seemed to be called the Reim and meandered on down halfway to Kishinev. We had not yet decided whether we would turn south to the capital, which seemed an unappetizing ex-Soviet troglodyte mini-metropolis of housing blocks, banks, shebeens and whorehouses, or head on into the unknown, crossing the Dniester either at Soroka or the picturesquely named Moghilev-Podolsk into Ukraine: en route for the truly mythical source of Morachwa, named by Grandma Judit, which Go Yuan has identified as a tiny spot on the map currently named Murafa." Deep in the steppes, in the direction of Vinnitsa, Hitler's forward headquarters in the invasion of the USSR in June 1942. Everything links up somewhere, to some disaster or other, until one somehow manages to peek behind the door…

But we are still in Moldova, the old Bessarabia, ever a stopgap between west and east… The old pressures that caused the sons and daughters of the rabbi, Avraham-Abba, with his Polish name of Gorwicz (as it was then spelled) to bring his wife, whose own birth name we do not know, towards this dubious shelter across the river, farther from the vengeance of czarist-leaning gentiles, to a new place, much the same as the old…

Andrei sped on, as fast as the road would allow us, some sections smooth, some virtually disappearing in a welter of gravel and stones. It was time for his preferred soundtrack, a CD of Moldavian folk music, the Zece Prajini band, which, he assured us, would take us all the way to Celovest. It was a manic sound, as if someone had given instruments to a group of people who had no idea how to play them, but were liberally supplied with vodka, so their enthusiasm never ran out. The music resonated with a savage joy and despair, and an indeterminate longing, probably for even more vodka, as well as the exquisite pain of the local soil. All the roots of our liturgy was somewhere in it, a kind of Scythian sound that had blasted across the limitless valleys and plains of the East.

Conveyed by the cacophony, we found ourselves driving through Balti, a conglomerate of Soviet block housing and indeterminate concrete, celebrating nothing, where we stopped for lunch after spying a large sign in blue and gold spelling Пица Италиано. It was surprisingly good, the plastic interior busy with young boys and girls jamming the tables, sipping Coca Cola through straws. I remembered that this was the town where the family photograph that had ended up in Cecil B. DeMille's collection had been taken, the Jewish urban center of the region. But whatever had been here of old was long long gone, wiped and replaced by the second city of the Moldovan Socialist Soviet Republic, which had slid into a bleak independence when Gorbachev's legacy tore it apart. Perestroika—that too is now the past.

With no reason to linger, we made our way down long, dismal avenues towards the east city exit, the sign that pointed towards Флорешть. Flicking on the Zece Prajini once more, Andrei took us over the line of the historic railway that continued parallel and south of the road. Go Yuan grew more pensive as we approached the destination, probably taken aback by the poverty of the few people we passed along the road: some workers in the fields, men in baggy pants and women in headscarves, small children with a few straggling goats, drivers of tractors or trucks that seem to have been culled from a museum of ancient agricultural implements, the by now familiar rickety carts, wobbling on small rubber wheels. Her first glimpse of a European peasantry, stuck in the time warp of fallen empires, a true shock for a stranger whose view of civilization is a solid curve up from the follies and deprivations of the past to a new dispensation, the battlements of an ascending east. The wailing clamor of the Moldavian tinkers, singing of God knows what in the wind...

The clashing chords almost made us miss the turn, a narrow road behind a scrubby glade with an arrowed sign pointing to Маркчлесть. Angling past a slow-moving cart piled with something that may have been an old car battery, and the usual curious look, the road swiftly crossed over the same railway track once again, with Go Yuan pointing towards a small hut in the distance that seemed to lean over the trace of a platform. Was this the place from which Uncle Kolya was whisked away to the czar's war? Bumping over the track, a crumbling silo to our right heralds a row of one-story village houses with blue-painted doors and fruit trees. Within a few hundred meters is a small gravel square and what might be a store, with two languid youths propped up against it, idly watching us pause, then turn left, towards a clump of small farming houses with peeling walls and corrugated iron roofs, set behind leaning wood picket fences amid wild grass and rough pathways.

Behind the fences, a few older women in loose smocks and some unshaven men in open shirts and rumpled trousers gave us the familiar brief look of vague contempt before glancing elsewhere, as if the day's diversions warranted something better than another bunch of lost tourists. But we had to stop short, as the road petered out at a hillock, in the midst of which a granite stone was set in a mound of earth bearing a plaque, beyond which an odd series of wooden poles topped with unlit light bulbs led downhill towards open fields...

At the house closest to the plaque a balding, sturdy old man in a string vest in which tufts of gray hair were tangled, his lower limbs rammed into army camouflage pants, leaned over his front gate, glowering at us. We waved to him but he remained impassive. I took the Canon out to start recording, and Andrei took out his film school camera as we trudged up to the slab. It bore a legend carved in three languages—Romanian, Russian and Hebrew, with one word spelled out in bold, center:

TRANSDNIESTRIA
ТРАНСДНИСТРЯ

Andrei read the legend aloud, from the Romanian: "In this location many thousands of people were killed in the years nineteen forty-one and nineteen forty-two by the fascists." And the same message spelled out in the Hebrew.

We walked up a few paces to look out over the hillock, towards the open landscape. The wooden poles marched off down the slope and then a plain of overgrown moss and grass, marshland stretching down to the river, two or three kilometers further west, beyond which was the next clump of houses, fences and rooftops. Close by the river, we could see a group of young men and boys paddling in the water, and as we watched one of the kids leaped off a small stone bridge, to a loud chorus of cheers. From the village came the sound of lowing of cows, and between us and them a lone horse, moved about in the low grass, flicking its mane.

Go Yuan turned her map over, puzzled.

"This is where it should be," she said, pointing.

Celovest. *Der heim.* But I could see, in the zoom of the camcorder, as Andrei filmed me filming, the name of the next village, carved on the stone fence of the small bridge: Baltinesti. There had been nothing between the marked village we passed through and the next, across water that seemed no more than a creek, except the tall poles with lights connected by a single wire, the horse, some sheep behind a thicket and a gaggle of geese that appeared from the grass to our left and cackled away through a break in the fence.

If I scanned carefully, I could see the stumps of some concrete blocks in the grassland, fallen steel girders, broken bricks, maybe some trace of a house that once upon a time stood on this ground.

Andrei walked up, waving us towards the old man. "Everybody speaks Romanian here. Bessarabia—it was Romania before the Russians came."

In 1812. Memories can be either as long as the Danube, or as short as the last bend in the road. The old man also spoke Russian, since he said he had been in the Russian army for forty years, retiring as an infantry Major, his last call to action having been on the Chinese border in the last years of Mao. Manchuria is never so far away. Go Yuan, intrigued, asked him questions in Russian, while Claire and I stood by as the eternal clients of translation, creatures of our own ragged limits. The old man was in charge, it appeared, of the monument, which was on the edge of his patch, which had been his father's before him. The monument was a stopgap before a new, proper monument that was going to be erected by the government. The Minister of Foreign Affairs had visited, along with an Israeli representative and two Romanians, to prepare a proper plinth, with national flags, and a large stone that would mark the wartime "lager."

Celovest, oh yes, there had still been some houses there, in the field, when he was a boy, but they were derelict; wild foxes lived in them, and children played there and smoked cigarettes out of sight of their elders. The Germans had built the lager on top of the ruins of the Jewish houses of both villages. The Russians had decided to leave the site fallow and not build on the bones of those who had died there, back when it was the Moldovan SSR. He had never heard the name Gurevits. Some Jews had come back to Marculesti after the war, but mostly there was just the graveyard. People used to come on bus tours from Romania, Bukovina Jews and others who were survivors and their relatives, they came to pray on the site. There was still an old synagogue, which was now a school. He pointed out the way to the graveyard. Go Yuan told the old man that her grandmother had been born here and then went to China, and that my father was born here. He nodded solemnly, saying, "Da, da, da." All the people who come here looking for ghosts, disturbing the horses, the cows and the geese.

We trudged a couple of hundred meters to the graveyard, back the way we had come, and around another bend of quiet houses. Across the gravel path from another row of farmer's houses was a crumbling stone fence, beyond which the old graves huddled close together almost buried in a mass of overgrown weeds and thickets that had been partially cut down, but not cleared, so that one plunged knee deep in broken branches and thorns. Some of the old graves were bent over; others had fallen completely, lost in the scrub. Others were still upright, bearing their chiseled inscriptions: The Revered and Learned R' Yitzhak Ben Shmuel... the Important Woman Hava Bat Gershon... the Man, R' Nathan Ben Ya'akov... a Woman Sarah Feige Fleishman... I looked down at the dates in the Hebrew count, but none seemed to precede 1930. In fact, there was a preponderance of two dates on many of the graves: אצרת and בצרת—5,691 and 5,692, i.e., 1931 and 1932, which, faint memory reminded me, were the years of Stalin's Ukrainian famine, which must have swept across this southwest corner of the same borderless swath as well. Another cataclysm, which postdated the departure of the last of the family nucleus with its charged protons to worlds this side of the mortal coil or the other, so none would have been left here of our own foreshortened annals. But somewhere underneath this clutter, perhaps in the deepest section of these remains, buried under two meters or more of brushwood, might be the stones of the progenitors: Avraham Abba and Leah Gurevits, the rabbi and his widow. Unless there was another, separate cemetery for the vanished village, somewhere out there in the ploughed-over and abandoned fields.

"What do you feel, Asher, what do you feel?" Her eyes tear-glistened, Go Yuan makes her way over to stand beside me on one of the jutting graves; there is no foothold on the tangled ground between them. For a Chinese person, it is a great calamity to be unable to attend the graves of ancestors. I now see that this is the purpose of her visit. "They should clear this ground, and make it right."

The valleys of the old dry bones. People like my brother Yitzhak felt strongly that they should be among the hosts of their progenitors. The line stretching as far back as the Word of God records and mandates. Jerusalem, apex of the return. Perhaps I understand why my father stopped short of the holy city when choosing to live and die in the homeland, while my brother had to be at the font. A secular refuge by the salt smell of the sea. The sea leads elsewhere, the mountain binds one to the spot. Here there is neither, only the open steppe. The soul has long wandered, slipping off into the boundless space. The rolling wheat fields, the old Slav tunes, the wailing threnody of intoxicated gypsies.

"There's nothing left here. Let's just take our pictures and go."

We stop at the small village store, buying a few tomatoes and apples, some strange salami, Romanian cola and bottled water to stave off our nagging hunger, as two youths on motorcycles buzz up and down the dusty main drag, swerving around two dogs lying unfazed in the middle of the town's only crossroad. We wave at them as we leave, but they continue dragging, growling up, growling down. Andrei stops the car for Go Yuan at the railway, getting out to take a few last shots: the tracks, from low angle, growing tufts of weeds, the train from nowhere to nowhere, empty fields east and west. Sergio Leone, without the action. Even the gunmen who should be hanging out in the station, enduring the flies that buzz at their foreheads, all left town long ago. More images that will not stay in the frame.

There was nothing here to be found but absence. Still, Go Yuan is determined to press on. Less than one day's journey of discovery is not even the first step in China. One must continue—over the next hill, over the next great range of mountains, over the plains, across the deserts of no return, on through the Taklamakan, the Kyrgyz, the Altai, the Hills of Manchuria... Even though we know the world is round, this is only true for our latterday frequent flyer. For the footsoldier, the Earth is plainly flat.

She has a whole new sheaf of Internet printouts of the motherlode, the ultimate source, Morachwa, the Shangri-la of the Gurevitses, the place from which the young rabbi and his wife were thrown by sack and pillage across the steppes, from peasant hatred to a place then of greater placidity, another haven that might last a certain time, until the next upheaval. Or was there a more mundane motive? Seeking a new post,for a young religious functionary, a different, mercantile, commonplace reason to choose Celovest? Or were they heading for a further destination, into Romania herself, newly liberated from Turkish Ottoman rule? Was it better to be a Jew among the Moldavians? Or did they just toss a coin?

It's three against one, with Andrei joining the go-ons. I have reached a stop, but Claire is curious. She always wants to know more. Onward, onward. If we found nothing here, where all the stories come from, how shall we find any other, from whence no tales of any kind, tempting, adventurous, poignant, tactile, mysterious, ambiguous, palpably untrue or inconsistent, have emerged at all?

Onward. Onward. Andrei and Claire have researched this. It is a bane to be married to someone with an rare ability to organize things. I knew many people like this when I was in the army, who had a plan for everything and could foretell to a reliable balance of probabilities what result would emerge from which action, and what the future might be, even factoring in the unforeseeable, acts of God and other uninsurable circumstances that might be expected to arise.

They said they had it all under control. They had even scouted out a hotel, in Soroka, on the river border with Ukraine, from which Go Yuan had put together a route up the backroads to the target. The main concern was that we should not risk tangling with Moldova's evil twin state, Transdniestria, unrecognized by anyone except Putin's Russia and its independent twin, Belarus. Indeed, none of the tourist maps we had brought from London showed any trace of its ethereal borders. As if it were a mere figment of the Russian imagination, carved out of the new Moldovan republic as the last bastion of the Leninist empire...

Soroka town then. A modest hotel, small bare rooms, bedding down separated as boys and girls. Andrei snored, afloat in chords of Romanian light, while Claire and Go Yuan plotted next door. A cat peeked in through the tiny window, though it might have been a fox or a masked Transdniestrian spy. In my confused dreams there were gravestones, a great freeway, an old Hasid weaving his way through a horde of hooting cars. In the morning, protocol required that we visit the old Polish fortress, established in 1499, Andrei tells me, by Stefan the Great, a Moldavian patriot, and rebuilt in stone under Petru Rareș in 1543. A perfect circle whose five great bastions stand exactly equidistant to one another. It was held against the Ottomans by Jan Sobieski and resisted Peter the Great in 1711. Andrei had to film it, in a slow wraparound pan, despite my advice not to construct a shot that couldn't be cut. Then we had pizza again, and moved on in the early afternoon.

The hazards of navigating by Go Yuan's cyber chart become apparent once we cross into Ukraine at Jampol; another hour between border posts, the good road gives way to a subsidiary heading north at Klembovka. The true Ukrainian steppe shows up directly, a great open space under the sun, scraggy trees lining the road at intervals along swaths of flat fields. Our vision blurred by the constant jerking of the car over the barely surfaced road, we make slow progress, occasionally slower when stuck behind an ancient tractor or cart, or a leather-clad motorcycle rider with a sidecar of Second World War vintage, with matching goggles and cap. A cloud of dust loitering in the road ahead resolves itself into a small herd of cows coming up from the verge, driven on by an old babushka. We have to stop and wait, while the cows amble around us.

Three hours later we limp into Sharhorod, the nearest substantive town to the target, close to 5 p.m., with no onward prospect of a night stop aside from the sleeping bags in the trunk. A clump of housing blocks with a main street unencumbered by any attempt to entice visitors to stop over, neither inn nor eating place apparent, a nondescript town hall with a few people milling by its entrance and then the road leads suddenly out, towards the east. Go Yuan has a sheet of data on the historic attractions: the largest and best-kept Jewish cemetery in the region, and a side street with some surviving examples of old shtetl-type buildings. But I point to the time and wave on Andrei, sighing like a fatigued pasha from the backseat.

Onward, onward, past a field of scrubby sunflowers drooping in the lingering heat. From here, the way stretches into the vast Ukrainian hinterland, hundreds of kilometers west to Kharkov and what once was Stakhanov, north to Berdichev, Kiev and into Belarus, to Gomel, Mogilev and Minsk, then five hundred miles northeast to Orel, Tula, Moscow and another five hundred miles to Perm and the Urals. The Great Mother, empire of princes and czars, party chairmen and other human beasts whose pitiless gaze stretched forever under the traveling sun and the moon. All from these shamefaced sunflowers, turned around, facing the Earth...

What do you feel Asher, what do you feel? Tired and battered, from the pummelling of the road, the leg cramps, the throbbing arse. But the goal approaches, such as it is, the wild Jew chase, the anticlimax, the place that can only wheel you around to the start, the old Joycean riverrun, past Eve and Adam's, bringing us back by a commonplace spiral to the first page, back again. Go Yuan had a sheet on Murafa too, a Polish website cyber-translated into both Chinese and Pinglish. It seems the village was known from the fifteenth century, as Morachwa, on land belonging to the "family Yazlovetskis... In the XVII century, Murafa constantly invade with Cossacks, and in the XVIII with Haidamaks and rebel." It had fortifications, churches and monasteries, of which three still remain, the largest being the "Murafsky Dominican complex church of the Immaculate Conception of the Virgin Mary." It included "house Abbot, cells, belfry, gardens, founding 1627... at worship, sounds great body, beautiful women singing, all amounting to sense of grace." There was a palace, built by a General Joachim Potocki. Until the Polish-Russian wars of the eighteenth century it remained, with all the surrounding region down to the Bessarabian border, an integral part of Poland but was subsumed by Russia after the Third Partition of 1795. During the Stalin period, the village was renamed Zhdanov—like several others in the Soviet Union—after the chairman of the Russian Soviet Republic and a major instigator of the Great Terror. A number of Polish Catholic priests of the church at that time were arrested and executed or disappeared in the gulags. Jews seem to have always been present in the village, as they were throughout the region. Their part of the village was known as Merachwe" There seem to have been equal numbers of Catholic Poles and Jews until the outbreak of the First World War. All specific records appear to have been expunged, and the entire area was among the first regions to fall to the German invasion in June and July 1941.

Driving into the village, past the standard monument to the fallen Russian soldier awkwardly holding a rifle, looking out over the Murafa River, which passes under an old bridge flanked by weeping willows, their lower branches caressing the rippling waters. On either side small individual houses anchored to the flowing wheat fields among pleasant groves, brightly painted white walls and blue doors and window frames under clean slate roofs. Just below us a cow and two goats laze on the green sward that leads to the river's edge. A picture of rural calm at the end of the day, with the sun's rays sharp on the walls of the three churches, the Immaculate Conception clearly recognizable from Go Yuan's printouts, a Ukrainian orthodox spire behind a low stone wall, and another further away, at the north end of the town.

Our cameras whir in the comfort of the Frame. Over by the church, we can now see a group of people gathering, coming out of the leafy lanes, heading for some service or a market. Two women with children wait by a bus stop and the bus rolls up, over the bridge, a squat boxlike thing in dusty khaki, growling and spitting black exhaust. The women and children climb aboard and are whisked away. No one seems curious about newcomers. This is, after all, the local road to Vinnitsa, fifty kilometers further on, over the fields.

Claire waves me over. At a house close by the river bank, an old headscarved lady has been watching us from behind a blue gate. Go Yuan has walked towards her, eager to try out her Russian, though Andrei has warned us that Ukrainian is a wholly different language, though he speaks neither. The house is surrounded by an exquisite garden of blue, yellow and red flowers. The lady is a textbook babushka, wrinkled brown face with a kind smile and rather mischievous eyes. She is taken aback that it is the "oriental", not the "occidental" girl, who speaks to her. She does cast me a somewhat suspicious look, a kind of recognition, as if she has seen my type before and knows what I am after, better than I do myself. I assume Go Yuan will ask all the wrong questions, innocent as she is of all the hidden layers that lie below the sun-soaked beauty of a summer's afternoon in Podolia.

Where are the Jews? Are they still living here? This is the homeland of my great-grandparents. Does the name Gurevits ring a bell? Do not ask for whom the bell tolls, it has no interest or attention or message of any kind for the likes of you. These people have their own ancestral pain.

I hear Go Yuan repeating the words "ebrei" and "babushka" and "dedushka," and "kladbushe," for cemetery. The woman is shaking her head. Not here, not here. She waves her hand on, over the beautiful garden, over the neatly fixed roof, over the shining green trees, over the hills and fields. Somewhere else, over there. Go Yuan has a copy of the strange photograph of her grandmother, my Aunt Judit, with her Chinese husband, in the garden of the Lu Xun House in Shanghai. The old lady looks at it and nods. "Ah, Sina, Sina." As if everything is explained. People come from afar. They look for things that are not here. Maybe they were never here. Maybe they were. It was a long time ago. Many things happened. Hard times. Life is good now. Only the young people don't like it, it's too quiet here. They go away, looking for jobs in the cities. They go away, but we are here. She is so happy that people have come from so far away as London and China to admire her flowers. We should all stay for tea.

I wave my watch at Go Yuan. The day passing. Soon we shall see a glorious sunset. The squatting cows. The ducks in the river. Trees swaying in light evening-coming breeze. You don't understand this, cousin. All these villages and towns. Each loiters with its own ghost beside it. The bickering twins, attached by the umbilical cords of their interwoven affairs. Business, commerce, the legal tangles with authority, the Lord, the "Schlachta," the czars. Each answering to a separate voice calling them to account in their heads. The church, the synagogue, the Name, the Christ. Each blasphemous to each other, uneasy, uncomprehending, their old folk searing with unforgotten grievances, the young forbidden to each other, the middle-aged trudging through their daily grind. They weaved here for hundreds of years, buffeted by winds of change, rising and falling empires, wanderers from west, east, north, south. They never liked each other, but life was a harder mulch even than faith or mutual suspicions, although it fell prey when the ground shifted to clashing battle cries of near and far, when hate engulfed reason.

In the end, it was Hitler who simplified the equation. There is no "x plus y." No Slavs, no Jews, only an empty land that would await its Aryan conquerors. Uncle Kolya trod this graveyard thoroughly in, I think, Volume 17 of the opus, with his usual merciless detail, no crime unrecorded, no pain untallied, no case for retribution discounted...

Babushka does not know the answers. Nor did the priest, whom Go Yuan and Claire approached, in the strange belief that the Provoslav Church would enshrine an appropriate memory. Nineteenth-century records? He had no idea where those might lie. He recommended the Jewish graveyard in Sharhorod. Many of the old gravestones had been moved there. They went back more than two hundred years, he thought. He had not himself visited there, he explained to Go Yuan. Two old women, who were cleaning the church, moved between us, wagging their heads and whispering as they wielded soft cloths to polish the icons, the doleful saints and the suffering God and the Virgin, who looked down on us from their golden frames.

"I've had enough graves," I told Claire, before leaving them in the nave to admire the images, Andrei filming on, while I took the Canon out into the garden. The afternoon had now faded to a classic sunset from gold to red over the river, with the treetops silhouetted against the sky. Too picture-perfect. The white-walled houses, chickens rustling and dogs barking from the yards. More babushkas peeking over the gates. Andrei films it all. The stoppage of time. Then the night question: far too late and hazardous to drive back to Soroka along those pitted roads. Go Yuan suggested that we could probably stay in the village; one or more of the babushkas would most likely invite us to stay. The old reliable peasant hospitality. The idea filled me with a kind of horror: hours spent listening to the Ukrainian narrative, from childhood Stalin days through the reborn nation, baptized in democracy's pure waters. The Orange Revolution. Was this a welcome too far? Andrei seemed uneasy too, in this alien language, too akin to the Russian of his own tormentors, old sores opening up in the breeze. We both firmly opted for the sleeping bags in the open, with Claire giving me the quizzical eye, and Go Yuan sighing. But Andrei still had the deciding vote. We had our provisions from Marculesti, with some extra salami and fruit from Soroka, apple juice, and even a few strange beers. A bottle of Moldovan wine, with a corkscrew somewhere in the car's toolbox.

We drove out of the village northward, leaving it in silence and dark. Rectangles of light shone from the house windows not obscured by the trees, a cow lowed somewhere, and dogs intermittently barked. Adieu, strangers. Come back soon. Never. We stopped about a mile out of town, the road flanked by a pleasant open field, leading to an expanse of tall wheat, the stalks practically man-high. "Better than any hotel," Andrei enthused. I could see this was his aim all along. Discomfort under the stars. They did appear, in full splendor, as the night deepened and the temperature dropped, but not sufficiently to deter the little animals that crept and crawled from their shelters and fluttered over the steppe. Andrei was fully prepared. He had mosquito balm, repellant, itching cream, and a bright battery lamp which, he said, would draw the worst offenders to its gleam. But this soon turned out to be a false premise, and we settled down in itchy darkness.

Unable to sleep, I wandered through the wheat field. How far could one go, and be lost, devoured in the breadbasket of the Ukraine? Claire was sleeping like a baby, Andrei emitting his Romanian rhapsody and my Chinese cousin emitting small pop-pop-pop sounds out of the hood of her pouch.

The moon was a thin crescent, and the starlight cast the palest glow over the wheat. I hadn't gone very far among the stalks before I stubbed my toe. I moved my shoe along the obstruction and found its contours smooth. I kneeled down and felt around it. It was without a doubt a gravestone. I cursed my lack of foresight in setting out without a torch. The classic sucker in a third-rate horror picture who is first to be dispatched. I felt along the ground. There were other fallen gravestones, and, looming in the dark, others, not quite upright but not yet fallen, all over the field, among the stalks. My fingers moved blindly along the stones, feeling out the chiseled letters. Was this an Aleph, or a Shin? I remembered the joke about the tomb of Louis Braille in the Pantheon in Paris: They just turn the lights off and let the visitors feel their way. This was, without doubt, the "kladbushe," the old stones of "Merachwe," the stetl's rest, the final source.

I wanted to go back to get a torch, but having stumbled and fallen and felt around over the graves, I'd lost my sense of direction, and the moon was too low, even if I jumped among the stalks.

It was a somewhat stupid situation. I tried to remember the constellations that I'd devoured in Dad's atlas. I could tell the Big Dipper from the Little Dipper, or Pegasus, just about. Or the Milky Way itself, never visible in urban skies, but that wouldn't help me either, as I had no idea which part of the sky all these signs signified. Defeated by the wrong knowledge. A caveman would be better off.

The graveyard seemed to stretch forever; the stalks were now a little shorter, and I could glimpse the taller stones dully in the soft glow. At Marculesti, I had noticed some of the stranger aspects of these monuments—pillar-like stones carved like tree trunks, apparently denoting the more eminent dead of the community, among which I had spent some time looking for the progenitor rabbi. Who knows who might be here, more generations back, and what their untold tales were? There's no end to it.

There was a flutter, around me, as if something had brushed past. I flicked my shoulder, but there was nothing there.

I figured out that if I retraced my stumbling and found the first stone I had tripped over, I would know the direction back. Or failing that, I could shout, something like, "Hallo! I am lost in a graveyard!" Which was sure to get me ignored. Claire in deep sleep would not wake for the last trump, Andrei I knew was a deep-ender. Go Yuan was the only unknown quantity. But if she came over to me, we could end up, both Gurevitses, locked in our ancestral time warp, rooting around among the dynastic sepulchres. She might never want to go home.

The best solution, it seemed, was to find the high ground, and the road wouldn't be far off. But, this region being what it always was, high ground was pretty hard to find. I would venture, cautiously, in two or three directions, from a centrally recognizable structure; the tallest tree-trunk shrine would do.

There was a slight rise in the ground towards it, but there was something else too. The flutter again. A trace of movement. Something flickering beyond the stone. A flap of some sort of clothing. Something dark, but not too dark, standing out in the gloom. A man's cape…

The head came peeking around the headstone. A white-gloved hand. And a top hat. The face, pale as a full moon, lighting up the weedy plinth, a thermos flask set down beside the grave. I knew it well, it had been staring at me for ten years since I had blue-tacked it up on the wall in our living room in Finsbury Park.

"*Bonjour, mon cher neveu,*" he said softly, putting his finger to his lips.

"Ah, it's you."

There was no reason for surprise. Like a benign Bela Lugosi, he twirled his hand and motioned me over. That "Doctor Livingstone, I presume" moment. He pointed up towards the sky.

"It's easy," he said, with still a strong trace of that Eastern, Yiddish, Pale of Settlement accent. "Up there, it's Cassiopeia. Down a little way, Cepheus. Well over there, Cygnus. Follow it down—Lyra, Hercules, Corona Borealis, Serpens Caput. Why 'serpents kaput,' I don't know. It's just one of those strange things."

"I used to know it all by heart," I said.

"The things we used to know! Tell me about it. I used to know everything out of five books in the house. There was the big railway digest, the gazetteer of the world, the book of Russian towns and rivers, and that French book your father got about Paris buildings and fashion designs. What else did we need? Later I had everything in the Rue Jacob. All the secrets of life and death: the tables of Isis, Trismegistus, the diagrams of the pyramids, Pythagoras, Faust's notebooks, the kabbalah, the keys to Dante, the Rosicrucian codes, the alchemical formulas. I had a handwritten notebook of Houdini's secrets that I found in a flea market in Clichy, but it was not worth the money. He was just an actor, he knew how to sell his deceits. In the end I believed in too many things. Then I finally came to trust the Great Void."

"My father always thought about you," I said, "more than all the others. I found the notes that Aunt Judit wrote to you, in tiny writing in the margins of the Little Red Book that was printed in the tens of millions in China."

"A bestseller. I always wanted to write one of those. 'Annals of a True Magician in the Other Spheres.' But you can only be a true magician in this one. What people believe, that's what counts. What you know, that's not important. It dies with you, and poof, it's gone."

"I looked for you all over the world," I said, "in France, in America, in New York, in Los Angeles, in Shanghai. I found Ace Harrington's tapes. But there was one missing."

"He talked about me? He was a good friend. A bit dodgy with the cabinet and the pulleys, but a good spirit. A *gute neshomeh.*

What were you looking for?"

"Your dreams. Everybody said you dreamed. Dad wrote about it, and Judit, and Sarah. Uncle Kolya didn't believe in dreams, because they made him into an assassin. I was only missing Zev. He vanished into the dream. Do you know what happened to him?"

"He didn't dream. He wanted to make money. Buying and selling. He went away. I thought Yuditel knew."

"He disappeared in Harbin, in Manchuria, some time in nineteen thirty-two. When the Japanese invaded."

"I did dream of going to Japan. I saw some pictures, wonderful pictures. Crashing waves and samurai warriors. And those Kabuki plays. I saw one in Paris. Everything was fixed to perfection. There was never a mistake allowed, only ritual. If the Jews had been like that, we might have made something in the world. But it would have been terrible."

"It's called the State of Israel."

"Ah, politics. There's no magic in that. Only tsuris."

"I thought if I understood where we came from, I would understand where we're going."

He waved his hand, at all the shadows, the dim contour of stones in the field.

"This is where we come from, this is where we're going. A woman cries, and a small child comes out. What does it know? What will it ever know? Not very much, I can tell you. How far back do you want to go? *Bobeh mayses*— Grandma's tales. Once upon a time. Moses went up the mountain and got his marching orders. Do this, don't do that. *A schoeneh metsiyeh.* Smashing the idols. Worshipping the Great Nothing. The idols come back. Pogroms, exile. They go here, they go there. Into bondage, out of bondage. The class struggle. I read Marx too. Your father, he was the reader. Proudhon, Bakunin, Kropotkin. He ended up with— what was that camera book?"

"*The American Cinematographer Manual.*"

"*Schoen.* Learning a trade. Nothing wrong with that. I learned my trade pretty well. You are quite right, I had a dream. Magic is the liberation from slavery. This was my release from bondage. Better than the sick urge for revenge. That was Kolya's fire. He burned up in it. But it also made him strong. Like a tall tree that can't be chopped down. I loved him most of all, you know, because he burned with so much passion. Passion to do good, passion to do bad, in the end you can't tell the difference. You have to hold back, find the silence. I was looking for it all the time, but the noise was too loud all around me. Even resurrecting the dead just produced some cheap applause."

"I have a Chinese cousin, down the road here. Judit's granddaughter. Your great-niece, I suppose. She would say that Buddhism is what you were looking for."

"Too many priests. We have one God, they have several billion. It's too much. There are great secrets there. People used to know them, and now they only know imitations. You have to start with nothing to arrive at nothing. I read that Lao-Tse too. He who says he knows the way does not know the way. It must make sense in Chinese. We developed Yiddish, you know. A language of people who are resigned to chaos. Hebrew was the language of commands. Yiddish is for disobedience. Nobody speaks it now. They follow the stupidest idols but they think they're free. I'm a magician, I know all about illusions. You have to have the right equipment, then you can make people believe anything. Today they call it technology. I know, I read some magazines occasionally. I like the gossip too. Kings, queens, movie stars, celebrities. *Gurnischt fun gurnischt*. Dust to dust. Do you want to know your future?"

"Not really, Uncle Yakov."

He moved his cape to reveal a crystal ball shimmering with a vague inner light. "I cut my teeth on this," he said, "back in the old days, with the Irish sisters. Their mother was the original gypsy queen. Mrs Maguire. She was a card."

"What about tea leaves?"

"Ah, yes. Zuleika was the great expert on those. She used the Chinese leaves, oolong and pu-ehr. She took no prisoners with her readings. A little slip of a girl, telling some hulky stevedore that he would fall under the crane two days later and be crushed like a beetle. I remember the man laughed and paid her double. Then we read it in the newspapers. A small item, on the New York docks. Three men were killed in the same slippage."

"Zuleika... She's on my list of questions. She's in Ace's monologues. It's there in the hints, but we never got the story."

"Well, it was before his time. It didn't last long. A whirlwind romance. She was with Haji Ali's acrobats. A class act, amazing things on horses. He was an Albanian you know. Fiery people, not to be crossed. I was risking my life every time I crept into the tent. Zuleika. She was a real magician. Then she disappeared. Too many jealousies. There were all sorts of rumors. I was only one of many people who would look for her all over the place, in new variety acts, big time, small time, when circuses and freak shows came to town. The dime museums. The bearded lady Annie Jones, the Siamese twins Chang and Eng, Pasqual the Two-Headed Mexican, Chang the Chinese Giant, the Horvath Midgets, Smallest People in the World. Houdini started out as the Wild Man of Mexico you know. He wasn't for real, always a faker. But he knew how to play the newspapers. Clever beast. Zuleika became the Queen of the Future. Then she changed her name and disappeared. I dreamed of her so often. Alma used to scold me, in the dream. Alma knew all my secrets."

"What happened to her? What happened to both of you, in Paris, nineteen-forty? What about the child? The one she was pregnant with?"

"I will tell you, boychik, after I tell you your future. Because this is your only moment. Who more than the Magician knows that the moment must be seized. Do you want to see it in pictures or shall I tell you?"

"I'll take it in pictures. If you have to."

"Na!" he snorted, shaking his head. "The glass is too fuzzy. You are in a hurry it seems. You spent too much time with images. Your own crystal ball, helping others to dream. But you see yourself as the Practical One. Born in madness to our wild breed, you thought life could be arranged in boxes. Here is reason, here is emotion. This is right, this is wrong. Here victims, there oppressors. Then you turned the glass upside down. First we were good, now bad. You were discouraged. So you stayed with the lenses. One really good thing, in all the brouhaha, you found a solid place, you fell in love in a good moment, when there was a balance of reason and emotion. That was good, you stayed with it. That was your great break from the family."

"This is my past, not my future."

"They are the same. As you start, so you continue. Fate, you cannot escape it. Does that sound old-fashioned to you?"

"I'll skip the future, thanks, Uncle Yakov."

"Not so fast. Thus speaketh the Great Gramby: I see conflict. I see a war. I see many wars. There is one raging as we speak."

"Lebanon, a repeat performance. As you said, the folly of politicians."

"This will not affect you directly. You think you are affected by these events that you watch on the public crystal, the television box. But your skin has been too hardened, and your tear ducts are dry. What makes you weep is memory. A great moment, a clear and balmy morning, a work of art, a stirring image, something that fires your thoughts. You traveled with your wife to an extraordinary country of strange echoes and landscapes, to find yet another piece of your puzzle. But you could not find meaning. It is illusion. This much I know. You do not wish the future to be as the past. That is man's great folly. Your dead brother speaks to you from the grave, shaking his head. What has been will be always. You will stay with your beloved—that is nice. But the glass is quite fuzzy. Life will provide many upheavals, as ever. Jehovah's time however, is linear; unlike the Buddhists, it does not run in cycles. The chain eventually wears out. I will not tell you further. As for the family: as they began so they will continue, in turmoil and confusion. A quarrelsome tribe, prone to self-delusion once it rediscovered violence."

"That's not very specific, Uncle."

"Call me Jake. Nobody else did, except the little black boy. So full of vim and vigor. Life threw everything at him, and he hurled it out of his horn. Such exquisite triumph. Pain transformed into truth."

He sighed, took out a white handkerchief and threw it over the crystal.

"I was never very good at this. Not enough Irish blood. Or gypsy. We are a practical folk, never more so than when we are being impractical. I was never good at verbal lying. I lied with myself, with my immortal soul. Master of mystery! Such a stupid phrase. If you are master, there is no mystery. There is only mystery in freedom. That's the most elusive trick of all."

"Did you succeed in it? In the end? In Paris?"

He looked at me sadly. Perhaps not sadly, but with some other emotion. Perhaps it was tiredness. Perhaps it was ennui. Perhaps it was a wider sorrow. Perhaps it was a kind of condescension. Perhaps, even, it was love.

"You are a persistent boy," he said. "Paris, at the end of time. They played out the "Marseillaise" on the radio. *Le jour de gloire est arrive*. But everyone knew the end was coming, and crowds of people were leaving the city before the Germans could encircle us all. Then it was strangely quiet. Alma said that the gypsy fiddler could hide us in the basement of the Hot Club. All the grand boulevards were completely empty. Nothing moved, and the birds stopped singing. There were no shows. We turned off the radio. I was interested in all this strange silence. I went out alone. I walked down the Rue de Clichy to Saint Lazare; there was a little café on the Place Saint Augustin where I used to sit sometimes, but it was closed. I walked down La Boetie towards the Champs-Élysées. In the stillness, I could hear a deep, heavy thunder. It seemed to come from under the ground, shaking the road. The closer I came to the avenue the more the road shook. I continued walking, and felt the shaking of the Earth in the soles of my feet, and then creeping up my legs, to my stomach. I came to the Champs-Élysées and saw the columns passing. The Panzers, big, ugly machines. The German soldiers were sitting up on the turrets, looking around them, as if disbelieving their eyes. There was nobody about except me, in my old cape and spats, and my spare hat, which was worn inside from the pecking of so many pigeons. I stood on the verge, and the soldiers turned towards me and waved. They shouted something, but it was lost in the rumble. A long column, coming down from l'Etoile, and heading for the Place de la Concorde. It was where the guillotine stood, during the revolution, do you know that? They chopped off the king's head, right there, and many more besides. And nobody was there to grow it back on. Magic was no use at all on that day, and I had left my wand back at the club. I looked at them, they looked at me..."

I leaned forward and waited for him to continue speaking. The crescent moon was rising above him, which was strange, because I thought it had been behind me. He sighed, and his wide limpid eyes looked straight at me, his lips pursed, the trace of a frown. Then he laughed, or rather gave out a chuckle, and shook his head ruefully. Then came the sigh again.

"No," he said, "I will stop here. Enough has been spoken. I will not tell you the rest of the story."

Boris (deceased):

OK, boychik? I don't like to haunt graveyards, so I'll drop in now and then in other places, when the wind is right and the muse nudges, and I see you with that forlorn look, gazing into the distance, wondering where it all went, the stream of youth, the bonfire of the desires, the banquet of possibilities, the gushing fountain of hopes. We sometimes come down, Hannah and I, during times when you're busy, to the little café on the corner of Shelton and Monmouth streets, close to your film school by Covent Garden, where on chilly days the two folding tables on the pavement outside are empty, and the customers crowd in to the shelf along the window. We sit there, sometimes just the two of us, sometimes with Yakov, when he drops in, shooting the breeze, talking of old times, watching the people pass to and fro...

Sometimes at lunch I see you coming, launching down the narrow road like one of those new-fangled heat-seeking missiles, marching up and sniffing at the line that gathers at this time of day, then ordering your signature snack, the Italian salami and cheese on ciabatta, with butter. Most times on your own, sometimes with a student, arguing some point of photographic law that appears so obvious to the adept, but so tricky to the novice. Learning is never easy if you want to do it properly. Everything is so relative these days.

Sometimes I go out on my own and sneak into the cinemas, mostly to retrospective screenings of the old classics, taking a spare seat or squatting in the aisle or just hovering, as Yakov has taught me. There is not much to appreciate in the current commercial cinema, where cinematography seeks to impress by technique of effects rather than by the song of light, though there are exceptions. I like to revisit the form of the great contemporaries, Harold Rosson's great work on *The Docks of New York* for Sternberg, Carl Hoffman's work on Murnau's *Faust*, Arthur Miller's modellng on *How Green Was My Valley*, Gregg Toland on anything, Jimmy Howe—he was still going strong on *Sweet Smell of Success* and *The Molly Maguires*, right up to 1970, Russell Metty, Karl Struss, Robert Burks' work for Hitchcock, Figueroa for John Ford, and Kaufman, who shot most of the young kid Vigo's Paris barge picture, which I could see complete for the first time. I want to thump my son on the shoulder and shout to him, You see how it's done—that's the ticket!

Water under the bridge. One sees the torrent, constantly gushing. We all started from somewhere and arrived somewhere else. It's not easy to stay focused, to avoid distractions, to gaze pitilessly inside the frame. Perhaps it is a form of blindness. When I told DeMille I was relocating to the State of Israel he told me that their film industry was much too primitive for my needs. "Thorold Dickinson went and made a film there," he said, "and it was pure shit." He was already planning the great remake of his *Ten Commandments*. He offered me a late comeback, but I passed. Sometimes you know when you're done. Too many things were beckoning. Ingathering our own exiles, joining Sarah and Kolya. Clutching Judit's Chinese faces. No hope of communicating there. Even DeMille met his match with Chairman Mao Tse Tung. There was a master of spectacle! The individual lost among the millions. But I carried on, made a home, watched the kids grow. The boys molded themselves so oppositely. The one diving into old waters, jumping back a full generation. The young one growing all angular, frantic and restless... As the first grew older, I saw my father in his face, but harder, chiseled from stone rather than carved out of oak... The finger of God writing his creed... In the movie, DeMille used a combination of his own voice and Heston's to boom out of the rock, as if Moses was speaking to himself. The covenant he knew only he could keep truly. One of my sons was a believer, the other a rebel. We always had to be one thing or the other. I saw a little of Kolya in both of them, and some Sarah, also in both, and Zev's recklessness and sense of adventure in Asher, and my mother's stalwartness in Yitzhak. And, I like to believe, so much of Judit in Asher. The youthfulness, the longing for something else, out there, beyond the horizon. Different journeys from the same sod to different destinations. But in many ways, the same trajectory. Like a dolly track that sees wonders along rails, or the Louma crane that soars up above. Perhaps my sons were the red and the blue of the three-dimensional spectacles, observing the same things in different ways.

About a year after *The Ten Commandments*, Otto Preminger approached me to do some second camera work for his new picture, *Exodus*, based on the book by Leon Uris, but I told him I was already retired. There was a character in the book called Akiva Ben Canaan, who I'm pretty sure was based mainly on Kolya, the zealous Irgun fighter who never gives up. I asked Kolya about this, but he said he never watched the movies. He was dedicated solely to his great opus, the minute and complete details of our historic pain. It was ironic that I came from Hollywood to Israel to be with him in our last days, but he ran off, back to America, because the state was too soft for his taste.

A stiff-necked people, we cultivate our sorrows and grievances. God commands us to love each other, but it is too difficult, with so many thorns. It's called the sabra, the national fruit, whose skin you could only peel off with heavy gloves. People used to sell it from stalls in the streets, but now you can't even get it in stores.

I knew Preminger well. He was an Austrian Jew, from Vizhnits, in Bukovina, some way west of our own local source. DeMille didn't like him, but he made some good pictures. *Anatomy of a Murder* was by far the best. *Laura* was his first big success, in 1944. Joe La Shelle won the Best Cinematography Oscar for that one... They don't make 'em like that anymore. I see the craft, but not quite the same art. I liked *Exodus*, but it was ponderous, too much politics over story... Asher went to see it three times. He was ashamed to admit it years afterward when I reminded him, when he was waving the other flag for the Arabs, they call them Palestinians nowadays. Once upon a time we were the Palestinians. Sarah used to call herself that for years, till she also made a right turn, with her party. But the truth was, boychik, I can remind you, that what you liked best were Westerns. Remember? One of the last films we saw together, at the Mugrabi cinema, was *Man of the West*. Anthony Mann. Ernie Haller shot that, beautiful mood pieces, exemplary composition, also in Cinemascope. Ernie also shot *Mildred Pierce*, which got a nomination for camera too, but he didn't get the award. You loved John Ford and Howard Hawks, and even those stupid Italo-rubbish films called *My Name is Trinity* and *A Fistful of Dollars*. You were an omnivore, you gobbled up everything. I think the truth was that you went to see *Exodus* so many times because of the girl— Eva Marie Saint, she played Paul Newman's blonde shiksa, not that he wasn't blond enough, too. How others see us, what the fuck!

Sorry Yakov, it just slipped out. What can I say? They are my boys, and I'm proud of them. They walked in their own path. One of them is still walking, *baruch hashem*. Hannah and I watch over him, but what do we know? We're just ghosts. We came and we went. He makes his own life. I don't peek into his bedroom, or poke around in the kitchen, as Anna would do. He gets on well with the English girl. They didn't want children. They saw too much of our squabbles maybe. I don't know. The Chinese girl, Judit's granddaughter, came to visit again, they all went to Paris together, it was a good trip. I can imagine. I still remember it in 1910. When the river rose and covered the boulevards, and people rowed down the Boulevard Malesherbes and Capuchines and St. Germain in small boats and rafts... But the summer! Oh, Yakov! You know what I'm talking about. You have to set aside those German tanks. They came, they murdered, and they passed. Human history. But somehow we endure. It is not all suffering and pain. The stupidity, the greed, that's always with us. What have we seen since then? More wars, murders, atrocities, crimes, financial disasters, more political skulduggery than you can shake a stick at, personal *mishigas, schweinerei*, who is immune? The massacre of innocents, revolutions, where is Kolya now, and Sarah? Why aren't they with us? They'll never sit in the same synagogue with us Unbelievers, will they? Or if we wait long enough, will they come? Will they join us? It's the old desert island joke—the rescuers come and find two Jews and three synagogues, so they ask them, what's this? And the first Jew says: That's my synagogue, that's his synagogue, and in that one—neither of us will set foot...

Zev is lost. Judit, it's such a long flight... You were the flyer, Yakov. As just a little *schmendrick*, you took off in the night. When you came back, you would tell stories, and sometimes you would not. Sometimes you had this look, very pensive, biting your lip, staring off into a distance only you could see. Or maybe you were seeing nothing? We couldn't tell. The magician already had his secrets. Mary Poppins you were not. Not so much spoonfuls of sugar. More of salt, and bitter herbs. At the Passover seder, where the empty chair was left for the Prophet Eliahu, you were always squinting at it, as if you saw someone sitting there. Somebody only you could see.

I have to admit to you, I still do some spying on my son. I told you a lie, I do go into his room sometimes. He keeps a secret book, which he wrote a long time ago, in his army days. They used to send him on assignments, from the army camera unit, to film special operations, border raids. Then there was the Six-Day War. He thought he might be killed. So he wrote about his thoughts, his schooldays, girls he dreamed about, juvenile stuff. Of course he wrote it in Hebrew, so he could keep it and Claire would have no idea what was written there. Of course she could have snuck off with it and copied it and got it translated by somebody else, but they trusted each other. So she just let it lie there, under a pile of camera sheets and film school papers, until he decided to tell her the story. But he never did. So I snuck in there, when he would take it out, as he did sometimes, late at night when she was asleep, and leaf through it, just to remind himself maybe what he used to be like. Kind of a corrective for late illusions. It was one of those blue-covered writing pads, 100 pages, 60 gram paper, from the "First Factory for Rulers, Note and Copybooks, Founded 1924, Jerusalem." It was blue-lined paper, and the handwriting was quite easy to read over his shoulder.

So this is what he wrote, in the summer of 1967, when he was just twenty years old:

> That day of 8th June was the day in which I saw the "Victory" for myself for the first time, as I joined the special bus of the correspondents who were being taken through the newly taken towns of Gaza and Rafah to El Arish. We passed through one great open air cemetery, and when we wound down the windows of the bus a strong smell as if of some stinking acid came through the air to almost choke our throats. This is victory. You pass kilometres of burnt vehicles and dead bodies lying inside and all around them, and after a few minutes it makes no impression at all. You become used to it. As a human being you should be shocked to the core by these sights. But you are not impressed. You just photograph. You point the lens and film and film and film. There is a

burnt tank, completely black, its turret blown a few meters away—you film. You see bodies of three dead Egyptians, fallen in attractive angles across the railway tracks—you film. And there are certain things you don't film—horrific sights that don't make an impression when you see them but return afterwards to your thoughts—the results of victory—a pile of torn body parts, a leg, an arm, a smashed torso, and a hand sticking right out of it. Something that was once a man, lying on its back with a completely burned face, and his inner organs spilled around him, half covered already by the sand. And his penis stands out of the destruction, like an accusing finger pointing to the sky.

Snapshots of the battle. An Arab man in the street in Gaza, as we pass, a wide smile on his face, but his whole body shaking, trembling that the smile might fall from his face and leave him defenceless. The look in the eyes of the Gaza residents as we pass by, that can't fail to show what they think of us, what lies hidden in their hearts. But these snapshots that we see are only a small part of the sights the fighters themselves saw, as they made the victory that we are seeing in its naked form. The guilt they don't talk about afterwards, that others died and they didn't, comrades and friends. The guilt that I would feel for having sat out the first days of the war in the film unit's office and in the editing studio getting the edited rolls of film that all the correspondents took in the battlefields and sending them out to all the foreign news companies, so that they should only see the war we wanted them to see. At least on this day of the battles I can smell the front line, the exquisite stink of victory. Skirmishes that were still going on, all around us. Soldiers would stop us on the way and say, Not here, please, they're still shooting. Some bastards are throwing grenades, we haven't finished with them all yet.

On the first day, we went down, the two of us, the chief cameraman J. and myself, into the empty streets of Tel Aviv, looking for the war that wasn't there. Driving around the deserted streets while the air raid sirens wailed all around us—the real sirens, the rising and falling calls that signified that this time it was not a drill. We walked the streets waiting for the bombardment, ready to film Tel Aviv in flames, the explosion of falling bombs, the destruction of our own familiar city. But it never happened that way. The bombs were falling elsewhere, and they were ours.

All the way to El Arish the same sights open up around us—the burnt tanks and trucks and armoured cars, the smashed bodies. No impression. We get out of the bus, arrange ourselves around the killing ground, look in the viewfinder for the best angles and compositions of destruction and death. We do what we are expected to do. Outside the city we are driven into an Egyptian air base. Smashed planes that lie wrecked on the bombed runways in the first minutes of the war. The Migs, with their razor thin wing tips. They looked like the broken and scattered toys abandoned by a giant, who has run away. Inside the administration building, the rooms are full of smashed furniture and glass and dust on everything. Personal documents and army i.d cards lie everywhere, spilled out of the cabinets. We each take a batch as souvenirs. Abdel this, Ali that, Mohammad so and so, staring faces, that may or may not be still alive. Soldiers are picking up souvenirs everywhere, mainly helmets. A helmet with a hole punched in it is a favourite prize. I heard later that one Major took home part of a skull crushed into a helmet. I suppose he wanted to show it to his family, his kids. They may be impressed, maybe not.

There are battles still raging, further south, as some Egyptian units are still fighting, near Bir Gafgafa, and further towards the Suez Canal. We don't know if the battles will stop there, or if we'll cross the Canal itself, towards Cairo. News comes over the radio that on the Jordanian front, our forces have completed the conquest of Jerusalem, the Old City. Soldiers are jumping about, shouting, hugging each other. I film it all, the moment of glory. Then we head off towards the south.

Whatever happens, as the skirmishes and wars and retaliation raids continue, I want to be sure that if I go too I don't want to be the subject of those rosy memorials that the journalists and military propagandists write about the soldiers who have fallen. It's always the same thing—all about the bravery of the fallen and how loyal and devoted you were to the army and your country and you family, and how many liters of tears were shed by your friends. Those people who always groan and sigh when they hear about disasters and deaths over the radio make me sick, because unless it touches them directly their supposed concern is only a fake, maybe they're just relieved that it hasn't happened to them, and in any case a few minutes later they've forgotten all about it and just get on with their lives. I hate all those state sponsored funerals with the flags and the rifle volleys and the politicians and generals who turn up to express their sorrow to the mourning families, so that they can perfume themselves with the odor of the hero, or the victim of the enemy's murderous impulses, who are fighting on their own side in the same way and for the same reasons as ourselves. And I hate all those fake praises for a person whom they all cursed and insulted when he was alive, particularly all the school friends who used to throw orange peels at you and copied from your exam papers and laughed at you but go all tearful when you have gone.

I don't want anyone to write how wonderful I was and how loyal and how they all miss me and cover their heads with sackcloth and ashes. I would like to know that somebody has the guts to say just what I was really like? I don't know if there's anybody who cares, since I've probably made more enemies than friends, because I never wanted to flatter anybody who wasn't worth it, and I never kissed anybody's ass, and I don't want anyone to kiss my corpse's ass when I'm gone. And if I do die in some stupid war for my country, it would really be the last big laugh, but maybe I can have the last laugh, after all, from these pages, which are the only monument that I want and the only memorial that I can accept, without spitting back in the face of the State, the People and their corrupt leaders.

That's all.

But there was one more thing. In the same section, as I was watching, my son inserted a new news clipping that he had scissored out of *The Guardian*, I believe, the same day or one or two days before, I couldn't catch the date. It was headed:

ATTEMPTED ASSASSINATION OF ISRAELI MINISTER: GUNMAN TAKES AIM AT PEACE CONFERENCE

Young man takes aim at conference in Jerusalem's King David Hotel during first meeting in the Israeli capital of representatives of new Likud government and Palestine National Authority officials.

As several newly appointed officials headed by the new Minister of Regional Strategy, Adir Gur-Arieh, met for preliminary talks aimed at averting a unilateral declaration of a Palestinian State in Ramallah, as part of the new peace initiative promised by Prime Minister Binyamin Netanyahu in Washington, a young man in religious skullcap and black coat broke through the security guards at the entrance to the hotel conference chamber and fired three pistol shots as the Minister arose for a handshake with Ahmad Corea, representing Palestinian President Mahmud Abbas. The first two shots hit Mr. Gur-Arieh in the shoulder and abdomen, and a third went wild as security personnel rushed forward and wrested the handgun from the assailant's hand. The delegates to the conference were rushed into a secure part of the building, and Mr. Corea and his retinue left quickly, in the care of their own bodyguards, to drive swiftly back to Ramallah, only twenty minutes drive from the capital.

The gunman was identified as Yakir Gurevits, a member of the Lions of Zion, an extremist Jewish settlers' movement responsible for a series of attacks on Palestinians in villages bordered by West Bank settlements in recent months. The group is also suspected of planting a bomb in the offices of a human rights group, Zechut, in Jewish west Jerusalem, on November 29 last year.

The gunman and his victim appear to be closely related. Minister Gur-Arieh is the son of the noted historian Nathan Gurevits, the scholar and ex-Irgun Zvai Leumi fighter (and terrorist in British eyes), who died in 1995 aged 99 years. Mr Gurevits was the author and editor of the multi-volume definitive history of anti-Semitism provocatively titled "Jew Hatred Down the Ages." The shooter, Mr Gurevits, is the great-grandson of Mr Gurevits's sister, Sarah Gurevits, who immigrated to Palestine from her native Romania and became a founding member of the kibbutz movement and the Zionist Labor Party, Mapai, which ruled the State of Israel from 1948 to 1977, though she never held any ministerial office. She died before the 1967 war in which the territories later settled by zealous right-wing Israelis were taken by force of conquest.

The gunman's grandfather, Zadok Gurevits, a Tel Aviv businessman dealing in agricultural heavy machinery (including the bulldozers used in clearing settlement lands and reinforcing the ongoing siege of Gaza), told the local newspaper Yediot Aharonot:

"This is a very Israeli and Jewish tragedy. We came here for love of our land but we are being torn apart by our hatreds. I am not a leftist, but when the shedding of blood becomes normal the boundaries of conflict and violence become too easily blurred. My grandson is my grandson and I will defend him. But the poison that afflicts so many is in the very atmosphere that we breathe. We are responsible for our own fate. I believe it is time that we look into ourselves and ask the crucial questions: Where have we come from, and where are we going? This rush to self destruction must stop."

A spokesperson for the Bikur Holim hospital in Jerusalem described Mr. Gur-Arieh's abdominal wound as serious, but called his prospects for a full recovery "reasonably good, in the prevailing circumstances."

Mr. Gurevits has been remanded for trial.

The Last Scene

Exterior, night. A barge chugs on up the river, its shape obscured by swirling mist, which is more accurately a fog, that settles on the river bank and almost completely swallows the wharfs, the warehouses, the nearest houses and streets leading up from the river to an unseen landscape experienced only in faint sounds of music and glimmering lights in the dark.

Encased in this black cloud, the barge slides across velvet ripples, to the soft pulse of its engine.

Interior: the captain (*le patron*) and his newlywed wife (*la patrone*) are asleep, cuddled up in their marital bunk in the compact cabin, wrapped in each other under a warm quilt, so that only the tops of their heads are visible, her blonde crown, his tousled black hair. In another cabin, the first mate (Pere Jules) is crouched over his tarot cards, fanned out on his workbench, hemmed in by a hoard of bric-a-brac culled from his long decades plying the flea markets of Paris, or from his service round the seven seas (whichever option you may wish to believe): rag and voodoo dolls, various magic gri-gris, broken musical implements, knives, a selection of puppets, children's show boxes, Punch and Judys, Indonesian shadow puppets, figurines from Okinawa and Easter Island, ships in bottles, the Kon-Tiki raft, cardboxes full of old postcards and photographs, his toolboxes, pushed under the bed, on which twelve cats of all shades of scruffy squirm about, trying either to avoid or to share the space with each other. Two of them leap over his shoulder, upending the beach and scattering the cards. He sweeps them away, with a clout of his thick calloused hand and several oaths in an indeterminate language.

Exterior: close shot on the barge, on the bridge deck, The Boy sits up, curled in a blanket, his hands hugging his shoulders, cackling to himself, gazing out into the fog. He is a fool, but not fool enough to leave his perch for the unknown.

Beyond, on the shore, the film crew cluster around each other, since they too cannot see beyond the arc lights set on the jetty's edge, pouring a yellow light pointlessly into the dark. An intense young man in a roll-neck sweater, the Director leans close to the Cameraman peering in the viewfinder of the great box-like Debrie camera, with its extended matte-box jutting out over the water. A cluster of young assisstants peer out too, trying to penetrate the fog. An older man in a scuffed jacket, the camera Consultant, walks over, commiserating with the crew.

"*Rien!*"

They look out into the darkness. The Consultant puts his arm around the Director's shoulder.

"Let them go their own way."

There is a sound behind them. A soft crunch of feet on the cobbles. The momentary rattle of a small drum. They look around. Silhouetted on the mist backed by diffuse lighting, three figures: A tall man in a cape, with a top hat, swinging on his back a clutch of musical instruments, the drum, a set of small cymbals, a horn, a slung banjo and a mouth organ set in a harness around his neck. A woman of indeterminate age, with a raincoat draped loosely around her shoulders. And a small boy, whom she holds by the hand.

The Consultant turns, taking a few steps towards them, but, as he approaches, a new, heavier bank of fog rolls in from the river and wraps around the group, shutting off all the lights behind them. The Consultant tries to brush the fog away, but he too becomes lost in it, climbing up the jetty's steps.

The Consultant: Are you there?

A figure scurries away from him, his face made out by the light from a window that briefly swings open. It is only a beggar, hunched in a torn raincoat. The Consultant looks at him for a moment, then turns back. Seen from behind, his figure recedes down towards the wharf.

The film crew is left alone on the jetty. The music swells up for the finale.

THE END